BANISHED
CHILDREN
OF EVE

PETER QUINN

BANISHED CHILDREN OF EVE

VIKING

VIKING

Published by the Penguin Group
Penguin Books USA Inc., 375 Hudson Street,
New York, New York 10014, U.S.A.
Penguin Books Ltd, 27 Wrights Lane, London W8 5TZ, England
Penguin Books Australia Ltd, Ringwood, Victoria, Australia
Penguin Books Canada Ltd, 10 Alcorn Avenue,
Toronto, Ontario, Canada M4V 3B2
Penguin Books (N.Z.) Ltd, 182–190 Wairau Road,
Auckland 10, New Zealand

Penguin Books Ltd, Registered Offices:
Harmondsworth, Middlesex, England

First published in 1994 by Viking Penguin,
a division of Penguin Books USA Inc.

1 3 5 7 9 10 8 6 4 2

Map of New York and Brooklyn, published by J. H. Kleefish
in 1859, courtesy of Map Division, The New York Public Library,
Astor, Lenox, and Tilden foundations.

LIBRARY OF CONGRESS CATALOGING-IN-PUBLICATION DATA
Quinn, Peter.
Banished children of Eve / by Peter Quinn.
p. cm.
ISBN 0-670-85076-4
1. New York (N.Y.)—History—Civil War, 1861–1865—Fiction.
I. Title.
PS3567.U3486B36   1994
813'.54—dc20   93-11184

Printed in the United States of America
Set in Adobe Sabon

For Kathy,
who taught me
to love is to persist.

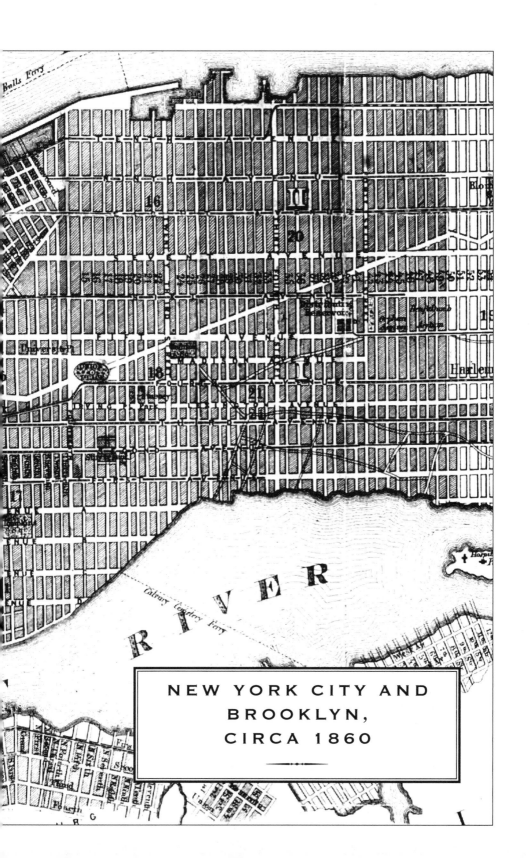

NEW YORK CITY AND
BROOKLYN,
CIRCA 1860

PROLOGUE

MUNSEY'S MAGAZINE

June 1904

The Mystery of the Bowery Sphinx

I

THE MORNING PAPER for February 21st last contained two items that could not help but arouse curiosity. The first, from Cairo, Egypt, recounted how a British archaeological expedition in search of the Lost Tombs of the Pharaohs had unearthed an ancient avenue lined with stone sphinxes. The second was from our hometown of New York. It, too, was concerned with sphinxes, in this case a singular one, the late Mr. James Dunne, a tavern keeper, whose death (from natural causes, we were assured) was reported under the caption "The Passing of the Bowery Sphinx."

Given our druthers, we would probably have booked passage on a steamer for the Mediterranean to unearth the full story behind that avenue and its enigmatic monuments. Alas, it was not to be. The directive that arrived on our desk described a quest of far shorter distance. "Who was this 'Bowery Sphinx'?" it asked. "How had he earned that appellation?"

The "Bowery" part seemed easy to explain. Like "Chelsea Joe," or "Broadway Mike," characters of our acquaintance, the mere fact of a long presence in a section of this city is enough to add a geographic qualifier to one's name. But "Sphinx," ah, there was the rub. In the loud, unending human chorus of the Bowery, who besides a mute could have gained that title for himself?

On a bright, frigid morning, with arctic gusts playing about our coat and pulling at our hat, we embark on our expedition. We walk up the great avenue called Broadway. The towering buildings on either side are as solemn and silent as any of those monumental guardians recently uncovered along the Nile. This is Sunday, and the usual rampage of money changers in and out of their temples is suspended for the day. The street is left to an occasional clerk or newsboy, his head bowed into the wind, his jacket and scarf bundled around him as tightly as the wrappings of any mummy.

We turn off Broadway into the narrow puzzle of streets where the magnificent thrust of the avenue dissolves into a jumble as confused as any found in the *qasbahs* of North Africa. In front of us pads a Chinaman, his pigtail swaying like a metronome, a distraction we welcome since all around us the hour has struck when sagging rows of lodging-houses are disgorging their guests.

It has been estimated that upwards of ten thousand souls a night seek shelter in these structures, the grandest of them providing a mattress and blanket for twenty-five cents, the lowest offering, for five to seven cents, a roof above and a floor beneath. Herein is an army as numerous as the one Cheops pressed into building his pyramid, but most find little employment beyond the annual ritual of Election Day, when, for a few drinks and some corned beef, the overseers of Tammany press them into the service of The Organization.

One recent observer counted over 100 churches, chapels, and places of worship of every kind in the lower quarter of this city, and 4,065 saloons, most of the latter clustered along and around the Bowery. This Sabbath morning, it is the saloons rather than the churches that are bringing in the sheep. The closer we come to the Bowery, the more there are.

Here is a typical specimen: a peeling, faded building that began its life perhaps as some respectable tradesman's domicile but in its dotage has been divided, subdivided, and redivided into an indeterminate number of "rooms" that are rented for the nocturn. At the street level is a sepulchral hole with a faded sign above that tells us we stand before JOHNNY MCCLUSKEY'S WELCOME INN. Ahead is a dime museum, one of half a hundred to be found in the vicinity. A tattered banner hangs outside and proclaims the marvels of freakdom that are to be found within. The door is open. But we resist the temptation.

We pass a used-clothing store, whose proprietor is standing

out front amid racks of secondhand coats that are swinging wildly in the wind. His face has the unmistakable physiognomy of the Hebrew, the same visage that Ramses and the priests of Osiris looked upon when Moses bargained for his people's freedom.

We move on. Our expedition has almost reached its destination. Up to the right, on the far side of the Nile, beneath the elevated railway, on the northeast corner of Bayard Street, is what has been reported to be the former place of business of "the Bowery Sphinx," Mr. James Dunne. Indeed, as we draw closer, our information is confirmed by the chipped and faded lettering on the front window. DUNNE'S SALOON, it reads. Below, in smaller letterings, is this: PROP. MR. JAMES F. DUNNE.

As we read, a squat, pug-nosed member of the Celtic race emerges. His bowler hat is pushed way back on his head; his hands are thrust into his jacket. His cheeks and nose are red, a color, we surmise, less inspired by the cold than the warmth he has already managed to imbibe. He regards us warily. We ask, "This is the establishment of *the* James Dunne?"

"Yeah," he answers, "may he rest in peace."

We continue: "Mr. James Dunne, 'the Bowery Sphinx'?"

"Yeah, that's the plug he preferred. 'His Holiness' was the cap I put on him. You don't look like no copper. What are ya? A reporter or somethin' like that?"

We confess, and our interrogee, having become interrogator, invites us inside to help us solve once and for all the riddle of the Sphinx.

II

THE ROOM WE ENTER is long and narrow. Along the length of one wall stretches a bar of dark wood. The walls are stained with tobacco smoke, but are relieved, at intervals, by the framed images of various Tammany pharaohs. Indeed, here are the hieroglyphs of the New Kingdom's dynastic succession! Without even a word from our would-be guide, we have part of the explanation behind the prominence of Mr. James Dunne, "the Bowery Sphinx." These wall paintings tell us that, though we may think ourselves in humble surroundings, the Immortals have watered here, supped and imbibed with their supplicants, writing down on a small papyrus the brief messages that when taken to an office of the municipal government may result in a job, a contract, or perhaps even a commissionership.

The rotund gentleman at our elbow signals to the barman, and in an instant two glasses of whiskey are set before us. We pull out some coins and drop them onto the counter, where they make, no doubt, a familiar ring. Our companion lifts his glass and says, "Here it goes under the nose." We put our glass to the lip, but take no sip.

The ritual done, we settle at last into fulfilling the purpose of this expedition. We mention that we saw in the paper several days ago a brief item on the passing of Mr. James Dunne, who was described as a longtime taverner known to customers and acquaintances by a title that had caused us no small wonder. How, we queried, did anyone in this cacophonous, garrulous quarter of the noisiest, most talkative town in the world get a reputation as a sphinx?

> Q. Was he a mute [we continued]?
> A. You mean, could he talk?
> Q. Yes, could he talk?
> A. Sure, he could jaw wid the best of 'em, when he wanted, but it was part of his beard that he handed out words like they was finniffs. It drew the crowds, I guess. Old man Dunne would run his velvet over his tombstones before he leans over and sez something like it's comin' from the gob of the Pope hisself.

At this point, we felt a twinge of sympathy with the first explorers among the antiquities of Egypt, who had been bewildered by the riddle of a language they had no key to understanding. What was a "finniff"? Why would one run velvet over a tombstone? The dilemma of those early adventurers was given a solution, of course, by some soldiers of Napoléon's who, digging the foundation of a fort near the Rosetta Mouth of the Nile, came across a stone of black basalt that carried on it the Greek equivalents of the Egyptian characters. The mystery solved!

The aproned figure behind the bar, a small, bald man, proved our Rosetta stone. "Mike," he said, pointing to our guide, "is a real Bowery mug. He thinks the whole world talks like they does around here." The gist of the matter was, according to our barman–Rosetta stone, that Mr. Dunne was given to silence, and, as is often the case, whether deserved or not, some saw silence as the same as wisdom, and sought Mr. Dunne out. Mr. Dunne, usually solemn-faced, could always be found in the same chair by the window. When someone would sit next to him and ask for advice, he'd move his tongue across his teeth ("run his velvet over his tombstones"), think for a moment, and give them some small, sage piece of wisdom, or what, on the Bowery, is taken for wisdom.

Mr. Dunne had been the proprietor here for forty years or so (neither guide nor barman–Rosetta stone could say precisely how long). A remarkable tenure, indeed. But what of his origins? What had he done before running this august watering hole for the tribe of Tammany? What of his family? Barman–Rosetta stone looked at our guide. There was perplexity in both their faces. It seemed we had touched upon a question they had not considered before our arrival.

Our guide spoke first: "Now listen here, I'm not out to flog old man Dunne's ground sweat, let him and all the 'faithfully departed,' as they sez, rest in peace, but to listen to all the talk you'd think it was some saint that died instead of a kiddie who stuffed the rhino and set hisself up in business before the booly dogs could lay a hand on him."

The confusion must have been evident on our face, because our barman–Rosetta stone started interpreting before we even asked. No one really knew about Mr. Dunne's past. Some said he had set himself up as a taverner with the proceeds of a criminal career ("stuffed the rhino") that he had landed before the police ("booly dogs") could apprehend him. But these theorists were merely maligning the dead ("flogging old man Dunne's ground sweat"). Nobody knew for sure.

"You could look it up," our barman–Rosetta stone suggested. "If he ever served time, the police must have a sheet." We considered it, but as we sat in the very seat where Mr. Dunne had sat for four decades and regarded the dull façades of ancient brick across the Bowery, we sensed that our expedition was coming to an end. The hard labor of that digging was best left to stronger backs than ours.

"There was a family," he concluded. "They lived up on the North Side. Dunne would ride the El home every night. When he died, the widow came down here once to sign the papers when the place was sold. I heard she moved. Anyways, that was the only time I ever seen her."

We bought a round of drinks for our hosts. The place was filling up, so we said our good-byes and went out into the cold sunlight that slanted down through the tracks above us. A train roared overhead.

The Sphinx could keep his secret, we decided. The city that bred him bore as little resemblance to the transriparian metropolis of our day as the mud huts of the primeval inhabitants of Egypt did to imperial Thebes. The sands of time had obliterated the landscape of his birth. And we, standing on the far side of that great desert, are unable to distinguish the truth of what was from the legend. Someday, perhaps, the archaeologists may turn up the bones of a creature with leonine as well as human features, and the Darwinists may draw from that discovery the ability to reach wider conclusions about the Sphinx and the world he inhabited. In this age, all things are possible. But for now, at least, the antiquarians and Egyptologists put aside their spades, and leave the Sphinx to his silence.

APRIL 13, 1863

. . . what is history anyway? Is history simply a matter of
events that leave behind those things that can be weighed
and measured—new institutions, new maps, new rulers,
new winners and losers—or is it also the result of moments that seem to leave nothing behind, nothing but the
mystery of spectral connections between people long separated by place and time, but somehow speaking the same
language?

—Greil Marcus, *Lipstick Traces:*
A Secret History of the Twentieth Century

I

JIMMY DUNNE FINGERED THE GLASS, revolved it slowly in his hand. Whiskey lapped gently against the rim.

One of Dandy Dan's rules: Never linger.

Sorry, Dan. No rule can't be broken. Said it himself and broke every one. Still, never tired of handing them out.

Outside the window of Mike Manning's Saloon, two currents flowed: the stronger away from the river, toward Chatham Square, Brooklyn trudging to work in Manhattan, ferry load after ferry load; the other, lesser current toward the river, workingmen mostly, gangs of longshoremen on their way to the docks. At the corner of Cherry Street, the two streams collided and created a turbulent mix, like the waters of the Hell Gate.

Another rule: Never drink on the job. *God, that one Dandy Dan didn't just break but slipped on, an icy roof in January, too much whiskey, an iron railing shoved up through his jaw, poking out of his mouth. They said it was a sight, the crowds fighting to get close and catch a view, the booly dogs pushing them back.*

The flow of the lesser current grew heavier, more longshoremen on their way to shape up for the morning shift. Those in need of a morning dose to get the shaking out of their hands and tame the confusion in their heads found their way into the warmth of Mike Manning's place. As soon as they arrived, Manning dispensed a line of shots. The whiskey rose to the rim, trembled, but didn't overflow. Without a word, Manning's customers lifted their glasses, the bottoms turned up toward the picture of Robert Emmet, Ireland's young martyr, his outstretched arm pointed toward the door.

Dunne watched the street. A cold, leaden mist clung to the waterfront and hung heavy with river smells, salt mixed with offal, smoke of coal furnaces and foundries, pungency of rotting fish. The customers, hunched over glasses that Manning instantly refilled, gathered at the end of the bar, close to the stove with its small pile of coals. An old man broke loose and ran into the street. He retched into the gutter, wiped his mouth on his sleeve, and came back in. Manning refilled his glass. The man threw down the contents, blinked, closed his eyes.

Frail-looking, his face as serious as a priest's, Manning walked to the end of the bar, by the window. He glanced at Dunne's full glass with a tavern keeper's smile: involuntary grin, small and insincere. " 'Tis a grim day on the River Styx," he said.

The whistle of the Catherine Street ferry gave three short shrieks.

Dunne nodded. *Christ, it was places like this Dandy Dan ended his days, shebeens that in better times he wouldn't have stopped to piss in.* A man is knowed by the company he keeps. *The Gospel according to Dan.*

Manning lifted the brimming glass in front of Dunne and wiped the bar with his rag. "Yer up early."

Dunne nodded again. He kept looking out the window. Could do it all day. The first thing he had done when he came back from the West was find a stool, pull it to a window, and stare. He drew a thrill from the continual press of people, the endless traffic, the ceaseless hurry, but what exactly that thrill was he couldn't say. Something to do with what the gold seekers found in California, whether they struck it rich or not: the assurance that, though poor, they lived amid great possibilities.

A woman carrying an umbrella strolled up to the window, stopped, and leaned forward, the plume on her hat touching the glass as she peered in. She had the face of a dockside whore, white as a ghost, a layer of Lady Emily Bowden's Face Creme and Emulsifier to cover the sores and pockmarks. Her lips were apple red.

Manning waved her away. She stuck her tongue out. "Bloody whores," he said. "A dog has more shame, and you'd be better in a dog's company. No dog ever caused a man to be robbed, his lifeless body tossed into the river." Manning shook his head. "The way they're multiplying, they'll soon be more whores in this city than men."

The tavern keeper's smile returned to Manning's face. He tapped the bottom of the whiskey bottle against the bar. "Drink up," he said. "The next is on me." He went back to the other patrons. When he returned, he said in an offhanded way, "Is it a job you're going to?"

"Coming from."

"Nights you work, is it?"

"Last night I worked the entire time, from the moment her husband left till the dawn's early light."

"Whose husband?" Manning asked. He seemed confused.

Dunne winked. "I'm not one to give out names. The seal of the confessional is what I work under, at least when it comes to the ladies. No names and never any addresses."

"Ach, you're one of those," Manning said.

"One of what?"

"A squiffer, that's what, all dressed up for the ladies, doesn't matter whether they're married or not, no respect for the state of matrimony."

"And you take no interest in skirts?"

"My younger days, well, I danced a few dances; but I've left the floor, prefer to sit and listen to the music. Far less dangerous, both for the soul as for the body." Manning turned and walked back to the other end of the bar.

Dunne stuck a finger into the glass, then sucked it. Bitter as oil, it stung his mouth. Knew he should have changed his clothes before he came. Be a gentleman among gentlemen. A workingman among workingmen. A Roman in Rome. Never stand out. But there hadn't been time to go back to the hotel. *More of Dandy Dan's advice disregarded.*

Manning pretended to gaze out the window, a vacant stare, but his attention was concentrated on Dunne, the mathematical brain trying to add up the several visits Dunne had paid to these premises. Most times he had come in the early evening; this was the only morning visit. First time he saw him, Manning thought he might be a detective hired by one of the employers' associations to spy on the longshoremen, listen to them talk, and take it back to the bosses. Or maybe an agent from the Provost Marshal's office on the lookout for deserters. Either case, an omen of these disturbed and troubled times. But he never seemed much interested in who came and went or what they said. Nursed a single drink while sitting on a stool by the window. Always turned aside a conversation. Hard to figure.

Manning ran his rag over the bar in the same unthinking way he smiled when he poured a drink.

Across the street, on the northwest corner of Cherry and Catherine, the clerks of the Brooks Brothers store stood in the doorway waiting for the manager to appear and let them in. They poked out their heads and looked at the sky.

"Could save them the trouble of looking," Manning said. "These bones of mine got the marrow of prophecy in them. They can tell whatever weather is coming, wet or dry, and can't remember a time they told me wrong."

"What'd they tell you this morning?"

"A stormy day, for sure." Manning crossed his arms and rubbed his shoulders. "And won't be just the skies fill with trouble. Mark my words, there's great botheration in this ward. Been building for some time, since prices started rising so fast and the men not being able to keep pace, their wives complaining that the children were going without. Talk of a strike is in the air. Last month, over on the West Side, was a strike on the Erie docks, and the railroad brought in a tribe of freed niggers to fill the jobs. Caused a fearful row. Two saloons looted, the owners wiped out, nothing left but empty bottles and shattered glass." Manning shivered. "Sure, that's the way with the Metropolitans. Fought to protect the property of the railroad, but left the tavern keeper to God's protection. Wouldn't be any different here." He pointed across the street. "Them there the Metropolitans would fight like terriers to protect. Me, well, the intervention of the saints is what I'd be left to call upon."

"Protect who?" Dunne said.

Manning jabbed his finger in the direction of the clerks. "There. Them there. The Brooks Brothers crew."

Dunne looked in their direction as though he hadn't noticed them before, hadn't learned their functions as well as faces, hadn't followed their routines as he browsed through the store, hadn't chatted with several as he contemplated making small purchases. They had been eager to help.

"There's a Brooks Brothers down here?" Dunne said. He stood and moved directly in front of the window to get a better view.

Manning came from behind the bar. "Are you blind?" he said, with annoyance in his voice. "The place is as well marked as Barnum's."

"Been to the Broadway store, but I didn't realize there was another down here," Dunne said.

"Have you now?" Manning's eyebrows lifted at the thought that one of his patrons was also a patron of Brooks Brothers on Broadway and Grand, clothiers to gentlemen. This was the first could make that claim. "I hear their clothes is awful dear."

"They're not cheap."

"Nothing is anymore, not in this city."

"Have they been here long?"

"Been here forever. The two Yankees started the business set up shop right where you see it. Over forty years that was the only place they had, then about five years ago they opened uptown. Fashionable people weren't coming down here no more, so the Yankees went and opened a new emporium on Broadway. Kept this store to catch the ferry trade."

His last visit, Dunne had purchased a felt hat. Only a limited stock of goods. Yellow oilskins, sou'westers, shirts, pants, hats sent down from Broadway and discounted to attract the clerks traveling to and fro from Brooklyn, catechumens who, if success smiled on them, might one day be received into the communion of the uptown store.

"Pack of thieving Protestants," Manning said.

"Who?" Dunne asked.

"The whole lot of 'em runs that store, Yankee bastards, the worst of the rat-nosed race."

The men from the rear of the bar filed past, happier than when they entered. Manning said good-bye to each by name. They walked in front of the window and almost instantaneously blended into the crowd.

"My mother sewed for them for years," Manning said. "Was all we had to support ourselves them first years in New York. Damn near starved, was never enough to eat, so she'd sew harder, and all the women like her done the same. The more they produced, the bigger the supply and the lower their wages fell. We wasn't much better off than we'd been in Ireland. Jesus, I think I was sixteen before I knew what it was like to have a full stomach."

It didn't seem to Dunne that it would take much to fill Manning's stomach. The tavern keeper was of a type. "Skinballs" is what they used to call them, a term borrowed from a card game of the same name, a version of faro. It wasn't applied to every kid who was as slight as a playing card (there were hordes of those), but to a special species: the stunted, small-boned boys who came over from Ireland and never grew to any size, a perpetually wizened look to them, sunken eyes and cheeks, an air of secrecy about them.

Dandy Dan's observation: The heart of a skinball is the shrunkenest part of him. *And the rule derived:* Beware the skinball. He'd sell his own mother.

In the orphanage on Randalls Island, the Irish born in Ireland fought the Irish born in New York for the right to run the place, a war fought out of view of the warders with fists, sticks, homemade knives. Dunne led the American faction. He boxed the leader of the Irish Irish, a strapping lad of twelve, two years his elder, beat him into the dirt, kneed him when he was down and broke two of his ribs. After that, the rest of the Irish fell in line. Except the skinballs. They had no leader. Each was a faction of his own, stayed to himself, devoting his time to acquiring and selling what the other boys wanted: liquor, tobacco, a deck of cards. If you wanted the loyalty of the skinballs, you had to conquer them one by one. Even then you couldn't be sure.

Manning stroked his chin. The face was smooth, the yellow skin as translucent as waxed paper, the veins clearly visible. It was difficult for Dunne to tell how old Manning was. You never knew with skinballs. As kids, they already seemed aged.

Manning let go his chin and pointed to the coat of arms mounted above the door of Brooks Brothers. "See that?" he said.

Dunne had glanced at it several times on his way in and out of the store. A sheep in a sling, Latin or French words around it. It reminded him of the lamb sometimes depicted in church windows. He had never given it much thought.

"Symbol of the Knights of the Golden Fleece, that's what I've been told, and a proper symbol it is for the likes of a store that's fleeced not only them who sew for it but the United States government as well, supplying uniforms to the Army that fall apart as soon as the soldiers put them on. The needleworkers are threatening to strike. 'Good luck to 'em,' says I."

The store manager appeared and opened the door. The clerks went in behind him. Dunne followed them in his mind: each clerk to his station, takes out his cashbox, removes his receipt book. The manager walks to the rear of the store, mounts a stairway to an office that looks out over the selling floor, kneels before a safe emblazoned with the sheep in a sling, symbol of the Knights of the Golden Fleece. The dial turns with an unfamiliar ease, no click of resistance. A pull on the handle. The door swings open to reveal an empty top shelf. The two stacks of paper that had been left the night before—gone.

The money was in one of the long pockets sewed into Dunne's pants, inner pouches that reached down to the calf, one on each side. In the other were the file and claw used on the store's FEDERAL CERTIFIED ALL-SECURITY SAFE. PATENTED. Broke open easier than a candy box. More security in a locked desk drawer.

"You'd think they'd forget about a store that small, and in this vicinity, when they got the likes of that palace on Broadway," Manning said. "But that's not the rat-noses' way. Where there's a dollar to be made, that's where you'll find 'em; it's a religion with 'em." He left the window and gathered up the glasses. "You're not in the clothing trade, are you?" he called over to Dunne.

Dunne kept watching out the window. Any minute a clerk should dash out the door and run up Cherry toward the precinct house. The crime discovered and reported. He didn't want to miss it.

"No, I'm not," Dunne called back. Still no sign of any clerk.

"You live around here?" Manning spit into each glass, rubbed it hard with the same rag he used to wipe the bar.

"Not far." Much too close. Pulling a job like this so near to Dolan's New England Hotel: something new, and dangerous. Some clerk passing in the street, remembering the face: *I can't tell you why I was suspicious of him, Officer, but there was an aspect to the visage that impressed itself upon me. Perhaps it was the Paddy nose and jaw, lineaments of criminality that cannot be hid by the respectable set of clothes. And yesterday, quite unexpectedly, I saw him only a few blocks from here, on Bayard, outside a hotel.* Was dumb luck like that brought the booly dogs most of their success. They liked to pretend it was hard work and persistence. But it was luck. They depend on it as much as any man, maybe more.

Manning rubbed the glass until it squeaked. He spit some more and kept polishing. He glanced at Dunne as if to ask another question, but dropped his head without speaking.

A clerk came out of Brooks Brothers, his hat jammed on his head, a hand holding closed the collar of his coat. He hurried up Cherry.

Dunne took up the glass of whiskey, put it under his nose, and dipped his tongue in. He took a deep breath and threw the liquor down his throat. *A toast, then, to the burgle of Brooks*

Brothers. Not exactly a crime to be remembered by the citizenry of New York, like the piracy of Albert Hicks, a True American pug shanghaied by the captain of an oyster sloop, the unsuspecting mariner unaware he had brought aboard a denizen of the waterside more deadly than any ever swam the deep. Returned to his senses, Hicks murdered the captain and the entire crew—slew them in their sleep—gathered up their valuables, and rowed a lifeboat to shore. Had a party for himself in the Five Points—a sailor's holiday, whiskey and whores—before the law caught up with him. They hanged him in the middle of the harbor, on Bedloe's Island, the July before the war started, a waterborne festival, the place crammed with boats. Barnum had a special one for him and his guests. So did the sachems of Tammany. Hicks gave the whole town a thrill. Newspapers ate it up, the crime and punishment alike. The crowds paraded in front of the Tombs to catch a glimpse of Hicks. The pickpockets said they never worked a more good-natured assemblage, not even when the Prince of Wales arrived. The day they hanged him, the city seemed to have lifted a burden from itself, as if it was done with everything undesirable in its midst. But the good feeling didn't last. One victory didn't win a war, everyone in the country knew that by now, and that's what it had become, war, what it had been since '57, when the Protestants up in Albany decided to throw out the Municipal Police, men who didn't care what was lifted so long as they got their share, and replaced them with the Metropolitans, a pack of hounds answering to the Governor and the Commissioners, a bite to match their bark, everyone lifted for breaking the law treated alike, kicked and manhandled, given a taste of the locust stick. No more holidays for the likes of Hicks, and no more shrugging off the pilfering of the city's merchandise.

Manning refilled Dunne's glass. Dunne tried to wave him off, but Manning poured it full. "On the house," he said with a regulation grin.

"I'm obliged, but this isn't an hour I'm accustomed to take a drink."

"Yer on your way to work?"

"In a bit."

"Well, if you've had no sleep, this will see you through to lunch."

Dunne didn't want to argue. He drank the shot in a single gulp and turned the glass over. He looked again to see if the clerk had returned, a platoon of embarrassed Metropolitans in tow, the job done right beneath their noses.

Manning set the glass right and refilled it. "Expecting someone?" he asked.

Dunne nodded. The whiskey burned its way across his tongue. His cheeks and ears reddened. What was it drove Dandy Dan to his ruin? Whiskey, for sure. But what was it drove him to whiskey? *A piece of advice delivered that day in the penitentiary on Blackwells Island, Dan's hands shaking, the eyes bulging out of his head:* Get out while there's time, Jim. Set yourself up in a saloon if you can.

Sure, Dan, first thing.

Manning went back to rubbing glasses. "Them streets are no place for loitering, not today, not with the mood hereabouts."

Dunne felt a little dizzy. He pulled a stool up to the window and sat. Still no sign of the Metropolitans. The pleasure of seeing their faces. They were getting used to having things their way, maybe not in the Five Points or Corlears Hook, where they only ventured to collect the dead, squads of them coming down the middle of the street and the people on the stoops and rooftops screaming, *Bloody peelers, go back where you came from! Booly dog sons of bitches!* But everywhere else they'd set to sniffing and barking, the watchdogs of the respectable quarters of the city, bloodhounds for the propertied classes. Had a special squad to patrol the dollar side of Broadway, and some of them didn't wear uniforms, just walked around, listening, spying, looking for the chance to pounce. There was the Strong-Arm Squad, or the Iron Brigade, as some had taken to call it, roaming the streets at all hours, climbing across rooftops or hiding in doorways or lurking in alleyways. After dusk, they'd be up the ass of anyone looked out of place. If you was lucky or seemed half-respectable, they'd let you give an explanation, but all the while they'd be wearing that smirk on their faces and tapping the locust sticks against the sides of their legs, like they was just waiting for you to finish so they could lay you out. And it didn't stop with the Metropolitans. Some of the storekeepers had banded together to hire their own detective force; so had the railroads and hotels. The pack grew bigger all the time, the worst of them your own kind, Paddies who barely escaped spending their days in the penitentiary now hunting the very friends they once ran with.

Manning stopped rubbing. "Tell me who you're waiting for, and there's a chance I can tell you whether you're wasting your time. Ain't trying to pry, wouldn't have lasted in this trade all these years if I got into such a habit, but I know most everyone around here. Rare the man frequents these paving stones ain't one time or other been a visitor to Mike Manning's."

On the wall above Manning, Robert Emmet continued to point to the street, arm outstretched, a martyr framed and frozen in his moment in the dock, his defiant legend in block letters across the bottom of the picture: LET NO MAN WRITE MY EPITAPH.

Dandy Dan made out of the patriot martyr's life a rule: Trust no one, least of all your own. Christ Himself learned that lesson on the Cross. Wasn't a Roman or a Greek sold Him for thirty sovereigns but a brother Jew. Emmet followed that same road to the scaffold. Trusted one of his own, forgetting that while the sons of Israel produced the true and original Judas, it was the Irish perfected the type, spewing forth rank after rank of Judases in every generation.

Dunne fingered his glass. Was that what drove Dandy Dan to drink? Fear of betrayal? In truth, he was never betrayed. Was himself he betrayed in the end.

"Rare the man passed this way ain't made my acquaintance," Manning said again. He twisted the bar rag around his fist. Most times, all he had to do was stand there as the whiskey flowed across the bar and wait until the backwash brought its predictable flood of stories, facts, confessions, the disappointments, hopes, hurts men nursed in their hearts, secrets they told no one else, not even a priest. He wasn't used to having to wring out bits of intelligence drop by drop.

"You probably know him," Dunne said. "Seems everyone either does or says he does."

"Ach, then, sure I know him, can't be a doubt of it." Manning came and stood beside Dunne's stool, his hands roped behind his back in the tight grip of the rag. He stared intently at the street. "Who is it we're watching for?"

"John Morrissey." A name like the Holy Name of God, source of terror and awe, to be invoked rather than discussed.

The rag went limp in Manning's hands. His mouth hung open. "*The* John Morrissey?"

"The one and only."

"John Morrissey is to meet you here?"

"The corner of Catherine and Cherry was what he said."

"And he made no mention of me?"

"It's him who recommended this place to me."

Manning's face radiated only delight. He stepped outside and surveyed the street. Seeing no sign of Morrissey, he reentered. "Your man will have a drink with me, I'll insist on that. He's no stranger to me. Sure, it's years since we last met, him traveling a higher road, defender of our race, knocking the stuffing out of every rat-nosed Anglo-Saxon Protestant bastard ever stepped into the ring with him, bringing honor on us all, but there was a time the distance 'tween John Morrissey and Mike Manning wasn't so great. We both started as runners back in the forties, fetching our bread by seeing to the immigrants right off the boat, making sure they had a place to stay or a ticket to Albany. Never was a fiercer competition on the face of the earth, with Awful Gardner and his like biting the ears off them who threatened to take a piece of the business. Thought that as True Americans the Constitution give them alone the right to cheat and abuse the immigrant. Morrissey showed 'em. He opened the trade to Irishmen. I'm not claiming we was any band of saints, but we was gentler with our own than the True Americans had been. Sure, most times what we took was less, and whatever gouging and stealing went on, many the Irish heart was lifted to hear the voices of their own race upon setting foot in New York. Besides, if there was cheating, and there's no denying there was, the worst of it was directed against the Germans."

A customer entered and went to the rear of the bar, by the stove. Manning went off to serve him. "Soon as you see Morrissey, give me a holler," Manning said. "I'm goin' t'insist he set a foot in here, raise a glass to the times we shared."

More customers entered, louder than the earlier ones, faster to finish their drinks. They kept Manning busy. He stood on his toes and shouted over their heads to Dunne, "Remember, the minute he appears, you let me know!"

Dunne had no date with Morrissey. He had invoked his name in the hope that it would silence Manning and stop his questioning. That was the usual effect. The agents of the House of Morrissey were everywhere. Most times they were congenial, just doing their jobs, collecting rents on the properties Morrissey owned, lending money at a rate north of usurious, seeing to it that at election times the ballot boxes were squeezed full with a near unanimous return for Tammany. But sometimes their duties were less civil. Sometimes they made examples of those who welshed on their obligations or failed to settle their gambling debts at Morrissey's uptown faro palace. Bodies were fished out of the East and North rivers, faces bruised but still recognizable, and for this reason Morrissey's men were cordially greeted but usually left alone. Any conversation was theirs to start or finish. They were never questioned on the activities of the boss or on his whereabouts. But here was Manning, back at the window, still jawing. "I knew Jack Morrissey when he was fresh from Troy, arrived as a deckhand on a Hudson River steamer, an Irishman ready to fight every rat-nose in the city. From the first day he set foot here, he was an inspiration to us all."

The men at the bar were talking so loudly that Dunne had to lean close to Manning to hear what he was saying. They yelled for another round and banged their glasses on the bar.

"O Christ," Manning said, "there's no telling what this day will bring, but that's why Morrissey is on his way, ain't it? He'll try to play the peacemaker. Maybe the men will listen to him. It's the nigger got the men so riled, bad cess to him. 'Tis a fearsome enough affair when any man be brought in to break a strike, but to bring in the nigger to do it is to spit in the face of every laboring man in this city. And what can John Morrissey do about that? Can he promise the men they won't be drafted and sent to free the niggers who'll take their jobs? Can he give each of 'em the three hundred dollars needed to buy his way out of the draft?" The shouting and banging grew louder. Manning scurried back to his bartending.

Dunne glanced at the clock that hung beneath the picture of Robert Emmet. It was almost nine. Still no sign of the clerk and his posse of Metropolitans, perplexity on their faces because the special gratuities they received from the management of Brooks Brothers were now in danger. They hadn't been alert enough to prevent a break-in, which is what they get paid for, and why reward a shepherd who fails to guard the sheep? Unfortunately, the two piles of greenbacks in the safe hadn't been what they seemed at first. The bulk wasn't notes but receipts, the one bundled on top of the other, a paper version of fool's gold. Enough to make your heart leap when the door swung open, before a quick thumbing revealed the truth: a grand total of twenty-eight dollars. At that point the decision made to stick around, seek some satisfaction from the embarrassment of the booly dogs.

Another crew of longshoremen made a loud arrival in the saloon. Manning worked feverishly to serve them. The stove contained only a skinball's portion of coal, a small pile in which each lump had been counted out until the minimum to sustain a fire was reached, but the room had become so crowded it felt warm and close.

A curtain of steam began to form across the window. Dunne put his sleeve to the glass and wiped a half circle clean. At first he almost looked for Morrissey, as though the story he had told

Manning were true. The Metropolitans were nowhere in sight, but Catherine Street was becoming thick with laborers.

"Christ," Manning said. "I wish your man would come."

"Patience," Dunne said.

Dandy Dan O'Neill's advice.

The first question he put: Can you cultivate in yourself a talent for waiting? *Hardly knew what he was talking about. The whole town in motion, nothing and nobody about to wait, everybody going about like they was in a walk-around in a minstrel show, packs of kids running up Roosevelt Street and Chatham Square, a drunken Negro sailor whose pockets had just been ripped open screaming at the top of his lungs,* Come back here, you Paddy sons of bitches, *and us taunting him,* Catch us if you can, nigger, nigger, nigger. *Us milling around McGirl's Ale House on Canal, where Anna O'Brien rented the second floor, the sounds of Anna's girls and their marks floating out into the street, picked up by our voices, echoed, a choir of moans and laughter. Us waiting at the corner of Houston to catch a glimpse of Big John Morrissey and his entourage as they'd start their nightly stroll down Broadway, swaggering along, copper-headed canes at their sides, looking for some band of True Americans to try to push them into the gutter, us trailing behind like gulls behind a scow, screeching encouragement,* Give it to the rat-noses!

Dandy Dan knew everyone, the whores, politicians, barmen, drovers, actors, the bare-knucklers and the sports, whether you was mighty or lowly didn't matter, he'd make conversation and listen to what you had to say. Always listening, watching, sizing it up. Never seemed in a hurry. Was outside the Atlantic Garden he picked me out, put his hand on my shoulder, a kind of ordination, like when the bishop puts his hand on the head of a man about to be a priest.

Just stood there dumb, not knowing what to answer, and stared up at him in his wide-brimmed straw hat, white coat, and flowing silk cravat, the wax in his mustache glistening in the light from the gas lamps at the Garden's entrance. In the background a band played that spittoon music the Germans love, all brass and blow, and the kids was running up and down the street, shouting and screaming, Runnin' a race wid a shootin' star, Oh! Doo-dah day!

Come on, Jimmy!

Didn't move. Stayed there with Dandy Dan. Says he, You'll have to work hard. Be prompt, alert, obedient. But you'll make a life for yourself. What do you say?

Yeah.

Manning was out from behind the bar. He wiped his forehead with the bar rag. "Holy Mary, Mother of God," he said, "there's gonna be trouble, no doubt it, there'll be no avoiding it now, not unless Morrissey can do something." Manning's breath smelled of cheese and onions, a skinball's breakfast, the same stale remnants he put out for his customers. "Are you listening to me, man?" Manning took grip of Dunne's arm. "It's a terrible mood the men are in, no telling the harm they'll do to themselves or others. Morrissey has got to try to stop them!"

The whiskey had settled on Dunne's brain like snow, muffling sounds, obscuring the world in a soft, fuzzy blanket, the hard edges made round and unthreatening. He had broken almost all of Dandy Dan's rules in a single morning. Lingering. Being conspicuous. Pulling a job in the same place you lived. Why? Maybe for the same reason Dandy Dan did, whatever that was. *Seen him that time right before Christmas, about a month before he died. Rode the ferry over to Blackwells Island. The cold was fierce, the trip only a couple of hundred yards, but it must have taken an hour, the ice was so thick. Got to the penitentiary half-frozen and it was colder in that hole than out. Dan was doing ninety days for stealing a bag of oranges. More a ghost than a man at that point, standing there in what looked like a gray sack, shivering. Held a stick with a clump of straw at the end of it, his hands fumbling as he tried to tie them together. Must have been ten men at that table making brooms. They all looked as bad as Dan. Don't know how they stayed alive in that cold. Dan's face was already as white and sunken as a dead man's, his eyes as flat and lifeless as a fish's. His hands shook something terrible. Slipped the booly dog a piece of silver so he'd look the other direction when Dan took the flask. Dan wrapped his hands in the big burlap sleeves of the garment he was wearing. He cradled the flask, lifted it slowly to his lips, but the shaking was so strong half the liquor poured over his chin.*

Your friends are asking for you, Dan.

My friends have written me off as dead.

The truth. Nobody wanted any part of him. Only one showed him any kindness was Mosie Pick, the gutter-rag fencer of old cups and dented silver. Her place was near the railroad station, on Twenty-third Street and Fourth Avenue, in the middle of the basement rooms where the whores worked so quick the travelers never missed their trains. As a favor, Mosie would occasionally fence watches or rings the whores lifted from their marks, but mostly she dealt in junk. A big lumbering Jewess, she let Dandy Dan sleep in the back room, with the score of stray cats she gave shelter to, but told him, Don't bring none of your loot back here. It'll only get me arrested.

At that point, Dan was lifting whatever he could get his hands on, nails, shirts, purses, pens, he'd stuff his pockets and go hurtling into a crowd, stumbling across streets and sidewalks, almost getting himself killed as he made his escape. That's how he landed on Blackwells Island. Mosie took him back when he was released. She's the one paid for the funeral. After Dan died, someone slit her throat, ransacked her place, took whatever money she'd stored up. Metropolitans didn't waste much time trying to find out who done it. More interested in protecting places like Brooks Brothers and collecting their tribute. Poor Mosie. But that's the way in this town: The good go to the grave, the greedy open their own bank, which is what Waldo Capshaw could do if he wanted. The worst of the lot. A nose longer and sharper than a rat's, him perched behind that uptown façade, the purple drapes framing the windows and the shades all drawn, the trappings of a respectability Waldo wanted the world to think he was born to. Liked to act like he was a gentleman, only everybody knew he

*was nothing but a fence, the tightest and meanest ever lived. Left
a note at the hotel last evening:* Must see you the day after tomorrow. Can you be at my place at four?

Maybe, Waldo. If there ain't anything better to do.

Manning was back in his position behind the bar. He fired
round after round of whiskey at the hordes in front of him. From
outside a shout went up. A group of urchins ran down the street.
"The boolys is coming!" they cried. "The booly dogs is here!"

The bar began to empty. The sidewalk was crammed with
people. They were quiet and sullen until a column of police turned
off the Bowery and headed down Catherine Street, then they
erupted into hoots and catcalls.

Manning went to the rear of the bar and lugged out a large,
flat piece of wood. "Give me a hand," he said to Dunne as
he dragged it through the front door. He tried to fit it across
the window but couldn't get it to stay in place. Dunne hadn't
moved. Manning rapped on the window and yelled at him,
"Please, man, give me a hand! They'll wreck everythin' once they
get started, won't matter who it belongs to!" His voice was muffled by the glass. It had a faraway tone. "For God's sake, man,
please!"

Dunne stepped outside. He grabbed the end of the panel and
helped lift it into place. Manning twisted two snap bolts to secure
it. The column of police had halted outside Brooks Brothers. The
head clerk rushed out and talked animatedly to the policeman in
charge.

"Ach," Manning said. "We're in for it now. Not even John
Morrissey can stop it."

Many of the men were armed with sticks, bottles, paving
stones, or baling hooks, which they held at their sides out of view
of the police. The children continued to frolic in the street, running up to the Metropolitans, taunting them, and then running
away. The chief policeman went on talking with the Brooks
Brothers clerk, seemingly unperturbed by the size and mood of
the mob.

Manning pointed to the corner of Cherry Street, where another column of police had appeared. "It's gonna be another Bull Run!" he cried. "It'll be ruin for us all!" He went back to the entrance of the saloon. "You better warn Morrissey!" He slammed the door shut behind him and pulled down a tattered green shade.

The two columns of police merged into one solid body of four ranks, ten men to a rank. Each Metropolitan held his locust stick in front of him. After a few minutes, the chief policeman gave the order for them to move forward. Men lifted their weapons and waved them at the police. There was a collective roar, and the crowd surged into the street. Dunne felt himself being dragged along. "Bloody peelers!" the man beside him yelled. The police halted a distance away. Dunne turned and pushed his way toward the rear of the crowd. He was almost free when an arm came around his neck, a bulky band of hardened muscle that pulled so tight he felt as if he might black out. He tried to reach into his inner pocket to grab the iron claw, but before he could, the arm released him and he was shoved so hard he lost his balance and slammed into the side of a building. When he got up, he was surrounded by dockworkers. The one who had held him around the neck, a hulking, clean-shaven man in a cloth cap, stuck his finger to the tip of Dunne's nose. In his other hand he held a baling hook.

"You're a newspaperman, ain't ya? Come down here to spy!"

"Stick him!" a voice in the crowd yelled. "Stick him in the balls!"

"I'm no newspaperman," Dunne said.

"Oh no?" the man said. "Then what are you? A bloody informer in the pay of the master informer, the chief Republican nigger-lover, Robert Noonan?"

Dunne slipped his hand into the interior pocket of his pants and gripped the iron claw. He marked the spot in the middle of the man's forehead where he would land it. "All I'm doing is trying to make a living, that's the only reason I'm here, as a drummer for Alton's Distillers, been trying to sell Manning on our stuff for weeks now."

"A lyin' shit is what you are. Manning ain't never sold anythin' but his own horse piss."

"Don't stop me from trying to sell him ours, does it?"

"I seen him in Manning's before today," another man said.
"He's telling the truth about that."

From down by the river came a swelling wave of shouting.
A boy ran up. "The men is stormin' the pier!" he yelled. "They're
gonna get the niggers! Come on!"

"Go try to sell that old stinkbug whatever piss it is that
you're peddling," the ringleader said. "Couldn't be worse than
the piss he already pours." He turned away and pushed his way
through the crowd.

At the bottom of Catherine Street, a mass of men pressed
close around the cast-iron façade of the pier. Those in front clambered up onto the grates that covered the entrance. They rocked
them back and forth until the hinges groaned with their weight.
More men climbed on and shook the metalwork.

"Get the niggers! Get the niggers!" the crowd shouted as
encouragement to the scores of men hanging from the gates. Several boys scampered to the top. Just as they reached it, the hinges
surrendered and ripped loose with a loud crack. Men jumped free
as the gates crashed down. The mob pressed ahead. Those on the
ground jumped to their feet to avoid being trampled. To the right
of the pier, a band of about twelve black men bolted out from
behind a metal door. They stayed as close together as they could,
running in a pack across South Street and up Catherine, toward
the phalanx of police.

The dockworkers in the rear of the crowd that had surged
onto the pier saw what was happening. "The niggers are getting
away!" a woman screamed. The dockworkers ran to block the
black men's path, their sticks and baling hooks poised above their
heads. "Get the thievin' sons of bitches, the boss's darlin's!" a
white-haired crone wailed from the second floor of a building on
the east side of Catherine. The flying wedge of blacks had gone
only a dozen yards when the dockworkers cut them off. Dunne
found himself between the two groups.

The black man at the front of the wedge was short and sturdy. He wore a canvas duster over his overalls that came down to his ankles. He reached into the pocket and pulled out a revolver. He pointed it at Dunne. Dunne put his hands in the air. He heard the scrape of hobnails on the paving stones behind him.

"Put it away, nigger." It was the ringleader's voice. "It ain't gonna do you no good. Your days of takin' the bread outta the mouths of workingmen is over."

"Get out of the way, Paddy bastard," the black man said. "I'm givin' you fair warning."

The scuff of heavy boots drew closer. The black man fired twice. Dunne threw himself against the wall. The ringleader and another man lay on the ground, writhing and screaming. Suddenly, the police charged down Catherine, flailing with their sticks. The front row of the mob offered resistance, tossing stones and bottles, hitting back with their baling hooks, but soon they broke and scattered into alleyways and buildings.

The Metropolitans formed a cordon around the blacks and the two wounded men, a ring that also caught Dunne and several dockworkers. A sergeant of police disarmed the black man. He had the wounded men carried away.

The old woman leaned out the window across the street. She pointed at the sergeant. "May God and His Holy Mother damn you to hell, Frankie O'Donnell! May They turn Their backs on you at the hour of your death! May They close Their ears to your pleas for water as the flames of hell devour your flesh!"

Sergeant O'Donnell walked about as if he didn't hear her. Finally, when she didn't stop, he told two policemen, "Go over there and get that witch out of that window." They ran toward her building.

"You bloody whore, O'Donnell! Selling your own into slavery, defending niggers while Irish women and children go without bread, you and the likes of you, the Noonans of this world! You're not worth my spit!" She let go a shower of it on the two policemen who were forcing open the downstairs door.

She shook her fist. "God's curse on ye all!" The two policemen suddenly appeared behind her and pulled her away from the window.

O'Donnell ordered the police to take the blacks back to the Bowery. Two of the dockworkers refused to give their names, so he had them handcuffed and sent along with the blacks. He looked Dunne up and down. He had a scowl on his face.

"Do I know you?" he said.

"Not likely," Dunne said. "I'm a Brooklyn man."

"What are you doing here?"

"Took the ferry over last night to go to a minstrel show, and you know how things are, Sergeant, one thing led to another and I ended up staying the night. Just coming to the ferry when I got caught in these proceedings."

O'Donnell squinted as he studied Dunne's face. "We ever met?"

"Not that I remember."

Dunne had been arrested only twice. First time, he was thirteen. Had flown the Orphan Asylum the year before. Was pinched for trying to lift some rat-nose's watch while standing next to him on the Broadway coach. Just a silly kid. He would have been sent back to the Asylum and been out again in a month if the Children's Aid Society hadn't gotten custody and shipped him west. Next time was on the day after the great battle in Paradise Square, the Dead Rabbits and the Plug Uglies in alliance against the Bowery Boys, the Paddies versus the True Americans for control of the East Side, the last stand of the rat-noses before the Irish sent them packing and claimed dominion. July 1857. A great day it was until the militia arrived, sealed off the streets, and the Metropolitans went door-to-door, dragging out suspects. He couldn't remember the face of the policeman who had found him in Tom Cahill's cellar, pulled him by his hair up the stairs. Perhaps O'Donnell had been the man.

"What's your line of business?" O'Donnell said.

"I sell tombstones at the Green-Wood Cemetery. Maybe you've family there, maybe that's where we've met."

"None of mine is buried in Brooklyn, thank you."

On the northwest corner of South and Catherine streets, a small mob had formed again. They screamed curses at the contingent of police that had stayed with O'Donnell. One of them threw a rock that fell far short and clattered across the paving stones. The policemen looked at one another uneasily. They were visibly anxious to rejoin the main body of men back on the Bowery.

O'Donnell said, "Maybe the best thing is for you to come along with us."

"O Jesus, Sergeant," Dunne said. "I'll be in trouble enough for missin' work, never mind if I'm arrested for nothin' more than the misfortune of walkin' in on a riot."

Another rock hit the pavement. It struck closer than the one before. A policeman called O'Donnell's attention to the crowd that was gathering on the rooftops of the buildings across the street.

"Goddamn it," O'Donnell shouted, "I ordered them roofs cleared and occupied." O'Donnell turned to Dunne. "Get out of my sight," he said. "If I see you again, I'll have you clubbed senseless. No questions, no conversations, just a good crack across the head." He marched the men toward the Bowery.

Dunne walked straight toward the Catherine Street ferryhouse. He stopped at the corner of South Street. Some boys had taken a bed sheet, laid it over the puddles of blood left by the men who had been shot, and then nailed it to a long stick. They scrambled up and down the street, waving it like a flag. From the rooftops that the police had failed to secure, a choir of women shouted encouragement. The boys followed O'Donnell's men up the street, running as close as they could without being grabbed. One of them ran ahead and fluttered the bloody sheet in front of O'Donnell's face. "Come on, you peelers!" he yelled. "Come on and show us how brave you are! Nigger-loving sons of bitches! Murderers of your own people!" O'Donnell lunged at the boy, who darted out of his grasp.

O'Donnell halted his men outside Brooks Brothers. A platoon of police came down from the Bowery to join him. O'Donnell paced back and forth in front of them. He never took his eyes off the crowd.

On South Street, from the direction of the Governors Island ferry, came another flock of street urchins. They ran at breakneck speed. One of them collided with Dunne and went sprawling. He clambered to his feet. The soldiers is comin'!" he yelled. "A whole pack of 'em!" He ran off, shouting his news.

Dunne saw them in the distance, a column of blue coats, bayonets fixed, campaign caps slouched forward over their eyes. The crowds that had filled South Street instantly parted to let them through, and the soldiers moved with an easy gait, muskets bobbing on their shoulders, seemingly oblivious to the uproar around them. Even at a distance it was obvious to Dunne that these weren't militia, skittish civilians whose uniforms couldn't masquerade their fear. These were real soldiers, part of the Governors Island garrison, many of them wounded veterans of two years of war. Dunne could see that once the column reached the intersection of Catherine and South, the mob would be caught in a vise, the police to the north, the soldiers to the west, a rout in the making. He hurried across the street toward the ferry-house. Three short blasts of a steam whistle warned him the ferry was about to depart. He ran through the ferry-house, his steps echoing through the emptiness of the cavernous interior. The boat was pulling out, already a few feet from the docking ramp, and Dunne took the distance at a leap. He caught on to the gate at the stern of the boat, and a deckhand grabbed hold of him and helped him aboard.

"Can't blame ya a bit for riskin' your neck to get out of there," the deckhand said. "A daft enough city when the sun is shining and the world is spinning in proper order, never mind when they're wagin' war in the streets." He took Dunne's fare. "I've never figured it out: Is it the people make the place crazy, or is it the place makes the people crazy? A little of both, I suppose."

A heavy rain began to fall. Dunne hurried toward the cabin. The deckhand followed him inside. "Me, I thank God I was born

and reared in Brooklyn," the deckhand said. "Only a river between us, but might as well be an ocean. Ain't two more different
races on the face of this earth than Brooklyn people and Yorkers.
We know how to behave, that's the gist of it, not regardin' lyin',
cheatin', and stealin' as the normal way. Tell ya this, as long as
we got this river between us, the good people of Brooklyn has
some protection, but it ever dried up, we'd be done for. The Yorkers would have the place overrun by noon of the first day."

Dunne took a seat by the window. Only a handful of other
passengers. He picked up a newspaper and pretended to read. The
ferry went ahead slowly, its whistle shrilling a warning to the river
traffic to steer clear and respect its right-of-way. Outside, all that
was visible in the gray-black mist were the gliding shadows of
other boats. It was a long time since Dunne had been on the East
River, not since he had gone to see Dandy Dan on Blackwells
Island. He put down the paper and watched the beads of rain
race down the glass, one into another, ceaselessly. Somewhere
north, beyond Blackwells Island, where the East River meets the
Harlem, was Randalls Island, his boyhood home, in the sense that
it was where he had been for the longest single stretch. *Fog and
rain mostly, at least that's the memory of it. Must have been
sunny, hot days aplenty over those four years, but it's not them
that stick in the mind. The cold and wet is what's there. Cold
gruel to eat. Cold tea to drink. The smell of damp sheets and
pillows, musty, moldy, the black lettering on the covering the first
thing you saw every morning:* THE NEW-YORK ORPHAN ASYLUM.

*The last year there, on a frosty, windy afternoon, the warders
brought everyone down to the south end of the island, from the
smallest kids who could barely walk to the biggest. They gave out
drums and flags. Only thing to ward against the cold was the thin
gray smock everybody got, boys and girls alike, no warmth in
them clothes of any kind. Walked back and forth as the sun got
hid by clouds and the wind off the river grew fierce, the little ones
crying and whining, the warders telling them to keep moving, till
finally the steamer appeared, a gleaming white boat trailing fat,
glorious plumes of creamy smoke across the darkening sky. Pulled*

so close to shore you could see the plush red cabin and the waiters carrying trays of drinks and food. The warders said that Miss Jenny Lind, "The Swedish Nightingale," wished to pay a visit to the orphan children that was the partial beneficiaries of the proceeds from her last concert at Castle Garden. Probably the only population in the city of New York, besides them in the lunatic asylum, didn't have a clue who Jenny Lind was, and some of the little ones expected she'd be a real nightingale, half woman, half bird, fluttering in the sky. No such creature appeared. The boat idled off shore. Been late leaving the city and the captain wanted to be through the Hell Gate before dark, so the only glimpse of Miss Lind came when she appeared briefly on deck, a shawl around her shoulders, and at her side a bulging figure who the warders said was the great impresario and bunko hisself, Mr. P. T. Barnum.

Hadn't been so cold, some of the kids would have been grievously disappointed to discover that the Swedish Nightingale wasn't covered with feathers, but they was too frozen to notice, jumping up and down, banging their drums, doing everything possible to fight off the cold. Boat only stayed a few minutes more, long enough for the newspapermen to scribble a fancy description of the city's gratitude for Miss Lind's generosity as demonstrated by the singing, dancing inmates of the New-York Orphan Asylum. Then it sailed off, leaving behind nothing but its tail of luxurious smoke, and everyone ran as fast as they could to the orphanage, the only time we was ever eager to get back behind its doors.

Next evening, two of the kids put a log in the water and tried to sail to the Manhattan shore. Couldn't have lasted long in water that cold, with the tides so strong. Was a month before the river gave them up, their bodies found floating in Deadman's Bend, across from Corlears Hook.

The ferry docked in Brooklyn with a loud thud. Dunne got off. He walked a block to the Swordsman Hotel. The streets were busy but seemed far removed from the battle scene across the river. The Swordsman was a faded wooden building that catered to the whores who worked the ferry trade. "No Sailors," read the sign on the door. Dunne paid the charge for a room. The clerk winked as he handed him the key. "Should any visitors arrive, I'll send her right up to your room, sir."

"Do that," Dunne said.

The room was on the third floor. It held only a bed and a dresser. Dunne took off his shoes. He put his claw, file, and the loot from Brooks Brothers beneath the mattress. The pillow had a large stain on it the color of tobacco. Dunne took a handkerchief from his pocket and covered it. He put his head down. As disapproving as Dandy Dan would have been of his conduct so far this day, of this Dunne knew Dan would approve. Rest, he was fond of saying, is the single most important thing a man in our line of work can get.

True enough, especially when scheduled to meet with Waldo Capshaw, a grudging, niggling croak of a man, the way all fences are, a Protestant True American to boot, the sharpest of that sharp race. An invitation to his house means a moneymaking scheme is afoot. Got to have your wits about you if you're not to be the goat.

Through the fragile walls of the hotel came the noise of huffing and grunting from next door, the mounting creak of bedsprings rising and falling, faster and faster, a momentary moan, then silence.

Well, Dunne thought, *there's one thing that's the same on both sides of the river.* In an instant he was asleep.

II

The rain scattered the small crowd in City Hall Park. The band of musician soldiers wrapped their bugles and drums in their canvas coverings. Men without umbrellas ran for the portico of the Hall of Records across Chambers Street, willing to risk pigeon droppings over rain. Stephen Collins Foster, umbrellaless, didn't run. He walked at his regular pace toward the Astor House.

As he went past the sagging, weather-beaten barracks that had been erected as a temporary measure two years before and had become a dreary and permanent part of the park, the music filled his head, the instruments still outside their canvas, the sounds forming themselves into notes and half notes, scales and bars, black marks on white paper, a three-cent royalty per sheet, thirty thousand in the first printing, a song for the nation's warriors, the printing presses never stopping, sixty thousand in the second printing, the presses *gwine to run all night, gwine to run all day, an' his rider's drunk in de old hayloft, Oh! Doo-dah, day!*

He stuck his hands into his pockets, the fingers numb and red. The traffic was heavy on Broadway, and he stood on the curb, the rain playing its own music in the puddle at his feet. *Dat, dat, dat, doo-dah, doo-dah.* A wagon went through the puddle, the monotoned rush of its wheels spraying red-brown water over his feet and pants. There was a break in the traffic. He ran across the street in front of a white omnibus with SOUTH FERRY in red letters on its sides. The driver pulled on the reins when he saw Foster, dragging the horses to a halt, and yelled an inaudible obscenity, but Foster was already on the pavement, running up the worn marble stairs into the rotunda of the Astor House. A throng of politicians, newsmen, brokers, and Army officers stood in front of the counters that encircled it. Behind the counters, men in white jackets carved steaming roasts and hams, sliced pies, shucked oysters and clams, laid portions onto white plates and pushed them across to the omnivorous crowd.

Foster listened: flatware clanging against dishes, dishes clanking against countertops, glasses clinking against glasses, a roar of voices echoing against marble walls and plaster ceilings. He rubbed his hands on his pants, blew on his fingers, and put them back into his pockets. He dug past the two nickels he knew were there, down to where a folded banknote could escape the touch of his benumbed fingers.

Nothing. Only the coins.

Most mornings, he groped his way out of the New England
Hotel, out of his cold bed, the sheets and blanket too thin to
warm his blood, down the Bowery to Catherine, into Mike Manning's Saloon, home to the cheapest whiskey outside of the Five
Points. He sat as close as he could to the cast-iron stove, the coal-
fired warmth pungent and piercing, going up his arms and legs,
into his bones, a penetrating warmth. But it was against the house
rules to sit there without a drink, so he put a nickel on the counter
for two shots of what the patrons called "Mike Manning's Revenge," colored camphine or rectified oil of turpentine, whichever
was selling cheaper, diluted, with a touch of beef broth to give it
the soft brown hue of real whiskey. Swill. But it let him sit there.
Manning would follow Foster back to his table by the stove, put
the shot glasses in front of him. Foster would lower his face almost to the level of the tabletop, tip the liquid into his mouth,
close his eyes, and swallow. A fire would start in his throat and
fall into his stomach. The warm glow would spread, kill the
thumping in his head, and still the tremble in his hand.

Money well spent, and Foster didn't begrudge Mike Manning
his nickel. Today he had gotten out of bed late and skipped his
visit to Manning's. He decided he would find refreshment elsewhere, in more convivial surroundings. But here, in the rotunda
of the Astor House, a nickel would buy only a glass of beer.
Access to the trays of food, too, yet two glasses of beer weren't
much to hold a man until evening, when the bar of the New
England Hotel would fill up and Jack Mulcahey or some other
soul, recognizing the nation's debt to America's first original musical voice, would advance him a loan and throw in a drink to
boot.

He was too wet and cold to think about going back out into
the rain. And if he didn't buy a drink and have something to eat,
one of the somber clerks would soon be over inquiring if he had
a room here or was waiting for a guest or required directions to
any of the city's numerous cultural and architectural points of
interest. No thanks. Two glasses of beer would have to do. Some
dry crackers. A slice of ham. Nothing too heavy. His stomach

rejected anything in bulk except beer or whiskey or Mike Manning's Revenge.

He stood and ate. He lifted the beer with both hands and licked the foam from the inner rim of the glass. The chorus of lunch continued around him. He walked straight ahead, past the potted ferns and the mahogany, marble-topped reception desk with its stern-faced clerks scribbling like music critics in the ledgers opened before them: *A Treatise on the Distemper of Current Popular Lyrics.* By Calliope. They loved anonymity. Clerks and critics. You rarely knew their names.

He sat in a lounge chair by the fire, stretching out his feet so close to the coals that the wet leather of his shoes hissed and steamed. He took out a pad of paper from his jacket pocket. It was soggy from the rain. He put it down by the side of the chair, facing the fire. Tomorrow morning he was scheduled to meet Daly at his publishing office on Grand Street with the song he had already been paid for. Something about summer and love. No, he had sold that one to Daly two years ago. "Our Bright Summer Days Are Gone." He printed the word *"GONE"* in large letters at the top of the page. Underneath he began to write, quickly, *"doo-dah, doo-dah, doo-dah."* He drew a line through it. Daly was a sympathetic type. Bumped into him by accident about a month ago. Hadn't seen him in over a year. Daly was waiting to catch the horsecar across Canal Street to the Hoboken ferry. Stepped into Sardmeister's. A glistening German place. Smell of beer and pickled meat. Bought dinner and put a twenty-dollar gold piece on the table. *Bring me a song. Something happy.*

Foster put the pencil tip on the paper. Nothing. Forget the war. Nobody wants to hear about it anymore. Tried that already. "We Are Coming, Father Abraam, 300,000 More." Music composed by Stephen C. Foster. Bad verse turned into bad lyrics. They wanted the music to save it. They paid for it, then said it sounded "too funereal." But they paid. He tapped the pencil tip on the paper. Morse code. *H-A-P-P-Y.*

Jane was working as a telegrapher at the Greenburg station of the Pennsylvania Railroad, a few miles outside of Pittsburgh.

Couldn't say he missed her. The pain he felt was not from absence but regret. He had put her through a decade of hell. At least for the first few years of their marriage, there had been money. And fame. Mrs. Stephen C. Foster, wife of America's minstrel genius. Those first days of their honeymoon in New York, the music publishers had fallen over themselves to entertain the couple. The reporters had written about them. At night, when they came back to the hotel, the clerk brought them to a small room behind the desk. It was filled with flowers, bottles of wine and liquor, gaily wrapped presents. "People have been dropping them off all day," the clerk said. "They read you were here in the papers." Foster picked up a small, bulky envelope. He opened it. Inside was a woman's black silk stocking with an address pinned to it. He and the clerk laughed. Jane blushed.

For the first two nights, he pretended to be so tired and filled with whiskey that he fell asleep. She lay with her breasts pressed against his back and her arm over his. He didn't move for what felt like hours. At dawn, he rose and went downstairs and ordered breakfast sent up. On the third night, she went up ahead while he uncorked a bottle and shared it with the desk clerk. He stayed longer than he should have. When he opened the door to the room, she was in bed with the quilt pulled up to her neck. *Close the door,* she said. She pushed down the quilt and knelt on the bed. She was naked. She cupped her breasts in her hands so that the nipples stuck out between her fingers. "Come to bed, my love," she said. She lay back on the bed, her legs open wide. In almost a whisper she sang, "Open thy lattice, love, listen to me! While the moon's in the sky and the breeze on the sea!"

Had she really sung that? The first song he ever published. The year before he left Pittsburgh. She had sung it to him once, but maybe not that night, maybe he was confusing that night with another time. What did it matter? Song or no song, he had dropped down on the bed beside her and put his hand over hers. What had he said? *I'm sorry, Jane.* His mouth was so dry his tongue felt as if it were made of cotton. He fell asleep. He tried many times after that. Usually after drinking heavily. A few times successfully. They made a daughter. But he came to their bed much as he had gone to milk the cow his father kept behind their house in Pittsburgh. Something to be avoided, if possible. A cloud that hung over you, a duty, a chore, another impediment to happiness. *Stephen,* Jane said, *what is it you want? Name it.* He had no answer. At least none he could speak.

He tapped out the letters of her name on the pad. A telegraph to nowhere. From outside he could hear the rumble of traffic on Broadway. Wheels, chains, horses, voices, peddlers, newsboys. Maybe a song about New York. No. New York had too much of its own music. It couldn't carry one tune. It would drown a single song, smother it. New York gave you freedom, indulged tastes and vices that could get you hanged somewhere else, but at a price. Silence. An inability to concentrate. And when you could no longer pay that price, what then?

Last night, he had walked with Mulcahey from the hotel, across the Bowery, down Catherine Street, to the ferry slip. They stood in the mist by the river. What did Mulcahey call it? The Swine-nee River. Sympathetic but sarcastic. As if he had a grudge against the whole world. A note of bitterness. All the Irish seemed to have it. Mulcahey sang in his tenor voice, "Way down upon the Swine-nee River, far, far from Rome." The stench of low tide hung over the entire area, from the river all the way over to the Five Points. It was always low tide in the Five Points. Muck and rot, the odor of lives left behind by a receding tide. But there was solace as well as squalor. Solace for everyone, for darkies and Paddies, for gentlemen and knaves, even for Stephen Foster: grandson of James Foster, one of Washington's soldiers at York-town; connected, through his sister's marriage, to the family of James Buchanan, former president of the United States; brother of William Foster, a vice president of the Pennsylvania Railroad. He had been born on the same day that Jefferson and Adams died, the fourth of July, a real live Yankee Doodle, born to write America's songs. Stephen Foster: wife-deserter; occupant of the attic room in a third-rate hotel; borrower extraordinaire from a host of Bowery habitués; musical has-been; drunk, cadger of drinks, swiller of Mike Manning's Revenge; indulger of unspeakable desires. In the Five Points, amid the tumbledown buildings, the alleys, the basement beer places, the attics and back rooms, there was a vice for every taste. The only question was price.

Foster had been in New York three years now, paying the price for his freedom. Six songs in 1860, the year he came for good, fifteen in 1861, seventeen in 1862, twenty-three so far this year. Most were swill. The musical equivalent of two shots of five-cent whiskey. The price kept going down, but there was always somebody willing to buy the name of Stephen C. Foster to print on music sheets. The world still waited for the songs. The people in the streets and in the armies, the men and women in the wagons pushing west, the bargemen, the fishermen, the firemen, they still expected a new tune, notes that would echo in their collective throat, the same song sung from coast to coast. It was only the snobs who hated his music. Workmen whistled it, they said. It had taken hold of the popular mind, particularly the young, repeated without musical emotion so as to persecute and haunt the acute, sensitive nerves of deeply musical persons. Such tunes were hummed and whistled involuntarily, they said, traveling through the populace like a mild form of the pox, breaking out like a morbid irritation of the skin.

He scratched his head. He dug his fingernails into the raw itchiness along his part. Lice. It could be. A gift of Dolan's New England Hotel. He ran both his hands over his hair, swept it back from his face. He propped his head in his right hand, the elbow resting on the chair, his fingers digging beneath his hair and playing against his skull, *tap-tap-tap, tap-tap-tap.* Nothing.

He felt a bump. Which one was this? His fingers ran over it, measuring. Dr. Mordowner, a friend of his father's and a leading Pittsburgh phrenologist, had felt his head when he was a child. Dr. Mordowner had pressed the palms of his hands into Stephen's forehead, run them back atop the boy's ears to the base of the neck, stepped back, and looked Stephen in the face. "Amazing!" he shouted. He put his right hand back on Stephen's head, the palm resting on his brow. He pushed down so hard Stephen had to close his eyes. "My good man," Dr. Mordowner said to Stephen's father, "the frontal ridges on this child's head are the most prestigious external disclosure of the Organ of Tune that I have ever encountered!" The palm of Dr. Mordowner's hand felt hot. The heat seemed to grow more intense. Dr. Mordowner pressed harder. He had his other hand at the back of Stephen's head. The vise of prophecy. Stephen sensed something melting in his brain. River ice in springtime, breaking, a force of nature coming alive, rising, sweeping everything before it. An industry was being born. Minstrels in every city strumming his music, schoolchildren memorizing it, lovers serenading each other, even pious congregations borrowing it to praise the God of their manifest destiny, all their rhythms indebted to the boy whose head is held so tightly by Dr. Mordowner.

Foster fingered the bump again. It was right on top of his head. It was sore, probably from the other night. A soldier did it. Having gotten drunk in McSorley's, across from the Seventh Regiment Armory, Foster reverted to the southern accent that he used whenever he was sufficiently under the influence. The cadences of a southern gentleman. An affectation from his days in Cincinnati. His minstrel songs led many people to insist he must be a southerner. He obliged, especially when liquor slowed his mind to a crawl. He wasn't talking politics, he never did, but this bear of a soldier came from behind, lifted him up, turned him upside down, and banged his head into the floor. He lay on the floor. The soldier stood above him. "Goddamn cracker," he said. "Go back where you came from."

Foster rubbed his head. He pushed more hair aside, ran his fingers down above his ear. Another convexity. Was this what the phrenologists called Matrimony, Desire to Marry? It was a very small bump. Next to it was a slight depression. More likely this was Matrimony. He moved his hand to the back of his head. A large bump. Dr. Mordowner had called this Amativeness, Sexual Love. "Unnaturally large in a boy this size," Dr. Mordowner told his father. "Make sure he is occupied in healthful activities and does not spend a great deal of time by himself. The dimension of these amative proclivities could lead the boy into danger."

A great deal of time by himself. Then and now. Lonely. George Cooper had joined the Army, their partnership dissolved, all their songs sold outright, no claim on royalties, or on each other. Daly the music publisher was nice enough, but hardly a friend. The diminutive Mr. Dunne, who lived on the second floor of the hotel, was cordial in his way. Offered his umbrella and was good for the occasional loan. But a secretive type. Very young, very quiet: an odd marriage of attributes. Like Mulcahey, he seemed animated by resentment. Mulcahey at least was talkative and attentive. Tall, slim, long-legged, with the body of a dancer, he was generous with his encouragement and his money. Foster felt affection for him. He could afford far better than the New England Hotel. But there between the Bowery and the Five Points, Mulcahey was safe to do what would be dangerous elsewhere. He shared a room with his mulatto mistress, Eliza. They paraded the hotel arm in arm. She was almond-eyed and beautiful, coffee-colored, with a deep wave in her hair. The fullness of her lips made her face look as if she were pouting. But she was sweet-tempered.

Sometimes, when Eliza sat in the small chair by the desk in the lobby waiting for Mulcahey, Foster would stand at the far end of the hotel barroom and stare at her. She was unaware he was looking at her. How much she resembled Olivia. Even the way she sat, with her hands folded on her lap. Olivia sat that way when she put him to bed at night. Her lovely face in the candle-light, the soft pitch of her voice as she sang him to sleep. He was four when his father brought her home, a colored girl of twelve to help his mother. Amid the tedious decline from respectability that his father's drinking inflicted on the family, amid the stifling respectability of their house in Pittsburgh, she was like a purple flower, luxuriant and exotic, wildly out of place, as if an orchid from Africa had been placed in the window of their austere, wood-framed house, its white curtains always stiff and starched and disapproving.

She chased him through the high grass by the river, her laughter a kind of music. On Sunday afternoons, without his parents' knowledge, she took him to the Negro church. He watched through the rear door. The people swayed and danced. He had never heard the human voice make such sounds. She never talked about her past, and he never thought to ask. When he grew older and went to school, her chores became cooking and cleaning. She slept in the shed behind the house, in a tiny room above the cow stall. He sold his first song for three dollars and gave her one. On the day he left to work in Cincinnati, his parents stood straight and formal on the porch. Oh, how Olivia cried and carried on. *Oh, don't you cry for me.* Dear Olivia. A long time since anyone had cried for Stephen Foster.

Suicide? Was there a convexity for that? He felt around his head. You had to think about it, alone in a hotel attic when the wind rattled the window, a continuous noise: the point in the night when the knowledge struck you suddenly, as if for the first time, that you'd sold the rights and royalties to most of a life's work for $1,800, all of it long gone. You had to regard the instantaneous solution offered by the symmetry of the razor across the windpipe, a neat line.

The line between a songwriter and a hack? Where was it? Or, to be more honest, where had it been? Foster pulled his legs back from the fire. The ragged threads on the cuffs of his pants were singed and smoldering. He held his hands close to the low, intense flame of the coals, which had a heavy layer of ash on top of them, holding down the heat. He picked up his pad from beside the chair. The pages were wrinkled from the heat. He fanned the coals with the pad till the ashes rose up the chimney and the flames jumped. He threw the pad onto the fire and it turned black, smoking, crumpling, consuming itself in a hum of combustion.

Ten-line musical verse in which nine lines are identical. Simple harmony. Simple melody. Music in three chords. Music that set people singing, that for all its clichés was new, music to work by, to travel by, to pan for gold by, to load a gun by, to run a machine by, to go to war by, music for the people, and if not *of* the people, then at least an echo in their heads of some older tradition they no longer had time to cultivate, new music for a new way of life, a new industry for an America of cities and railroads, America in a hurry, with Stephen Foster stoking the engine of progress.

For "Old Folks at Home," Firth, Pond & Co. had kept two presses running all day, but even that hadn't been enough. They had to add a third, then a fourth. Up till that point, three thousand copies of an instrumental piece and five thousand of a song had been considered a great sale. "Old Folks" hit ten thousand in a month. *Gwine to run all day.* It raced ahead of "Oh! Susanna!" for which he'd received a flat payment of one hundred dollars. "Camptown Races" had sold more than five thousand copies at two cents a copy, and earned him just over one hundred dollars. *I keeps my money in an old tow bag.* The publishers were staggered by the success of "Old Folks." Desperate for money at the time, he sold the title space to E. P. Christy for fifteen dollars. "Old Folks at Home, an Ethiopian Melody as sung by the Christy Minstrels/Written and Composed by E. P. Christy." Still, Foster got the royalties. One hundred thousand copies at two cents a sheet. The Sutter's Mill of American popular music.

You write, a composer of operas once told him, in words of one syllable, with harmonic textures as naïve as the melodies. Your musical vocabulary is so impoverished that you repeat yourself over and over again. Foster stared into the grate. The pad became bloated with fire and began to collapse in on itself. Never claimed to be a composer of operas. Only said the songs were what people would want to sing. And that's what they did. Naïve melodies in ten million throats. You better listen. The people are telling you something. *All de world am sad and dreary, ebrywhere I roam.*

Feel these bumps: Causality, Desire to Know Why; Comparison, Perception of Resemblance; Sublimity, Love of Grandeur. They stood out on Foster's head. Because of them he could see what nobody else could see. Sheet music and the two-cent royalty were just a beginning. When he thought about it, his brain raced so fast that he couldn't keep up. Drink helped slow it down, but too often brought it to a halt. He sought balance. Last night, he had it—enough drink to slow rather than stop him. He told Mulcahey what he saw: a cast-iron box in every house, sound coming out of it at the turn of the tap like Croton water, song after song in succession, an unlimited profusion, beginning and ceasing at will. You pay a charge once a month, the same as for water, and you can turn the spigot on or off, at will.

They were standing at the end of a pier. River noises all around. Whistles, horns, screeching of gulls. Mulcahey dropped pebbles into the black water of the East River. It's no longer enough just to write music or to sing it, Foster said. You've got to know how to sell it, to create as well as to meet demand. Wed Hermes to Polyhymnia. Mulcahey dropped more pebbles. The circles rippled out toward infinity. The future belonged to the salesman. The country is overrun with inventions and inventors. The Patent Office can barely keep up. Machines for sawing, reaping, canning, digging ditches, cleaning streets, binding books, stitching shoes. The ones who grow rich won't be the inventors, but those with the ability to feel the bumps on the national cranium, decipher the shape of the people's desires, form those desires into a single vision of happiness, and go out and sell it.

Plug, plug, plug: That's the future. The lesson of a songwriter's career. Don't just wait for the public to decide what music it likes. Listen carefully as it hums. Measure its bumps. Anticipate the songs it wants to sing. The science of anthropometry has shown that despite all its variations, mankind comes in three basic sizes: small, medium, and large. Now all things are possible! Ready-made shirts, pants, jackets, dresses, blouses. Ready-made books, ideas, philosophies, politics, religions, music, culture. The world has become a marketplace. The same challenge for the philosopher as for the politician, the ironmonger, and the songwriter: Sell or die.

Mulcahey kept his eyes on the circles that widened out from the pebbles he dropped into the water. He dropped some more.

Plop, plop, plop. He started to sing: *Beautiful dreamer, wake unto me; starlight and dewdrops are waiting for thee.*

Foster watched the water. The East River. But it was not a river at all. Merely a column of water connecting the upper harbor to the Sound. Yet everyone called it a river. They chose not to think about it. They clung to the surface of things. Enough to drop a few pebbles and make the smallest of waves. A ship sounded its foghorn. *Over the streamlet vapors are borne, waiting to fade at the bright coming morn.* He could see the river for what it was. He could see through the vapors to the other shore. Not a dreamer at all, but a man waiting for history to catch up with him. He knew where the column of water led. He wasn't mesmerized by tiny circles, nor did he confuse ripplets with waves.

His problem was the same as his maternal granduncle's, Oliver Evans. Foster had never met him, but he heard the story repeated over and over again by his mother, one of the few that drew out any sign of passion or excitement in her. She was there the day Evans drove his steam engine out of the yard near the Schuylkill River, a clanging, banging, puffing monster, its copper boiler sticking a thick thumb of smoke into the air. Behind this engine Evans pulled a steam dredge mounted on a scow—the "Orukter Amphibole," he called it. He transported it through the quiet streets, scaring horses and dogs, sending a rush of birds into the air, the noise and smoke causing men and women to fear that the Last Judgment had arrived. A freewheeling steam engine that turned corners and climbed hills and pulled another ton of steam-driven machinery behind it. One more in a long line of Evans's inventions. A mill that ran itself, free of any human hand. A machine for carding wool that could turn out 1,500 cards a minute. A pump to bring enough water to satisfy the daily requirements of 25,000 people. He could have brought America into the Age of Steam a generation before Stephenson put England on rails. But he was dismissed as a dreamer until the day came when the waters of history caught up with him, lifting the notion of the "Orukter Amphibole" on its crest, carrying it into the future. A horde of salesmen now jumped in, infringing his patents, stealing his ideas, growing rich by selling what he had created and suffered for. *Sounds of the rude world heard in the day, lull'd by the moonlight have all passed away!*

"Beautiful Dreamer." Firth, Pond & Co. had paid for it and had the plates engraved for printing, but they'd never used it. Maybe Daly would be interested in buying it from them. Then he would have his song. But would Daly want his twenty dollars back? Foster sensed someone standing behind him.

"Are you waiting for a guest, sir?"

A face bent close to his. A long nose and chin, side-whiskers running to the lips, the hair parted in the middle, greased down close to the skull, smelling of pomade. Foster kept his eyes on the fire. A new layer of ash was forming over the coals.

"I'm digesting my lunch."

"Sir, these seats are for our guests and their visitors. If you wish to digest your meal, I would think a walk in the fresh air might help." The nameless clerk-critic stood next to the chair, his shiny black boots reflecting the golden-red coals. Foster sat still. The clerk didn't move. "Sir," he said again.

Foster got up. Without looking at the clerk, he walked across the lobby. Men and women hurried past him. They shook their umbrellas and folded them.

You never knew where an idea would come from. In the summer of 1849, the cholera struck Cincinnati. Iron tubs filled with charcoal burned at street corners and crossroads, the thick smoke a presumed antidote to the invisible vapors that carried the disease. The worst of it was among the immigrants and the Negroes. Their bodies piled up in the streets before the authorities could muster the men needed to bury them. Stephen moved out of the city to a small farm owned by a Mrs. Dodge. The landlady was thrilled with her tenant: Cincinnati's musical poet. Soon she had turned Stephen into a specimen. He couldn't eat a meal alone. There were always guests, friends of hers she wanted to introduce to the young and famous songwriter.

On a wet, cold day in September, a few days before he was scheduled to return to the city, Mrs. Dodge told him she had an acquaintance coming to tea who had recently lost a child to the cholera. She was in very great need of cheering up. Her husband, Calvin Stowe, was a minister and scholar. He taught at the Lane Theological Seminary. She came from a family of preachers. Her father was Lyman Beecher. Her brothers were preachers back east.

He expected a shy, proper, quiet woman. Mrs. Stowe surprised him. When he came into the room, she was standing by the window with Mrs. Dodge. Mrs. Stowe was a woman so small that her growth seemed to have been arrested in childhood. She walked over to Stephen without waiting for Mrs. Dodge to make the introductions.

He bowed slightly at the waist. She barely reached his chest. He stared down into her small, pale face. "Mr. Foster," she said, "while I find your music enjoyable, I find the lyrics to be offensive and vicious." He burst out laughing. He couldn't help himself. The incongruity of it, this diminutive woman in black striding over and, without the smallest amenities, launching into her sermon. His laughter didn't stop her. "You make the Negro an object of ridicule," she said. "You confirm the white man in his silly notions of a divinely conferred superiority." She had a piece of paper in her hand. She read from it:

> I jumped aboard the telegraph,
> And trabbled down de ribber,
> De 'lectric fluid magnified
> And killed five hundred nigger.

"You should know better, Mr. Foster. A man of your talents should be filling the country with the uplifting music of brotherhood, not such inanities. The Negro is not someone to be laughed at, Mr. Foster. For his suffering, God will exact a price. The laughter will stop. There will be tears instead."

Mrs. Dodge interposed herself. She handed them their cups

of tea. Foster smiled at Mrs. Stowe. He wasn't insulted. He liked
her direct way, always liked that in people, not having to figure
out where somebody stood. The Negro as a figure of tragedy. She
was on to something. The sadness of the Negro. The only one he
really knew was Olivia. A girl of sadness. Others never saw that
part of her, but he had. The way she cried. Such pain. And there
was also Uncle Ned, the free Negro who swept out the office. An
ancient, stooped man with a great air of tragedy, he died at the
beginning of the summer from the cholera. *No more hard work
for poor old Ned, He's gone whar de good niggers go.*

Sometimes, after work as a clerk in the steamboat office in
Cincinnati, Stephen would go down to the docks and watch the
gangs of Negroes load and unload the boats. They were men. He
had never given it much thought before. Never looked at Negroes
with any intent of figuring out who they were, no more than he
tried to distinguish the individual horses in the work teams that
endlessly hauled wagons to and from the docks. Now he watched
them. When the work stopped, they stood together in a group,
talking and looking over their shoulders at the white men who
oversaw them. Their whole way of speaking and gesticulating
changed when they were by themselves. There was a litheness to
their step, an energy and gracefulness, that they lost when the
whites returned. They threw back their heads and laughed. Loud
laughter. Rhythmical, playful, high-pitched. Yet there was something sly and mocking in it, conspiratorial. White people were
unnerved by it. They were sure it was at their expense, Sambo
and Cudjo making sport of their master, aping his walk or man-
nerisms, returning his contempt.

"Come over here, boys," the white man would yell, and the
Negroes would come. They could be coaxed into singing or commanded to dance or made into the butt of a joke, but they kept
the secret of their laughter to themselves, a subversive glare lingering above the broad, innocent smile.

What did they talk about among themselves? Foster thought
about approaching them but knew they would respond to him as
they did to all white men. The free Negroes were even more

guarded than the slaves. They hurried to end any conversation and get on their way. It had been impossible to talk to Ned about anything but the Bible and, once he was started on that subject, equally impossible to stop him.

Foster was astounded when a few years later Mrs. Stowe became the world's most famous author. Shrewd as well as outspoken, a true daughter of New England, she pushed aside Maria Monk's *Awful Disclosures of the Hôtel Dieu Nunnery,* with its exposé of popish sexual depravity, as America's favorite reading. In its place she put her noble Negro, patient, saintly Tom. Foster read the book. Which was further away from the real but impenetrable humanity of these black men and women? His Uncle Ned? Or her Uncle Tom? Still, he admired her. He never spoke to anyone about Negroes, never asserted what observation had confirmed to him: These are men. Mrs. Stowe had. Better yet, she had made a fortune at it. Good luck to her.

When he finished reading her book, he began writing a song based on it. The tragedy of the Negro. A man sold away from his family. He wrote it in the accounting ledger where he wrote the rough drafts of all his songs:

> *Oh, good night, good night, good night*
> *Poor Uncle Tom*
> *Grieve not for your old Kentucky home*
> *You're bound for a better land*
> *Old Uncle Tom.*

He crossed it out. The new opening came to him whole, in an entire sentence: *The sun shines bright in the old Kentucky home.* He called them darkies instead of niggers. The darkies the white man liked to see, *merry, all happy and bright,* but Mrs. Stowe's darkies also. The Negro of tragedy taken away from his family and home.

> *The head must bow*
> *And the back will have to bend*
> *Wherever the darkie may go . . .*

He heard that it was among the favorite songs that Confederate military bands liked to play. Rebels marching to a Negro lamenting that *the time has come when the darkies have to part.* Sentiments by Harriet Beecher Stowe. Music makes for strange bedfellows.

Foster stood by the doorway of the hotel, next to a potted palm. Wished he could remember what he had done with Dunne's umbrella. He glanced quickly in the direction of where he had been sitting. The clerk was standing in the middle of the lobby, staring. Foster walked outside. The clock atop City Hall said 4:00. The rain had changed into a soundless mizzle.

On the other side of Broadway, down to his right, was Barnum's Museum, its façade already ablaze with gaslight, a riot of banners bearing the images of birds and beasts and mermaids. On the balcony, above the door, five men in white gutta-percha coats with red-plumed hats sat on chairs and tuned their instruments. They prepared their siren song for the early-evening crowd. Pay attention, New York.

Oliver Evans had been a genius of steam and iron, of the mechanical arts. He lived with a lonely vision of the future, with ideas the people couldn't share, at least not in his lifetime. Barnum was a genius of tears and laughter, of the emotions. The shrewdest of the shrewd race of Connecticut Yankee peddlers, he understood the people in their multiple desires. No need to guess. He thought their thoughts as the child in the womb thinks its mother's thoughts. Barnum waits contentedly in the womb of his public, lets its thoughts and tastes shape him, and then, at the moment of parturition, emerges to give them the very things they knew they wanted but couldn't articulate. *Hurry, hurry, hurry, step right up, here for your viewing pleasure, the one, the only, the object of your desire!*

Three times Foster had left his name with the museum manager. Once, a brief note. *You may remember me. We met during a trip I made to New York ten years ago. I would like to discuss a business proposition of possible benefit to us both.*

No answer beyond "Mr. Barnum has your note."

The band struck up "The Star-Spangled Banner." Two years ago, the traffic and pedestrians would have come to a halt. Now they moved on, iron-covered wheels rattling over cobblestones, draymen shouting, a cacophony of conversations, no melody, no harmony, a thousand different songs being sung at once. *A few more days for to tote the weary load.* Doo-dah, doo-dah. After two years of war, even Barnum was having a problem getting the people's attention. But the people still needed to be entertained. The song industry wouldn't die. It was only a matter of listening, hearing the faint chord of the future, giving the people what they wanted.

Foster walked out into the pavement, into the middle of the two-way river of pedestrians that was pushing north and south. He stood and listened to the shuffle of wet feet. Two years ago, the bombs bursting in air above Fort Sumter, *whiz, crash, bang,* a strange new music to the nation's ears. A woman bumped into him. She gave him a startled look and walked on. Tramp, tramp, the troops are marching. The papers advertised a substantial reward for anyone who could produce "an American *Marseillaise* or a suitable Tyrtaean hymn." What was the song they were waiting to sing? *"Willie, My Brave, Our Willie Dear Is Dying, Willie's Gone to Heaven."* Not that. The song of the future. He would hear it. If anyone could, he would. From the direction of the North River came the long piercing stab of a steam whistle. Poor Oliver Evans.

> *Hey mister, you're blocking the way.*
> *Watch your back.*
> *Doo-dah, doo-dah.*

Barnum's band could barely be heard.

The song was there. Somewhere. He would find it. Just you wait, New York. Just you wait.

III

Jack Mulcahey claimed to be, in his own words, "a born minstrel," a claim that was true enough since, to begin with, he was born in 1832, the same year as the industry. But it was Tommy Rice who created the industry, which was why they called him "Daddy" Rice, a Yankee Doodle Irishman born in the Seventh Ward on Bancker Street, in the year before the Bancker family had petitioned to have the street renamed in honor of someone who either couldn't see or didn't mind the immigrant horde that had turned a dignified, elm-lined lane into a treeless, refuse-strewn, overpopulated confusion. That someone was the former president of the United States, James Madison, who offered no protest when Bancker was renamed Madison Street.

Rice was born on Madison (née Bancker) Street, in 1808; the industry came into being in either Louisville or Cincinnati, the location varying according to the level of alcohol in Daddy Rice's veins when he repeated the story in the bar of the New England Hotel, on Bayard Street, in those last performances of his life, while syphilis raced John Barleycorn for the honor of committing to eternity the man who'd done for the stage what Fulton had done for steam.

> First on de heel tap, den on de toe,
> Ebery time I wheel about I jump Jim Crow.
> Wheel about and turn about and do jis so,
> And ebery time I wheel about I jump Jim Crow.

Daddy Rice had suffered his second stroke in 1860, when Mulcahey first saw him do that immortal chorus, a limping old man, his right eye practically closed, his badly shaven face and neck spotted by tiny nicks and cuts amid gray stubble. But the old man came alive with that chorus, the limp disappearing, the left foot moving forward, *heel tap*, the right foot backward, *den on de toe*, a circular motion on one foot until he had his back to you, *wheel about*, and a leap into the air, perhaps not with the dramatic intensity of twenty years before but into the air nonetheless, *jump Jim Crow*. Everyone would clap because as people whose livelihood was the stage they knew, no matter how pathetic the old man or how repetitive his nearly nightly rendition of his original act, this was history, a living tableau of a moment that nobody in the room, except Daddy Rice, had been there to see.

If Daddy Rice was just setting sail on the mighty sea of whiskey, the location was definitely, positively, don't let anyone tell you different, Louisville. He remembered everything about it. The stable next to the redbrick hall on the dusty street directly opposite the Andrew Jackson Hotel. If the journey was more advanced, the sails filled with wind, the waves sweeping over the forecastle, it was Cincinnati, and Rice didn't care what you'd heard to the contrary. But if he wavered on *where* it happened, Rice never changed a detail of *how*. The version Jack Mulcahey heard for the first time in 1860 was, essentially, the version Rice always told.

Daddy Rice started in the theatre as a carpenter's apprentice at the Park Theatre on Park Row, and one night had to fill in for an actor who was drunk. It was a two-line bit as a British soldier. He never went back to carpentry. He did scores of small parts and then, in the fall of 1831, joined a company on circuit as actor and property man. The troupe played every small town it ran into, some not even on the map. A potpourri of stuff. A scene from Shakespeare. Some song and dance. Or maybe a play like Robinson's *The Rifle*, in which Daddy Rice, as a Kentucky cornfield Negro, first found himself in blackface.

They were at it six dusty, rainy, hot, cold, snowy, sunny months in churches, halls, saloons, and the only success Rice had was in a filler he did between acts, Paddy with the shillelagh and the shovel, the standard dumb Mick of the transatlantic, pan-Anglo stage who wouldn't know the difference between one end of a fork and the other unless he sat on it. It kept people in their seats, and Rice had no difficulty doing it because all he was doing was imitating his old man, an immigrant whose difficulties in America his son turned into parody, made the brogue thicker, the mind weaker, the ambitions fewer, the stoop steeper, the emotions sillier, the clothes raggier, until the audience recognized the universal Paddy. It went over fine, but Rice grew quickly tired of it. Then he walked in on the darkie idea. An industry was born!

The darkie was brushing and rubbing down a horse in the stable yard next to the theatre in Louisville (or Cincinnati), and Rice, on his way to a performance, noticed him right away because of his twisted shoulder. It was the same thing Rice's old man had, the shoulder turned in toward the chin and drawn up toward the ear, as if he had been born a hunchback and the hump had slipped inside his body and was trying to come out the other side. A queer resemblance. Rice was amazed two people could have an affliction so strange yet so similar, and he followed the charcoal replica of his old man into the stable, watched him shuffle across the stone floor, *heel tap, den on de toe,* singing his little song, and if those weren't exactly the words, well, *jump Jim Crow,* they were as close as Rice could come to understanding them.

He did the act the next night after practicing all day in his hotel room. Didn't tell a soul. Slapped on the charcoal paste just before he went on, Jim Crow instead of Paddy dancing across the stage, the audience at first surprised and quiet, maybe a little threatened by the novelty of this singing, dancing darkie, until they saw the shuffle and the jump, heard the funny little rhyme, adjusted to the sight of a white man's nigger pantomime, and brought the house down, ovation after ovation, shouts and yells, minstrelsy and the darkie song industry all born that evening in Cincinnati (or Louisville). Daddy Rice never played another part in his life until very near the end, when he couldn't dance anymore (except for the few seconds he would reenact the historic moment in the bar of the New England Hotel) and was signed up for the role of Uncle Tom in the eponymous play's Bowery production, in December of 1860.

He lost the role the second night. Mas'r George leaned over his pillow during the climactic death scene and said, "Oh, dear Uncle Tom! do wake—do speak once more! Look up! Here's Mas'r George—your own Mas'r George. Don't you know me?" Uncle Tom slept on, snoring.

Mas'r George whispered through clenched teeth, "Rice, you son of a bitch, wake up." He poked and prodded. He slapped his face, but Daddy Rice, having enjoyed a pre-performance celebration and reassured by the familiar feel of the burnt cork on his skin, slept on. The audience hooted, whistled, and laughed. Rice was fired. The next night, when Mulcahey made his debut with Brownlee's Minstrel Parade, he came back to the New England Hotel specifically to see the old man dance: Daddy Rice, the former stage Irishman, Jim Crow, and Uncle Tom. An American legend.

Rice died soon after that, a month or so after Stephen Foster, another legend down on his luck, moved into the hotel. Foster arranged the funeral. He talked to Mulcahey and George Holland and Frank Lynch and Dan "Dixie" Emmett, the city's leading minstrels, and they all contributed to meet the expenses, everyone except that notorious plagiarist and tightwad, Edwin Christy. It was the biggest theatrical funeral since Jack Diamond's in 1857. Another Paddy raised to prominence by the stage, Diamond had been America's greatest dancer of Ethiopian breakdowns, signed to a contract by P. T. Barnum himself, the first performer to command a salary of over one hundred dollars a week, until the drink did him in; his funeral had been paid for, like Rice's, by popular subscription.

"These men deserve monuments," Stephen Foster said to Mulcahey as they came down the church steps after Rice's funeral. "They've made an industry and given work to thousands."

Mulcahey moved into the New England Hotel once he was signed to an extended contract with Brownlee's. It was an actor's hotel. Names from the past and, some occupants hoped, from the future, living in a part of the island that ran from the Bowery to Broadway, from Chambers to Canal, where the country that surrounded it could find all its conscious and subconscious desires and fears conveniently located in one place: drink, whores, racial amalgamation, catamites, opium, sexual titillation, foreigners, unbridled debauchery, the wages, rewards, and consequences of every conceivable sin. Here the rules the young democracy had imposed on itself were, within limits, suspended, and Mulcahey found himself living in a room next to a mulatto woman, an actress, with a beautiful cocoa-colored face, whom the proprietor described as "the *Cuban* thespian" Señorita Therese La Plante. Therese couldn't speak a word of Spanish. It was said that she was really from Louisiana, a highborn octoroon whose father, a white cotton merchant, had shipped her off to a convent in Baltimore for her education. Therese played Eliza in the same production of *Uncle Tom* that Daddy Rice had lasted one night in; "Eliza," the broadside said, "as Mrs. Stowe described her: 'Rich, full, dark-eyed, with long lashes, ripples of silky black hair. The brown of her complexion gives way on the cheek to a perceptible blush, which deepens as the gaze of the strange man is fixed upon her in bold and undisguised admiration.' "

"Eliza" is what Mulcahey always called Therese and what she had come to call herself. He had planned only a short stay in the New England Hotel. Once his star was in the ascendancy he would move to the St. Nicholas on Broadway. But he stayed because of her. Eliza of the oval eyes and high cheekbones, Therese, Indian blood mixed with black and French, her brown pupils deep and lovely, her curly hair in deep waves around her face, black framing brown, the way it fell onto her shoulders, down to the top of her breasts, ah, Eliza, no minstrel boy ever wanted anything more, Eliza, drop your shift, the candlelight lineaments of your body without the hint of blush as the minstrel from next door, the man who bought you drinks and waited to meet you, serendipitously, in the hall, now invited, thank you, Eliza, to your bed, gazes intently on all your naked brownness.

Mulcahey walked up Broadway to the theatre past Meecham's Minstrels, the Coliseum Minstrels, and Mechanics' Hall, where Dan Emmett first played his song "Dixie," past the posters plastered on Canal and along the Bowery, "BOB BUTLER'S THE-ATRE (MALE ONLY)" in red letters across the top, and beneath it a woman in pink tights, ripe, her bosom in delicious bloom, her thighs fully blossomed, her posterior curved like a full-grown melon, her petal-like feet covered by a white banner with black letters: SOLD OUT.

The finger of Nebuchadnezzar was moving on those walls, filling out those shapes. Hello, girls. Good-bye, Mulcahey. *Mene, mene, tekel, upharsin,* a bevy of white boys dressed as darkies.

The war was killing minstrelsy. Emancipation. Long lists of dead and wounded. Now the draft. The specter, north and south, of the black face, real and corporeal, owing nothing to burnt cork. *White folks, I'll sing for you no more.* And something else was killing it, too. Mulcahey couldn't put a name on it, but he could feel it and hear it and see it. The press of the traffic on Broadway. The crowds in the stores and restaurants. The nonstop banging from the factories, the gaslight on all night, men assembling revolvers and reapers and thresher and shoes and shirts, faster, faster, faster. Make it quick. Next. We ain't got much time. No time for shuffle, shuffle, shuffle, or slow-as-molasses soliloquies. The country had found its different drummer all right. And a one, two, three, heel, kick, heel, kick, get those legs up, girls, let's move it, *look a-way, look a-way, a-way,* make room for the next act.

Mulcahey came up the back steps of the theatre on Crosby Street. Up the block, at the corner of Spring, he could see a mob of soldiers waiting outside the Adelphi. *Living Tableaus! Moments of History! Cleopatra in Her Bath!* He hurried inside. Squirt had everything set out for him. Mulcahey rubbed Squirt's head for luck, the same way he always did, the head of America's lurking nightmare, an amalgamationist kid, shanty-Irish mother, no-count Negro father, part of the nigger-Paddy colony on Roosevelt Street that deprived the directors of the Association for Improving the Poor of their sleep. Mulcahey took off his jacket and shirt in a rush, wet a cloth in the tin basin Squirt had set out for him, washed his face and neck and quickly dried them.

He sat down at the mirror. The chaos around him was building, people putting on their jackets and pulling on their wigs, white men blackening their skin. Brownlee's Minstrel Parade. A Rainbow of Shining Darkies. New York's Finest Ethiopian Review. Last night, Stephen Foster had asked him to walk down to the Catherine Street ferry. Foster talked the stuff that drunks are made of, uninvented inventions, unachieved success, unrequited everything, the lost opportunities that only the magic of alcohol could temporarily restore. But he also talked sense.

"Jack," Foster said, "this darkie thing isn't going to last much longer. It's like the whaling industry. First it booms. The age of Daddy Rice. The public can't seem to get enough. Then it disappears. Twenty years ago, every clerk and widow in the country was trying to buy a share in a whaling ship, and you know where those ships are now? They're sunk in the mouth of Charleston Harbor, the whole damn bunch of them filled with stones and sunk as part of the blockade. The style is changing, and it's not enough to change with it. That'll be too late. You have to change ahead of it."

"What should I do, Foster, grow a pair of teats?"

"Ladies are a part of it, Jack. But only a part. Success demands more than that. Take songwriting. It's not enough to write words or lyrics anymore. The future is in wholesale. Producing song after song, getting those songs to the people in bulk. Selling, Jack. You have to know how to sell. Plug, plug, plug, that's the future. Pay the stores to carry your sheets and put them in their windows. Print your music on candy wrappers or on the backs of daguerreotypes. The old days are dead. You can't just produce, you've got to know how to sell."

Squirt pulled the curtains closed around Mulcahey's cubicle. Mulcahey looked at himself in the mirror. *Hello, Jack.* Veins of red in those flashing blue eyes. Got to start keeping a cork in the bottle until the performance is over. Mulcahey always did his own makeup. It was bad luck to let somebody else do it for you, but he let Squirt lay out everything he needed, he depended on him for that. The kid never failed. The burnt cork was there and a small dish of water and a piece of cheesecloth. Jack made up the paste, rubbing the cork around the dish until the residue of water and ash became thicker and thicker.

In the mirror, Squirt's brown face came into view. "Jack, you keep getting here later, pretty soon they gonna go on without you."

"No way, kid, I'm the show."

"You the show until you don't show and somebody else gonna be the show." Squirt pulled back the curtain and went out.

Mulcahey pushed back his hair and dipped the cloth into the paste. He drew a black line across his forehead. "So long, white man," he said. He drew a great black circle around his face, picked up a small brush, dipped it, and leaned toward the mirror, circled his mouth beginning an inch above his lips, holding his right wrist with his left hand, whispering to himself, "Steady there, white man, steady." He rested his elbows on the table and worked on his eyes, leaving a small white area around them, getting as close as he could to the mirror and dabbing away with his brush.

He leaned back. "Squirt," he yelled, "Come here." Squirt appeared in the mirror once again.

"How's that?"

"Perfect."

Mulcahey picked up the cloth again and in broad strokes filled in the rest of his face, down his neck, behind his ears. He put on a wig of black curls. The curtain opened again, as if on cue, and Squirt came up behind Mulcahey with a hand mirror. He held it up as Mulcahey pulled and tugged on the wig, picked up the cheesecloth and went over a few spots on his neck and ears. Squirt moved the mirror to give Mulcahey the view he needed.

Mulcahey rolled his head back and forth, from left to right, and the curls danced. He picked up a second brush, dipped it into a small, flat metal tin, brushed on the pink greasepaint, filling in the space around his lips, and gently rubbed them with a swab of cotton. He smiled at himself, and his teeth looked white and large in the black oval of his face and the pink ellipse of his mouth.

"You're all set," Squirt said as he ran out.

Mulcahey put on his white gloves, held them at each side of his face, with the palms toward the mirror, the fingers spread out like fans. Mulcahey, "The Ethiopian Impersonator." His name at the top of the bill. The blackened white man stared back at him, frowning, smiling, the gloved hands waving. "Why, you ol' darkie," Mulcahey said to himself in the mirror, "what would da ol' folks at home think of you now?"

It was twenty years since Mulcahey's first performance, the first, that is, he could remember. He couldn't have been more than ten. He stood with the others on the great stone pier. The lord's yacht was late. The lord had stopped in view of Cruit Island, off the Donegal coast, to watch a flotilla of small leather boats filled with people on the way to the *Leacht Mór*, the Big Stone blessed by Saint Columcille himself. The yacht stayed for an hour as the people came ashore to touch the stone and pray for a cure, a procession of idiots, the old, cripples, the dying. The lord's agent for his Irish estates was on the deck with his employer. "They do it once a year, my lord, on the feast of Saint John the Baptist. It's a kind of crusade."

"Crusade? I think you mean a pilgrimage."

"Pilgrimage, yes, that's it, that's what they call it."

"Is it efficacious?"

"Pardon, my lord?"

"Is anyone ever cured?"

"Some have claimed to be."

"Good God, I suppose one would have to travel to the Ganges to see anything as bizarre."

The tenants were drawn up in rows on the pier. Jack stood next to his father in the first rank. In front of them, seated on a milking stool, was Jack's granduncle, Malachi, who had wept bitterly when the agent came to their cabins with news of the lord's first visit to his estates. "He'll evict us all, that's what he's come for, so he'll have the land for his cows."

Like most of the other tenants, Malachi had no English. But Jack's father was proficient at it and translated for them. "They want you to play for his lordship, Malachi, that's all. They want him to hear our music and feel welcomed. They don't want your cabin."

Malachi was unconvinced. "Why would a great lord the likes that lives in London want music from an old blind man? No, he wants the land. Mother of God, he wants the land."

The white yacht sailed into the harbor, its rigging ablaze with flags. The lord stepped out of the boat that had rowed him ashore and slowly mounted the steps of the pier. Two other boats followed with his luggage. The agent rushed ahead and tapped Malachi on the shoulder. "Play, man. Play." Malachi's sightless eyes stayed fixed ahead. His pipes rested on his lap. Jack's father stepped forward. "Malachi," he said in Irish, "they want a tune." But Malachi sat rigidly, not moving.

The lord was in front of them. "What seems to be the problem?"

"No problem," the agent said. "It's simply most of these people, my lord, don't understand the language."

The lord gestured at the pipes on Malachi's lap and the bag that was strapped under his arm. "These are different from the Scottish pipes?"

"Yes, my lord, they are called 'uileann' pipes and played manually, the piper using these bellows strapped to his arm, instead of blowing with his mouth, as is done in Scotland."

"This seems more primitive."

"Many things here are, my lord."

The agent turned to Jack's father. "Speak to him in his tongue. Tell him it would greatly please his master if he could hear a song on these pipes."

"Malachi," Jack's father said, "the man here says there'll be whiskey and tobacco for all the tenants if his lordship can only hear the music that even the people of London speak about so highly, the music of Malachi the piper."

Malachi began to play. The lord stood and listened. "What is he playing?" he asked.

The agent said to Jack's father, "Ask him the name of the song."

"Malachi," Jack's father said, "the lord wants to know the name of the tune."

"It's the 'Lament for Red Hugh O'Donnell.' It was taught me by my teacher Moriarty, who learned it from McDonnell, the piper from the Isles. When Moriarty taught it to me he was an old man, nearly eighty, and McDonnell himself was an old man when he taught it to Moriarty, who came here from Kerry to learn the pipes from McDonnell." Malachi was relaxed now. The story of the music came easily to him: "McDonnell himself was the pupil of Patrick O'Malley, and it's said that O'Malley's father saw the O'Donnell himself ride out against the English and that he was there when the earls, O'Donnell among them, set out from Lough Swilly for Spain, and O'Donnell was still strong and young and swearing vengeance, and there was little doubt he would have had it but the English poisoned him, as is their way."

"This must be the longest song title in history," the lord said.

"He is giving the history of the song, my lord," Jack's father said. "It's a long story."

"Most stories here are, my lord," the agent said. "You become accustomed to that."

When Malachi finished, the lord dropped a large silver coin into his lap, a thing so heavy, the engraving so fine to his fingers, so intricate and so interesting, that Malachi refused to let it out of his hand, feeling the crown and the profile of a face and the letters that no one could understand except for the English name "George."

It was two weeks later that Jack performed for his first audience. He led his granduncle, Malachi, by the hand to the Great House he had seen from a distance but never visited. The piper's hand was wet with perspiration, and Jack could sense his nervousness and it added to his own excitement. "Don't ye move so fast," Malachi said to him. "Ye cost me my breath." Jack walked alongside him, and the small pebbles of the carriageway felt strange under his bare feet, a tingling feeling on the rough, hardened skin of his soles, mysterious, a carpet of fine stones.

At the end of the carriageway, Jack could hear the hubbub of voices ahead, the *woo-woo* sound of English. There was a group of people on the stone porch, round men in red and blue and green coats, their boots all shined and bright, and women in long dresses, long curls around their faces, red circles on their cheeks. Jack described them to his uncle. "What are they doing?" Malachi said.

"They're staring at us, Granduncle."

"O Holy Child Jesus, have mercy on us."

Malachi slowed down, but Jack was in a hurry to see these people up close and he began to move faster and drag Malachi with him, and as his granduncle tried to restrain him, a tall man in a blue coat saw them and came down the stairs. It was the lord. There was a servant behind him.

"The piper!"

"I led him here as I was told," Jack said in English.

The lord rubbed Jack's head. "You're a good boy." He gestured to the servant behind him. "Get two chairs ready. Put them here, by the window, not too close to the food." He walked back up to the porch and clapped his hands. "The treat I promised you is here. The music, purely played, of a former age, the savage, plaintive tunes of the instruments that once called this island's natives to war."

The guests gathered around them. "Tell your uncle," the lord said, "to play the 'Lament for McDonnell'; tell him to start with that."

"O'Donnell, you mean, sir."

The lord looked down at Jack and smiled. "Yes, boy, you're quite correct. O'Donnell it is." Jack spoke to his granduncle in Irish, and Malachi played. He finished that and immediately started to play a reel, and Jack got up and began to dance, as he always did when Malachi played his song. He stood on his toes, his knees pumping up and down, his feet moving in the intricate patterns he had learned by heart. Not a touch of stage fright. The crowd began to clap, and some of them laughed with delight. The lord began to tap his foot and beat time with his hand against his thigh. One of the guests, a short, stout man, stood next to the lord. He roared with laughter. "This is rich," he said, "too rich."

When Malachi and Jack finished, the lord sent them around to the back of the house and they were given food on plates so white, Jack told his granduncle, that they must never have been eaten off before. They each got a breast of chicken and a great mound of potatoes with a thick gravy over it. And for all the years since, Jack never lost the taste of that debut dinner, the association of the stage with a full stomach and the Great House and the handsome people, the carriageway of white stones, so watch out, you minstrel boys, because here comes one Paddy who, jump Jim Crow, is out to have it all.

Mulcahey stood in front of the dressing-room mirror. He went up on his toes, the muscles in his calves tightening. He walked on the tips of his toes toward the door, arching the upper half of his body backward, strutting across the floor. "Jesus," Tommy Rice told Mulcahey that night they met in the New England Hotel, "I could dance before I could walk, wasn't any step I couldn't get the hang of in no time, because it all came naturally from listening to the sound of my old man's fiddle, and dancing in the middle of Bancker Street with all those other Irish kids."

Squirt came back into the room from the direction of the stage. "You is crazy, Jack. The show is about to start and you not even finished dressing." Mulcahey heard the twang of banjos, a chorus of voices. He sat down, and Squirt wrapped a paper collar around his neck, did it slowly, carefully, while Mulcahey held his chin high in the air.

"How's the crowd?"

"The house is half full."

"That's a nice way of putting it, Squirt."

Mulcahey slipped the red ribbon around the collar and tied

a big bow. He stood, and Squirt held up the silver jacket with the satin lapels and Mulcahey put his arms into it. He picked up his banjo and walked to the door. The smell of stage lights filled the corridor, calcium heated to incandescence, a sharp, acrid, familiar odor. At the end of the corridor the half-moon of shining darkies was in place on the stage.

Mulcahey went ahead. The curtain was going up. He drew a deep breath and sang softly to himself as he went: "The minstrel boy to the war is gone, in the ranks of death you will find him."

IV

"YOUR MASTER, I suppose, don't keep no dogs?"

"Heaps of 'em. Thar's Bruno—he's a roarer, he is, and why 'bout every nigger of us keeps a pup of some natur' or uther."

"I don't want no nigger's dog."

"Ours is good dogs, Mr. Haley, and I don't see no use cussin' on 'em, no way."

Eliza stood in the wings and adjusted the shawl on her shoulders so she could toss it over her head quickly. The slave-catcher was getting ready for the chase. A stagehand knelt next to her, holding a big red dog with one hand, stroking it with the other. He had his face next to the dog's ear and was whispering into it. Eliza took her handkerchief out of her sleeve and pressed it lightly against her forehead to absorb the perspiration. The dog was panting, drops of saliva dropping from its mouth onto the floor. "Here, Bruno," the black-faced actor yelled. The stagehand took his hand off the dog's collar and slapped it gently on the rump. The dog ran into the center of the stage.

"We're off!" the slave-catcher yelled.

The stagehand ran back to a trunk by the wall and took out a doll wrapped in a plaid blanket. He came back and put it into Eliza's arms. "Don't throw the little nigger," he said. She had once, accidentally. Tripped on the wooden blocks painted to look like ice, the doll careening away from her down between the blocks.

She adjusted the blanket around the doll. A round wooden head painted dark brown, big white eyes with black pupils, wide mouth with red lips that stretched into a grin. The white people's nigger baby. She couldn't have been more than eight weeks' pregnant with Mulcahey's baby when she visited Mrs. Dumas's on Bond Street, the downtown version of Madame Restell's, abortionist to the respectable, an establishment that operated in a mansion close to the unfinished cathedral. Mrs. Dumas shared space with a dentist and a newspaper, her offices in the basement, wooden shutters permanently closed against the street, like a whorehouse. Hanging over the sidewalk was a wooden sign with a large white tooth painted on it. Printed beneath in tall black letters was the word "EXTRACTIONS."

Eliza bled badly after it. She drank the medicine Mrs. Dumas gave her. It smelled like camphor. She ripped up a sheet and put the rags between her legs and slept as much as she could. Mulcahey didn't seem to notice anything wrong until he tried to make love to her. He reeked of alcohol. She had fallen asleep waiting for him to leave the hotel bar and come upstairs. He was kissing her shoulder and rubbing her thigh. She was cradling a baby in her dream, an infant with big brown eyes. It took her a minute to get her bearings. Mulcahey's hand was underneath her nightgown. She pushed it away. "Jack," she said, "I'm sick."

He sat beside her, grinning the way he always did when he had had too much to drink.

"Something you ate?"

"Women's problems, Jack."

He lay down and in a few moments was snoring. She went back to *Uncle Tom's Cabin* the next night. Although weak and tired, she got through the initial scenes without any problems. Then came the escape across the ice, the doll in her arms. She held it tightly, stroked its head, kept in mind the directions in the script: *Eliza strains her child to her bosom with a convulsive grasp, as she goes rapidly forward.* The grotesque face stared at her. Brown eyes, not blue; eyes like hers, not Mulcahey's. "Eliza, move it!" Regan, the chief stagehand, said in a harsh whisper. Stagehands in both wings were pulling on ropes in a kind of tug-o'-war, moving the wooden blocks back and forth, making a river of roaring ice. She jumped onto the first block. From behind her, offstage, the slave-catcher yelled, "Thar she is! Don't let her get away!" She jumped to the second block, then to the third. She was in the middle of the stage. The dramatic leap was next. The stagehands paused in their tugging. "Count to two," Regan reminded them. The script repeated itself in her head: *Eliza pauses and looks behind, and then, nerved with the strength such as God gives only the desperate, with a wild cry and a flying leap, vaults across to the block that is momentarily stationary. She turns in disbelief to view her desperate achievement, and lifts her child up to heaven in a gesture of triumph.*

Her foot hit the rim of the block and she fell forward. The doll and blanket went flying, bounced off the far end of the block, and fell into the make-believe river. The audience gasped. She crawled on her hands and knees. Regan gave the order to get the blocks moving again. The river ice churned wildly. She reached down between the blocks. "Oh, God," Regan said, "the bitch is gonna get her arm broke." She pulled the doll out before the blocks banged together. The blanket was gone, and one leg was missing. She clutched the doll to her so the audience couldn't see it.

Not once in the hundred-odd leaps since then had she fallen, but Regan insisted on bringing up her mishap at every performance. She stepped onto the first block and looked down into the doll's face. The same silly smile. From behind her came the cue: "Thar she is! Don't let her get away!" She was off and running, one block, two block, three block, pause, look behind, ice stops, jump, a two-footed landing, baby lifted into the air, a burst of applause, exit stage left.

She put the doll down and took off her shawl. Her blouse was wet with perspiration. Nothing to do until the shoot-out with the slave-hunters, then another break until the last scene when

Eliza and her husband, George, would be reunited with Madame de Thoux, George's sister, and Cassy, Eliza's mother, the whole cast Africa-bound, a convoluted ending but, since everyone had already read the book, one everyone readily grasped. Coming as it did after the respective death scenes of Eva and Uncle Tom, it drew some tears but soft, hopeful ones, not like the sobbing that attended the ends of the little girl and the Christian slave. "Mrs. Stowe should try her hand at comedies," said Mulcahey. "She has a gift for endings that go past the happy to the hilarious."

"There's nothing wrong with happy endings," Eliza said. "They happen sometimes."

A crowd of barefoot black-faced actors in ragged clothes walked around Eliza to the stage. A musical interlude. Nothing crude or in the fashion of a minstrel show. The audience was mostly country types, families from Ohio, Pennsylvania, Indiana, young soldiers, the fresh-faced kind on their way from upstate New York to their first taste of war. They were here to be uplifted. Eliza went out the stage door into the alley. The rain had stopped. The night air felt cold. She pulled the shawl close around her.

A group of actors were playing crack-loo against the wall of the theatre, pitching half-dollars that bounced against the brick and rang loudly when they hit the pavement. Carrie Drew, Aunt Ophelia in the play, had her hem hitched into her belt. She stood with her legs apart, her knees slightly bent, and pitched a coin in a high arc that barely kissed the wall and fell closer to it than any of the other coins scattered about. She did a little dance and picked up her winnings. A stagehand appeared at the door and shouted, "Girls, you're on next." Carrie unhitched her dress and let it down. She was a woman in her thirties made up to look older. On her forehead was a set of India-ink wrinkles, drawn with a camel's-hair brush, and covered with a dusting of fine chalk. There were gray streaks in her hair. Behind her were the actresses who played Eva and Topsy: Eva, a woman of twenty in a blond wig with pigtails, wearing a long white dress; Topsy, a woman of about the same age, in blackface and a black wig with tufts of hair tied in red rags, and clothed in a faded, torn calico dress. The audience was required to believe that they were pre-puberal incarnations of some of America's most cherished verities. "Representatives of their races," as Mrs. Stowe described them: "The fair, high-bred child, with her golden head, her deep eyes, her spiritual, noble brow, and prince-like movements; and her black, keen, subtle, cringing, yet acute neighbor. . . . The Saxon, born of ages of cultivation, command, education, physical and moral eminence; the Afric, born of ages of oppression, submission, ignorance, toil, and vice!"

Eva took a deep draw on her cheroot, dropped it, and crushed it with her foot. "Let me see that," she said to Carrie. Carrie tossed one of the half-dollars high in the air. Eva caught it.

"How do I know this is the one you used?"

"Just gotta trust me."

"Do I look that stupid?"

"Want an answer?"

They laughed and went up the stairs.

"Well, Eliza," Carrie said, "I'm glad to see you escaped the slave-catchers. How was the trip across the river?"

"Uneventful."

"And how is our devoted audience this evening?"

"A full house ready to weep."

Carrie turned her head and said over her shoulder to Eva and Topsy, "Come, my younglings, we mustn't disappoint."

Eliza watched them go in. The two younger actresses were new in their roles. This was only their second week. Carrie had been there almost six months. For these three, as for the other migratory creatures of the stage, *Uncle Tom* was a convenient refuge that served as a resting spot between more promising engagements, a perpetually running play in which the cast was always changing, all except Señorita La Plante, the actress from somewhere in the South, whom everyone called Eliza.

*

Several nights before, Stephen Foster had shown up to stand in the wings and watch the play. It was not the first time he had done so, but he was drunker than usual, swaying from side to side and forced to hold on to the curtains to keep his balance. He was so loud that Regan came over and threatened to toss him out.

"Eliza," Foster said, "I must talk to you."

She took him to a corner where the dust hung like Spanish moss on abandoned props and scenery. He had been in Jim Ryan's on Cherry Street, the lowest dive on a street lined with them, watching people dance—sailors, whores, thieves, soldiers. Darkie musicians were playing banjos and drums in the corner of the room, and the white trash was moving to it, legs pumping rapidly, arms swinging, people who had just met swaying together, sometimes dancing so close, and in such a frenzied way, their pelvises seemed to grind together. The music kept getting faster, and its pulse, its regular metric beat, was hypnotic.

"It made you want to move," he said.

"What made you want to move?" Eliza asked.

It was the music he had heard on the Cincinnati docks, Olivia's music as she moved so naturally, so fluidly, when they stood outside the Negro church and listened to the voices inside. An ancient whore with lips and cheeks farded with red paint had come over, taken his arm, and moved him out onto the dance floor. He tried to go back, but she dragged him to the floor once more. He felt humiliated, but when he looked around, he realized no one in Jim Ryan's was watching anyone. They were each involved in the excitement of their own movement. The floor was moving up and down with the pounding of the dancers. It felt as if it might snap. The whore started to move furiously, flailing her arms.

"Uncle Tom," he said. "Uncle Tom with music. New music. A new way to dance." He moved his feet in a little jig. "Do you understand, Eliza?"

He could tell by her face that she didn't. He had gotten too drunk. But in the morning he would be able to explain. *Uncle Tom's Cabin* with music. Not an opera. But a play interspersed with singing and dancing. Not minstrel music. But real Negro music. And real darkies. Up until now, Eliza had one of the few roles that a colored person could aspire to: Mrs. Stowe's mulatto girl who could almost pass for white. The American stage had darkies galore, from the tragic Othello, with Edwin Booth in blackface, to the dimwitted Tambo, played by any number of burnt-cork minstrels. It also had Coal Black Rose and Little Yaller Gal, the high-struttin', dark-as-midnight, big-as-a-barrel mammy and the silky, smooth-moving, coffee-colored siren. But the universal conventions of minstrelsy ordained that darkies need not apply. All roles were reserved for transvested white men, sometime pretenders to another sex as well as to another race.

Foster staggered, and Eliza took him by his arm. "I have it," he said to Eliza. He tapped the side of his head with his forefinger. He found what he was looking for in Jim Ryan's: a new moment in the history of the American stage. *A Play by Harriet Beecher Stowe. Musical Direction by Stephen Collins Foster. And a Cast of Real Negroes Singing Real Negro Songs and Dancing Real Negro Dances.* He would do for the stage what he had done for the popular song. *"Susanna, don't you cry."*

Eliza said, "I'll see you back to the hotel once I'm done here."

He sat for a minute until he saw Carrie Drew, another neighbor from the New England Hotel, and tried to talk to her. A thick-browed, cretinous-looking stagehand shushed him. He walked away and held the curtains for support again. He could see the faces of the audience in the first few rows. They watched solemnly as Eliza and her husband pledged their love. They laughed at the antics and language of Topsy. He knew that when the time came for Uncle Tom to die, they would weep—less violently than at the death of sweet, white, innocent Eva, but weep nonetheless—as innumerable audiences had wept at the suffering and death of Uncle Toms played by Daddy Rice or one of his many counterparts, every black countenance in the play, field niggers and house niggers alike, a true pale face underneath. Except

Eliza. When she came off the stage, she kissed Foster on the cheek, and he saw the powder that was spread on her face to lighten her tan skin, the Negro equivalent of blackface. He didn't say anything more to her. He kept listening to the music from Jim Ryan's that was in his head. A thing no respectable audience of white people was prepared to hear, no matter how sympathetic to the cause of anti-slavery. He could sense the aspirations of the people in the seats: Give us black people devoid of any blackness, a spiritual and cultural cipher, black people in whiteface. Here is the trademark of the black race that we will accept: orphans devoid of history or memory, free at last to seek the values, traditions, history, culture, morals, religion, customs, ambitions, and presumptions of Anglo-Saxons, the lowest and darkest beginning their long evolution into the full stature of the highest blankness. Otherwise, let us have our mad and merry minstrels, everything about them, der big lips and dem big words and all dat clowning to remind us of the impossible gap between the black species and the white. There was a story in circulation that in an attempt to save money, the Christy Minstrel Show had hired *real* Negroes for the chorus, but they had been required to spread the burnt cork on their faces, big red ovals around their lips, until they resembled the true nigger, an innovation that was soon stopped when the white men in blackface refused to countenance such a seditious assault on the art of Ethiopian Impersonation.

Foster didn't stay to let Eliza take him home. He borrowed a dollar from Carrie Drew and went to Mike Manning's. The next morning he didn't remember much beyond having danced with a whore at Jim Ryan's.

The stagehand called Eliza back in for the gunfight with the slave-catchers. She went through the scene perfectly, her lines flowing on cue, without her having to think about them. When it was over, she sat by the back wall. No Foster to bother her tonight. She waited until it was time for Little Eva's death. Two stagehands sat on the rafters behind the proscenium, ready to crank their winches and lift Eva from her bed into heaven.

The extraction hadn't been exactly a death. No chorus in the background, no guy-wire ascension, just a *plop* in the pail that Mrs. Dumas held under the sheet. A noise, not a face. Would Mulcahey have objected? She couldn't be sure. Once, in the bar of the hotel, he had raised the issue of marriage.

"There's no law against it, at least not in New York, and as far as the world knows, it could be a Cuban-Irish nuptial, not one that would be celebrated by the city's hoi polloi but neither would it call for tar and feathering."

"We could live on Roosevelt Street," Eliza had said, "along with the Paddy women and their nigger husbands."

The Irish around it called it "Loose Belt Street," the black men impregnating their Irish women at a prodigal rate. It was a street shunned by other Irish and blacks, an amalgamationist community of the lowest order, denizens and employees of the dives and dance halls of the Five Points living in some of the city's most decrepit and squalid rookeries.

"That's not the only street in New York."

"It's the only one where colored people and Paddies aren't at each other's throats. And a lovely place it is, too, Jack. A garden spot for children. We could have a son just like Squirt who'd one day, perhaps, earn the right to clean up after white men in blackface, or maybe a daughter who could inherit my role as Eliza."

She had wanted him to say that they would figure out the details later, that he wanted to be with her, that there were places in the world where the races intermarried and their offspring weren't treated as lepers, places where skin color was overlooked, and together they'd find them. She had wanted to say, *Go ahead, Jack, put down the drink and wipe away the grin, say you love me in this room full of white men, show them I'm not just the mistress who you'll one day leave behind, but your woman, Jack, for good or for bad, your wife.*

But she hadn't.

Mulcahey's mood turned grim. He ordered another drink. "This is no place for arguing such matters," he said.

What place, then, Jack?

"We have plenty of time to work out the details."

We have this one moment in this one place. We have nothing more.

"You've got the ceremony over, and you're already worrying about kids. Slow down, Eliza, one step at a time."

The next step in time is Mrs. Dumas's, Jack.

When she was a girl, Eliza's aunt had explained to her the secrets of the female's body, told her everything in detail, and even explained the workings of the man's body. In every drop of semen, her aunt said, is a perfectly formed person so small it can't be seen by the naked eye. It had everything but a face and sexual organs. The mother created those after she received the seed, her dreams and thoughts determining which sex the child would be. When the time comes, her aunt told her, you must be very careful to think beautiful thoughts and to dream only of boys if you want a boy and of girls if you want a girl. Don't be careless the way Tiny Tom Butler's mother was, watching kittens being drowned shortly before he was born and thereby causing her baby to be marked as a dwarf. Happened all the time, women witnessing events that deformed their unborn children.

The painted doll in her arms: What sex was it? It never stopped smiling. Supposed to be a boy. Did Mrs. Dumas see a smile on a perfectly formed little man as he fell into her pail?

Above the stage, the winches bearing Eva heavenward squeaked slightly as they began to turn.

"Eva," the actor playing her father cried. "Oh, Eva, tell us what you see! What is it?"

The winches creaked louder. Eva's mattress left the bed. She raised herself and pointed to the rafters, "Oh! Love . . . joy . . . peace!" She fell back. The chorus of darkies hummed. There were sobs from the audience. Eliza had read the book. Mrs. Stowe knew little about black people. They were, Mrs. Stowe insisted, kinder, better, more intelligent—more human—than most of the country was ready to admit, but even in her eyes they were still a lesser breed, creatures whose greatest asset was the Anglo-Saxon blood they had been forced to absorb. But Mrs. Stowe did know about the death of a child. It wasn't something she learned about through reading or conversation. Here was the central event of the play, the mystical chord that resounded through the audience. Slavery and the black man remained an abstraction for most, a white man in burnt cork serving as a summation. But the dead child was everywhere, in the past, the present, the future, cholera, scarlet fever, typhoid, a continual slaughter of the innocents.

The thought consoled Eliza. No such grief lay ahead. Her mother had watched four of her babies die. Each born, cherished, raised to the age of three or four, then ravaged by fever and diarrhea until death came as a kind of mercy. It sucked the life out of her mother, death by death, each of them laid in the graveyard next to the church, on the hill overlooking the sea, the wind tearing at her mother's hair, her father showing no emotion, his face as expressionless as brown clay.

Topsy was lying on the floor. She cried, "Oh, Miss Eva! Oh, Miss Eva! I wish I's dead, too—I do." She looked up as Eva ascended into the rafters. Her blackface glistened in the glare of the stage lights. From her position behind the stage, Eliza watched Topsy as she kicked her legs into the air. A white imitation of black grief. She could be the real-life mother of the black doll Eliza carried in her arms.

The previous actress who played Topsy had been far more emotive, screaming, yelling, throwing herself to the ground. During one of her performances, a stagehand standing next to Eliza had asked her half-distractedly, "Do all darkies act like that? Or is it only the southern ones?"

Eliza said nothing. Darkie grief was grief, as well in the North as in the South. She knew that for sure. Eliza had never seen Cuba or New Orleans or even Baltimore, never been closer to Dixie than the southern shore of Staten Island, where she had been raised. Midian's Well is what its inhabitants called their collection of houses, or rather what their preacher, Benjamin Enders, named it when he led them out of New York City. He had been their pastor in the Church of Zion on Albany Street, not far from Trinity Church, the congregation drawn from the black waiters, porters, and seamen of lower Manhattan. They left en masse in 1815, almost the entire congregation, over thirty families and a smattering of single men and women. The year when Eliza's grandmother Rose Harris was hanged for arson and attempted murder. She had been a member of the Church of Zion. The Reverend Mr. Enders had assaulted the city fathers with his pleas and cries to spare her life. None of it had done any good. She was hanged. The Sunday afterward he rose in the pulpit and told them that, whether slave or free, black men had no hope of finding either peace or freedom in Pharaoh's land. They must do what Moses had done when, as a young man, he slew Pharaoh's servant: flee Egypt and dwell in the land of Midian, by a well, until God brought the rod of His judgment down upon the evildoers.

Eliza's grandmother Rose Harris was descended from a slave who arrived in New Amsterdam in 1639, imported from the West Indies as part of the household of Willem Kieft, Governor of New Netherland, and advertised in the colony's newspaper as *Male negro, 15 or 16 years. Skilled as a carpenter. Cato (Kieft's)*. New Amsterdam traded its slaves at the foot of the East River and by the town's protective palisade, which became known as Wall Street, and when Kieft was recalled after provoking a bitter war with the Hackensack Indians, he sold Cato to a tea merchant named Vandervort. The English seized New Netherland in 1664. They changed the colony's name to New York and reaffirmed the institution of slavery. Vandervort rented Cato's services as a carpenter to Dutch and English alike. Cato's work was admired and sought after.

The following year, Cato fathered a daughter by one of Vandervort's indentured servants, a Scottish girl named Mary Munro. Cato and Mary Munro both died in the typhoid epidemic that struck the city in 1670. Their daughter, Elizabeth, was sold at age fifteen to a family named Pruit. *Female negro, 15 years. Seamstress. Betty (Pruit's)*. She was raped by Elias Pruit several weeks after he purchased her. She bore him a son, whom she named

Elias, but Pruit forbade her to call him by this name, and when she persisted, he struck her with his fist and broke her nose. Pruit sold Betty and her son, whom he renamed Cuffee, to the Holcombs, who owned a large farm on the city's outskirts. Betty served them as a cook and seamstress, and in 1682 was allowed to share quarters over the stable with Caesar, a slave who served as chief groom. They had no children of their own. Betty was pregnant several times but never let Caesar or the Holcombs know. She visited a slave woman named Obie, who was rumored to be a witch. Obie gave her a vile-tasting potion to drink and told her to stand on the small hill behind the Holcomb farm when the moon was full.

"You must curse the name of Jesus three times," Obie told her.

"I can't do such a thing," Betty said. "I'm a Christian."

"Then you will have the baby."

"There is no other way?"

"No."

Betty did as she was told. The miscarriages came soon afterward. But she grew despondent about the way she had used the name of God, and when Caesar was kicked by a horse and bled to death, she saw that as her punishment. In 1692, Cuffee, her son, was sold by the Holcombs to Andreas Kortrecht, a lumber merchant. *Male negro, age approximately 20 years. Laborer. Cuffee (Holcomb's).* Betty became silent and withdrawn. She disappeared in December of the year Cuffee was sold. When her body was found in the frozen marshes of the East River, the death was ruled an accidental drowning.

Cuffee spent the rest of his life with Kortrecht. He became the overseer of the lumber operations and lived in a small house on the North River with Nina, a mulatto woman from Barbados who served as the cook in the Kortrechts' home. Cuffee lived to be seventy. He died in 1740. He had two sons. The older one was bought by an Albany merchant. After several years in that city he was allowed to purchase his freedom, and he moved to Canada at the end of the Seven Years' War. The younger, Plato, was made an assistant to his father and became manager when Cuffee died.

Plato kept to himself. He was noted for his silences. A grim, sober, hardworking Negro, Plato lived in his father's house. He had a daughter, Maria, by a woman who died in childbirth; the baby was raised by Nina, Plato's mother. Times were hard. The weather was as fierce as anyone could remember. The city was frozen in ice for three months. Competition from Philadelphia and Baltimore hurt New York's position as a grain entrepôt for the British Empire. Exports fell. Mills closed. Men lost their jobs. In a city where one fifth of the population was slaves, the whites grumbled about how the niggers ate better than they did and were taken better care of. With a hostile Spanish Empire to the south and a French one to the north, they also worried about a Catholic alliance that would crush their colony and claim all of North America for the papists.

The fears grew. In 1739, four black slaves and an Irish Catholic indentured servant successfully fled New York and reached Florida, where they were fêted by the Spanish. The slaveholding Spanish even issued a proclamation offering "Freedom to all Negroes, and other slaves, that shall Desert from the English colonies." A few months later, outside Charleston, South Carolina, there was a slave rebellion along the Stono River. It was put down quickly and brutally, but its aftershocks reverberated north and south. In New York, there was a feeling of dread, of expectation, a sense some horrid secret was about to unfold. Plato left the house where he lived with his daughter and mother. He moved into a fishing shack that protruded over the river. He spoke only when he had to and kept his contact with whites to what was required by business.

The city's fears came to a head in March 1741, when Fort George, at its southern tip, burned to the ground. The smoldering ruins wrapped the city in a pall of smoke. More fires followed. Suddenly the city began to apprehend the outlines of a plot to destroy New York's defenses and welcome a Spanish fleet into the harbor, a Negro plot that involved an untold number of slaves. The roundups began. Across the river, in Hackensack, two slaves were caught in the act of setting fire to a barn. They were tortured and then burned at the stake, and although they admitted no motive beyond hatred of their master, the implication was clear: There was a conspiracy afoot that involved not only illiterate, ignorant slaves but some central mastermind, some evil genius in the pay of the papists.

The city had faced a slave revolt years before, in 1712, when Adrian Beekman and other prominent New Yorkers had been murdered in their beds by their slaves. Retribution had come quickly. Fourteen slaves hanged. Two roasted over a slow fire. Nineteen whipped and chained in a public place, where they were left to die. In 1741, the lesson was still green: Act swiftly, with no mercy. More slaves were arrested, mostly young men with a history of troublemaking. It wasn't until the city had spent another week in anxious anticipation of some new outrage that Tom Kramer, the owner of a lumber business on the East River, began to talk about Plato. Such an unusual Negro, living alone, so quiet and unfriendly, an air of arrogance about him. Even knew how to read and write, strange skills for a slave. Kortrecht offered no protest when Plato was arrested. In jail, Plato was whipped and kicked. Three of his ribs were broken. Christopher Bancker and Philip Vandervort, two prominent members of the colonial government, came to his cell at night and pleaded with him to save himself by confessing. He said nothing. He was put on trial with two other slaves. They were quickly convicted and sentenced to be burned at the stake. Plato died silently, offering no response to the final call for a confession. The other two broke. They named names and gave dates. They talked so fast that their interrogators had trouble keeping up. When they were finished, they too were burned.

The Negro Plot took on a life of its own. A number of whites were implicated, one an Irish servant girl, Peggy Kerry, another a teacher accused of being a Catholic priest. Irish troops in the city's garrison fell under suspicion. In the end, four whites and seventeen blacks were hanged; thirteen blacks were burned at the stake. Kortrecht sold Plato's mother and his child. *Female negro, age*

approximately 60 years. Cook and nursemaid. Nina (Kortrecht's).
Female negro, age approximately 9 years. Skilled in all domestic
tasks. Maria (Kortrecht's). Note: Owner prefers to sell these girls
as a pair.

In the great Bible that Eliza's father kept by his bed there
was a brief list of names entered on the back flyleaf. Brown faded
ink on thick yellowed paper. At the top was the first entry, written
by Maria herself in 1801, when she was a woman in her seventies:
"Maria Montgomery, b. 1731, daughter of Plato and Maria, baptized in the freedom of the Lord Jesus Christ, 10th day of April,
A.D. 1743. Purchased her earthly freedom, 24th day of December,
A.D. 1753. Married to James Cooper the following day, 25th of
December, A.D. 1753, the birthday of our Savior."

Nina and Maria were purchased as a pair by Thomas Montgomery, a Scot who had arrived in New York as an indentured
servant. He had earned his freedom and became a brewer, one of
the city's most successful, and built a fine house for himself on
Cherry Street above Pike. His wife was dead, his two daughters
raised and married, by the time Nina and Maria arrived in 1742.
He let Nina run his kitchen and made Maria her helper. He kept
his servants and slaves under such loose supervision that the city
fathers complained. Montgomery ignored them. "I'm rich enough
not to have to worry about meddlesome burghers," he said.

In matters of religion, Montgomery was a freethinker. He
belonged to no church and required no worship by those who
worked for him. But when Nina came to him and told him Maria
wished to be baptized, he had no objections. On the day she returned from her immersion in the waters of the Collect Pond, he
presented her with the Bible she would keep all her life and pass
on to her children. Maria had been taught to read and write by
her father and had salvaged whatever printed matter she could
find to create a small library of battered books and tattered broad-
sheets. Now she threw them away. She would never read another
book except her Bible.

As Nina grew older, Maria took over her duties in the
kitchen. Montgomery told Maria that so long as she completed

her tasks she was free to rent her services as a cook outside his house and to keep the money she earned. He told her he would let her buy her freedom, and set a price. "I will not simply give you your freedom," he said, "because then you might take it for granted. You will earn yours the way I earned mine, and you'll never forget how precious it is." Nina died in 1749. She was buried in the Negro cemetery. Maria worked hard. Her services were sought after. She saved what she earned but made only slow progress toward Montgomery's price. In 1752, while working as a cook in the home of a family near Cherry Street, she met James Cooper. He was a free black from New Rochelle, a skilled wheelwright who had only recently arrived in the city. He was working in the yard outside the kitchen and came in and asked her for a drink of water. "What's your name?" he said. She blushed and walked away, saying nothing. A few days later he appeared at the Montgomery house and was hired to refurbish the wheels on a carriage.

When James Cooper finished his work, he kept returning. Maria became comfortable with him, eager for his visits. She told him she was working for her freedom and had saved nearly half of what she needed. He offered her the other half and asked her to marry him. "The one does not depend on the other," he said. "I will give you the money with the certainty you shall repay it. But I want you to be my wife." She said yes. They went to Montgomery with his offer and he accepted it. Cooper's money was as good as any man's, he said, and Maria had already learned the worth of her freedom.

With the start of the Seven Years' War, boom times returned to New York. The harbor was choked with warships. Soldiers filled the streets. Wheat and wood and hides poured through the port on their way to the British armies in Europe and India. New York went from being a colonial grain depot to an international port, surpassing Boston in its ability to attract European trade and becoming the American terminus for the British transatlantic mail boat. One of the signs of the city's new status was the proliferation of imported coaches, luxury vehicles that announced the social arrival of their owners and drew the ire of the American carriage makers. For Cooper, however, the rising number of coaches on the streets meant more work, and he prospered at his trade.

He and Maria rented a small house. They had a son, named James, in 1759, and a daughter, named Miriam, in 1760. Another daughter, Elizabeth, died of fever at age two in 1764 and was buried in the Negro cemetery alongside Nina. The Coopers lived among whites and went about their work quietly, never bothered but never embraced. They ignored as best they could the growing tumult leading up to the Revolution, but James junior was involved in several scuffles with Tory sympathizers.

When the British drove Washington off Long Island and invaded the city, James junior fled with the American army. A few days later, word reached Maria and James senior that their son was a hero. It was brought by Jacob Valentine, a young boy from a Tory family who although too young for military service had trailed along with the retreating army and then slipped back into the city. He told them that as a party of British soldiers had approached the American rear guard, James, who had been lying in a forward position on a stretcher, his leg badly swollen from a musket ball that had passed through his calf, had spotted the British as they stole up, seized a musket, and killed one of the redcoats, alerting the Americans to the danger. That was the last Maria and James ever heard of their son. They could never find anyone who knew what had happened to him after that. They were told a lot of wounded men had fallen by the wayside. Left behind by the retreating Americans, they crawled into the bushes and rocks of northern Manhattan, where they died and were never discovered. Maria prayed that was the case with her son. But she nursed a fear that some Virginians or Marylanders had taken him as a slave, ignoring his status as a freeborn, and that he was living his life in shackles on some southern plantation. Her husband said that Maria's apprehension was foolishness, but she held it nonetheless, and it troubled her.

The Coopers lived for the next five years under the British

occupation. Half the city had gone up in flames soon after the British entered, an act the Tories blamed on a revolutionary arsonist, and the revolutionaries on British vindictiveness. Like many New Yorkers, Cooper did work for the British army. The city had the air of a fortress, redcoats everywhere, frigates and warships riding at anchor in the harbor. British officers took over the house James and Maria rented, and for a while they lived in a tent before they found lodging in a farmhouse on the northern outskirts of the city near Richmond Hill, in an area populated mostly by free black tradesmen.

By the time the British left, Maria and James's daughter, Miriam, was twenty-one. A strikingly handsome young woman, she married a baker named Charles Harris, who lived with his mother not far from the Coopers. The city came alive again after the occupation, commerce and trade slowly reviving, the flow of goods from the interior resuming. And as the members of the state legislature met to put in place a new government, the free blacks petitioned that the institution of slavery be abolished in New York. The legislature decided against it. The special slave courts were abolished and private manumission was made easier, but there was no emancipation, a decision that made it easier for the city to serve as the seat of the new federal government created by the Constitution.

The city filled up with members of the Congress and the executive branch, and with their slaves, hundreds of them, maids, footmen, cooks, drivers, seamstresses, servants in every possible capacity. Their masters found it inconvenient or impossible to distinguish between the blacks they imported and the ones they found living in New York. When Cooper finished working on the coach of a congressman from Georgia, he knocked on the front door of the man's house to tell him he was done and to present his bill.

A young black girl opened the door. "What you doing coming to this door, boy?" she said. "Mr. Jarvis see you coming in this way, he'll have your hide."

"My hide doesn't belong to Mr. Jarvis."

"Don't matter who it belongs to, he'll give it a good kick he sees you coming to the front door."

"I don't care what he sees. He owes me money. I want it."

She tried to close the door. He stuck his foot in it. "Tell Mr. Jarvis that Mr. Cooper is here for his money and isn't going away till he's paid." The girl screamed, and a stout, red-faced man suddenly appeared behind her and opened the door wider. He looked Cooper in the face.

"What in God's name do you think you're doing?"

"Mr. Jarvis?"

"Yes."

"My name is James Cooper. I'm the wheelwright who was asked to work on your coach. I've completed the work and am here to be paid."

"Cooper?" Mr. Jarvis seemed to relax. "Nobody told me you were a nigger. They said you did good work, but they forgot to mention you were a nigger."

"I'm freeborn, Mr. Jarvis; so were my parents."

"Well, Mr. Freeborn Nigger, you scoot down the alley to the rear of the house and I'll have one of the servants deliver your money."

Cooper turned on his heels and walked away. He shouted over his shoulder, "Keep your money, you big-mouthed suckfish, I wouldn't soil my hands with it."

Jarvis stepped out onto the stoop. He pointed at Cooper and yelled, "You worthless nigger son of a bitch, don't ever dare set foot near this house, you hear!"

Cooper made a fist with his thumb between his fingers, a gesture he had learned from an Italian wigmaker on Pearl Street. "Don't worry, I never step near shit," he yelled back at Jarvis.

In 1798, James Cooper and his son-in-law, Charles Harris, were part of a delegation of free blacks that traveled from New York City to Albany to petition the legislature, once again, to abolish slavery in New York. With the federal capital now moved elsewhere, the time seemed ripe to end an institution already made economically obsolete by the state's rapid-growing industrialization and the growing pool of cheap immigrant labor. The following year, the legislature acted. All children of slaves in New York born after July 4, 1799, were declared free, but they were required to work for their masters until the costs of their upbringing were paid for. Slave marriages were legitimized retroactively, and the right of blacks to own property approved. The status of slaves born before 1799 was left unchanged. For the time being, they would remain slaves.

During the trip to Albany, the delegation of free blacks was refused lodgings in Kingston. No hotel would have them. They slept in the coach. In Albany, Governor John Jay sent word he was too busy to receive them. They sat an entire morning in the lobby of Assemblyman DeWitt Clinton's hotel before he sent down word that he didn't have time either to listen to their requests.

In the summer of 1800, while working in the choking dust of Canal Street to repair a broken wagon, James Cooper had a stroke and died. Maria moved in with Miriam and Charles. They lived in a house near the Minetta Brook in Greenwich Village that had been built by a speculator who had gambled that the postwar prosperity of New York would bring the city right to Greenwich Village and multiply the value of his property. He lost his gamble. The city grew, but not that fast, and the new owner gave Charles and Miriam the chance to live in the house for a year at a low rent. He said that after that time, if they wished to stay, he would raise the amount they paid and apply it toward the purchase of the house. In twenty years they would have full title to the property.

Charles and Miriam had three daughters. The oldest two, Elizabeth and Nina, died as infants, one from the croup, the other from fever. The third daughter, named Rose, was born in 1790, and although thin and sickly, she lived. The family lived quietly in their house. Miriam took in sewing and Maria helped her. When Rose was old enough, she helped, too. Charles worked in a bakery by the river that shipped its products to the rest of the city by boat. At night, Maria read aloud from her Bible. She would start at Genesis and night by night read on, a few pages at a time, until they heard the whole book; then she would start again.

In 1809, when Rose was nineteen, a French music teacher moved in a few doors from them. He taught in homes throughout the Village. He walked past the Harris house every day, whistling to himself, and sometimes he stopped to talk. He didn't seem to notice Rose's color. His heavily accented English sounded lyrical and charming. He was tall and thin, with a sharp handsome face, and he walked in a loose, graceful way. Gradually it dawned on Rose that he stopped by so frequently because he was attracted to her. Her parents were wary of him, as they were of all whites, but they seemed to relax a bit as they grew accustomed to his visits. He talked with them about everything—politics, religion, music—and listened attentively when they spoke.

The first time the Frenchman and Rose were alone together was on an August night when Rose was too hot to sleep and she stepped out onto the house's small porch. The moon was so bright it was like day, and she was amazed to see the Frenchman walk toward her. Something in her heart had told her he would appear.

"I couldn't sleep for the heat," she said in a low voice.

"Yes, the heat, I could not sleep either."

He put his hand over hers and kissed her, and she felt as if a seed inside her were budding, coming to life, unfolding. He took her hand and led her away from the house. They lay down behind some bushes, on soft grass, and he was gentle and reassuring, telling her how beautiful she was as he made love to her.

He never stopped at the house after that. He waved as he walked by and shouted a greeting, but he never stood and talked the way he had. In a few weeks Rose knew she was pregnant. She prepared to tell her mother, but just as she was ready, her father was brought home from work; his right hand had been mangled by one of the new kneading machines. Within a week, he was dead from blood poisoning, buried in the Negro cemetery with the other members of the family, and Miriam was so sunk in her grief, Rose didn't have the heart to tell her.

The landlord stopped by to give his condolences, and Miriam told him that without her husband's income it would be hard to keep up payments on the house, but that she and her mother and daughter would do their best. She asked how much was left to pay before the house was theirs.

"Left to pay?" the landlord asked.

"Yes, before the sum we agreed upon when we moved in is completed and we have finished paying what we owe."

"Madam, I have the dimmest of recollections of discussing once, many years ago, some sort of arrangement with your late husband, but it never went beyond the realm of words. I will do what I can to arrange a convenient schedule of rent payments to see you through your period of grief, but, please, dismiss the fantasy from your mind that you have some claim of ownership on this property."

Miriam trembled with rage. Her lips became pale. "Get out of this house, you white bastard," she said. She took the landlord to court, but the case was dismissed before trial; afterward, the landlord served them notice to quit the premises. They moved to the city, to basement rooms on Washington Street, near the Negro church; the pastor, the Reverend Mr. Enders, helped them find their quarters. One day Miriam looked at Rose and said, "My God, you're with child," and she wept.

Maria was growing feeble. She spent all day with her Bible, and after they moved to the city she became confused, sometimes speaking to her dead husband and long-vanished son as if they were in the room. She died quietly in her sleep the month before Rose had her baby. At her funeral, the Reverend Mr. Enders said that Maria was a woman whom all New Yorkers of African descent should take pride in, a woman who had never asked for anything, who had earned everything she had in this life, even her own freedom, and who had never let life's trials shake her faith in Jesus. He said that Maria Montgomery Cooper was a name to be remembered as a source of hope and inspiration.

Rose named her daughter Elizabeth. Rose was sick for over a month after the baby was born, and Miriam had to try to support all three of them with her sewing. They moved to smaller quarters and sold most of the furniture they had brought with them from Greenwich Village. They barely had enough to eat. When the baby was six months old, Rose began to look for work. She found a position in a house on Prince Street as a live-in maid. The woman asked Rose if she was single. Rose said she was. She would be free from Sundays after the afternoon meal until the next morning, the woman said; otherwise, she would be required to be fulfilling her duties. She could eat after the family had been served and was entitled to meat once a week. She would be paid every two months.

Rose lived in an attic on the fourth floor, a cramped room with sloping walls; cold in the winter, stifling in the summer. She lit the cooking fire in the morning and put it out at night, shoveling out the cinders and washing down the floor. She prepared the meals and pumped the water and drew the baths and swept the rugs and made the beds. In the winter, she rose early to break the ice in the washing bowls. She cleaned out the chamber pots and scrubbed the privy and boiled tubs of water in which to wash an endless traffic of clothing, drapes, and sheets.

The mistress of the house rarely talked to her except to complain about something undone or done incorrectly. The master was a solemn-faced merchant who never acknowledged Rose's existence except once, when his wife was away and Rose was serving him dinner, and he put his hand on her rear and began to rub. She dropped a ladle filled with hot soup into his lap. After that, he never bothered her. On Sunday nights she returned to the room where Miriam and the baby lived. She brought a small basket filled with sugar and pieces of dried fruit and vegetables and portions of meat, leavings carefully salvaged from the meals she had cooked and served. She played with the baby, then went back to work in the morning. The pay Rose received was pitifully small, but with it Miriam and the baby were able to survive.

Miriam saw a noticeable change in her daughter. Rose became frail and haggard-looking and began to stoop like an old woman. On Sunday evening she would just sit there and ignore the baby. She complained of constant headaches and fevers. One night she giggled and took her mother into a corner of the room and said she had a wonderful secret to tell her.

"What is it?" asked Miriam.

"Mother, the angel Gabriel appeared to me and said he knows where a hoard of gold is buried and will soon reveal its location to me."

"You were dreaming, child."

"It was no dream. He was right there in front of me, white wings and a blue robe with gold buttons. I could even see his sandals and the white linen wrapped around his ankles."

Miriam spoke to the Reverend Mr. Enders. He said the girl was overworked and that Miriam should be sympathetic. In time she would come out of it. She was an intelligent girl who was seeking some solace in her hard situation. Better she saw angels than took to drink. Rose never mentioned the angel again. But she seemed distracted and moody, crying one moment, giggling the next.

It was the Reverend Mr. Enders who brought Miriam the news her daughter had been arrested. Miriam had been waiting on a Sunday afternoon for Rose to appear. There was a knock, and when she opened the door, the Reverend Mr. Enders was standing there. She watched his lips move, his white beard go up and down, saw the crinkles in his brown face around his mournful eyes, but the words didn't seem to make any sense. *Rose has been arrested for theft, arson, and attempted murder. She is being held in chains in the city jail and the possibility of bail has already been ruled out. Her fate is important to every Negro in this city. If a harmless innocent like your daughter isn't safe from persecution, none of us is.*

Mr. Enders insisted Miriam gather up her things and take Rose's child to his house. He said that some white men were already talking about *teaching the niggers a lesson and making sure no nigger would try what Rose tried.* They threw some clothes into a basket, and when they reached Mr. Enders's house, he sat Miriam down and explained what had happened. The evening before, when Rose had finished her chores, she had gone to her mistress to collect the last two months' of salary she was owed. The mistress told Rose that she had become aware someone had been stealing from her kitchen, had observed Rose for the past several weeks, and had seen her leave every Sunday afternoon with a basket of food. As a consequence, she felt she owed Rose no pay at all; indeed, it was Rose who owed her, and she had half a mind to bring charges.

"I stole nothing," Rose said. "I saved scraps from plates to feed my child."

"A child? You told me you were single."

"I am."

"Then you're a whore as well as a thief, and a liar to boot."

The mistress ordered Rose off the premises. Rose gathered her things and left. In the middle of the night, the mistress smelled smoke and came downstairs and found the kitchen on fire. She ran out and screamed, "Fire!" The alarm was sounded in time. Her house was saved, and when she told the city watchmen and the fire volunteers what had transpired that day with Rose, they all agreed the girl must be found immediately. They didn't have to look far. One of the volunteers went down into the basement of the house to see if there was any damage to the flooring, and there was Rose, sitting in the dark, her small pile of possessions on her lap.

They brought her before a magistrate the first thing in the morning. A large crowd was gathered in the courtroom.

"Girl," the magistrate said, "do you know that in seeking revenge against your mistress, you threatened this entire city with destruction?"

Rose's hands and feet were chained. A phalanx of watchmen surrounded her. "They took bread out of my child's mouth and condemned us to starve. They had given up their right to be alive."

The crowd groaned. "Hang the nigger!" someone shouted.

"You would punish all for the supposed sins of one?" the

magistrate asked her. "And you would burn a whole city to cover the crime of pilferage?"

Rose said nothing.

"The charges against you are shocking in their enormity. If you be guilty, hanging is too easy an end."

Miriam saw Rose once in jail. Her daughter barely spoke, but when the jailer left, Rose giggled. "Gabriel is with me every night," she said, "but he says that he needn't tell me where the gold is buried because I shan't have any use for it."

The trial took two days. Rose had no lawyer. The Reverend Mr. Enders asked permission to speak on her behalf. The judge denied it. Mr. Enders started to speak anyway but was dragged from the courtroom. Rose was condemned to be hanged.

"You have admitted this crime," the judge said. "Your only defense is that your deed was justified by what you allege to have been the poor treatment you received at the hands of your mistress, as if that were sufficient reason to take her life and set fire to the city. You showed no mercy; now you shall receive none. And as you have no remorse for the act, I have no remorse in imposing the sentence it requires."

The verdict was handed down on a Saturday. The next morning Mr. Enders took Rose's child, Elizabeth, who was now a girl of three, to the Baptist meetinghouse on Mulberry Street, near Chatham Square, and sat in the upper gallery, from which Negroes were allowed to watch the service. In the middle of it he arose and said in his loud, commanding voice, "There is innocent blood about to be spilled in this city! A confused, agitated woman is to be hanged for a crime she didn't commit!" He picked up Elizabeth and presented her to the congregation. "This child is to be made an orphan!" The sexton came up and told him to be quiet. Mr. Enders continued. The sexton reached out to push him into his seat, but two other Negroes intervened. The minister watched from the pulpit. He recognized Mr. Enders and addressed him: "You are a man of God, sir, and should know better. This is the Lord's house. You know what is required!" Mr. Enders shouted, "Mercy! That is what is required and what you refuse to show! You show no mercy toward colored people, and the longer I live among you, the more I believe you are incapable of ever doing so!"

"Sir," the minister said, "I order you to be quiet and to cease disturbing the worship of this congregation!"

"Glad on it! By the name of Jesus the just, it ought to be disturbed."

Born a slave in Virginia, Benjamin Enders had escaped when he was twelve and been raised by Quakers in Ohio. He had been a minister for ten years in New York, tending his small congregation on Albany Street, and never attracting much notice. But he made the case of Rose Harris a crusade. With the child Elizabeth in tow, he haunted the city's officials and paraded through the streets and thundered on corners and on the steps of public buildings. A few of the city's more prosperous Negroes approached him in private and asked him to stop. They said Rose's guilt was beyond question, she had confessed, and besides, why keep poking a hornet's nest and risking everything on this one woman's fate? "Rose is out of her senses," he told them. "She would confess to setting fire to London if she were asked to. As for hornets, they are forever astir and are as likely to sting you as to sting her, and if you think your modicum of wealth or respectability protects you, think again."

On the day Rose was executed, a great mass of people gathered beside potter's field, where the city's gallows was located. The day before, another fire had occurred in the house of Rose's mistress. It was in the kitchen, as the first had been; and when the fire laddies pulled down the wall, they found a faulty chimney. Believing that this discovery might have some bearing on the previous incident, the captain of the fire brigade sent for the magistrate who had arraigned Rose. When the magistrate was seen entering the house, the rumor spread that another Negro had been caught setting the fire and that the magistrate had been called to investigate the possibility of a Negro plot to burn the city and free Rose. Fire bells rang throughout the night. Any Negro seen on the streets was detained and questioned. When dawn finally arrived, an ill-rested city streamed to witness the cause of its apprehension being sent to her eternal punishment.

They wrapped Rose's legs in heavy chains to ensure her neck would break quickly and so spare her the torture of dangling at the end of a rope. The sheriff asked her if she had any last words, and she said in a small voice that carried across the silent crowd, "I am satisfied with my fate. If it wasn't this, it would be something else." She bounced when the door went from under her feet. The crowd cheered.

Rose's death was Elizabeth's earliest memory. Mr. Enders had taken her by the hand and led her to the front of the crowd. Sometimes the whole thing would come back to mind: the sheriff in his official dress, the blue coat and gold buttons, his fat legs enmeshed in white hose; the chains around Rose's feet; the pressure of Mr. Enders's hand around hers; the bang of the trapdoor and the way her mother's body had gone down and then shot up again. When she was old enough, Elizabeth wrote in the family Bible, next to where her great-grandmother Maria had recorded Rose's birth: "Murdered by the City of New York."

After Rose's execution, Mr. Enders told his congregation that New York was as much a part of Egypt as Virginia or South Carolina. "The Lord's wrath is coming on this people," he said, "all of them, in whatever province of Egypt they might dwell. And until that day comes, let us remove ourselves, as Moses did, to Midian's Well, and await the day of His command." Mr. Enders had no family. Miriam became his housekeeper. Elizabeth was raised in his house. Some of the congregation resisted leaving. They asked what would happen to the old cemetery. "Let the dead bury their dead," he said. The majority followed him. Quietly, they sold whatever they had. In conjunction with the elders of the congregation, Mr. Enders purchased an expanse of land on the south shore of Staten Island. They built a church. One by one, the families built small houses. They farmed and developed a thriving business as oystermen. They avoided as much as possible any contact with "Egyptians," as Mr. Enders called whites, and waited patiently for the Day of the Lord's Instruction to arrive in the unincorporated village of Midian's Well.

Eliza was born there in 1840. She was called Maria Rose after her great-great-grandmother and her grandmother. She was the only child of Elizabeth's to survive. The four other names were entered in the Bible in her mother's small, neat script, the dates of their short lives inscribed underneath. Only her name was without a second date. *Maria Rose Pryor / Born this 20th of January, the year of our Lord 1840–*

Perhaps by now her father had already entered a date, chosen one at random or used the day she disappeared into the city. A few times, in those first days after she left Midian's Well, she went in the early mornings down to the market at Catherine Street and stood in the shadows, watching the men from the village unload their oysters. Occasionally, her father was among them. The oystermen had as little contact with the white merchants as possible. One man handled the money. The rest did the unloading. Then they sailed off into the mist, a small company of black men in broad-brimmed hats, their eyes turned skyward as if they were expecting a messenger from heaven to descend. They stopped coming sometime in 1857, after the financial panic. She asked the merchants in the market about them. Nobody knew. Maybe they had all gone to Canada. Mr. Enders had talked about it. Or Africa. Maybe one of the recolonization societies had learned about Midian's Well and decided to finance transporting the entire community back to Africa.

Men and women in blackface were on the move all around Eliza. The final scene. A compact version of Mrs. Stowe's happy ending: All the darkies gather behind George Harris, Eliza's husband. Uncle Tom is dead. Eliza and George have left Canada or Europe, and now, in the finale, they stand on the deck of a simulated ship. Everyone is reunited, slave sons and slave mothers, slave brothers and slave sisters.

Regan, the chief stagehand, walked by Eliza. He clapped his

hands. "Let's move it," he said. Eliza slipped the shawl over her head. It saved her the trouble of putting gray powder in her hair. George had slipped on a gray wig. He was played by Tad Bigelow. This was Bigelow's last night in the play. He had landed a part in a play at Laura Keene's Theatre—*Our American Cousin*. It was a comedy. He tugged on the ends of the billowing wig and ran his hands over it, pressing it to his head. His face was a light brown, shoe polish mixed with wax. He pressed a large white mustache onto his upper lip. He extended his lower lip and exhaled. The mustache lifted toward his nose. "Damn thing," he said. He turned around and faced Eliza. "Can you do something with this?" Eliza wet her forefinger, gently lifted the mustache, and ran the finger underneath. She put the mustache back and pressed it with her thumb. Bigelow extended his lower lip again and blew. The mustache stayed in place. "Sweet girl," he said, and patted her face. "I wish I could take you with me." He looked a little bit like a lion.

"*Our Negro American Cousin?*" Eliza said. "Somehow I don't think Miss Keene would welcome such a change."

Bigelow laughed. "I guess not." He turned around and faced the curtain. Eliza stood behind him, and the rest of the darkies behind her. Next to Bigelow was a captain's wheel, and above them all was a sail. He rested one hand on the wheel. Regan raised his arm and then brought it down quickly. The stagehands pulled on their ropes, and the curtain rolled up smoothly.

Bigelow pointed off in the distance over the heads of the audience. "There it is, at last," he said in a loud voice. "Africa!" Eliza came forward and stood next to him. A second-rate actor, she thought. When he wished to indicate sincerity, he raised his voice. The mark of bad preaching and bad acting. Stamp of a born amateur. Maybe he would be better at comedy.

"O sweet land of my ancestors." His voice went higher. "My soul thirsts for thee, and it is with the oppressed, enslaved African race that I wish to cast in my lot. Indeed, should I wish anything, it would be that this skin be two shades darker, rather than one lighter." He raised one of his gloved hands to his face and ran a line down the side, careful to keep his finger an imperceptible distance from his cheek.

"The desire of my soul is for an African *nationality*." His voice rose another notch. "I wanted a people that could have a tangible, separate existence! Some pointed me to Haiti. But what is Haiti? A stream cannot rise above its fountain. The race that formed the character of the Haitians was a worn-out, effeminate one. Its people will be centuries in rising to anything."

In the balcony, the ushers were already cracking the doors open in anticipation of the play's ending. Eliza kept her eyes on Bigelow. The first man she had ever given herself to was a Haitian sailor. He came up to her outside the old A. T. Stewart department store on Chambers Street as she was looking in a window. A beautiful coal-black face, strong, intense, with a thin, carefully trimmed mustache. He followed her to where she lived. Returned a week later. Took her to a restaurant on William Street. It was filled with white people, and most of them seemed to know him and nobody stared at them when they ate. She had her first glass of wine with him. He made love to her in the bare, small room where he lived. It was spring. The air was warm and she could hear the traffic as it moved through the streets. A musical sound.

They lived together for a month. She loved the clean sparseness of the room. They had a wooden chest for their clothes. On a nail above the chest, the sailor hung a pair of rosary beads: black pellets and a silver crucifix. One morning she woke and he was sitting on the bed stroking her hair. He was dressed and there was a canvas bag at his feet.

"I am leaving," he said.

"Leaving?"

"Going to sea."

She sat up. "And what about me?"

"What about you?"

"Where am I to go? How am I to pay the rent?"

He put a five-dollar gold piece in her hand. "Stay here," he said. "I have talked to the landlady, and she will allow it."

Eliza tried to clear her head of sleep. "But I thought I could go with you, that we might be married and find a place to live, a home, someplace you would always come back to."

"Go with me to sea?" He laughed, and Eliza saw again how good-looking he was and she felt a hollow ache inside herself.

"I will find a place, and someday I will take you there," he said.

"Haiti?" she asked.

"You would be freer there, but hungrier, too. And Haiti likes foreigners even less than this place does."

"Where, then?"

"Child, I don't now. I'm still looking. There are places where the free colored man is welcomed but only so long as he is few in number and usually without a wife and family. The colored in any number makes the white man nervous. For the time being, you are safe here, at least in this part of the city. Stay to yourself. It will only be until I return."

When he left, she stared at the empty space on the wall where his rosary beads had been. She knew he was gone forever.

"Oh, not Haiti!" Bigelow's voice had risen to a scream. "But Africa!" Eliza took his arm. He would probably be just as bad at comedy as at tragedy. "On the shores of Africa I see a republic formed of picked men, who, by energy and self-educating force, have, in many cases, individually, raised themselves above a condition of slavery. Having gone through a preparatory stage of feebleness, this republic has, at last, become an acknowledged nation on the face of the earth. And here it is we shall go. Here it is we shall find ourselves a people!"

The theatre rocked with applause. So long, George. Goodbye, Eliza. Farewell, Cato, Betty, Cuffee, Nina, Plato, Maria, Miriam, Rose, Elizabeth, nine generations of Negroes who somehow managed in their struggles and travails to establish no claim to any part of the American continent. When your descendants have all been freed and returned to Africa, we'll have our burnt-cork actors to remind us of you!

The doors behind the balcony were fully opened. The light

from the hallway beyond streamed in. The night a few weeks before, when Mulcahey had brought up the subject of marriage, he could see that he had upset her. He tried to comfort her. He was always that way with her, gentle and reassuring, and she loved this about him. For all his talking and pretending, for all his drinking and theatrics, he was kind.

"Look, Eliza," he said, "when the war ends, maybe we can move to Cuba. The races live together down there just fine, that's what I'm told. You want to rush everything. Go slow, Eliza. It ought to come naturally to a southern girl. Trouble is, you're trying too hard to fit into this city. Everybody here wants what they want *now*."

The darkies in the background linked arms. Eliza continued to stare at Bigelow. The sweat was rolling down his cheek onto his collar. The wax he mixed with the shoe polish stopped the color from streaking. "*Our nation,*" he cried, "shall roll the tide of civilization and Christianity along its shores, and plant there mighty republics, that, growing with the rapidity of tropical vegetation, shall be for all coming ages."

The entire cast took a step forward. She let go of Bigelow's arm. He stepped closer to the audience. "We want a country, a nation, of our own. Our African race has peculiarities yet to be unfolded in the light of civilization and Christianity, which, if not the same with those of the Anglo-Saxon, may prove to be, morally, of even a higher type."

More applause.

"To the Anglo-Saxon race has been entrusted the destinies of the world, during its pioneer period of struggle and conflict."

Applause again.

"To that mission its stern, inflexible, energetic elements have been well suited. But as a Christian, lo, I look for another era to arise. On its borders I trust we stand, and the throes that now convulse the nations are, to my hope, but the birth pangs of an hour of universal peace and brotherhood."

The darkies began to hum and move their feet as if they were marching.

"We go to *Liberia*!" Bigelow shouted.

Eliza heard real passion in his voice. Bigelow was free at last. Tomorrow he would be rid of George, the wax and shoe polish, and in a part that might win him some attention.

The darkies stopped their humming and said in chorus, "We go not to an Elysium of romance, but to a field of work!"

"To work *hard*!" Bigelow said.

"With both hands!" the chorus answered.

"Against all difficulties and discouragements!"

"Until we conquer or we die!"

Bigelow lowered his voice and threw open his arms. "This is what we go for. And *we* shall not be disappointed."

"Drop it," Regan yelled. The curtain rolled down. Bigelow called over to Regan, "Bring it up twice, no more, I'm not going to stand here all night." Uncle Tom and the other members of the cast came on stage. The curtain came up. They bowed. The applause continued. Bigelow walked into the wings and returned with Bruno, the slave-hunting hound. There was a burst of laughter from the audience. He looked down and saw that Bruno had Eliza's doll in its mouth. He tried to pull it loose, but the dog held on and snarled. He bowed his head as if to signal the dog's victory, and the audience laughed again, their applause unabated.

APRIL 14, 1863

In reading the history of nations, we find that like individuals, they have their whims and their peculiarities; their seasons of excitement and recklessness, when they care not what they do. We find that whole communities suddenly fix their minds upon one object, and go mad in its pursuit; that millions of people become simultaneously impressed with one delusion, and run after it, till their attention is caught by some new folly more captivating than the first. We see one nation suddenly seized, from its highest to its lowest members, with a fierce desire of military glory; another as suddenly becoming crazed upon a religious scruple; and neither of them recovering its senses until it has shed rivers of blood and sowed a harvest of groans and tears, to be reaped by its posterity.

—Charles Mackay, *Extraordinary Popular Delusions and the Madness of Crowds*

I

Den I walks up and down Broadway wid my Susanna.
And de white folks will take me to be Santa Anna
Hey get along, get along Josey,
Hey get along Jim, along Joe!

A refrain Dunne couldn't get rid of. Over and over it ran through his mind. A deckhand on the ferry from Brooklyn whistled the tune, and the words floated up from nowhere. Couldn't remember where or when he learned them, but there was no getting free.

Hey get along, get along Josey,
Hey get along Jim, along Joe.

Get along is right, Dunne thought. It was his third time around the block, and he knew he made an odd sight: a lone figure in the northern reaches of the city taking a stroll around the outside of a half-finished church, picking his way across a row of broken planks, the local version of a sidewalk, in a rain as heavy as horse piss.

Anyone gazing out a window had to wonder, *What's that jack up to? Been circling the block several times. Check and see the door is locked. Get a good look at him, height, dress, make a note for the Metropolitans.*

The shade on Capshaw's front window, the one next to the door, was still pulled down. In his note, Capshaw had given Dunne a signal to wait for: *When the shade in the window nearest*

the door is raised, then and only then will you know it's safe. Be
there at four.

It was half past that now.

Dunne halted in front of Capshaw's stoop. A solemn row of
houses, but nothing more than another of Capshaw's swindles.
Started as a dry-goods clerk, selling the stuff he lifted, until he
decided to go into the fencing business and graduated to richer
stock than pants and shirts. One of the first to learn that Archbishop Hughes—"Dagger John," as the Yankees called him—
planned to build America's largest church up in the wilderness.
Tipped off by a fellow True American in the architect's office,
Capshaw bought all the land he could around where the Paddies
were set to build their church. He told the old farmer who owned
the adjacent lots that the city wanted to use the land for a hospital
to treat victims of cholera. The old man practically wept with
gratitude at Capshaw's kindness in taking the property off his
hands.

Waldo Capshaw laughed the time he told Dunne the story,
at least close to a laugh, a choking noise in the back of the throat,
half cough, half laugh: "I got the whole block for a song, and old
farmer Greene goes off thinkin' I'm a real live Father Christmas!"

Dunne imagined it was the old farmer who must be laughing
now. The houses Capshaw built on the land he swindled enjoyed
a direct view of the biggest hole in Christendom, half-built walls,
a field of mud, all of it surrounded by a tumbledown wooden
fence plastered with peeling broadsides for minstrel shows and
remedies for the aches and pains of the female condition. Might
as well be a cholera hospital for the good it had done him. Took
the corner house for himself; the rest he couldn't sell and had to
rent.

The shade went up, came down again, and shot skyward.
Capshaw's face was pressed up against the glass. Had a nose as
prominent as a bird's beak. He beckoned impatiently with his
hand. His lips moved silently behind the glass. Dunne ignored
him. He decided to walk and circle back, strolling like it was in
the May sunshine. Get a little wetter, drip all over Capshaw's fine

rugs and sit in one of his soft chairs without removing the soaking coat, letting the water seep out. Nobody worried about the condition of his furniture as much as Capshaw did. Let him see the hand go through the hair, as if combing the wetness out. Make sure it was all greased up with pomade, then rub it across the upholstery. The hair atop Capshaw's head would bristle like a cockatoo's crest. But he'd hold his tongue as long as they were talking business.

Back in front of the house, Dunne went slowly up the stoop. He was sure this was some kind of test, letting him rot in the rain. But a test for what? How eager he was. Sure, let the Paddy almost drown, and every minute he stays out there proves how hungry he is for what Capshaw has to offer. Expects he'll walk in with drool on his chin.

"Come in, come in." Capshaw opened the door but kept his body half behind it, shielding himself from the rain. Dunne pushed past him, shook like a dog, spraying water in every direction. Capshaw stood back.

"Can I take your coat?"

"Little good it'll do. I'm wet right through."

"Couldn't be avoided. I had business to be done before we could talk." Capshaw led the way into the parlor. "You can stand by the fire," he said.

"I'm tired of standing. I'll just pull up a chair and sit awhile."

"Suit yourself. Care for coffee or cocoa?"

"Nothing stronger?"

"You know the position I takes in regard to spirituous liquors."

"I'm afraid I do." A temperance man. See you in hell before he'd stand you to a drink.

"Damn rain," Capshaw said. "It's the war that's causing it. It's a proven scientific fact. The smoke from the gunpowder been shot off rises into the atmosphere and forms into clouds that condense and cause the rain. They almost drowned in Europe the year after Waterloo. Rained steady for months before the air cleared and people got a peak at the sun. No telling how long it will take before things get back to normal in this country, at least as regards the weather."

"Maybe it ain't the smoke at all. Maybe it's the noise of all them rifles and cannons." Dunne ran his hand through his hair until his fingers were streaked with grease. He rubbed them across the silk-flowered armrest of the chair. Two could play at this. Be glad to sit here until midnight and talk about the weather if that was Capshaw's game.

"Just wish it would stop, that's all. Bad enough tryin' to rent properties in this part of the city when the days is dry and bright, but with the mud and the floodin', people steer clear of here, and that ruin across the street don't help things. A bloody disgrace the way the whole area been allowed to deteriorate. The city fathers are afraid to do anything about it, afraid of what Dagger John will do."

"Don't worry, Waldo. I hear old John has told the nuns to open a home for paupers with the syph right on the spot where he'd once planned to build his rectory. Soon the neighborhood will be crowded with them, and won't be so lonely up here no more."

"I ain't lonely, Dunne, and though I might be vexed by the current state of things, ain't worried neither. In the long run, you can't lose money on real estate in this town, not if you stick with it. Reductions in price is always temporary, and if the upper class avoids the place, the lower class will find its way here. Won't buy, but they'll pay dearly in rent. Somebody will live here, don't matter if they opened a home for lepers across the street."

Capshaw continued with his speech about the eternal value of real estate. Dunne settled into the chair. He pulled out a bag of tobacco, patted it. Damp but not wet. He reached into his pocket and got the square gold case with the rolling papers. A memento of the first job with Dandy Dan. Went in through the coal chute, down into the basement, came back upstairs, and let him in. Picked up the case on a table in one of the bedrooms. It was atop a book. Lit a locofoco to see what else there was to lift. The cover of the book caught Dunne's eye. Red velvet with the words ARETINO'S POSTURES embossed on the cover. Couldn't imagine what it was until he opened it. Jesus, never seen pictures like it, at least not back then. A drawing of a man with a big stiff member plowing into a woman with legs spread wide as a train tunnel. All sorts of pictures like that, so he lit another loco and the next thing Dandy Dan had him by the throat and shook him like a rag. "Don't you ever strike a light again," he said. "Do and you're through, you hear. Damn stupid mistakes like this is what'll wind you up in jail."

Dan never missed a trick. Soon as the match was out, put the book in his coat. Thought Dunne didn't notice, but he did. Dan could be like that. Generous, sure. But not above keeping the best for himself. Never mentioned the gold case to him. Figured that made them even.

Dunne rolled a cigarette, tapped it on the case, struck a loco on the heel of his shoe, and lit it. Capshaw finished with his real estate talk. Spoken with such conviction it sounded to Dunne like preaching. Protestants: They loved their sermons.

Across the room, the glow from the fireplace flickered on the highly polished floor. The big standing clock in the corner ticked loudly. Leaning forward, Capshaw put his face so close he seemed about to whisper in Dunne's ear. Yet he spoke in a strong, clear voice. "Have any idea why I asked you here? What it is I want to discuss?"

Dunne turned slightly, so that Capshaw's beak was almost touching his, and exhaled right in his face. "Not real estate?"

"No." Capshaw straightened up, coughing. He moved his hands like a fan, dispersing the smoke.

"And not the weather."

"No."

"I give up, unless there was no reason other than to watch me paddle around like a duck in that pond outside."

"Couldn't be otherwise. Had a person here stayed longer than I thought he would. Didn't want no one else knowing he was here. Was particular about that. Said he'd be here at three, so I figured he'd be gone before you arrived. Turns out he spent more time with me than he planned. Left by the back door only a few minutes ago. Went over the fence through them empty lots toward Lexington Avenue."

"This a man or a cat?" The ash drooped on the end of the cigarette. Capshaw hurried into the hall and came back with a small copper urn. He put it in Dunne's lap. Dunne flicked the ash onto the rug.

"Oh, this was no cat, and not any ordinary man neither, no sir, this was a gentleman!"

"Don't sound like a gentleman to me, not if he's in the habit of slithering out back doors and shimmying over fences."

A choking noise came from Capshaw's throat: a laugh. He cocked his head to the right, opened his eyes wide. With that big beak of his, he looked to Dunne a little like the parrot they kept on the bar in Harry Hill's. Feed him a cracker and he'd angle his head the same way. "Hang Abe Lincoln," the parrot would say.

"That's because you're a Paddy and ain't had no real exposure to gentlemen. See 'em in their big coaches and fancy clothes and thinks they belong to another order of creation. Well, let me inform you of somethin', ain't nobody better at back doors and quick escapes than gentlemen. Someday when you've time to, go down to William Street, right off Broad. Watch the gentlemen skulkin' in and out of the Coal Hole, them with their somber black suits and silk hats, tryin' not to be noticed, like a bishop enterin' and leavin' a goosing slum. What a sight! All of 'em lookin' this way and that, then slippin' into a basement no bigger than the one McGloin uses to stage his cockfights. Only our Knickerbocker aristocrats ain't there to get goosed or to bet on chickens. No sir, they're there to bet on gold!"

The hair on top of Capshaw's head was flaxen, dry and straight as straw. Protestant hair. He pulled at it with his hand and it poked up from his skull. Harry Hill's parrot in the flesh.

"*Gentleman.* What the hell is the word supposed to mean?"

"Ain't got a clue."

"Maybe I never had the proper schooling or made the right marriage, but I never bet on my country losing the war. Never

made a penny on this war. Matter of fact, I'm a monthly sub-
scriber to the Sanitary Commission, donate regular, never missed
a pledge. But these gentlemen, them with all their patriotic talk,
well, the minute the war starts going bad, they start putting their
money in gold. Every battle the Union loses, up goes gold. If the
Rebels take Washington, there'll be nothing in this world as
worthless as government paper. So our gentlemen friends ain't
taking any chances. But they're embarrassed by all this gold in-
vesting. Don't look good, them putting their money on a Rebel
victory while they're sitting at patriotic dinners toasting the Union
and victory! So they ban gold trading from the Exchange for 'the
duration of the hostilities,' then slip around the corner and trade
gold in a room so dark they can barely make each other out. Go
see for yourself, Dunne, 'the pestilence that walketh in darkness,'
as the Good Book says, all rigged out in kid gloves and cravats
from Brooks Brothers. And now that the war is going worse than
ever, the pestilence has emerged into noonday. They're running a
regular gold market in Gilpin's News Room, right up from the
Exchange, charging a twenty-five-dollar membership fee. Most of
'em use proxies, but everybody knows who's behind the game.
Gentlemen, that's who! They're doing volume of over five million
dollars a day. *A day!* The Union forever, and if not forever, then
be sure you're in gold!"

"Your visitor a goldbug?"

Capshaw's head was cocked so that only the right eye seemed
aimed at Dunne. The eyebrow was lifted high, arched in anger.
He didn't seem to have heard Dunne's question. He stood there
and didn't say a thing. An odd bird. Dunne half expected to hear
the parrot's voice: *Hang Abe Lincoln!*

After a pause of several moments, Capshaw said, "No, he
ain't, though he probably wishes he'd placed his bets on gold
instead of with John Morrissey. A big loser at the faro table, that's
what he's been, and now Morrissey is starting to turn the screws."

"Why's he coming to you? Never heard it rumored you got
any influence with Morrissey."

"Morrissey's the lowest of the low. Got the morals of a rat

and the manners to match. I wouldn't shake his hand or breathe the same air. He's a lyin', murderin', cheatin' son of Satan.''

Capshaw lowered himself into the chair facing Dunne's. Sat ramrod straight, hands on knees. On the back of his right hand was the tattoo of an eagle, its talons near the knuckles, wings spread wide, in its beak a writhing serpent, around its head the initials OSSB. The mark of the secret brotherhood of oath-bound True Americans, the Know-Nothing Order of the Star-Spangled Banner, which was no secret at all, least of all to the Paddies battling it for control of the streets. Was Morrissey helped put them in their place. Made his name barging into their clubs and smashing up their meeting halls. A bear of a man, he broke their noses and ripped off their ears, and one famous day he stormed into the lion's den, the American Club on Water Street, and challenged Tom Hyer, the heavyweight champ, and Bill "the Butcher" Poole. They almost killed him. Morrissey's eye was hanging on his cheek and Poole was set to cut his throat when they decided to let him live as a lesson to all of Paddydom of what happens when you attack a True American. Only Morrissey wasn't cowed. As he limped out the door, he shouted, "Yankee sons of bitches, I'll be back!"

Back he came. Fought the True Americans for every polling place. Put out the word that ears and noses would be regarded as prized trophies, bring 'em back as proof of what you done, Morrissey said, and he'd take care of you. The Tammany chiefs made him their number one brave. They saw that the Paddies had the votes, and if Dagger John owned their minds and souls, was Morrissey had their hearts, so the chiefs gave him anything he wanted, and he led the boyos of the Five Points against the True American gladiator of the Bowery. He always reminded his men that if they proved cowards in front of the Star-Spangled gangs, they would have him to deal with and he would give them a worse thumping than they would get at the hands of any American.

The even, anxious ticking of the clock echoed through the room. Dunne rolled another cigarette, running his tongue slowly along the glued edge of the brown paper. It had begun to sink in that the secret visitor and Morrissey were tied together with the reason for Capshaw's invitation. Key in hand, Capshaw approached the mystery and seemed ready to unlock it.

"You trust me?" he asked.

The smoke caught in Dunne's throat. He coughed until his eyes grew wet and bleary.

"I'm like you, Dunne, the word *trust* makes me choke. Be in Sing Sing a long time ago if it didn't. But what exists between us ain't trust at all. It's the mutual knowledge that we're each looking out for our own good. Won't allow ourselves to be cheated. You bring me what you have and I pay what I think is right, maybe sometimes less than you expect, maybe sometimes more."

"Always less," Dunne said.

"Ain't no fraud or pretense or illusions between us, and that's a rare thing in this life, very rare."

"Sounds like you're asking me to marry you."

"Like that about you, too. Got a sense of humor. No, I ain't proposing matrimony, but I am lookin' for a partner. Somebody got your skills. Somebody steady, quiet, sober, who'll take the profits might come from the undertakin' I have in mind and use them sensibly, in a manner not guaranteed to draw the bulls down our necks. I know you take a drink, and you know my feelings on the subject, but I've never seen you drunk or under the influence. You ain't much like most of your kind, and I don't mean that in a deprecatin' way, but it's true and everybody knows it's true that the worst characters in this trade are the foreigners."

"Sorry, Waldo, but I don't work with partners. Dandy Dan was the first and last."

"Neither do I. But what I got in mind is too big for me to handle alone, and what I'm proposin' is a one-time partnership. We're in, we're out, each our separate roads. Can't work no other way. If it works, both of us be assured the gelt to get outta this business. Don't know about you, but that's one exit I'm ready to make. This was once a profession. Now it's Pandemonium itself. Never sure if the next gip through the door ain't gonna cut your throat. Look at poor Mosie Pick. Talked to the Metropolitan who found her body. Her throat wasn't just slit, he said. Her head was taken off. Well, I don't intend to be found someday with a severed windpipe or my brains beat out. I'm not content to sit and wait until that fate comes through my door. No sir, I'm set to strike the mother lode, get out and set myself up in some safe and respectable country place. But I need a partner."

The bird's eye fixed itself on Dunne: "Well, which is it? In or out? Can't say no more less I know I'm talkin' to my partner." Capshaw's Adam's apple bobbed up and down as though he were trying to swallow a worm.

"Hardly told me much. I need to hear more before I decide."

"Told you all there is to tell for now."

Dunne was poised to rise but didn't. He was tired from walking around in the rain all that time, but it went beyond a single afternoon: ten years since the first job, the big, fat watch hanging from the vest pocket of a red-faced, barrel-bellied gent. The others egged him on. They were riding for nothing, hanging off the back of the Broadway coach. The driver ignored them, and all the fancy people in their finery pretended not to notice, afraid of the rowdies and the ruckus they made.

The watch hung there, ripe as an apple.

Go on, Jimmy. Grab it!

He reached and caught it in his hands, pulled so hard a button came off the vest. *Run, Jimmy, run!* He jumped off slam into the arms of a Municipal. The others scattered, laughing and singing as they went:

> *Hey get along, get along Josey,*
> *Hey get along Jim, along Joe!*
> *So long, Jimmy!*

Going back to the Orphan Asylum or being locked up would have been easy time, all the while with people he knew. But the judge commended him—that's the word the judge used—to the Children's Aid Society, and it was off to the West. Made it back in three months. That's when Dandy Dan spotted him. Never understood why Dandy Dan picked him out from all the others. Then once, toward the end, when Dan was sunk in drink, Dunne asked him directly.

In a flash, Dan seemed to sober up. "That first winter I landed in New York, it wasn't much better here than in Ireland. Know what saved us? Rats. Not the fat ones with the glossy coats. They were used to dining on the scraps of the city's finest restaurants. But the runts. We fought them for control of the garbage mounds by the North River. Beat them off with sticks. But the runts clung to those heaps. Gradually we came to realize: Wherever they were, that's where we'd find the meat bones and discarded vegetables. Follow them and find a feast! Wasn't for them runts, we couldn't have survived. Ended up, we felt not only gratitude but comradeship, and when I first saw you, Jimmy, was a brother runt I saw, quick, alert, a snout for survival, knew in an instant: There's the boy for me!"

Dan fell off the roof onto the iron-pointed railing in front of the house he was trying to break into, was impaled on it, the point driven up under his chin and sticking out his mouth like a rat-catcher's spear.

"I'm in, Waldo," Dunne said.

A triumphant grin spread across Capshaw's face. He got to his feet again, put his hands into his back pockets, and pumped his elbows back and forth, like wings. "You'll never regret it, Dunne! I promise you that."

"Now tell me what I'm in."

"Tell you as much as I know. My gentleman caller has been here before. He's a man of considerable means. Or was before he backed himself into a corner and tried to escape by means of the faro table. Remarkable, ain't it, the stupid things smart men do. Dug a hole for himself gamblin', and not just any hole, mind you, but a hole in the House of Morrissey. Of course, that bastard lent him the shovel and let him dig deep as he wanted, but the day arrives when the hole is so deep our gentleman can't climb out and that's when Morrissey announces the days of diggin' is over. Now is the time for fillin' in!"

"How'd you find all this out?"

"Don't matter. What matters is I know what I know. Our gentleman friend wakes up one day to realize that if he can't pay, he faces the less-than-tender ministrations of Morrissey's henchmen. He can't just dump his clients' stocks on the Exchange. Word of what he done would spread fast and furious among that club. So he starts takin' their bearer bonds, which he holds in trust, and looks for someone who can fence 'em, which is me."

"Neither the Exchange nor the House of Morrissey holds an attraction for me, Waldo. Steer clear of both."

"Just listen, please, a moment more, I'm getting to the point. Our gentleman is amassing a great store of cash, little of which, I have reason to believe, he's paid to Morrissey. Before long he'll make a run for it, I'm sure of it. And think what it means. A small fortune sitting somewhere in this city, the owner of which can't go to the Metropolitans should it be stolen from him. What's he gonna say? 'The money I stole been stolen from me'? And he can't tell Morrissey either. 'Oh, Jack, by the way, I had what I owed, but somebody took it away.' Fortune or no, he's gotta fly quick or face prison or an unmarked grave. And we're left in possession of a fortune no one knows we have!"

"Sounds perfect, like one of those military plans for trapping General Lee. But perfect as they are, they never work. Suppose, for instance, our friend don't steal the money but borrows it legitimate. Then he runs to the police the minute it's missing. Or maybe he'll arrange some schedule for repaying Morrissey. Or maybe he'll make a killing on the Exchange and not have to borrow nothing. Maybe he'll skip town tonight with what he's already got. Even if he does what you say, even if he loots his company or his friends of everything they got, how are we supposed to nose out where he stuffs it? And one thing more. Should Morrissey ever suspect you or me of scheming to do him outta what he was owed, he'll feed us to his pit dogs."

"You ain't listenin'. The whole idea is that Morrissey never knows a thing. Sets his dogs on the trail of a former patron of his faro table while we're sittin' as quiet as the dead."

"Quiet as the dead is right. Morrissey would see to that."

"If there's one to worry, it's me. I'm the American. You're one of his, and they can say what they like about the Paddies, but there's no denyin' they stick together tight as Chinamen. We Americans could take a lesson from you, stead of slaughtering each other over whether the niggers should be free."

"Don't fool yourself, Waldo. Morrissey will do what he has to do to protect his realm. Was a Protestant mayor first set him up in a gaming house of his own. Was a gang of True Americans arranged the fight with the Boy Heenan. Morrissey has been loyal to his own, ain't no doubt, but don't mean he won't join hands with a Protestant to make money or kill an Irishman tries to take it from him. Send us both to the same grave. Maybe he'd enjoy killing you and regret having to do it to me, but it'd be done all the same, very democratic-like."

The parrot turned into an owl: Capshaw sagged back down into his chair. He stared intently into space, solemn-faced, sad-eyed, unblinking. He said nothing for a few minutes. When he spoke, there was anger in his voice. "They shoulda hung the bastard a long time ago," he said. "That's the problem with this city, we stopped meting out justice. And when you do that, it's the rabble takes over. That's what happened in ancient Rome, and that's what's happened here, and I don't need no history book to read about it because I seen it happen with these very eyes, seen it from start to finish. Was there the night they done in Bill "the Butcher" Poole. Thousands make that claim, but I really was. Stanwix Hall had just opened, all marble, cut glass, copper fixtures, and a brass plate right by the door: NO FOREIGNERS OR DOGS ALLOWED. Morrissey took it as an invitation, struts in with Monkey Maguire, the self-crowned King of the Newsboys, the lowest specimen of street scum you ever set your eyes on, blazing red hair set atop a face as flat and thick as a nigger's. Shoulda been an exhibit in Barnum's. Respectable women ran when they saw him, which is why Morrissey brought him along, of course. Grins that big Paddy grin of his and walks Maguire right through the bar into the back room. They start playin' cards, spittin' on the floor, and singin' awful Paddy songs. Morrissey was enjoyin' it all, and Maguire even more so, the fact of enterin' a True American stronghold and pissin' on our shoes.

"I was standin' at the bar when the Butcher come in. Was like General Washington himself had returned. A mighty cheer went up. Morrissey comes out to see what all the huzzahin' is about, and Monkey Maguire is cavortin' behind him, and straightaway you can see on their faces the shock of findin' the Butcher had arrived to spoil their fun. All of us stand back, and in an instant Morrissey walks up and spits in the Butcher's face, and the fat ball of it runs down his cheek. The Butcher don't even blink. Simply strikes a fightin' pose. 'When I'm finished with you,' he says to Morrissey, 'there won't be enough left to bury.'

"The Monkey is crying and pleading, 'Oh, Johnny,' he says, 'let's get outta here.' Me, I thought Morrissey and Monkey would run out the back door. Instead, Morrissey, that treacherous dog, pulls out a gun. Didn't see what happened next, took refuge under a table, but heard it sure enough.

"*Click. Click. Click.*

"Three times Morrissey pulls the trigger. Three times nothing happens. The Butcher never flinches. Stands there as rock solid as a statue. Then he pulls out a revolver of his own. 'I shoulda killed you the first time, you stinkin' Paddy cuss,' he says to Morrissey as he puts the barrel right to the tip of his nose. But he don't pull the trigger. Why, I'll never know. We were all expectin' it, hopin' for it. God knows, Morrissey had earned it. With that shot the Butcher might have saved this city and rallied the native workingmen to the defense of their homes.

"But he didn't. Just stands there, holdin' the gun and smilin', and in an instant Monkey Maguire is jumpin' up and down, screamin', 'You wouldn't shoot a defenseless man, would ya? That ain't the American way, is it?'

"God bless him, the Butcher never stopped smilin'. He puts the gun down on the bar and picks up the carving knife lyin' next to the roast that's set there. 'This is the tool of my trade,' the Butcher says, and holds it up for all to see, 'the instrument with which I cut the meat that feeds the True American yeomen of this city. What better tool to cut the balls off a shit-assed foreigner?'

"Justice at last! A chorus of voices calls on the Butcher to do the work. A couple of lads grab hold of the Monkey and stuff a rag in his mouth. Beads of sweat have broken out on Morrissey's head. He crouches as the Butcher approaches. And right then, as the Butcher swings the knife at Morrissey's throat, in come the Municipals, them two-penny hirelings of Tammany that laughingly called itself a police force. They form a circle round Morrissey and whisk him out the door.

"I wasn't there when Morrissey's henchmen came back and gunned the Butcher down, and glad I wasn't. Them that seen it were never the same. The tragedy stayed with 'em forever, the Butcher lyin' there in a puddle of his own American blood, a bullet in the heart. Woulda killed an ordinary man in an instant. The Butcher lasted two weeks. His true heart beat on until it could take no more, and then he bid us farewell in them most famous of last words: 'Good-bye, boys: I die a true American.'

"Five thousand men trudged behind the Butcher's hearse, and a dozen brass bands escorted him to the Brooklyn ferry. The streets was everywhere lined with people, men and women weepin' like little children, some fallin' prostrate as the coffin come by, rich and poor united in their grief. That night, George Law and the gentlemen of the United Order of Americans had a dinner in the Butcher's memory, and it seemed that the decent God-fearin' people was finally as one, that they wasn't gonna take no more, that men of all classes was gonna stand together, no matter what. But it didn't turn out that way. No sir, we was never as strong as we were that day in March of '55. Justice was never done. Tammany rigged the jury so Morrissey and his fellow murderers went free. The foreigners kept pourin' in. The gentlemen abandoned the workingmen, retreated to their neighborhoods and formed a police force that was able to protect them. The True Americans were left to fend for themselves, and after the panic of '57 the fight went out of people. The American workingman just picked up and moved wherever he could, someplace away from his tormentors, to Brooklyn or Westchester or Jersey, and he left the city behind, a carcass to be devoured by Morrissey and his fellow hyenas."

The room had filled with shadows. Burdened by the sadness of his story, Capshaw's head drooped, the beak pointed toward his breast. Poor owl.

Dunne rolled another cigarette and lit it. The flash of flame seemed to snap Capshaw out of his reverie.

"Pardon me," Dunne said, "but you think the John Morrissey you've just described is the same man gonna let you and me get away with his money?"

Capshaw got up and turned the valve on the gas lamp. The shadow retreated. "Ain't paid attention to a thing I said, have you?"

"Haven't missed a word."

"I'll say it one more time: Morrissey ain't gonna know we got his money. He'll be after our gentleman swindler, and even if he catches him, he ain't never gonna believe the man ain't got the money hid somewhere. But I doubt he will catch him. If it goes right, we'll be rich, Dunne. Set yourself up in business. Look around, boy. Ain't no old men in this business. One day you'll read about me being found with my head bashed in, or maybe I'll hear that you ended up like Dandy Dan, fallen from some rooftop with a pike through your jaw."

"You keep talking like you're offering me gold, but it adds up to a lot of gas. A man who *might* steal a fortune and, whenever that *might* be, *might* stash it where we *might* get our hands on it, or, rather, where I *might*, since I'm the one being nominated to carry out that part of the arrangement, the difficult part, the breaking-and-entering part."

"You're good at it. Got a reputation for being smooth."

"Supposin' I say no?"

"You're too smart for that."

"Supposin' I'm loyal to my own kind and go to Morrissey and tell him I talked to someone who's out to jump his jack?"

"He'd thank you. And then, just like you said before, Paddy

or not, he'd have you killed for having had such a conversation."

"Supposin' I do some investigating, find this gentleman for myself—it shouldn't be hard—and pop the beans alone?"

"Then I'd kill you. Track you to the ends of the earth if I had to."

Dunne took a draw on the cigarette, held the smoke, blew an O at the ceiling. It hovered over Capshaw's head. A halo. Saint Waldo the Fence. Capshaw waved away the crown of saintliness. Probably had the same feeling toward tobacco as alcohol.

"I'm not gonna beg. Don't want to be a part of this, just get out. Keep your mouth shut. Mind your own business. Forget we ever talked. But I thought you was smarter than that and had more ambition. Wouldn't have invited you here if I didn't."

"How do you plan we split it?"

"Fifty-fifty, right down the middle."

"Seems to me that the man who actually has to do the job has the greater risk."

"Wouldn't even know where to look or when if it wasn't for me. Fifty-fifty. Ain't no use a-hagglin'. I ain't gonna budge."

One of Dandy Dan's observations: The Yankees are a race born to bargaining. You can rob them with gun or knife or bludgeon, but never with the tongue.

"Fifty-fifty it is."

"I knew it, boy! Knew you wouldn't let me down! I have an eye for character."

"What now?"

"Patience on your part, persistence on mine. I must help our friend along. Tighten the screws a little at a time. Push him down the proper path. One day he'll do it. Ain't no doubt. Take his bundle and skip-toe. That's the moment we strike. We're in, we're out, get the bundle, and off he goes with the Metropolitans and Morrissey in hot pursuit!"

"Can't wait forever. Got my own business to attend to, and I'm no glad leg goes in a place without first lookin' it over and gettin' an idea of what's inside."

"That's why I picked ya. Got a reputation for bein' careful.

Enter a house in some disguise, as a tradesman or the like, before you pull a job. That's the kind of preparation I admire. For now, sit tight, that's all."

Capshaw reached down and removed the urn from Dunne's lap. A signal their meeting was over. Next gip, please. Dunne took a final draw and blew a last O. It circled Capshaw's head, grew wider, and descended around his neck. A noose. Protestants might not believe in omens, but wasn't a Paddy didn't know the truth they held. It was Dunne's turn to wave the smoke away.

"You want me to leave front or rear?" Dunne said.

"Up to you."

"When should I come back?"

"Sit quiet until you hear from me. When the time comes, I'll have another message left at the desk of the New England Hotel. It'll say, eh, 'Father is dead. Please come home instantly. Mother.' "

"One last thing. How'd you know I'm living at the New England?"

"I know mine, and mine know me."

They stood together by the door. Capshaw opened it, and gave his eagle-marked hand to Dunne. They shook. The rain had stopped, but the sky was still threatening, the wind stronger than before. Across the street, the half-built church loomed over the ragged fence, a rain-stained shell.

"Be patient, Dunne. Don't do anythin' foolish."

"Never have."

"Don't start."

Dunne started down Madison. A lone carriage moved up the avenue. He looked back once. Capshaw was at the window, preening. Dunne knew Capshaw was up to more than he had revealed. Had to be a trick in there somewhere. Not sure what. Have to find out for himself, no other way, poke around, listen, ask, play it carefully. A dangerous combination, Capshaw, Morrissey, the Metropolitans, but hit it right, and *hey get along Josey, get along Jim,* no telling what might come.

II

THE WIND SWEPT IN from the harbor, up the long corridors of
stone, shaking the coach as it turned the corner of Thirty-fifth
Street onto Madison Avenue. As they came over the crest of the
hill, Father Corrigan looked out the rain-streaked window across
Forty-first Street at the massive sloping wall of the collecting reservoir, the flag on its rampart standing out straight, pointing
north. The coach picked up speed as it rattled and jolted down
to Forty-second Street. Corrigan leaned forward to look out the
other window at the hill that brooded over the street's east end.
Its slopes were covered by a ragtag collection of shanties. Smoke
rose out of the crooked chimneys that poked through their roofs,
white wisps trailing north with the wind. St. John's parish. Mis-
erably behind in its contribution to the building of the cathedral.
People with goats and small yards full of potatoes, old women
who smoked clay pipes and spoke in Irish. A place to be avoided.
Corrigan sat back in the seat, and turned to his right. The old
man, shrouded in his black cape, was more silent than usual.
Probably been drinking. But didn't smell of it. Could be the
weather. Two days of it now. A burden on even the sunniest
temperaments, never mind those suffering from inordinate mel-
ancholia. Corrigan put his hand gently on the sleeve of his companion's cape. "Your Grace," he said, "don't think it would be
wise to leave the coach. It would be better, I think, if we drove
around the site without exposing ourselves to the elements."

There was no response. The old man's face was up close to
the window, his nose almost pressed against it. A lone figure
moved down Madison Avenue, his head bowed into the wind.
The coach turned onto muddy, rutted Fifty-first Street. Corrigan
felt the weight of the old man fall against him. More shadow than

man. At the corner they turned onto Fifth Avenue and came to a halt.

"Your Grace, we're here." Corrigan grasped the strap by the door and pulled his bulk forward. His cassock came up over his socks. He raised himself off the seat and straightened it. "I'll tell the driver to circumvent the site." He reached up to the small glass panel set high in front of them and knocked on it. It shot back. A red face appeared.

"Yes, Father?" the driver asked.

"Turn around here and slowly circle the cathedral."

The coach rocked as the door swung open. The old man jumped to the ground. Corrigan slid across the seat and crouched at the door. The wind almost blew his hat off. The black cape was already moving away. Corrigan looked up at the panel. The face was still there. "For God's sake, Heaney," he said, "give me a hand." The coachman climbed down slowly and held up both hands. Corrigan took them and lowered himself. He stood and righted his hat. The black cape was moving on. "The mud, Your Grace," he shouted, "be careful of the mud." He turned to the coachman. "Not a word of this to Mrs. Rodrigue, do you hear me, Heaney."

The coachman took off his cap and stuck it in his pocket. There was a smirk on the red face. "Your man has a mind of his own, no doubt about it, a powerful mind of his own." He pointed at the old man. "Better stay close to him. I'll be waiting for you here, Father. And be sure of it. Not a word to the Archbishop's sister." He put a finger to his lips. "Not a word." The smirk spread into a smile.

Corrigan looked to make sure the Archbishop was still in sight. Him a kind of coachman, too. The same roughness. The same undertone of insolence. The edge in his voice that always sounded like a challenge. The Archbishop's sister, as well. Married to the son of a wealthy planter from Santo Domingo. Servants, a French tutor. Her husband's successful career as an architect, with the Archbishop of New York, her brother, as his patron. The mansion on Lexington Avenue. Silk drapes. A cellar full of wine. And still she looked and sounded like one of those crones from the shantytown on the hill above Forty-second Street. Peasants, all of them. An indelible stamp, like the priesthood. Corrigan lifted his cassock at the knees. He walked on the tips of his toes to where Archbishop Hughes looked up at the cathedral. The Archbishop's cape billowed around him, and he kept one hand on the back of his head over his zucchetto, the purple skull-cap the Pope had given him.

"It could start raining again any minute, Your Grace."

The Archbishop started to move again. Corrigan resisted the urge to grab him by the arm and hold him. A fine sight. Archbishop Hughes and his secretary wrestling in the mudhole surrounding the cathedral. They walked along the tall wooden fence that cut the construction sight off from the avenue. The watchman came out from his hut, tipped his hat, and opened the gate. Hughes went past without acknowledging him, his pace quickening. Ahead was a great puddle. Corrigan called after him, "Watch out!" But he went ahead, striding through it, his cape trailing through the water, the mud splattering his slippers and the bottom of his cassock. The parted water closed behind him. Corrigan stepped around the perimeter of the puddle as quickly as he could. The mud sucked at his shoes. Hughes had stopped in front of the great portal, an empty arch with water dripping from its stone.

"Your Grace," Corrigan said as he came up behind Hughes, "please stand back, the wind might blow some debris down; please don't get too close."

The wooden framework that enshrouded the cathedral sagged in places. It had been two years since any workman had used the cranes or climbed the scaffolding. First they had gone on strike. The winter before the war. The Catholics had gone out with the others. Hughes had threatened to find out their names and have their priests order them back to work. An impossible task, the priests told him. It will only embarrass the Church. *Embarrass the Church.* "And what was it called," Hughes asked, "when Irishmen put down their tools and abandoned the con-

struction of a monument to the suffering their race had endured
for the sake of that Church?"

Corrigan watched the parapet above them. Some ropes had
come loose and were swinging wildly in the wind. He moved
closer to the Archbishop. He should take him firmly by the arm.
He should insist they return to the coach. If anything should happen, he would be held responsible. The wind played on the scaffolding. The ropes made a snapping sound, and a piece of one
came loose and sailed over their heads toward the avenue.

"Your Grace, please!"

Corrigan heard the desperation in his own voice. He reached
out to grab the old man's arm. He couldn't. The sanctity of his
office. A successor to the Apostles. Crude at times. Always cold,
distant, exacting. Sometimes cruel. Never at ease, nor concerned
whether anyone else was. Occasionally an embarrassment. A relic.
A bishop who despite his unwavering declaration of loyalty to the
Holy See still saw himself as sovereign in his own diocese, an
equal of the Pope's. That was why the red hat had never been
placed on his head. He had wanted to be the first American cardinal. He wouldn't be. Rome needed him but did not trust him.
His old-fashioned independence and his public avowals of democracy. Cardinal Barnabo of Propaganda had said as much to
Corrigan that final day in Rome. You understand Rome, he said,
because you have been educated here. You have the spirit of a
Roman, Father Corrigan. You will need that very much when you
return home. You must serve Archbishop Hughes as best you can.
He is a great man, and I would not like to see him fall prey to
those in Rome who would destroy him. But he is . . . *the Cardinal
held out his hand with the palm down and gently rotated it* . . .
how shall we say, incautious. He says things that are, eh, hard to
comprehend. So, my friend, you must . . . *the Cardinal put a finger
to his eye* . . . and you must . . . *the Cardinal put a finger to his
ear* . . . and you must . . . *he made a gesture as if he were scribbling on a pad.* We must know what is happening in New York.
Someone must be the eyes and ears of Rome.

Archbishop Hughes stepped forward under the scaffolding and put his hands on the wall. He could have settled for Belleville or Dorchester stone. It was cheaper, said the architect, Mr. Renwick. And just as durable. Mr. Renwick was a Protestant. They tended to be practical in all things. But the worship of God wasn't a practical matter. It was a mystery, sorrowful, joyful, glorious. And this was an edifice that would house the greatest mystery of all: wine into blood, bread into flesh. Protestants didn't believe that. They preferred logic to mystery, Dorchester stone to white marble.

"It may rain again, Your Grace. It will aggravate your rheumatism," Corrigan said. He felt himself sinking into the mud. He lifted his left foot, and the mud almost pulled off his shoe. Water dripped from the scaffolding onto his hat.

The Archbishop stood with his hand against the wall. He seemed not to hear. Corrigan cleared his throat. In the time he had been the Archbishop's secretary, Corrigan had never raised his voice to him. As unthinkable as Peter raising his voice to Our Lord. But now he had no choice.

"Sir, I must insist." He said it so loudly he felt himself stiffen from the sound. Hughes didn't move. Corrigan repeated himself. "Sir, I must insist you step out from here." Nothing. "Sir, Your Grace, your sister gave me specific instruction: 'Keep the Archbishop out of the rain.' "

She had stood by the door, arms folded beneath her small bosom, like a mother superior talking to a novice. She had all the haughtiness of her brother. "Madam Archbishop," some of the priests had taken to calling her since Hughes had moved into her home on the top of Murray Hill, a three-story town house with a commanding view of Brooklyn and the lower city. At first it had seemed a good idea. When they had returned from Rome in February, the Archbishop had been sick. His sister said the old residence on Mulberry Street was drafty and the neighborhood unwholesome. It was hard to argue with her. The squat brownstone cathedral and its grounds were wedged in the narrow streets between Broadway and the Bowery, an insignificant collection of buildings lost amid the tenements, factories, and saloons that surrounded it.

The Rodrigue house was only twelve blocks from the new cathedral. A short drive. The Archbishop can visit it when he wishes, Mrs. Rodrigue said. It will lift his spirits. Besides, this is a home more like the one he will occupy when the cathedral is finished. She was right. Stately, tall, with a corner location that let its rooms fill with southern light, it was a home fit for an archbishop, a long way from the cramped quarters downtown. It was enjoyable at first. The fine carpets, the warmth, the private chapel. Only gradually did the visitor begin to detect the uniformity in Mrs. Rodrigue's voice: She addressed priests and houseguests as she did the light-skinned Negro servants. She and her husband used French with the servants; but it didn't matter, the tone was the same. Clipped, unpleasant, an undercurrent of annoyance.

In the vestibule under the cut-glass chandelier, she had unfolded her arms and put her hands on her hips. Her gray hair was pulled back severely from her face. Always the peasant wife talking to the spalpeens, acting as if she were better than they. Corrigan struggled to maintain an impassive face.

"The Archbishop is not to get out of the coach. He is to be kept out of the rain. Is that clear, Father?"

"We must return to the coach this minute," Corrigan said.

Hughes didn't move. He ran his fingers over the wall. The stone was wet and cool, like a tomb. The day wasn't far off. They would carry him in procession to his grave. The priests in black chasubles with gold crosses embroidered front and back. The altar clouded by incense. But where? Not here. No altar, no roof, no floor, no windows, no vault with the chiseled words ✠ JOHANNES, ARCHIEPISCOPOS PRIMUS NEO-EBORACENSIS ✠ Would he be put beneath the floor of the old cathedral on Mulberry Street? Forgotten. Left behind. When Hughes's sister Mary had died in county Monaghan, the law had forbidden Catholic priests to enter the gates of a cemetery. The procession had stopped at the stone wall, and the priest had reached down and scooped a handful of dirt from the road. The priest blessed the dirt and poured it into Hughes's hands. It made a sad, empty sound when he dropped it onto his sister's coffin. They never raised a marker above her grave. They began leaving the next year. His father went first, to a place called Maryland, a place where they had been told Catholics could live well. A long time ago. Mary waiting all these years beneath the wet grass. No stone to remind passersby to pray for her soul. Her family gone, the last of them driven out by the Famine and the Orangemen. The wind moved through the doorless portal of the cathedral. A sad, empty sound.

"Your Grace, please, I am begging you." Corrigan gently touched Hughes's sleeve. "Step out from here." Large drops of water continued to drop from the scaffolding onto the broad rim of his hat. He kept his hand on Hughes's sleeve. The Archbishop walked away from the wall. Corrigan followed behind him. More rain was imminent. To the west, heavy clouds were skirring low across the sky, their black bellies seeming to scrape the earth as they approached the horizon. There was a long, distant rumble. Lightning crossed the sky.

Corrigan circled the Archbishop like a dog herding sheep. He stayed at his side, directing him toward the wooden fence, then moving him back toward the gate. Corrigan realized he was perspiring. But slowly they were moving in the right direction. You must help guide the Archbishop, Cardinal Barnabo had told him, and he put his hands together like a ship and moved them in a zigzag fashion. Keep him on the narrow path. The Cardinal's hands moved smoothly ahead in a straight line.

They walked side by side back to the gate. Corrigan relaxed a bit. The cheek of Heaney. Sitting in the coach and leaving him to escort the old man alone. Always so polite with the Archbishop, a fawning, cloying, false man. As lazy as any Negro. He always reeked of horse manure and whiskey. His favorite tactic was to engage in conversation as a way of avoiding work. The sort who give the Irish a bad name among the Protestants. He would have to bring this up with Mrs. Rodrigue again. Simply refuse to take him as driver. But Heaney now had this incident to use against him. *Father Corrigan left your brother, His Grace, to wandering in the mud and rain, and it's a miracle he didn't catch the death of it.* Heaney would employ any tactic. Shameless as well as shiftless. They approached the lake of mud. Corrigan began herding the Archbishop away from it. But it was useless. The Archbishop seemed once again determined to part it. Corrigan looked down at the Archbishop's shoes. They were caked in mud. So were the bottoms of his cape and pants. Mrs. Rodrigue would know right away. Corrigan felt small beads of sweat run from his armpits down his sides.

The Archbishop stopped at the edge of the puddle and turned around. In the distance, over the fence that ran along Madison Avenue, he could see the upper stories of a row of brownstones sited where a farmhouse had once stood. Thirteen years ago, before the rumor of the new cathedral led to a fever of land speculation, before Mr. Renwick had been consulted, a stooped, hatless man had come out onto his porch and raised his hand to shield his eyes from the sun. An ancient, solitary Yankee with a white beard, he stayed there for nearly an hour as the three strangers had walked across a field of wildflowers. He watched them as they got back into the coach and drove away.

He was a well-known character in this area, said Mr. Curran, the diocesan lawyer, on the trip home. Amos Greene. As a boy of six or seven, he had helped his mother fill a wagon with food and cider and drove over to the Bloomingdale Road to feed Washington's soldiers as they retreated up Manhattan away from General Howe. His mother had hoped to find her husband amid those men. But he had been captured in Brooklyn. At one point, as they were doling out their food to the retreating Continentals, an advance party of redcoats came up on them, and, Greene claims, he grabbed a musket and fired it at them, killing one of the British soldiers and alerting the Americans. Says he was the youngest person to fire a musket in the Revolution. He's been telling that story forever. Mr. Barnum has agreed to sign him up as an exhibit at his museum. "THE YOUNGEST HERO OF THE REVOLUTION."

Someone to go alongside General Washington's Negro wet nurse.

Nothing left. No farmhouse. No fields. No Amos Greene. Who remembered him, the youngest soldier of the Revolution?

Corrigan stood behind the Archbishop and waited. The wind cut through his clothing. The sweat was a cold film against his body. He would be the one who would end up getting sick. It was Heaney's fault. He shivered. At least the Archbishop was wrapped in his black cape. At the base of the Archbishop's skull, Corrigan noted, were two slight indentations, as if the flesh had wasted away. Hughes was a small man but had the thick, hard body of a laborer, the result of a childhood and young manhood spent as a hired hand. An awkward strength, too concentrated in the arms and chest, it had made him seem larger than he was. But the muscle was disappearing, the Archbishop's body sagging like the framework around his cathedral.

The year he had come over from Rome and taken up his duties as the Archbishop's secretary, Corrigan had driven up from Mulberry Street with Hughes for the laying of the cornerstone. They had put on their vestments in an old farmhouse across from the field. It had been sold by its owner, the boy hero of the Revolution, to a speculator, who had rented it to the diocese for the day. An exorbitant price. But they had no choice. Thirty priests were to be in the procession. They needed someplace to dress. When they had vested and come out on the porch, they were shocked at the size of the crowd that was still gathering. People were streaming up Madison and Fifth. A vast throng already filled the field, a sea that lapped around the wooden island erected near Fifth Avenue on which the dignitaries were to sit.

The Feast of the Assumption. August 15th. It was not yet midmorning, but the heat was blistering. On the fringes of the crowd, the odd tent sprouted up where beer and whiskey were being sold. Hughes called over the Commissioner of Police and demanded it be stopped. But as soon as the police closed one tent, another would open somewhere else. One German beer vendor, with a cask roped down in the back of his wagon, began to scream loudly when the police moved in and tried to lead him away. The crowd surged around him, and the police backed off. Hughes stood motionless on the porch. From behind, Corrigan could see the muscles in the Archbishop's neck as they tightened. Above the white of the stola, his skin was crimson.

Corrigan walked next to Hughes as thurifer. There was barely enough room for them to pass. The people in front pushed back against the solid wall of humanity behind them. There was shouting, and it seemed as if the crowd might surge forward and overwhelm the Archbishop and his priests. Hughes kept moving at a deliberate pace, turning right and left to give his benediction. One man fell to his knees as the Archbishop drew near. The sway of the crowd sent him sprawling. Hughes stepped over him and moved on.

A layer of brown dust began to cover the white vestments of the priests. It filled their mouths. Corrigan thought he would have to put the censer down. With the smoke and the dust, he could barely breathe. He kept moving, his eyes down, and followed the silver-tipped spike on the bottom of Hughes's crosier as it struck the dry, brittle earth. It was frightening to look up. The flushed faces covered with matted hair. Mouths of broken teeth. The smell of a barnyard. Some of them were reeling drunk. Their heavy woolen pants and jackets, hideously ill-fitted, were soaked with sweat. An old woman with a heavy black shawl and a pipe stuck between her teeth held up a pair of rosary beads. She put her face into Corrigan's. "Bless me beads, Father," she said rapidly as she stepped backward. She repeated it over and over. "Bless me beads, Father." The stench of her breath almost made him vomit. He kept the censer in his right hand and blessed her beads with his left.

They drew near to the platform. The crowd was thicker than ever. As people shuffled backward to make way for the procession, others were pushed against the platform. They screamed loudly. Hughes went up the wooden stairs first. When he reached the top, a thunderous cheer went up. Corrigan came up behind him. Governor King was standing there, holding his tall hat in his hand. Behind the small silver circles of his spectacles, his eyes were wide with fear. The dignitaries all stood and crowded around Hughes, as if for protection. In the middle of the platform was the cornerstone. It sat there like an altar. The priests came up behind him and filled the platform. Corrigan stood directly behind Hughes and swung the censer. A priest came forward and opened the book from which Hughes was to read the prayers.

The constant motion of the crowds continued to stir the dust. The sun was at its height and seemed to be burning away what little air there was to breathe. Corrigan kept his eyes down. To his left he could see a portion of the crowd, their heads pressing up against the platform, pain and anger on their faces. Corrigan inched closer to Hughes. He had been in Rome since he was twelve. When his father died, his mother had sold the family's livery stable, on Washington Street, and gone to Rome, where her brother served as rector for the Irish Franciscans. It was the Famine winter. Corrigan remembered the people coming up to the stable door and begging food or work. More and more of them every day. They filled up the neighborhood, cramming into basements and cellars unfit for habitation. Their children took over the streets. At night they scoured the garbage piled up by the river. His mother forbade him to go out. She gave them food, but they stole from her anyway. *They are a disgrace to our kind,* his mother said, *a living, breathing disgrace.*

"O Jesus, I'm being crushed," yelled one woman positioned directly at Corrigan's feet. Her face was scarlet from the heat and her screaming. Other voices competed with hers. Together they made a deafening roar. Only gradually did Corrigan make out a steady insistent sound beneath. A creaking. Wood bending. The platform was beginning to sway. Corrigan looked over at Governor King. His eyes were bulging. "My God," Corrigan heard one of the priests behind him say loudly.

Hughes stood perfectly still. When they had put on their vestments that morning in the farmhouse, a priest had said to Corrigan, "You'll meet your sheep today, Father, the entire flock." Hughes had laughed. "Some of them are a little wild, but they know their shepherd and he knows them." Corrigan had nodded. When they saw the size of the crowd, Hughes lost his humor. "We will proceed slowly," he said. "This is a day of dignity and celebration. The people will not let me down. There will be no cause for scandal. They will not give justification to our accusers. *I know them.*"

The creaking continued. The sway of the platform grew more pronounced. Hughes continued to look down at the book held in front of him. But his eyes were closed. The muscles in his neck were taut and prominent. Suddenly he lifted the crosier above his miter. He clenched it in both fists. Corrigan watched the bulk of the Archbishop's shoulders as he held the staff over his head. He seemed about to hurl it into the crowd. In a strong and steady voice, he intoned, "*In nomine Patris, et Filii, et Spiritus Sancti.*" The noise diminished. The pushing began to stop, those behind gradually making room for those in front. Far back, at the edge of the crowd, the noise around the refreshment tents seemed to become louder as the people near the platform grew quiet. But in a moment it too ceased. Hughes held the stick aloft, a coil of silver at its head. The chieftain's rod. He waited for silence. When it came, he brought the crosier back to his side and began to read the prayers from the book.

Corrigan felt another chill. It made him shake violently. No doubt about it now. He was getting sick. He looked behind him. The watchman had come out of his hut and was staring at them. Corrigan motioned for the watchman to approach. The two of them could quickly escort the Archbishop back to the coach. One on each side for the short distance that was left. There could be no escape. When Corrigan turned around, the Archbishop was already in motion, the wind filling his cape as he sailed forward.

"This is quite enough, quite enough. I am getting sick, Your Grace," Corrigan shouted after him. Hughes moved toward the cathedral. He didn't look behind. The watchman came up beside Corrigan.

"Is there something wrong, Father?"

"Something wrong?" Corrigan said. "Something wrong?" He sputtered with anger. Goddamn Heaney. And Mrs. Rodrigue. And this incorrigible old man. An impossible burden. He didn't deserve such a trial. When he had been about to leave Cardinal Barnabo's apartment, the Cardinal had put his hands on Corrigan's shoulders. "You will have a cross to carry, Father. A heavy cross in a wild and untamed country where heresy is strong. But as the burden is great, so shall be the reward." The Cardinal had gently patted his face.

"Come with me," Corrigan told the watchman. "When His Grace turns around, you walk on one side of him and I'll be on the other. We'll go straight to the coach."

"Yes, Father."

Another drone. The cousin, nephew, brother, of some priest. Poorly shaved. Hairs sticking out of his nose and ears. Cracked and stained teeth. A dull look in his eyes. Another Heaney. Corrigan felt tired. Sometimes the burden was almost too heavy to bear. Hughes was walking up to the wall again. He went under the scaffolding. Corrigan felt the droplets of rain on his hat. It grew more steady. Goddamn.

Hughes walked up a short set of wooden stairs. He stood at what would be a side door into the still roofless cathedral. Inside was a field of mud, planks of wood thrown about. Weeds pushed out from beneath the large blocks of marble that sat squat and forlorn. A ruin like the thousands of ruined churches and abbeys of Ireland. Save for the cathedrals the Protestants had taken for themselves, the rest had been destroyed, their roofs torn off, the lead melted into bullets for the Protestant armies, the old vessels and chalices smelted into bullion for Protestant merchants, the land taken for the Protestant gentry. A nation of Catholic ruins and Catholic serfs. Hughes's father had stood in the road after Mary's funeral, the tears running down his face. But when the coach of Lord Osborne had hurtled past, Hughes's grieving, distracted father had lifted his hat in respect. The habits of servitude.

As a small boy, Hughes had gone with his mother and sisters to the place where they heard Mass. The men walked ahead. They talked in hushed tones. It was around the time of the Union with Great Britain. He must have been four or five. The Protestant yeomanry still rode around the countryside intent on driving home the lessons of 1798: *Rebellion will be punished! Traitors will be executed! Croppies, lie down!* The Catholics had contemplated building a chapel, but they were afraid it would be seen as a provocation, so they decided to wait. They would hear Mass as before. In the fields, the priest stood beneath a *scáthlán,* a wooden canopy, and the people knelt in the wet grass.

The priest said the holiest of words. "*Hoc Est Enim Corpus Meum.*" He raised the Host, then genuflected before it. Into the silence came the thud of approaching horses. They were moving quickly. The men stayed on their knees. There was nothing illegal in what they were doing. Lord Osborne had given them the wood for the *scáthlán.* Big men, with strong backs and powerful arms, they were afraid. Young John Hughes clung to his mother. She wrapped her shawl around him.

Suddenly a fox bolted from beneath a hedge. It came across the field, darting from side to side, absorbed in its own terror. In a second it was out of sight. From the other side of the hedge came the wild barking of hounds. One came under the hedge. Two more followed. The whole pack raced behind on the scent of the fox. The sound of horses filled the air, and a great black horse soared over the hedge. The red-coated rider had one hand pressed flat on the top of his black hat. Horse and rider seemed to shudder as they hit the ground. They took off in a shower of torn earth. One by one, other horses and riders followed. They splattered mud everywhere. When they were gone, the men stood in the chewed-up field. There was relief on their faces.

Hughes turned to his right. Three planks had been nailed across the entrance to the workmen's stairway that zigzagged to the top of the scaffolding. He grabbed the top plank and pulled. It held. He pulled harder. It came out with a groan. He tried the second plank. It gave way easily. He entered the stairway and began to climb.

Corrigan heard the crack of wood. He rushed ahead and

looked around in bewilderment. Hughes was gone. From above he heard the pounding of planks. Through the platforms and ropes he could see the Archbishop two levels above him, moving higher. The watchman was nowhere in view. He must be outside. Corrigan started off to get him. He stopped. There was no time. He entered the stairway and grasped the rail. It shook in his hand. He blessed himself. He took the stairs two at a time and stopped at the second landing to catch his breath. All he could see of the Archbishop were the muddy shoes and the bottom of his cape. Corrigan felt his thighs tightening. His heart had always been weak. Cardinal Barnabo's physician in Rome had warned specifically against the ill effects of exertion. It pumps too much blood into the heart, he'd said. Corrigan kept his eyes on the stairs. The tightening in his legs grew worse and extended into his stomach. He felt a powerful pressure on his bowels, as if he might have to evacuate them. He took three flights without stopping, and when he reached the last, he went sprawling. His heart felt ready to explode. He raised himself to his knees. One more flight. He looked down. Through a wide space in the planks he could see the ground below. A fatal distance. He stood and gathered up his cassock in his left hand, took the rail in his right, and went up as fast as he could.

When he reached the top of the stairs, he saw the Archbishop walking along the broad parapet to the cathedral's northwest corner, where one of the spires would stand. The scaffolding was about a foot from the wall. Corrigan sat on the landing and took off the round, broad-brimmed hat he had bought in Rome, a hat like Cardinal Antonelli's, the Pope's secretary, and wedged it under the step, safe from the wind. When he stood, the wind flipped his short cape up against his face. His foot slipped into the space between the wall and the scaffolding, and he tumbled forward onto the wall. He lay on his stomach with his eyes closed. When he opened them, he could see down to the ground. The pressure in his stomach became irresistible. For a moment, he wasn't sure whether he would vomit or defecate, and then the volcano inside him erupted and he threw up over the side of the building. The stream of vomit sailed through the air, and it seemed a long time before it hit the ground. Corrigan wiped the water from his eyes with his sleeve. He pushed himself to his feet and tried to steady himself. His legs were quivering with pain. It was another hundred or so feet before he would reach the Archbishop. The old man was at the edge of the wall, and a violent burst of wind, which seemed to make him stagger, ripped off his zucchetto and, with it, the hairpiece he was wearing, the new one he had bought in Paris before seeing the Emperor. Hughes turned and looked at Corrigan. The Archbishop's skull was shiny and knobby, his cheeks sunken. He was smiling. He beckoned to Corrigan to come forward. Then he turned around again.

As a young man, with the priesthood still a distant dream, Hughes had gone ahead of his people. The first trickle in the massive exodus that would follow. In the hold of the ship, the "superfluous inhabitants" mentioned in the parliamentary reports on conditions in Ireland were given far less air and space than the animals. One of the women from Donegal lost two of her three children to fever and sickness on the voyage. She begged to be allowed to keep their bodies until they reached Philadelphia and she could bring them to a priest for burial. The captain said that it was out of the question. They were buried at dusk, after the cabin passengers had finished their post-dinner walk around the deck. The first mate read from the Book of Common Prayer, and the two small sacks weighted with paving blocks were dropped overboard. The mother keened after them, and the other women joined in. The captain sent down word to have the "savage noise" stopped, and the women were taken below. The women cried all night, and in a corner a small gray man said over and over in Irish, "God is abandoning us, God is abandoning us." Hughes told him to be quiet.

In Maryland, a family of Catholics hired Hughes to work on their plantation. Haughty people proud of their English descent, they made him sleep in the barn. He took his meals with the slaves. As soon as the harvesting was done, the overseer called him to the porch of the house. We have no more need of you, he said. With food and lodging taken from his wages, his pay for a season's work came to less than a pound. That afternoon he set out walking to Harrisburg, where his father was working as a laborer on a new turnpike. On the way he fell in with four other men who had also been let go at season's end and were going north in search of work. Three were from Galway, one from Cork. At night they sat in silence around the fire they made in an open field. No one spoke until the Cork man, a thickset laborer with a shock of wiry red hair, said, "When the boat bringing us over came near to land, I fell to my knees. I thought I'd reached the Promised Land." He laughed. The others stared into the fire.

In the first winter of the Famine, the same year he brought the Jesuits to Fordham, Hughes spoke at a meeting for Irish relief at Castle Garden. He was famous now. "Dagger John," as the Protestants and nativists called him. A feared opponent. He said that while there were those who saw this calamity as a judgment on the Irish, as God's punishment, the truth was that it was God's judgment on the English, a final testament to the wicked results of their centuries-long oppression of the Irish. The crowd roared its approval. But he was left feeling empty. Where was the will of God in this? A people who had suffered and died for His Church, who had become serfs for Christ's sake, were suffering a crowning indignity of starvation, their remnants tossed across the sea to a land that had no use for them.

When he had left Castle Garden, he walked up Broadway to the Astor House, where the organizers of the meeting were holding a small dinner. It was February, and the wind off the harbor was brutal and penetrating. As he approached Bowling Green, where the Americans had toppled a statue of George III at the beginning of their Revolution, he heard the sound of a fiddle rising and falling with the wind. A small crowd was gathered. He pushed up behind them to see what they were watching.

A young boy in his teens was sitting at the base of the fence. He was wrapped in a blanket and had a crudely woven cap on his head. He was playing the fiddle with hands wrapped in burlap.

A girl his age was dancing a jig to the music. She had a shawl over her head, but her face was visible. It was red and pock-marked, and there was a half-healed wound on the bridge of her nose that was an ugly shade of purple and yellow. People stopped and then quickly moved on. Hughes moved closer. The girl's feet were wrapped in burlap, and there were dark stains of blood around the toes. The fiddler was off-key. Either his fingers were numb or he was drunk, or perhaps both. But Hughes recognized the music. "The Bride of Annologhan." *Annologhan.* His village.

They were coming by the thousands now. What was once a thin stream of immigrants had turned into a river, the river into a raging torrent, an entire nation on the move, or the remnants of a nation, the final stage of a defeat suffered long ago and con-firmed in every generation until this was all that was left: tattered, exhausted dervishes bleeding away into the gutters of history. Ire-land had became a wound that would not clot.

The emptiness inside him was physical, as if his heart and liver and lungs had been removed. He wanted to move on, but he couldn't. The emptiness had become a kind of paralysis. And then he understood. The years of resentment and bewilderment had confused him, but in this moment he saw a truth so obvious he didn't know how he had missed it. *God had chosen this peo-ple.* He had steeled them through centuries of persecution, and now He was taking them from Egypt into the desert, preparing them to spread the faith across the face of the continent that He was raising to preeminence. Their suffering was a mark of being chosen. Their temples were ruined. Their possessions taken. Hun-ger and servitude their lot. But for a reason. Israel in the desert. Israel coming into the land of Canaan. God making the last first and the first last.

Corrigan didn't move. He cupped his hands and shouted through them, "Your Grace, step back, in the name of God . . ." The wind whipped the words away. He dropped his hands to his side. He had done all he could. Hughes shouted something back. Corrigan couldn't make it out. Hughes pointed west across the old terrain at the city's edge to the Palisades beyond. He shouted

again. Corrigan strained to hear, but couldn't. He looked helplessly at the gaunt figure silhouetted against the clouds, his cloak
and cassock fluttering around him like a flag twisted on its pole.
In the distance a single slash of lightning cut the sky in half.

A pillar of fire.

III

AUDLEY WARD BOWED HIS HEAD in prayer. He felt the presence
of the divinity in this room more than anywhere else in the house,
more even than in church. The table he sat before was as hallowed
as any altar. Shipped by Andreas Vandervort from Holland to his
home in New Amsterdam, it arrived in January 1651. Over the
years, it had survived the Anglo-Dutch wars, Indian uprisings, the
British seizure of New Amsterdam, the fires set by rebellious
slaves, the Battle of New York and the conflagration that followed, the British occupation, the Great Fire of 1835, the migration over two centuries from wooden farmhouse to brick town
house to here. The faces on the walls had once been real presences
at this table, supped here, argued, deliberated, communed, generation after generation. Ward envied them their ignorance of the
fate that had befallen the city they had helped found.

Charles Bedford bowed his head also. No prayer came to
mind. He looked up. Ward was still conversing with the Deity.
No wonder. A lot he should be thankful for. The use of this
house, Bedford's house, its food, drink, servants. The carriage at
his disposal. Ward's head dropped a little lower. The reverence
of an aristocrat, the respect for Him who put the few above the
many. Still, Ward prayed. Bedford felt his impatience shading into
anger. He picked up his soup spoon and banged it twice on the
table.

Audley Ward raised his head, and said softly, "Amen." The
maid ladled soup in his bowl from the tureen she carried on her
tray; she then filled Bedford's bowl.

"Will ya be wanting the wine now, sir, or should we wait until dinner is served?"

"Now, bring the wine now," Bedford said.

He lifted a spoonful of soup to his mouth, blew on it, sipped it carefully. He sat silently, but the silence unnerved him. Capshaw. Morrissey. His debts. His mind wandered to the things he was trying not to think about. Better to talk. It provided a distraction.

"You're wrong, Audley," Bedford said. It was a conversation they had begun in the drawing room before dinner. Bedford had cut it off. Now he began it again.

"The draft is not only necessary, it's desirable," he said. "The South already has it. They started this conflict, and neither the spirit nor the substance of their efforts seems to have suffered in the slightest from the imposition of compulsory military service." He put the spoon down. The soup was watery and tasteless. When Mrs. Bedford returned from Europe, he reminded himself, the first piece of business would be the hiring of a new cook.

Ward hadn't touched his soup. He wasn't hungry. He wouldn't be able to eat until tonight's lecture was over. A little wine, that's all he would take for now.

"I wasn't talking about the military success enjoyed by the Secessionists," Ward said. "I was talking about the future of the country. The draft may help win the war, such an eventuality is outside my purview. Yet if a republic is unable to defend itself except by the mass impressment of its citizens, then even though it may win a war, it has shown itself bereft of the qualities it needs to continue."

Bedford put his elbows on the table and tore a piece of bread in half. "You're talking philosophy again. I'm speaking about practical matters, Audley, the here and now, the stuff of survival." He pointed a piece of bread at Ward. "The side with the most men and the biggest guns will inevitably wear down its opponent. We have the guns. We need the men."

The maid poured Bedford's wine. He gulped it.

"The roast will be out in a minute," she said.

"Fine." Bedford picked up his fork and shook it at Ward. "War isn't philosophy. It isn't filled with complexities, subtleties, nice distinctions."

"I didn't say it was."

"What did you say?"

"I said the fact that we must force our citizenry to defend the Republic means that no matter whether we enjoy victory or defeat, the Republic is doomed."

"Would you be happier if Congress had voted down the three-hundred-dollar exemption, if it had decided to draft everyone regardless of their value to the country, if they planned to surround Wall Street and impress the financial community of this nation into the infantry? Would that satisfy you?"

"No, not at all. The three-hundred-dollar exemption has a certain wisdom to it. It extends the principle of substitution, which is an ancient one, and allows the men conducting the nation's commerce to stay at that work. I am not worried about the men of substance. Those that can will do their part. They always have. It is the men of no substance who disturb me. We no longer have a yeomanry to fight our wars, the solid farmer or craftsman who serves the Republic out of a sense of duty. With the draft, we have shown that we must ultimately rely on a military force composed of those with nothing to defend, with not even a simple spirit of patriotism to inspire them. We have brought the barbarian across the Rhine in order to help defend our frontiers. A terrible mistake."

"Impressment has never seemed to weaken the British. They manned their navy with it." Bedford picked up another piece of bread, ripped it in halves, then quarters, and dropped them into his soup.

"Britain is not a republic. It rests on a philosophy of aristocracy. The nobility may make concessions for the sake of maintaining order, but British institutions have never drawn their authority from the voluntary subscription of the lower orders."

"And ours do?" Bedford asked, his voice rising.

"They did, until the draft."

Bedford dropped his spoon into the bowl. He looked down the table at his wife's uncle, a small man in an old-fashioned frock coat, bald, a half circle of white hair combed forward in the Greek Revival style of some years before, a head that looked as if it were made to be cast in bronze or molded in clay, a soft Dutch face, full but not fat, the blue eyes behind two silver half frames, a beard that ran under the face, two creases in his cheeks that made his nose seem noble and important. He bore more than a passing resemblance to Horace Greeley; Ward was an older, shorter, plumper version of the editor of the *Tribune*. It was a comparison Ward despised.

Ward's niece, Sarah, had been no richly endowed bride. She brought to Charles Bedford a few small lots, some land outside Albany, a minor interest in a moribund trading company, some stocks, portraits, silverware, ancient furniture. It was the dowry of a Knickerbocker family that had been foolish enough to sell off its ancestral farm, a hundred acres of meadows and woodlands, to a syndicate of buyers who eventually turned it into blocks of houses and shops, harvesting a rich annual crop of rent. The family had invested what it had been paid, a pittance in retrospect, into a series of languishing ventures, and its fortunes went into a steady decline, especially in comparison to the new wealth that was making its appearance in the city.

What Bedford had really obtained by marriage was a great fortune of names and dates and dead ancestors, a genealogy he could never keep straight. But it was an asset for a boy from the clam beds of Long Island, the son of a farmer, to have these portraits on his walls, heroes of the Revolution, mayors, merchants, men and women with round, substantial faces, serious and dignified, the Lares and Penates of commerce and civic duty. They stared down at his dinner guests. They said, Here is continuity and carefulness, an ability to make money in war and peace, to preserve wealth from generation to generation without interruption. An illusion, but a useful one.

"It seems to me," Ward said, "that the recent passage of the

Enrollment Act will be remembered as the moment in our national life when spiritual bankruptcy was translated into political bankruptcy, when a disease of the lower extremities finally spread upwards and inflicted itself on the brain of the Republic, a fatal transference."

"You use two metaphors there, Audley, one financial, one medical. You should stick with the latter. It is more within, as you put it, your 'purview.' "

Bedford sat back in his chair. He rubbed his napkin back and forth across his lips, restraining himself from saying what he wanted to say: This is my house. I paid for it, for the servants, the wine, the food, the coal and ice, the gas, the water charges, the tax assessments, and I won't be lectured about finances by a man who if left to his own income would find it hard to afford a second-rate boardinghouse.

"The metaphors are unimportant," Ward said. "They are peripheral to truth."

"Perhaps."

The maid came into the room with a platter of sliced beef. She put it down on the table next to Bedford, and removed his soup bowl. He lifted three slices of meat onto his plate. Ward held up his glass. "More wine, please."

When the tray was brought to him, he took one small piece. He watched Bedford cut his meat and eat it. A voracious appetite, omnivorous, suitable for a bear. Ward had spent the afternoon preparing his talk to the New-York Historical Society. After drinking Bedford's wine and eating a small portion of his food, he would ride in Bedford's coach to the Society's building, on Second Avenue, near Astor Place. There was no loss in inviting Bedford to go, especially since Ward knew he wouldn't.

"Will you accompany me this evening?"

Bedford scooped potatoes from a serving dish onto his plate. He chewed and swallowed before he spoke. "I'm afraid not. I have financial matters that require my attention." He put more potatoes into his mouth, a forkful.

Ward stood up, placed his napkin on the table. "I have to put my notes in order. I worked this afternoon, but some little bit remains to be done on the ending."

"What's the subject?"

"The Battle of New York as seen through the eyes of its citizens." Ward pointed to the portrait on the wall behind Bedford. "Anne Vandervort Holcomb was one of them."

"Your mother?" Bedford asked.

"My grandmother. Sarah's great-grandmother. This table comes from her house, a part of her dowry as a Vandervort."

Bedford swiveled halfway in his chair and looked at the painting. He really should commit these faces to memory. "Yes, I know, of course, Sarah's great-grandmother, but I never knew she participated in the Revolution."

"She was an observer, not a participant."

Ward turned his head from Bedford and stared at the portrait, a large picture in an ornate gold frame, the corners chipped, the white molding showing through. Anne Vandervort Holcomb, his paternal grandmother, the great-grandmother of his niece, Bedford's wife. She had been born on the Vandervort farm, near Cherry Street, her marriage to John Holcomb bridging an old division, Holcombs and Vandervorts, English gentlemen and Dutch tea merchants, the ancient grudge between the city's first settlers and their usurpers finally forgotten. She was no longer a bride in her portrait. A heavy woman in her middle age, she wore a blue velvet dress, her hair drawn up in a brown hive. In the corner of the portrait was a large window, and through it was visible the outline of Mount Pitt, the northern border of the Holcomb farm. It had stood on what was now Grand Street, another part of the intricate terrain of this island's landscape that had been reduced to an unremitting sameness, farms, ponds, hills, forests, meadows, villages, streams, fens, all bowing to the relentless leveling imposed on the island's topography, a surveyor's grid, streets meeting avenues at perpendicular angles.

"I have my last paragraphs," Ward said.

Bedford went back to his food. "Your what?"

"My last paragraphs for tonight's lecture. They've just come to me."

Bedford took a drink of wine, wiped his lips with his napkin. "Where did you find them? In your wine?"

Ward walked toward the foyer, down the length of the old oak table where two centuries before Dutch burghers had discussed how to secure their city against the designs of the English. He looked at the portrait as he went, and almost crashed into the maid as she entered the room with a dish of pudding.

"Pardon me, sir," she said.

"I found them there." Ward pointed at the portrait. "Behind my grandmother."

Bedford turned once more in the chair. Anne Vandervort Holcomb looked down at him, scowling.

"A formidable source of stimulation, your grandmother." Bedford returned the scowl with a smile. He admired the bulk of her body, the plump contours beneath the dress, solid and sensual, like the two stone goddesses that supported the pediment of the building where he had his office. Caryatids of commerce and prosperity. Their arms above their heads, their full breasts pressing prominently against the folds of their robes. Some days he had been tempted to reach up and rub those breasts, round and round, gently, two at a time, just for luck. It couldn't have done any harm. Maybe he should have. He straightened himself in his chair. Sarah had breasts like her grandmother's. Firm, voluptuous. When she straddled him in bed, a knee on each side, he pushed her nightgown up slowly, navel, stomach, the ascending curve, the hard nipples, round and round he rubbed. Not much left between Sarah and him now, but occasionally, like the night before she left for England, he tried her door to see if it was unlocked. It swung open noiselessly. They didn't speak. Each knew what to give the other, and what to take. Bedford pushed his spoon around the pudding in his dish. It quivered when he touched it. He ran the spoon around its surface, as if to caress it.

Ward waited a moment by the door. He watched Bedford toy with his pudding and supposed he was enjoying a merchant's reverie: the mental abacus never stopping, the counters sliding eternally along their rods. He crossed the hallway to the stairs and went up slowly, stopping at the first landing to catch his breath. A weak heart, another Vandervort inheritance, like the table and the portrait. At the second floor, he paused again before he went down the hallway, past the child's room that had never been occupied, to the back of the house. Entering his room, he lit the paraffin lamp on the table by the door and carried it over to the desk. He noticed that the wick hadn't been trimmed or the reservoir filled, another sign of the incorrigible inattentiveness of the servants, a chronic problem that seemed only to grow worse. He sat, picked up his pen, hesitated a moment, and began to write rapidly, stopping only to dip the pen into the inkwell, the blackened metal point scratching across the surface of the paper.

Long before the Revolution, the Indians had a settlement near where the Holcomb farm would be. From this village of Rechtauk, on the East River, there was a sylvan trail that led to Werpoes, the chief settlement of the savages, on the western shore of the Collect Pond, where the city prison, the Tombs, now stands. Rechtauk was situated between the river and a small sweet-water lake. The trail to Werpoes began in the high-grass fields near the river. Somewhere below Grand Street it entered a wood and moved in a straight line until the vicinity of Canal Street, when it meandered eastward, in true Indian fashion, toward Werpoes.

For centuries this trail was barely more than a faint imprint upon the grass and the forest bed, a slight presence on the land, like the Indians themselves. When the white man came, he trod the savage's forest path in boots rather than in bare feet. Instead of a leather quiver on his back, he carried his implements, guns, plows, clocks, in heavy-wheeled carts pulled by oxen or horses. He cleared the trees and planted wheat in the fields where the savages had grazed on blackberries and wild onions. Eventually, the trail became a country road, the road a city thoroughfare, Division Street, as it is now called.

By the time of my grandmother's childhood, the savages were long gone. But though Rechtauk had disappeared and the forest been hewn down, the land was still soft and undulating, still green. The steeples in the city rose in the distance. This is where Anne Vandervort Holcomb came that September morn when she first heard the report of heavy musketry from across the river. A servant hitched up a wagon and drove her the short distance to Mount Pitt. She scaled its steep side in breathless haste. Her husband of four months was over there somewhere, and now the British assault on Brooklyn Heights was under way. The smoke and sound told her the day of reckoning had begun.

Today it is still possible to stand where she once stood. But Mount Pitt has been shaved away. It is now nothing more than a small rise in Pitt Street as it proceeds from Delancey to Grand. If you look to the east, you may catch a glimpse of the river, but the landscape my grandmother saw on a late summer's day in 1776 has disappeared as completely as Rechtauk or Werpoes. The street makers have torn down the past. They have left nothing in their way.

All that is left to connect us to the past is the imagination. With it, we may try to banish the dirt and the confusion that surrounds us as we stand on the busy corner of a street not very different from the streets all around it. In our minds we may re-create a vanished dignity and grace. We may dismiss the ugly, peeling façades of these immigrant barracks. We may raise again the hillocks and dig the vales. We may envision a sole farmhouse built of stone in the Dutch fashion where now there is only crowded shabbiness.

If we wish, we may take out a small map and draw upon it. We may mark Indian villages. We may pencil in the forest and the ponds. We may imagine the route of the stout settler as he set out into the woods, an apostle of civilization in a continent of savagery. We may close our eyes tightly against the ramshackle buildings all about and transpose ourselves to the top of Mount Pitt. A young woman stands next to us. Together we look across open fields to the heights of Brooklyn, where the smoke of cannons and muskets lifts above the trees. In the river, the oarsmen

*of Massachusetts strain to row boats top-heavy with retreating
American soldiers to the safety of the Manhattan shore.*

*Alas, we may try. But be careful of the Hebrew who will
come out of the door we are standing in front of and demand we
stand aside and not block the way of those who wish to enter his
store. Or if it is a Sunday, prepare to withstand the mob pouring
out of the church behind us, a communion of foreign drudges
swarming to the plethora of whiskey dispensers that line the
street.*

He put down his pen. He read what he had written. Once.
Twice. There was no time for editing or rewriting. Rain struck
the window, first softly, then harshly. It had been raining inter-
mittently all day. In the late afternoon there had been a crashing
thunderstorm—rare for the cold beginning of April, but a suitable
orchestration for the second anniversary of the surrender of Fort
Sumter. The rain would keep the audience small this evening. And
the topic of war, even the Revolution, was no longer as popular
as it had once been.

The rain grew louder. Ward gathered his papers, inserted
what he had written at the back, carefully numbering each page.
He stood and went to the window to draw the curtain. He stared
at the darkness. Two years before, in the spring the war began,
he had glanced out this window as two washerwomen brought
the laundry out to the yard behind the kitchen. Both of them were
large women, hips and bosoms swollen from years of childbear-
ing; hair drawn back in buns, faces and arms red and flushed from
the hot water they had been working over. Each of them carried
a tub of wash, the steam rising out of the clothes up into their
faces so that they had their heads angled to the side, and the veins
and muscles in their necks stood out.

Ward had almost turned away. It was a scene he had witnessed many times before. But some instinct had told him to stay.
He watched them as they worked. Unaware they were being observed, the women giggled and laughed. He couldn't hear precisely what they were saying, but he could catch the rise and fall
of their Irish voices. They strung the wash out on the wire, pressed

clothespins at the end of each piece. When they had it done, each picked up a pole of about seven feet in length and, catching the wash line in the small notches at the ends of the poles, lifted the wash into the April sky, bracing one pole against the yard wall, the other against the house. They handled the poles easily, picking them up and lifting the line in one motion, wielding them like weapons, not gracefully but with assurance and purpose, each acting in concert.

He kept watching. He was filled with the sense that he was gazing down Godlike on more than some insignificant, isolated moment in a familiar routine. He was above history. He was seeing the process of history, the past, present, and future, all as one simultaneous event. The women stood and talked for a moment with the wash flapping above their heads, their faces still red. They bent over, picked up the empty tubs, held them by one handle, the other handle touching the ground. Shields, Ward thought. First they used their poles like the *poissardes* of revolutionary Paris waiting to march on Versailles. Now they have taken up their shields and moved further back in history, a tribe of viragoes readying for the hunt. In a moment they shall get down upon their hands and knees and yap and snarl at each other like animals.

Here was the unchangeable nexus of history, one age linked to the next by this human chain of brutes, the *levée en masse* of barbarism that burns libraries and smashes marble statuary, that beats down the thinker and tears out the heart of the philosopher, and consumes it.

Once the Republic had been an Athens. The poorest of freemen had been independent and strong. The progeny of a common ancestry, they shared with the gentry an instinct for patient industry, a sound practical sense, and an ancient love of constitutional freedom that set them apart from other races. Gentry and yeomanry alike had left their farms to secure their liberties against the mercenaries of the British king. But Athens was only a moment. The men who created the Republic had not understood this. Wise in many things, they didn't understand the barbarian, even when he raised his head in France and turned the theories of self-government into the carmagnole, a drunken orgy of bloodlust and retribution. They thought the savage had been banished to the periphery. They tore down his crude village of wattles and mud, and raised their temples and markets in its place.

From his Godlike prominence, Ward could see the truth: Athens cannot outlast the barbarians. No frontier can withstand their infiltration. They are forever. The spirit of Rechtauk and Werpoes, of superstition, of brute ignorance, of savagery, is amongst us, growing stronger. The barbarians surround us, and we have become dependent on them; and when they raise their hands to destroy us, how shall we defend ourselves?

The rain struck hard against the window. Ward picked up the book that he had spent the afternoon reading: *The Races of the Old World,* by Charles Loring Brace, the founder and director of the Children's Aid Society. New York's noblest soul, living his life among ghastly want and depravity, faces festering with diseases of the body and soul, creatures cast out from everything but God's mercy. Brace had been leading the effort to ship the offspring of this human refuse to the West, to spread the compost festering in the city's lower wards across the prairies and mountains, where, someday, its noxiousness diluted and rendered harmless by the strength of American soil, it might nurture a thing less fearsome and repulsive than the rank corruption so rife in this city. But now even Brace had come to understand. The blindfold of noble sentiment had loosened and slipped, one eye opened finally, free of what Carlyle had called "the gossamer gauze of sentimentality." Brace saw the true face of what he had pitied and tried to reform.

Ward opened the book to where he had left a leather marker. The paragraph he wanted was underlined: "The Negro skull, though less than the European, is within one inch as large as the Persian and the Armenian, and three square larger than the Hindoo and the Egyptian. The difference between the average English and Irish skull is nine cubic inches, and only four between the average African and the Irish."

Cubic inches. Brain size. The iron judgment of measurement. This wasn't the prurient delusion of the phrenologist, a theory for fools, a superstition of bumps. This was truth. Science. The mob was a race. The race was a mob, its conduct no more variable than that of an insect or a fish. Bedford did not understand that. He refused. He clung to his faith in progress. His investment in it was stronger than Brace's. It involved not philanthropy but profit. For Bedford to carry on in his work it was necessary that he believe trade would transform the world. The barbarian would be converted into a loyal purchaser of cloth, paper, glass, iron, whatever the merchant had to offer. The savage would lie down with the stockbroker. The gospel of commerce depended on the ability of all men to buy and sell the banausic trinkets of civilization. It could not entertain the notion that the barbarian's wish was deeper and more primitive, that in the very act of possessing what he wanted, the barbarian would destroy all those who created it.

Ward put his face closer to the window and peered down into the darkness. Below, the lights from the kitchen flared across the yard. The wash line swung in and out of the darkness. He understood what progress was: Progress was luck. The luck of those who lived in the interstices, in the brief moments of light between the coming and going of the barbarian, the convulsive agents of dissolution and destruction. History, the evangelists of progress preached, was a journey from one place to another, a steady sojourn from the savannas of savagery to the highlands of civilization and contentment, the air getting purer the higher one goes, the sunlight becoming perpetual. But they had forgotten the lesson the traveler learns when he climbs to the mast of a ship. Seeing another ship approaching over the curve of the horizon, he comprehends the cyclical nature of his journey, the destiny of all who travel the earth's straight lines, inch by inch circling back to where they began.

There was a knock at the door. "Come in," Ward said. Another of the maids. Face a mass of freckles, wisps of red hair sticking out from underneath her cap.

"Beggin' ya pardon, but Mister Bedford told me to inform ya dat da coach will be at da dour in a minute, sir."

"Yes, Bridget, I shall be down in a moment." He put the papers into a cardboard folder and tied it with a red ribbon. He still needed a flourish for the ending. One or two lines. Perhaps he would think of something in the coach. The maid was still at his door. "I shall be down shortly. You needn't wait." He smiled at her.

"Margaret, sir."

"What?"

"Me name's Margaret. You called me Bridget."

"Margaret, yes. Go ahead. Tell the coachman I'm on my way."

IV

THE HOUSE WAS QUIET. Bedford went into the library. A coal fire made the room stuffy, the way he liked it. As in so many other things, Sarah liked the English style of living, in this case rooms with a slight chill to them. Bedford loved the heat. Even with the furnace on, he had the servants put coal in the grates of most of the rooms. Sarah had complained, "It is unnatural to live in such a temperature."

"Comfort is unnatural," he told her in reply. "It is an achievement, a victory over nature. The denizens of Shantytown live in a natural way. Their bodies are cooled by the winds that blow through the ill-fitted boards that serve as the walls of their homes. Unable to afford coal, they sit and stare at an empty grate. And so, they fall sick and die, naturally. God save us from nature."

Bedford had a special contempt for nature, the obsession of so many of Sarah's English friends as they went west or north into the American continent. Nature as the Prince of Wales had seen it on his trip to the United States, through the windows of a railway car, roast beef and whiskey on the damask-clothed table before him; nature as Mr. Olmsted had contrived it in his Central Park, undulating lawns and picturesque rocks, a plaything for city dwellers, its naturalness the unnatural creation of crews of sweating, mud-splattered Paddies set to work on a project vaster than the Pyramids.

He picked up the *Tribune,* went into the hallway and up the stairs. He stopped on the first landing and opened the paper to check the gold prices. Steady. That told him all he needed to know about the war: no movement anywhere. Hooker wasn't stirring, nor Lee. When they did, gold would move: up with a Union defeat, down with a victory. He put the paper underneath his arm and went up the stairs to his room. Another point of difference with Ward, whose resemblance to Greeley didn't go beyond the physical. "Mr. Greeley is absurd, and his paper is the gospel of fools," Ward said. Bedford spent little time on the fine points of that gospel, but he felt a bond with Greeley, enjoyed the pervasiveness of the vision that filled his paper, the country on the move, the unfolding of a people across a continent, wild land yielding new wealth, the glories of a second Eden, idle and improvident tribes and classes disappearing, a new race appearing, nobler and happier, moving steadily forward, every man capable of forging his own success, nature itself chained and tamed, and put to some productive purpose.

Greeley made money. The *Tribune* was read in Washington, in the Army, on the frontier. It was carried by trains and steamboats, its circulation expanding, new presses being added, facts, statistics, and opinions made into a commodity as valuable as coal or cotton, the demand continually rising. Greeley had come east to grow up with his country, walking along the banks of the Erie Canal, against the rush of westward traffic, away from the hardscrabble existence of his father's Pennsylvania farm. In ten years, he was editor and publisher of the *Tribune,* and a rich man. Charles Bedford, a boy in the village of East Hampton, walked behind his father's plow in the scorched, sandy soil of Long Island. Sometimes, on a Sunday afternoon, in the long, empty space between the morning and evening church services, he loitered in the office of the New York–Montauk stagecoach. The men sat in chairs by the wall. Taciturn men, faces like old leather, cracked and brittle from lifetimes in the sun and salt air, they worshiped the God of the Old Covenant, God the Punisher, His displeasure made continually manifest in the weather: one year too much sun, the next too much rain, great gales from the north, hurricanes from the south; crops ruined, boats overturned, steeples blown down, trees uprooted, men drowned. Judgment Day eternally hovered above them in the Atlantic sky. When they talked, it was foremost about the weather, their animals, their aches and pains, the price of everything. A boy of sixteen, Charles sat on the bench by the window. He turned the pages of the *Tribune*. He heard the thunder in the distance. Squalls moving up the coast. The air was electric. His mind raced as he read of the uprisings in Europe, the fall of kings and dynasties, the news from California, gold, changes everywhere, the roar of great winds, the rush of water as it reshaped the shoreline, nations disappearing, new ones being built, and gold, big nuggets of it, there for the taking, wealth in unlimited supply.

The contagion spread slowly at first, almost unnoticed. East Hampton was accustomed to its sons going to sea and being away for years at a time. This time it was different. The boys left pell-mell, with the cows unmilked, the kindling unbundled, the horse untethered. No forwarding address. No sign they would ever return. Coming out of the stage office, standing next to his father in the cool April dusk, Charles realized he was infected. The heat radiated from his loins. He put his hands in his pockets so that his father wouldn't see them shake. He felt the same desire as when the girl-longing seized him, the obsessive imaginings that sent him to the dark recesses of the barn, where he unbuttoned his trousers and took his secret pleasure. It could not be resisted. And although as he walked next to his father back to church he couldn't remember a solitary sentence from the *Tribune*, the single-word message couldn't stop reverberating in his head: *West!*

From the pulpit, the minister prayed for the young people of the village. Most of them are damned, he said. But it was not too late for the community to undergo the awakening that had occurred when Lyman Beecher had preached from this same spot and helped their ancestors turn away from sin. Charles watched his feet. They tapped slowly, almost imperceptibly, beyond his control, to the lyric that repeated itself incessantly in his head: *Oh! Susanna, oh, don't you cry for me; I come from Alabama, wid my banjo on my knee.*

In July of 1849, Charles and two friends signed on a fishing smack bound for New York City with a cargo of porgies and blues. He didn't tell his parents. He rose in the darkness. When he closed the door behind him, he knew it was forever. He met his friends in the small wood outside the village. The three of them would go together, first west, down the coast of Long Island. When they earned enough money, they would book passage around the Horn to California.

Charles had never experienced heat of the kind that hit him the morning they tied up at South Street. It consumed the entire atmosphere, left men and animals struggling to breathe. This wasn't the heat felt in East Hampton, where relief came as soon as you stepped out of the sun into the shade, or sat in the dunes by the ocean and felt the ocean wind in your face. Here there was no wind, only a deathly stillness. And the sun was not a blazing whiteness that filled the sky, but a red disk that lurked behind clouds of smoke and dust, its presence seemingly unconnected to the choking heat.

They landed on a Sunday. They took their wages and walked away from the river. The city was dead. Shutters closed. Doors locked. They thought it was because of the Sabbath. They found a building marked LODGINGS on the corner of Gold Street. A good omen, they thought. The proprietor looked out a small hole in the door before he opened it. He rented them the attic, a room with sloping ceilings and unspeakable heat. They paid for two nights and said they intended to find work in the morning, when the city reopened. The proprietor laughed. "Reopen?" he said.

"Boys, this city ain't closed on account of the worship of God. It's shut up because of the cholera. The Paddies have infected the whole place. Keep pouring off boats, piling on top of each other, breeding like rats in a granary, and spreading sickness wherever they go. They live like animals, and I don't ever open my door to them. This place is for Americans and them that knows how to conduct themselves like civilized men. That's why you're safe here."

In the morning, the streets were still empty and quiet, but the docks bustled with life. Ships came in and out. Cargo was landed. Immigrants disembarked. Men shouted and sweated beneath the blanket of unremitting heat. The three boys were hired to haul paving blocks out of the hold of a ship and toss them onto a wagon. They worked next to big, unfriendly Irishmen who spoke English with such heavy accents that the boys were barely able to understand them. For two weeks they labored like horses, rising early, walking to the docks, working all day, coming back to their room with bread and milk they bought in a corner grocery. Their clothes were soaked with sweat, their lives sustained by the thought of California. They were exhausted, drained, and then, at the beginning of the third week, Bill, the youngest of them, started to vomit violently. He held his stomach and cried out in pain. Charles went downstairs and brought up a pail of water from the pump in the backyard. In the meantime, Bill had lost control of his bowels. His pants and mattress were awash in diarrhea. By morning his face was dark and pinched, his feet and hands cold and blue. He babbled incoherently.

The landlord shut his door and would not speak to them. On the third night, Bill died from the cholera. They wrapped his body in a sheet and carried it down to the street. They left it on the curb to be carted away to the potter's field. When Charles awoke the next morning, Bill's body was still there, the flies in a thick, noisy cloud around it. But his other friend, the third in their trio, was gone. He had quietly gathered all the money they had earned, everything Bill left, everything Charles had, and run away.

Charles wandered the streets in a daze. He was aching with

hunger, alone, frightened, bewildered, without money or friends in the streets of a city polluted with foreignness and disease. His only hope was to return home, to face his father's wrath. He leaned against the side of a building for support. There beside him, tacked up on a long corkboard and framed in glass, were the familiar pages of the *Tribune*. He was on Spruce Street, outside the paper's offices. He peered inside. Men were moving quickly, with purpose. He could hear the rattle of the presses. Somewhere in the building Mr. Greeley was penning his visions of the future. Charles felt a surge of hope. He thought about going inside and asking to see Mr. Greeley. But he couldn't summon the courage. He looked at the sheets once again. In the corner, just at his eye level, was a column of notices. He began to read them. He got no further than the first one. *Wanted. A reliable Protestant boy. Able to read and write. Needs to be industrious. The firm of Stark and Evans. 51 Cortlandt Street.* He stopped a stranger and asked where Cortlandt Street was. The man pointed west. Charles ran as fast as he could. He arrived out of breath and in a lather. Mr. Stark said he liked to see such haste in a boy. He hired him on the spot.

Charles began to dig for gold with a broom. He swept out the offices that evening, slept in an alleyway, washed in the public fountain near City Hall, and was waiting at the door when Mr. Stark appeared at eight the next morning. They set him to running errands, storing and fetching account books, making sure the inkwells were filled. He finished all his work and walked up the stairs to Stark's office and asked for more. Stark looked at Charles over his spectacles. "A commendable request, my boy," he said. The third day, Charles asked for a key to the office so that he could start his work as soon as he arrived each morning. Stark said he would take it under consideration and went back to his work. At the end of the day, Stark called Charles over, reached into his pocket, and pulled out a long, heavy key. "A great trust is given you," he said. "Be worthy of it."

Charles stayed until the last clerk had put out his lamp and gone home. He swept and dusted and replaced the books. When he was sure nobody would return, he raised the trapdoor to the basement. He took a tattered piece of canvas he had found discarded by the docks, put it on the dirt floor, and used it for his bed. He knew he would have to be up by six, so he left the trapdoor open and listened for the *gong* of the big clock mounted at the bottom of the stairs next to Stark's office. The chimes reverberated through the silent building. He never overslept. With the money he saved, he bought a respectable set of secondhand clothes on Chatham Square. He lived in the basement until the middle of January. The cold in the building became so intense that he awoke one morning with feet and hands that were purplish and numb. He came down with a fever and a painful cough, and decided he had to find some appropriate lodgings. He rented a bed in a boardinghouse on West Street, three single beds in his room, the other two occupied by clerks, old men who drank too much, their entire earthly treasure stored in the beaten leather trunks at the bottom of their beds. He was still the first one in the office every day. "I couldn't expect a better record of punctuality if you resided in this building," Stark said.

Every morning at a few minutes before ten, Stark put on his coat and hat and left the office. On a warm, windy morning in April, he approached Charles and told him to come with him. They walked with their heads down, each with a hand on his hat, Stark one or two steps ahead. At the corner of Thames Street and Trinity Place, Stark took his watch out of his vest pocket and looked up at the clock atop Trinity Church. The chimes began to ring out ten o'clock. Stark put his watch back into his pocket and patted it. He walked down a small flight of stairs. Charles went behind him. He felt temporarily blinded as they entered a dark, low-ceilinged room whose air was thick with the smell of mutton and musty ale.

They sat in the back, at a table set against the wall. "I've come to Old Tom's midmorning for the past thirty-six years," Stark said. "I make no decision till I've eaten here and filled my stomach with a substantial meal that draws off some of the blood which accumulates in the brain during sleep and sets it to the work of digesting my food. Be sure to fill your stomach every morning and drain some of the blood out of your head. A wise and necessary act for every man of business. Many a firm has been ruined by decisions made by fevered brains and empty stomachs." Mr. Stark ordered a mutton chop and fried potatoes and a cup of hot coffee with a shot of brandy in it. He ordered the same food for Charles but no brandied coffee. "At your age," Stark said, "you have no need of stimulants in order to start the day."

The waiters were all old colored men who moved with an air of dignity. One of them put a basket of hot bread on the table. Stark began to devour it. He pointed at the basket and gestured for Charles to do the same. When they had eaten all the bread, Stark said, "Charles, you're a remarkable young man. I have high hopes for you. And because of this I confess to a certain interest in your origins and background, an interest I don't usually take in the errand boys we hire. You obviously come from good solid stock, but tell me about yourself, boy, about your parents and education and how you came upon your ambitions."

Stark sat back in his chair as the waiter served their food. He set immediately to work cutting and eating the chop, drawing the blood away from his brain. Charles stared down at his food. His stomach tightened. He became flushed and confused. The tale of a Long Island runaway, a thwarted traveler to California, the son of a hand-to-mouth fisherman-farmer, was not one he wanted to tell. The story in one way or another of all the American boys crowding among the immigrants in the attics and basements near the docks, it did not speak of extraordinary ambition nor foretell success. He had to do better than that. He reproached himself for not having thought of something before. Stark kept his head up as he shoveled the food into his mouth. He arched his eyebrows and waved his hand, as if to say, *Begin, boy, let me hear.*

Charles searched his head. He remembered the morning edition of the *Tribune*. It was all that came to mind. Stark was waiting. Charles felt as if he were drowning. He struggled to find some limb with which to pull himself to safety. A heading from an

article was all that floated into view: MORMONS SPLIT OVER GOLD
RUSH. BRIGHAM YOUNG DENOUNCES THOSE WHO LEAVE THE
"KINGDOM OF DESERET" FOR THE "FLESHPOTS OF CALIFORNIA."

"Mr. Stark," Charles said, "my parents are Mormons."

Stark stopped eating. He put down his knife and fork. "Good
God," he said.

Charles felt his foot scrape sand. He wasn't going to drown.
The story came to him as he talked. He was from upstate, outside
Albany, the only son of a prosperous farmer and his wife. (Albany
was the only city in the state outside of New York whose name
he knew. Charles prayed Stark wouldn't ask for details. He
didn't.) Stark seemed mesmerized as Charles told his story.
Charles's parents were pious and uneducated folk. They had never
ventured any distance from the farm. Occasionally, his father
went into Albany, but he never took Charles or Charles's mother
with him. Theirs was a peaceful, quiet, uneventful life until about
a year before, practically to the day, when at around dusk two
strangers rode up to their farmhouse. They looked like respectable
men. They said they were tired of traveling and wanted to hire
some lodgings for the night. Father took them in. Mother cooked
for them. In the evening they came into the parlor with their
Bibles and read in silence. Mother and Father joined them. After
a while the men brought out another book. A Mormon bible.

"You mean the Book of Mormon?" Stark said.

"Yes," Charles answered. "I could hear them talking from
up in my bedroom. Not the words, but their tone. At first, Father
sounded angry. He was arguing with them. I heard my mother
crying, soft sobs. Their voices settled down. After a bit, I fell
asleep. When I awoke the next morning, the men were gone, but
Mother and Father were different. There was a flatness to their
voices, a hardness in their eyes I had never seen evidence of
before."

Charles had his feet now. He was treading on dry land. Stark
had forgotten his food. He was listening raptly. Charles began to
relish his tale, sensing that here was the greatest privilege a city
could offer: a man's right to decide who he would be. The city

gave what no village would. The ability to disappear and reappear, to die and to be born again. If a man assumed a role, the way Barnum or Greeley did, if he pretended to be a prophet or a showman, all the city cared about was that he succeed. The city applauded its successes and dismissed its failures. Nothing else mattered. And Charles sensed something more: The water he was emerging from was the river of baptism.

Charles told Stark that before he knew it his parents had become Mormons in their hearts and joined with other converts in the area, not merely to read the Mormon scripture but—as painful as it was for him to say—to indulge in the plurality of wives. They were like strangers to their son, and when they announced their intention to sell their farm and join a company of Mormons headed for the Great Salt Lake, Charles decided to run away. He took the small amount of money he had saved and bought passage on the Albany steamboat. He left at night and arrived in New York City the next morning, alone, almost penniless, struggling to believe that God would sustain him. And He had. On the second day in the city, he had wandered by the *Tribune* and seen the advertisement of Stark and Evans. Stark sat motionless, his mouth open, his food untouched. The story's ending came effortlessly to Charles.

"Mr. Stark, I have a confession to make."

"Something else?"

"Charles Bedford is not the name I was born with. My real name is Ezra Van Wyck."

Ezra Van Wyck was the name of one of the clerks Charles had shared a room with. The man had died in his sleep two weeks before.

"Why did you change it, boy?"

"Two reasons, sir. First, because when I left my parents, I felt it a kind of death. The family I had been part of was gone. The name no longer had any meaning for me. Second, because on my first night in the city I had crept into a livery stable on Charles Street near the docks and slept on a pile of straw. I prayed for God's help but awoke hungry and bereft of hope. I began to wander the streets aimlessly. I had no money. My hunger became so great my legs shook. I thought of throwing myself into the river when suddenly I heard a voice speak to me. 'The Lord feeds His lambs,' it said. I looked around but there was no one to be seen. Suddenly I realized my hunger was gone, and my despair. I stopped the first passerby. *Where am I?* I said. *What street is this?* I took hold of his arm. He pulled away, frightened. *Bedford Street,* he said.

"Sir, it was as if I'd entered the world anew. My prayer on Charles Street had been answered on Bedford. Charles and Bedford. I had entered the Jordan on one street and emerged on the other. I knew now that I stood on solid ground, and not an hour later I passed the offices of the *Tribune* and was soon on my way to you. But now I was no longer Ezra Van Wyck. I was a new creation. Charles Bedford."

Charles wanted to order a brandy and drink it in one gulp. A celebration. He had taken his name and made it his own, turned it to his own use, put himself on the map. *Hurrah Charlie!* He cut slowly into his chop. It was cold. He was seized by an elemental hunger but made himself eat slowly. He didn't look up for a few minutes. When he did, there were tears in Mr. Stark's eyes.

The next day, Charles was given a desk and a stool. They were set up outside Stark's office. For the first time, the clerks addressed Charles Bedford as something other than "boy." Charles learned the business quickly. Stark and Evans had been founded by Stark's grandfather and a Mr. Evans, two round-faced, red-cheeked men whose portraits smiled down onto the counting floor. It was an old-style firm that dabbled in all sorts of transactions: loans, insurance, investments in canals and roads, imports and exports, and money exchanges. The workday was long but leisurely, a continuation of the polite, intimate world of the firm's founders, business conducted in coffeehouses and taverns among gentlemen who had known one another all their lives, money accumulated slowly, without haste. Every day, after breakfast at Old Tom's, Charles accompanied Stark to the Merchants'

Exchange Building, a stately Greek temple on the block between Wall Street and Exchange Place and Hanover and William streets. The two men stood in the room rented by the Stock and Exchange Board. Stark always took up the same position, in a corner with his back to the wall, his elbow resting on a windowsill. Silence, said Stark, is a wonderful weapon. It makes other men nervous. They are distracted by the absence of noise and try to plug the hole with their chatterings. Often they'll reveal things they otherwise would not.

Gradually the room filled up with stout, gray men like Stark. They moved deliberately around the room, never raising their voices. Around noon, an auctioneer would mount an oaken rostrum that was carved and polished like a pulpit and call out prices on securities being offered for sale. A brief bidding would go on, accounts settled, entries made in ledgers, papers exchanged, hands clasped, and the men would leave as they entered, slowly filing out, sometimes alone, sometimes arm in arm.

Charles paid attention. He stayed close to Stark's side. Stark would pull slips of paper from his pocket, lean over on the windowsill, and scribble on them. He would fold a slip and say "Groesbeck" or "Thorne" or "Lockwood" or "Van Zandt." He would point to the recipient, and Charles would move quickly to deliver it, press the paper into the man's hand, and whisper, "From Mr. Stark." Often he simply stood next to Stark in silence, and listened. The room hummed with the soft tones of privileged conversations. But from outside came voices that seemed to grow louder and more raucous each month, voices that seemed to have no secrets. Charles watched from the window. To someone who didn't know better, what he saw might seem a minor civil disturbance, hundreds of men milling in the street, waving their arms, shouting and pointing, their faces crimson from exertion. The sound of the curbstone brokers arose every morning, no matter how wet or cold or hot the weather, their enthusiasm never diminishing. Once in a while, Stark looked out the window and a pained expression came over his face. "The tribe of speculators," he said, "is more dangerous than any tribe of red men."

The tribal war whoop grew stronger. Gold from California fed the frenzy. Lands seized from Mexico gave life to the tribal dream of empire. The corner outside the Stock and Exchange Board became more crowded. New men appeared, no gray in their hair. "Nobodies," Stark said. They traded wildly in mining stock and railroads, in steamships and telegraphs. They hired rooms and ran telegraph wires out of them, looking on the hinterland beyond the Hudson as one great market, one immense gold mine. They moved about the narrow, crooked streets of the financial district reading printed sheets as they went, their fingers running down the columns of price quotations, trading a million shares a day among themselves while the daily auction among the members of the Board barely reached five thousand.

Stark grew tired of pushing his way through the crowded street. He lingered over his coffee and brandy in Old Tom's, ordered a refill, and sent Charles ahead. He preferred to tend to his social duties, and became more prominent in the city's philanthropies. In December of 1855, he brought Charles along with him to a lecture by Mr. Charles Loring Brace, of the Children's Aid Society, at the old Dutch church on Nassau Street. "Involvements in charity are an important part of a gentleman's life," said Stark. "They speak of a responsibility that extends to all things." The crowd was mostly brokers, but Mr. Greeley was there, the first time Charles saw him in the flesh, and Frederick Law Olmsted, the editor of *Putnam's Monthly*.

Stark introduced Charles to Cornelius Roosevelt, a director of the Chemical National Bank and a legendary stalwart of the financial community. Roosevelt put his head close to Stark's and said something. Both men threw their heads back in laughter. Charles felt uncomfortable, afraid that the comment might have been at his expense, but as he and his employer moved toward their seats, Stark said, "Roosevelt just observed that it must be a powerful temptation to divine justice to gather so many brokers under the Lord's roof." He laughed again. They entered a pew, and Stark reached over and tapped a man on the shoulder.

"Audley," he said. The man turned around and started to

rise. Stark put his hand on his shoulder. "Please, stay seated."

Charles had seen the man several times in the office. Mr. Audley Ward, a client. He looked as if he could be Mr. Greeley's brother. Ward showed no sign of recognition when Stark said, "This is Charles Bedford, an associate of the firm."

"And this," Ward said to Stark, "this is my niece Sarah."

Beside Ward was a young woman with wide, round eyes and a complexion that was silky and unblemished.

"Good gracious, Sarah," Stark exclaimed, "you were a little girl when we last met, and now you are a woman, and such a soothing sight for eyes as overworked as mine."

Sarah let her chin fall toward her chest. Charles saw her blush.

Mr. Brace had mounted the pulpit to begin his lecture. He opened by reading a quote from Carlyle.

" 'Sansculottism will burn much; but what is incombustible it will not burn. Fear not Sansculottism; recognize it for what it is, the portentous inevitable end of much, the miraculous beginning of much. One other thing thou mayest understand of it: that it too came from God; for has it not *been*? From of old, as it is written, are His goings forth; in the great Deep of things; fearful and wonderful now as in the beginning: in the whirlwind also He speaks; and the wrath of men is made to praise Him.—But to gauge and measure this immeasurable thing, and what is called *account for it,* and reduce it to a dead logic-formula, attempt not! Much less shalt thou shriek thyself hoarse, cursing it; for that, to all needful lengths, has been already done. As an actually existing Son of Time, *look,* with unspeakable manifest interest, oftenest in silence, at what the Time did bring: therewith edify, instruct, nourish thyself, or were it but amuse and gratify thyself, as it is given thee.'

"*Look!*" Brace said. "*Look around thee!*"

Charles couldn't take his eyes off Sarah, the profile of her face. He stirred in his seat, unable to get comfortable.

"Is something wrong?" Stark asked in a low voice.

"No, I'm warm, that's all."

Stark covered his hand with his hat so that only Charles could see the finger he pointed toward Sarah. "A suitable cause for heat." He winked.

From the pulpit, Brace warmed to his subject. "In the space of a single decade, a generation of darkness has been raised up in this city. The specter of Sansculottism! Ten thousand children a year born to superstition and poverty, their destiny to become prostitutes, burglars, shoulder-hitters, pickpockets, purse-croppers, garroters, short-boys, murderers!"

Sarah turned her head slightly, as though she had become aware of Charles's staring. He looked down at his shoes and tried to concentrate on Brace's words.

"The intervention represented by the Newsboys'-Lodging-House, which your generosity made possible, cannot suffice to meet this threat. Yea, if we recognize the thing for what it is, we shall see that there is only one influence capable of exorcising forever the rise of Sansculottism. I speak not of a man nor a party but of a place. The land. The countryside. The American farm and the race that inhabits it. It is here that we find the repository of the extraordinary promise of our nation. It is here that we find a laboring class that respects itself more than the corresponding class of any other country, even England. Anyone coming among this class and violating its characteristic habits—thrift, courage, sobriety, hard work, faith, fairness, self-reliance—soon receives the most severe punishment a workingman can feel: the contempt of his own fellows. No one living in a rural district can altogether escape the indirect power of these influences. The necessity of education, the reality of religion, the purity of intentions, the consciousness of being a citizen with political power in a great Republic. These ideas are so profound among the laboring classes of our advancing frontier that no one, however low, utterly fails to be affected by them."

The pressure Charles felt was painful, a throbbing stiffness that bulged against his pants. He put his hat on his lap. Elsa Jones had been his first. A hired girl on a neighboring farm. She barely got enough to eat, so the boys used to pay her with food. She said he was different. "I like you, Charlie. You're sweet. Don't need no payment from you." Once in the loft of the barn, they had gone at it all afternoon, over and over again, and he kept becoming erect, and she moaned so loudly the cows below got nervous. It was as much relief as pleasure when he had felt himself entering Elsa.

Sarah sat up in her seat. He could see the outline of her breasts, firm and prominent. He averted his eyes to the pulpit and tried again to concentrate.

"It is here, then, in the progress of our countrymen across the vast expanses of the continent that we find reason to fear not Sansculottism. Already, with the cooperation of our courts, we have had success in transporting the abandoned youngsters of our streets, or those whose depraved circumstances mock the very word *home,* to a new life in our rural districts. Some predicted that the inhabitants would resist the appearance of the children of our dangerous classes in their midst. But the readiness on the part of farmers to receive such children has been edifying.

"Indeed, an announcement through circulars or rural papers of the intention to supply children almost always brings a speedy response in the form of hundreds of applications from farmers and mechanics. On the day the band of children arrives, faces shining, boys and girls made clean and properly dressed, the greeting received is universally enthusiastic. Crowds wait at the station, and under the close supervision of the agent who has escorted the young travelers on their trip, the children are quickly disposed of for the night. The next day, a meeting of the people, irrespective of religious sympathies, is addressed by the agent who informs them of the benevolent objects of the Children's Aid Society, and relates, in brief form, the history of the children.

"Soon, prospective parents come forward. The childless are usually first. They are followed by those, moved by what they have seen and heard, who apply for children they hadn't planned on taking. There are also those who see the opportunity to gain an extra set of hands for their homestead while in the same stroke fulfilling the godly injunction to care for the least of our brethren.

"At length, the business of charity is finished and the former wayfarers and waifs find themselves in comfortable and kind homes, with all the boundless advantages and opportunities of the western farmer's life about them."

There were two coal stoves in the church, one in the front, the other by the vestibule, and the room had become exceedingly hot. The sweat rolled down Charles's back.

"I ain't got anything left," he had told Elsa after the third time he had mounted her. She sat on his chest, bent over, and put her breasts next to his face. "I'll help you, Charlie." She reached back and took him in her hand.

He shifted position. Stark poked him with his elbow. "It should be over soon, my boy."

Brace was appealing for funds.

Charles glanced at Sarah. She seemed enrapt with Brace's words. A girl just entered into womanhood, the last awkwardness of youth gone. A flower come to blossom. But Sarah had more than Elsa's physical ripeness. She had grace and refinement; she was a lady as well as a woman. She and her uncle left by the center aisle. Charles had no chance to talk to her before she left.

A few weeks later, on New Year's Day, the city's traditional day for paying visits to friends and acquaintances, Charles stopped at the Ward home. It was a tall redbrick house with a fan-shaped window over the door. But the neighborhood was no longer fashionable. There was a grocery on the corner with pug-nosed Irish children loitering outside it. In the middle of the block, two houses had been subdivided into flats. Rags were stuck into broken windows. The smell of boiled cabbage hung in the air.

Inside, the Ward house vibrated with life and voices. The furniture was old but tasteful, the walls hung with portraits. When Charles came in, he saw Sarah on the other side of the room, surrounded by four young men. She looked at him. No sign of recognition in her eyes, she looked away.

Ward came over to him. "I don't believe I've had the pleasure," he said.

"Several times, Mr. Ward. Twice at the offices of Stark and

Evans, where I'm an assistant to Mr. Stark, we were together in
the same room for the purposes of going over your account. And
then, three weeks ago at Mr. Brace's lecture, I had the pleasure
of being formally introduced. My name is Charles Bedford."

"Quite so."

A servant helped Charles take off his coat. Ward didn't
move. "Are you here on some matter of business, Charles?"

"I'm here to wish you good cheer."

"Quite so."

Sarah didn't speak to him that day. Once he caught her looking at him from across the room. He didn't call again. He found
a bagnio on Greene Street with a young Irishwoman who bore
Sarah a fair resemblance. He made love to her every chance he
could. He moved out of his room on Albany Street, a private
room he had taken after leaving his shared quarters in the boardinghouse, and leased two rooms in a hotel off Union Square that
catered "exclusively to gentlemen." Soon after, Stark announced
he was giving up the daily running of the office and retiring to
his estate on the Hudson, above the Spuyten Duyvil. He told the
assembled clerks that Charles would direct matters in his absence.
"He is youthful," said Stark, "but he is graced with discerning
judgment and foresight, golden attributes that he has dug out of
the coarse earth of experience." The clerks stood silently, dismay
on their faces. As he headed for the door, Stark paused and put
an arm on Charles's shoulder. "Charlie," he said, "the day we
met, I said to myself, 'Here's the boy I never had.' I thought from
the start I saw something remarkable in you. Still do. I have great
expectations, Charlie, great expectations."

Charles gloried in his position for the first few weeks. He
stood silently in the same corner of the Stock and Exchange Board
as Stark had. He made no attempt to treat the older brokers as
his peers. He knew they snickered behind his back, but he believed
that they would eventually accept him as one of their own. Only
gradually, as he adjusted to his new responsibilities and made a
careful examination of the firm's books, did he realize that the
laughter wasn't directed at his age but at his gullibility. Charles

had imagined Stark as the captain of an old but seaworthy vessel. After years of guiding it through seas rough and smooth, the old man had decided to go ashore and put his ship in younger hands. But now Charles learned what the other brokers had known or suspected all along: The ship had been leaking for some time, and the captain had taken all his money and valuables, put them in his own skiff, and rowed a safe distance from his ship. In his place he had left a junior mate. If the ship went down, the captain would blame it on the mate's inexperience; if it survived, then perhaps at some later date he would come aboard and take command again.

At night, alone in the office, Charles pored over the books and felt a growing admiration for the way Stark had dexterously skimmed off a significant portion of the profits for himself. He had been persistent rather than greedy, never looting outright a customer's account, simply adjusting the fractions in his own favor. Over the years, he had let some of the larger accounts leave the firm. They were ambitious for gain and apt to want a careful look at the books. Stark and Evans preferred volume, a roster of comfortable, reliable clients who looked for a steady income and were satisfied when it was provided.

Charles remembered the tears in Stark's eyes that first morning in Old Tom's. Was it possible that as far back as then, the old man had laid out his plan? Had Stark known from the beginning that the story of the upstate boyhood was all an invention? Had he even cared? Was he crying out of gratitude? Perhaps, as he listened to the story, he was formulating his own design for getting out before he was discovered, overwhelmed by the thought of escaping with both his profit and honor intact, a heaven-sent innocent to be sacrificed in his stead.

There was the possibility that Charles could expose the long history of illegal gain by Stark and Evans. But Charles understood this was precisely why Stark had put *him* in charge. Charles was like one of those faceless, nameless creatures whom Stark watched from his position at the window of the Stock and Exchange Board. The pack of hurrying, striving, pushing men, their nostrils filled with a first whiff of real wealth, they were like wolves on the trail of a wounded deer. Along with his peers on the Board, Stark disdained them. But unlike many of his colleagues, Stark also saw in the outsiders something irresistible, an inevitable triumph, a force of nature, a source of energy as new and as potentially revolutionary as the oil that was being drawn from the fields of Pennsylvania. Stark would never have walked down into that crowd to seek a partner. His fellow brokers would think him drunk or mad. But fate had put into his lap one of the ubiquitous nobodies. Whether his parents were Mormons or Millerites or Myrmidons, who cared? Here was a boy who could not only be molded and prepared to take over the firm but who possessed the appetite of his class, the belly-seated hunger that no gentleman could admit to. Such a boy would never destroy his own future by revealing peculations that would undermine the reputation of Stark and Evans, and send it into bankruptcy. He would play the cards he had been dealt and, grateful for finding himself in the game at all, would employ his skills and instincts with a concentrated desperation.

When the shock of realizing how skillfully he had been manipulated wore off, Charles found himself without any bitterness toward Stark. After two months, he received a letter from the former director inviting him to take the train up to Spuyten Duyvil. Stark wrote that he would pick him up at the station.

On the agreed-upon day, Charles walked up to the terminal on Chambers Street and boarded the Hudson River Railroad. An investment that Stark hadn't favored. He had been suspicious of railroads. "The public has a passion for them, no doubt," he had said back in 1851, when Charles had timidly suggested that the firm take a position in railroad stocks. "But I see railroads as more a fashion than an institution. They'll never match the speed and convenience offered by steamboats, and there's something incurably vulgar about them."

The cars were pulled by horses until they reached Thirtieth Street, where the clot of buildings and traffic thinned, and a locomotive was attached. The car was soon rocking along the track.

Charles read the *Tribune*. When he looked up, the train was roaring past the cluster of shantytowns that filled the wild precincts north of the city. Children stood on hilltops and waved as the train went by. Charles went back to his paper. In 1851, the Hudson River Railroad had reached Albany. Passenger growth was explosive. Finally, in the following year, Stark had allowed Charles to handle the firm's initial investments in railroads, small sums that had brought quadruple returns. Now it was rumored that Cornelius Vanderbilt, whose immense holdings in sailing vessels, ferry service, and steamships had earned him the title of "Commodore," was liquidating his shipping interests to take control of the railroads. An intriguing prospect, if true, and Charles, having already decided to watch the Commodore carefully, had surreptitiously retained one of the grumpy Dutchman's clerks to share any information that might come his way.

Stark was waiting for Charles by the train platform. They rode in Stark's coach a short distance to a local tavern, a dingy, dirty place owned by an Irishman named Ahearn who seemed overwhelmed by the presence of two gentlemen in his establishment. They had mutton chops, fried potatoes, and coffee with brandy in it. When they were done, Charles handed Stark an account book containing a summary of the last two months' transactions. Stark put on his spectacles and examined it. As he thumbed the pages, he said, "Well, Charles, what do you think?"

"Of what?"

"Of the responsibility I have given you."

"I think that I was lucky to have found you, and that you in your turn were even more lucky to have found me."

Stark's eyes widened. This time there were no tears in them. "Luck has little to do with it, my boy," he said. "I don't deny it plays a role in human affairs and an especially important one in the making and unmaking of men's fortunes. But luck is more than mere happenstance. Luck is the fruit of hard work. It is the result of patiently striving to put the odds in one's own favor, of long preparation to take advantage of the opportunities that circumstance may present." Stark closed the book. "Are you frightened?" he asked.

"A little, I suppose. Stark and Evans is undercapitalized. Most of our lucrative clients have gone elsewhere, and your departure robbed us of both wisdom and financial resources."

"You mean *robbed* in the poetic sense, I take it." Stark smiled.

"I mean *robbed* in whatever sense you wish to interpret it. Stark and Evans is meeting its obligations thanks to the general prosperity in the markets. Gold and credit are plentiful. Interest and dividends are paid with regularity. There is a strong demand for new issues of stocks made by banks, railroads, mines. But we have no margin. We are using all our strength to stay afloat, and when the flood comes we will be the first to go under."

"The flood?"

"A wave of bank failures and ruined companies, a dramatic plunge in the value of stock, a general disappearance of credit."

"You're still a cub, but you reason like a bear. I have always thought caution was a creature of memory. It's been almost two decades since the panic of '37, and I'd imagined time and California gold had cleansed the national consciousness of bitter recollections."

"My caution comes from a simple observation: All bubbles burst, even the prettiest that catch the light of the sun and sail on summer breezes."

Soap bubbles, small orbs of brilliant colors, they rose out of the steaming tub as his mother pulled the clothes out. She spent the entire day at the washing, months, years, a lifetime. He was a small boy sitting in the yard of their house. He watched the bubbles all morning as they rode the wind out of the yard. None escaped very far. The next day, his father would bring the carefully folded clothes to the people in town and return with more bundles to wash, and his mother would be bent over the tub and bubbles would rise again in the air and travel only a short distance before they disappeared. A first lesson in the ways of Wall Street.

"And should the bubble burst, how will you save the firm?"

"I shall not wait until the bubble bursts. I shall begin by reducing Stark and Evans to the point at which it can survive on a handful of nuts and apples. I shall dismiss most of the staff, and close the numerous accounts that bring little or no profit to the firm."

"You will be ostracized. No gentleman will welcome you into his house."

"I shall make only infrequent appearances at the Board. I shall move our offices to cheaper quarters, perhaps on Pearl Street."

"The clients will resent it."

"Not the ones interested in making money, and they're the only ones I want. I shall also begin trading at the curb as well as at the Board."

"At the curb? Good God, you'll be immediately dismissed from the Board, deprived of your seat and your trading privileges. Men will speak of you in the way they speak of sodomites or papists."

"Let them. Besides, I won't trade in person. I'll do what several others of the august members of the Board have done, and hire a proxy to trade at the curb for me."

"Where is that bright-eyed young boy who heard the voice of God on Bedford Street?"

"He is grown up and been educated by a master."

"I take that as praise."

"You should."

"But be careful. Many a cub never lived to be a bear. Be patient."

"I trust my instincts. I have come to understand that despite all the figuring and calculating that surrounds the money trade, those who succeed do so because of their sense of sight and smell, their ability to discern changes in the weather, to sniff out the future."

"Your instincts are keen, that I don't doubt, but even men with keen instincts have been known to end up in the poorhouse.

Timing is the key. When to get in and when to get out, that's what separates the victims from the victors."

"My timing will be right. For the present I shall stay out of the market. But as prices continue to go up, and reason gives way to fancy, as it must, I shall lift my nose to the wind. At the heavy scent of salt, the first sign of a great storm at sea, I shall contract to deliver stock at its current price but set the date for delivery at some point in the future, when the storm will have hit hard and values will have plummeted along with the barometer. I shall then buy the stock at its low price and present it to my clients, who will be obliged to pay me the high price. And when the storm has finally passed and blown down the dreams and designs of the incautious, I shall come back into the market as forcefully as I can and have for a penny what formerly cost a dollar."

"Buy low, sell high. An admirable if unoriginal formulation. But tell me, how does a boy from Albany know so much of the sea and its storms?"

"It came to me in a dream." Now it was Charles's turn to smile.

"You were the new Noah, floating in the Ark with the debris of the wicked all around you?"

"Yes, the new Noah, I like that."

"Well, Noah, I pray to God your nose is trustworthy." Stark picked up his coffee mug and gently tapped it against Charles's. "Here's to the Deluge," he said. "Ruin to the foolish and wealth to the wise."

The storm came in 1857. It struck suddenly, with the failure of a single bank. It was as if a solitary cloud had been punctured and all the water of the heavens had spilled through it. Charles had heard the word *panic* used to describe what happened when men began to realize that the paper they held in their hands wasn't an invitation to new riches but a one-way ticket to pauperdom. But he found himself unprepared for the terror that actually descended. Crowds gathered everywhere, in front of banks, the Merchants' Exchange, the telegraph offices. Pushing led to shoving, shoving ended in fistfights. Serene, self-confident brokers turned

into wild animals, screaming and ranting in the streets, the froth
of madness on their lips. For days the crowds poured into the
streets. When the police proved unable to handle them, the militia
was called out. Gradually a ghostly calm descended, but the newspapers reported the progress of the storm as it swept across Aus-
tria, France, Britain, Scandinavia, bubble after bubble bursting,
the sheer scale of the disaster leaving the world amazed and gov-
ernments concerned with their very survival.

One morning, when Charles stepped out of the Broadway
stagecoach and walked to his office on Pearl Street, Wall Street
was empty and quiet. It reminded him of East Hampton after one
of the great winter storms had blown away trees and flooded the
land, the shore looking as it must have on the morning after the
Deluge receded, all fresh and scrubbed and ready for new life.
Many offices were empty. One small, elegant granite-faced structure, formerly the headquarters of a respected brokerage, had
been turned into a soda dispensary. The Mining Exchange, which
had been set up on William Street to compete with the Board,
was a ruin, its doors ripped off their hinges, windows broken,
papers strewn everywhere.

The Board itself, housed in its new headquarters at Lord's
Court, was deserted. A handful of brokers appeared each day for
the sake of keeping it open. They whispered among themselves,
then left. Passing on the other side of the street from the Board,
Charles ran into Morris Van Shaick, a friendly rival of Mr. Stark's
and a former elder of the Board. Van Shaick was standing in a
doorway, staring across at the façade of the Board's building. His
firm had been in decline for some time. The panic had put it out
of its misery. Charles said hello. Van Shaick tipped his hat. That
afternoon the old man drank arsenic in his office and died. Two
days afterward, a letter from Van Shaick arrived on Charles's
desk. It had been written the day Van Shaick committed suicide.
The script was a spidery scrawl. It read:

*Bedford, keep the spring in your step. But in your mind
the poet's thought—all that wealth e'er gave—awaits alike*

the inevitable hour—the paths of glory lead but to the grave.

M.V.S.

As the months passed, activity began again. New faces appeared, most of them young, around Charles's age, many of them former members of the tribe of nobodies. The Board's membership committee, eager to fill the depleted ranks, ignored for the moment the traditional requirements of lineage and pedigree. What mattered now was the four-hundred-dollar initiation fee.

The results of the debacle were far more extensive than Charles had expected. Overnight he had gone from being a small-time broker, the youngest member of the Board, to being one of its veterans, not only a survivor of what had occurred but a beneficiary. Men who had recently found it difficult to acknowledge his existence now sought his advice. One of the Board's former titans, a fourth-generation broker, stood in Charles's cramped, shabby office and wept. He begged for a loan, the words interspersed with sobs, money enough to keep himself afloat until, as he said, "some order returns to the world." Charles gave him a hundred dollars to pay some immediate expenses. But he knew that the "order" this man hoped to see return was gone forever. Anyone who thought otherwise couldn't be trusted with a larger sum. Soon after the broker left, a telegram arrived from Stark: AND GOD BLESSED NOAH AND HIS SONS AND SAID UNTO THEM BE FRUITFUL AND MULTIPLY AND REPLENISH THE EARTH.

Before the panic had struck, when he had moved the Stark and Evans offices to Pearl Street and dismissed three quarters of the staff, Charles had informed a large number of clients that the firm could no longer handle their accounts. He wasn't interested in the penny-ante game of percentages that Stark had played. But the account of Audley Ward, as insignificant as it was, he would keep. He had visited Ward at his home to inform him about the changes at Stark and Evans, and to reassure him. Ward had met him at the door and invited him in only as far as the front hallway.

"Mr. Bedford," Ward said, "I'm pleased to see you because the most dreadful rumors have reached me about the condition of Stark and Evans. It is said the firm is failing and has had to dismiss most of its staff and move to near the East River waterfront, in the same building as a chandlery."

"The firm is in solid condition. We are only making it stronger. It is our opinion that difficult times are ahead, and we intend to protect our clients and ensure they prosper."

"And the chandlery? Is it true you have taken up residence with a hawker of common ship wares?"

"Mr. Ward, you make it sound as if I'm committing adultery."

Ward talked on. He said he wasn't sure he should keep his account with Stark and Evans. Men he respected were advising him otherwise. Charles stopped listening. He looked past Ward at the portraits that lined the wall leading to the staircase. The one closest was of a dignified-looking gentleman and a young girl. The girl had Sarah's lips and eyes. It must be she. She was probably upstairs at this moment. Charles had given up his regular visits to the Irish whore on Greene Street. Her resemblance to Sarah had diminished with each visit. He inclined his head slightly and tried to see up the stairs. Maybe she was standing above, listening to what they said.

"Mr. Bedford, what assurance have I that my funds are safe in your hands?"

"You have my word."

"Your word?"

"The word of a gentleman."

Ward looked perplexed. "I suppose I must rely on that. Quite so."

Charles continued to pay occasional visits to Ward's home. The third or fourth time he appeared, Ward invited him to sit in the parlor. They had tea. Charles asked after Sarah. She was in England, Ward said. She had been there for the past month. She went every few years to renew the ties she had formed several years before. Her father had sent her to boarding school there as

a girl. Ward dropped his voice to a whisper: "In my humble opinion, Sarah is not so much interested in old relationships as new.
I believe she's in search of a husband."

Sarah returned unwed, and a few weeks later joined Charles
and Ward for tea. Charles had his first real lengthy conversation
with her. He was surprised by the strong English inflection in her
voice. Several times after that she joined them. She spoke a great
deal about poetry. Charles had little to add.

"Are you inclined toward poetry?" she asked.

"I am, but my inclinations are outweighed by my obligations,
and I can rarely find the time."

She looked at him in such a way that he couldn't tell if she
was angry or sad. "No one should be too busy for poetry. It is
the truest expression of a sincere heart."

In the springtime, Charles asked Ward and Sarah if they
would like to join him on a carriage ride into the country. They
accepted. He rented a driver and a four-in-hand for the occasion.
As they drove out of the city, Ward said, "We should avoid the
Harlem Lane. It has become little more than a racetrack, a place
where the lowest types trot about on their flimsy one-man traps,
vying with each other in velocity and ostentation." Charles told
the driver to mind Ward's instructions. "We shall follow the route
of retreat that General Washington took."

Charles sat across from Sarah. Her face was framed by her
Pamela bonnet, a nimbus of straw trimmed with pink ribbons and
blue silk anemones. She dressed in a simple style that had mostly
gone out of fashion in New York. Her skirt lacked hoops or
flounces. It hung close about her body. Her long, graceful neck
curved into the round, firm line of her bodice. They rode in silence, watching the scenery, until Ward announced, "This is the
spot where the Americans turned and fought a rearguard action."
Charles told the driver to stop. "It is a good place to rest," he
said.

They were on a rise in the road that gave them a dramatic
view of the city to the south and the Palisades to the west. Charles
got down first. He helped Ward out of the coach, and held his

hand up to Sarah. She took it, and with her other hand lifted her dress at the knee, exposing the black silk stocking above the top of her shoe. Charles felt the warmth of the sun on his face. He closed his eyes for an instant and pictured the silk as it ran up her leg, enfolded it, the black ending at the perfect whiteness of her thigh.

"You know," Ward said, "this is near where that imposter Amos Greene claims to have shot a British soldier dead and saved the American retreat. Youngest hero of the Revolution. Absolute bunkum. Everyone knows it was Jacob Valentine who fired the shot."

Sarah bent down and picked a dandelion, a ball of soft fluff at the end of a stem. She held it to her lips and touched it gently to her tongue. She blew on it, and the ball exploded. A shower of white particles traveled on the wind. She picked another and handed it to Charles.

Ward had his back to them. He looked at the city in the distance. "Mr. Barnum even went so far as to make Greene one of his exhibits. Posed him in a uniform with a musket in front of a wax image of General Washington. A perfect marriage of scoundrels, Greene and Barnum."

Charles blew on the dandelion. The white down shot away from him in a long spray.

"If some future historian ever wished to chart the decay of this Republic," said Ward, "all he'd need do is recount the origins of Mr. Barnum's museum. Think of it. When Tammany was founded at the end of the Revolution as a patriotic society for artisans and mechanics, it created, as part of its aspirations to knowledge and self-improvement, a collection of art and specimens of nature. But since Tammany very quickly surrendered such aspirations, it turned over the nascent museum to its caretaker, who sold it to John Scudder, who sold it to Barnum. Here we have the history of the Republic itself! A collection of exhibits formed from a native spirit of patriotism becomes in two generations a circus, a collection of two-headed calves and bogus mermaids and false heroes exhibited for the enjoyment of a gross and ignorant mob."

When they reentered the coach, Charles sat next to Sarah, with Ward on the seat across from them. Ward continued to lecture. Charles rocked with the motion of the coach, falling gently against Sarah, their shoulders and legs continually touching. Sarah was quiet. She nodded in agreement with whatever her uncle said. Ward pointed north, across the Harlem River, to wooded hills in the distance. "Over there lies the Van Cortlandt estate. A good family, they suffered much for the cause of the Revolution, and afterwards were strong supporters of the rights of property. It seemed obvious to them, as to others, that men of property had a natural interest in order and stability, and that men of no property had an equal interest in overturning such order. The Van Cortlandts were men of common sense, I'd say, a moral asset increasingly lacking in this age. Of course, they had the advantage not only of having good breeding but of coming from good stock, a mixture of English and Dutch blood. Mr. Stark tells me that this is your ancestry, too."

"Yes," Charles said. He had barely been listening. The touch and scent of her body so close, the thought of those black stockings, white thighs, two bodies entwined, she so willing and eager, breathless, *Oh, Charlie, Charlie, Charlie!*

"An unbeatable mixture of bloods," Ward said. "From the English come the boundless spirit of individual enterprise, the solid courage, the sense of civility and propriety, and the instinct for self-government. From the Dutch, the sound practical sense, the patient industry, the willingness to persist, and, not least of all, the respect for women. The Dutch blood comes from your mother's side, I take it."

"Yes, she was a Van Vliet."

Mother. A worn and silent woman from the earliest he could remember, withdrawn, eternally tired, empty of emotion. Maiden name was Payne. He had no idea of her blood. English, he supposed.

"The Van Vliets of Brooklyn?" Ward asked.

"Of Albany."

"Albany? I didn't know there was a northern branch of the family."

"Albany is overrun with Van Vliets." The coach jolted. Charles put his hands on the seat to steady himself. He felt Sarah's hand beneath his. She didn't pull it away. She turned and smiled at him.

On the way home they passed a wrecked coach. Baggage and bodies were strewn across the roadside. Sarah turned away. Ward shook his head as they drove slowly by. "Such disasters are commonplace now," he said. "We see them every day. Smashed and ruined vehicles, broken bodies thrown about like child's toys. Yet scenes such as this fail to bring any alteration in conduct, and the addiction to velocity seems only to become more severe with each passing day. God knows what it will take to cure us of such a dangerous and destructive passion."

When they reached home it was dusk, and the street looked shabbier than ever. Sarah went up the stoop into the house. Ward stood on the sidewalk and shook hands with Charles. On the other side of the street a disheveled Irishwoman with a ragged woolen shawl pulled over her head was sitting in front of a decaying wreck of a house. She was singing in a loud voice, but the words were indecipherable.

"Can you believe that the French ambassador to the Republic once lived not far from here?" Ward said, shaking his head as if to answer his own question.

"I should like to call again soon to take a drive to some other point in the country. In no time I shall be educated in the history of this city."

"Quite so. I should like to do it again myself. In a fortnight, let's say."

"A fortnight it is."

For the next two weeks Charles wrestled with his emotions. He would have to declare his love to Sarah. He was sure that she felt something toward him. Love? He hoped so. If it was, sooner or later he would ask Ward for her hand. The question of his family would come under closer scrutiny. He would have to do better than claim some mythic family from Albany. There would have to be portraits, artifacts, papers, some silverware, an officially prepared record of his ancestry. Charles was certain it could be done. A few judicious purchases in the pawnshops, a writer paid to invent a history, a craftsman engaged to produce some authentic-looking documents. Somewhere in the city there were people to provide all these things. He couldn't be alone in his need for a past, not in New York.

As the day approached, Charles practiced in his mind what he would say, how he would tell Sarah about his growing affection. He wouldn't use the word *love,* not yet. In a building on Frankfort Street, right in the middle of the Swamp, the city's leather district, he found an antiquarian shop that sold reproductions of old maps, charters, certificates, parchments. The proprietor, Mr. John Allan, sat at a counter carefully turning the brittle pages of what seemed an ancient book. Without looking at Charles, he said, "We can do most anything. It will cost, but it can be done." He pushed the book he was examining across to Charles, his finger holding it open to the title page. The words were in Latin and Charles couldn't understand them, but below the words were the Roman numerals MDCX. Allan raised his spectacles to the top of his head and put his face close to the page. "Sixteen ten," he said. He tapped the date with a yellowed finger. "But in truth this is as fresh as today's newspaper." He lifted his head and smiled. His teeth were as yellow as his finger. "Yes indeed, for the right price, we can do just about anything." Charles smiled back. A deeply felt smile. His spirits soared. Now he had an ancestry, as noble and extensive as he wished.

He showed up at Ward's home excited, with a sense of the importance this day would hold in his life. As soon as the carriage pulled up, Ward came out the door and down the steps. They shook hands. "Well, I've been looking forward to this," said Ward.

"I too."

Ward motioned to the carriage. "Shall we?"

"What about Sarah?"

Ward's face showed his surprise. "Sarah? Sarah left for England three days ago."

They got into the carriage. Afterward, Charles would remember little of the hours that followed, only the drone of the old man's voice. He resolved to be through with Ward. He would notify him that his account could no longer be handled by Stark and Evans. He would forget Sarah. New York teemed with women. He threw himself into his work. The task of making money seemed a kind of revenge. It comforted him. And three weeks later, before he could get around to discontinuing Ward's account, the panic struck. He was in the office from morning to the late evening, calling in his chips, tallying up his victory.

The train stations were filled with brokers and investors returning from the country in the hope that they could salvage a part of their fortunes. Americans streamed home from abroad, entire families on European tour discovering that in their absence their quickly accumulated wealth, the privilege and position they had obtained almost overnight, was gone. The sellers' market was now a buyers' one. New money replaced by the still newer. The pages of the *Tribune* devoted to "Houses for Sale/To Let" doubled and trebled. One day Ward appeared in the offices of Stark and Evans, and Charles supposed he was there to offer thanks for the salvation of his property. But Ward was glum. "Some of the oldest and finest families in the city are ruined. A terrible thing to see. They come to me for help or advice. Some even come right out and ask for money."

"The poor usually do."

"Where will all this lead?"

Charles opened the *Tribune* across his desk and waved his hand over the long columns of real estate notices. "It will lead wherever you wish it to. My advice is to have your present home subdivided into three or four flats and rent them. It will be a nice source of additional income. You are now in a position to buy a fine new house in a rising part of the city. The market is overwhelmed with such bargains. Mr. Ward, you should be celebrating. You have survived the Flood. The tide that has sent other men to the bottom has lifted you up. You are a true son of Noah. Multiply your holdings in real estate as fast as you can."

"I shall consider it. But real estate is not what brings me here. Sarah has returned from England. She thought perhaps you might wish to renew your generous invitation to escort us into the country for a day's excursion. It would be salubrious for all of us, I should think."

More than mere happenstance, luck is the result of patiently striving to put the odds in one's own favor. Stark's formulation. Charles felt the truth of it. It was luck that he hadn't gotten around to closing Ward's account. But the victory he now felt on the verge of winning flowed out of the time and care he had invested in cultivating his relationship with Ward. A long time since the night he had run into Ward and Sarah at the lecture by Charles Loring Brace. He barely knew Sarah. Their conversations had hardly gone beyond the tritest pleasantries. Except for the electricity he had felt between them that day they went to the High Bridge, she had never given any indication of her feeling toward him. But the pull he felt toward her wasn't something that yielded to reason. It was something he felt in his gut. An absolute confidence that what was about to happen had to happen. He had been patient. She was his now. He felt it was a certainty.

When he knocked on the door, Sarah answered. He greeted her stiffly and stood silently by the stairs. She was as beautiful as he had remembered.

"I have bad news," she said.

Charles felt his chest contract. Could he be wrong about what must happen? "What is it?"

"Uncle is feeling unwell and shan't be able to accompany us."

"But you still wish to go?"

"Of course."

They drove up Fifth Avenue in Charles's new coach, a London-made brougham bought for a song from a distressed broker. Charles sat across from Sarah. He asked her a few questions about England but not about with whom she had stayed or whether she had been entertaining the proposition of some wealthy young Englishman whose fortune had disappeared when the panic crossed the Atlantic. He suspected this might be the case but no longer cared. What he cared about was having her.

The conversation died. Their silence filled the coach. He couldn't wait any longer. He rose from his place and sat again, beside her. "Sarah, I missed you."

"And I you, Charles."

He put his hand on her breast. She put her hand over his and pressed it. He took off his hat and threw it onto the opposite seat. He kissed her on the cheek. She turned her mouth to him and he kissed it. She unbuttoned his shirt and put her hand inside. He pulled away.

"What's wrong?" she said.

"Nothing." He knelt on the forward seat and slipped back the panel that fronted on the driver's seat. He knocked on the roof, and the driver's face appeared. "No interruptions. Drive on until I tell you to stop, and go slowly."

He put his hands on the inside wall of the coach to steady himself. She wrapped her arms around his waist and pulled him down on top of her as she spread her body across the length of the seat. He sat back onto his knees and undid her bodice. She unloosened his belt and opened the buttons of his fly. He knelt on the floor and pulled off her petticoat. He got back on top of her, the rhythm of their rise and fall conforming with the motion of the carriage. He ran his tongue down her neck. She sighed. He put his face beside hers and said softly in her ear, "Let us be fruitful and multiply."

A few weeks later, Charles asked Ward and Sarah to join him for a ride up to see the work on Central Park. Since a new superintendent, Mr. Olmsted, was now overseeing the construction, a real park had finally begun to emerge from the swamps and squatters' settlements that the city government had acquired for over five million dollars.

They went up Fifth Avenue until Charles suddenly directed the driver to turn left. The driver stopped the brougham in the middle of the block without having to be told. Charles got out. He asked Ward and Sarah to follow. As Sarah stepped down and looked at the monumental brown façade, she seemed to know immediately what this detour meant. The house was his gift to her. Built in the latest Italianate style, five stories tall, clad in close-grained Triassic sandstone—lately known as brownstone—it was barely two years old, the former home of one of the panic's many victims.

She held a hand over her mouth, and with the other took Charles's arm. Ward looked around, puzzled. "A whole new quarter of the city, and I haven't even been aware of its existence." He stood behind Charles and Sarah. "You know, I can remember walking up to the top of the steeple of the new Trinity Church the year it was completed and taking in the view of the entire city, a neat, well-ordered, redbrick town dotted with green; nothing imperial or decadent about it, an American place, modest, sensible, hardworking, ambitious, filled with hope, the prosperous merchant living next to the industrious mechanic. That was just four years after the Croton Water Works were finished. Such a sense of the future, of what our city would become. Who would have thought that in barely more than a decade we would come to rival the Romans in our taste for the monstrous?"

Sarah and Charles went up the imposing stone stoop, her arm on top of his. He opened the unlocked door to a vestibule with rosewood paneling and a burgundy tiled floor. Ward followed, still unsure of what was happening.

"Do you know the proprietor?" Ward asked.

"Exceedingly well," said Charles.

They entered the hallway and peered up the stairs. Far above there was a skylight of stained glass, its reds and yellows on fire with sunlight. To the right was a parlor with more rosewood paneling. They could see their reflections in the polished hard-wood floors. Between two floor-length windows that opened onto the street was a piano covered with a sheet. Charles threw back the sheet and lifted the ebony cover on the keyboard. He bent over the keys and ran his fingers over them. He pounded one or two keys with his index finger. "Someday I will learn to play," he said. He stood with his hand on the top of the piano and sang in a loud, off-key voice:

> 'Tis the song, the sigh of the weary:
>   Hard Times, Hard Times, come again no more:
> Many days you have lingered around my cabin door;
>   Oh! Hard Times, come again no more.

Sarah and Ward continued to look around as Charles sang. His voice echoed through the empty room. Sarah clapped abstractedly when he finished and took him by the arm. They wandered each floor. Sarah touched every wall, ran her hand over the woodwork, examined the closets and looked out the windows. Ward, aware at last that this was more than a visit to the house of an acquaintance of Charles's, complained of the effect the stairs had on his heart.

Charles went into the water closet on the second floor and closed the door behind him. He turned a brass handle above the sink and hot water came out. He pulled the chain above the commode and there was a rush of water. In the boarding house he had lived in there was a privy in the backyard. Ward's house had a hand pump in the kitchen, and though there was a small, recently added toilet under the staircase, there were still chamber pots in the bedrooms. In East Hampton they had gone in the fields, whatever the weather. Here was privacy, warmth, comfort—everywhere.

Ward knocked on the door and entered without waiting for an answer. "I must sit a minute, please." He used the commode as a chair. Charles opened the window.

"Are you all right?"

Ward nodded. "I merely need to gather my breath."

"Would you like some water?"

Ward shook his head. "All I needed was a moment's rest." He stood. "You know, in his chapter on the Roman Empire in the age of the Antonines, Gibbon points out that the addiction of the wealthy to opulence had both good and bad effect. The good derived from the distribution of property that the patricians brought about when they lavished their money on hiring artisans and laborers to build their villas, palaces, and baths. The bad was the pervasive and inevitable corruption of morals and manners that accompanied such a compulsion for the luxurious. The age of indolence, as Gibbon called it, sucked the strength out of the noblemen and -women of the Empire, erasing the last vestiges of republican Rome, so that when the barbarians pushed on the gates of the Empire, they discovered to their surprise that such a magnificent and imposing edifice was guarded by a race of moral and physical pygmies."

"Very interesting," Charles said. "Now let me show you your room."

"My room?"

"If you wish. With your permission, Audley, I'm going to ask Sarah to marry me, and I expect that her dear uncle will live with us."

It was the first time Charles had ever called the old man anything but "Mr. Ward," and he savored the small triumph. The clerk whose name was beyond—or beneath—recall now asked for the hand of Ward's niece and offered the old fool a room.

"Quite so," Ward said. He seemed dazed. They went down the hall to the rear of the house.

Charles sat on the windowsill as Ward poked around the room. Down below, in the next yard, a maid was stringing white sheets on a clothesline; they snapped in the wind. Flags of surrender. The city's surrender, and Sarah's and fortune's. All hail the conquering hero. The maid looked up. Charles waved. She waved back.

"One wonders if one can grow accustomed to such comfort," Ward said.

Bedford lay on his bed for a long time. He didn't take off his clothes. He heard Ward return from his lecture and close the door to his room. He stared at the ceiling. He should be at the Trump. He was scheduled to meet Halsey. He wasn't up to it. He got up and put the *Tribune* under his arm. He went into the bathroom. Despite all the disappointments and unexpected twists of the last several years, he still drew a sense of security from this house and its comforts. Seemed like a lifetime ago that he walked up the stoop with Sarah for the first time. And the days on Gold Street, how long ago had they been? In antediluvian times.

He leaned toward the mirror above the basin. The face he saw was tired and haggard. He had allowed himself to believe that time would only add to his success, year by year, a steady accretion, a stalagmite of good fortune. But time didn't just pass in New York, it ran like a trotter on the Harlem Lane, legs pumping, sweat and snot lathering across its face, the rider balanced on his flimsy platform trying to maintain his headlong pace so as not to be left behind and yet avoid one of those bumps in the road that would send him flying in the air to break his neck or be trampled by those close behind. Go faster or get out of the way or be trampled: the only choices.

Bedford unbuttoned his fly, slipped off his galluses, and sat down on the commode. He had fallen dangerously behind. But he must not lose his head and try to make up the distance all at once. That was a certain recipe for breaking one's neck. The object was to gain speed at a steady pace, paying attention to the road, keeping a resolute hand on the reins, sustaining an acceleration that will pull you away from the pack into the safe open space ahead. It would be difficult but not impossible. He opened the *Tribune* and spread it across his lap. A great naval attack on Charleston had been made. The seat of the insurrection. But it had apparently been repulsed. *Immense Strength of the Enemy,* the caption said. The war had taken him by surprise. It shouldn't have. He should have grasped that it was indeed an irrepressible conflict. But that was easier to understand now than it had been then. The southern merchants and agents had come to New York right up until the fighting began. In December, after Lincoln was elected, a group of South Carolinians had thrown a chevaliers' ball at the St. Nicholas Hotel. The men came dressed in plumed hats, capes, and Elizabethan pantaloons. They hired the Brownlee Minstrels to entertain. The minstrels paraded across Broadway and came into the lobby singing and dancing; it was as though a crew of plantation darkies had spontaneously descended on the hotel. They performed their famous walk-around for the ball-goers, assembling in the middle of the floor and dancing in their raucous way, all the while clapping their hands or playing their instruments.

The Mayor of New York, Fernando Wood, made an appearance. His cronies went around the room telling everyone to be quiet. The Mayor stepped out into the middle of the floor. A former grocer from Rector Street, at twenty he had gone bankrupt trying to run a cigar store on Pearl Street. At twenty-eight he was a wealthy merchant and a member of Congress. Wood began his political career as a nativist True American but trimmed his sails, tacked with the wind that brought ashore the endless influx of immigrants, and was now a full-blown panderer to the Paddy vote.

A thin, elegant man with shifty eyes and a high, unpleasant voice, Wood exuded a restless, hurried air. He thanked the gentlemen from South Carolina for once again reminding New Yorkers that southern hospitality was a truth rather than a legend, and he said that he wanted his southern friends to be assured that the evening's bonhomie wasn't a passing emotion, a warmth generated by excessive imbibition, but a genuine expression of the deep and abiding ties between this metropolis and the South. "These ties," the Mayor said, "are not only commercial but also moral and political. Moral because of the shared commitment of New

Yorkers and southerners to protecting a man's right to the ownership of his property and to the disposition of that property as
he sees fit. Political because New Yorkers understand what it is
like to see their prerogatives as a free people assaulted by an aggressive and despotic legislature."

The Mayor said that when New York looked to find the
cause of its oppression, it was to Albany, not Alabama. The
crowd cheered. He promised that if war should ever come, New
York would declare itself a free city rather than participate in an
attack on southern liberties. There was more cheering. The minstrels paraded out in the same boisterous way they had come in.
A colonel from the militia offered a toast. Someone called for
three cheers for Francis Pickens, Governor of South Carolina, and
three groans for Abraham Lincoln. The chevaliers and their guests
drank and danced until the early morning hours. At dawn, a
group of them, still in plumed hats and capes, made a clamorous
arrival at a whorehouse on Canal Street. Bedford walked arm in
arm with a man he didn't know, a big, friendly southerner with
a thick drawl who sang lines that the rest of the group repeated
in chorus:

> Dar's a niggar in de tent, keep 'im in, keep 'im out,
> Dar's a niggar in de tent, kick 'im in, kick 'im out,
> But he ain't paid de rent, throw 'im out, throw 'im out.

They woke up the women with their banging and singing. The
madam poked her head out of one of the upper windows.
"Quiet," she said. "We're coming." Bedford's companion yelled
up to her, "Not yet! Wait until we get there!" They all burst out
laughing. War with such men seemed an impossibility.

The square tiles on the bathroom floor were laid black next
to white, like cards on a faro table. Bedford held the paper up in
front of him. He didn't need any reminders of his folly. ORDER
BY GENERAL HOOKER AGAINST INCORRECT INFORMATION FROM
PICKET LINES, AND LOOSE DISCIPLINE GENERALLY. Maybe Hooker
would prove the man. Perhaps he would smash across the Rap-

pahannock and take Richmond. But despite the blockade and the Confederacy's loss of manpower, Secessiondom seemed stronger than ever. FROM CAIRO AND BELOW. Grant was still mired in the mud before impregnable Vicksburg. The *Tribune* tried to put the best face on it. *Whether General Grant succeed or fail in the end, it must forever be acknowledged that he and his army are making heroic efforts.* An unfamiliar note of fatalistic caution. *Whether General Grant succeed or fail.* Where was the envoi *On to Richmond!?* Half a page of ships captured by Rebel privateers. DEPREDATIONS ON OUR COMMERCE. Bedford read down the list. How much longer could the Union's merchants sustain such losses? RIOT AMONG THE 'LONGSHOREMEN. COLORED LABORERS ASSAILED BY IRISHMEN. More labor troubles. The war-induced inflation was fueling a growing number of strikes. The employers were determined not to be intimidated by combinations of their employees. In this instance they had tried to bring in colored workers to replace the striking Irishmen, and the docks turned into a battlefield. *Without the least provocation or word of warning the rioters commenced hurling stones and brickbats at the unoffending colored laborers, shouting "Drive off the d—m niggers," "Kill the niggers," etc.* Such were the men Lincoln and Stanton were proposing to conscript. Ward was right. God help the Army. *One of the colored men, in self-defense, drew a pistol and fired, the shot taking effect upon the person of one of the rioters.* The mob assaulted the police and tried to maul the colored man, whom the police had taken into custody. The clear purpose with which the war had begun was now a hopeless muddle. Another set of defeats or another Secessionist invasion of the North, perhaps sometime in the late spring, by August at the latest, and a negotiated peace would be unavoidable.

The night before last, Sunday, the Union League Club had held a dinner at the Maison Dorée, a restaurant near its headquarters, which were still in the process of being refurbished. One hundred and fifty guests had been invited. In the middle of the room was a great triple-tiered cake. On top was a confectionary incarnation of the goddess Liberty. Beneath, eight marzipan infantrymen acted as supports, and the layer they stood on was supported by twelve marzipan ironclads in a sea of blue sugar rippled with whitecaps. Most of the guests were older, but there was a representation of younger men from the financial community. Everyone understood that a merchant or businessman could leave his company in order to take a commission in the Army, and that his firm, under the stewardship of his assistants, would suffer no disruptions; many of the city's younger men of substance had followed such a course. But it was also understood that this was not true for those who labored in the financial markets. A well-run commercial concern was like a train moving along the rails. Once running properly, the engineer might turn it over temporarily to an assistant, but the financial markets were a roiling, raging river, a swollen, savage, treacherous course: The vessels that set out on it required a helmsman of experience and stamina who never left his post. This was almost universally recognized by the propertied class, most of whom had investments and none of whom wanted them placed in the hands of the eager but unseasoned. Few quibbled with the decision of those on Wall Street to serve the nation by continuing to add to its wealth.

Bedford was invited to the dinner in recognition of the money he had helped raise among his fellow brokers for the work of the Sanitary Commission. Two weeks before, at a ceremony on the pier at the bottom of Fulton Street, he had formally turned over to the Army's Medical Bureau six ambulances that had been purchased in England with the funds he had helped raise. A small platform had been set up. Dr. Bellows spoke for an hour and a quarter on the purposes and methods of the Commission. He emphasized the responsibility of men of property and wealth in supporting the national cause, but he never mentioned Bedford by name. The officer from the Bureau was briefer and more gracious. He thanked Bedford and asked him to stand. Bedford stood to acknowledge the applause. He took his hat off and bowed slightly. This was the pier where fourteen years before he had hauled paving blocks out of the holds of immigrant ships.

For some time he had had the feeling that life was coming to a close, that the permanence he thought he had achieved was an illusion, that the curtain was coming down on him as surely as it had come down on so many others. Several months before, one of the English visitors Sarah filled the house with had sat next to Bedford at dinner and talked interminably about the Hindoos and their wisdom. Bedford half listened. It seemed so much gibberish: the illusion of all material things, the eternal cycle of existence, a constant transmigration of souls. But standing on the platform and listening to the clapping, realizing that this was where he had started his climb, Bedford felt the resonance of the Englishman's words. His spirits lifted and he wished he had listened more carefully. The Hindoos were right. Nothing was forever. Life was a great wheel, around and around we go, continually, and if the curtain comes down on one act, another one soon begins. The Englishman had said something about resignation, submitting to one's own fate. Bedford made little sense of that, then or now. You resigned yourself at death. Before that moment you struggled, worked, planned, plotted, pushed, never giving in. You shaped your own destiny, and if circumstances took you from the top of the wheel to the bottom, you began over again, renewed, in a different incarnation, wiser than before.

Bedford had tried to maintain that inner confidence that had illumined his mind on the Fulton Street pier. But the true nature of his dilemma constantly threatened to extinguish it. His problems were financial, and the debts he owed were ruinously large. Yet far worse than *what* he owed was *to whom he owed*. Morrissey. A murderer and professional thug, with a small army of Paddy retainers ever eager to execute his wishes. And now Bedford had added embezzlement and the illegal sale of securities to his worries. He was stuck as deeply in his own swamp as General Grant was in his. Bedford lifted the paper again and made an effort to keep reading. He sought some solace in the immensity of the Union's military problems but found none. He had expected that the dinner at the Union League Club would be an uplifting affair, even perhaps renew the surge of confidence he had felt a few weeks before. But it had cast a pall that had still not lifted. Yes, he had drunk too much at the dinner and kept drinking afterward until he had to be helped into a coach, but the effects of *that* had worn off a day ago. The problem was not a mere case of katzenjammer.

He had been seated at an obscure table with two men in their dotage and one young man whom he knew vaguely from Wall Street, a small dark-eyed character whose furtive looks suggested he was about to steal the silverware. On the other side of the room was the head table, at which were seated A. T. Stewart, the department-store prince; George Griswold, the tea merchant; Franklin Delano, the son-in-law of William Astor; and a group of high-ranking military officers. In the middle of the group was George Templeton Strong, a man Audley Ward detested. A year ago, they had engaged in some sort of a debate over the war that had escalated into a shouting match over matters philosophical and theological. As it was related to Bedford, Ward had called Strong "a degenerate Puseyite whose pretensions could never totally erase the smell of raw fish that clung to his family's origins in some Long Island backwater." Strong, in turn, dismissed Ward as an "atrabilious relic of Nieuw Amsterdam who belongs in Barnum's Museum next to the *What-Is-It?*"

The room was noisy with conversation, but no one spoke at Bedford's table. One of the two older men slurped his soup. Bedford tried to remember the name of the young man sitting across from him. *Gold, Ghoul, Gouge.* Something along those lines. He had been a leather merchant and a tanner, and had been involved in some disreputable affair. A partner had been murdered or committed suicide. Bedford couldn't remember the exact details of all the rumors he had heard because Wall Street was continually rich with rumors. The trading of rumors was the only bull market that never flagged. But whatever was said wasn't complimentary. Rumors never were.

Bedford grew more uncomfortable with the silence at the table. He felt people looking at them. He half rose from his chair and held out his hand to the young man across from him.

"Charles Bedford," he said.

The man took his hand; Bedford was surprised by the firmness of his grip. "Jay Gould," he said.

Gould. The name he had searched for. Gould stared off into a corner of the room. He made no attempt to use Bedford's introduction as an opening for conversation.

"Whom are you with?" Bedford asked.

"With?"

"What firm do you work with?"

"Myself. I'm with myself."

Gould picked up a knife. He held it at both ends and ran it between his fingers. He stood it on its handle and nervously tapped the table. Bedford had heard it rumored Gould was an Israelite, a co-religionist of August Belmont's. But he obviously didn't share Belmont's Democratic politics, not if he had been invited here, and it seemed equally improbable that Gould could be a Jew and have been asked to share this company.

"What brings you here this evening, Mr. Gould?"

"Here?"

"To this dinner."

"You mean, why am I here?"

"Yes."

"I was invited."

Gould picked up the spoon. He put it through the same drill as the knife. Bedford felt the wine taking effect. The two older men said nothing. One excused himself and went off to the toilet. The other, the soup slurper, stared at his hands. Gould kept his eyes averted. The wine relaxed Bedford, made him less intimidated by the silence.

"I don't think you answered my question," he said to Gould.

"Your question?"

"Yes, why are you here? Are you a member?"

"A member of the Union League Club?"

"Yes, a member."

"No, I'm not."

"What brings you here, then? What is the reason you were invited?"

"The reason?"

"Yes, the reason."

"Contributions. I am a contributor to the cause."

Bedford found Gould's evasiveness an enjoyable distraction, and the man's obvious discomfiture made Bedford feel an insider. He was about to ask about the nature of Gould's contributions when A. T. Stewart rose and asked the entire company to stand. He proposed a toast: "To the Union, one and undivided, now and forever." This was followed by toasts to the President, General Hooker, the Army of the Potomac, General Grant, the Navy, and Admiral du Pont.

Bedford noticed that Gould held the glass to his lips but did not drink. Standing, Gould seemed even younger than when seated. He was so short and slight that except for his piercing, feral eyes, there was a boyish air about him, an adolescent's manner. They sat down to eat. Bedford forgot the question he wished to put to Gould. Gould pushed his food around on his plate. Bedford had more wine. He searched for something to say to his dinner mates, but the old men seemed lost in their senescence, and the boy-man locked in his shyness. Bedford's sense of ease began to give way to a darker mood. He had worked hard to raise money for those ambulances and been publicly honored for his achievement by a representative of the Medical Bureau. They had applauded him on the pier. Perhaps he hadn't expected to be seated in a place of honor, not on the dais with Stewart and the club's nestors, but he *had* expected to be placed somewhere up front, in proximity to the prominent.

The old man got up to go to the toilet again. The soup slurper was no longer staring at his hands. He was now asleep. Dessert was served. Bedford's piece of cake was topped by half a confectionery ironclad. He pushed it away and asked for more wine. When the old man returned from the toilet, he tapped Bedford on the shoulder and gestured for him to stand. The old man drew Bedford aside, to the corner of the room. He pointed to his ear with his forefinger. "The hearing's gone," he said. "Didn't catch your name before, but just now someone stopped me and told me that I was sitting with Charles Bedford."

Bedford nodded, unsure of what to say.

"I'm Jacob Valentine," the old man said.

"Of course," Bedford said. "I should have known." He searched his mind for some clue as to why he should know Jacob Valentine. Was he a client of the firm's?

The old man said, "Eh?" He pointed to his ear again. "You must speak up."

Bedford raised his voice. "I said I should have known."

"Known what?"

"Known who you are."

"I thought I just said who I am. I'm Jacob Valentine."

Bedford spoke even louder. "Of course, of course, I should have recognized you."

"But I don't believe we've ever met."

"No, but I've heard a great deal about you."

Valentine nodded. "From Audley, no doubt. He does go on. A trait of the Vandervorts. Incurable talkers, with a theory on everything. You married into a fine family, and from what I'm told you're bringing new honor to that escutcheon."

"It's kind of you to say that."

"Eh?"

Bedford leaned close and repeated himself into Valentine's hairy ear.

"Kindness has nothing to do with it. It's the truth, and I'm grateful for it. Sometimes I think the manliness, the virility, is going out of our race, and it's encouraging for a *senex* like me to see that there are still men of honor in the world."

They returned to their seats. Stewart rose again at the dais and thanked them for coming. He said that this commemoration of the surrender of Fort Sumter might induce melancholy thoughts in some, and while an element of sadness was certainly attendant to the disruption of the Union and the ensuing bloodshed, they should keep in mind two things: "First, in our presence tonight is Jacob Valentine, the son of one of the youngest participants in the Revolutionary War. As a boy of twelve, in the hills above the city, with the Americans in retreat from what seemed a decisive defeat by the British, Jacob Valentine, the namesake of our tonight's companion, had left his family's house to see what he could do to help. Wiser and older men would have eschewed such a course, putting self-interest and safety before the interests of what seemed already a lost cause, and some did. But Jacob's wisdom was not the world's, and he put courage ahead of caution. He shouldered a musket that was undoubtedly taller than he, and as the exhausted, defeated Americans fell down in the grass, desperately trying to get some rest before they resumed their retreat, young Jacob stood guard over them. When the British approached, thinking to silently surround and overwhelm the remnants of the American forces, young Jacob fired the shot that awoke them and saved not just the day but the Revolution."

Stewart asked Jacob Valentine, son of the boy hero, to stand. Valentine was facing the dais, but Bedford realized the old man hadn't heard a word. He leaned over and said into Valentine's ear, "He wants you to stand." Valentine looked puzzled. Bedford put his hand under Valentine's elbow and gently nudged him up. "The Valentines are still with us," said Stewart. "Like the father, the son seeks not the path of comfort but of commitment, and there are thousands, nay, millions, like them, a race of Jacob Valentines, adolescents, adults, and the aged, who will never— *never*—desert the Union, no matter what course others may take."

The room rocked with applause. Bedford tugged on Valentine's sleeve. The old man sat. The other point to ponder, said Stewart, was that if the war had turned out to be a more bitter, costly, drawn-out affair than could have been anticipated, and if the nature of the struggle had demoralized and discouraged some, in far more cases it had inspired a new fervor and determination, a fiercely formed patriotism, implacable, unquenchable, unstoppable. There were an endless myriad of instances of this new patriotism, both on and off the battlefield, and in mentioning one he hoped he wouldn't be interpreted as slighting the many, but he felt the work done by Mr. Charles Bedford on behalf of the Sanitary Commission deserved at least a mention. He asked Bedford to stand. Bedford heard no more of Stewart's words. He felt a ringing in his ears and his eyes blurred with emotion as he stood with hands folded in front of him, the Union League Club's cynosure.

When Stewart was finished, the entire audience rose to sing "The Star-Spangled Banner." They were then directed to the lyrics of "We Are Coming Father Abraam, 300,000 More," printed on the back of their dinner programs. They sang it also.

Bedford switched from wine to brandy. A kindly-looking, white-haired man came over and introduced himself as Rodney Atkinson. Atkinson expressed to Bedford his profound admiration and said how important the support of men like Charles Bedford was to the successful conclusion of the war. He thumped Bedford on the back. "My apologies about the seating arrangements," he said.

Bedford waved his hand as if the lapse were a trifle.

Atkinson continued: "I'm afraid the dinner was oversubscribed, and since the object was to raise money, that was the prime criterion for admission. Unfortunately, this required us to seat some of the nobodies amid the Charles Bedfords and Jacob Valentines." Atkinson gave Bedford another thump on the back and walked away.

Nobodies. Bedford stood alone and put his drink down on the table. He had an image in his head of Mr. Stark looking down from the window of the Merchants' Exchange Building on the crowd in the street. That was the race he belonged to, the race he had risen from, numerous as the stars of the heaven or as the grains of sand upon the seashore. Charles Bedford had changed into Ezra Van Wyck and back into Charles Bedford so as to molt his nobodiness and put on somebodiness. He picked up his glass of brandy and took a mouthful of it. Suddenly he understood that what he had felt earlier wasn't anger at being relegated to a table with the likes of Jay Gould, but fear. The race of nobodies could never be stopped. It was endowed with an endless capacity for multiplication and a remorseless urge to advance. *We are coming Father Abraam, three hundred thousand more, / From Mississippi's winding stream and from New England's shore; / We leave our plows and workshops, our wives and children dear, / With hearts too full for utterance, with but a silent tear.* Come they would, the war would only accelerate the process, and just as the somebodies became secure in their somebodiness, the nobodies would arrive to overthrow them, assuming their trappings and their airs, purchasing their presumptions as well as their furniture, possessing their daughters as well as their houses, growing secure in their somebodiness until the new wave of nobodies descended on *them.* Bedford suspected the process was as old as time, but he was too little acquainted with history to be sure. What he did know from experience was that if it hadn't been the rule of existence, it was now.

The room was clearing out. Bedford looked for Gould but didn't see him. He had no idea when Gould had left. He had sensed the raw energy in the boy-man across from him. He had felt it in his handshake. Gould couldn't be all that much younger than Bedford, but it was as if a millennium separated them. Bedford saw he had made the mistake all somebodies make, presuming that somebodiness was an indelible grace, and like most nobodies-turned-somebodies he had imagined that he still understood the appetites and aspirations that drove the nobodies. Gould's touch, Gould's eyes, Gould's restlessness, punctured such illusion. Bedford knew: A whole new race of nobodies has arrived, is arriving, will arrive, hungrier than even those who had come before, more aware of the opportunities around them, boy-men with bigger plans and fewer scruples, ready to rewrite the rules whenever it was to their advantage. *We dare not look behind us but steadfastly stare before. We are coming, coming, coming.*

Bedford felt a loosening in his bowels. His stomach grumbled. His irregularity was becoming chronic. The cook didn't help. Perhaps he shouldn't wait until Sarah returned to replace her; perhaps he should do it now. He knew he wasn't being quite fair. The disruptions he was suffering from weren't entirely due to his cook's lack of culinary skills. He broke wind loudly. He pulled the chain that hung above his right shoulder. *Swoosh,* the water came down from the tank above his head, surged around the bowl, and gurgled down the pipe. Bedford left the paper across his lap. He put his elbows on his knees and rested his chin on his fists. The floor filled his view, black tile laid next to white.

He had been playing faro on margin, using his debts as security on new debts, double or nothing, with only nominal payments required by the house. Sometimes Morrissey himself would come over, put his arm around Bedford's shoulder, a fraternal embrace that also demonstrated the iron strength in his arms. He told Bedford that no man's bad luck lasted forever, that if you stayed at it, if you believed in luck, luck would return that belief. Morrissey loved to talk. The wheedling garrulity of the Irish, coachmen, servants, tradesmen, they were all skilled at creating an enshrouding fog of words, as though they were always trying to hide something. Bedford tried fervently to believe in his luck, but he kept losing.

"O ye of little faith," Morrissey said to him. "You're not trying hard enough to believe."

"Luck is more than faith," Bedford said. "Luck is the result of patiently striving to put the odds in one's own favor. Luck is what happens when you have gained a position from which it's possible to take advantage of the opportunities that circumstance may present."

"That sounds too complicated for me," Morrissey said. "I'm a man of simple faith. I'll leave the higher reasoning to the likes of yourself."

The chits mounted steadily, month after month of losses, until the night Morrissey put his arm around Bedford's shoulder, the pressure slightly greater than usual, and offered not encouragement but an ultimatum. "Charlie," he said, "we need for you to make a settlement of your account."

Sarah was of the opinion that he drank too much. They

hadn't been married a year when one day she announced she was leaving for England in order "to renew acquaintances." Bedford had no objections. The day she left, he found a pamphlet on his desk. *The Drunkard's Disciples; Or, Twelve Brief Notices of the Dissolution and Death of Once Happy Men.* A slip of paper marked the sixth chapter: *A Young Man of Promise, Bound for Prominence in the World's Financial Matters, Is Dragged to Ruin By His Addiction to Rum, An Affliction that He Is Unable to Discern Until He Has Lost Everything, His Wealth, His Wife, His Friends, and Must Die Alone. Herein His Rise, His Fall; The Awfulness of a Discovery Made Too Late.*

When Morrissey's arm had fallen on his shoulder, the phrase had come back to him: *The Awfulness of a Discovery Made Too Late.* "Old Smoke" was what people called Morrissey behind his back. When he was a younger man, he had been in a barroom fight. A stove of red-hot coals had been knocked over. Morrissey's opponent pinned him to the floor atop those coals. The smell of burning flesh filled the room. But Morrissey neither flinched nor screamed. He slowly worked his way out of the hold the man had on him, grinding the coals into his back in order to do so, and, once free, pummeled his antagonist into a bloody, lifeless lump, punching away as the remnants of his pants and shirt smoldered. The name "Old Smoke" invoked in Bedford an image of the Devil, the Great Tempter, leading the sinner to hell, usually through Drink. But Drink had never been his problem. Sarah's father had been a drunk, one in a long line, a condition that the portrait painters had brushed out of the august faces on the walls, nothing more than a slight ruddiness on the nose and cheeks. Sarah saw drunkenness everywhere. But leaving no trace on the breath, never impairing speech or inducing a slight stagger, faro had escaped her view.

Faro had been a form of relaxation from the uncertainties of wartime. After Lincoln's election, Wall Street had been afflicted with neurasthenia. In retrospect, despite the night of festivity at the St. Nicholas Hotel, it seemed impossible that so immense and cataclysmic an event as the war could have taken any broker by surprise. Looking back, the portents of what was to come seemed unmistakable. Some bears had hunkered down the minute Lincoln was elected. Others had taken the firing on the federal supply ship *Star of the West,* which was bound for Fort Sumter, as the signal that war was inevitable. But in the end, Bedford had found it impossible to believe that men would choose the ruin and devastation of war over the amassing of profits, and he continued putting together the pieces he had picked up after the panic of '57, fitting together what he envisioned as an impregnable financial empire. He speculated that the markets would go through a ten-year period of steady growth before the boom-time delusions would reappear and the wise bulls would begin to transmogrify into ever more cautious bears. He was still hard at work when the Secessionist barrage opened on Fort Sumter, the shells falling with deadly accuracy on the last remaining bulls, a direct hit on their magazines, men left groping amid the smoke and confusion. As the heroic commander of Fort Sumter had done, the directors of the Board walked calmly amid the shot and shells in order to reassure the troops. Steady, they said, it will all be over soon. Order will be returned. The world made right again. But when the smoke cleared, Bedford knew that the fort was done for. Southern merchants defaulted on three hundred million dollars in obligations. Over six thousand northern firms went bankrupt. The banking structure seemed to teeter on the brink of ruin.

The early days of the war were a blur. Bedford went for his usual breakfast at Old Tom's. He found it hard to leave. The cavelike atmosphere was cool and secure. From where he sat, below street level, he could see the feet and legs of brokers and messengers as they flew past Old Tom's windows, men running a footrace that seemed to grow more frenetic each day. The trading on the curb outside the Board resembled one of those famous minstrel-show walk-arounds, a crowd of men pushing and sidestepping, faces contorted, arms waving with rowdy gestures. A mob gathered outside the offices of the *Journal of Commerce,* which had been steady in its insistence that the South be allowed to depart in peace. They broke in, smashing windows and doors and draping a flag out a second-floor window. Bedford stood among the crowd. He recognized some brokers who he knew shared the same opinions as the *Journal,* but that no longer seemed to matter. They were looking for something on which to vent their confusion and frustration, and they went at their work with real enthusiasm. Afterward, they stood together in the street, on a carpet of torn and shredded copies of the *Journal,* and lustily sang "Hail Columbia."

The summer was brutally hot, and, along with the news from Virginia, it drove men to the edge. *Bull Run.* One broker tried to make a joke out of it. "Next time we fight the Rebs," he said, "we should look for a place called Bear Run." Nobody laughed. Men strove to maintain their composure. The Board continued to try to conduct business as usual. Despite the burst of new businesses generated by the demands of what was obviously going to be a prolonged conflict, the Board stuck to its practice of two auctions per day and rejected the notion of continuous trading. After the morning session, waiters brought around glasses of Saratoga water with spikes of Adirondack ice. Men drained the water and held the ice to their foreheads. From outside they could hear the roar of the curbstone brokers. Bedford's representative on the Curb said he was too busy to handle Bedford's business anymore. He suggested that maybe Jim Halsey would be available and promised to introduce him to Bedford.

Bedford disliked Halsey the minute he set eyes on him. Halsey was in his twenties. He had the thick upstate nasality of an apple-knocker. He kept his hat pushed back on his head, stood with his hands in his pockets, and rocked on his heels. A cocksure pose. He wore a tan jacket, green vest, and soft felt hat, the clothes of a clerk on holiday. Said he wanted 2 percent of all the business he handled.

Bedford laughed. "Do I look like a yokel?" he said.

"Gaze around," Halsey said. He opened his arms to the milling mob of curbstone traders. Some of them looked as if they had come directly from a county fair. "It's the yokels who seem to be raking in the gelt."

Bedford declined Halsey's services. He would see him occasionally on the street, and Halsey would give him a loud hello. Bedford had sustained substantial losses in the post–Fort Sumter turmoil. He held his own in the months that followed, but he felt unnerved, off balance, and it left him tired and depressed. He had thought he had taken the measure of the market, had understood its mechanisms, had discovered the physical laws it ran by, then the thing he hadn't counted on happened, war, and he groped to find a new set of laws. As he left his office at the end of one particularly unsuccessful day, he bumped into Halsey. For once, the man's brashness seemed diminished. Without being asked, Halsey volunteered that the day's business had gone badly for him also. Bedford offered him a ride in his coach, and Halsey said he was going to Morrissey's. When they reached there, Halsey got out of the coach and held the door open.

"Come with me," he said.

"No thanks, I have work waiting for me at home."

"To Lucifer with work. It can wait."

"It can't."

Halsey leaned into the coach. He cupped his hand next to his mouth and said in a soft voice, "It's a whore, ain't it? That's who yer so anxious to see. Where yer going to? Greene Street? Or are yer off to Mrs. Woods? Can't blame yer. Whores are about the only thing can settle a man's nerves after a day like today."

Bedford didn't smile. "You're delaying me," he said.

Halsey rocked on his heels and kept his hand on the door. "Thing about faro is it's less work than plowing a whore, more fun than watching rats, and gives yer better odds than yer ever gonna find on Wall Street. Come on, worse can happen is I'll drop a bundle and you'll get to gloat. Might stop yer from feeling sorry for yerself."

Bedford reached over to grab the door. Halsey took hold of his wrist. "Ain't no fun in losing money less you got somebody to watch yer do it." For an instant Bedford felt a twinge of sympathy for Halsey.

"For Christ's sake," Bedford said, "let go of my wrist. It will give me pleasure to watch you go to ruin."

Bedford followed Halsey into the House of Morrissey. Halsey purchased a handful of copper chips from an attractive woman in a décolleté gown who sat in a wooden booth behind an iron grille. Each chip was stamped "$100." It was early, and the place was nearly empty. The curtains, rugs, and wallpaper had a faded, dingy look; the walls and ceilings were discolored by the residues of ammonia and sulfur given off by the gaslight, which although left at a low level burned from dusk to dawn, as long as men believed their luck would change or hold out. Halsey went directly to an empty faro table and stood in front of the green cloth, its surface enameled with a representation of a full suit of spades. He wiped his hands on his trousers, blew on a hundred-dollar chip, and put it on the 4. The dealer stood before a pack of playing cards laid faceup in a dealing box. He drew the top card and laid it off to his right. It was the "soda" card, and out of play. The next card out of the box was a "loser," and lay next to the box. The following card, facing up, was a "winner."

Halsey's bet stayed on the 4. The first card, the "soda," was a 7. The second card, the "loser," was a 3. The card still in the box, the "winner," was a jack. Halsey left his bet. He wouldn't lose unless a 4 came out a "loser." On the next draw, a 4 was the card on top. He won. He put a copper on the queen and then another copper on the first one to signal that he was playing the queen to show up a "loser." He left it there for two turns. On the third deal, the second card out was a queen. He had bet on a "loser" and won.

Bedford didn't play, but Halsey gave him a sheet so that he could record each card as it came out and was retired. Bedford watched Halsey simultaneously play some cards as "losers," others as "winners," his bets spreading across the table, chips laid between cards and in the corners of cards, each marking a bet split to cover two or more cards. Bedford lost track of the permutations. He stopped trying to grasp the subtleties of Halsey's maneuvers and surrendered to the beauty of the game, the soft green cloth, the copper disks, the steady flow of the cards out of the box, the small snap they made as the dealer drew them out, the constant motion of hands, the reshuffling of the cards, a reel of black and white. As the game went on, trays of champagne came by, and Bedford drank as much as was offered. A crowd gathered to watch Halsey. When his earnings reached $10,000, they applauded. Morrissey himself appeared. The room was filled with people and conversation, and in the background was the constant snap of cards being dealt. The gaslights flickered softly, and as the time passed the surroundings no longer seemed faded and threadbare but rich and sumptuous.

Halsey kept playing. He lost a part of his winnings before he finally cashed in but was still left with over $8,500. Bedford felt the urge to have a go but suppressed it. He had had too much champagne, and had too little grasp of the game. After they left Morrissey's, Halsey suggested they stop at the Trumpeter Swan, a concert saloon generally known as the Trump. Halsey told Bedford to have the driver drop them on Clinton Place, at an alleyway that led to the rear of the Trump. Halsey knew the pug stationed at the back door, who let them in without a word. Bedford followed Halsey up a flight of stairs, where Halsey knocked on a door. A tall black-haired woman in a purple robe opened it. Bedford was stunned by how beautiful she was. Halsey embraced her, kissed her lips and neck, and drew back her robe to kiss her breasts. She pushed him away. "What's got you so excited?" she said.

He put his hands into his pockets and rocked on his heels. "I've been bucking the tiger, riding high on his back, and rode the monster into the dust." He took out of his pocket the bank draft from Morrissey, unfolded it, and stuck it between her breasts. She retrieved it, glanced at it, and put it into the pocket of her robe. Now she embraced Halsey. He looked over his shoulder at Bedford. "I forget that an introduction is in order," Halsey said. "Charlie Bedford, I want you to meet the Trumpeter Swan herself, the eyeball attraction of the metropolis, the nonpareil of every gawking Cyclops in the city of New York, Miss Eleanor Van Shaick."

She formed her arm into a V, her milk-white hand hanging limply at the end. She obviously intended it be kissed, not shaken, and Bedford obliged.

"It's a great pleasure," he said. Behind her, hanging on the door, Bedford noticed a floor-length cape of white feathers.

"Ellie keeps this place afloat," Halsey said. "What has the Trump got to recommend it over any other concert saloon except for the Swan herself?"

Bedford had heard of the Trumpeter Swan's "special attraction," the lure that distinguished the Swan from the city's other saloons. Especially popular with soldiers, the "attraction" was located in a small chamber on the second floor surrounded on three sides by eight closet-size booths, each containing a peephole. Several times an evening, for a fee ranging from three dollars to ten, depending on how wealthy or eager the customer seemed, invitations were given to enjoy the view from one of those booths. A waiter girl would lean over and whisper, "How'd ya like to see the Trumpeter Swan herself?" In a while she would return and escort the patron to a rear staircase. At the top she would lead him into a booth and pull the curtain shut behind him. There he'd sit alone for several minutes, staring at an empty porcelain bathtub on lion's paws, with nothing but a chair beside it. Finally two Negro boys in turbans and baggy pants would enter with a barrel labeled CHAMPAGNE and pour its contents into the tub. After they left there would be another pause before the door opened again and a tall, gainly, black-haired woman entered: the Trumpeter Swan herself! She wore a cape of white feathers that she slowly removed to reveal her nakedness. She walked around the tub, stopping at various points to bend over and stir the water—or champagne—with her hand. She stepped into the tub and, after a quick dip, got out, stood, and rubbed her body with a soft white towel, fondling her breasts, drying each nipple between her fingers, bringing the towel down between her legs and pulling it back and forth. Once dry, she put her cape back on and was gone.

The Negro boys pulled back the curtains, and one by one the booths' occupants went downstairs into the crowd without ever seeing their fellow viewers. Occasionally, one of the Trump's regulars darted up the stairs during the time between baths and rubbed a piece of charcoal around a peephole. At first, the management had threatened to find those responsible and have them thrashed, but with the war and the proliferation of soldiers, it became a house joke to let some officer sneak back downstairs, his eye circled in black, and be asked by half the house, "How'd ya like the bird?"

Ellie Van Shaick lay back on a divan. Bedford sat across from her. The room was small but well furnished. Halsey went over to the dresser, poured from an open bottle of champagne into three glasses, and handed them around. Bedford had paid occasional visits to the Trump but had never been upstairs "to see the Swan." Looking at Van Shaick as she stretched out on the divan, her shapely ankles protruding from beneath her robe, he regretted his oversight.

She raised her glass. "To luck," she said.

Halsey started to recount his triumph of earlier in the evening: the applause of the crowd, Morrissey's attempt to appear unfazed.

"Maybe Mr. Bedford brings you luck," she said to Halsey.

He scratched his head. "I never looked at it that way. Why, Charlie, from now on I ain't goin' nowhere without yer."

The room was warm and perfumed. They had more champagne. Halsey droned on, describing every bet he had made. Bedford noticed that Van Shaick was staring at him. He felt himself growing excited and tried to think of some way to dismiss Halsey. Halsey paused in his storytelling, and Van Shaick said, "Mr. Bedford, I believe we've met before."

"I wish it were so, Miss Van Shaick, but you are not a person I would forget."

"Time changes us."

"I could not imagine what change time wrought in you that I should not be able to conjure up some clue as to our meeting."

She saluted him with her glass.

"Charlie," Halsey said, "I didn't know you were so well known among the ladies. I thought yer were one of them went home after work."

Bedford ignored him. Van Shaick said, "Do you recall a Christmas reception at the home of Robert Schuyler?"

The day after Christmas, Robert Schuyler, the president of the New York and New Haven, the New York and Harlem, and the Illinois Central railroads, had annually held open house for the proprietors of the most prestigious investment houses, filled the rooms with food and drink, and invited his guests to bring their children or friends. One year, Stark had taken Bedford along. It was Bedford's first time in one of the homes of the great families. He had never been amid such opulence.

"Yes, I have a vivid memory of it."

"Do you remember talking for some time to Morris Van Shaick?"

Bedford recalled the house and its trappings. In the entrance hall there was a full-length portrait of Philip Schuyler, Major General in the Continental Army, would-be conqueror of Canada, Hudson Valley patroon, a founder of the Republic. The servants still wore the livery of the General's day, breeches and powdered wigs, and the house was filled with precious-looking crystal and china. Above the mantelpiece in the main parlor was the sword that Congress had presented to the General. But Bedford was terrible with names. He suspected such a talent was developed among those who grew up in large towns or cities and who from their earliest childhoods were required to keep track of the endless number of new people they were exposed to. Either that or, like Audley Ward, they were preoccupied with keeping track of bloodlines and social position. Bedford had grown up in a town where strangers were rarely encountered. He had no real interest in anyone's ancestry. Often he even had difficulty remembering the names of clients or of other brokers. He would look at them as they talked and, while trying to recall their names, miss everything they said. It was a deficiency he had promised himself to work on correcting but had yet to do anything about. He decided not to lie.

"To be honest, my only recollection is of the surroundings. I'd never been in such a place. I felt intimidated, in awe, and I let the man whose guest I was, Mr. Stark, do the talking."

Van Shaick looked saddened. A film of water covered her eyes. "At one time," she said, "men used to boast about knowing my grandfather."

Bedford heard the hurt in her voice. It was obviously important to her that he remember her grandfather.

"Yes, now that I give it some thought, I recall having a conversation with a very distinguished gentleman. I had forgotten his name, but it comes back to me now. Morris Van Shaick was your grandfather?"

"Yes, and of all his grandchildren I was the favorite. He took me with him that day. I shall never forget it, nor you."

"Me?"

"I thought you were the handsomest thing I had ever seen. The whole time Grandfather talked, I couldn't take my eyes off you. When we left I told Grandfather you were the man I wanted to marry, and he gave a great laugh."

Halsey laughed. "There yer go, Charlie, Ellie's grandpappy knew better than letting the likes of yer near his women."

"I was twelve at the time," Van Shaick said. Halsey was standing over her. She reached up and patted his cheek. "Hardly a woman, my dear bumpkin, although in the rural precincts of our Republic female children may often be treated as such."

"Twelve!" Bedford said. "That explains the hesitancy of my memory. By God, the scene returns to me with some clarity!" He was surprised he still had no recollection at all of either of them. "Let's see, it must have been 1854 or '55."

"I think you're trying to establish my age," she said.

"It was 1853," he said, "yes, it had to have been. It was the

Christmas before Schuyler left for England with two million dollars in notes he'd embezzled from friends, partners, and family." Bedford had a clear memory of the day the news had struck that Schuyler had absconded. Stark had laughed until his face was so red it seemed ready to explode. "The little scamp," Stark had said, "I always counted him a mouse, yet he's proved himself a rat."

"Never heard of Robert Schuyler," Halsey said.

"He ruined my grandfather," Van Schaick said. "The poor man had placed a great deal of trust in Robert Schuyler. He held on until the panic of '57. Did the best he could until then, but he was never the same."

"Never heard of your grandfather, either."

"This city forgets the good with the bad; all are consigned to the same oblivion. Nothing matters but the present ability to pay, and once that disappears you are dead, gone, forgotten."

"Ain't that the gospel truth."

It came back to Bedford now. The old man standing in a doorway a few days after the panic. A friendly rival of Stark's. Morris Van Shaick. Poisoned himself. Bedford received a note from Van Schaick a day or so after his suicide. Something to do with the grave.

"Your grandfather was a gentleman," Bedford said. "I've never forgotten that."

"He was. But after he died and the firm was in ruins, his so-called gentlemen friends turned their backs on my family. My father tried to keep the firm afloat. He was sure he could rely on Grandfather's acquaintances for at least some measure of help until he got back on his feet, but none was forthcoming. The day after our house was taken from us, he left. We never saw nor heard from him again. My mother went to some of those same gentlemen and told them what had happened. They suggested she go to the almshouse. *The almshouse!*" Her eyes became as cold and merciless as the winter sea. She put her feet on the floor and sat up. "We moved to a boardinghouse on Washington Street, a place filled with immigrants. My mother took in laundry like a common Irish washerwoman, and her hands bled from the work.

She didn't last a year. My younger sister, Edwina, a girl of talent and true musical sensibility who had been planning to study in Europe, was reduced to playing stringed instruments at the lowest sort of affairs, for the worst riffraff you could imagine."

"I don't know what to say, Miss Van Shaick," Bedford said. "It is a tragic story, but if it is of any comfort, I would say this city is filled with such."

"It is not comfort, Mr. Bedford, although you are kind to try to offer some. But I have learned the lessons to be learned." She reached into her pocket and took out the bank draft. "This is the first lesson. Always have a lot of it." She put it back. "And this is the second." She reached up and took hold of Halsey's lapel and pulled him down to her. She kissed his lips and rubbed her hand over his chest. "Always have someone you can trust, someone reliable, preferably a good farm boy, a man of strong instincts and rough tastes, as far from being a gentleman as possible."

"I've been accused of being many things," Halsey said, "but ain't nobody accused me of being that."

There was a tapping at the door so gentle that at first Bedford didn't hear it.

"Who's there?"

"Mr. Bedford, sir, it's Margaret."

He pulled the chain above him. The water rushed down.

"What is it?"

"Mr. Bedford, I was just closin' up da house and wonderin' to myself if you was all right in dere or maybe had fallen asleep or needed somethin'. You've been in dere a terrible long time."

"Everything's fine," he said. "I'll be out in a minute." He found it impossible to be harsh with the servants, to see them as part of some separate order of existence. He left that to Sarah. They were afraid of her. He noticed how attentive they were when she was in the house, and how that attentiveness waned when she was away. They would never knock on any bathroom door *she* might be behind, that was for sure. They would wait.

Bedford placed the newspaper on his lap. Should have gone

to meet Halsey at the Trump. No use hiding. Sooner or later it would all have to be faced. He reminded himself again: Don't panic. He glanced down at the paper. The obituary notices. He wasn't tired. His stomach rumbled once more. Although his taste for food hadn't diminished, his insides were a ruin.

In the early autumn of the first year of the war, he had closed the office for several days. Had sat by himself at his desk for an entire day. He had remembered the contempt he had felt for the victims of '57. How pathetic they had seemed at the time, how weak, their eyes blazing with fear, like trapped animals. He had imagined that their weakness and fearfulness had led them to destruction. They had chosen to ignore the brute nature of the struggle they were involved in, and as a consequence the struggle devoured them. Sitting there in his empty office, Bedford had come to understand that perhaps their fear was the outcome of their ruin, not its origin.

On his second day alone, Bedford had done a mental inventory. He had played his instincts and bet that the country would walk to the very edge of civil war but recoil from the abyss. However foolish they had come to seem, his instincts had been widely shared. But others had hedged their bets, especially after Lincoln's election. They had liquidated investments, invested in gold and foreign assets.

When war came, his losses had been devastating. As he recovered from the shock, he decided to approach the matter more rationally, not suppressing his instincts but tempering them with a reasoned judgment as to what lay ahead. The war, he calculated, could last only a year. At the end of that time, the North would have either crushed the South or realized that such a victory could not be achieved and negotiated a peace. In the meanwhile, the withdrawal of southern investments, the absence of cotton for northern mills, the destruction of shipping, the loss of crops, the possible sacking of border cities and ports, and a halt to railroad construction would all leave the economy in a shambles.

In the evening, Ward and Bedford dined together at home.

"The war will ruin the economy," Bedford said.

"Quite so."

"It is a clear lesson of history?"

"I thought history didn't interest you."

"I am asking a question."

"Ah, history always tells us several things. For example, in the case of war, history tells us the economic energies of a nation can be either vitiated or invigorated."

"Depending on whether it wins or loses?"

"In history, nothing is so simple."

"Could you get to the point?"

"Well, in the case of war with another country or power, a nation may well find that the requirements of its military efforts strengthen its commercial prowess no matter what the outcome. Britain lost its struggle with the American colonies, but the exercise of fighting such a distant war stimulated its productive capacities."

"And you believe this war could do the same for us?"

"This isn't simply *war*, Charles, a struggle such as Britain fought against Napoléon, waged by both sides on the territory of other nations. Nor is it of the type the English and the Dutch fought, waged mostly on distant seas. Nor the kind of *pique-nique* we had with the Mexicans. This is civil war, and civil wars are ipso facto destructive for all involved. The French civil war lasted for half a century and ruined the country. The English civil war lasted nearly a decade and left scars that have perhaps never healed."

"Those were religious wars, were they not?"

"Charles, you know more than you let on. Yes, religion was one of the issues, and one might well understand the decline of the Gaul and the rise of the Saxon by recognizing that in France it was the Catholic forces that triumphed, but in Britain the Protestant. Yet whatever the issues, the universal results of civil wars are the same, and were pointed out very nicely by Gibbon in his summation of the struggle that brought Constantine to the imperial throne. The first is a ruinous expense of blood and treasure.

The second, an oppressive escalation in taxation. I don't see any reason to believe that we shall escape such a fate, do you?"

Bedford didn't. He abandoned the market and decided to wait until it reached bottom before he reentered. The country seemed to sink into a depression, just as he thought it would. For a few weeks, the atmosphere on the Street was quiet, almost tranquil. But slowly at first, then with astounding rapidity, the war turned into the single greatest engine for production in the nation's history. Contracts for rifles, wagons, uniforms, boots, corn, ammunition, artillery, and ships poured out of Washington. In the East, the factories ran all day and all night. In the West, the railroads expanded across the newly laid track, and the trains ladened with grain and meat and lumber came puffing eastward. Government bonds were issued in massive amounts, an unprecedented flood, and hawked with an unheard-of urgency and success by Jay Cooke and his ubiquitous agents. More and more business was done on margin, the buyer putting up a small part of the purchase price of a stock. The pace of business swirled and gathered like the gush of a spring thaw, a roaring volume of water that grows stronger and stronger until it obliterates the riverbanks, pouring down the valley, carrying all before it. A new Deluge, different from the last. A new day. New exchanges sprang up for trading stock and they were filled with new faces, men even younger-looking than Halsey. These newcomers trotted through the streets—nobody seemed to walk anymore—waving papers, shouting at the top of their lungs. Many of them followed only one stock, in rails, or canals, or petroleum, or banks. They seemed not to know that anything else existed, nor to care. Bedford found them crude, impudent, and contemptible, but he realized they were becoming masters of the market.

Old Tom's was deserted. The colored waiters stood around solemnly, with their white towels draped over their arms. Bedford knew them all by sight but had never exchanged more than pleasantries. He wondered if they resented the war for bringing in a new order that was depriving them of their livelihood. For the first time in all the years he had been going there, he made an effort to engage them in conversation. They were polite but distant. He gave up after a few tries. He ordered another coffee with brandy. One thing was for sure: The war had disproved Stark's theory of the relationship between a full stomach and a successful broker. That notion was being trampled into the earth by a thundering horde that barely had time to eat. In place of the colored peddlers who had wandered the district selling hot corn or oysters, coffee stands sprang up, sidewalk booths that offered quick food and drink, which was devoured by men who blew on their coffee as they gulped it and consumed a roll in two mouthfuls.

In the first winter of the war, the administration made its initial issue of "greenbacks," paper currency backed by neither gold nor silver but only by the good word of the government. A whole new speculative game was born. Everyone on the Street instantaneously understood the rules. If the North were to lose the war, the greenbacks would be worthless, and the demand for gold would become insatiable, its price skyrocketing. But if the North won and could redeem the greenbacks in specie, the opposite would be true: In relation to paper, gold prices would drop. Within a few weeks of the greenbacks' appearance, there was an intense competition for exclusive rights to telegraph lines, and some of the roofs around the district sprouted rookeries for carrier pigeons. The race was on for news of the campaigns in the West and along the James, news of Union victories deflating the rise in gold prices, rumors of defeats inflating it again.

After several months in which a number of brokers bet openly on the defeat of the Union, gold sales were banned from the Board's activities. But Gilpin's News Room opened across from the Board in Lord's Court, and the gold business was carried on with an even greater intensity. Brokers fled Lord's Court and dashed in and out of the News Room. The trading was so heavy that it also supported another gold exchange, farther down on William Street. The Coal Hole was located in a poorly lit, badly ventilated basement. There was a steady traffic through its doors all day. Bedford avoided the News Room altogether, and on the one visit he made to the Coal Hole, he stood in the back. With

its haze of tobacco smoke hanging over everything and the constant clatter of voices, it reminded him of a concert saloon. There
was a raised platform at the far end with a long blackboard
mounted to the wall, on which a line of clerks entered and erased
the ever-changing prices of trades. Men jostled and pushed to see
what was happening. A fistfight broke out, and one man was
knocked, unconscious, to the floor. The trading never stopped. In
a corner of the room was the slight figure of Jay Gould. Men
were running up to him and then scurrying away. As Bedford
watched, he realized Gould was conducting a network of trades
throughout the room, dispatching runners in every direction,
sending and receiving bids, keeping track of it all in his head.

Bedford had the feeling that fate had turned against him, that
no matter what he invested in or didn't invest in, it would be the
wrong decision. He went home most nights. The war had interrupted Sarah's periodic visits to England, but a steady stream of
traffic came the other way. Usually there were two or three British
guests in the house, most of them self-styled poets or philosophers
who always seemed to find the house too stuffy or the streets too
dirty or the help too forward and familiar. At dinner they prattled
on about the war. Bedford barely listened, and Sarah grew angry
at his inattentiveness. Some evenings they put on theatricals in the
parlor, elaborate productions that required weeks of rehearsals.
Bedford would stay for a few minutes, then go to his room. He
didn't despise Sarah, but he understood that his desire for her had
been flamed by her inaccessibility. Like success, wealth, a fine
home, his own firm, Sarah had dangled at the end of the branch,
far out of reach. But eventually it had all fallen into his lap, and
Sarah with it. She was more calculating than her uncle; Bedford
had always understood that and didn't resent it. If she had fallen
into his lap, it was because she had climbed into the tree and
taken aim at where he sat below. He could provide her with the
things she wanted and had no other way of obtaining. But he had
come to find her tedious. In this, too, she surpassed her uncle.
Her conversation always dwelt on the arts, aesthetics, the realm

of the beautiful and the true, and in it was the implication that Bedford spent his days in the basest of activities.

Morrissey's was a place to go instead of home. Bedford couldn't remember precisely when he began to make a nightly visit. He came for several weeks just to watch Halsey, who never matched his performance of that first evening. Gradually Bedford learned the game. Once in a while, he placed a bet. The first time that he waged heavily, he held his own. Across the next few weeks he continued to stay even, losing one night, winning the next, never straying too far in either direction. Faro absorbed more and more of his attention. At the office, he played faro in his head. On an evening in early June, he won close to $3,500. In August, he and Halsey traveled on the *Rip Van Winkle* to Albany and hired a coach to take them to Saratoga. They spent a week at the place Morrissey ran there in the summer, and both of them were stung by the size of their losses. On the night boat back down the Hudson, Bedford couldn't sleep. He sat on the deck and smoked cheroots. The sky was starless. The paddle wheel slapped steadily, softly, on the water, a happy sound. Bedford felt a surge of hope. He wouldn't despair. Look at the twists that fate had taken in the past fifteen years. He lived under a lucky star, which although locked for a moment behind the night clouds was up there somewhere, shining. Something would come along at the right moment, the way it had done that day on Spruce Street when he saw the advertisement for Stark and Evans outside the *Tribune* offices. He fell asleep on deck. In the morning he woke up with a painful stiff neck. His clothes were soaked with morning dew and the river mist. When the boat pulled into the berth on the North River, the city was barely visible through the cloud of heat and dirt and coal dust that enveloped it.

A crowd at the end of the pier waved the boat off. The engines went into reverse and turned the water into foam. There was a small knot of policemen hauling something out of the water. Bedford stood at the railing. At the end of the policemen's rope was a body so bloated that it had burst the seams of its clothing, which hung on it like so many rags. A deckhand stood next to Bedford. He said, "Never fails, we get one of these almost every time. If they gotta kill 'emselves, I wish they'd do everyone a favor and jump into the Hell Gate, where they wouldn't interfere none with the river traffic."

Back in the office, Bedford pored over the books. His own finances and those of the firm were sinking even faster. He began going to Morrissey's every night. His luck had to change. Instead, he piled loss on top of loss. Halsey did the same, and soon their names were linked. *The Faro Twins. Broadway's biggest losers.* It was Halsey who started swiping bearer bonds from some of the brokers he represented on the Curb and fencing them with somebody he knew uptown. Bedford resisted as long as he could. He kept waiting on luck. Finally he asked Halsey for the name and address.

He had been to Capshaw's several times now. He had the feeling that Halsey had spilled his guts out to him, which meant that Capshaw knew all about their indebtedness to Morrissey. That afternoon Capshaw had pointed out a man walking up and down on the other side of the street from his house.

"I think it's a copper," said Capshaw. "Maybe he followed ya."

"A Metropolitan? Impossible," said Bedford.

The man was walking in a driving rain, his hat pulled down so that his face was obscured.

"Then maybe he's someone's henchman come to make sure you'll be getting what ya need to satisfy his boss. Either case you better leave me something I can give 'em if they come knockin' and askin' questions."

"Something to give them?"

Capshaw slid one palm across the other. "Oil upon the troubled waters. Gelt."

Capshaw sent him out the back door to avoid whoever it was keeping guard in the front. There were only a few rows of houses in back of Capshaw's. East of Lexington Avenue, except for scattered settlements of squatters, empty fields ran down to the river. He climbed to the top of the fence and looked around to see if there was someone keeping watch there as well. It seemed clear. He swung his legs over the fence, but his right boot got caught and he tumbled into the mud. Capshaw was going to try to blackmail him. He had dug a deeper hole for himself. He lay there for a minute to get his breath. If the Hindoos were right, if life were truly a cycle, this must be the lowest point of the wheel. He could fall no farther. He picked himself up. There was a message from Halsey waiting for him when he got home. They had to meet at the Trump this evening. It was urgent, the note said.

Bedford stood. He pulled his trousers back up and buttoned his fly. To hell with Halsey. He had to find the money to repair his business and to pay off Morrissey. Then one way or another he would have to deal with Capshaw. He pulled the chain that hung down from the water tank. He listened to the water course down the pipe into the bowl beneath.

Here was wealth.

Water that flowed through the Croton system from upstate to the distributing reservoir at Forty-second Street, water from the mere turn of a tap or the tug of a chain, water at ten dollars a month flowing down tubes to sweep away the body's waste and dirt, water to drink, to wash with, to let the children splash in. Water: a result of New York's wealth and a cause of it. Wealth created by the mingling of the waters when Clinton's canal united Lake Erie and the Hudson, the Great Lakes and the Atlantic, the harvest of a virgin continent flowing west. Water to carry barges filled with coal, driving down its price, affordable coal for factories and for homes, the source of a new and better heat, coal to make water into steam, driving new engines and new machines, generating new industries and new ways of transport, coal gas to light homes, to banish the shadowy light of candles and whale oil. Water on every side. East River, North River, the Harbor, the Sound. Water brought down in frozen blocks from Saranac and Champlain, cut and sold, delivered to homes for the preservation of food, shipped as far south as Cuba. Water to skate on in the winter, to sit by in the summer. Water: the great divide between the haves and the have-nots, the washed and the great unwashed, the primeval source of life, the spawning pond of the bourgeoisie.

He understood wealth because he had been born without it: The rich didn't stay rich because of some inner quality, of some God-infused nobility. They had their hand on the chain. They controlled the flow of whatever it was the people needed or thought they needed or were persuaded they needed.

Wealth wasn't a question of blood. It was a question of water. He put the *Tribune* on the washstand next to the toilet. His eyes fell to the bottom of the page. *There was a sharp advance in gold this morning on the news from Charleston and Vicksburg.* If defeat came, if it came by summer, whoever had bought gold low would have his hand on the chain. A defeated North would cry for it, Cooke and his cabal sent packing, federal bonds and greenbacks as worthless as fish wrappings.

It would be a gamble. The greatest game of faro ever: winning a personal fortune by betting everything he had that the Union would be a loser.

He grasped the chain and pulled it down.

No, the gambling was over. Here was the dictate of fate, a voice as clear as the water sounding through the pipe: *Buy gold —all you can get your hands on.*

MAY 15, 1863

There are two large sections to society: those with more dinners than appetite, those with more appetite than dinners.

—Nicolas Chamfort

I

HE STROKED HER HEAD, mussed and smoothed the hair, dug deeper, down her back, elasticity of skin, hard muscle, steady hum of pleasure, *don't stop, don't stop, don't stop.* The vibration rippled across lap and legs down into his crotch. Suddenly she turned and looked at him.

Cat's eyes.

Dunne stopped. The cat shifted about on his lap, clawed at the woolen nubs of his trousers. Unblinking eyes, as emotionless as a whore's. Why was it that he noticed their eyes? Others didn't. Took their pleasure, in and out, and it was enough. Not that he hadn't, but why wasn't it enough? The cat muzzled Dunne's hand. He raked his fingers through fur the color of weak tea, brown, red, golden tint of gaslight. He moved his hand in long, slow strokes. The tautness in her body flowed away as the weight of her body sank into his lap.

Across the lobby of the New England Hotel sat two military officers, one reading the *Tribune*, the other puffing a cigar and staring at the passing whores. A red-haired girl, her hair piled atop her head beneath a hat the shape of a butterfly, noticed him watching. She tapped on the window, pulled back the lapels of her jacket, exposing the top of her well-formed breasts, ran her tongue over her painted lips, and made a stroking motion with her hand, up and down, up and down. Without a word to his companion, the officer stood and went out the door. In an instant, he returned, whispered something to the face behind the paper, and stuck the cigar back into his mouth. He strode across the lobby and, like a locomotive pulling into a station, left a fulsome wake of smoke as he went up the stairs. A moment later the whore followed.

The cat rolled onto her side, stretched, put a paw across her eyes. Dunne scratched beneath her chin. She seemed to smile.

Down the same stairs the officer had just gone up came Jack Mulcahey, the minstrel performer, arm in arm with his cocoa-colored mistress, Eliza, a Cuban or a nigger depending on whom you talked to. They walked toward the bar, Mulcahey with that slight exaggeration to his step, up on the heel, down on the toe, a strut he carried with him on and off the stage. Behind them was Squirt, the nigger kid with freckles and kink the color of brick, who always stuck close to Mulcahey, usually seeing to it that the star of Brownlee's Minstrel Parade, "The Nonpareil of Ethiopian Impersonation," made it to the theatre on time. Dunne had heard it said that Squirt was Eliza and Mulcahey's son, but if he were, he had none of his mother's fine looks. More likely he was the result of a Five Points' amalgamation, a few minutes' worth of in and out on the floor of some dive.

Mulcahey stopped at the entrance to the bar, a few feet from Dunne. "You go ahead," he said to Squirt in a loud, theatrical voice.

"Come on, Jack," Squirt said. "You can stop later. We ain't got much time."

Eliza took her arm out of Mulcahey's. "You should leave now," she said. "It's already late."

"Among my many talents is that of telling what hour it is. There is enough time to allow a moment of refreshment."

Eliza said nothing. She walked out the door.

Dunne moved his hand down the cat's chin and neck into the tufted fur of her belly. She stiffened, clutched his hand between her paws, and sunk her teeth into his knuckle. He pulled away with such force that his elbow banged loudly against the wall.

The cat jumped to the floor, darted through the legs of several passersby, and disappeared into the bar.

Mulcahey laughed. "Your first encounter with Cassandra, I take it?"

Dunne knew Mulcahey from passing him in the lobby. No names, just a nod.

"Our house feline has taught you two valuable lessons. First, before you touch a woman, always get to know her. Second, if you touch her where she doesn't want to be touched, be prepared to pay the price."

"Oh, Jack," Squirt said, "quit your gabbing and come on."

"Go ye and prepare a place for me," Mulcahey said. He turned to Dunne. "And you, my friend, come with me. I'll give you a proper introduction to Cassandra and show you how to touch her without losing a finger."

Dunne sucked the wound on his knuckle. Cassandra had drawn blood. "Got an engagement to keep," he said. "Some other time."

The crowd in the barroom had caught sight of Mulcahey and called for him to come in. He put his hat and gloves in the chair where Dunne had been sitting and entered with a flourish, jumping to his right, sliding to his left, going up on the heels, then on the toes, and singing in a deep baritone:

> *Oh, boys, carry me long; carry me till I die!*
> *Carry me down to de buryin' groun'.*
> *Massa, don't you cry!*

Cassandra was on the bar. She meowed when Jack sang. He picked her up, cradled her in his arms, put his face in hers, rubbed his cheek on hers, the whiskers brushing across his nose. He scratched chin, neck, belly. She lay limp and content in his arms. He held up his unwounded hand for Dunne to see and shouted, "Come on! I'll show you how it's done! You'll never be bitten by the feminine animal again!"

Dunne shook his head. The whore in the butterfly hat came past him and grabbed the arm of a woman who stood by the door, a short, thickset whore in a black cape whom Dunne hadn't noticed.

"Oh, those military men!" the whore in the butterfly hat said, her voice distinctly Irish. "Give me one every time. Come quicker than a gnat can blink!"

"God's gift to the trade!" said the other whore. "So ready to shoot and no time to reload." They went out into the street, their laughter echoing behind. Dunne followed them as far as Canal. Thought about stopping at Tomoline's for a shave, eighteen barbers amid acres of marble and glass, open twenty-four hours. Always seemed to be busy. He decided not to dawdle. The scene with Mulcahey had left him uneasy. A Dandy Dan commandment: *Avoid boardinghouses and any establishment that caters to clerks and salesmen. Such places are the antechamber to the penitentiary. Either the landlady will rat you out or some nosing jake will sell you out. Stick to hotels, preferably the theatrical kind.* But even in a theatrical hotel, people got to know you, started wondering, questioning, prying in a cordial kind of way.

The whores Dunne had followed out of the hotel each picked up a soldier on the corner of Canal. Dunne walked to Broadway. In the middle of the traffic, only a few yards away, was the swaying bulk of a Broadway stagecoach. When it drew close, he darted out, pirouetted around the mounds of fresh horse droppings, grabbed the vertical iron bar on the rear, and swung himself up. Inside, the seats were taken by the usual complement of flour-faced clerks in ill-fitting coats, just now setting out for some distant northern quarter of the city. Once they married, this is what they did, migrated to the barren outlands, where a house could be bought for what it cost to rent a single room in or near a respectable part of the city. A few read the paper, squinting in the lantern light at the columns of figures on the back pages. Most stared at their ink-stained hands, as smeared as any ditchdigger's, and shuffled their feet in the mud-colored straw spread across the floor. None looked up at Dunne or took any notice of the sidewalks outside, noisy with the hubbub of theatregoers and the patrons of minstrel shows. They might as well be traveling across the emptiness of the western territories, Dunne thought, and yet he envied the destination they had, a warm, familiar place where they would be welcome and secure, wives to look after them, no worry that the Metropolitans would soon be banging on the door.

As the coach approached Houston, the fare collector made his rounds. Dunne jumped off before he had to pay his half dime. Always a pleasure to avoid further enriching the owners of the coach and horsecar franchises. He walked east, past Mulberry and the headquarters of the Metropolitans, a purpose to his step. There was no more time to waste. Little sense in moving again to another hotel. He would put all his energy into finding what it was Waldo Capshaw was really up to, and short of approaching Morrissey himself, there was only one man to talk to, one endless source of stories, rumors, news, facts, and fables, one ceaseless chronicler of the sins and passions of the metropolis: One-Eyed Jack Cassidy.

"Cassidy is to talk," Dandy Dan used to say, "what Niagara is to water."

Cassidy and Dandy Dan had grown up together. "FIGS" is what they called themselves: First Irish in Greenwich Street. Their families lived above the same stable, picked their food from the same refuse heaps, the children watching out for one another. As youngsters Jack and Dan were inseparable, but where Dandy Dan went on to make his way in the world through quiet and studious attention to the details of his work, One-Eyed Jack had no occupation except talk.

Originally Cassidy had been dubbed by those who knew him Rat-a-tat Jack, his mouth going all the time like one of those floorboard castanets the minstrels continually banged. He became One-Eyed Jack in the summer of '57, the time of the Battle of Paradise Square. Everybody knew it was coming. Dandy Dan warned Dunne to stay away, but there was no way he could. On July 4th, the Paddy gangs did what they had long threatened to do. With Brickabat Bob Sweeney at the head of the Dead Rabbits and Savage Sam Foley at the head of the Plug Uglies, they descended on the headquarters of the Bowery Boys and the Atlantic

Guards and wrecked the places. Forgetting for the moment whatever bad blood there was between the Rabbits and the Pluggies,
Sweeney proclaimed a final victory over the "shit-scum Yankees"
and concluded his speech, "May Bill 'the Butcher' Poole rot in
hell forever!"

It was too much for the True Americans. Although badly
outnumbered, they counterattacked, a hard wedge of enraged
combatants, catching the Paddies by surprise and driving them
back to their haunts around Paradise Square. The next day the
Paddies retook the offensive, wrecking a favorite watering hole of
the nativists on Broome Street, hauling down the American flag
and raising in its place the trousers of a Yankee who had been so
frightened he had befouled himself. A force of True Americans
stormed across Centre Street toward Paradise Square to revenge
the insult and stumbled upon the Metropolitans. It was a first test
for the new police force that had been created by the Governor
and the legislature to replace the Municipals, the police loyal to
Tammany. The month before, the Metropolitans had fought a
pitched battle with their rivals for control of City Hall. Metropolitans and Municipals whipped one another with locust sticks.
Bodies lay everywhere, and the fighting continued until the militia
arrived, seized City Hall on orders from Governor King, and
routed the Municipals.

The police war went on all month, Municipals and Metropolitans contesting a possession of every precinct. Gradually the
Metropolitans got the upper hand, and once aware of the continuing turmoil in the Bowery, they determined to assert authority
and demonstrate their ability to bring the gangs under control.
On they came, a parade of bluecoats and plug hats, their locust
sticks cradled like muskets. The force of two hundred men
marched with pride and confidence until Paddies and True Americans, temporarily abandoning their own hostilities, fell upon the
policemen's flanks and sent them into headlong retreat.

It was soon after the rout of the Metropolitans that Rat-a-
tat became One-Eyed Jack. He was sitting in the parlor of Theresa
Boyle's brothel on the corner of Mulberry and Bayard when a

squad of True Americans burst in intent on evicting the Irish
whores. Cassidy tried to run, but they caught him on the stairs
and dragged him outside, where Mike Poole, a cousin of the late
Butcher, put his foot on Cassidy's throat and, using his thumb as
lever, gouged out Rat-a-tat's right eye. He was about to do the
same with the left, but the whores had taken refuge on the rooftops and their screaming brought a flying wedge of Rabbits and
Pluggies. Poole straddled Cassidy's body like a lion with its prey.
He called for reinforcements, and they came, the street filling with
men and the battle spreading in size and intensity until it seemed
to fill the entire Sixth Ward. Poole finally abandoned Cassidy
when a gunman opened fire from the window of a nearby hotel.

On the Bowery, immigrant and nativist alike joined in the
looting of brothels, saloons, stores, and homes. The battle and its
attendant disorders went on for an entire day before the militia
arrived and laid down a series of volleys to clear the streets so
the fire laddies could get to the buildings that were burning and
prevent a conflagration of the type that would consume half the
city. Afterward, they began a house-to-house search of the area
around the Five Points.

Dunne was arrested the next morning. He knew he should
have stayed away, but he also knew that those who did would be
despised by all the gangs, the ruling ones like the Dead Rabbits
and the Plug Uglies, and their vassals as well, the Buckaroos,
Slaughter Housers, Daybreak Boys, Hookers, Swamp Angels, and
Patsy Conroys. Although more witness than participant, Dunne
made sure the Rabbits and the Pluggies saw he was there.

Under the protection of the militia, the Metropolitans raided
the basement shebeen where Dunne was holed up. They arrested
everyone there, chained them together, and threw them into a
single dungeon in the Tombs, a cell without light, the walls wet
with slime, water oozing up through the floor, the remnant of the
Collect Pond, which the city had filled in and built a prison on.
They sat in silence, their eyes adjusting to the darkness, when,
suddenly, a figure emerged out of the deepest shadows of the cell,
a ghostlike apparition, face wrapped in a swath of dirty linen, a

great blot of dried blood where the right eye used to be. Dunne felt the hair on the back of his neck stand up. The man next to him said in a loud voice, "Sweet Jesus, save us!"

"No need for prayers, boys," the apparition said, "it's only Jack Cassidy, you all know me, and I'm alive, not dead, no thanks to Mike Poole and his like, the craven Protestant horde calls itself patriots but in truth is unworthy of being called civilized men." Cassidy talked most of the two days they were housed in that cell, chronicling the battle that had taken place, and Dunne and the others were grateful for it, his words a welcome distraction from the uncertainty and dread they felt.

On the afternoon of the second day, a militia officer appeared. He had the cell door opened and stood among the prisoners. "In the judgment of the civil authorities, there is scant evidence against you and even less space for holding you. Scoundreldom has multiplied beyond our ability to contain it, a historic day for New York! That means you are free to go, so do it quickly before I succumb to the inner voice that implores me to shoot the lot of you. God knows, posterity would bless me for it."

Dunne had met Cassidy many times since they shared that cell. It was hard not to encounter Cassidy somewhere, since he was constantly on circuit from concert saloons to alehouses to hotel bars. His favorite haunt was Harry Hill's, on Houston Street. For several years it had been the busiest of the concert saloons, where sooner or later every politician, sport, actor, squiffer, and jackanapes passed through. Hill's was located in an old, rambling wooden-frame house built decades before by some prosperous farmer. The fields were long gone. In their place a solid row of brick façades pressed the old building tightly on each side. An aged, battered, peeling wreck in the day, at night it seemed a place of incessant movement and gaiety, the band never stopping, the dance floor constantly filled, the waiter girls in their red-tasseled boots and low-cut dresses swirling about with drink-ladened trays. The noise from Harry Hill's was audible a block away, and a huge gas lantern, as powerful as any harbor beacon, bathed the entire area in its glow.

Old Harry Hill himself usually tended the door. He was a man of few words except when he mounted the stage to recite his poetry, a weekly event that emptied the place for an hour or so. Mostly he said nothing, devoting all his attention to making sure the bartenders weren't doling out free drinks or pocketing the profits. Some said Harry Hill was the wealthiest man in New York, richer than A. T. Stewart. An exaggeration, for sure, but despite his ragged appearance—the same unkempt look as the old men who slept in the waiting rooms of the ferry terminals—there was no doubt that Hill was exceedingly rich, and he employed a small brigade of bodyguards to protect his person as well as saloon.

Tonight Harry Hill wasn't at the door. A bored-looking bodyguard sat in his chair. The place was less lively than usual. The stage was empty, no line of waiter girls kicking their legs up, flash of leg and stocking, din of voices and cheers.

Perched on the corner of the bar was Harry Hill's parrot. It preened itself, turned its head, and screeched, "Hang Abe Lincoln!" No one seemed to hear.

One of the waiter girls came over. Anna O'Brien was a second-generation whore, not as pretty as her mother had been, thinner, with a small bosom, and without her mother's good cheer.

"Jimmy," she said, "haven't seen you in a while."

"Been busy."

"Wish I had that excuse." She gestured with her head at the half-empty room. "There's more life in potter's field."

"I'm looking for One-Eyed Jack."

"Haven't seen him in a good bit, a run of luck I hope will continue. Business is bad enough without having to suffer Cassidy's mouth."

There was a puffiness in Anna's face, especially around the eyes, that Dunne had never noticed before. Rumor said she lived with a Chinaman on Pell Street, in the opium-smoking dive he operated. Dunne had known Anna since they were runts together running the streets. Lost touch with her for several years, but then bumped into her on Broadway. She was a runt no longer. They talked a few moments. Dunne was drunk, one of the few times. He bent over and kissed her right there beneath the gaslight, and she took him to her room, and they were at it for hours before they fell asleep. Woke in a tight embrace, her leg entwined in his, her arm around his chest. He worked his way out slowly, without disturbing her.

He knew she did it for a living but wasn't sure if she expected to be paid. It hadn't felt like an encounter with a whore, a quick, mechanical in and out, the next customer waiting outside. When he saw her again, he blurted out, "Anna, do I owe you anything?"

"Do you think you do?"

He felt his face turn red.

"Where love is, there are no obligations," Anna said. "A saint wrote that. Little he knew about either love or obligations, little any man does."

Did he owe her or not? He was never sure. Could never talk to women, never had the knack for putting them at ease. No different tonight. Anna said nothing more. He stood next to her, not knowing what to say, until he said good-bye and walked back into the street. He stopped in several other saloons before he reached Clinton Place. No sign of Cassidy in any of them. Up ahead, in the middle of the next block, was an immense gaslit transparency of a wild swan. Carriages were lined up two-deep at the curb.

A group of soldiers pushed past him on their way out. They were reeling drunk. Dunne went down the stairs they had just come up into an immense smoke-filled room. To the right was a bar that ran the length of the wall; behind it, a dozen bartenders served the insistent crowd. To the left was a stage. The space between stage and bar was filled with tables, and darting in and out among them was the same species of waiter girls as could be found at Harry Hill's in similar outfits; low-cut red blouses, black skirts that came only to their calves, black stockings, tasseled red boots with tiny bells around the laces. There was little visible in the place that would explain why Harry Hill's should languish while the Trump thrived, especially since the Trump seemed the smaller and less well appointed of the two.

Dunne stood at the bar. An army officer was next to him, his eye encircled with a faint black mark. Dunne peered past him, through the thick wreath of gray-blue smoke, toward a voice that carried over the din, a constant drone, like the engine of a ferry. There at the far end was Cassidy, talking with two men Dunne didn't recognize. They were short and stocky, the thick folds of their necks bulging over their collars.

"Ah," One-Eyed Jack said when he saw Dunne approach, "young Dunleavy! A welcome sight to this single sore eye of mine, which can never see enough of the faces from days just passed but seem gone an eternity."

The name jolted Dunne. *Dunleavy.* Been so long since he had been called by that name, it was like hearing himself being summoned from the dead: the name of the boy who had been shipped west by the Children's Aid Society, the image of a deceased relative as captured in a daguerreotype, standing motionless on the deck of the boat to Albany, a tag tied to his too-small jacket, the same bold lettering on it as had marked his clothes at the Orphan Asylum. DUNLEAVY, J. Dropped that name first thing, soon as he got back, but kept a part of it, a small piece of the only thing the old man he had never known left him when he walked out on wife and child.

"But you're no more Dunleavy," Cassidy said. "Dunleavy is dead! Long live Dunne! And what's the difference except some letters dropped or rearranged, a false scent for the booly dogs? You proceed, young man, according to an ancient precedent, for wasn't the tactic of rebaptism first employed by the great Ulysses? 'Nobody' he called hisself when he entered the Cyclops's cave, though what he done to that one-eyed soul is more than any Christian could bring hisself to forgive." Cassidy winked with his one eye and burst into laughter. The two stout men with him kept their same stone-faced expressions.

"Come," Cassidy said, "let us toast that great solo-sighted ancestor of mine with ruddy wine, a vintage of nectar and ambrosia distilled." He signaled the bartender, who refilled the glasses of Cassidy and his companions, and poured a brimming shot of whiskey for Dunne. Cassidy turned away and distributed the drinks. Dunne paid.

On the other side of the room, three waiter girls dragged a reluctant lieutenant on stage. One of the girls sat down at the piano. The other two hung on the lieutenant's arms. The trio began to sing, but the din in the room made it impossible to hear. Cassidy took his whiskey in a single gulp. The others did the same. Dunne motioned to the bartender, who refilled their glasses again. The two with Cassidy still looked on impassively. One had a mustache, the other was clean-shaven, but their builds and profiles were so similar it seemed obvious they were brothers.

On stage, one of the waiter girls had gotten down on her hands and knees. The lieutenant was astride her, mimicking a horseman. The melody of "Camptown Races" rang out on the piano.

"Let me give you a riddle," Cassidy said. "What has five eyes, six arms, one tongue, six legs, and two ears?"

Dunne shrugged.

"The three of us!" Cassidy put a hand on each of his two stout companions' shoulders. "These are the Gallagher boys, Dunne—now, surely you've heard of them—a most famous pair, the Romulus and Remus of Greenwich Street."

Dunne shrugged again.

"Don't tell me our city has grown so big and lacking in memory that there are them have no acquaintance with the likes of these two stalwarts!"

The bartender stood behind Cassidy. He slapped the bar, but Cassidy ignored him. Dunne paid for the drinks. "Don't believe we've ever met," Dunne said.

"Never met, sure that's one thing, but never *heard* of them, that's another!"

The brothers appeared unconcerned about what Cassidy had to say. They stared over his shoulder at the stage, where the waiter girls had coaxed the lieutenant to get down on all fours. The two girls sat on his back, and the one at the piano handed the rear rider a strap. She raised it in the air as the piano player banged the keys and the crowd began to take up the refrain:

> *De Camptown ladies sing dis song,*
> *Doo-dah! doo-dah!*

On *Doo-dah!* the rider brought the strap down on the lieutenant's rear. It made a loud *thwap*. The lieutenant bucked like a horse.

> *De Camptown racetrack five miles long*
> *Oh! Doo-dah day!*

Thwap.

The Gallagher brothers didn't join in the singing. They stared across the room. Their large, protruding eyes gave them a hang-dog look.

"They're deef," Cassidy said, "deef as stone. Could shoot a cannon off right in their ears and wouldn't bother them a bit, and they've no speech either, not a word, deef and dumb as the dead. The Protestant missionaries was always trying to take them from their mother when they was pups, said she couldn't care proper for them and the other twelve children with no father about, came once with a court paper empowering them to remove the twins, but Mrs. Gallagher was a Galway woman, with the gift of guile the people of those parts so naturally possess, and she hid them beneath a pier, kept them there for near two months, out of sight, before the Protestants gave up. The boys didn't disappoint her. Went to work as stokers on a steamboat, the infernal noise of the engines that drives some men mad never bothered them, their ears sealed by God, and once the traveling urge got in their blood, they never stopped moving, becoming cabin boys and porters and finally going into a trade of their own as a pair of wandering gips, working all routes west, rail as well as steam, relieving the unsuspecting passenger of whatever valuables they can and doing it with such noiseless grace he's none the wiser till the twins is long gone."

The twins watched closely the proceedings on stage, where the lieutenant, red-faced and sweating, was struggling to get out from beneath the riders and the rain of blows. He grabbed the front rider by the boot and twisted. She screamed. The rear rider reached back and put her hand between his legs and squeezed. He cried out and heaved himself to his feet, spilling both girls to the floor. He stormed off the stage, and the crowd cheered.

Dunne studied the faces of the brothers. The only deaf and dumb boy he ever knew was Grover O'Higgins, a runner for the Dead Rabbits. Moved quick as a fly. They all knew he was deaf but shouted for him as if he could hear. Someone turned it into a ditty:

> Grover, come here,
> Grover, come here,
> Stand there, stand here,
> Or I'll stick me foot up your rear!

It was true: He got kicked when he didn't come. A face filled with eagerness and fear, eyes that studied every face with searching intensity.

" 'Tis a terrible fate befallen us," said Cassidy. "Days past, the Paddies of this town all knew one another or knew someone who knew someone who knew them, a great iron circle of unbroken bonds that the rat-noses could never dent, but now there are so many of us we live in ignorance of one another, traveling about like the followers of Ulysses clinging to the underside of thick-fleeced sheep. To think there are those your age, Dunne, that is unacquainted with the Gallagher brothers, it's a thing to lament most grievously."

Cassidy went on with his lament, his voice competing with the barroom noise. "His gift for talk," Dandy Dan once told Dunne, "is from his father, one of those scholars of the Irish tongue who taught in fields and barns, a 'hedge schoolmaster,' as they was called, skilled in Latin and Greek and the ancient stories. A man of learning, though in the things of the world as lacking as those he taught. Unlike most of the scholarly kind, Cassidy the Elder was married. Barely able to keep his family from starvation, he brought them to New York same time as my old man came over with us, during the famine of '32, and they met each other working on the laying of Croton pipe. Was a hard thing to watch, my old man said, poor Cassidy with a shovel, so unskilled was the scholar in the ways of the spade, but he did his best and amused the other men with his stories and his learning till one day, in the middle of a tale, Cassidy the Elder sits down and holds his head. Someone asks what's wrong but he never answers, just keels over facedown dead in the bottom of a watery ditch, dying *bás gan sagart,* as the old people say, without a priest, and was carted off to potter's field leaving nothing to his family but his learning and his talent for talk, the latter a legacy all the Cassidys share in."

Cassidy ordered another round of whiskeys. He handed the Gallagher brothers their glasses and stepped aside so Dunne could pay.

"We aren't the people we once were, no doubt of that," Cassidy said, "a nation of poets, warriors, and priests, our royalty showing through our rags, the most ancient race of Europe, our country conquered by the treachery of an English-speaking rabble but our souls and spirits free. What have we become? Just look around. A broken, dispirited, anonymous mob of pleasure seekers cowed by the likes of Robert Noonan, that lickspittle calls himself a provost marshal, the greatest traitor of the day!"

"We still have men like Morrissey," Dunne said.

"Thank God for it," Cassidy said, rapping his knuckles on the bar.

"None can cow him."

"The man hasn't been born yet."

"Nor show him disrespect."

"None."

"Nor dare to cheat him."

Cassidy took his drink in one gulp and wiped his mouth with

his sleeve. "Well, some have tried, no doubt, but paid the price."

Dunne ordered another round. "Always a price to pay for crossing John Morrissey," he said.

"Always."

"Seems to me only a fool would take the risk." Dunne passed around the drinks.

" 'Tis true, but such are always in abundance, especially in New York, the mecca of fools everywhere."

The Gallagher brothers took their drinks without removing their eyes from the stage. Three waiter girls were singing a soft melody. The words were inaudible; every few minutes, as they bent at the waist and the low cut of their blouses practically exposed their breasts, a cheer went up.

Cassidy leaned close to Dunne, and seeming to forget that it was only the Gallaghers who might overhear (and couldn't anyway), whispered to him, "They aren't hard to find, the kind of fools you spoke about; indeed, you need go no farther than these premises: One of the cabal of the rat-noses that owns this place is as big a fool as God makes and has traded away his future at the faro table. Morrissey is breathing down his neck for payment, a hot and discomforting breath it must be."

"Is he a gentleman?"

Cassidy laughed. "A crude hayseed of a Yankee is what he is, an original apple-knocker from some upstate backwater, one of those crossroads calls itself a town. Made a bundle on Wall Street and, from what I hear, lost it too, and is now in danger of losing more precious things, like life and limb."

"And he owns the Trump?"

"A part. He was the one brought in the spectacle of the lovely Anatid, a sight even Barnum can't match. The Trump was just another concert saloon until Halsey came up with the notion of offering private viewings of the Swan, found her, too, a girl worth ogling. A pimp's work, but the house rewarded him with a proprietary interest in the place since it was him who raised it to prominence."

"Halsey know the danger he's in?" Dunne asked.

"Does the mouse fear the cat? The man may be a speculator and pimp, but he's got ears and eyes. He knows what Morrissey will do to a welsher and knows too that when his luck was running high and the cards running his way, he boasted about putting Morrissey out of business and taking the faro palace away from him. Morrissey will never forget the slight. He'll do to Halsey what Achilles did to Hector, not just destroy him but subject his fallen form to shameful outrage."

Cassidy called for more drinks. Dunne turned and watched the stage. A line of waiter girls were kicking their legs. He wouldn't press Cassidy any further. He had what he was after. A lead. *Halsey.* Didn't sound like Capshaw's gentleman visitor, but it was a place to start.

The waiter girls moved back and forth across the stage, their arms locked together, an identical half-moon smile on each face.

A waiter girl came up beside the Gallagher brothers. "Would you like to see the Swan?" she said. Neither of the brothers looked at her.

"How about One-Eyed Jack?" she said.

"Little need have I of such foolishness," Cassidy said.

"You'd come sure enough if you could get someone else to pay. How about your friend here? Maybe he'd like a view and will take you along."

Dunne shook his head, turned, and paid for the last round of drinks. He felt beyond such boy's stuff, peeking through holes at a naked woman. Look but don't touch. He wasn't averse to the pleasures the likes of Anna O'Brien could offer, but in his heart was a desire he never spoke about, a desire few denizens of the Bowery or the Five Points ever seemed to think about, a desire for what seemed out of reach, not merely a woman, but a wife, children, a home. Lying abed at night in the cold, damp darkness of the New-York Orphan Asylum, he had thought of that warm and distant world, closed his eyes, and tried to keep it there until the occasional coughing from the other beds, the sleepers' cries for mothers who would never come, the sound of the whistles on the river, night noises, distinct and lonely, drew him back to where he was.

He had his first woman when he was fourteen. Been out of the orphanage almost two years. Left one day on a scow, hidden beneath a canvas tarp, landed in Manhattan, gone back to the old neighborhood he had been taken from six years before, when his mother died of cholera. Ran with a pack of Paddy urchins like himself till he landed in the arms of a Municipal and was hauled before a rat-nosed judge.

"Mr. Dunleavy," said the judge staring down at him, "you have committed a theft while riding a public conveyance. You deserve to go to jail." The judge glanced at a tall somber man who stood at the side of the bench. "What do you think, Mr. Scott?"

"I think what I have always thought, Your Honor," Mr. Scott said. "It is a waste to send a boy such as this—and despite his crime, that is what he is, a boy—to a penal institution in which he will be further schooled in criminal depravity. What boys like this one need are Christian homes free of superstition, ignorance, and drunkenness. In the proper setting, surrounded by habits of thrift, piety, and honesty, divorced from the influences that have misshapen them, it is possible they may one day grow into mechanics, farmers, taxpayers."

"I doubt it, Mr. Scott. In my experience, few things short of hanging can change the direction of a youth set out on a life of crime. His is invariably a felon's doom. But if the Children's Aid Society promises that this criminal will be removed to a distance not less than a thousand miles from this city, I will consent to put him in your custody."

"Your Honor, I cannot promise the distance to which he will be removed, but I can aver that as we have done with a myriad of his ilk, the Society will provide this boy with the chance for a new and productive life."

Jimmy Dunne left in autumn, part of a company of forty-three boys and girls. He was among the oldest, the majority being between the ages of six and ten. Jimmy was brought by Mr. Scott from jail to the Hudson River pier on the morning of the departure. The agent in charge was the Reverend Edgar Potts, a visitor of the Society, who was assisted by two matrons. He had the children line up in rows. He searched the clothes and sacks of the boys, the matrons those of the girls. They confiscated scapulars, rosary beads, religious medals, several knives, and a small vial of gin. Each child was then given a Bible. "This is the greatest protection and comfort you will have on our journey," Mr. Potts said. "Cling to it." He told them to kneel, and said a prayer over them. The boy kneeling next to Jimmy was small and frail. He was clothed in a silver-buttoned tunic several sizes too big for him. "O Holy Mother of God," he said over and over again in a thin voice, "we're going to Kansas, and the Indians will eat us."

They traveled up the Hudson overnight. Mr. Potts locked the older boys and girls in a cabin. Most of the children were Paddies, but there was a contingent of Germans who spoke to one another in their own language until Mr. Potts forbade any conversations except in English. In Albany they were given breakfast and put aboard a train for Buffalo. For many of the children it was their first trip on the rails, and there was an air of excitement as they got aboard. But Jimmy and the older children were locked in a windowless baggage car, and their excitement soon turned to tedium. In Buffalo they boarded another boat. By now the novelty of the trip had disappeared for everyone. The little children were crying constantly, and the older ones were sullen and withdrawn. Mr. Potts and the matrons were rarely to be seen. They arrived in Detroit before dawn, walked through dark, empty streets to another rail station, and climbed onto a train for what seemed an endless journey through great forests that gradually gave way to a flat, treeless land. At several stops, Mr. Potts and the matrons removed small groups of children to a nearby church or hall. Mr. Potts invariably carried one of the little ones in his arms, tousling his hair, hugging him, making it seem as if such playfulness were a usual part of their relationship.

A crowd gathered at each place, farmers and their wives

waiting in their wagons until the children appeared. They looked the children over the way they would a horse, examining teeth, feeling limbs, turning heads this way and that. "Good children all," Mr. Potts said each time. "I've come to know every one of them in special ways. I envy your chance to suffer these little children to come unto you."

The older children were no longer kept under lock and key. Jimmy sat by the window of the rocking railway car as it traveled across open country, the land brown and flat, rolling waves of grass beneath a sky that curved down to meet the ground at what seemed a continent's distance away. Jimmy was part of the next-to-the-last contingent of children to be given away. They left the train and walked down a street flanked by a dozen or so wooden buildings, a small interruption on the dull, uniform terrain. It was as remote and lonely as any place Jimmy had ever imagined. They were lodged in what looked like a church, but a church without an altar or statues or decorations, just a pulpit and pews. It seemed to match the territory in its plain and unforgiving appearance. Mr. Potts and the matrons left them in the church and went to stay two doors away, in a hotel. The wind blew hard all night and carried the high moan of animal noises, wolves or coyotes or whatever was about, and the small boy who had knelt next to Jimmy on the Hudson River pier sobbed himself to sleep.

The next morning Mr. Potts roused them early. They washed at a pump behind the church, and each child was dressed in a clean shirt. About noon they were lined up in front of the pulpit, and the matrons opened the rear doors. People filled the church, couples mostly, some with their own children. Mr. Potts gave his standard talk from the pulpit, at one point reaching down to put his hand on Jimmy's head. "Good children all," he said, "perhaps not blessed with the intellectual gifts of our American youth but capable of being molded into men and women of industriousness and obedience." Jimmy studied the hard, weathered faces of the crowd, thin-lipped wives and husbands with skin the sun had tarnished the same color as prairie grass. Their clothes hung loosely on their frames, drab coats and washed-out dresses covered with a film of dust. They looked to Jimmy like the inhabitants of the poorhouse who were brought periodically to sweep and clean the grounds of the New-York Orphan Asylum: grim, silent, in need of a good meal.

When Mr. Potts was finished with his speech, the people left their pews and crowded around. A man with a fringe of beard around his face came up and looked in Jimmy's ears, poked him in the ribs and chest. Jimmy pushed the man's finger away.

"There, there," Mr. Potts said as he took Jimmy by the neck. "Let's not allow the rigors of our long journey to cause in us an uncharacteristic outburst of ill temper." He ruffled Jimmy's hair. "He's a fine boy, for sure, just brimming with ambition!"

The small boy from the pier was led away by a gray-haired woman. Halfway up the aisle he tried to run back to the other children. The woman grabbed one arm, a matron the other. They dragged him screaming from the church. The man who had poked Jimmy took Mr. Potts aside. They had an animated conversation that Jimmy caught only snatches of: "one of the strongest" . . . "not to be given away." They stepped outside. Jimmy watched them through the window of the church. The man reached into his pocket and handed something to Mr. Potts, who quickly stuffed it in his coat. As soon as they came back in, the man strode over to Jimmy. "Boy," he said, "come with me."

"Dunleavy," Mr. Potts said, "this is Mr. Ellingwood. He is offering you the refuge of a Christian home. Go now, in true gratitude and with true determination to make something of yourself."

Ellingwood said, "Ain't got all day. Come on."

Another couple had selected an eight-year-old girl and were leading her away. She was screaming and crying, begging not to be separated from her younger sisters, three-year-old twins who stood in quiet amazement at the commotion. The matrons helped remove the older sister.

Jimmy walked outside with Ellingwood. The wind was rising

again, rippling across the sea of grass and spraying the churchyard with dust. Jimmy got up next to Ellingwood on the creaking seat of an old wagon.

"That all yer got?" Ellingwood said. He pointed at the canvas bag in which Jimmy carried the shirt he had worn on the journey, a pair of extra trousers, a bar of soap, and the Bible that he, like the other children, had been issued.

"Yes."

"Ain't got a hat?"

"Nope."

Ellingwood shook his head. "City folk," he said. "A grasshopper got more sense." He snapped the reins, and they drove off across the prairie under a sky that was rapidly becoming gray and stormy. Jimmy looked back at the town. Lights glowed in the windows. He fought the urge to jump out of the wagon and run toward them.

It was pitch-dark before they reached Ellingwood's homestead. Ellingwood went in first. "Watch yer step," he said to Jimmy. He stepped down to a dirt floor two feet below the threshold. Ellingwood's home was a one-room sod house. A bench ran along one wall; there was a table in front of it. In the far corner was a sagging bed and a cupboard. The stove, which was beside the door, was glowing red.

"I got us a boy," Ellingwood said as he entered.

"Praise God," said a voice over by the bed. A woman stepped forward into the light. She was thin and small. Her hair was parted in the middle and drawn back from a round, pretty face. She wore a faded plaid dress that was buttoned to the neck and had a tattered red towel tucked into her belt like an apron. "Let's see."

Ellingwood led Jimmy to the center of the room. "Ain't exactly Samson come back to life, but he's got two hands and two legs and seems fit enough. Name is Jim."

"Well, Jim," she said, "how about something to eat?"

Jimmy watched her at the stove. She moved with a quick, lively step and sang to herself. She seemed to be about twenty or so, at least a decade younger than Ellingwood, and had none of his sourness. She served them a dinner of coffee, beans, potatoes, and salted buffalo meat. They ate in silence. When dinner was over, Ellingwood took a lantern and a blanket and led Jimmy to the shed attached to the side of the house. Amid a clutter of farm implements was a wooden bunk.

"This is where you'll stay," Ellingwood said. "Be careful not to break nothing."

Next morning, Ellingwood woke Jimmy before dawn. They had a meal of beans and coffee. Ellingwood gave Jimmy a thick woolen coat that came to below his knees and a fur hat with ear patches sewn on. "Weather is crazy this time of year," he said. "Ain't telling how fast winter will be on us." They rode in the rickety wagon across the prairie until they reached a railroad track. Ellingwood drove beside the track for some distance, not telling Jimmy where they were headed. The day was surprisingly hot. Jimmy's nostrils filled with a sickening smell before Ellingwood stopped the wagon. "Here we are," he said.

Across the prairie in front of them were thousands of animal carcasses, some little more than skeletons, others swelling masses of decaying, putrid flesh. "This is where the buffalo cross the tracks," Ellingwood said. "Trains get forced to sit here until the herds are past, so to make the time go faster the passengers take target practice on the beasts." He handed Jimmy a burlap sack. "Everythin' is left behind for the pickin', fur, meat, and bones, tons of 'em. Bring a good price as fertilizer at any railway station." Jimmy worked all morning at collecting bones, a rag soaked in cottonseed oil tied across his face to keep out the terrible odor. Toward late afternoon, a strong wind came up and the sky clouded over. Ellingwood tied the horses to the track. He and Jimmy lay beneath the wagon as a barrage of hailstones beat hard on the planks above. In a short time, the sky cleared and the day turned warm again.

They worked at bone-gathering all that week. On Sunday, Ellingwood hitched up the wagon. Mrs. Ellingwood sat next to her husband; Jimmy on the floor in the rear.

"We're goin' to church," Ellingwood said.

"I won't say no Protestant prayers," Jimmy said. In the orphanage, the Catholic children, who were 90 percent of the inmates, had stood with their arms folded during the compulsory prayer services. The little ones followed the lead of the big ones, who remembered the admonition of mothers, fathers, uncles, aunts, grandparents, the people of the neighborhood: *Don't give in to the rat-noses' ways. Don't let them take away the faith.* Jimmy's dim memories of his mother were mostly of her praying, saying her beads, him kneeling next to her in St. Mary's on Grand Street, the soft, repetitive murmur of the Hail Mary. Little of the faith had he learned since. Mass heard amid a crowd of boys packed into the rear vestibule of a church. More a social gathering than anything else. In the orphanage, a priest visited them every month and said Mass. "Your people have suffered for the faith," he said each time in his sermon. "They tried to starve us out of it in Ireland and shame us out of it here in America. But we've never allowed ourselves to be separated from it, not then, not now, not ever."

"Suit yourself," Ellingwood said. "Stay in the wagon and mumble your hocus-pocus." Jimmy sat where he was through the hour-long service, and for the next several weeks, each time the three of them drove to church, though the weather grew colder and the snow began to fly, Jimmy remained outside, wrapping himself in the coat he had been given. He never set foot into the church, even to get warm.

Soon the snow made it almost impossible to venture very far from the house. The bone-picking ended. Their daily fare became an unchanging round of beans, potatoes, and coffee. One day in January, Ellingwood rode a horse to town to buy some provisions. The sky was clear when he left, but by early afternoon the clouds rolled in, and soon the snow swept down in a solid mass, an obliterating descent of white that lasted well past dark. Jimmy joined Mrs. Ellingwood for dinner, something he had never done before. She had banged on the door of the shed and told him to come in. He was surprised at her thoughtfulness. She had always been polite to him, but it seemed to Jimmy that she regarded him as little more than a cat or a dog, an unthreatening and almost unnoticed part of the domestic complement.

Jimmy dug into the beans as soon as he sat down. He was ravenously hungry. She didn't touch her plate. "You're from New York, Jim?" She rested her head on her palm.

He nodded and went on eating.

"Must be something to see, the women in their silk dresses, hair all done up and wearing ornaments of gold, and the men in their fine frocks, smelling like spice, the whole town driving around in big fancy coaches, with their servants in tow."

"There's a lot of that in New York," Jimmy said. He shoveled more beans into his mouth.

"My husband says it's a wicked place, noisy, dirty, impious. Says that most of the people don't work, live off politics, and that criminals abound and whores and drunkards are everywhere. It belongs to the foreigners, he says, and let them have it. America's got no use for it."

"Could be," Jimmy said, "but I ain't never given it much thought." The wind swept past the sod house with a steady scream. Jimmy felt his physical hunger subside, but another kind of hunger filled him, hunger for the bustle of Manhattan streets in wintertime, lighted store windows, tinkle of shop bells, the evening crowd stepping out on the Bowery, the echo of women's laughter. Suddenly, for the first time since he'd left, he understood that he would return, that he had always intended to return, that although he had grown used to thinking of himself as a footloose Paddy without a hometown, he had one all along: New York.

"Like to see it for myself," Mrs. Ellingwood said. "My husband is probably right, it might well be a fearsome swamp, but at least I'd know for myself."

They sat for a while with no other sound than the wind. Jimmy toyed with what was left of the beans. The hunger inside for going home turned into an ache. He felt as if he would cry. Mrs. Ellingwood stood up and walked over to the bed.

"Jim," Mrs. Ellingwood said, "come here." She unbuttoned

her dress and let it fall around her feet. Underneath was a white shift. She let that fall, too. She folded her arms across her naked breasts. "Jim," she repeated, "come here."

He didn't move. He studied the dark triangle between her legs. He had taken pleasure with himself on occasion, imagining naked women as he did, riding up into them, his hand simulating what he thought the tug of a woman's body must feel like, but he had never been with a woman before, never seen a woman's body in its full fleshiness. He was aroused.

Mrs. Ellingwood got into bed and pulled the covers up to her chin. "Come to bed, Jim. Don't be afraid."

His excitement was mixed with fear. He felt his heart pound. He hesitated, then rose and walked over to the bed.

"Take off your clothes," she said.

He removed his pants and shirt, becoming fully erect as he did. He climbed in. The bed was warm from her body, like the glow of a soft fire. She took him in her hand, stroked him. In an instant there was an uncontrollable flood in his loins, an unstoppable surge. He rolled on top of her the second before it happened, spilling his seed on her leg and stomach. He was embarrassed and didn't know what to say. She got up and fetched a rag, wiped herself clean, and did the same to him. Neither of them said anything. She put her arm around him. They lay there silently until he fell asleep.

He wasn't sure how long he had been asleep when he felt her hand between his legs, rubbing gently, stirring him erect. He rolled toward her. "This time we'll make it last," she said. He kissed her on the lips. Her mouth opened. He put his tongue in. He cupped her breast in his hand, squeezed the nipple between his fingers. She closed her eyes. "Suck them," she said. He put his mouth on her right nipple and drew on it, caressing it with his tongue. After a few minutes he did the same with the left. She took his hand, brought it down to the opening between her legs, separated his index finger from the others and rubbed herself with it. "Like this," she said. "Do it like this." He slipped his finger into the tight, wet space, and rubbed. She moved with the motion of his hand, her firm stomach undulating up and down. She took his hand away, pulled him on top of her, and he slipped into her, his buttocks pushing him in, in and out, the surging feeling returning to his loins, the mattress springs groaning with the movement of their bodies until a shudder of release ran through his body and she cried out with pleasure. They slept after that. At the first light of day, she woke him as she had before, and they did it again.

Ellingwood returned in the late morning. Jimmy was sitting in the shed sharpening a scythe. He worked hard at it, drawing the stone back and forth across the blade. He was sure that his guilt was splashed all across his face, and he felt helpless to do anything to remove it.

"We won't be needin' that for some time," Ellingwood said. If he saw any clue in Jimmy's demeanor as to what had gone on in his absence, he gave no sign of it.

"Just staying busy," Jimmy said.

"Good thing. Winter lingers in these parts. Having nothin' to do can drive some to distraction and also land 'em in trouble." Ellingwood spoke in a flat, impersonal voice, his usual tone, and betrayed no suspicion.

There were times after that, snatched moments when Jimmy lay with Mrs. Ellingwood, but that first night after Ellingwood returned, Jimmy was racked with remorse and fear. He stretched out on his bunk, unable to sleep, said an Act of Contrition, and promised himself that if he escaped detection, he would never go near her again. Soon his anxiety gave way to the overwhelming desire to be with her. He wondered at her ability never to reveal the slightest disquiet in front of her husband. Once, Ellingwood came home unexpectedly, and the lovers barely had time to get their clothes on before he was through the door. She greeted him in a calm, disinterested way, as though she were in the middle of her chores. Jimmy left as quickly as possible, afraid that Ellingwood would notice his burning red face.

In the spring they planted wheat and potatoes, and the weather was fine, with just the right amount of rain. Jimmy began to think about how he could sneak away and make his way east. He had no money, nor did Ellingwood ever mention the possibility of his being paid. He thought of telling Mrs. Ellingwood about his desire, but the more he was with her the more he noticed how little interest she had in him outside of bed. He suspected that the attitude of casual indifference she assumed toward him in front of her husband wasn't a pretense but her true feeling.

Returning from a day of bone-gathering with Ellingwood, Jimmy saw a horse and buggy tied up in front of the sod house. Inside the house they found Harold Karst, the owner of the stable in town. A tall, muscular man with thinning blond hair, he was one of the few people in the area who seemed prosperous. Ellingwood didn't appear surprised to find Karst there. They shook hands and stepped out into the yard. Mrs. Ellingwood busied herself in a corner of the room, saying nothing. When the two men came back in, Ellingwood said, "It's all settled, Jim, you'll be staying with Mr. Karst from now on. Town is a better place for a boy like you than a lonely farm like this."

"I'll take the horse back into town," Karst said.

"And we'll bring Jim in the morning," Mrs. Ellingwood said, "in the buggy." She smiled at Karst, and Jimmy knew that the buggy had been given in exchange for his indenture to the livery owner but that there had been an even more intimate exchange between Karst and Mrs. Ellingwood.

"We'll miss you," Ellingwood said. "You've been a good hand, more than I hoped when I first laid eyes on that poor waif from New York City."

"Boy," said Karst to Jimmy, "there'll be none of the pampering with me that you've had here, a fine lady to cook and care for you. With me you'll learn but one lesson: the value of hard, honest work. And let me warn you now, first thing, to put out of your head all thoughts of running away. There's been a lot of that among the children brought here, and the good people of this territory are fed up with such ingratitude, and determined to put a stop to it."

"Don't worry about him," Ellingwood said. "Jim is as loyal as a dog."

Jimmy hardly slept that night. He thought about stealing a horse and running away but had neither money nor any idea of where to go. He was dressed and sitting on the side of his bunk when Ellingwood came in.

"Want some coffee?" Ellingwood asked.

Jimmy shook his head.

"Suit yourself. We'll be leaving in a bit."

Although it was early, it was already a hot, still day. The sky was empty and almost white. Ellingwood hitched up the buggy and brought it to the front of the house. Mrs. Ellingwood came out and walked around it, caressing it with her hand. She got in next to her husband. Jimmy sat next to her, the small bundle containing all his possessions on his lap.

They were about half a mile from the house when the sky darkened: In the distance, a low cloud spread like black ooze. "What's that?" Jimmy said to Ellingwood.

"What's what?"

Jimmy pointed. "That cloud."

Ellingwood squinted at the horizon. "Oh my God," he said. He dragged on the reins and drew the buggy around, flaying the horse with his whip. They dashed back toward the house. The wind began to blow, grass and dust whipping ahead of them as though fleeing the black cloud. The light faded, and it seemed night was coming on. Ellingwood beat the horse savagely. Ahead loomed the low profile of the sod house. Mrs. Ellingwood was screaming, but the noise of the wind had become so tremendous it devoured her words. They were only a few hundred yards from the house, and Ellingwood began tugging on the reins to slow the horse but the terrified animal was out of control. He grabbed the brake, pulled, and the buggy went into a wild skid and turned over. Jimmy jumped just before the vehicle flipped. He rolled across the grass and lay for a minute in total, unrelieved darkness, the wind roaring in his ears. He got up and ran toward where he thought the house should be. Suddenly he found himself at the front door. He kicked it in, threw himself on the floor and rolled under the bed.

The earth itself seemed to be writhing, and the wind invaded the house, smashing crockery and glass, tossing the cupboard to the floor, and flinging iron pots against the walls. After a few minutes the noise diminished, and gradually it died away, but Jimmy lay there for a long time before he crawled out from under the bed and looked around. Half the roof was gone, and the sun was shining in. He walked outside. A short distance away was the overturned buggy, but there was no sign of either the horse or the Ellingwoods.

Jimmy went back in and searched the house. He took a rifle and a blanket and set out walking, opposite the direction of town. In the early afternoon a farmer stopped his wagon and offered Jimmy a ride. The man was dazed. He was looking for his two sons, who had been out scavenging bones when the storm struck. He drove Jimmy a long distance to a town where the railroad stopped. They never saw any sign of the man's two sons. In town, Jimmy sold his rifle to a German teamster. With some of the money he got, he bought a piece of pie and a cup of coffee. The coffee was rich and strong, not like the watery, bitter brew Mrs. Ellingwood made, and the smell stirred in him the memory of New York, open doors of restaurants, smells of food and good coffee everywhere. He was going home. He purchased a train ticket with the money he had left. It was only enough to take him a few hundred miles eastward, but he knew he would find someway to complete the journey, would do whatever it took, and that sooner or later he would be in New York, the old gang on the Bowery celebrating his return.

Cassidy ordered another round of drinks. "Sure, the real thing ruining this city is the war, no doubt about it. It's turned everyone dishonest, made speculation the only religion, and raised the nigger into a god on whose altars the Irish are to be sacrificed by the high priests of True Americanism and abolitionism."

Dunne paid for the drinks. One of the Gallagher brothers squeezed past, practically pushing Dunne into the other brother's arms.

"Nature's call," Cassidy said to Dunne, "even the deef must answer it."

Two officers came down the stairs, and many of the Trump's patrons began to jeer and hiss.

"One in every generation," Cassidy said. "One Judas to sell the Irish to the Devil." He dragged up a gob of phlegm from his throat, rolled it around his mouth, and spit it onto the floor. "There's our Judas, Colonel Robert Noonan."

Noonan walked with a slight limp. He went through the room to the tables in the rear and took no notice of the jeering.

"He sold hisself to the Republicans," Cassidy said. "Took their silver and gave them what they thought they'd never find, an Irishman willing to enforce the draft and coerce other Irishmen to free the very niggers who'll steal their jobs."

Noonan took his place at a table with other officers. The jeering grew louder. "The cheek of him," Cassidy said, "the bloody arrogance of a true peeler. On the docks of this city the niggers are killing innocent Irishmen, and the Army protects them while they do, and there's the man responsible, Pontius Pilate Noonan, washing his conscience with whiskey."

Dunne decided it was time to go. Cassidy would talk nonstop about the war and the draft, subjects Dunne had no interest in. He knew few who did. Except for the early days, when the Bowery had shared the city's delirium, the sporting crowd generally held that what happened in Virginia or Tennessee might as well be happening in Mexico. Of course, the newspapers were filled with it, and the docks, railyards, and whorehouses were jammed with soldiers. But save in places like the Union League Club or in the wealthy Republican neighborhoods or in the homes of those with sons, brothers, or fathers in the Army, the war seemed an increasingly distant echo that only occasionally commanded interest. The news of the draft was stirring things up, but in Dunne's opinion, only the slow-witted would let themselves be ensnared.

Dunne excused himself, said good night to Cassidy, nodded to the Gallaghers, and went upstairs. Tomorrow he would start finding out everything he could about Halsey. He walked down Broadway. Across from the towering façade of the Haughwout Building, a structure in which the builders had installed a "vertical railroad" to reach the upper floors, he stopped to see the time. He reached into his pocket to check his own watch against the building's clock, but it wasn't there. He searched his clothes, and as he did the image of the Gallagher brothers bumping him flashed into his head. An old trick, but they had performed it flawlessly.

Dunne was content to let them keep the watch. It was a small price to pay for being reminded never to put down your guard, a lesson that the likes of Capshaw and Morrissey wouldn't hesitate to teach in far more lasting ways.

II

SITTING ON THE THRONE in the middle of the semicircle of darkies, three to each side, Misters Fossil, Fingers, and Flossum to the right, Misters Bones, Blossum, and Biglips to the left, Mulcahey put his foot on the board that was raised slightly from the floor and fastened with a spring, pressed it down with a tapping motion, *tat, tat, rat-a-tat, tat,* strummed his banjo, and looked around at his fellow minstrels: Each sat bent forward with head inclined toward center stage, hand poised above banjo and tambourine, bow resting on fiddle strings, ready to go, waiting only to hear the music the interlocutor had chosen and joining right in at the opening notes of the "Clem Titus Jig," an Ethiopian minstrel version of the Irish reel "Young Arthur Daly," all rising in one well-rehearsed motion, rocking back and forth, swaying, shuffling, until ol' Mister Bones could take dis standin' still no mor' and let his feet follow the relentless metrical banging of Mulcahey's self-invented floorboard castanet, *rat-a-tat, rat-a-tat, rat-*

a-tat-tat-tat-tat-tat. When Bones reached stage right, he stopped with his back to the audience, turned slowly, and strutted in the opposite direction, a broad, exaggerated walk, his shoulders rolling from side to side, his knees reaching up to his chest, and the others fell in behind him, still playing their banjos, Mulcahey taking up the rear, a confusion of discomposed, gyrating marchers, which is why Daddy Rice used to insist, "Say what you like about minstrel music, ain't nobody ever going to get men to march off to war to it," and why Dan Emmett was so surprised when "Dixie," the walk-around he had written for Bryant's Minstrels, became the grandest military anthem of them all. It seemed nobody recognized its martial potential until the month the war started and the owner of the Varieties Theatre in New Orleans, lacking an audience for his production of *Pocahontas,* added a concluding extravaganza: a drill and march of *Forty Female Zouaves!!!,* the high-stepping chorus crossing the stage singing, "*Look a-way, look a-way, look a-way, Dixie's Land.*" The song swept across every corner of the South, the anthem of the Confederacy, the *Volkslied* of its people, a Broadway ditty.

From the other side of the footlights, Mulcahey could hear the murmuring beneath the noise of the music and the dancing. Hadn't been more than a dozen sold-out houses in the last year. Just his luck. No sooner had he climbed to the top mast of minstrelsy than the whole damn ship began to fill with water. The first week he had signed on with Brownlee's, the troupe had been hired to play at a ball at the St. Nicholas Hotel, a costume party with the Mayor present and the ballroom packed with people stamping their feet and clapping. The troupe paraded across Broadway in the Advent twilight, a slender, hesitant light, playing their banjos as they went, the traffic coming to a halt to let them pass, a pack of prancing children trailing behind, the whole city seeming to enjoy the frolic, and out of the corner of his eye Mulcahey saw, plastered on the side of a building, a playbill for Brownlee's, his name in big black letters.

There had been good months after that. Until the spring almost every night had been a full house, and business had been brisk even after the war started. But it was that one night that summed up all the others, his name there on the wall in front of him, the St. Nicholas up ahead, half of Broadway stopped to see "The Ethiopian Sensation."

A long time since Mulcahey had to work at minstrelsy: It came easy now, and even the ritual of the burnt cork seemed as natural as putting on clothes. Still got that flutter in his stomach when the curtain came up, but it left soon as he spoke his first line. For a while he drew his enthusiasm from the audience. He could sense their anticipation on the other side of the footlights, hayseeds and apple-knockers reveling in their first experience of the Rialto, workingmen anticipating some fun, journalists, politicians, pugilists, financiers, the habitués of Broadway, men in search of stories, laughter, noise, music, movement. They were still around, but now they spent their time socializing in concert saloons, or in theatres where they could see the likes of Edwin Booth, or whore-hunting in goosing slums like Jim Ryan's, or rubbing elbows with the riffraff in Bob Butler's Theatre (MALE ONLY) or the Adelphi (LADIES MUST BE ESCORTED). The heart of the Rialto was moving north, to Fourteenth Street, and minstrelsy was being left behind like one of those wagons that broke down on the trek west, the occupants trying to decide whether to try to repair the thing and get it back on the trail or to hop aboard some other wagon, if they could, before night fell and the savages did them in.

A week ago, Mulcahey had visited the Adelphi at the invitation of Bill Wehman. He stopped by on his night off, was let in the stage door, and stood in the wings. The show opened with a short minstrel skit performed by two noodles in third-rate blackface, the paste erratically applied around their eyes and lips. One had a thick German accent. They shuffled their feet and bent their knees like amateurs trying to imitate what they had seen at a real minstrel show. The audience was mostly soldiers; they hooted and cheered. The minstrels were followed by a quartet of "Swedish Serenaders," four females in blond wigs who had never been north of Central Park. They sang a medley of songs until the audience got restless, and then Bill Wehman, who rivaled Daddy Rice in his love of the grape, came on as "Paddy Murphy," paragon of the hod-carrying race, in battered hat and threadbare coat. He stopped in the middle of the stage and gave a start, as though surprised to find himself in front of an audience.

"Faith," he said, "sure, dere ye be! And ain't I been searching da place fer ye! I'm comin' from havin' da most illigant time at da Astor House itself. Sure, dere were five gentlemen counting mesilf. Dere was me, for one; the Kelly brothers, for two; Terry Moran, three; and Jack O'Leary, four."

He lifted his hat and scratched his head.

"By Saint Patrick, now I know dere were five, yerra dere were." He held up his hand and counted with his fingers. "Mesilf, *one,* an' Moran, *two,* an' O'Leary, *three,* an' the two Kellys, *four.*"

Wehman went on with his impersonation of Paddy for as long as he drew a response, and once he sensed the audience had had enough, he took off his coat and threw it on the ground. The minstrels reappeared and played a hornpipe, and old Wehman did some vigorous leg- and footwork, jumping so high that the audience broke into applause. When he stopped, he put one hand on his heart and stepped up to the edge of the stage. He dropped his Irish voice and spoke slowly as he struggled to catch his breath. "Gentlemen, we come . . . to the part . . . of the . . . show . . . that will take . . . *your* breath away."

He moved off the stage, and the curtain behind him rose to reveal the first of the evening's *Living Tableaus from History and the Bible,* a tree of papier-mâché in the center, an apple hanging on one branch, a large snake of black cloth coiled around its trunk, and a woman in flesh-colored tights standing on one leg and reaching for the red fruit, her breasts bulging forward, her hefty thigh arching up into the fullness of her rump. Stood as still as she could until the curtain came down. The boisterous crowd settled into silence. There was a procession of tableaus: *"Queen Bathsheba," "Helen of Troy," "The Slave Girls of Babylon," "Es-*

ther Before Ahasuerus," "The Abduction of the Sabines," "Cleo-patra in Her Bath," all composed of stock-still assemblages of women in tights, straining, grasping, reclining, every posture revealing the convexities and concavities of their bodies. It was a public display less explicit than what was available on the second floor of the Trump but considerably cheaper and far more accessible.

After the show, Mulcahey and Wehman went to Tom Kingsland's, New York's minstrels' bar, on Broome Street. Men in blackface threw down a refresher before returning to their roles. At the far end of the bar stood Henry Wood, the Mayor's brother, a promoter for the Christy Minstrels. He patted backs and bought drinks, working the room in political style. Mulcahey pushed his way to a small booth in the rear. Wehman shook so badly he held his glass in both hands. "Christ," he said, "sometimes I ain't too sure I'm going to make it to the end of the evening, but it's a funny thing, I been in this all my life and never once have I seen anyone die on stage—not for real, anyways—and I've seen the walking dead themselves go out there, men you'd figure could never take the strain, but somehow they never cashed in on stage. Seems like it's some kind of rule of nature, and I suppose it applies to me same as to the others."

"You had a good house," Mulcahey said. "Full up."

"I don't know where it will all lead." Wehman wiped some whiskey off his chin with the back of his hand, then licked it as a cat does its paw. "When I started in the business, you had the Broadway Circus, the Park Theatre, the Anthony Street Theatre in the Five Points, and the Chatham Garden, period. They built the Bowery Theatre the year I got my first real part. It was in *Othello*. Edmund Kean played the Moor. I was Cassio. Nobody wanted the part of Iago because those were the days before they'd imported Drummond's limelight from London. They used floats, big tubs of oil with wick-holders coming out of the bottom, and the light they gave wasn't particularly strong, at least not enough for Kean, who regularly took his anger out on Iago, every night half strangling him to death with the audience thinking it was part of the play and cheering him on. I've seen a lot of changes in my day."

"But minstrelsy is here to stay," Mulcahey said. He threw back his whiskey and waved the bartender over. "Leave the bottle," he said. He poured Wehman a full glass.

"Nothing's here to stay," Wehman said. "No memory, no man, no manner of doing things, not in this town." He lifted his glass like a chalice, hands a little steadier than before, and poured the contents down his throat.

Wehman started telling a story he had told many times before, about how in '49 he landed the biggest role of his career as Banquo in *Macbeth,* starring England's leading tragedian, William Charles Macready, at the Astor Place Opera House. Wehman was a man full of stories and reminiscences, but sooner or later he always came back to this one.

"I thought that sharing the stage with the likes of him would lift me into the pantheon of America's illustrious actors. But Edwin Forrest used this occasion for his own ends. Claimed to have been slighted and insulted as an American actor in London, and since he'd already planned his own production of *Macbeth* for the new Broadway Theatre, he said Macready was spitting square in the eye of Cousin Jonathan. He and his cronies got the city all fired up about this affront to American manhood, and the next thing you know, before Birnam wood did come to Dunsinane, a screaming, howling mob of assorted riffraff, sailors, thieves, fishmongers, and the worst sort of scum surrounded the Astor Place Opera House. They heaved paving blocks through the windows, and when the police tried to escort us out, the mob drove them off. We figured we were done. Then the militia arrived. Turned into a massacre. Twenty-one killed, twice that number wounded, scores arrested. Macready snuck out of the city dressed as a woman. And it was sworn among all true Americans that none of the traitorous dogs who appeared with Macready would ever be allowed again on an American stage. They circulated the playbills from *Macbeth* with skull and crossbones next to my name. And you know what? Three months later nobody remembered I'd been in the play, and six months later I was playing opposite Anna Bishop in *Esmeralda* at the sold-out opening of Tripler Hall. In other cities, the people would have never forgot. But this town ain't got no taste for what was. Ain't nothing you can count on except the fact that you can count on nothing, and that ain't going to change ever, not in New York."

Wehman had a thin, worn face, the remnants of his good looks still there in his high cheekbones and pale blue eyes. He had played in comedy, tragedy, minstrel shows, whatever was available, but had never come closer to glory than Banquo to Macready's Macbeth. The whiskey relieved the tremor in his hands. He sipped it instead of gulping it.

"The war's the problem," Mulcahey said. "All this jawing about slavery and the draft, but once it's over and things get back to the way they were, minstrelsy is going to be bigger than ever, I'm sure of it."

Mulcahey drummed his fingers on the table, *tat-tat, tat-tat, rat-a-tat-tat-tat*. He had invented the floorboard castanet. Minstrelsy was his life. The first time he appeared on stage was in 1848, with Jack Diamond. He was right off the boat, trying to figure out how not to starve to death and how to get out of Boston, a town he detested from the moment he set foot in it. The Yankee disdain and disgust for papists and Paddies was as thick as the fog that enfolded the harbor. He got a job sweeping out a saloon and was allowed to sleep in the carriage house behind it. Right across the way was the rear of a theatre, and for the first month Mulcahey was at his job, the theatre was empty. But then the bills went up announcing the appearance of "THE GENIUS OF HEEL AND TOE—JACK DIAMOND—THE NATCHEZ NIGGER BOY."

As Mulcahey crossed the alley that first night, he could hear the banjos, loud, happy, and see the light as it spilled out the windows and doors to turn the darkest corner of this dourest of cities into a place of happy expectation. The music washed up against the redbrick walls and rose into the nocturnal emptiness.

Even before he reached the stage door and was bathed in its rectangular glow, even before he caught his first glimpse of black-faced Jack Diamond gliding in front of the footlights, arms outstretched, he knew he wanted to be a part of whatever this was, a feeling that resonated from the depth of his soul to the soles of feet, a baptism by desire. He watched every night for two weeks. Made living in Boston almost tolerable, and on the afternoon of the last day of Diamond's scheduled appearances, just as the grim realization that this light was about to go out of Mulcahey's life, the only light he had, he overheard two stagehands as they stood by the back of the theatre and discussed what Diamond would do now that his fellow heelologist and minstrel partner, Danny Byrne, had gotten so drunk that he had fallen down the stairs in his hotel and broken his foot. Mulcahey's hand trembled as he took axle grease and spread it across his face, an impromptu blackface, some of it getting on his tongue and leaving a foul, oily taste in his mouth. He ran to the hotel, people turning and pointing at the crazed, grease-smeared urchin tearing through the streets, another symptom of the immigrant influx that had turned Boston Harbor into an American version of Botany Bay, a polluted depository for the diseased and disorderly Irish, 37,000 of them invading the city of 115,000 in the single year of 1847.

Mulcahey flew past the desk and the startled clerks to the room where the stagehands had said he would find Jack Diamond. He made the sign of the cross and knocked. There was no answer. He knocked again, harder. He could hear footsteps coming up the stairs. It had to be the desk clerk. He banged with the flat of his hand. The door opened. Diamond was scratching his head and yawning. Mulcahey started dancing, imitating what he had seen on stage, leaning forward with his hands almost touching the ground, shuffling backward, his arms starting to sway from side to side, the momentum building, the pace picking up. Diamond told the clerk to stand back. *Give the boy room, that's it, heel, toe, shuffle right, shuffle left, rat-a-tat-tat-tat.* Mulcahey got the part. They left Boston the next day.

*

"Everything has its own modicum of days, a beginning, a middle, and an end," said Wehman. "Trouble is that the days go so fast in this city that it's over before it begins." There was a globule running from the right corner of his mouth down to his chin, a pendulous dribble of spit and whiskey, the product of a mouth trained to project a voice into the metropolis's auditoria. He wiped his chin once more, and again licked the back of his hand. Mulcahey poured him another glass.

"The trick is, Jack, finding what people will pay to see. Garbage ain't much different from gold as long as people are willing to pay for it. Willingness to pay! That's the Philosophers' Stone, the thing that can turn lead into gold. If people are willing to put their money down to see or possess or let something, then that thing has value, no matter its size, shape, condition, or smell."

The dribble was back on Wehman's chin. They stood up to leave. Wehman almost fell. "My leg's asleep," he said. He held Mulcahey's arm and shook his leg. After a minute he sat back down. "It'll take a little bit of time before I can walk on it. Nothing serious. Happens pretty regular."

"I'm in no hurry," said Mulcahey. He looked down at the top of Wehman's head, strands of hair pulled across the freckled skin, the skull of a tuckered old man who risked a burst blood vessel every time he put himself through the paces of his tired routine. Banquo's ghost. Here but not here. A broken-down player in a back-alley theatre with an audience that barely paid him any attention.

"You okay?" Mulcahey said.

"Sure," Wehman said. "Just a minute more."

Mulcahey could see the aura of death around the bowed head, a clear, pure light that seemed to emanate from inside it. *Caveat histrio:* the has-been's fate, a lonely death, on stage or off, his haunted head a mirror for Mulcahey to peer into.

This afternoon, Mulcahey and Eliza had gone down to the Methodist church on John Street for Wehman's funeral. A church without kneelers or statues, a bare place made barer by the small number of mourners sprinkled about. Wehman had been right about actors not dying on stage, but just barely. Wasn't more than a foot or two off stage when he keeled over dead. The minister obviously hadn't known him. In a Catholic service, with the incense and vestments and the Latin, that wouldn't have mattered much. A funeral Mass made even the humblest jack seem important, especially when it was sung, the priest in his black chasuble intoning the Dies Irae as if the Almighty were rearranging heaven and hell over this one death.

The main part of the service consisted of the minister's sermon. He kept referring to Wehman as a tragedian. He seemed to think the departed had never played in anything save *Hamlet* or *Macbeth*. He never mentioned the hundred-odd roles Wehman had played—singer, dancer, minstrel, comedian—or the Adelphi or the Astor Place Riot, the tragicomic olio that brought Wehman to the grave. On the way out of the church, Mulcahey rapped three times on the coffin lid. "More luck to you in the next world, old-timer," he whispered.

Tonight, the Adelphi had opened as usual, Wehman dead, buried, and replaced, and those unable to get in had come to Brownlee's. They were filled with alcohol and desire, the thought of what they were missing, every curve and motte, every mountain and crevice, the lay of the female landscape, women the likes of which you would never find in country towns. They moved in their seats. Restless. It was an itch Mulcahey couldn't scratch. The noise and motion of the opening parade kept their attention, but you couldn't keep that up all evening; and when the darkie dialogues began, the stories and the jokes, the noises from the seats grew louder, the shuffling of feet, an anxious, angry energy, the occasional shout, *Come on, nigger boys, let's see some leg, bring on the girls!*

At the end of the strutting and dancing, the minstrels came back to their chairs, Bones and Biglips squabbling over who sat where. Mulcahey pulled a big red satin handkerchief from his pocket and dusted off his throne with a broad sweep. He put one foot up on his seat, polished his shoe with the hanky, then did the other shoe. When he was finished, he blew his nose loudly into the satin square.

"Be seated, gentlemens," he said.

Squirt's head was framed in the prompter's box directly in front of Mulcahey. Mulcahey placed three fingers on his lips, and Squirt signaled back the same way to indicate he had the appropriate script. Mulcahey had never needed a prompter's support until recently. Usually he improvised, randomly starting stories, skipping from joke to joke, presuming the end men had a full command of the repertoire, but there had been times, only a very few but they had happened, when his mind stood still like one of those old horses that the cartmen used, a horse that pulled faithfully for years till one day it stopped dead in the middle of Broadway, refusing to move despite the merciless urgings of the whip.

"Well, dere, Mister Bones, I hear you been trabelling," Mulcahey said.

"Oh, yeah, I trabel all de time," said Bones.

Mulcahey watched Squirt follow the text with his finger. Eliza had taught Squirt to read. Mulcahey thought she was wasting her time, too much of the squirming, fidgeting darkie in the boy, but Squirt had amazed everyone with the ease and skill he demonstrated. Read everything he could get his hands on. Nothing seemed too difficult for him.

"Where you trabel dis time, Mister Bones?"

"I was up at de famousest resort in dis whole world. Got de best food I eber tasted, and de accommonations was widout paralong."

"Oh, I see, you been to Saratoga!"

"Saratoga? Who say dat? I been in Sing Sing!"

One of the minstrels strummed his banjo. Mulcahey pumped his floorboard castanet. *Rat-a-tat, rat-a-tat.*

They weren't laughing, at least not very hard. Mulcahey strummed his banjo and tapped the castanet again. Give them another song. *All you delineators of the Sable Race of the South, up! Out of your seats! Move dem feets! Keep the show movin'!*

The minstrels moved in unison, a synchronized shuffle, up on the toes, slap the left foot on the floor, slide the right foot forward, back, without lifting it from the floor, now the other way around. In chorus they sang:

> *We New York niggers thinks we's fine,*
> *Because we's drink de genuine,*
> *De Dixie niggers dey lib on mush,*
> *And when dey laugh, dey say, "Oh, Hush!"*

Mulcahey put his banjo on his chair. He moved out in front of the other darkies, right in front of the prompter's box, and let his legs follow the music that came from behind him. He spun around in a circle and fell to one knee:

> *I'se de nigger dat don't mind no troubles,*
> *Cause dey ain't nuffin' mor' dan bubbles*
> *De only ambition dat dis nigger feels*
> *Is showing de science of da heels.*

He got back on his feet, and they all made another parade around the stage. When they returned to their seats, there was a new altercation over who sat where, Flossum and Fingers trying to squeeze into one chair, and Flossum landing on his rear. Mulcahey looked down at the prompter's box. At first he thought his vision had retained the intense whiteness of the footlights, creating the glow that surrounds the first object seen after looking into a bright light. He closed his eyes for an instant, then slowly opened them. The glow remained around Squirt's head, that same incandescence that had hovered around Wehman's. Mulcahey realized that the stage was silent. He picked some notes on his banjo. He waited for something to come to mind. From inside the prompter's box, Squirt whispered something. Mulcahey looked at him. The light came from inside Squirt's head, that's the way it seemed, hovering around his skull, a perfect outline. Mulcahey searched his brain for a joke, but there was only a translucent blankness.

Squirt raised his voice: "Mister Flossum, you eber been in lub?"

Mulcahey repeated it.

Flossum said, "You means, has I eber felt my heart burn?"

Mulcahey knew the next line by himself: "I don't means does you likes yer gal's cookin', I mean lub . . ."

The light persisted. Mulcahey the Prophet. The Boy Seer. He had been born with the caul, the inner fetal membrane had covered his head at birth. The women attending his mother had rushed out to tell his father, and the news spread throughout the whole village: a child born with the veil. His father buried the membrane beneath the doorstep. A blessing on this family. A child who could see things hidden from mortal eyes.

"Be a long time since I been in lub," said Flossum.

"How long?"

"Oh, since about half past eleben dis mornin'."

"But how you know it lub and not infatunation?"

"When I'se in lub, I'se always does de same thin'. I goes over to de gal dats caught my fancy and I'se whisper somethin' soft in her ear."

"Somethin' soft?"

"Yes, siree, I'se put my big lips rights next to her pretty little ear, and I sez, 'Mashed pertaters.' "

"And dey likes dat?"

"Likes dat? Why, my gals lub mashed pertaters!"

Squirt was mouthing the words, looking down at the text, then up at Mulcahey. Squirt's head was in constant motion, but the light remained.

At first Jack Mulcahey had been a disappointment to the villagers. Although born with the caul, he could tell them nothing about the future. At night, when they came back from the fields, some of the old men and women would sit by the fire in his father's cabin and wait for the small boy to start uttering prophecies, or at least to tell them what kind of weather or crops to expect. But the infant Jack never rewarded their patient silences, and in time they stopped coming.

The summer he was twelve, his father died of pneumonia and the following fall Jack joined men from the townland in the annual migration to Scotland for the potato harvest. The morning they left, the men were silent as they gathered in the yard in front of the chapel, but Jack and the other boys his age were filled with excitement. Some of them had received their first pair of brogues for the trip, and ran ahead amazed at how heavy and awkward their feet felt. They walked all morning carrying their small bundles of clothes and food before they reached the port where they were to find passage to Scotland, the newly shod already limping because of the way the leather rubbed against their skin. They waited by the pierside in the sunshine, the boys wrestling with one another, the men sitting and smoking their pipes. A procession of livestock was loaded into the hold, and when the loading was complete, the crew called to the migrants in English, and they ran up the gangplank and sat in the middle of the deck, out of the sailors' way. One boy had brought his fiddle and played a tune. A few of the gentlemen passengers stood on the upper deck and watched them impassively.

About an hour away from land, the sky became dark and the sea began to roll. The migrants lay down on deck, and the crew flung them a huge piece of canvas, which they held above their heads. The sea grew more turbulent and the waves began to break over the deck. The rain lashed the canvas. From down below, in the safety of the hold, they could hear the fearful lowing of the cattle and the constant movement of hooves as the animals tried to keep their balance. Jack became wet to the skin, and grew so cold that he shook uncontrollably. One of the men gave him a drink of whiskey, but he vomited it. They put a blanket around him; it was soon as soaked as everything else. He was in a stupor. They were talking to him, but he couldn't understand what they were saying. The man who had given him the whiskey went up and pounded on the door of the pilot's house. A mate stuck his head out and said he was sorry but there was nothing he could do, regulations were regulations, and none of the potato pickers was to be allowed anywhere but on the deck of the ship. The others huddled around Jack to give him the protection and warmth of their bodies, and rubbed his arms and legs. He surrendered to an overpowering exhaustion. He lay in utter darkness. Slowly he became aware of a soft hiss, the inhaling and exhaling of something so close that its warm breath touched the side of his face. He sensed that whatever it was was hunched close to the ground like an animal set to pounce, and he held himself perfectly still, sure that the slightest sign of life would be a provocation. When he awoke, he was next to a fire. The others had taken him into a fishing shanty on the Scottish pier where the boat had landed, wrapped him in a dry tarpaulin, and put him as close as possible to the fire.

In the morning he felt weak and light-headed, and there was a buzzing in his ears that would persist for several days, but otherwise he was recovered and walked with the others in search of work. They broke into groups and spread across the countryside to offer themselves to the local farmers. It was a good crop and there was plenty of work. They moved from job to job. Most times they were allowed to sleep in the barns, but one farmer insisted they stay in an old half-wood, half-brick bothy, or shed, that had iron bars on the windows. The first night, after they were inside, the Scotsman barred the door behind them. They threatened to quit. The farmer said that being locked in was for their own good, that there was a great deal of local resentment in the neighborhood over the horde of ragged pickers, some of whom had stolen money and goods from their employers. They could be the objects of a misdirected retaliation, he explained. The men insisted that they wouldn't stand for being caged. They said that they weren't criminals and wouldn't be treated as if they were. Then begone, said the farmer, and since their work was unfinished, he would pay them nothing.

In the end they agreed to stay. There were nineteen of them, twelve men and seven boys, including Jack. They worked hard to get the harvesting done and be on their way. On the day they finished, they went to the farmhouse to be paid. The men went ahead, and Jack followed with the other boys. It was dusk, a red-black sky with a long, low streak of final sunlight on the horizon. Too tired to talk, they walked with their heads down. When Jack first saw the glow around the other boys' heads he thought it was from the twilight, but as they moved on he realized it was radiating from each head. The men took their pay, and tired as they were, rather than suffer the indignity of another night in the latched bothy they decided to set out on the road and sleep in the fields. The boys chose to stay. They would catch up with the men in the morning. Jack stood with the men. *Aren't you going to stay with us, Sean?* the boys asked. *We'll have some singing tonight, a good sleep, and tomorrow we'll be ready for the road. Come join us, Sean.*

He could perceive the presence of death. The thing ready to pounce. He knew who its victims would be. The judgment was already sealed. It couldn't be appealed or changed, he understood that as well, and the very fact that he could choose to leave meant the verdict didn't include him, that all he could do would be to stay and see it executed on the others. He left with the men. Reaching the ridge of the far hill, he stopped and turned. In the last light he could see the farmer barring the bothy door. *God's mercy on them.* In the morning the news reached them on the farm where they had found work that six young pickers had died in a fire in a bothy, a tragic accident.

On the way back to Ireland the weather was clear, the opposite of the journey over, and the men sat and smoked and talked about the boys who had died. They dreaded bringing the news to the families. We'd all be better off in America, one of them said. Such things don't happen there, unless of course the Indians should get you, but even then you'd die a free man defending what belonged to you.

They had a little money in their pockets and enough to eat. The sea was calm. They dreamed the bigger dream of a journey across the Atlantic, a place where they would no longer be migrant pickers, papists, tenants, men with a value less than cattle. In America you would own the land and everything it produced. In America there were no landlords, no tithes, no rent. The great open spaces of America lay over the horizon, exile in a distant, foreign land away from everything they knew, the people, the earth, the sky, an unreal place, a place that existed only in stories, and even if they would go, where would the passage money come from?

The Famine began the next year, and it killed any speculation about America. The people clung to what they had, desperate to keep it. Jack's family survived the first winter on what could be salvaged from the potato crop and on the livestock they slaughtered. The following winter Jack's mother died from the fever, and his two youngest brothers and sisters, and his granduncle, Malachi. The light was everywhere he looked, a country filled with people marked for death, and Jack feared he was marked as well. He kept a broken shard of mirrored glass that he had found and looked anxiously every day to see if the helmet of light had formed around his head. All he saw was his thin face, a soft down forming on his forehead, his sunken, fearful eyes.

The people passed beyond panic and anger. As the deaths mounted, a resignation settled over many of them, there was no way out, God's will be done. Occasionally wild rumors about an approaching army of Young Irelanders, a well-armed force with abundant supplies of food, would rouse the neighborhood, but the rumors were invariably false, and though they continued to circulate, they ceased to be listened to. Only a miracle could save them from starvation, and in the middle of winter, with the government relief stations shut down and the potato crop totally putrefied and every chicken and pig long ago consumed, the miracle arrived. His Lordship's agent offered passage to America to all those of his tenants who would surrender their holdings. It was a gesture of His Lordship's concern over the reports of the grievous distress on his estate that had reached him in London, a two-year-long series of reports that had gone unanswered until the agent had appended a note explaining that under the operation of the amended poor law, His Lordship was personally responsible for poor rates on all holdings below a four-pound evaluation. The agent explained that by his calculations it would cost the estate three pounds per annum to support a person in the workhouse, while for a single charge of five pounds that same person could be transported to North America. His attention drawn at last to the suffering of his tenantry, His Lordship, remembering their innocent and happy ways when he had visited among them several years before, authorized the offer of emigration to Canada.

Jack and his remaining younger brother and sister were in the first group to go. They were loaded on the *Duke of Cumberland*. A rotting antique hull that had been launched in the last year of the Seven Years' War, the *Duke of Cumberland* in its prime had carried a company of 120. Given the exigencies of conditions in Ireland, 230 of His Lordship's tenants were put aboard.

The weather was bad from the day they embarked, rain and clouds obscuring the land so that they barely had a sense of leaving. By the second day the pitching seas left most of them sick, and willingly forgoing the ration of barley and pease they were given to eat. By the end of the first week the deaths started. *Fiabhras dubh,* typhus, the black fever. People's skin turned dark; they appeared to be drunk. The quarters became rank with liquid stool and vomit. The crew disappeared and then one morning reappeared and roused everyone out of their wooden bunks and splashed the place down with buckets of seawater. Jack's sister died that night; his brother the next afternoon. They were put in a single canvas sack, which was weighed down with Belgian blocks, ballast intended as paving stones for the streets of Montreal, and tossed overboard. People lay listlessly in the bunks, rolling back and forth against one another, and since they had ceased reporting deaths to the captain, there was a daily inspection by the crew to find and dispose of the corpses.

Jack lived on deck. The mates kicked him and tried to force him to go below, but every time they threw him down he climbed back out until they finally gave up and simply ignored him. He slept under the stars and spent all day watching the sea. One of the mates befriended him. He gave Jack an apple to eat, and when he was on the night watch he allowed Jack to stand with him. In the beginning Jack found it hard to understand the mate's speech, but gradually it became easier and he came to love the sound, American speech, faster than the English spoken in Ireland, more clipped and to the point, and spoken through the nose. The mate came from a city called Troy, on the river Hudson. He was the man who baptized Sean Mulcahey "Jack." "Sean," he said, "ain't a name for an American boy, and John ain't much better, you'll never meet an American boy going around calling himself John. No, it's going to be Jack, that's what you are going to be from now on."

In late June, five weeks since leaving Ireland, they saw land. Forty-eight people had died on the passage over, one fifth of those who had sailed. Many were still sick, but everyone came on deck to see the coast of North America, the shores of Canada. They carried up the infirm and those too frail to walk, and their spirits were lifted by the sight of the green shore, the wooded headlands of the great continent. When they entered the mouth of the St. Lawrence they could see the land at close range, and the trees seemed so much larger than anything in Ireland, the forest so untamed, that they watched with equal parts awe and anticipation. The American mate told Jack that before they proceeded to Quebec they would have to stop at the quarantine station on Grosse Isle, where the sick would be treated and those well enough transported westward.

They arrived at Grosse Isle while the river was covered with mist. It was morning and the weather had turned extremely warm. Jack saw the masts of other ships poking above the mist. They dropped anchor. The air was filled with a foul odor that Jack assumed was a river smell, stagnant water, rotting leaves, and wood. Anyone who was still fit came up from below. Strung across the rigging of the nearby ships was what looked like a collection of pennants that had been shredded into rags by the wind. Jack climbed up onto the railing of the *Duke of Cumberland* for a better look. The pennants turned out to be trousers and shirts and shawls and skirts, the laundered tatters of the other ships' passengers. The *Duke of Cumberland*'s captain, who had hardly been seen through the voyage, appeared on deck. He ordered a boat to be lowered, and four crewmen rowed him off into the mist.

The stench of the river had become almost overpowering. Jack yelled over to the nearest ship. Nobody answered. He yelled again and heard the echo of his own voice. There was a ghostly quality to the other ship as it rode at anchor and slipped in and out of the mist. Jack put his legs through the railing and sat with his chin resting on his forearm. After a few minutes, someone appeared on deck. Jack called out. A boy his own age appeared on the opposite railing, a redheaded skeleton, shirtless, his trousers tied with string.

"What ship are ye?" Jack yelled.

The boy stood silently. Jack yelled louder. The boy stepped up onto the rigging. He stayed there for a moment, then let go and went down feetfirst into the water. Jack leaned over as far as he could to watch the boy swim, but the mist was thickest above the water and obscured his view. He listened, but there was no sound of swimming, only the water lapping against the sides of the ships. He waited and watched a long time, but there was never any sign of the boy.

When the captain returned, he had a loud argument with the crew. They demanded to be paid and allowed to make their own way to Quebec. They said that their work was done and they wouldn't go near Grosse Isle. The captain refused to pay them, and they disappeared into their quarters.

The passengers had brought up from below everything that they could carry, and the deck was littered with clothes and bedding. The sick lay all about. In the late morning, the sun burned away the mist and they could see that the river was crammed with ships, as many as thirty between them and Grosse Isle. The sun became burning and intense, and a swarm of flies and stinging insects descended, driving the people back down to the quarters they had just left. An official in a blue jacket arrived and went about the entire ship, poking into every corner, sweating profusely as he went. He went over the passenger lists and wrote down names in a small book he carried. He said that a boat would be sent to bring the sick to the island, where they would be temporarily held in quarantine, but that the bodies of the dead must be brought there immediately. The captain said that the crew wouldn't go, so the official suggested enlisting some of the passengers. Jack and three others volunteered. They brought up the bodies of a small boy and an old woman who had died the night before. The bodies were wrapped in canvas and tied tightly with thick rope. The volunteers put the bodies into the bottom of the boat and rowed toward the island. They didn't have to strain, the current moved them along quickly, and Jack kept turning to glimpse where they were headed. He could see a large number of tents that stood out against the trees and made the place seem festive and inviting. The river smell became sharper as they neared the shore.

There were three rows of bodies laid by the spot where they landed, twenty bodies in a row. From a distance Jack had thought they were black men, but when he jumped ashore and helped pull the boat up, he could see the swelling, darkened corruption of bodies left too long in the sun. The flies made a frenzied hum in the air. Jack and the others took the canvas-covered bodies from the boat and moved up a slight incline toward the tents. The ground was covered with bodies. Jack presumed they were all dead, but then he saw that many of them were breathing and moving. Another man in a blue jacket walked down to meet Jack and his fellows. He asked what ship they were from and ordered them to follow him. They picked their way through the maze of bodies on the ground until they came to a shed, where the official gave them shovels and led them to a tent with open sides. Inside were rows of crudely made double-tiered bunks, two, in some cases three, people sharing a single space. The official went over and lifted a man by the shoulder. He told Jack to grab the feet. The man was dead, and so was the woman next to him. Above was a woman delirious with fever, praying and cursing in Irish.

Her bedding was soaked through with diarrhea, which had dripped down onto the corpses beneath.

Jack and his shipmates tried to dig graves in a field behind the tent, but the ground was so stony that they couldn't dig past the topsoil. They scraped and clawed at the earth with the shovels, rolled the bodies into shallow graves, and piled dirt and stones on top. The official said to keep at it, that he would return in a short while. As soon as he left, Jack and the others dropped their shovels and walked quickly back to the boat. The current was against them and they had to row hard before they reached the *Duke of Cumberland*. Jack lay on the deck. He ached. He knew it would be only a matter of time before he got sick.

That night, Jack made a raft of three planks lashed together. He stole a canvas bag, into which he put his shoes, and a tin of dry biscuits he had taken from the ship's hold. He had hoped to talk to the American sailor about Troy and how to reach it. He loved the sound of it: *Troy*. The mother of exiles. Great stone towers above a great river. But the American had disappeared with the rest of the crew. Jack would find his own way.

A bright, white moon made the river shine. Jack tied the canvas bag to the raft, which he then threw off the back of the ship. He ran the length of the deck and climbed up onto the railing. The raft turned in a slow circle, collided with the side of the ship, and moved into the current. Jack jumped, feetfirst, into the water, the blackness enveloping him, the brutal coldness stunning him. He sank helplessly for a few seconds, then he moved his legs and feet as rapidly as he could and pulled with his arms toward the surface. The moonlight surrounded him. He sucked in air, flailed around for the raft, and sank back into the darkness. He moved his arms and legs, struggling to rise, breaking into the moonlight again, gulping for air and getting a mouthful of water that made him choke. The river drew him down. It grew colder as he sank. His lungs felt as if they were about to burst. He reached up with his arms, his legs scissoring the water, and felt the raft sliding by. He lunged for it, grabbed the wood, and pulled himself up. He lay gasping. After a few minutes he began to shiver violently from the cold. He lay on his stomach and kicked his legs, gliding down the river, steadily moving closer to the southern shore.

He was exhausted, and fell asleep in the tall grass along the riverbank. The heat of the sun woke him. He stood up. He couldn't see the ships. He ate some of the biscuits he had stolen and set out on his way, southward, on a wide dirt road; he hid in the bushes whenever a wagon went by. He had already made up his mind that he wouldn't stop moving as long as he was in a country where the Union Jack flew: the double crosses of Saint Andrew and Saint George, the empire of hunger and servitude, the realm of eviction and emigration, a kingdom where the ability to discern the presence of death had ceased to matter because death was everywhere, around every head, death from starvation, fever, dysentery, from a sheer unwillingness to face any more of life, death in workhouses, on roadsides and in ditches, in the holds of ships, the dead lined up along the shore, in canvas bags weighed down with paving blocks, the anonymous dead already as forgotten as his brothers and sisters or the red-haired boy, Her Majesty's superfluous Paddies.

He slept in the fields, and although the days were hot, the nights were chilly. The country was immense, a landscape unlike anything he had ever seen, great forests that spread out as far as the horizon, endless meadows of wildflowers, with farms only rarely to be seen. He drank water from streams and husbanded his biscuits, walking until he lost track of the days, always half expecting to see the towers of Troy sticking out above the tree-tops, the American flag flying from the highest spot. Finally his biscuits ran out. He debated what to do. He was sure that a farmer would take one look at his rags and alert the authorities that some diseased immigrant from Grosse Isle had drifted into the area; they would try to send him back. But he knew he had no choice. It was either make himself known or starve to death. He decided to stop at the next farmhouse but walked all after-noon without seeing a sign of any settlement. He stopped by the roadside, exhausted and starving. The sun was setting. He sat with his back to a large rock and fell asleep.

When he awoke, it was pitch-black; he had no idea where he was. He lay still and listened. He stood up. Off in the woods, a few hundred yards away, he could see a campfire. He started walking toward it and caught the smell of roasting meat; the scent killed any sense of caution. He called out "Hello!" and walked faster until he was running. There was a silhouette standing before the flames, and just as he got near, he felt an arm around his neck. Someone had come behind him and pressed the sharp point of a knife into the flesh beneath his chin. The figure in front of him approached, silently. Neither did the person holding the knife speak. They brought him over by the fire and forced him to lie down. One of them knelt with his knees on Jack's back, and the other went through Jack's pockets and shirt.

They spoke in Irish. "The boy has nothing," the one searching his pockets said.

Jack said, in Irish, "I'm starving."

The knees came off his back. A hand grabbed him by the back of the neck and dragged him close to the fire. The smell of the meat was intense. He could hear the sizzle of fat dripping onto the hot coals. On the pile of rocks set around the fire was a tin plate with cooked meat on it. He reached for it. One of the men grabbed him by the hair and jerked his head back. Jack cried out in pain. The knife was right in front of his face, and the metal reflected firelight.

"What's your name?" one of the men asked.

"My name is Sean," Jack said. The man tightened his grip on Jack's hair.

"And what are you looking for, Sean?"

"Food. I'm starving."

"And where are you from?"

"Donegal," he said.

The hand tightened its grip on his hair. "Where are you walking from? How long have you been following us?"

"I haven't been following you at all. I was sleeping by the roadside and I saw the light. I'm starving."

"A terrible thing, starvation, we've all seen a lot of it, but this isn't a relief station, boy, so why don't you be on your way, and may God be with you."

The man let go of his hair, and Jack put his hand on his head and rubbed the soreness on his scalp. He got up on one knee, then stood. He was almost lifted off the ground by a kick that caught him square in the middle of his rear.

"You heard me," the man with the knife said. "Be on your way."

"I need food," Jack said in English. He started to cry, he couldn't help himself, and he blurted out the English words, unthinkingly, in a flood: "I'm desperate, please, anything, I'll go but just give me some scraps, I'll die out here unless you help me, in the name of Jesus, all I'm asking for is just a mouthful of food."

"You have the English, do you?" one of them asked, in Irish.

"I do," Jack said. "I speak it as well."

The man grabbed Jack by the shoulder and pulled him back over to the fire.

"Do you know where we are?"

Jack lied. "I do."

"Where?"

"The border is twenty miles to the south. Over to the west is a town called Cumberland." He made it up as he went along. "I was working there, but the authorities came searching for any of the Irish who ran away from Grosse Isle, so I set out to reach the United States."

The man pressed the knife against Jack's temple. "Don't lie to me."

"I'm not lying."

"If you've been working, why do you still have these ship's rags on you?"

"Was only there a day or so before I had to flee. I left in the middle of the night, without food or my pay. I had no choice."

"And you know where the border is?"

"I know the way and where to cross. It was explained to me by an Irishman in Cumberland, a safe route so I wouldn't be stopped. It's fearsome, he said, the way the Americans are guarding their border, turning back any immigrant who doesn't have money or a bond guaranteeing him against becoming a public charge."

"You know where to cross?" The knife pressed so hard against his skull that Jack cried out again.

"I swear by the Holy Trinity I do."

The other man said, "He might really know. Besides, he speaks English like he was one of them. We've got nothing to lose by finding out if he's telling the truth."

They let him have some meat. He ate, then lay down by the fire. In the morning he could see that the two men were as ragged as he was. They carried a canvas sack filled with provisions that Jack guessed they had stolen in the same way he had stolen the biscuits. They made him walk in front of them, and they ducked into the woods at the sight of a house or a horseman. On the second evening of their walking, they told Jack that the border had better be close or they would teach him about the consequences of telling lies. He swore once again that he was telling the truth. He woke while it was still dark and went through the sack they were carrying. He took some of their biscuits and a piece of cooked meat. He ran to the road and kept moving as fast as he could, alternately running and walking, until the sun was high overhead. He stopped in the woods to let a wagon go by. It was drawn by six horses and carried a great pile of logs. He ran behind it, pulled himself up, and hid among the logs. He rode all day, and when the wagon stopped at an inn he jumped off and slept in the woods. In the morning, unseen by the teamster, he jumped back on for another day's full journey.

He saw that the settlements of houses were closer together and the farms seemed more prosperous. On the third day they came into a valley, and the wagon stopped at a mill outside a substantial village. Jack started walking again. He climbed a hillside, hoping to see the American flag flying from some mast, but saw the Union Jack fluttering above a redbrick building. He kept walking. That afternoon he stole a shirt and a pair of pants that were strung out from a line in back of a farmhouse. He threw his rags into the woods. He put on the stolen clothes. The shirt was too big and the pants too short, but they were comfortable and clean, unpatched, without holes, and Jack felt less conspicuous than before. He ate apples from an orchard, the first he had had since the sailor had shared one with him on the ship.

The next morning he passed a small, neat cabin. A pair of boots were on the porch. He crept up to the porch and tried them on. He left behind the lumps of cracked, torn, perforated leather that had been his shoes.

He walked across meadows full of cows and through fields of furrowed earth, and his boots made him feel tall and fully grown and he imagined himself a Yankee farmer striding across his lands, a journey that would take all day. He found another road, and after about a mile he came around a bend. There was a white building with a steep roof and a pole jutting from it with a banner of red and white stripes, and white stars on a field of blue. Jack danced right there in the middle of the road, his boots kicking up small clouds of American dust.

There were wagons and carriages pulled up around the building. Jack looked through a window: Some sort of auction was going on inside. Men stood around what looked like a courtroom; some draped themselves over chairs, their legs dangling over the arms. They talked in loud voices and walked around as if they owned the building. They displayed none of the cap-in-hand hesitation that any tenant farmer in Ireland would have shown in entering such a place, eyes cast down, a proper deference in his voice, *Yes, milord; no, milord; I beg your pardon, milord.* These men sounded like the sailor from Troy, but there was an even more pronounced twang to their speech, and also something more American, even more direct and clipped and assertive.

The auction ended, and the men strolled out of the building and began to get into their wagons. Jack walked away and stood by the roadside, where the driveway met the road. A farmer with a gray-streaked beard pulled up next to him.

"Where ya headed, son?"

"Troy," Jack said.

The farmer laughed loudly. "Better get started. I'd say you got a ways to go." Jack nodded. He didn't know why *Troy* should sound so funny. He started to walk to hide his embarrassment. The farmer said, "Get in." He held out his hand and helped Jack onto the driver's bench.

"Where ya from?" the farmer asked.

Jack tried to imitate the tone of the men he had just heard talking, tried to speak like an American. "From Cumberland."

"That a town?"

"A small town. Most people never heard of it, even in Canada."

"Where ya from before that?"

Jack realized he hadn't done a very good job of disguising his accent. "I was born in Scotland. I came to Canada with my parents three years ago. Cumberland is mostly Scots."

"Where your parents now?"

"Still in Cumberland but my father's been sick and can't work, so they sent me to stay with my uncle in Troy."

The farmer looked over at Jack, then snapped the reins and made a loud *cluck cluck* noise. The horses moved faster. "Them parents of yours didn't send you with much, did they? No clothes but what's on your back? No food?"

"Oh, they did, but I was robbed."

"Robbed?"

"Two men with a knife. Happened day before last. They came on me at night. I offered to share my food, but they took everything I had, said I should be grateful they didn't slit my throat."

"Paddies, I'll bet anything. They were Paddies, am I right?" He looked at Jack again. Jack nodded. "For sure," he said.

"Pug-nosed louts, ain't a farmer in the country hasn't had

something swiped by them, clothes, food, boots. They'll take anything."

Jack looked the farmer in the eyes, unblinkingly. He was unsure whether the farmer was playing with him the way a cat does with a mouse. He considered jumping off the wagon and running away, but decided against it.

"Know the worst part of it?" the farmer said.

"What might that be?"

"They're a warning from God, a plague sent on us so we might learn to hear His word: 'Yea, there came a grievous swarm of flies into the land, and into its houses, and the land was corrupted by reason of the swarm of flies.' It's the plain truth. Swarming in our ports, swarming over the border, no doubt about it, and unless we return to godly ways of thinking and acting we'll be struck down just as sure as old Pharaoh was."

Jack let him talk. Obviously, the farmer had no idea of who was sitting next to him. They came to a crossroads, and the farmer stopped the wagon. He pointed straight ahead. "I'm going this way." He motioned with his thumb to his right. "That way is Troy."

"How far?"

"Two hundred miles, more or less, if ya run your finger straight across a map. Three hundred, I'd guess, on the road."

Jack was exhausted. He wanted to lie somewhere and sleep, sink down and not think about getting up. He was tired of being hungry, of walking, of seeking the walls of Troy. He remembered the emotionless plunge of the redheaded boy down into mist and water, no sound of struggle.

The farmer seemed to know what was on Jack's mind. "You got most of the state of New Hampshire and all of Vermont. Didn't your pappy give ya some idea of the distance ya had to go?"

"He said it was a long way, but I don't think he knew the distance."

"Well, I got a proposition for you. Been looking to hire a hand. Can't pay much, but I can give ya a place to sleep and your meals. Maybe ya can save up something to make up for what them Paddies stole."

Jack accepted the offer. The farmer, who lived alone, worked him hard, but he had a place to sleep in the barn, and there were milk and eggs to eat, peaches and apples, bread and cornmeal and chicken. He ate whatever he was given, gobbled it down, lying back afterward to enjoy the sensation of a full stomach.

One day, after the midday meal, Jack was on the barn roof hammering on new shingles when he saw two men coming up the road. He knew right away who they were. He flattened himself against the roof. He heard the farmer come out the front door of his house. He peeked over to watch. The farmer was carrying a musket, and his dog raced ahead and ran circles around the men, who stood there, their hats in their hands, their eyes on the dog. They looked older and smaller than Jack remembered. They were caked with dust, and their shirts were stained with dark pools of sweat. They were shoeless.

"Sir," said the one who had held the knife to his throat, "could you spare us water?" Jack heard the obsequiousness in the voice, the tentativeness of someone speaking in a language not his own, the man's eyes traveling from the dog to the farmer to the ground, his hand worrying the brim of his relic of a hat.

The farmer cradled the musket in his arms. "Sorry, boys," he said, "ain't got nothing I can spare." He shooed them with his hand, as if they were flies. "This is private property, so you best be getting along."

They walked back the way they had come. The farmer trailed behind them. He stood by the gate until they disappeared around a turn. He came back into the yard and called Jack down from the roof.

"Jack," he said, "there are Paddies in the neighborhood, so you have to keep an eye out and make sure none of them tries to sneak around and steal what he can."

By September, Jack felt rested and strong. He told the farmer he thought it was time he resumed his journey to Troy, and he asked for his pay. The farmer gave him two dollars for two months' work. Jack felt he was being underpaid to the point of being cheated, but he was eager to be on his way and said nothing.

"I got good news for you, Jack," the farmer said the next morning as the boy prepared to leave. "A cousin of mine is hauling freight down near Boston. He says he can take you as far as Manchester, and that will leave you in shooting distance of Troy. Says he'll do it as a favor to me."

The cousin came by in his wagon in the early afternoon. He introduced himself as O Ahaziah Fry. Jack climbed aboard. They traveled a pitted, rutted road and were jolted up and down. Jack wasn't sure he had heard the name correctly. The cousin repeated it. "O Ahaziah Fry. Second Kings, chapter nine, verse twenty-three," he said. " 'And Joram turned his hands and fled, and said, "There is treachery in the land, O Ahaziah." ' "

The roads were so bad that Jack thought the wagon might break apart. O Ahaziah said nothing more until they reached a smooth stretch.

"This will cost you a dollar."

"Your cousin said it was free. Said you were doing it as a favor to him."

"My cousin don't speak for me, nor me for him. And that dollar is payable now." Jack handed it over.

"I got apples and cheese in the sack behind you," O Ahaziah said. "Since you're a paying fare, you got a right to help yourself."

O Ahaziah said little over the next few days. They lived on apples and cheese, and slept under the wagon, O Ahaziah reading his Bible by the light of a lantern. When they reached Manchester, O Ahaziah said, "Might be better if you just stay aboard for Boston, that is, if you ain't going to keep any of your relatives waiting in Troy. I figure they probably gave up on you by now."

Jack hesitated. He had no idea how he would reach Troy. He had only a dollar in his pocket.

"Plenty of work for an enterprising boy in Boston," O Ahaziah said.

Jack knew nothing of Troy except that it was the home of

the first American he had ever met, a city on a river, walls, towers, great pennants atop them.

"Troy is still a distance," O Ahaziah said.

Jack told O Ahaziah he would travel with him to Boston. When they had passed through Manchester, O Ahaziah said, "I got to charge you an additional fare since you only paid for as far as Manchester. It will be another dollar." Jack handed over his second dollar.

They settled back to the rhythm of their journey, eating apples and cheese, sleeping under the wagon. Jack sat next to a silent O Ahaziah through the day. The roads were good. He took cat-naps and dreamed of Troy. His mother and father and brother and sisters were on the walls, their heads surrounded by light. An enormous wooden horse was being brought through the gates. His granduncle, Malachi, was weeping and pumping the bellows underneath his arm, but no one paid attention.

"This is as far as I go," O Ahaziah said. He poked Jack in the ribs to wake him up. They were atop a small hill, and in the distance was a vast compass of roofs and steeples, and a great gold dome blazed with sunlight in its midst. Jack thought he was still dreaming. O Ahaziah said, "I don't go no closer than this." The two of them sat and stared at the city. It was grander, bigger, more beautiful, than Jack's vision of Troy.

O Ahaziah closed his eyes and said, " 'And the children of Israel did secretly those things that were not right against the Lord their God, and they built them high places in all their cities, from the tower of the watchmen to the fenced city. And they set them up images and groves in every high hill, and under every green tree; and there they burnt incense in all the high places, as did the heathen, and wrought wicked things to provoke the Lord to anger.' " He opened his eyes. "Second Kings, chapter seventeen, verses nine through eleven."

Jack jumped down. He felt a surge of apprehension as he left the familiar surroundings of the wagon. The urgency of finding his next meal hit him.

O Ahaziah reached behind himself and took an apple and a

piece of cheese from his sack. He handed them to Jack. "Be careful," he said. "Was Cain built the first city, and it's his sons and daughters who inhabit it." He snapped the reins and moved off to the east.

Jack sat on a tree stump and watched the clouds race over the city toward the sea. As the sun passed in and out, the dome went dull with shadows and then blazed again with light. It seemed to match his mood, dark one minute, bright the next, a mélange of hope and fear. He walked down the hill toward Boston, and after a short distance he came to a cluster of houses and stores, a neat, prim-looking village on the outskirts of the city. He walked into one store, and the clerk came from behind the counter. He had been cutting meat and wiped the bloody knife on his apron. He blocked Jack from coming in any farther. He held the knife at his side.

"What you looking for?" the clerk said.

"I was wondering about the possibility of finding work."

"Keep heading to Boston, there's work there for them who are willing."

The clerk stood where he was. Jack walked out of the store. Three doors down, there was a small building with a printing press and a board outside filled with notices. Most were broadsides for meetings and political rallies. Jack stopped to read them.

A voice behind him said, "Ain't nothing there of interest to Paddy shits like yourself."

Jack turned to look around. There were three boys about his own age standing there. They all held sticks. Jack said, "I'm looking for work, that's all."

"Ain't that wonderful," one of the boys said to his companions. "A Paddy looking for what he can earn instead of steal." The boy whipped his stick around and smacked Jack on the right calf. "Get moving, Paddy, this is American territory, off limits to pigs."

Jack held up his hands. "I'm just coming from Canada, that's where I'm from."

One of the others lashed out with his stick and sent a sharp pain up Jack's left leg. "And I'm the Emperor of China," the boy said. Jack hopped around, the hot pain shooting up and down his legs.

"Canada, is it?" the first boy said. He hit Jack across the thighs. Jack put his hands down and stepped closer to the boy, who was just then raising his stick. Jack drove his fist into the bridge of the boy's nose, sending him sprawling. The two other boys came at Jack with their sticks, beating him relentlessly until he stopped trying to find an opportunity to hit back and simply tried to protect his face. The two boys threw away their sticks and pinned Jack's arms, and the boy he had struck, his nose dripping blood, pummeled Jack's face with his fists.

Blood ran into Jack's eyes and blinded him. He felt he was about to pass out when the blows abruptly stopped. A man had pulled his cart over, jumped down, grabbed the boy who was punching Jack, and threw him aside. The man kicked at the other boys, swatting one across the back of his head. They ran away. The man picked Jack out of the dusty street, took a rag out of his back pocket, and handed it to him. "Wipe your face," he said.

Jack looked at the blood on the rag, and tasted the blood in his throat. His ears were ringing, and his face ached with pain. He started to cry.

"Don't give them the satisfaction of your tears," the man said. He led Jack over to the cart, helped him up, and drove off at a rapid pace.

"My God, boy," the driver said, "you should know better than to stray into a Yankee place the likes of that."

"Didn't do a thing but ask for work," Jack said.

"Look at you, boy, in them ragamuffin's clothes, somebody's discarded shirt and them pants two sizes too small for you, right away they knew you were a Paddy, before they even caught a look at your face or heard you speak. You're lucky one of your own was passin' by when it happened, or you might not have gotten off as lightly as you have." Jack felt a lump in his pocket. He reached in and found the apple and the piece of cheese O Ahaziah had given him. The cheese was broken and crumbled.

He took the apple and hurled it into the roadside, and threw the cheese after it.

"Where are you from?" the driver said.

"Canada," Jack said.

"Before Grosse Isle, boy, what part of Ireland are you from?"

Jack told the whole story, from the time he had left Ireland until that moment. He concentrated on getting it all straight, and the effort took his mind off the pain he felt in his legs and face.

"These Yankees are the sharpest people on the face of the earth," the driver said when Jack had finished.

"What do you mean?"

"O Ahaziah and his cousin. They played a game with you. Pretendin' they didn't know you were Irish and havin' you work for nothin' but two dollars and then makin' sure they got the two dollars back. That's how the Yankees play. It's their way with everyone, even with each other, but when it comes to we Irish, they see us as some sort of punishment for their sins and cheatin' us as an atonement. The whole city and state is run by them, and they'll ship the lot of us back to Ireland if they have the chance, but not before they've made sure they've wrung us dry."

They drove through streets that grew narrower and more crowded. They came to a squalid area of sagging wooden houses that looked ready to sink into the muck that surrounded them. "You'll be safe here," the driver said. "It's our own kind." Across from where they came to a halt was a one-story tavern, a peeling, weatherworn place with a crowd standing around outside, idle men in patched and soiled clothing. On each side of this building was a taller, even more disreputable-looking building with a pitched roof. Strung between these two was a clothesline laden with the same kind of tattered garments that had hung from the lanyards of the ships at Grosse Isle, the semaphores of the Irish.

Jack was three months in Boston when he walked across the alleyway to see the minstrel show that had come to town. As it had for Saul, suddenly there shone around him a light as if from heaven. When Jack had finished his performance in the hotel hallway, Jack Diamond had taken him to dinner and got him a room. Jack told Diamond his life story, and Diamond told him his, two immigrant sagas, the same yearnings and hunger. Jack got drunk for the first time in his life.

Heel, toe, round you go, heel, toe, come on, move those feet, watch me, follow what I do. They practiced together for hours, Diamond never seeming to show the effects of the alcohol he continually consumed. He treated Jack like a son. Good-time Jack Diamond. The great heelologist, his red hair under a black wig, Irish skin and Irish face all covered in soot, Paddy parodying a black man and receiving his first welcome in America, thunderous applause, two curtain calls a show.

"It's a funny thing," Diamond used to say after a couple of drinks, "but I didn't stop being a Paddy until I became a nigger. Once I put the burnt cork on my face, I was all right with everybody."

All right with everybody.

They pay to see us sing and dance. Wehman's definition of the Philosophers' Stone: Willingness to pay.

Mulcahey led the parade of self-melanized performers around the stage, *Listen, you darkies, no more sitting around telling stale jokes.* This was the third dance he had called for in a row, the pace never slowing, sweat dripping down their faces, their eyes wide with astonishment at this breach of the sacred canon of minstrel ritual, a spontaneous interjection of *wheel about and jump about* that snapped the audience out of its fidgeting inattention.

The minstrels fell into their seats.

Rat-a-tat, rat-a-tat, rat-a-tat-tat-tat.

Mulcahey's foot worked the floorboard castanet. The signal for another dance. The minstrels groaned, but in an instant they were all up and moving. Biglips stopped trying to keep up. He swayed slightly in a vague attempt at movement but was panting for breath, one hand on his chest. He seemed ready to test Bill Wehman's assertion that performers never died on stage.

Squirt had left the prompter's box and was standing in the wings. The light had disappeared from around his head.

The power of the caul had returned suddenly. In the year before he was signed by Brownlee's, Mulcahey had gone on tour with Joe Lunty's troupe, the Manifest Destiny Minstrel Show. The agent in New York had booked them not only in Illinois, Ohio, and Iowa, but also in Kansas. They hadn't appreciated what he had gotten them into until they found themselves on trains being stopped and searched by bands of armed men, participants in the opening act of the Civil War. One night, while they were doing the show, a gang of Border Ruffians pushed its way in. As they stood in the aisles, one of them started shouting about how they didn't need northerners coming into the territory acting like a bunch of silly niggers.

Old Joe Lunty walked right up to the front of the stage and said, "Gentlemen, I must ask you to move because the owners of this hall have requested that we make sure no trash accumulates in the aisles." The audience roared, and the man who had done the shouting pulled out a huge Navy revolver and started blasting away at the stage.

The only damage done by the pistoleer was to the interlocutor's chair, two big holes in its frame, but the minstrels canceled their stay and took the next train east. Mulcahey sat across from Lunty, and they laughed about what had happened the night before, and then Mulcahey saw the light around Lunty's head, the first time the benefaction of the caul had reappeared since he had left Ireland. Two mornings later they found Lunty dead in his berth. His destiny manifested, he had passed away in his sleep.

Wehman was next.

Now Squirt.

He felt genuinely sorry for the kid. But he had learned a long time ago that you couldn't be sentimental about death. Did no good to concentrate on it as though it were something you could influence or change. Get away from it if it wasn't for you, keep moving, *heel, toe, slap that knee, stamp that foot,* keep learning to beat the Yankees at their own game, and if minstrelsy proved a bust, *hey, I'se de nigger dat don't mind no troubles, cause dey ain't nuffin mor' dan bubbles.*

III

THE THING ABOUT JACK MULCAHEY was that you never knew.

"There are two Jacks," Squirt had once said to Eliza. "Black Jack, he's a hurricane in a bottle, all these clouds and wind and rain swirlin' around, and it's always nighttime, no light nowhere. And Jack Jack, him a dancin' and laughin', always smilin', the sunniest Paddy you ever seen."

The minute Mulcahey came through the door of the New England Hotel, Eliza knew the weather had changed. Black Jack had given way to Jack Jack. The silent, somber man who had moped about the room all morning was now grinning, garrulous, ready to entertain. Squirt was right behind him, and they went directly into the bar. Jack bought a round of drinks for the house, put his arm around Eliza and kissed her on the neck. In the creases of his ear were the remnants of the burnt cork that could be removed only by a good bath. In the morning she would push his head under the hot, soapy water and hold it there until he threw his arms about in a mock struggle, splashing water on her. Kneeling beside the tub, she would work the inner S of his ear with a facecloth. So long to "The Ethiopian Impersonator." He was like a boy at times and Eliza loved that about him, the way he tilted his head when she poked the facecloth into his ear, the grunts and complaining, his playfulness. Jack Jack. She hadn't known white men could be like that, so devoid of arrogance, self-importance, condescension. She recognized the first time she met him in the hallway of the hotel that he wanted her, that their supposedly fortuitous meeting was the result of his deliberate planning, but she hadn't tried to avoid him. She liked his reticence. Enjoyed his attentions. He had none of the typical white man's silly expectations, the presumption that she secretly desired to wait on his whims and wishes. He courted her the way she imagined a boy courts a girl, trying to get her attention, and when she pretended not to notice, he tried harder, and even after she returned his interest, smiling at his antics, holding his hand, he seemed innocent of her responses until, in the end, she felt that she was doing the seducing.

Jack Jack was no amateur in bed. He said that his mentor, Jack Diamond, had seen to that, making sure he had the best training in the romantic arts that the young Republic could provide. Unlike most performers, Diamond had preferred to tour the wilder, less settled parts of the country, the fringes of the frontier, where, he had told Jack, the women were given to amorous acrobatics that their counterparts in the East were incapable of, especially in the vicinity of Boston. But Eliza found in Jack a knowledge that she knew wasn't imparted by whores, an interest in her response, slow caresses stoking her desire.

Black Jack had no interest in lovemaking. He tossed around at night, unable to sleep but unwilling to tell her why. She knew he worried about money. He was well paid, and the accommodations in the hotel were far cheaper than he could afford. He put his money in the bank or hid it somewhere. Never told her how much he had. But he talked about hard times the way sailors talk about bad weather, as if it were a looming certainty, if not today then tomorrow, a storm of wind, rain, and hail that would flatten the improvident and sink the spendthrift. No matter how brightly the sun shone, he lived in despair over what lay ahead until, suddenly, motivated by reasons she could never fathom, the clouds would lift, and instead of going directly from the show to their room, Black Jack would give way to Jack Jack, bosom friend of everyone in the barroom, congenial host, standing round after round, a fountain of stories, songs, drinks; her gentle, attentive lover.

When they left the barroom, it was late. They made love. He rolled off her, both of them expended, and she felt the soft exhalation of his breath on her neck, the rhythm of sleep. It was not her time of the month, and she had not asked him to withdraw before he ejaculated. She lay in the dark, and his semen flowed out of her. Sexless creatures, without faces. Her aunt's superstition.

"Do you believe in signs?" he said. She was surprised that he was still awake. She turned her head toward his. Their faces almost touched.

"Signs?"

"Omens. Portents."

"It depends."

"On what?"

"On what's being portended and who's doing the portending. I believe the prophecies in the Bible and what the prophets said, but I'm not much for the fashion of the séance and the knock-knocking of the spirit world."

"You don't think it's possible to foresee a death?"

"I never thought about it."

"In Ireland we believed it was, and among the old people there were those believed I had the power."

"To tell who was going to die?"

"Yeah."

"Did you ever?"

"Sometimes I thought I saw a light that surrounded a person's head, and, sure enough, he was usually dead before too long."

She knew he was superstitious. All performers were, the Irish ones especially, with their medals, scapulars, holy water, and beads. Most of it was foreign to the stark religion she was raised in at Midian's Well. Jack had two holy cards tucked into the mirror over the bureau. On one the figure of Jesus pointed at his exposed heart, which was crowned with thorns; on the other was a prayer that Eliza loved to read. She found comfort in its cadences, its promises. Mercy, clemency, love, the fruit of thy womb. She had repeated it so often she had it memorized.

Hail, holy Queen, Mother of mercy;
Our life, our sweetness, and our hope.
To thee do we cry,
Poor banished children of Eve;
to thee do we send up our sighs
mourning and weeping
in this vale of tears.
Turn then, most gracious advocate,
thine eyes of mercy towards us;
and after this, our exile,
show unto us
the blessed fruit of thy womb, Jesus.
O clement, O loving, O sweet Virgin Mary.

"You don't believe me?" Jack said.

"People die by the hundreds every day in this city. And you can tell which ones?"

"Not all. Some. A few."

"Anyone I know?"

"No, it ain't happened since I left Ireland."

He was quiet again. He rolled onto his side and draped his arm over her. In a moment he was asleep. Eliza lay still. She loved the night. As a child she had gotten out of bed when her parents were asleep and snuck up the hill behind the house. She could see the sea from there, the lights of ships as they glided across it, and hear the sounds that carried with magical clarity over the water, words, laughter, songs. She looked up at the stars but never found in them a clue to what lay ahead. The only premonition she ever had was the one that kept her from sleep: Sooner or later, Jack would leave her. As much as she appreciated his gentleness with her, as oblivious as he was to race, she had come to understand that his kindness was an attempt to keep her at a distance. And beneath his indifference she sensed his fear of losing what he had, his talent, his money, minstrelsy, as the burden of a family dragged him under as he tried to stay afloat.

*

In December of 1860, when Eliza left her own room and moved in with Jack, Stephen Foster performed a mock wedding in the barroom of the hotel. Jack had just made his debut with Brownlee's: Jack Jack in his prime. He made the champagne flow, and spun around the room dancing with different partners. Foster stood on a chair and demanded silence. He fell off once and everyone laughed, but Jack helped him back up, and wobbling a bit as he spoke, Foster said that no matter what the politicians claimed, there was but one real democracy in the world, one true society of equals, and this room encompassed it.

"The dancer, the singer, the balladeer, the minstrel, the thespian, whether comedian or tragedian, those of us who compose music and those of you who play it, we know no qualification but ability! We accept no distinction save talent!"

Foster almost fell off the chair again, but Jack caught him. Foster called Eliza to come forward. She was standing in the back of the room, and when she didn't move, the others pushed her forward. Foster took her hand and put it in Jack's.

"Neither Greek nor Jew, nor slave nor free! Can anyone tell me why these two should not be joined in holy matrimony?"

"No!" the crowd yelled.

"Get me a ring," Foster said.

Someone rushed to the hotel dining room and came back with a large napkin ring, which he handed to Foster. Eliza was embarrassed but excited. She had just started her role in *Uncle Tom* and was new to the company of entertainers. She felt Jack's hand tighten around hers until it hurt. He said under his breath, "Foster, stop this." She glanced at him. Black Jack. Squirt had it right: It was as if there were a storm bottled up inside him.

Foster held up the ring. "This is the symbol of the union we celebrate, a new race to be procreated, talc to whiten the black, the cork to blacken the white, appearances only, the inconsequentiality of the accidental beside the shared essence of what flows through their veins—greasepaint!"

There was more cheering. Foster rocked unsteadily on the

chair. Jack pressed his foot against the leg and pushed. Foster went backward, his arms outstretched and spinning in circles. He crashed into a table. Those standing nearby helped him up, and Eliza lent a hand. When she turned around, Jack had disappeared. His money was still on the bar, and the party continued, the increasingly loud camaraderie celebrating the truest democracy of all: the dispensation of free drinks.

Eliza stayed and drank champagne, but with Jack gone the others lost interest in her and she found herself at a table alone. The room was still crowded. A man with thinning gray hair plastered to his scalp came over and poured champagne into her glass.

"Do you mind if I sit?" he asked.

Eliza shook her head. He introduced himself as Bill Wehman.

"You're Miss La Plante, I presume. People are talking about you, which in our profession is a thing to be desired."

"Yes, I'm Therese La Plante, but everyone calls me Eliza. Jack started it, now everybody does it."

"Eliza it is. You're new to the city?"

"Fairly."

He held up his glass. "I wish you luck. The rest seems to have been taken care of. I'm told you have talent. I can see you have beauty, and it's all wrapped in mystery, a combination that is nonpareil."

"There's no mystery, Mr. Wehman."

"Bill," he said. "Never been called nothing else. Call me Bill."

"What is so mysterious, Bill?"

"Well, in case you don't know it, there's a storm of speculation about you. There's one story says you're the illegitimate daughter of Santa Anna, the conqueror of the Alamo and a late resident of this city. There's another says you're a Negress, the first ever on the New York stage."

"Nobody's business but mine, is it?" Eliza stood up. She had been warned that even as her presence helped draw in audiences, it could lead to suspicion, a disquiet about "the niggers taking over." Let them have their mystery. She wasn't going to solve it for them.

He put his hand on her wrist. "Miss La Plante, Eliza, hear me out. Please, this will take but a minute." She sat.

"At my age, I ain't got much interest in people's origins. Never interested me, even when I was young. But there are people mightily interested."

He poured champagne into his glass and put it next to her ear. "Listen, Eliza. Effervescence. Escaping gases. Someday a philosopher of some sort will undoubtedly write a book explaining the sudden popularity of this bubbling brew, why at this particular moment it should conquer New York, sweeping aside the taste for whiskey and ale."

The glass was so close to her ear that she could hear its fizz and feel its sparkle. "I have no idea," she said.

"Nobody knows why, not even our yet-to-be-born philosopher. But he'll make up a reason, invent some theory about the era we live in and then use champagne to prove it. Philosophers do it all the time. Matter of fact, everybody does it, finds facts to fit his theories. It ain't just the philosophers."

He put the glass next to his own ear. "Double, double, toil and trouble; fire burn and cauldron bubble."

Eliza stood up. The man was obviously drunk. She was too tired to humor him. "I have to go," she said.

"I know I sound like a raving old lunatic, but just a minute more." She stood where she was. "I'll get to the point. People got all sorts of theories about Negroes, about whether to free them or not, about how much like the white man they are, about whether they can be civilized, about whether they belong back in Africa. Some are sure that one day we'll learn to live together, peacefully. Could be. But that's a theory. Let me tell you a fact. In the summer of '34, I was appearing at the National Theatre in a play I can't even remember the name of. Was brutally hot, typical for New York at that time of the year, the city was seething with trouble, and before too long gangs of immigrants were fighting gangs of Americans for control of the streets. Got so bad the city watchmen hid themselves for fear of being killed.

"Well, somehow in the middle of it all, both sides got it in their heads to go after the abolitionists. New York never had many abolitionists, not then, not now, but the mobs decided that hordes of free blacks was about to be imported into the city, so they went wild, pausing long enough in their warfare to attack the homes of the abolitionists and beat up any colored they found on the street and wreck some colored churches.

"We never closed the theatre, even when the whole city seemed run by the mobs and they had barricades up in the streets like Paris during one of them French revolutions.

"One night in the intermission, when the heat was wringing the life out of me, I went out the back of the theatre and stood in the street, still in costume, my hair all white like I was an old man. Odd, when you think about it, that I don't remember the play but recall how I was made up. Memory's like that. Anyways, I'm standing there next to this colored boy who used to move the scenery. Quiet boy, polite as can be, and as light as they come, so much so that, sometimes, if he was standing in the shadows, you'd swear he was white. But that night he wasn't in the shadows. Was right out there in the street, and I was talking to him just like I'm talking to you when this crowd starts coming up the street, maybe two, three hundred people, and before either of us knew what was happening, they were all around us and this colored boy is struggling to get free and people are tearing at each other to get at him.

"No need to go into what they did, because the truth is I don't like thinking about it. They treated that boy the worst way you can treat a living thing, and then strung him up from this withered, spindly tree that bent with the boy's weight.

"I tried to stop 'em, but there wasn't much I could do. Matter of fact, if I hadn't a been made up as an old man, I think they woulda mashed me up almost as bad as they did that poor boy."

Wehman poured more champagne; the bubbles foamed to the top of his glass. He held it up in front of his face. "I've never cared for this stuff. Whiskey is my drink, and I suppose one day the fashion of champagne will pass and some new concoction will take its place, because that's the way this town is, fashion following fashion, but I'm not sure that the feelings toward the colored is going to follow that pattern. The colored seem to be in a category all their own. I've been here all my life and never seen it change."

In the church in Midian's Well, the Reverend Mr. Enders had constantly reminded his congregation not to show any emotion when they came into contact with white people. "It is the Lord who has hardened their hearts," he said. "You can't change them. Only the Lord can." Eliza could see that Wehman was trying to be kind, but it was a white person's kindness, an inescapable if unintended note of superiority, as if any Negro in any part of America needed to be reminded of the danger he was in. Wehman was sitting with his mouth open, drool at its right corner. He thought she was a total innocent, Mrs. Stowe's Eliza in the flesh.

"I must be going, Bill," she said, "but I thank you for your note of caution."

Wehman stood up and walked with her to the hotel lobby. "For all I know, maybe you *are* Santa Anna's daughter, but it's best to be on your guard. Be careful."

Jack Mulcahey was the only white man Eliza ever met who talked as if color were of no consequence. He had told her several times the story of how when he was a boy in Donegal a man from his village had come running back from the coast, breathless and frightened. People gathered around and asked him what was wrong. The man said he had just seen the *Góban Saor* himself, Goban the Wright, his tongue a hammer, his eloquence a bellows, his skin as black as the grates on which he beat the red-hot irons, *fir dubh,* the dark man the storytellers described. The villagers said that the man must be drunk. But Jack and some other boys slipped away and went down to see for themselves; and sure enough, there he was, *Góban Saor,* standing in an alehouse, amid a crowd of sailors, in striped pants and blue jacket, his head bare, his hair tightly curled and glistening. The boys watched him through the window while he drank porter. A demigod from the land of the stories.

Jack said, "I don't think that black man had ever seen such a collection of ragamuffins as he did that day. He gave us each a shilling. Paddy as the object of a nigger's charity. You don't get much poorer than that." But like marriage, race was something Jack usually preferred not to talk about. For Jack it was as if his and Eliza's life were confined to the New England Hotel, as if this were all the past they had, the only future they should expect.

Eliza never volunteered anything. When Jack asked, she would tell him everything, from her childhood in Midian's Well until the day she met him, but only when he asked, only when he expressed interest. And she would tell only Jack. She would tell no one else. When Josie Woods had taken her to the theatre and told the manager that Miss Therese La Plante would be a perfect Eliza and would bring an element of exotic to the flagging stage version of Mrs. Stowe's novel, the stage manager had been skeptical.

"What is your background?" he asked.

Eliza said nothing. She knew he was looking for some reason to dismiss her, any excuse.

Mrs. Woods broke the silence. "What is *your* background?" she asked him. "Or *mine*? And what does background have to do with acting? Are you a parson or a stage manager?"

"I mean, what experience?"

Eliza spoke up for herself. "I studied under Mrs. Euphemia Blanchard at the Fulton Academy."

The manager agreed to give her a try. When they left his office, Mrs. Woods said to her, "You never mentioned anything to me about studying acting. Is it true?"

"Yes."

Eliza always considered it her first successful bit of acting, the authority with which she invoked Mrs. Blanchard's name, a bluff that neither the stage manager nor Mrs. Woods called. It wasn't a total lie. Mrs. Blanchard not only rescued her from the streets, clothed, and fed her, but taught her about the supreme artifice of the coloreds who lived among the whites, the necessity of dissembling, the acting required of those who would survive.

She had left Midian's Well on a Sunday, done it suddenly, although she had yearned to leave for as long as she could remember. She had gone to a dock a few miles down the road from Midian's Well, in the white folk's town. Her father and the rest of the community were in church, where they would be for most of the day. He would be looking back at the door, growing angrier by the minute, working himself into a rage that would explode once he came home.

A white man in an oyster boat that was pulled alongside the dock called to her. "Girl, here's a nickel, run up to that shed and fetch me some tobacco."

She had been in the presence of whites before but had never talked to one. The men of Midian's Well were the only ones who did, and only when necessary. He reached up and handed her the nickel. She ran to the shack by the dock and asked the white man behind the counter for tobacco. Her heart was racing with excitement.

"Ain't you from Niggertown?" he said.

"Midian's Well."

"Yeah, Niggertown."

The forbidden word. Sometimes, alone in their play, the children of Midian hurled it at one another. *Nigger, nigger, nigger.* The men of Midian never seemed to notice when the whites used it. Their faces were impassive. But the children got a beating when *they* used it.

The man took a canister from beneath the counter and asked her how much she wanted. She put the nickel down, and he poured some of the contents into a small cloth pouch and drew it closed.

"Don't go tellin' that head nigger up there what I done. I don't want him comin' here threatenin' to cut my ears off." He put the pouch in her hand. She juggled it in her palm. The first purchase she had ever made, and in a white man's store. The

Reverend Mr. Enders would make her stand before the pulpit and use her as an example of the wickedness and faithlessness that existed even among the chosen of the Lord. Her father would fall on his knees and pray. He would call out the name of his dead wife and hide his face in his hands.

She tossed the tobacco to the man in the boat.

"Where are you sailing to?" she said.

He motioned over his shoulder with his thumb. "The city."

"Take me."

"You got family there?"

"My grandmother. She's sick real bad, and my poppa doesn't want me to go, but I got to see her before she dies."

He stood with one hand on his hip and one hand shielding his eyes. "You ain't foolin' me, girl. I'll take you along, but you ain't foolin' me."

"I ain't lyin'." She looked down at the gray planks, the green sea visible between them. Speaking each line with the same tone of sincerity, brazenly, no fear in her voice, looking into their eyes: tricks she hadn't learned yet.

He held up a hand. "Get in," he said. She took his hand and climbed into the boat. "We're goin' to the Fulton Market. After that you're on your own."

Eliza hadn't eaten for two days when the vegetable seller found her poking around in the garbage and grabbed her by the neck. "Why, you little nigger," the woman said, "what are you lurking around here for?"

It was early morning, and the market was filling up with customers. Eliza squirmed. She tried to shake herself loose, but the woman only tightened her grip, pulling Eliza along the stalls until they reached the end of the row. "You back there, Effie?"

A soiled blanket that served as a curtain parted, and a small, fierce-looking black woman with a bandanna tied around her head came out. "Who da sonofabitch makin' all dat noise?" she said in a loud voice.

"This belong to you?" the woman holding Eliza asked.

"Why you think every nigger in dis city belong to me? Every

piece of white trash belong to you? Hell, no, but anytime some nigger be caught doin' anythin' at all, dey brings 'em right to Effie Blanchard like I'm momma to every livin', breathin' one of 'em." She was talking at the top of her voice, and people were coming over to see what the fuss was about. She was as short as a child, and her eyes bulged out of a deep-brown face that was webbed with wrinkles. She put her hand under Eliza's chin and moved it back and forth.

"What mischief you up to?"

"She was rummaging in my refuse pile," the vegetable seller said.

Mrs. Blanchard suddenly dug her fingers into the sides of Eliza's cheeks and screamed in her face, "Stay outta other people's garbage, you hear?"

Eliza began to cry. She tried to stop, but couldn't. She was weak from hunger and filled with fear. From the moment she had landed at the bottom of Fulton Street, the recklessness of what she had done had overwhelmed her. She sat on a piling and watched the hubbub on the piers, white people everywhere, men cursing and groaning as they loaded and unloaded cargo, carts moving quickly up and down the street, their iron-rimmed wheels making an earsplitting noise. A man came over to where she was sitting and said, "Move it, nigger, we got a ship comin' in here." She crossed the street and stood against the wall of a building. A man stopped and asked, "How much, sister?"

She smiled. "Sister" was what the Reverend Mr. Enders called all the women in Midian's Well. The man stood in front of her. "Well," he said, "how much? I sure as hell know you ain't givin' it away."

"How much for what?"

"Nothin' exotic. Just a straight lay."

"A straight lay?"

"You got it, sister." He took her by the hand. She pulled it away. "You're new to this business, ain't you?" he asked.

"I'm waiting for my mother," she said.

"And I'm Jesus Christ." He grabbed her hand again. "Listen,

I'm gonna introduce ya to some people who can help. Believe me, ya not gonna last long otherwise. They'll set ya up in a room, make it easy." He started to tow her along.

She yelled so loudly she hurt her throat. He dropped her hand. "Hey, ain't no need for that." She screamed again. Nobody stopped, but some people walking by turned and looked.

"Suit yourself," he said. "You're gonna learn the hard way." He left her there.

That night, Eliza slept in an alley. She didn't awake until the sun was already up and the noise of carts and voices was impossible to ignore. The sidewalks were so crowded that people walked in the street, dodging the growing crush of vehicles. Eliza walked out of the alley, unsure of which way to go. People bumped into her and pushed her out of the way. There were peddlers everywhere, and hordes of bedraggled newcomers walked up from the docks carrying bundles and trunks. These people were set upon by packs of boys with handcarts who took their possessions, often wrestling with them to do so, and led them to the rickety-looking boardinghouses that lined the side streets. Eliza wandered around the whole day, afraid to stand still, letting the flow of the traffic move her along. She wanted to strike out for some other part of the city, the marble and granite streets of her imagination, the porticoes she had seen in the frontispiece of the family Bible, Saint Paul preaching in Athens, the paving stones immaculately clean, tall, slender trees ringing the hills in the distance. But this squalid dockside was the only part of the city she had seen, and as terrifying as it was, it was at least familiar and less terrifying than what lay beyond.

She slept a second night in the same alley, and in the morning, while rummaging in a pile of half-rotted vegetables, was grabbed by the neck and hauled to Mrs. Blanchard. When Mrs. Blanchard stopped screaming, the vegetable seller walked away and left Eliza standing there. Mrs. Blanchard walked behind the curtain. She came out with a box of fish.

"Stop your cryin'," she said in a softer voice. "Go home to your momma, if you got one." She adjusted a metal scale that hung by a chain from a rafter. She went behind the curtain and brought out another large box of fish, their dead eyes open and fixed on some distant point. Eliza wiped away her tears.

"Where you from?"

Eliza didn't answer.

"You got a tongue?"

Eliza stuck it out.

"Don't be silly with me!" Mrs. Blanchard's voice rose again. She came out from behind the stall. "Now, I axed you a question." She was at least three or four inches shorter than Eliza and had to stand on the tips of her toes to put her face into Eliza's.

"I'm from Jersey."

"What you doin' here?"

"I ran away from home."

"Well, run back just as fast as you can, 'cause you don't belongs here. Go back and stop worryin' your momma and pappy. Ain't nothin' here for you but trouble, and plenty of dat."

Mrs. Blanchard went back to work. The market was flush with people, the aisles filled. She took a long sharp knife from a sheath beneath her apron and began cutting fish, chopping off head and tail with quick strokes, slicing open the belly and back, peeling out the fillets, laying them on a bed of salt, and spreading more salt on top. She had the last stall in the market, and Eliza stood in the space next to the wall to keep out of the way. Mrs. Blanchard ignored her.

Set into the wall was an iron grate that was lifted up and hooked to the roof like the hatch on a ship. Outside, in the street, stood a man on a box, his back to the grate. He had a Bible in his hand, and in front of him was another man handing out pamphlets.

A small crowd gathered. The man on the box began to preach. He had some of the same sentiments as the Reverend Mr. Enders but none of his eloquence, none of the fiery lakes and skies dripping with the burning tears of a merciful God forced by the wickedness of men to wreak acts of vengeance. The man raised his voice to imitate the anger of the Lord, but it conveyed only noise, not the soul-seated anger that resonated in the Reverend Mr. Enders's speech or even the passionate annoyance of Mrs. Blanchard's. And then, suddenly, from inside the stall, came a thunderous explosion that startled Eliza and echoed across the market.

"Fresh fish!" Mrs. Blanchard said in a voice that seemed beyond the capacities of her slight build. "I gots dem all!"

The tract men, the retailers of the word of God, stopped their preaching and pamphleteering, and turned and looked. The rest of the market went about its business.

"Fresh fish, right from de water! No fresher anywhere 'cept in the sea!" Mrs. Blanchard chopped and cut as she shouted, barely pausing to draw a breath.

"All de creatures of de deep! Speckled redmouths, long-finned harvest fish, blunt-noses, iron-skins, yellow mackerels, calico bass, bills, spots, shark suckers, mooneyes, gold-eyes, thimble-eyes, conners, siscos, chubs, shiners, pumpkins, yellow-fins, glasseyes, blennies, hair-fins, redfins, rounders, spots, spotted-fins, spotted threads, blows, puffers, horse mackerel, sheepheads, needlefish." The poetry of fish: a monologue shouted at the rafters, the great bellows of Mrs. Blanchard's lungs going all day. She seemed to have only five or six varieties of fish, but she repeated the litany over and over, and the customers who came all seemed to know her and not be bothered by the small selection they found; some of them stood around just to attend to her litany. Eliza lingered by the stall. In the early afternoon, Mrs. Blanchard stopped pretending not to notice her and told her to go back behind the curtain and bring out a box of fish. Eliza jumped to the work. When the market was ready to close, she helped Mrs. Blanchard wash down the stall. Eliza scrubbed as hard as she could. Mrs. Blanchard stood back and watched.

"You a stupid little creature for sure."

Eliza put down her rag. Mrs. Blanchard was speaking in a loud voice, and although no one else seemed to take notice of her words, Eliza was embarrassed.

"What you leave home fer? What you think you gonna find here?"

A scarlet city, the Reverend Mr. Enders called it. City of whores. An abomination in the eyes of God. The dwelling place of the Egyptians. From atop a hill on the other side of Staten Island where Eliza and her friends went to gather blueberries, they could see the distant outline of the city, a wall of masts around it, slender steeples rising above them. The sun blazed down on the red brick, not scarlet at all but ocher, the color of earth in spring. She sat as the others went on gathering. The wind that came off the sea was soft and fragrant. Overhead, a flock of blackbirds lifted out of the trees and flew toward the city.

"I wasn't happy where I was," Eliza said.

"Happy?" Mrs. Blanchard said. "Girl, you more stupid den I thought. Happy? You wasn't happy? O Lord, you got lots to learn." She put a raggedy shawl over her shoulders and began walking to the street. After a few steps she stopped and turned. Eliza hadn't moved from the stall.

"Where you gonna stay?"

"I'll find a place," Eliza said.

"I don't doubts that! And pretty soon dey pull you outta de river like some fish!" She shook her head. "Come wid me, child, I puts you up for de night, 'cause it look like dat what de Lord sent you to me fer."

They stood in the street. After a few minutes, a two-wheeled cart came whipping around the corner. It pulled to a stop in front of them. Mrs. Blanchard gestured to Eliza to get on and climbed up after her. They sat with their backs to the driver, their feet dangling over the rear. Mrs. Blanchard reached up and opened her hand. "Mister Flynn," she said, "here my two pennies, and two fer de girl here." The driver turned around and grabbed the pennies. The cart reeked of horse manure, which was splattered everywhere on the floor and rails. Eliza tried to find something to hang on to that wasn't smeared with it. Neither Flynn nor Mrs. Blanchard seemed to care. Flynn brought his whip down on the

horse with a loud crack, and the cart jerked into motion. Flynn
threaded his way through the narrow streets, whipping the horse
constantly, cursing at the drivers of other coaches and wagons
and carts. When they came to an avenue lined with imposing
buildings, he turned right and they raced for a block before they
were caught in another maze of traffic and pedestrians, a hopeless
tangle of vehicles. They crept past a band playing on the balcony
of a building hung with banners, and a park with a fountain, and
buildings that looked as if Saint Paul could have preached beneath
their columns. This was a city more like the one Eliza had imagined; noisier, dirtier, and more chaotic certainly, but massive and
imposing, exciting, women in beautiful dresses, men in fine clothing, more people and movement than she thought could exist in
one place.

They kept moving slowly up the avenue, and finally, after
they passed a second park, the congestion dissolved and Flynn
beat the horse until the cart raced along. He swung left and went
down a street of towering houses that had doorways framed by
columns and immense windows; endless acres of brown granite.
He turned onto another avenue, went up it several blocks, then
left again up a street of stables and small brick houses. Eliza could
see the North River and the Jersey cliffs in the distance. The driver
made another left, and after traveling past rows of iron-shuttered
warehouses, they came to a hilly terrain that was occupied by
wooden shanties. Some stood alone; others leaned against each
other. The cart halted. Mrs. Blanchard got off and slapped
Eliza on the knee. Eliza hopped off, and without a word Flynn
moved on.

A mud lane led from the avenue up a slight rise. Mrs. Blanchard walked ahead of Eliza. People sat in the doorways of their
shanties, and children clad only in short shirts, boys and girls
alike, ran around the yards. As at Midian's Well, here everyone
was black, but this was a shabby place, the people sullen, the
shacks they lived in looking as if they were ready to collapse. Mrs.
Blanchard acknowledged only a few of those she passed, but everyone's eyes followed Eliza. At the top of the lane was Mrs.

Blanchard's shanty. Outside, it was as decrepit as the others, but inside, it was exceedingly neat, a table and chairs in one corner, a bed in another, a cast-iron stove in a third.

Eliza slept on the floor. The next morning, when it was still pitch-dark, she and Mrs. Blanchard repeated, in reverse, the trip they had made the night before. The cart stopped. They got on. Mrs. Blanchard paid the pennies, and they rode to the market. Then they went to the docks, where Mrs. Blanchard haggled with fishermen on their boats over the price of their catch. The two women carried the wooden boxes back to the stall. Eliza worked all day beside Mrs. Blanchard, and when it came time to leave, the older woman said, "Where you goin' tonight?"

"With you."

"Dat a question?"

"I have no place else to go."

"Go home."

"I can't."

By now the Reverend Mr. Enders and her father would have gone down to the dock and talked to the shopkeeper, suffered his rudeness in order to find out what had happened to her. When they were finished, they would have gone back to Midian's Well, walking in silence, uncomprehending of how any child of God could choose to live among such evildoers, and certain of her damnation.

"I don't run no orphanage."

"I'll do whatever work you say."

"Can't pay you nothin'. You can have a place to sleep, and food, and I'll pay for Flynn to bring us back and forth, and since you ain't got no clothes but what's on you, I'll see what de rag-man got to sell. But I can't do better den dat."

Eliza settled into the work. She told herself she could learn as much about the city from working as she could from watching and listening. Mrs. Blanchard was merciless to her while they were in the stall, screaming and cursing, her voice a regular part of the market's noise. But the abuse stopped as soon as they got on the cart. At night Mrs. Blanchard hardly spoke, and if she did it was never in a harsh way. She cooked their food and stood by the door to smoke her pipe.

Eliza once asked her where she was from.

"Don't matter where. What matters is we survive, child. Remember dat."

Coming home one night they passed a church. A wedding party was just coming out, the bride in a dress of white silk with delicate satin flowers rimming the bodice, the groom in a black suit, both of them smiling and shaking hands with the guests. Eliza couldn't stop talking about it. She said that she would have a ceremony like that one day, and a dress just like the bride's.

Mrs. Blanchard interrupted her. "Quiet, child," she said. "I can't stand listenin' to such nonsense. Sometime I wonder what country you growed up in. Ain't nothin' like that fer colored people, not here, not anywheres I ever heard of."

Twice a week, before it got dark, Mrs. Blanchard and Eliza took a canvas sheet down to the river and collected firewood. They laid the wood on the sheet and hauled it home. North of them, white people did their own scavenging.

"Stays away from dem," Mrs. Blanchard said. "Dey all Irish from de shanties in de hills over dere. Lowest of de low. Times was never very good for colored people in dis town, at least not so long as I been here, but dey never so bad until de Irish people come, and sometimes it seems dere no end to their comin'. My husband, Robert, Mister Blanchard, he was as light as you, child, and he was born in dis town, and his pappy before him. He worked servin' tables from de time he was a little boy, but when de Irishmen come, dey take most of dem jobs away from de colored, and dey kill a colored person if he get in dere way."

The Irish shanties covered the hills to the north. Flynn, the cartman who transported Mrs. Blanchard and Eliza to and from the Fulton Market, lived there. So did the city's ragpickers, cinder gatherers, and shit haulers—an army of casual laborers.

At dusk one evening, as Mrs. Blanchard and Eliza were dragging home a sheetful of wood, a group of children on a hill above the railroad tracks threw rocks at them. Mrs. Blanchard took a stick and went after them, and they ran away. When she came back, she sat by the side of the tracks and smoked her pipe. "A few years back," she said, "colored people wasn't allowed on de omnibuses at all, and even if dey pay dere fare on de horsecars dey had to stand on de outside platform; and den Miss Jennings and Reverend Pennington, dey refused to be treated like dat anymore. Dey said if dey pay dere fare, same as de whites, dey should get de same treatment. And dey went to court and de judge say dey is right, colored should ride like everybody else. Some colored got so excited, like it was de day of de Lord's return, and my Robert says dat it meant colored people goin' start be treated like men instead of dogs. He really believed dat. We was livin' on Minetta Lane back den, and Robert was workin' down in Old Tom's, waitin' tables, and right away he started ridin' de Broadway omnibus to work. I worried so much, yeah, I told him de white man ain't goin' let de colored raise his head without tryin' to knock it off. I told him, Don't you ride in dat omnibus. But he don't listen, and de second week he doin' it, sure enough, two of dese big Irishmen gets on and dey demand Robert's seat, and when he won't give it, dey pick him up and throw him off de back onto de pavin' stones. He broke his arm and three of his ribs and was never de same after dat. He never really got better. And den he died and I moved up here."

In the second month Eliza was working with Mrs. Blanchard, business fell off for the entire market. There had been a crash on Wall Street, which was only a few blocks way, though at first, except for a greater crush of traffic than usual on Broadway, it was an event that made no impact on the fish and produce sellers. But as brokerage houses closed and businesses failed and unemployment grew, the market people quickly felt the effect.

One day Flynn the cartman pulled up at the bottom of the lane in the early-morning darkness and said to them, "I think maybe ye be better off stayin' where ye are. Dere's been fightin' down on da Five Points, a regular ruction among the gangs, and I'm told it's spilled over da Bowery and Broadway, and da Dead Rabbits is drivin' da Bowery Boys right into da river. It don't concern colored people, but once things get started there's no tellin', and if I was you I'd stay outta da city today, I would."

Mrs. Blanchard thanked him for the advice but said she wanted to go anyway. Flynn took them down the West Side. They rode past Castle Garden, then circled up the East Side to avoid coming near Broadway or the Bowery. Mrs. Blanchard took the fish-cleaning knife from its sheath and laid it in her lap. She sang in a loud voice as they went. Eliza was frightened, but for the first time she understood the theatricality of Mrs. Blanchard's temper, the act she put on in front of white people to keep them at a distance and off balance. Somehow, in the face of their hostility, she had gotten a stall for herself in the market, something no other colored person had done, and kept the white people from taking it away from her. Eliza stopped regarding her as a changeable old woman, perhaps half-mad, and saw the strength she had, the cunning she employed against the world, the mixture of courage and intelligence. They went to and from work that day without being bothered.

By the time winter came, business in the market was half what it had been. The weather was cold and bitter. The morgue wagon made frequent visits to both the Irish and Negro shantytowns to pick up the dead, most of them children. The shore was stripped bare of firewood. Eliza and Mrs. Blanchard followed their neighbors up to where Forty-second Street crossed the railroad tracks on its way to the ferry. To the north they could see a wild tract of land stripped bare of trees, a terrain of squat, barren hills and gray-black rocks covered with an endless jumble of indistinguishable wooden shanties, some of them with roofs made of straw and mud; the domain of the shanty Irish.

They waited along the south side of the badly rutted street, and kept moving to stay warm. The traffic came up from the ferry, the horses laboring to gain momentum, the heavily laden coal and lumber wagons rocking crazily as they bounced over the ruined roadway and the railway tracks, often spilling a small part of their load. If the pickings were small, there was usually a fight over them, a wild mêlée between the Irish and Negroes that lasted only a few seconds. The rest of the time the two groups ignored each other.

On one gray Sunday when Mrs. Blanchard was sick with a fever and stayed in bed, Eliza went up to the street with the people from the neighboring shanties. The roadbed was covered with ice; the wind off the river was a sharp, penetrating shiv. A small crowd of Irish loitered on the other side of the street. From the ferry came a coal wagon jolting its way over the jagged, icebound surface. When it reached the slight grade at the tracks, the driver drew the horses to a stop. He started again. The wagon skidded sideways. He whipped the horses. The wagon suddenly jolted forward and swayed wildly as it careened over the track bed. The driver leapt off. The wagon went on for a few more yards before it pitched over and crashed onto its side, taking both horses with it.

From both sides of the street, people came running. The driver was brushing off his clothes and limping toward the wagon. He looked up and saw them coming. He raised his whip. "Get outta here, you dogs," he said.

Eliza ran to the other side of the wagon. She took off her shawl, put it on the ground, and used her hands to shovel coal into it. The driver hit an Irish boy with his whip. He tried to push people away. But from the north side of the street, down the icy, debris-strewn embankment, poured an army of shanty Irish, children and adults bundled in blankets, shawls, patchwork coats. From the south came a steady flow of shanty Negroes, some of them carrying tubs and cans. The driver turned and fled. The crowd covered the wagon. When the coal was almost gone, a man with a red beard walked over to the prostrate horses and clubbed them unconscious. Another set to carving them up. A black man drew a knife and started to hack away at a haunch. The red-bearded man kicked the Negro in the side and waved his club at him.

"Get your hands off, ye nigger thief," the Irishman shouted.

"Paddy shit," the black man said. He cut the air with his knife. A handful of black men ran to help him. More Irish came running with clubs and staves in their hands. They stared at one another, waiting to see who would begin the fight. Steam rose from the horses' entrails as they spread in a puddle on the pavement.

From down by the ferry came the shout of voices. The driver was returning with a small band of ferrymen and railroad police. Two of the coppers had their revolvers drawn, and as they drew nearer and the crowd didn't disperse, one of them fired a shot into the air. People scurried up the embankments. Eliza had her shawl filled with coal and slung over her shoulder like a sack. When she reached the top of the embankment, she turned to see if the railroad police were in pursuit. They had formed a broken circle around the wagon. One of them fired another warning shot. On the other embankment, an Irish girl of about twelve was carrying a small boy on her back; she ran up the incline with a steady, graceful gait. The boy's arms were around her neck. He had no legs. At the top of the rise, the girl turned and saw Eliza staring at her. "Niggers go to hell!" she yelled.

Mrs. Blanchard's fever didn't break. She was violently ill. Eliza gave her tea and tried to keep her in bed. Mrs. Blanchard insisted on dressing and going to work. She only got halfway down the lane before she had to turn back. Eliza went alone. It continued like that for a week. Sometimes Mrs. Blanchard seemed to be getting better—the fever would almost disappear and she would take some small nourishment—but she was soon sick again. She became so weak that Eliza felt she should stay with her. Mrs. Blanchard wouldn't hear of it. "White people take my stall first chance dey get," she said. "Dat for absolute certain."

In the late afternoon, when Eliza came back from work, she saw from the bottom of the lane that the door to the shanty was open. She ran up to the shack. Inside was a shambles, the few pieces of furniture smashed, the stove overturned, the bed ripped apart. The floorboards had been torn away and the earth underneath dug up. There was no sign of Mrs. Blanchard.

A voice from behind Eliza said, "Come away, girl." An elderly man from one of the shanties down the lane was standing outside. He beckoned to her.

"What happened?" Eliza said. "Where's Mrs. Blanchard?"

"She's with us. Now come, girl." He waved his hand impatiently, gesturing for her to come with him.

She followed him to his shanty. His wife sat at a small table by the door with a Bible opened in front of her. There was a sagging double bed in the corner near the stove, and on it a body covered by a sheet. The old man went over and lifted a corner of the sheet. Mrs. Blanchard lay there with her knees drawn up near her stomach. She seemed smaller, as if death had already shriveled her.

"My wife went up about midmorning to see how Mrs. Blanchard was faring," the man said. "Knocked and knocked but weren't no answer, so she come and got me. I banged and called her name but got no answer either. I busted the door in. Didn't take much. Figured maybe she was dying and might need help. I was right, except she was no longer dying, she was dead. Once people heard the shouting and saw the door being busted, some of them come to find out what's happened, and as soon as they see Mrs. Blanchard is dead, there's a few grumbling about how she mostly kept to herself and they start wondering about what she done with all that money she took in down there at the fish market."

"By the time she bought her supplies of fish and paid the rent on that stall, there was hardly anything left," Eliza said.

"I'm sure that's the truth, but people believe what they want to believe and don't let the truth stand in their way. I told them to hush. 'Respect the dead,' I said. But I could see what was going to come about. These are hungry people, and the hungry don't know no laws, not even the laws of God, so I said to my wife, 'Helen,' I said, 'let's take this woman to where she can rest in peace,' and Helen and me took a sheet and we wrapped the body in it and carried it here, just the two of us, no one else lent a hand. Weren't in the door a minute before we heard them ripping

her place apart. You saw what they did. Don't know if she hid
money away or not, but if she did, it ain't there anymore."

The old man left Eliza with his wife. He said he was going
to walk to a police station and see about getting Mrs. Blanchard's
body taken away. He told his wife not to light a fire. "Keep the
room cold," he said.

He was gone over two hours. When he returned, he was
shivering. "The police said if no one killed her, they ain't interested." His wife lit a small fire in the stove, and he pulled up a
chair right next to it. "They said they'd notify the morgue, and
the wagon should be by in the morning. 'Leave it at the bottom
of the lane,' they said, 'because the wagon ain't going to go a-
hunting all through Niggertown.' "

"What time will they be by?" Eliza asked.

"Didn't give no time. 'Tomorrow' is all they said."

Eliza helped them move the body to near the door, the
coldest place in the room. She slept on the floor, beside the couple's bed. Just past dawn the old man and Eliza carried the body
to where the lane met the avenue. There was no sun. It was bitter
cold. After an hour, the old man said his feet were numb. He
went back up the lane. Eliza walked back and forth, trying to stay
warm. A skinny dog, its ribs clearly visible, skulked nearby, its
snout raised in the air. Eliza threw rocks at it, and it went away.
In the late morning the old man came back and told Eliza to go
to the shanty to get warm. They spent the afternoon taking turns
guarding the body. They were both standing in the dusk, about
to carry Mrs. Blanchard's corpse back to the shanty, when they
saw a wagon approaching. It stopped across the avenue and circled around to where they were standing. Two men in heavy coats
with fur hats that had flaps to cover their ears got down. One
went to the back of the wagon, which was enclosed in canvas,
and brought out a stretcher. They took the sheet off Mrs. Blanchard and put her corpse on the stretcher.

"Who wants to sign?" the driver asked. He waved a sheet of
paper. Eliza took it. Her hand was so numb she could barely hold
the pencil.

"Been waiting all day," the old man said.

"Oh yeah?" the driver said. "Well, we've been *working* all day." The two men bent over to pick up the stretcher.

"Count your blessings," said the other attendant. "This could be summer." They opened the flap at the back of the wagon. There were eight slots, four on each side. The soles of seven pairs of feet faced them; six of the pairs looked as if they belonged to children. The two men slipped Mrs. Blanchard's small body into the bottom slot on the right. Her feet, too, looked like those of a child.

"Where does she go now?" Eliza asked.

"If she's lucky, heaven." The driver brushed past her and jumped up onto the wagon.

"I mean, what they do with the body?"

The other attendant mounted the wagon. "Don't worry, she'll go to potter's field. Ain't exactly the Marble Cemetery, but earth is earth, and she'll be in a place where the rent collectors never go."

The driver snapped the reins, and the wagon moved away.

On the second day after Mrs. Blanchard's death, Eliza stood in the pre-dawn darkness waving for Flynn the carter to stop as he came down the avenue. She told him Mrs. Blanchard had died, and he took off his hat. "May her soul rest in peace," he said, "and perpetual light shine upon her." Eliza gave him her two pennies, and he said nothing more. Once arrived at the market, Eliza found that Mrs. Blanchard's fish stall had simply vanished; the stall next to it had expanded into her space. There were boxes of salted fish piled up in the corner. On top of one were the remnants of Mrs. Blanchard's possessions: a soiled blanket, some knives and trays, pieces of rope. The scale was gone. Eliza left without taking anything. The other sellers ignored her, simply pretended Eliza wasn't there, looking away when she went by.

Eliza walked up to Catherine Street. This was the market where the men of Midian's Well brought their oysters. She asked after them and was told they had stopped coming a few months before.

In the evening she went back with Flynn to the shantytown. She didn't know where else to go. Her small store of possessions had been taken when Mrs. Blanchard's shanty had been ransacked. The old man and his wife said Eliza could stay with them until she made permanent arrangements somewhere else. There was no letup in the cold, and Mrs. Blanchard's shanty was torn apart by the people on the lane and used for firewood. The next week there was a great snowfall, and when it melted there was no trace left of the shanty.

The old man worked as a barber on the North River piers. He carried a wooden crate that served as a chair. When the weather permitted, he set up shop in the open air by the paddle-boats, offering the immigrants a quick cut before they left for Albany and the West. If it rained, he stood under the protruding roof of the ticket shed, but the desk clerk charged him half a dollar for that privilege, which meant he had to service ten customers before he turned a profit.

He told Eliza that he had owned a shop of his own on Canal Street, but that the rise in rents and the arrival of the Italian tonsorial palaces, fifteen barbers in a room of gilt and mirrors, had forced him out of business. "I used to have some of the best customers in the city," he said. "They all came to my place, the important people did. I cut Governor Bouck's hair. He had a mane like President Jackson's, and there were even some who used to mistake him for Jackson. And Governor Young, too, I cut his hair. Both Bouck and him worked in the Treasury on Wall Street after they left Albany. You'll never see a politician die poor, that's for sure. And I cut Jack Diamond's hair, the dancer, there was never anybody tipped as good as him."

Eliza helped the old man's wife with her seamstress work. Mondays they walked to Sixth Avenue and took the horsecar down to Houston Street. They picked up two bundles of shirt pieces, paid a deposit, and spent the rest of the week sewing on sleeves and buttons. They worked all day. Saturdays they brought the finished work back and waited in a long line of women, mostly immigrants, until the piece master had inspected every shirt and haggled over a final price. There were children everywhere, playing in the street and in the alleyway, a legion of laborers set loose for a few hours of play until the next consignment of garments was received. Sometimes, after they had been paid, Eliza stayed downtown by herself. She walked to St. John's Park and sat on a bench facing the church, its great spire rising out of the uniform horizon of imposing homes. Of all the places in the city that she had seen, this was the one that most approximated her vision of what she had hoped to find in New York, the quiet dignity of the church and the homes surrounding the park, the men and women in their tailored clothes, servants walking with the children, a place of substance and permanence, and in the distance the weak echo of traffic and crowds, the reminder of the excitement that was nearby.

After sitting for a while, Eliza liked to walk east to Broadway and then down to A. T. Stewart's Marble Palace on Chambers Street. Most times she stood looking at the windows. Once she went in. There were rows of counters behind which were stacked dresses, skirts, shawls, and bonnets. There were floor-length mirrors at intervals around the room, and clerks roamed the aisles, tall, thin men in well-cut clothes constantly inquiring if they might be of help. Eliza saw one of them coming toward her. She turned and left.

One Saturday in early June she studied a window filled with blouses that were blazingly white. There were flowers stitched on the bodice and blue ribbons drawn through the cuffs. Each one must have taken hours to make, but the racks behind the window were filled with boxes of them. It was in that window that she first saw the face of the Haitian sailor, his image standing next to hers, his smile losing nothing in its reflection. She walked away when he talked to her. He followed her. When she boarded a Broadway coach, he did too. He sat next to her. She stared at her feet. He talked incessantly. She refused to tell him her name or where she lived. He said that she could be as silent as she wished or walk anywhere she wanted because he wasn't going to leave her until he knew where she lived. In the end she talked with him.

They walked west from Broadway to the lane. She pointed out the shanty where she lived. He put his arm around her waist and kissed her on her mouth. He said he would come back in a few days to see her.

A few days turned into six. He didn't come back until the following Friday. Eliza felt real despair for the first time since she had landed in the city, the fear that she had traded the closed, drab, strict world of Midian's Well for something worse, a lifetime of needlework until the morgue wagon arrived at the bottom of the lane. She prayed the Haitian would return but was certain he would not. On the seventh day he did. His name was Joseph. After several months she moved in with him, into a house where all the other boarders were white. They were the first white people Eliza had ever spoken with at any length, songwriters, actors, singers, musicians. Joseph mingled easily with them.

Joseph said that before he went to sea he had been a professional singer in Haiti, but that Haiti was a poor country and the people could not afford many amusements or support many artists. "You are always better off among artists," he told Eliza. "They are the easiest of the white people to get along with. But don't be deceived. Even among them it is always best to be the only colored in their company. Never more than two. And always be careful in your attitudes. Never be sad for extended periods. Never be moody. They find that difficult to understand, and they are made uncomfortable by it. Be of good cheer as much as you possibly can. And remember, they will forgive you more than most because you are beautiful. But don't be fooled, you are a colored in their eyes. That will always matter more than your beauty."

After Joseph left her, Eliza stayed in the room for two days without coming out. She slept most of the time. The five-dollar gold piece Joseph had given her lay on the table beside the bed. The nail on which his rosaries had hung was covered by the blouse he had presented to her when he had returned to the lane, blue stitching on the bodice, blue ribbons drawn through the cuffs. In the afternoon she sat by the window. It was autumn, but it already felt like winter. Across the way, a line of prostitutes paraded up and down the sidewalk. Until recently they hadn't made their appearance on the street until after the lamplighters' rounds, but the disaster on Wall Street and the hard times it caused had made them diurnal as well as nocturnal. With every factory that closed and business that went bankrupt and immigrant boat that arrived, the prostitution industry's labor supply grew. At every hour, all day, all night, a growing number of the female unemployed twirled parasols in summer and swung their muffs in winter, members of the city's first twenty-four-hour-a-day enterprise. Along Canal Street a battery of cigar stores displayed a few crumbling, sun-bleached Havanas in their windows. Behind the counters the willing sales help, young women in loose-fitting blouses, suggested that the gentlemen customers have a look at the "select stock" kept in the room upstairs. For less than a dollar, there were the depraved and degraded haunts of the Five Points as well as of Corlears Hook, where Manhattan Island bulged out into the East River, its aggressive "hookers" competing for each customer. Around the railroad terminal on Twenty-sixth Street, a basement trade in quick-as-a-wink service promised that no customer would miss his train. Farther west, at the corner of Seventh Avenue and Twenty-third Street, were "The Seven Sisters," a septet of adjoining brownstones lining a block built on speculation on the eve of the financial panic and quickly turned to commercial use. On Washington Street, Maria Casey's staff of white women catered to a clientele composed mostly of black sailors. Shanghai Sally's off Peck's Slip promised its patrons "pleasures in the Oriental style," but its lights were kept so low and its women were so taciturn that it was hard to tell where the whores were from. At Josie Woods's establishment on Clinton Place, near the Trump, only men who were referred by other clients and then interviewed by Mrs. Woods were accepted. The membership was said to be limited to a hundred, and each of the staff of twenty possessed an instrumental or vocal skill that she employed in nightly entertainments. The cheapest champagne that was offered was ten dollars a bottle.

The epicenter was Greene Street, from Canal to Houston—
"Love Lane," as it was sometimes called—its east and west sides
occupied by brick houses entirely devoted to the trade. The homes
were shuttered day and night, and the lamplighters were paid to
leave the lamps unlit. After dark the street's only light came from
the gas bulbs mounted over every door, bowls of tinted glass,
mostly red, the name of the establishment etched in white: "Xan-
adu," "The Pied Piper," "The Forget-Me-Not," "The Alps,"
"The Garden of Eden," "The Highland Fling," "A Bird in
the Hand," "The Devil's Own," "The Greek Gals," "The
King's Pleasure," "The Parisian," "Sin Bad the Sailor,"
"The Whip," "The Heavenly Rest," "Lulu's Place," "It's
Always a Pleasure," "Queenie's," "Once More," "Flora's,"
"My Lips Are Sealed," "The Kissing Corner." There were
patrons padding up to the doorsteps at all hours, but the heaviest
traffic was at night, a slow-moving river of customers flowing up
and down the street, its tributaries snaking in and out of the
houses.

On the third day after Joseph had left, Eliza came down from
the room. She sat at dinner with the other boarders. They never
mentioned Joseph, nor asked her where she had been. Eliza smiled
and laughed when the others did. She was too distracted to follow
what they were saying. The landlady stood next to the serving
table, between the boarders and the food, bantering with them
while making sure that no one made more than one return trip.
She stared at Eliza. The rent for the week ahead was due the
next day.

After dinner the landlady stopped Eliza as she was going upstairs. "I gotta know how much longer you plan to stay."

"Least another week."

"I only rent two weeks at a time."

"Wasn't that way before."

"Is now." The landlady was drying her hands with her apron.
"Look, dearie, I'm not tryin' to throw you out on the street. I know
Mister Joseph is gone, but you're not the first been left."

"He'll be back," Eliza said. "He's not left forever."

"Sure. He's been gone before and will come back again, a free spirit, and we all have an affection for him on account of it, but there ain't no tellin' when that day will be, and it just ain't possible for you to stay here till he *does* come back. Single women in this city that ain't with their families, most of 'em got but one way to pay the rent, and that's not the kind of place I run." She reached into the pocket of her apron, took out a piece of paper, and handed it to Eliza. "I feel sorry for you. Ain't easy making your way in this city, nobody knows that better than me. I wrote down the address of a woman might be of help. Colored like yourself."

Eliza glanced at the note. *Madame Julia Gates. The Arms of Love. 53 Greene Street.* "Go at midday," the landlady said. "It's the only time a girl would be safe."

"I'm not a whore," Eliza said.

The landlord folded her arms across her ample bosom. "Watch your tongue, girl. I never used that word. Whatever it is that goes on at Madame Julia's—and I ain't never tried to find out, 'cause that's her business like this house is mine—there's a regular staff of domestics, all colored, I'm told, and it's not easy for the colored to get that kind of work anymore, not since the Paddies overrun the town and drove 'em out of it. If I was you, I wouldn't overlook that fact."

Eliza went. A black boy of about twelve answered the door. He was wearing old-fashioned breeches with white stockings. He brought her into the front parlor. The room was shuttered and dark. It had an overpowering smell of must. The boy turned up the gaslight and left. Eliza heard a rustling sound from the hallway, the crisp swirl of taffeta, and a moment later an immense white woman entered, a mountain of flesh wrapped in a purple dress. She walked past Eliza and lowered herself onto a settee. She filled most of it. She gestured to Eliza to sit. The boy came back in, placed a drink on the table next to Madame Julia, lifted her slippered feet and put a footstool beneath them.

The woman sipped from the glass. "You were told Madame Julia was black?" she said as she put the glass down.

Eliza nodded.

"They tell all the colored girls that. Hope it will make them feel more secure. You see, if I hire you, the woman who sent you will get a small fee, so she was eager for you to come here. She lied, but we all do that when it's convenient. Have you worked at this before?"

Eliza shook her head.

"And the woman who sent you said you might perhaps find work here as a maid?"

"Yes."

"She lied again. There's no end to the lying that goes on in this town. New York depends as much on lies as on Croton water. Now, there *are* maids here but they're all old and plain, and you're neither. You're someone men would pay to be with, and I offer such women the chance to lie in my beds, not make them."

Madame Julia shifted her leg, and winced. She picked up her drink and took a long draft.

"Gout," she said. "It's very painful at times, but this helps." She held up the glass. "Quinine and laudanum in Saratoga water. It softens the edges. Life would be intolerable without it."

"I'm not interested in being a whore," Eliza said.

"Who is? No woman I ever met, at least not in the way a man likes to imagine, the delusion of women deriving some pleasure from the gratification of his desires. Thing is, you needn't be interested in being a whore to be a good one. You must be interested in prospering and accumulating the wherewithal to take up some other livelihood, that's what's important, and as long as you are working, you must avoid addictions such as this one." She lifted her glass, and took another drink. "The fact that you are here shows you are interested in having enough to eat and a place to sleep, and for the time being such interest is enough."

Eliza was perched on the edge of her chair. Her knees were pressed together. She was aware of how uncomfortable she looked.

"Please, sit back," Madame Julia said. "I'm no pimp, and I'm not going to eat you." She winced again and bent over to touch her foot but was unable to come near it. She called for the boy, and he came in with ice packed in a towel and put it on the foot.

"All my girls are colored. The specialty of the house. You've seen how crowded this street has become. Every place has to have something to distinguish it, some unique attraction, and the colored girls are mine. We do a good business. Every girl in The Arms of Love makes a living, which is more than you can say for the employees of some of the sinkholes on this street. Customers like to visit here. They think they're breaking some taboo, and a man who thinks that gets twice the pleasure. You been with a lot of them?"

"Who?"

"A stupid question. Just look at you. But some men would find your inexperience attractive. Don't ask me why, but they would. Others would demand their money back. Men are fairly consistent in their inconsistencies. The only thing you can count on is that each in his own way will be capable of a whole lot of silliness. Anybody sits where I've sat these last years and listens to them whispering their requests soon comes to realize there isn't another creature in God's kingdom capable of such silliness as a grown man."

The narrow slits of Madame Julia's eyes closed. She bit her lip and winced once more. "This Goddamn foot. The price of the life I've lived. Oysters and beef—stay away from them if you can." She drained her glass. "I haven't been out of this house in four years," she said. "But you know, sitting in a house such as this, you get a better idea of what's happening in this city than if you walked the streets all day and read all the newspapers. Men reveal themselves here. Take the passion for orality. I'm not talking about the right or wrong of it. I never talk about the right or wrong of anything because it doesn't have much to do with the way men live, and besides, one man's taboo is another man's taste. I'm just talking about the *universality* of it, the way it's swept everything else aside. I started in this business in '44 and it was the odd man asked for such a thing, mostly sailors. Now it's demanded here and everywhere on this street, and sitting here hearing such requests you realize something has changed in this city, the nature of manhood nowadays. I don't think it has the vigorous energy of former days, the pump, pump, pump it once did. There's too much European influence around. Consider all the eau de cologne being sprayed around necks and ears. What does that tell you about the level of masculinity in this city? If you ask me, all the real men in New York are dead or left for California. It's the soft ones that's left."

In the hallway a clock's chimes rang twice. Neither Eliza nor Madame Julia spoke. Eliza wanted to get up and walk out, but she was unsure of what to say to excuse herself.

Madame Julia broke the silence. "You're a little bit confused, but that's because I talk too much. Don't feel bad, though. Nobody ever entered this profession wasn't confused. I left Albany in '43, ran away from home and got as far as here, and when I began I was more confused than you are now. But don't bother yourself with too many questions. They answer themselves most times. For now all you need to know is it will cost you ten dollars a week for a room, meals, and laundry, and on top of that the house gets half of whatever you do. The rest is yours, and you work hard, develop a steady group of patrons, and in a few years the money starts to add up. One other thing. If you decide to work in The Arms of Love, you'll have to see my doctor, not that I expect any problems on that account, at least not yet. Now go make up your mind."

Several men looked at Eliza as she came down the front stairs. She walked toward Broadway as quickly as she could. A city of whores, the Reverend Mr. Enders had called it. A woman arrayed in scarlet, decked with gold and precious stones, in her hand a cup full of abominations and filthiness, the fruits of her fornication. Eliza knew she could go back to the barber and his wife in Niggertown. They had been sad to see her go and would welcome the extra set of hands; their livelihoods were increasingly threatened by the tide of cheap immigrant labor, an endless obligation to drink from the bitter cup of poverty, the fruit of their nigrescence.

Eliza packed her few things and left the boardinghouse. She wandered the streets. She looked in the windows of the shops. Not a single Negro clerk in any of them. What would they say if she asked for a job? Would they laugh? Or throw her out? Or stand in speechless wonderment? She kept walking.

The same boy opened the door of Madame Julia's. He reached to take her carpetbag. She held on to it.

"Suit yourself," he said.

He directed her into the parlor. Madame Julia was sitting where Eliza had left her. Her eyes were closed. Eliza stood motionless for a moment, then let her bag drop. Madame Julia opened her eyes slowly.

"You here to work?" she asked.

"No."

"Them that won't work, neither shall they eat. The Good Book says that."

"I'll work. I'll clean up."

"I already told you, I don't need more bed makers."

The ice in the towel over Madame Julia's foot had melted. There was a puddle on the rug. Her glass had been refilled. She seemed to be having difficulty keeping her eyes open.

"What time is it?" she asked.

"About six," Eliza said.

"They'll start arriving in steady numbers soon. The soldiers first. They're the eagerest." She pointed at the chair where Eliza had sat earlier in the afternoon. "Sit."

Eliza sat with her bag in her lap. She was perched in the same position as before, as if she were waiting for a train.

"I was as good-looking as you are now when I started. The men wanted me in the worst way, and I quickly learned to pretend likewise. I imitated their hunger, and that drives them wild, when they think you want it as bad as them. Of course, a man in the grip of his own desire will believe anything. That's what a whore learns better than anyone. Now they laugh when they see me. 'Mount Julia,' one of them called me. Thought he was being smart. Said I was as big as one of those Catskill mountains. 'You wish you could mount Julia,' says I, 'but the kind of man could make such things worth the doing has long since disappeared.'

"How they love to talk when they come down from upstairs. How calm and capable of conversation they are. But before they go up it's a different story. It's hard for me not to laugh in their faces when I bring them in to find out what they're after and to explain the rules. A nightly procession of love-hungry pups masquerading as pleasure hounds, reeking of alcohol, nervous, so damned anxious to get it done, so impatient, as though the fate of the Republic hung between their legs. I like to sit them right where you're sitting. Just sit and watch them squirm. They're worse than schoolboys, and all of them got it in their heads the colored women are going to show them something they've never seen before."

"I don't know where to go."

"Don't go anywhere. I never forced a girl into doing what she didn't want. But I guarantee you'll get used to it. Doesn't take much more effort than to ride a horse. If you're good, maybe I'll recommend you to Josie Woods. She's always had a colored girl on her rolls, and her girls don't have but one customer a night. It's not much worse than being married."

Eliza lived a month in The Arms of Love, in an attic room with a bed, dresser, chair, mirror, and a wardrobe for the dresses Madame Julia provided and for which she added two dollars to the weekly charge. She sent Eliza the youngest and most inexperienced men, the ones who squirmed the most. "They'll be done before they start," she said.

The routine dulled Eliza's revulsion. She had an average of six or seven customers a night, all nervous and quick to satisfy themselves. They were hayseeds, tourists, young clerks, soldiers with boys' faces. "Be sure not to let them fall asleep," Madame

Julia said. "They're filled with liquor, and once they're asleep it's like trying to wake the dead."

Eliza slept most of the day. There was a cook who prepared the girls' meals, and Madame Julia insisted they eat in the kitchen and not bring food to their rooms. There were five other women who resided in The Arms of Love. Four spoke with southern accents. They were not openly hostile to Eliza, but they never went out of their way to make conversation.

"Don't expect help from anyone in this house," Madame Julia told her. "This business is already crowded, and you can't blame them for not wanting to encourage the competition. Money means more than color. Negro or not, you might end up taking business away from them, and nobody is gonna abide that eventuality, not in this town. But if you're here long enough, they'll warm up."

In the room next to Eliza's was a girl her own age who said she was from Pennsylvania. She had been sent to the Quaker School in New York to be trained as a teacher. She had run away. Most afternoons she stayed in her room and cried. On Sundays she went to the French church on Twenty-third Street to hear Mass. She tried to get Eliza to go with her. "The ceremony is so . . . so . . ." She threw up her hands, "I am tired of all that is drab. I want a world of beautiful colors." She said she was saving her money so that she could move to Europe. "Negroes are accepted as equals by the French," she told Eliza.

"I worry about that girl," Madame Julia said to Eliza. "She has more delusions than a man."

Madame Julia spent the greater part of the day sitting in the parlor, drinking, napping, talking to the guests, her great bulk bathed in the weak light that seeped through the shutters. Each Monday the inhabitants of the house stopped in the parlor to pay their rent. On the fourth Monday that Eliza was a resident, Madame Julia had a female guest with her when Eliza entered, a slim, attractive, middle-aged white woman in an elegant velvet dress and a hat with a green plume.

Madame Julia introduced her to Eliza as Mrs. Josie Woods.

"Your employer speaks highly of you," Mrs. Woods said.

Madame Julia nodded in Mrs. Woods's direction. "You could hardly tell we started in this business together. We had the same figure once. Josie expanded her interests. I expanded my size."

Mrs. Woods said, "Tell me, what do you think of this profession?"

"I try not to think about it," Eliza said.

"That's a mistake. Thinking is essential to all success. '*Cogito, ergo prospero.*' I've had that motto placed on my coat of arms. 'I think, therefore I prosper.' "

"Your coat of arms?" Madame Julia laughed and clapped her hands. The fat on her arms shook. "We've come up in the world, haven't we, Josie?"

"It's either up or down," Mrs. Woods said. "No one stands still."

"Most days I'm as still as can be. The gout makes sure of that. I sit here and watch the world go its own skittish way, and as far as I can see the great majority of people is traveling sideways. A portion may be going down, but very few are going up."

"Ah, my dear Julia, the problem is that you can't see much from this self-imposed Elba of yours. Come for a carriage ride with me, and have a look at the city. It's changing every day, the buildings and ambitions growing higher at the same time, new faces, new businesses, new notions, expectations increasing, capital expanding, investments growing, the panic is over, the country is on the move again. There are fortunes to be won. This is an age made by God for the industrious."

"I get tired just listening to you talk, Josie."

"And you," Mrs. Woods said to Eliza, "have you ambitions?"

"I thought so once."

"And now?"

"I'm not sure."

"Are you freeborn?"

"Does it matter?"

"Of course it matters, or I wouldn't ask. We are entering a period of such progress that even the Negro shall share in it. Emancipation is only a matter of time, and the freeborn will be the leaders of their race."

"You sound like a Republican," said Madame Julia.

"I am a Republican, and proud of it. The party has my financial support, and the day that our sex is enfranchised, a day I pray for with some urgency, the Republicans shall have my vote also."

"Please, no politicking on these premises. I do not permit the discussion of politics in The Arms of Love. It bores me and distracts my customers."

"You're the one who raised the issue, but I respect your wishes." Mrs. Woods turned in her chair to face Eliza. "Besides, my real reason for coming was to see if you were as pretty and alluring as Madame Julia told me you were, and having seen for myself, I would, with the permission of our hostess, like to offer you a position with my establishment."

"I'm not a Republican," Madame Julia said, "but I never stand in the way of ambition. As I told you before, you may offer her whatever you wish."

Mrs. Woods said to Eliza, "Do you know the difference between a whore and a courtesan?"

"The price she's paid," said Eliza.

"That's a consequence of the difference, not the difference itself. The real difference is here." Mrs. Woods tapped her forefinger against the side of her head. "In the mind. A whore sees herself as a commodity. A courtesan understands that what she is selling is not herself but her services. She respects herself as a member of a profession, the way a lawyer or a broker does, and she never allows her patrons to ignore that fact. Have you ever heard of Theodora?"

"Another Republican?" asked Madame Julia.

"She was the empress of Byzantium, the wife of Justinian, and she'd been the most famous courtesan in the imperial city."

"Any of your girls ever marry emperors?"

"One married a senator, another the president of a railroad. Should an emperor ever appear on the scene, I wouldn't hesitate to offer one of my girls as a suitable candidate for his attentions." Mrs. Woods directed herself to Eliza again. "Can you play a musical instrument?"

"No."

"Can you sing?"

"Yes."

"You read and write, I presume?"

"Yes."

"Certain of the gentlemen who patronize my establishment have a predilection for women of color."

"Are they all Republicans?" asked Madame Julia.

"For a woman who bars politics from her establishment, you nevertheless seem incapable of divorcing yourself from its associations. No, they are not all Republicans. Some are Democrats. But it is not color alone that interests them. They look for poise, gentleness, refinement, a facility for conversation, a delicate nature, and an educated sensuality devoid of the gross and distasteful. You," she said to Eliza, "seem possessed of these or, at least, capable of mastering them, and since I am at present lacking a woman of color, I'm glad to offer you the opportunity to join my staff on a trial basis."

"Old men will ask you to beat them with whips," Madame Julia commented, "and you shall see for yourself that no matter what his age, a man is always a boy. But the pay is good and the demands are few. My advice is, Take it."

"Julia, you are the prisoner of your cynicism. It is what keeps you locked up in this tomb."

"There isn't a better view of the city to be had than the one from this chair."

Eliza took the offer. The best part of Josie Woods's establishment was the library, a whole room of leather-bound books that the staff was free to use; novels, histories, poetry, a complete set of Shakespeare. The other women ignored Eliza as much as they could. With their coldness they made it clear that if some of the clients had a taste for the dusky, it wasn't shared by the staff. The only one to be friendly was Ellie Van Shaick, a young woman with thick black hair and deep green eyes. She and Eliza sat in the library during afternoons and read aloud to each other. Sometimes they would enact an entire play, each taking several parts, and speak with such verve and enthusiasm that a few of the girls would stop outside the door, where they didn't think they could be seen, and listen.

At night, the girls would receive the customers in the parlor. Certain men maintained their anonymity, entering and leaving by the rear entrance, especially men of political stature or of the cloth. But a significant number of the older men enjoyed sitting and listening to a recital or a dramatic reading. They drank champagne or brandy, and then one by one they slipped away with their escorts for the privacy of the upstairs. Eliza had a roster of six. One a night. They were not inexperienced like those she had encountered in The Arms of Love, and she learned their preferences very quickly and did what was expected of her in an expert way, her mind detached from the mechanics of her work, the poetry she had read that day in the library repeating itself in her head.

Ellie Van Shaick left after two years. She said she was going to California and would write Eliza when she got there. She never did write. Six months after Ellie had left, Mrs. Woods discovered that Ellie had never left the city.

"I can't believe it," Mrs. Woods said, "but from what I'm told she trusted a man with her money. She always impressed me as smarter than that. It seems he was from a good family, and Ellie fell in love with him, which is understandable, I suppose, but to have let him take charge of her finances, such foolishness on the part of an intelligent girl! The boy did what you might expect him to do. He fled to England with Ellie's money and has married a British woman—titled, of course."

"Where is she now?" Eliza asked.

"This is the strangest part. She is working in a concert saloon just around the corner. A concert saloon! I sent word that she was welcome back here but never heard anything in response. Ellie has her pride. She comes from one of the city's ancient families, and I respect that. I know that she might feel some embarrassment at the consequences of her naïveté and wish to avoid old acquaintances, but a concert saloon!"

Eliza thought about going to see Ellie, but she knew that Ellie must feel humiliated by her mistake. Eliza remembered the enthusiasm with which Ellie had left Mrs. Woods's, and her high hopes for finding a new life in California. Eliza had felt her own expectation rise with Ellie's. She had seen Ellie as a pioneer who would open paths that even a colored girl might follow. She had no desire to cause any embarrassment to Ellie or to aggravate Ellie's sense of disappointment, so she never approached her.

In the early fall of 1860, Eliza told Mrs. Woods that she would soon be leaving, that she had saved a sum of money. Mrs. Woods said that she was sorry to lose Eliza. "Where do you intend to go?" she asked.

Eliza had no idea. Were the French really without racial attitudes? What would Haiti be like? Or Cuba? Eliza had read in the *Tribune* of a colony of Negroes from the United States that had been established in Montreal.

"I'm going to Canada," Eliza said.

The last week Eliza was at Mrs. Woods's the Prince of Wales paid a visit to New York, and except for the sullen hostility of the Irish, the event turned into an immense holiday, with businesses closing early the evening he arrived, and spectators lining Broadway from the Battery to the Fifth Avenue Hotel on Twenty-third Street, where the Prince was staying. Like many other homes and shops, Mrs. Woods's establishment had the Union Jack draped out of a window. Mrs. Woods herself went to the ball held in the Prince's honor at the Academy of Music. Her ticket was sent with the compliments of Edwin Morgan, the Governor of New York. Since all of her gentlemen clients were also to be in attendance, Mrs. Woods had given her employees the night off.

Eliza was in her room when she heard Mrs. Woods return

from the ball. It was still early, not yet eleven o'clock, and Eliza
was surprised that Mrs. Woods hadn't stayed longer. She could
hear Mrs. Woods yelling at the servants, something that never
happened in the house. Eliza opened her door and stood by the
stairwell. "He's coming! He's coming! My God, he's coming!"
Mrs. Woods's words echoed through the house. She came flying
up the stairs, her gown billowing around her, a crown of flowers
tilted off the side of her head.

"How many of the girls are home?"

"I've no idea," Eliza said. "I've been in my room all night."

"Get dressed immediately. The best you have. If you need
jewelry, go to my room. There's no time to waste. I'll see who
else is here."

Mrs. Woods ran past Eliza and began banging on doors.

Eliza said, "Who's coming?"

Mrs. Woods turned quickly. She covered her eyes, and with
the full force of her voice screamed, "The Prince! My God, the
Prince is coming *here*!"

There were six of the girls in the house. Once dressed, they
waited in the parlor. They didn't talk. Mrs. Woods kept fanning
herself and pacing near the window. She held on to the drapes.
After a few minutes, she told all the women to stand. She inspected each one like an officer at a dress parade, adjusting
clothes, straightening shoulders, rearranging hair.

"The city was disgraced tonight," she said as she went about
her inspection. "Absolutely disgraced. It was a riot, not a ball.
Half the guests were intruders who forced their way in without
an invitation. Rabble, the lot of them. At one point, part of the
floor collapsed. I was ashamed to be a New Yorker. Ashamed.
But then I found myself squeezed into a corner with this magnificent specimen of a British officer, Captain Grey, one of the royal
equerries, and once I was introduced to him, he said, 'I have a
good friend who has spoken very highly of a Mrs. Woods, but
I'm sure you couldn't be the lady of his acquaintance.'

" 'Who might that friend be?' said I.

"Says he, 'Colonel Percy of the Irish Guards. He was posted

for a year at the embassy in Washington and managed to spend
a good deal of that time in New York.'

" 'Bootsie Percy?' I asked, and the Captain near jumped out
of his skin. We spent the next hour talking about Bootsie and
other things until Captain Grey informed me that he had to rejoin
the royal party.

"I extended an invitation to him to visit these premises, and
he said that he would do everything in his power to see that he
did, but would I mind if he, perhaps, brought along another
guest? *Would I mind?*

" 'Bring along anyone you like,' I said. 'Why, bring the Prince
himself!' I was trying to be humorous, of course. Never did I
dream. But he pressed my hand and said, sotto voce, 'Ah, Mrs.
Woods, I shall try. Nobody would benefit as much from what
you offer as our young friend.' My God. *Our* young friend. The
Prince *here*. Among us. I shan't believe it until it happens, until I
see him here in the flesh."

They sat for another half hour. Mrs. Woods kept getting up
to look out the window and fidget with the curtains. The room
was warm, and the women began to yawn. They listened to the
sounds of approaching wheels on the pavement, wheels that then
moved past. At last they heard wheels that stopped. Mrs. Woods
ran to the window. Her voice quavered. "The Prince is here," she
said. She smoothed her hands down the front of her dress, and
walked toward the door.

Eliza went to the window with the other women. They jostled one another to see out. A landau was pulled up to the curb.
The driver was sitting on his raised seat smoking a pipe. The
women couldn't see if anyone was inside. Mrs. Woods reappeared
with a tall man in a suit of hound's-tooth check. He wore a mon-
ocle and had a luxurious mustachio, glistening with wax and
twirled at its ends.

Mrs. Woods introduced the women to Captain Grey. He
bowed slightly to each one. The madam took him by the arm and
they went back to the door. Captain Grey went outside. A servant

came in and said that Mrs. Woods wanted to see Eliza upstairs, that she was waiting on the first landing.

"They are pulling the coach around to the stables in the back," Mrs. Woods said. "He can't be seen by anyone. Captain Grey impressed the need upon me. He needn't have. I understand, of course."

For the first time, Eliza felt nervous. Until now, she hadn't taken the Prince's appearance among them very seriously. But now she knew not only that he was there, but that she had been chosen to be his.

Mrs. Woods took a deep breath. "He wants an Indian," she said. "That's what the Captain insists. Nothing else will do. All other possibilities are available in London and Paris."

"An Indian?" Eliza asked.

" 'An American aborigine' is how he put it."

"What did you tell him?"

Mrs. Woods bit her knuckle. "Well, I told him that, well, yes, I had a young woman who was half Indian. Her mother, I said, was a princess of the Montauks. He came in to see for himself. He thought you looked splendid." Mrs. Woods was a step above Eliza. She put her hand on Eliza's shoulder. "I shall be eternally indebted to you. Whatever I can do for you, I will." Her crown of flowers was askew again.

"What is my name to be?"

Mrs. Woods let go of her shoulder. "Running Deer. Princess Running Deer."

They went to Mrs. Woods's room. Mrs. Woods took a length of red ribbon and tied it around Eliza's forehead, like a headband. "Remember one thing. You must not speak unless spoken to. Captain Grey was adamant about that." She kissed Eliza on the cheek and left. Eliza sat on the bed and waited. Her heart was racing. After a few moments she heard footsteps outside the door. She stood. Mrs. Woods entered without knocking. A young man stood behind her. He was short and a little plump, with a round face and a receding chin. He reminded Eliza of the many clerks and mechanics she had met at Madame Julia's, nondescript, un-graceful, unable to hide their nervousness.

Mrs. Woods said to him, "This is Running Deer." Eliza curt-sied. Without saying another word, Mrs. Woods turned and left.

The Prince had his hands in his pant pockets. He walked over to the window and parted the drapes to look down at the street. With his back to Eliza he said, "This is Captain Grey's idea. Mil-itary men have trouble thinking of anything else." He kept look-ing out the window.

Eliza wasn't sure whether the remark had been directed at her, whether it was something she should respond to, or whether the Prince was merely thinking out loud. She kept silent.

The Prince stepped back from the window. He looked di-rectly at her. "Are you really an Indian?"

"Part."

"You are part Negro also?"

"Part."

"Many Americans seem to have Negro or Indian blood, a result, I suppose, of the preponderance of men among the settlers. They took squaws for wives, I'm told, and produced a mixed race. Even when their skin is white, you can see they often have thicker lips than is normal. Many also seem to have a discernible slant to their eyes. The Lord Mayor of New York, whom I met tonight, had a distinctly aboriginal cast to his eyes. There also seems to be a prevalence of brachycephaly among the laboring classes." He pressed his hands against his skull. "You know, the kind of short, broad heads you find among the non-Teutonic peoples, especially the Irish. And prognathism seems to predominate as well."

Eliza wanted to say something, but was at a loss. The Prince said, "When I was in Canada last month, I met a number of pure-blooded Indians. Ferocious-looking fellows. Chippewas, they were. Turned out that despite all their feathers and war paint, they were the cordial sort. We smoked a pipe together. It's often the case, you know, at least from my experience, that people aren't as bad as they first appear."

The Prince continued to stand across the room from Eliza.

He launched into a description of his visit to Niagara Falls and to the fair in St. Louis, two of the sights along his trip that seemed to impress him most, and as he kept talking, he began to stammer.

"We toured Mis . . . Mis . . . Mister Barnum's today," he said, "and I saw the most dread . . . dreadful creature! What-Is-It?"

"Pardon me," Eliza said, "what is what?"

"No, no. That wa . . . wa . . . was its name: 'What-Is-It?' Mis . . . Mis . . . Mister Barnum claims it's the missing link. Claims it was cap . . . cap . . . captured on the coast of Africa. Says it's ha . . . ha . . . half man, half gorilla. Looked like . . . looked like a poor deformed nigger to me."

Eliza didn't say a word. The Prince took his watch out of his vest pocket and glanced at it. Eliza saw there was a tremor in his hand. He walked to the door. "This is not the time," he said. "I'm fatigued." And then he left.

Eliza untied the headband and took off her dress. She wrapped herself in the sheet and rumpled the pillows. Several minutes later, Mrs. Woods came in.

"He was quick," she said.

"Very."

"But he seemed pleased."

"I hope he was."

Mrs. Woods never spoke openly about the Prince's appearance in her establishment. Sometimes, perhaps, she might hint at it in an indirect way, embellishing her invocation of the Empress Theodora with a veiled reference to her intimate familiarity with the amorous instincts of a certain royal person. But she left the rumors that surrounded the Prince's visit to the city's raconteurs, who fabricated an elaborate myth of a princely debauch in Manhattan's lowest dives. Eliza kept silent, too. She had no interest in becoming the object of attention of every man in New York who wanted to share the Prince's pleasures. She knew what she wanted from Mrs. Woods, and concentrated on getting it.

Mrs. Woods often talked about her financial stake in a local theatrical production of *Uncle Tom's Cabin*, which she saw as an investment in the fortunes of the Republican party. Lately, she had been complaining about the return of her investment. Attendance was way down. Eliza had seen a notice in the paper that the management was seeking replacements for most of the major roles.

There was no precedent for people of color appearing on New York stages, and she expected Mrs. Woods to express shock at her request, but she had been made a promise. *Whatever I can do for you, I will.*

She knocked on the door of Mrs. Woods's room in the early evening, before the patrons began to arrive. Mrs. Woods invited her in.

"I have a favor to ask," Eliza said.

"Anything I can do, I will."

"I should like to try out for the part of Eliza."

"Eliza?"

"In *Uncle Tom's Cabin.*"

"You wish to appear on stage?"

"Eliza is a person of color."

"So is Uncle Tom, in fact of a far deeper color than Eliza, but no one has ever suggested that he be played by a real Negro. It isn't done."

"I'll say I'm Cuban."

"I'll have to think it over."

In the morning, Mrs. Woods gave her decision. "I've considered your request," she said. "Matter of fact, it kept me awake half the night. I will see what I can do, but you shall say nothing about your race. We'll let people wonder. The mystery is what draws them, the possibility that they're seeing something they're not supposed to see. In this, the theatre has much in common with *our* business. We'll let them decide for themselves what you really are."

Mrs. Woods was as good as her word. She took Miss Therese La Plante to see the manager of the theatre. He was resistant. She was insistent. "The wind is gone out of the sails," she said. "This production is becalmed and is rapidly taking on water. It's in danger of sinking."

"They'll rip the theatre apart if you put a nigger on stage."

"Who says Miss La Plante is a Negro? Perhaps she's part Spanish, part Indian, a native of Louisiana, an exotic. The distinction between the races is often blurred. It is not the science some pretend. Let them guess what she might be. People will admire their own daring in going to see such an intriguing figure, a woman who might well be a Negress. Let them believe whatever they want to believe."

"This is a theatre, not Barnum's Museum. We're not in the business of displaying freaks."

Mrs. Woods said the issue of race was closed. She had no intention of debating it further. She was exercising her prerogatives as the major investor. The only question left to consider was, Could Miss La Plante act?

"What is your background?" the manager asked Miss La Plante.

She invoked Mrs. Euphemia Blanchard, and the Fulton Academy: a university education in the theatrics of survival. The manager shrugged. He had her read from the script. "Well, you can act, there's no doubt about that," he said when she was finished.

The theatre filled again. The war and the crowds of soldiers in the city brought in new audiences, even after the question of Miss La Plante's identity faded from the city's conversations.

She met Jack soon after she got the part of Eliza.

Their first night together, after they made love, he stood in the dark by the window of the hotel room. Eliza felt herself drifting off to sleep. Jack smoked a cheroot, and she watched the tip flare brightly as he drew on it. He sang softly, in a lovely tenor:

> *Come where my love lies dreaming,*
> *dreaming the happy hours away,*
> *In visions bright redeeming*
> *The fleeting joys of day.*

She dreamed she was on a boat, traveling from Staten Island to the city. Her father was at the tiller. Her mother sat in the bow, facing her. They were both smiling, and as they neared the shore, they saw that all the people lining the docks were colored and were shouting welcome.

JUNE 1, 1863

Beware the ingratiating stranger, whether comely girl, genteel woman, decorous gentleman, or sincere and friendly tradesman! Beneath the polite veneer and winning smile may lurk the blackest of hearts and vilest of intents. Guard the portals of the home as you do your own life! *Never* admit a guest whom you have not been told to expect. *Never* give entry to a laborer, artisan or tradesman without specific instructions from your employer. Failure to heed this injunction can result in consequences too terrible to describe.

—Mrs. Sarah Benning Oswald, *A Decalogue for Domestics:*
A Primer of Rules, Regulations and Suggestions
for Those Engaged in Household Service

MARGARET O'DRISCOLL FLIPPED the skinlike pages of her missal. Holy sounds: people turning their prayer books and missals as Mass progressed, rattle of rosaries against the pews, drone of the Latin prayers. She found the page she was looking for and marked it with one of the ribbons sewn into the spine of the book. *June 1st. The feast day of Saint Angela Merici.* She rested the missal on her bed, and covered her face with her hands. A habit: first thing in the morning, down on her knees, the book open to the prayers the priest would say in honor of the saint or sacred event to which the church dedicated the day. So easy to fall back to sleep. She said a Hail Mary, and her eyes went back to the same place on the page.

June 1st. The feast day of Saint Angela Merici. Virgin. 3rd class. White.

She rested her head on the bed sheet. *White.* The color of the vestments the priest would wear this day. White for virgins, red for martyrs, black for funerals. She raised her head and turned the pages forward to a place marked by another ribbon.

August 28th. Her father's birthday. *Saint Augustine. Bishop. Confessor and Doctor.*

White for Augustine, too, the missal said. A great saint, but he was no virgin. A great sinner before he was a great saint. Why white for him? The Church had reasons that only the theologians could understand, and even they had trouble sometimes. Augustine himself, it was said, almost went mad trying to figure out the Trinity. But *3rd class,* what did that mean? Why was Saint Angela *Virgin. 3rd class*? Either you were or you weren't. Virginity wasn't the Trinity, a mystery only theologians could understand. The great bull in the field outside Macroom, the way he mounted the cows, his masculinity jutting out beneath him, there was no 2nd or 3rd class about that, all the cows got it the same way. Wasn't a virgin among them. Unless, of course, you were one of those always wanting a man and never getting one, like Miss Kerrigan, a virgin by default, because no one would have you. Maybe that's what it meant: *Virgin. 3rd class.* But anyone who spent her life wanting it, but not getting it, she would be no saint, certainly not one to whom the Church would give a feast day.

Probably *3rd class* had some significance she didn't know, something to do with how the Church ordered its calendar. Another mystery. Mystery on top of mystery. Mary was, at once, a virgin and a mother. Some mysteries you could ask the priests about. They might look at you a little quizzically, surprised that you were questioning holy truths, but they always tried to answer, even if the answer was invariably the same: *There is no explanation, only faith.*

True enough. Who could hope to understand all the works and wonderments of God and His saints? The Church drew its existence from them. There was no explaining. Besides, who would approach a priest and ask, *Father, what makes a virgin 3rd class?* You could never utter such a thing to a priest.

From downstairs she heard the soft, muffled *bong* of the standing clock by the staircase as it struck six. She crossed herself quickly and read the first prayer.

O God, through Blessed Angela You caused a new society of holy Virgins to flourish in Your Church; grant through her intercession, that by living angelic lives and detaching our hearts from earthly joys, we may merit enjoyment of those that are eternal. The prayer ran down the left side of the book. On the right was the Latin. The priest's language. An unintelligible jumble, but holy words, the very sound of them far holier than English, a Protestant language. Under Saint Angela's name was a brief biography. *She founded the Ursuline Congregation to undertake the education of Catholic girls. She was fond of saying that the disorders of society were the result of unsanctified families, and that there were too few Christian mothers. Saint Angela died at Brescia on January 24th, 1540.*

Odd, a nun worrying about mothers, since she would never have a family of her own. *A new society of holy virgins.* There was something to be said for it. Frances Kelly, Betty O'Connell, and Molly Foley, all Cork girls, were now in the convent.

In the days when he was still proud of the sobriquet "Pagan" O'Driscoll, Margaret's father had railed against the convent, the same way he had railed against everything connected with the Church. "A waste of human fecundity," he called it. "Another priest-driven nail in the coffin of the Irish nation." There were things her mother would listen to in silence. This she wouldn't. "God Himself commanded it," she said. "Blessed are the women who take it upon themselves, never having a family and living in rooms by themselves, praying all the time."

"In this country, a woman needn't be a nun to end up alone. Emigration sees to that."

"There's no telling the suffering we've been spared—and will be spared—because of their prayers and intercessions."

"What we've been *spared*? What other curses could Jehovah send against the Irish besides subjugation, persecution, famines, exile, and death? He's already been harder on us than any save the Jews. What's left for Him to visit on this island?"

"Maybe if we weren't such a vicious tribe of spiteful, back-biting sinners, we'd have been spared these things. Archbishop Cullen himself said that the Famine was a calamity sent by God to purify the Irish people, and there's no denying the return to religion in this country since it happened, and now, with the con-secration of so many lives to God, maybe we'll finally be a people that find some favor in His eyes."

"Archbishop Cullen is a swine," Pagan O'Driscoll said.

Margaret closed the missal. A farewell present from her mother. There was never any time during the week to go to Mass, only on Sundays, at one o'clock, when she got off from work. But she knew her mother was saying these same prayers, kneeling every day in the Dominican church in Cork City to hear Mass, always in the same pew next to the Fourth Station of the Cross: *Jesus Encounters His Mother.* Prayers linked to prayers. The confidence that they would meet again after this, our exile, in another life, all of them gathered in by the Virgin Mary, no one left out, not even her father.

There was a sharp rap on the door and muffled words she couldn't hear. She didn't have to. They were the same every morning. *Get a move on. The world won't wait for you.*

Margaret went to the washstand and poured water from the pitcher into the basin. She pulled her shift over her head and threw it onto the bed. Bending over, she rubbed a bar of soap in the water, between her hands, and glanced up at the small mirror on the wall. It contained a portion of her nakedness, breasts hanging down and, framed by them, the triangle of pubic hair. She kept rubbing her hands. It was a woman's body in the mirror, the breasts larger in this bent position than if she were standing straight, her hips full and well formed. She had once confessed to a priest the pleasure she took in looking at her body. He had been silent for a moment. "Try to practice modesty of the eyes," he said. Gave one Hail Mary as a penance. Not much of a sin, with a penance that small.

She took a cloth, wet it, and rubbed it beneath her arms, lightly touched her breasts with it, wiped it across her stomach, and brought it down between her legs, cleaning herself quickly. *Detaching our hearts from earthly joys.* Holy women who would spend all their days atoning for sins. But it wasn't for everyone, not for those who admired the heft and strength in a man's body, the feel of his arms when you danced, joys not eternal but as real as any to be found on this earth. When she finished dressing, she brushed her hair, bending over so that it fell in a great mop toward the floor. She held it with one hand and brushed it with the other, quick, hard strokes that pulled through the knots until it was smooth and tangleless. As she stood, she flipped the mass of hair to the top of her head, worked it into a rope, laid strand upon strand, tied it with a small black band, and stuck in pins to secure it. In the convent they had their hair cropped like sheep. Molly Foley with her great mane of black silk. Such a sacrifice. And why? It was all covered anyway, hidden beneath veil and wimple, not a strand showing. Who would know if the nuns kept their hair? She reached down to the top of the small bureau that stood in front of the window and picked up her cap. A silly-looking thing. Round plate of white linen with a high, full crown and a short rim that was starched and corrugated. The washer-woman hated to iron them as much as Margaret and the other maids hated to wear them. But Mrs. Bedford had brought them back with her, mobcaps of English make, and insisted they be worn.

Margaret stuck the cap onto her head, worked it down until it was settled just above her ears, and tucked the loose strands of her hair beneath its stiff circumference. She bent her knees to lower her body, a crude curtsy, and stayed in that position as she adjusted the cap in the mirror. Except for above her ears and at the nape of her neck, her hair was invisible. "Such hair is a glory," her mother had said to her when she was a child, as they sat before the firelight, in the hour before bed, the brush running through Margaret's hair, rhythmic strokes, her mother's hand fol-lowing the brush. "It's your great-grandmother's hair. They sang about it at the fair in Macroom. They probably still do."

> *Kate of the red-yellow tresses*
> *That river of crimson gold*
> *So lightly on your shoulders rests.*

Margaret hummed the tune to herself and tried to remember the words, but she found herself recalling something else. *I dream of Jeanie with the light brown hair, borne like a vapor on the summer air.* A snippet from somewhere. Where? The picnic the Cork girls held in Jones's Woods on a Sunday two weeks before, the five of them sitting on the grass on their afternoon off, and the boys in their blue army uniforms leaning against a nearby tree, harmonizing. *Many were the wild notes her merry voice would*

pour; many were the blithe birds that warbled them o'er. American boys, they had stood around but never approached. Sounded
like one of Tom Moore's melodies, but it was more likely an
American song. Beautiful, whatever it was. She gave the cap a
final tug on both sides. Might as well be a nun as a maid. Small
room. Hair hidden away. A life of rules. It was blasphemous to
have such a thought. She crossed herself. *A society of holy virgins.*
God's grace on them, but she hadn't traveled all the way to America for that. She shut the door to her room quietly. It wasn't yet
six-thirty. "Before nine and after ten"—that was the rule—"the
servants should be careful not to disturb the family's rest." One
of many rules, all of them written down in the booklet given her
at the office of the Society for the Encouragement of Faithful Domestic Servants. A bare room with benches that looked like pews,
it could have been a Protestant church except that the seats were
filled with Irish-Catholic girls. She had been nervous waiting for
her name to be called. "Nothing to fear," the girl next to her said
in a voice thick with the accent of West Cork. "Ach, they're desperate for help. Every upstart squireen in the city of New York
has to have at least two skivvies or he doesn't feel he belongs.
This is me third job in six months. Get rid of me one place, I'll
find work in another, quick as that."

In the room Margaret was called into the clerk sat behind a
battered desk, watching intently as she entered, making no effort
to disguise that he was examining her clothes and deportment.
Once she was seated, he barely glanced at her again; he stared at
the folder on his desk and talked rapidly, in the Yankee style. She
was used to it now, the nonstop monotone, but had trouble with
it then, the clerk's face pointing down, his eyes evading hers, his
words running into one another.

"You have little real experience, which under ordinary circumstances would be a serious impediment to employment as
anything save a laundress or scullion, but these, as we are all well
aware, are anything but ordinary circumstances, and I have several positions for maids-of-all-work that would normally be un-
available to someone like yourself."

He glanced at her for an instant, then shot his eyes back to the desk. His hands were folded in front of him, long white fingers with carefully tended nails. He unfolded them and reached into a drawer and took out a blue pamphlet.

"We shall keep your name on file here, and enter the comments of your employer. Those whose diligence and dedication win them praise, and are with one employer for a period of not less than three years, shall be awarded a certificate of merit from the Society, an invaluable aid in the obtainment of future employment."

With his slender index finger, he opened the pamphlet to the back page. "Here you will find a facsimile of that certificate, a reminder of what you should be working toward." He handed her the pamphlet. *A Decalogue for Domestics: A Primer of Rules, Regulations and Suggestions for Those Engaged in Household Service. By Mrs. Sarah Benning Oswald.* He removed from the folder on his desk the sheet she had filled out earlier. Under the space marked *References,* she had entered three fictitious names and addresses. She would have left it blank, but the girl from West Cork wouldn't let her. "Fill it in," she said. "They're sticky about these things. Doesn't matter what you put down, so long as there's something. They know it's a lie, but it gives them comfort that you tell it. It's the way the Yankees are."

"Everything's in order." He handed her a slip of paper. "Here's the name and address of your prospective employer. All the particulars, wages, hours, responsibilities, will be settled with them." He extended his hand. She shook it. A weak grasp, as though the long fingers had no bones in them. "Good luck," he said with a smile as unsubstantial as his handshake.

Two and half years since then. Six months away from her certificate of merit. Little she wanted it. Margaret went down the stairs slowly. Today would be quiet. Mrs. Bedford had left for Long Branch. Be away until September, glory be to God. The other two maids, Minnie and Eileen, had been dragged away with her, swept up in the torrent of trunks, hatboxes, carpetbags, cartons, and parcels. It had taken half a morning to pack the coach, which then had to be unloaded at the pier and repacked on the boat. Mr. Bedford had grown exasperated watching the whole affair, and yelled at Andrew, the coachman, a thing he never did; speaking harshly to the help wasn't Mr. Bedford's way.

On the second landing, she stopped outside his door. She could hear his snoring. Last summer, when he and Mr. Ward had joined Mrs. Bedford in Long Branch, they had left her behind. Mr. Bedford was staying only a few days, and didn't want the city house closed or left unattended. The first summer, the summer the war started, they had closed the house, taken down the drapes, rolled up all the rugs, covered the furniture, and all the servants had been dragged into the Babylonian Captivity of the Jersey seashore, a pitiless sun, swarms of mosquitoes and flies, a cramped house, the help condemned to an attic where the heat turned the candles into puddles of wax. But Mr. Bedford had never decamped. His business kept him in the city, and Margaret and Miss Kerrigan had been sent back.

Margaret was glad to stay in New York. Miss Kerrigan said that Margaret was left behind was because Mrs. Bedford had no regard for her. "She won't have you with her because you're more a bother than a help," she said.

"And she won't have you," Margaret said, "because she wants to remember what life without stomach pain can be like."

Miss Kerrigan prided herself on the way she ran her kitchen. "Wellington of the pots" was how she said one former employer had described her. Margaret would watch Mr. Bedford's face as she served him his meals. He wore an expression of resignation, like Wellington's adversary at Waterloo. Mr. Ward picked at his food; he never seemed to have much of an appetite. Mrs. Bedford was away so much and ate so little when she was home that she didn't seem to take much notice of what came out of the kitchen, and the guests were few these days.

When Margaret had started working at the Bedfords' in December of 1860, the house was always filled with dinner guests, many of them from England. There were dinner parties three or four times a week. The cook then was a former assistant kitchen master at the Astor House, a small Welshman with a vile tongue and a knack with the cookstove that brought renown to the Bedfords' table. Margaret couldn't remember exactly when Mr. Bedford began missing those dinners, but it had been sometime shortly after the war started. At first, she and the other servants hadn't given it much thought. The city was in an uproar, and the likes of Mr. Bedford, with all their duties and responsibilities, and the demands of the money trade, were no doubt awash in work. Yet even after life had returned to its routine, and when except for the content of the newspapers and the presence of so many soldiers on the streets the war had faded into the background, Mr. Bedford stayed away.

One evening, as she prepared Mr. Bedford's bath, Margaret heard him arguing with his wife, and not the usual kind of argument, hushed and angry tones, each of them trying not to shout and draw the attention of the servants. This time you didn't have to lean your ear against the wall or crack the door just the slightest to hear what they were saying: Their voices echoed through the house. Standing next to the tub, even with the water running, Margaret didn't miss a word.

"It's another woman, Charles. I knew your drinking would eventually lead to this, that's what keeps you from this house. Tell me the truth, and at least spare me being made a laughingstock; don't add *that* to your sins."

"Sins?" You could hear the rage in Mr. Bedford's voice. "I consume my life in the task of providing for you and that drone of an uncle of yours, and you have the Goddamn gall to speak of *sins*? My *sins*?"

A month later, Mrs. Bedford hired Miss Kerrigan as cook. Whether or not Mrs. Bedford had done so to spite her husband, that had been the effect. Whatever had been keeping Mr. Bedford away from home had lost its—or her—grip. He came home most nights to eat his evening meal. He was almost always unfailingly polite, and hadn't any of the contemptuous airs of some of the guests that stayed in the house; nor did he call you by a wrong name most of the time, in the manner of Mr. Ward, as if it didn't matter who you were. He also paid a bit above average, even if there wasn't much left after Margaret sent her monthly remittance back to Ireland. And Mr. Bedford wasn't like some of them she had heard about, running his hands where he shouldn't, always pressuring the girls to grant him privileges that weren't included in *A Decalogue for Domestics*. Yet there was a distance to Mr. Bedford that had always made him seem more a boarder in the house than its master.

This morning there was no sound from behind the door save the buzz and growl of his snoring. When he went to Long Branch for a weekend and Margaret was left to keep the house in order, turning on lights in the evening to discourage burglars, she would wrap herself in one of Mrs. Bedford's robes. There would be no need to use a chamber pot, or wash from a pitcher or bowl, or dash down four flights to the water closet next to the kitchen. She would lie in the tub in the evening, and when the water grew too tepid, she would turn the handle with her foot and let more hot water in. As she had the previous summer, Miss Kerrigan would howl in protest, and threaten to turn her in. "A sin against your employers," she called it. Mrs. Sarah Benning Oswald agreed. Commandment No. III in the *Decalogue:* "Under no circumstances shall any servant violate his trust by in any way availing himself of those quarters, amenities and conveniences reserved for the exclusive use of his employers."

She forgot what she had done with the pamphlet. Put it in her bottom drawer, probably. There was precious little Mrs. Sarah Benning Oswald knew about a domestic's life, the small opportunities to relax, to share in the amenities and conveniences, and as long as you cleaned the tub and put everything back in its place, what was the harm? It would take more than Miss Kerrigan's scoldings or Mrs. Sarah Benning Oswald's pontifications to convince Margaret otherwise.

In the kitchen, Miss Kerrigan was standing at the cookstove. She didn't turn when Margaret entered. Margaret took down the teapot, cups and saucers, and two plates. The same fare every day. One coddled egg for Mr. Ward, lightly toasted bread, a slice of ham. An hour or so later, nothing save coffee and two fried eggs for Mr. Bedford, who was in the habit of eating a large meal at midmorning, when he was at work. There wasn't much Miss Kerrigan could do to ruin two eggs.

Still facing the stove, Miss Kerrigan said, "Well, praise be to God, Her Royal Highness has reported to work."

Margaret yawned loudly. Miss Kerrigan looked over her shoulder, her eyebrows arched in disapprobation, and took down a small pot. She put it down with a clang.

"You want to know what's wrong with you?" Miss Kerrigan asked.

"No, but I suppose I'll be told anyway."

"Same thing wrong with your whole generation, with all the Irish girls coming over here now, and you know what that is?"

"Can't it wait until I've had my tea? Tea softens the blow of bad news."

"You're spoiled. Think the world owes you something. Come over here on one of them big, fancy steamships in ten days flat, your meals provided." She filled the pot with water and put it back on the cookstove. "And your heads filled with fantasies."

"Put the kettle on, too."

"Do it yourself."

"It's right beside you."

"I'm not the tea maker, I'm the cook."

And not much of one, at that, Margaret thought but did not say. She went over next to Miss Kerrigan, lifted the kettle high into the air, and brought it down slowly.

"There we are," Margaret said, "and a mighty effort it was."

Miss Kerrigan was hunched over her pot and didn't seem to notice. "Not in my day, it wasn't like that at all. It was hunger we were fleeing. Real hunger. And we came without any royal notions of what we'd find, and them that had any fancies didn't keep them very long, not after five weeks in the hold of a packet ship, people dying every day, the fever leaving some of them raving mad, and the runners on South Street, some of them our own kind, robbing whatever they could, and the Yanks spitting on us when we went to look for work."

Margaret opened the door to the dumbwaiter and put cups and saucers, silverware and plates, on the tray inside. She wasn't without memory of the hunger. As a girl of four or five, she had watched her mother stand at the door of their house in Cork City and give food to those who stopped, shadowy creatures who quickly moved on. Once she looked out the window and watched a steady stream of people move through the street toward the center of Cork and the harbor beyond. It was twilight, the weak, washed-out eventide of winter, and although she hadn't been concentrating then on watching the passersby, she could recall now the impression they made on her, the straggle of slow-moving strangers, the air of some terrible defeat hanging over them. At night, after they said grace, her mother ended with the same petition: "And we pray especially for God's mercy on the poor starving people of this country."

"And we had no contraptions such as that," Miss Kerrigan said. She motioned with her head toward the dumbwaiter. "We carried everything up and down the stairs, didn't matter if it was a dinner for forty, up and down we went all night, and if we dropped anything, it came out of our pay."

The kettle began to steam and sputter. It gave out a shrill whistle. Margaret made the tea. Miss Kerrigan handed her the cup with the coddled egg, a plate with a slice of ham, and two burned pieces of bread. Margaret turned the bread over. It wasn't as badly burned on the other side.

Miss Kerrigan stood by the cookstove with her arms folded. Margaret formed her mouth into the shape of a smile and turned it on the cook. Miss Kerrigan glowered back. A thin, short, gray woman, no breasts or hips.

Margaret went up the stairs into the butler's pantry, hoisted the dumbwaiter, and took the tray into the dining room. The room was cool and dark, the portraits on the wall hidden in shadows. She drew back the curtains, and the faces on the wall seemed for a moment to be startled by the light. She set Mr. Ward's place.

The cup, saucer, and plate sat forlorn on the great table. She had barely finished when Mr. Ward appeared. Punctual as ever, he always wanted his breakfast on the table when he sat down.

"Good morning," he said. He glanced up at the portraits as if the greeting were as much for them as for Margaret.

"And a good morning to you, sir." She curtsied slightly.

Ward put the book he had brought with him next to his plate, and began to read and eat at the same time. With Mr. Bedford, it was the newspapers. Sometimes, when they dined together, the two of them sat at opposite ends of the table, the one with his book, the other with his paper, and they would scarcely speak a word. It was hard not to be nervous in a situation like that, with every sound, from putting down a plate to collecting the silverware, echoing through the room. Margaret preferred when they talked and argued, which with Mr. Bedford and Mr. Ward was usually the same thing, Mr. Bedford becoming red in the face, and neither of them taking the slightest notice of what was going on around them.

"Would you like your tea now, sir?"

Without looking up from his book, he nodded. "Please," he said.

She left him alone, went into the butler's pantry, took her own cup and saucer off the tray, and poured herself a cup of tea. She decided to wait in the pantry until Mr. Ward wanted his second cup of tea, and not return to the kitchen for another lecture on the slothful state of her existence, more of Miss Kerrigan's comparisons, her life as the standard for all others. Little wonder at Miss Kerrigan's constant state of grievance if she took life under the *Decalogue* for her ideal, every coming and going prescribed, every hour of the working day given over to routine. Service was better than a rented corner of a tenement, at least for the amenities it offered, no matter if most of those were forbidden to the help, yet the possibilities were as narrow as the attic beds the servants slept on; this was a life chosen not in the manner a nun chooses the convent, certain that the bare, celibate boundaries of her cell are the thresholds of eternal happiness, but one that unfolded like age itself, minute by minute, hours turning into days, years into decades, until the mirror reflects a face that is old, unwed, unweddable, a virgin by default, a permanent Irish domestic, 3rd class.

In the end, famine or not, they had all come to America for the same reason: There was nothing else. At home the prospects were not so much bleak as nonexistent. Servant or shopgirl, the whole of life would be determined by your accent and religion. If it could be arranged, a match with some farmer; if not, celibacy. Ireland was a country haunted by the memory of hunger, by the ghosts of its starved children, by a final and terrible humiliation.

Some rebelled—that was part of the country, too, hands raised against the English, or against custom and tradition—and tried to act out their own romances. But Ireland was more comfortable with tragedy. Margaret's parents had tried for romance. Her father, Augustine O'Driscoll, had come to Cork City as a small boy, the year after his parents had been swept away in one of the local potato-crop failures that drew little notice outside the affected area. He and his two sisters had been divided among their relatives around Baltimore, a fishing village on the coast of Cork. The uncle he was sent to was scraping by as it was, and could barely feed him. In the mornings, Augustine ran down to the fishing boats and begged for what they could spare him. He roasted the scraps they threw him on the end of a stick held above the pitch fire that served as a beacon for the boats. Afterward, he washed his face and hands in the seawater so that his uncle would not smell the fish.

In the last years of his life, when he had abandoned politics and come back to the Church, as ferocious in his devotion as any man in Cork, there was hardly any spark that could light the old fires that had blazoned his reputation as "Pagan" O'Driscoll, nor any that could rekindle the burning oratory of his Irish Confederation days, except when he wandered into the subject of his childhood, the ache of hunger that never went away, the one-room cabin with the farm animals living beside the family, the constant fear of eviction.

When he was ten, he set out on the road for Cork City, alone, with nothing. He got a job in a linen mill as a glider, and ran across the wooden frames in his bare feet and reached into the clattering apparatus to stop the cloth from bunching or tangling. Some gliders lost a limb, a few their lives, but Augustine O'Driscoll, save for the loss of a toe, escaped unharmed. At fourteen, he was made a full-fledged hand, and at eighteen, a foreman in charge of several looms. That was the year he met Catherine Murphy, from Macroom, who had been sent by her father to work in the shop of some distant relatives. It was her father's hope that since he couldn't give her a dowry of any worth, she would become skilled in the ways of the townspeople, and make a suitable candidate for marriage to some shopkeeper in Macroom. But it was in Cork City that she met Augustine O'Driscoll, fell in love, and eloped, a girl of seventeen, and was disowned by her father.

Margaret always liked to imagine them in their first days together, her mother young and beautiful, so in love with the tall, lithe foreman that she was willing to defy custom and her father, to be turned away by her family in order to marry him. Self-educated and so well spoken that he was looked upon by many as a representative of the Cork City's laboring class, Augustine O'Driscoll achieved a stature no workingman had ever held before. He voiced the anger of his peers against the conditions under which they worked, and insisted that even if relatively few in number, they suffered as much as anyone from Ireland's colonial status.

Although he consented to marry in church, Augustine O'Driscoll had already earned the nickname of "Pagan" from his alehouse denunciations of Christianity, and his political radicalism. Eventually, alehouses and politics would prove to be his undoing, but all that was as yet unknown to the two lovers who took up residence in a crowded, noisy lane. Catherine sometimes wondered if she had done the right thing, but seeing her husband come through the door assured her that marrying him was the only thing that her heart could have let her do.

In the end, after years of estrangement, Catherine's father had relented. Old and sick, he had sent for his daughter, and she went to him in his last illness. Seeing her for the first time in all those years, he had stood back, both hands clutching the knob of his thorn stick, and said, "Sure, Catherine, you've become an old woman."

Small wonder. First came the babies, six in eight years, Margaret the eldest. They were good years at the mill, and Pagan O'Driscoll had rented a cottage in a newly constructed row of workers' residences on the outskirts of Cork City. More and more, however, Pagan was caught up in the political agitation that was sweeping across Ireland. A local organizer in Daniel O'Connell's Repeal Association, and a fervent advocate for untying the knot of union with Great Britain, he was less enthusiastic in his devotion to O'Connell himself, "The Liberator," the man who had pushed through Catholic emancipation. At a rally outside Blarney Castle, Pagan proclaimed, "You can repeal a union, but you can't a rape, and the truth be told, that's what has been done to Ireland and to her people. And even though England can be forced to recognize that it can continue its depredation only at the cost of continually multiplying the size of its garrison in this country, even though it accepts the inevitability of Ireland's intention to regain its honor in the eyes of the world, an equally important question shall remain for us: What to do with the landlords? These are the servants of injustice, who held the robe of our ravager, and who to this day collect the spoils of criminal accomplice. What justice shall be meted to them?" His words were widely quoted in the loyalist newspapers, and that embarrassed the Association. Pagan was reprimanded by its leadership in Cork City. In private he said, "O'Connell is a landlord himself, and their fate will be his."

In 1847, with the Famine raging in the countryside, Pagan joined the Irish Confederation, the militant embodiment of the Young Irelanders' desire to deal with the catastrophe of hunger by forcing an immediate restoration of Irish self-government. Margaret would remember him in the green uniform he wore to the Confederation meetings, a heroic sight in her eyes, but all the while her mother busied herself with the children, never seeming to notice the uniform or rhetoric of her husband, yet praying in her heart that the condition of the country could rectify itself before any harm could come to her husband.

In March of 1848, when John Mitchel and Thomas Francis Meagher, two of the most fervid of the Young Irelander firebrands, were arrested for treason along with William Smith O'Brien, the organization's leader, there were speeches and torchlight parades. Later, Margaret remembered being at an outdoor meeting when her father spoke. She had no recollection of what he said, only an image of her mother with her head bowed, her hand raised to her forehead, as if praying or in pain. Whatever he said, he was subsequently dismissed from his job. That summer, habeas corpus was suspended, and the country proclaimed. Her father and a handful of others in Cork were arrested. In Tipperary, O'Brien, acquitted of the charges on which Mitchel had been convicted, led the remnants of the Irish Confederation in a "rising" that left two dead. Some of O'Brien's followers escaped to France or to America. O'Brien, Meagher, and several others were tried for treason, this time convicted, and sentenced to be hanged, drawn, and quartered. The sentence was commuted to transportation.

The trials of O'Brien and the others were a sensation. They were men of wealth and substance, landowners with university degrees, and yet their words and deeds were redolent of the age-old excesses of the "wild Irish." Where the grim, inexorable depopulation of the island through three years of starvation, disease, eviction, and emigration had failed to rivet the attention of the British reading public, the courtroom performance of the Young Irelanders did.

Pagan O'Driscoll didn't share in their fate. He languished in jail in Cork, but was never brought to trial. Margaret accompanied her mother to the jail each afternoon. It was a looming,

featureless building not unlike the mill where her father had
worked. Margaret and her mother stood behind one set of bars,
Pagan behind another, and a jailer paced up and down the space
between them. Her parents argued. Once, her father pointed at
her and said to Catherine, "You'll upset the child if you talk like
that." Catherine became subdued. "If you gave a ha'penny for
your children, you'd have not allowed yourself the words that put
you behind those bars," she said.

Her father's friends helped pay the rent. After three months
in custody, he was finally released. They moved to the cellar of a
drapery store owned by a former member of the Confederation,
and although the Famine receded and the country adjusted to the
calm that followed in its wake, Pagan remained a committed revolutionary. He ate and drank politics and, as time passed, drank
it more than ate it, an admired figure in the pubs of Cork, not
allowed to pay for his own drinks, yet without any offer of work.
While Margaret cared for the other children, Catherine went to
work cleaning the homes of young clerks, Protestant newlyweds,
mostly, who in the interests of domestic economy were willing to
spend the early period of their careers without live-in help.

In 1853, when Margaret was twelve, Catherine became pregnant for the seventh time. By this time, Pagan shook so badly in
the mornings that Margaret shaved him. She sat across from him,
drew the razor across cheeks, chin, and throat. He held the chair
with both hands, his eyes closed, grimacing when she nicked him.
Sometimes she did it deliberately, out of anger at his drinking, at
his stumbling home in the middle of the night, waking the children, making her mother cry. They lived on bread and tea. Finally, Catherine wrote to her father and explained their plight.
He sent back an envelope containing no letter, only some pound
notes. Pagan was furious when he found out.

That morning, Margaret finished shaving him and put the
blade into the bowl of soapy water. A thin spume of blood trailed
off. There was more blood on Pagan's chin. He had his hands
shoved into his pockets so that they wouldn't shake, and he was

shouting, demanding to know where the money had come from to fill the house with food.

"Not from you, that's for sure," Catherine said.

He grabbed her by the collar of her dress, and a button at her throat flew off and ran in a wide circle around the floor. He twisted the dress in his hand and lifted her to her toes. "You bloody whore," he said, "don't you ever talk to me like that."

Margaret retrieved the razor from the bowl and held it tightly, open, in a fold of her dress. She moved toward her father, her hand trembling.

"Let go," Margaret said.

He took his hands off Catherine, turned, and went out the door. He didn't come back that night, nor in the days that followed, and Margaret was glad for it. They heard reports that he was drinking heavily, sleeping in alleyways, but he was never mentioned except when they said their prayers and her mother put his name in the litany of those she asked God's mercy for.

When he came back, he stood in the stairwell that led down from the street to their door. The shadows hid his unwashed, unshaven face. Holding the door open a crack, Margaret thought he was just another beggar.

"It's me," he said, "your father."

Margaret put her shoulder against the door and braced it with her knee. Her mother came from behind her. She gently pushed Margaret out of the way and stepped outside.

Neither Catherine nor Pagan ever made mention of what was said, but when they came back inside, he sat on their bed and wept. He got a job as a porter in a bakery. It required him to work nights. He slept most of the day, and to the children became little more than a curled, sheeted figure behind the curtain that served as the wall of their parents' bedroom.

When the second O'Driscoll daughter was old enough to look after the younger children, Margaret joined her mother cleaning houses. In January of 1858, Catherine went to Macroom for the first time since her father had died, and she took Margaret with her. Catherine grew excited at the prospect of the trip, chattering away about her girlhood, the dances at the crossroads, the pilgrimages to the holy well, the boys who risked her father's wrath by flirting with her. They stayed with Catherine's brother, Jeremiah Murphy, a big, bearded, taciturn tenant farmer who lived alone in the whitewashed cabin where he and Catherine had been born. Catherine and Margaret did their best to bring some sort of order to the place, and to get rid of the barnyard odors that pervaded it. Catherine had brought sheets from Cork City to cover the straw mattresses.

Approaching fifty, and in the process of bargaining for a wife, Jeremiah seemed pleased. He invited his neighbors to come see his sister, and after Mass on Sunday they came, some to see the prodigal daughter returned, to mark the changes in her since she was a girl among them, and others to set their own daughters on display, eager for a match that would join their fortunes to Jeremiah's. In the old days, before the Famine, it was only a handful of prosperous tenants with the biggest holdings who would postpone marriage so long, but now such procrastination was increasingly the fashion among all levels, save the Irish-speaking and the poorest of the poor, which were usually the same thing. On the way back from Mass, Catherine pointed out to Margaret a field where a cluster of cabins had once stood. "The people there were all musicians and singers. Laborers by day, at night they filled the air with their melodies. But it's a different country now. The life is gone out of the land. Half the people I knew as a girl are gone, God knows where."

The men entered Jeremiah's cabin first, the nails in their big leather shoes scraping loudly on the floor. They held their hats in their large, red hands. Their wives followed. To Margaret, the women resembled nothing so much as the dwellings they inhabited—squat, thick-walled, the shawls over their heads as bulky and rough as thatch. Last came the daughters, girls with none of their mothers' girth, but wrapped beneath the same kind of shawls, and as shy as calves. Moving around the room in a store-bought dress from Cork City that was bordered at the cuffs and neck with lace and drawn in at the waist, Catherine seemed from a different world. It was hard for Margaret to believe that her mother had lived her youth as one of these timid girls, or that if she had stayed she would have turned into one of these solid, stocky peasant wives. Catherine glided about the room with lovely grace, serving tea. It was also difficult for Margaret to think of her mother as a clerk's skivvy.

The husbands tried not to look at Catherine but couldn't help themselves. Even with her graying hair and the lines in her face and around her mouth, Catherine Murphy was still near to the girl they remembered from their youth, same body, same smile, same way about her. The wives, their eyes hard and fixed, looked at their husbands, but they, too, thought mostly of Catherine, the easy life of city women, the luxuries they had, the clothes they wore, and the airs they assumed even though they had been born and reared under thatched roofs. Only the daughters made no attempt to hide the awe in which they held Catherine, an apparition from another order of existence, like the visitors from Dublin or London whom they caught glimpses of in Macroom, the wives of government officials or military officers on their way to some other part of the empire.

Margaret and Catherine stayed for a week with Jeremiah. At first, Margaret took delight in the novelty of what she saw. She enjoyed walking the lanes, the look of the countryside in high summer, and the talk of the people, the accents so thick that if you didn't listen carefully, you might think they were talking Irish instead of English. But by the middle of the week, she was already growing tired of the place, cow droppings everywhere, flies swarming around them, the remorseless routine of her uncle's life, the same chores done the same way every day. It took less than a day to see the sights there were to see, a ruined castle, the remains of an abbey, a new church, the tree from which, it was said, Cromwell himself had hanged Bishop Boetius Mac Egan—martyr's scaffold or not, it was a sorry-looking tree.

Jeremiah employed two spalpeens. Young men with no English, dressed in ragged clothes, their mouths already half empty of teeth, they never came near the cabin. There were scores of men like them in the area, but they lurked in the background like half-domesticated dogs, living tentatively on the edges of the community. Jeremiah worked beside them, and spoke to them in Irish, but his tone was usually harsh, and Margaret felt sorry for them.

When he had been drinking, Pagan O'Driscoll had been vitriolic on the contrasting fates of the spalpeens and of the tenant farmers, who had not only survived the Famine but increased their holdings.

"Calluses on the arse of landlordism," he said. "When the Hunger was at its height, they closed their doors to their own people, Irish like they were, serfs to the same masters, and then, when it was done, they feasted on the carcasses of the dead and the departed, licking their master's hand when he threw them the crumbs of lands that had been seized from the starving. Fat and prosperous now, they're like crows back from a battlefield."

It was hard for Margaret to think of her uncle and his neighbors as prosperous. Their cabins were spare and stark, and whatever surplus they had they hoarded, scared the landlord's agent might raise the rents to levels they couldn't pay, and perpetually afraid that the potato blight might strike again, destroying whatever margin they had managed to amass. And although the Famine was never mentioned, although there was more talk of Cromwell's presence two hundred years before than of the events of the previous decade, the memory of what had happened hung over the countryside like the morning mist that shrouded the stubby remnants of cabins in fields and on hillsides, clusters of shattered walls where cows now grazed.

On her last night at her uncle's, Margaret attended a dance in Macroom. It was held in a hall brightly illumined by gaslight and filled with many of the same girls she had met the Sunday she'd arrived. They all stood to one side of the room. On the other side were boys who looked as if they had just stepped out of the bogs, red-faced and heavyset, with hands like their fathers'. They reeked of whiskey. The music was the kind heard coming out of the lowest shebeens in Cork City, the fiddle tunes that emanated from cellars and back rooms choked with tobacco smoke. The next morning Margaret awoke happy with the thought of going home.

It wasn't until her uncle married that she and her mother returned on another visit. They came down at Eastertide. Jeremiah's wife was in her twenties. She was shy, sitting by the hearth to have tea with them but saying little. Jeremiah, however, was more talkative than he had ever been. At one point, he suggested that Margaret accompany his wife out to gather some eggs, and she did, glad for the chance to get away from the stinging smoke of the turf fire.

That night, when they went to bed, Catherine told Margaret that her uncle had made a proposition. "He wants to arrange a marriage for you."

Margaret had been on the edge of sleep, her back to her mother. She opened her eyes.

"He said that he looks on you as he would a daughter and is willing to settle a dowry on you."

"What did you tell him?"

"That I'd talk to you."

"That you'd talk to me?" Margaret sat up. "What kind of an answer is that?"

"A good one. Ireland is hard on its children, hardest of all on its daughters."

"Especially on them that spend their lives scrubbing out troughs."

"The man he has in mind owns a grain store in Macroom. His name is Murphy, too, but no relation. Not the worst sort. I knew his father."

"Not the worst sort? Well, now, *there's* a recommendation. How could I resist such a match?"

"I thought that you should at least know of your uncle's offer."

"Now I know."

"There aren't a lot of choices, Margaret."

"You refused to settle for such a life. What do you expect of me?"

"I don't offer my life as a model. You can go back to Cork City; no one will stop you. Spend the rest of your days sweeping out other people's houses. But, to be honest, if *I* knew that lay ahead, I might think twice about being the wife of a grain seller in Macroom."

Margaret threw her head onto the pillow. She put her hands beneath it and shut her eyes. "I'll go to America." She had often had the thought, a fleeting, indistinct desire. This was the first time she had spoken it.

"And do what? Clean the houses of Yankee Protestants instead of staying home and cleaning those of Irish ones? Small reason for such a great journey."

The vision Margaret had of America was always of the West, tall men with faces turned so brown from the sun that they were practically indistinguishable from the Indians. And rivers. Rivers that poured over mountains and plains, torrents of raging water, untamed.

Catherine put out the candle. She rolled onto her side with her back to Margaret. "It's no holiday in America. Some of them that went over are already coming back. It's as hard for the Irish there as here, they say."

Margaret faced the window. Her tiredness was gone. Outside, moonlight bathed the far hills and turned the land to a single shade of gray. One girl had come back, that's all, and she to enter a convent. Molly Foley had spent a few years in New York. She had returned with boots for her father, a silk shawl for her sister, and a sewing machine for her mother. Pious, sincere, quiet Molly. If she wasn't so kind and sweet, Margaret would have hated her. But none of the others had come back, and the remittances they sent home had become a regular part of life for many of the families the O'Driscolls knew, money that paid the rent and put food on the table. The blessings of the Yankee dollar. It brought more comfort to Ireland than all the deliberations of the Parliament in Westminster ever had.

It was on that night in bed with her mother that Margaret decided she would leave Ireland for America. She didn't sleep. It was as if she were leaving the next day. In the morning she still felt sure of her decision, but, perhaps because she was so tired, she was less enthusiastic than she'd been the night before. Her uncle was unusually talkative, bantering with Margaret and Catherine when he came back from the fields for his breakfast. Margaret was sure that he supposed the offer had been conveyed to her. She was sure also that he believed she would jump at the chance to be a townsman's wife, the opportunity her mother had lost. And he'd generously settle the dowry, happy to help his niece—and not ignorant of the benefits of a personal tie with Murphy the grain seller. In bad times it was such connections that could make the difference between holding your land or being turfed out. But Jeremiah was also happy for Murphy, maybe for him most of all, a girl from Cork City as his bride, with her city ways and city dresses, and her grandmother's hair, *Kate of the red-yellow tresses*. Such things were important to townsmen, especially those determined to rise in the world as Murphy was, a lovely girl on his arm, the envy of the other merchants, *that river of crimson gold so lightly on your shoulders rests.*

Margaret wasn't sure of when her mother told Jeremiah of Margaret's refusal to avail herself of his offer. Probably late the next afternoon. He was still friendly and full of talk at breakfast. But he didn't come home for dinner. His wife said that he had gone to look at a cow that was for sale. "He's a great one for seizing an opportunity," she said. He was there the next morning, but had little taste for conversation. He barely spoke a word to Margaret for the rest of the visit.

Catherine didn't mention the offer again, and when they returned to Cork City, neither did she bring up Margaret's announced intention to emigrate. They went back to their work as day-hire domestics, and instead of handing over all her pay to her mother, Margaret began holding back a few pennies from each job, determined to accumulate what she needed for a passage to America. It would take time before she had enough, but it would allow her to find out more about where she was going, to give some thought to what she would do and with whom she would stay. She was in no great hurry.

Walking home one night from a triduum in honor of Saint Monica, the mother of Saint Augustine, several months after they had come back from Macroom, Catherine finally brought up Margaret's plans.

"How much have you saved?" she asked.

"Saved?"

"Don't be coy, you're just after leaving church."

"Near half a pound, I should think."

"You're a long way from ever seeing America."

"Eight pounds isn't all that much."

"Eight pounds, is it? And what will you live on after you land? Do you think the Yanks provide free room and board?"

Margaret hadn't given it much thought, not yet. As determined as she was to go, she hadn't made much headway in fleshing out her plans. America was still so indistinct a place, rivers of roaring water, men panning for gold in them. The Mississippi. The Hudson. The Swanee.

"I'm making plans."

"Plans, is it? Well, people make their way there same as here; 'by the sweat of thy brow shalt thou earn thy bread.' You keep saving your money, all that you can. You may need it to carry you over once you land. I'll see to the fare."

"And where will you find eight pounds?"

They were standing at the top of the street, and down below the Lee moved swiftly but gently. No one had ever looked for gold in it.

"Your uncle."

"Jeremiah? He wouldn't give me the tail from a pig, not after I went and ruined his grand alliance with Murphy the grain seller."

"Never *give* you anything, 'tis true. But perhaps he'd lend it to you at a small rate. He never turns his back on such propositions."

A few weeks later, Catherine returned from Macroom with the money. Suddenly the distant possibility of America was near, but along with a growing excitement Margaret felt hurt at the ease and speed with which her mother had made the arrangement, as if she couldn't be rid of her fast enough, one less person to crowd the basement where they lived, a daughter to send them remittances from America, whatever she could afford after dispatching her uncle his monthly payment. It wasn't until the night before she left that Margaret grasped her mother's desire to have it done with as quickly as possible; her eldest child, the one she was closest to, sent on her way without a prolonged leave-taking, the equivalent of a slow dying. Few ever returned. They went by the thousands, sometimes whole villages, swearing never to forget. And yet their eyes and voices, their merriness or sadness, their marriages and spouses and children, were all reduced to the occasional letter, fewer as time went on, until the small death of emigration was eventually enveloped in the greater final one.

The last night, Catherine sat apart as Margaret's girlfriends buzzed about. The relatives had yet to appear, and the girls were still too excited by the thought of Margaret's departure to dwell on the loss they would feel, a truth they would comprehend only at the end of the evening. Catherine held her apron to her face and tried to stifle her sobbing. The girls stopped their talking and stood around her, each trying to offer some comfort. Then she began to keen: the cry of the country women, their shawls thrown over their heads, a low moan that gradually ascended to a shriek. The girls kept talking, trying to muffle the sound of the cries, but eventually gave up. Margaret hadn't thought her mother capable of such a thing, but then she began to sob too, which is most of what she would remember from that last night, tears and sobbing, her mother's keening, singing and music, the raucous sound of men with too much to drink suddenly coming to a stop for a song or more crying. Margaret stood like an observer at her own wake, and understood why her mother wanted it over as quickly as possible.

*

Margaret looked up at the clock on the wall of the pantry. Twenty past seven. "O Christ," she said. Mr. Ward would have expected his second cup of tea long ago. She jumped up from her stool, grabbed the pot, and put her hand on its side. Tepid. She should have brought it back to the kitchen and kept it warm, should have poured it ten minutes ago, should have cleared the table by now. No time to warm it. And she had no intention of giving Miss Kerrigan more inspiration for her speeches. She went into the dining room. Mr. Ward was sitting with one elbow on the arm of his chair, his hand propped beneath his chin. With the other he held open a book that rested on the table; his spectacles were laid atop it; his dishes had been pushed to one side.

"More tea?" she asked.

He seemed startled.

"More tea?" She gestured with the pot.

He looked around the room as though he were getting his bearings. From the walls, the images of his ancestors gazed serenely into the distance. Recovered from his surprise, his expression seemed similar to theirs. Reposed. Thoughtful.

"Tea, of course. Yes, please."

She poured it and went about gathering up the dishes. As she was about to reenter the pantry, he said, "When you're through, please bring me pen, paper, and ink."

She went into the library and brought back pen, paper, and an inkwell. She had planned to clean the dining room first thing, or at least get a start before Mr. Bedford came down for his breakfast. But the old man could very well spend the whole morning scribbling at the table and throw off her schedule. She put the writing materials in front of Ward. He picked up his spectacles, fitted the wire arms around his ears, and began to write. She stood at his elbow and read, mouthing the words to herself. *The manly pride of the Romans, content with substantial power, had left to the vanity of the East the forms and ceremonies of ostentatious greatness.* The script was large and legible and flowed across the page. He stopped and dipped the pen into the well. She wondered whom he was writing to, but then she saw that he was copying from the book he had been reading. His finger sought out the line where he had left off. He started to write again. *But when they lost even the semblance of those virtues which were derived from their ancient freedom, the simplicity of Roman manners was insensibly corrupted.* He paused. She waited for him to continue. Without looking up he said, "That will be all, thank you."

"Of course, sir."

She hurried out of the room, embarrassed that he had caught her reading his words. But what was the harm? It wasn't a letter to his mistress, not that Mr. Ward was the kind that would have one. Mr. Bedford, maybe, there was no telling, but Mr. Ward was wed to his books, as faithful a spouse as there was. She shouldn't have been peering over his shoulder. Privacy of the eyes, it could be called. Something she had to practice. But not much of a sin, not when all she saw was merely words copied from a book. Hardly worth a Hail Mary.

Margaret put the breakfast dishes in the dumbwaiter and tried to decide whether she should wait for Mr. Bedford to come down for breakfast before she began her cleaning. That was the trouble with the Bedford household. No instructions. She away so much, and he not caring, and no housekeeper to run things, although Miss Kerrigan liked to imagine she had that job. It was worse with Minnie and Eileen in summer exiles. Margaret had to deal with the disorder left behind. Closets to clean and put right. Rooms to maintain until the house was in full use again in the fall. Every hallway, corner, and cranny to be dusted, swept, wiped, mopped, polished, so that the dirt and soot blown from the street through the windows or tracked in on boot bottoms would never go unchallenged.

She decided that she would begin with Mrs. Bedford's room. She could start and stop when she wanted, without worrying about leaving it unfinished. She went through the dining room as quietly as she could. Mr. Ward never looked up. He was poised pensively over his paper. When she reached the top of the stairs, she could hear Mr. Bedford in the water closet. He would be in there awhile, for sure.

Mrs. Bedford's room was still in disarray from yesterday's packing, clothes tossed onto the bed and chairs, boxes strewn across the floor. After two and a half years, Margaret was still impressed by the sheer profusion of things. Not merely the quality of the things the Bedfords owned, but the multiplicity. A mountain of things. In the bedroom, quilts from Belgium, rugs from Persia, sheets from France, blankets from Scotland, armoires so full the doors would barely close, shelves crammed to capacity, dresses and jackets and petticoats crushed together, hatboxes piled one atop another and more under the beds, drawers packed tight with silk shifts, silk blouses, silk handkerchiefs, silk scarves, silk stockings, a cedar chest filled with intimate silk apparel from Paris, lavender paper between the layers; in the attic, standing trunks in which hung winter capes, coats, jackets, more dresses; in the basement, more clothes and the overflow of shoes, racks going from the floor to the ceiling jammed to capacity; in the kitchen, a tall, broad cabinet overflowing with everyday china, flowered cups and plates from Nanking, serving dishes, tureens, bowls; in the dining room, two more sets of plates and utensils: the ancient pewter plates and cups and flatware brought from Holland by Mrs. Bedford's first American ancestor, each piece kept in its own felt purse, and, in the towering china cabinet against the wall, the formal dinner service, Limoges plates edged in gold, and gold flatware. An endless number of possessions to be cleaned, polished, pressed, tucked away, retrieved, a seasonal flow of raiment and instruments that were impossible to catalogue fully. As grand as the house was, it strained to contain all inside it.

Margaret picked up a dressing gown from Japan that was the color of jade. It had been thrown in a ball onto the bed. Next to it was a jewelry box, the lid opened, and necklaces, earrings, and brooches spilled across the damask coverlet. She worked at putting things away until she heard Mr. Bedford leave his bath. She went back to the dining room. Mr. Ward was nowhere to be seen. She cleared the table. In the kitchen, Miss Kerrigan was sweeping the floor.

"Mr. Bedford will be down in a minute," Margaret said.

"Sure, I know what time it is." Miss Kerrigan put the broom aside and went back to the stove.

Mr. Bedford was easy to serve. He read the paper until his food came, and then devoured both at the same time, his chair set sideways to the table, turning pages with his left hand, eating with his right. After he gulped his coffee, he would be gone. He did his lingering in the water closet, not in the dining room, but this morning he sat at the table a little longer than usual, taking more time with the paper than was his custom. Whatever it was that he read, it seemed to make him happy.

He left at half past nine. Margaret handed him his hat and gloves in the vestibule. Andrew, the coachman, stood below, holding open the door to the brougham.

Mr. Bedford surveyed the street from the top of the stoop.

"A lovely day, sir," Margaret said. She hoped he would take these as parting words and be on his way, but he didn't move.

"I should take the victoria today," Bedford said. "No sense in being cooped up when I could be enjoying the day."

Margaret was afraid he was going to send Andrew back to get the victoria. It could take another half hour to unhitch and rehitch the horses, and she would be left standing around, kept from her work, perhaps fetching more coffee. But Bedford was only thinking aloud. Finally he started down the steps.

"Better yet, I should take the trap, hook up the trotter, and race downtown on my own, in and out of traffic, to the Devil with all obstructions, be they men or monuments."

Margaret knew there was no chance of that. He kept the trotter in a stable up near the shantytown. He got into the brougham. Andrew tipped his hat, shut the door, climbed into his seat, and off they went. Margaret went into the dining room and set to work. She stripped the table, washed it, dried it with a cloth, poured on wax and rubbed it in, rubbing hard until it had a sheen. Yet the sheen couldn't hide the table's age, its tally of dents, chips, scratches. Margaret didn't understand why people with the Bedfords' means didn't buy a grand table of cherry or mahogany, and put this relic in the basement. Eileen said it was because they wanted something for the help to do. "Making the old look new, isn't that what we spend most of our time doing?" she asked.

Finished with the table, Margaret emptied the glass-faced cabinet in the corner, wiping each piece as she took it out: wide-mouthed goblets with hollow knopped stems, Dutch fluted glasses etched with roses, candlesticks with baluster bases, bucket-shaped crystal bowls with intricately faceted rims, fruit dishes that stood on elegantly molded feet, a serving platter in the shape of a fish. When everything was returned to its place, she swept the rug. On Thursdays, the silverware was polished. Fridays, the parlor and music room were dusted and scrubbed. Mondays, the hallways were swept, the doorknobs shined, the curtains taken down, and the windows in the bedrooms cleaned. Tuesdays, she did the windows in the library, glass crisscrossed with bands of lead that divided the panes into diamond patterns, each to be washed inside and out, then rubbed dry. An endless cycle. But still, she preferred to be here than with Minnie and Eileen in the dunes of Jersey, cramped quarters, bloody mosquitoes, and sand in everything.

The day was getting warm. She felt herself perspiring. She swept the stairs. She polished the banister, fetched a duster from an upstairs closet, and worked over the pictures that lined the stairs. Men in togas. Temples in flames. Young women in white robes holding a garland. Romans and Greeks. Pagans, by the look of them, the genuine kind, not like her father. He had always been a Christian at heart, her mother said. " 'Tis this cursed country hardened his heart, but they are few it hasn't done that to, in one degree or another."

When she reached the first floor, she dusted the pictures along the hallway. Men in red coats, horses, hounds, the hunt in progress, flying across the countryside, a fox turning to look behind him. One day in Macroom, she had been walking with her uncle up a boreen when a troop of hunters had come cantering from the other direction. The riders took no notice of them, and they had to scamper up the steep side of the lane to avoid being trampled. At the top, her uncle quickly turned, removed his hat, and

smiled in a tense, unnatural way. "A fine day for it, Your Lord-
ships," he said. "Good luck to ye." The horsemen never looked
his way. In the picture, the fox was still ahead of the hounds and
their masters, a thundering pack of landlords. Margaret hoped he
got away.

She turned the tap in Mr. Bedford's bathroom and leaned
over to take a drink. There had been a few blistering days in May,
but the heat hadn't settled in yet, not the way it did when summer
arrived with full intensity, the gritty, grinding heat that sat on the
city day after day, the night bringing no relief. On the boat over
from Ireland, they had hardly noticed the change in temperature
until they had come through the Narrows and it suddenly felt like
the steam engines were all throwing off excess heat and cooking
the atmosphere. People were crowded on deck for their first
glimpse of New York, but the seamless curtain of gray, lifeless
air blocked their view and left them panting for breath. The men
took off their woolen coats. The women removed their shawls
and unwrapped their babies. It was a heat they had never felt in
Ireland, steamy and inescapable. Margaret felt her clothes grow
wet with perspiration. Out of the mist came a small tender that
chugged up alongside the ship. A rope ladder was thrown down.
Margaret and the others watched as a man in a blue coat with a
single row of gold buttons pulled his way up and climbed onto
the deck. Their first American. He took off his cap. His round,
fleshy face was crimson and dripping with sweat. He pulled a
great red handkerchief from his back pocket and wiped his brow.
He looked around the deck at the wilted passengers, and chuck-
led. "Well, ladies and gents," he said, "welcome to hell."

Margaret made the bed in Mr. Bedford's room. She hung up
his robe and made a pile of his soiled clothes and the towels he
had used. Mrs. Bedford wanted him to have a valet. They had
even interviewed one. But Mr. Bedford had never gone any further. He was too preoccupied with his business to be bothered.
Margaret dusted the armoire and the nightstand next to the bed.
The first time she had entered the Bedford house, she had had the
feeling of being in a church, a place of quiet and peace, unchange-

able, a fixed refuge from the noise and crowds that filled the rest
of the city. At the top of the front stairs was a skylight of stained
glass. Holy colors. She stood in the hallway, nervously fingering
the latch on her handbag, rubbing it like a rosary bead, trying to
contain her nervousness. Suddenly Mrs. Bedford appeared; her
footsteps had been inaudible on the thick carpeting. She wore a
white dress with blue ribbons at the throat and cuffs. Our Lady's
colors. She was a handsome woman, with a passing resemblance
to Molly Foley, Margaret thought, but she had a fuller figure and
a commanding way about her. The house seemed especially suited
to her, as if built with her in mind, a permanent shelter for her
loveliness and beauty, a space where she would always be safe.
That impression lasted for the first few weeks of Margaret's employment. But one afternoon, while serving tea to Mrs. Bedford
and a guest, she couldn't help but overhear that Mr. Bedford was
contemplating building a larger home, somewhere nearer to Central Park. "This time," Mrs. Bedford said, "we'll employ an architect of our own, instead of relying on some contractor's version
of metropolitan elegance." She waved her hand in a circle, an
indictment of the entire premises. "We hope to get started as soon
as possible." The war had made them postpone their plans. But
Margaret's perception of the house had changed. She realized that
neither Mrs. Bedford nor her husband regarded this as their home,
a setting in which to live out their lives, year following year, accumulating memories as numerous and substantial as the furniture. Both of them in their own way lived here in the expectation
of leaving; and despite all its size and grandeur, the house had no
more claim on its inhabitants than the tenements or shanties that
filled other parts of the city.

Margaret went to Mr. Ward's room. She knocked. There was
no answer, so she opened the door slowly and stuck in her head.
Sometimes, when he didn't answer, he was in there poring over
his books, and would be annoyed by the disturbance. The room
was empty. She made his bed and dusted the furniture. The windows needed washing, but they would have to wait their turn.
She dusted the windowsill. Down below, Miss Kerrigan was

standing in the yard talking to Mrs. Flynn, the washerwoman. They had their arms folded in the same way, fists tucked into the elbows. Mrs. Flynn came down every day from Shantytown to do the washing. Her sleeves were rolled up, and her arms were red and beefy, like a man's. A head taller than Miss Kerrigan, she leaned down toward her, busily nodding in agreement with what was being said.

They prided themselves on their travails, on what they had survived. Margaret was sure they were talking about her; Miss Kerrigan was no doubt using her as a measurement of the indolence and ease that had crept into the world since the days of their youth, the lack of seriousness and purpose in these girls nowadays, them with their fancy ways and fear of hard work. Mrs. Flynn's head rose and fell in continual agreement. Margaret pulled the drapes. Mr. Ward liked it that way, rooms in darkness during the day. He said it kept them cool.

Miss Kerrigan was right: Margaret had come with bigger hopes than those who fled the Famine. America was more than just enough to eat, the alternative to the workhouse or to being laid, coffinless, in a mass grave. America was the things Molly Foley had returned to Cork City with: store-bought clothing and a sewing machine, money of her own, possibilities that it was hard to put a name on. But perhaps these expectations made the disappointment bitterer. The money that had poured into Ireland from America had created a false impression. To the families that received it, it fell like manna on the Israelites, an excess of abundance, God's sustenance. But to those who earned it, it came hard, the fruit of heaving, hauling, digging, cleaning, sewing, serving, low-paid work of which the very numbers available to do it drove down wages even further, and what was sent to Ireland represented, in most cases, not a sharing of what was left over but the breaking of a single loaf, food taken from one mouth to feed another. When Molly Foley returned, she hadn't spoken much about New York. They thought she was being shy. A girl suited to the convent. But Molly had come to New York at the beginning of 1857, and although Miss Kerrigan was never willing to admit that there was anything worse than "Black '47," the year of her arrival, the year of the Famine exodus, even she said that the winter of 1857–58 was the bitterest of all.

"Many the girl had to do what she had to do in order to survive, and I say God's forgiveness is on them because they had no choice. Was that or starve."

Molly gave Margaret rosary beads. She sent them from the convent with her sister on Margaret's last night in Ireland. The beads were next to Margaret's bed in the attic. She hadn't much time to use them. Lying in bed, she would start a decade, but she never got very far before she fell asleep. On the journey over, aboard the *New World,* a four-decker of 1,500 tons, she had used them every evening. All the women had, led by an Irish-speaking girl from Killorglin, in Kerry, who was going to America with her mother. Everyone was attentive to their prayers. Afterward, there was dancing and singing in the men's compartment. The music drowned out the steady thud of the engines.

Margaret hardly slept during the voyage. The bunk she occupied was a top one. There was only a small space between her and the ceiling. But it wasn't the engines' noise or the sense of confinement that kept her awake. No one slept well. They each had an address of someone in New York, a cousin, an aunt, a brother, a former neighbor, a friend of a friend, a guide to the strange land of America. But they had also heard stories about the size of New York, and stories of people moved or dead or simply disappeared by the time their immigrant relatives arrived, of addresses that weren't there anymore, a hotel or store in place of the house or tenement they had expected to find, of wrong addresses, Third Avenue instead of Third Street, or even the wrong city, lost souls looking for addresses in New York City that were actually in cities named Brooklyn or Yonkers. They had been told to be careful, a cautionary note that was sounded constantly in the letters that came from America, a reminder that as each ship disgorged its own quota of bewildered Paddies, individuals and entire families, there were those who would wander the streets for days, even weeks, before they got even a rudimentary sense of where they were, and some who would never find the places they had come looking for, becoming instant and permanent additions to the city's vagrant population.

Margaret had the address of a friend of her mother's from Cork City who had left Ireland in 1853. Domitilla O'Sullivan. A dim memory to Margaret. A slight, soft-spoken woman standing in the street as her boys ran wild. Her husband had gone to England in search of work, but had been killed in a train wreck soon after he arrived there, a car full of Paddy laborers splattered against a retaining wall. Margaret remembered Mrs. O'Sullivan sitting in a chair while Catherine tried to comfort her. Catherine and Mrs. O'Sullivan had exchanged a few letters after Mrs. O'Sullivan left for New York, and Catherine had written to explain Margaret's plan to emigrate. They waited and waited for an answer. Finally, a week before Margaret was set to depart, it came, brief and to the point: *I will be glad to do what I can, but she should have no silly notions of what she shall find here.* "I knew Tilly wouldn't let me down," Catherine said. The reply, as short as it was, made Catherine happy. She went on about Tilly's humor and good-naturedness, but the memories were of a general sort, distant impressions. Margaret knew it was relief her mother felt, the assurance that however attenuated the tie, there was *somebody* for her to go to. Margaret felt a sense of relief, too.

Tilly's address was sewn into the pocket of Margaret's dress. *65 Jackson Street. The Seventh Ward. The City of New York.* When Margaret disembarked in New York, she had her rosaries in her hand, and though she worked them steadily, what was running through her head was not the Hail Mary but Tilly O'Sullivan's address.

The last days before they had arrived, they had talked of nothing else but the landing. Margaret couldn't touch the cured meat they were served. At most, she had a cup of tea and some hard bread. The girl from Killorglin didn't ease the nervousness. She said that her cousin in America had written to tell her to look as healthy and alert as possible when she landed, that it wasn't like in the old days when the ship simply docked and the immigrants spilled off to make their way. Now there was a depot with government inspectors wanting to see what physical condition you were in, and to count how much money you had, and to demand to know where you intended to stay. Those that didn't satisfy them were detained a few days and then shipped back to where they came from.

They spent their last night aboard ship at anchor in the harbor. At dawn the next morning, they docked and were formed into a single line. They proceeded from the dock down a short lane lined with sheds, and through a dark passageway into the largest hall Margaret had ever been in, a vast circular concourse under a wooden roof. At the center of the roof was a cupola, and directly beneath it, in the middle of the room, a fountain that shot a small column of water into the air. The sun streamed through the high circle of windows the way it did in the pictures on holy cards, but instead of shining on virgins and martyrs, it fell on immigrants in baggy, badly wrinkled clothing, and officials in blue caps and jackets. The dust swirled in the shafts of light. It grew thicker as more people entered the hall. The noise of shuffling and coughing grew louder, and the barked commands of the officials reverberated off the Castle Garden ceiling, echoing loudly, the unintended beneficiary of the acoustics of what had been the city's largest auditorium, the scene of Jenny Lind's great triumph, the voice of "The Swedish Nightingale" filling the hall, bringing thousands to their feet.

Most of the time they stood. One by one, they approached a long counter onto which they set their baggage, which a clerk proceeded to open and inspect. At another counter they laid down the money they had, and it was counted and returned to them. The clerks were either emotionless or gruff and irritable, especially with some of the country people whose English was poor and who, in their nervousness, usually managed to spill the contents of their bundles across the floor or send a handful of coins careening across the countertop. As the morning went on, a steady flow of immigrants entered, some in embroidered clothing that was beautiful but strange, women with braided hair the color of cream, men with tasseled hats, children covered from head to toe with billowing dresses. The clerks' voices rose, the words blending into the indistinguishable din, a chorus of babble. The lines snaked around the room, one for baggage inspection, another for the medical officer, and Margaret found herself standing next to a broad-faced man in short pants and a feathered hat. She tried not to stare. Farther on, she waited beside a neat, scrubbed-looking girl her own age who was intently reading what appeared to be a Bible. The girl looked up to check the progress of the line and caught Margaret's eyes.

"Are you saved?" the girl asked.

Margaret smiled, uncertain of what she had been asked and aware that the people around her were listening.

"Safe?"

"No, *saved,* do you know the Lord?" She had a flat way of speaking, an English accent, but not one that Margaret had ever heard before. Margaret felt her face turn red. She sensed people waiting to hear her answer.

"I pray."

"But do you read God's word, and know His will?" The girl held up her book. "It's here in the testament of the prophet Mormon, the truth of God's plan for us."

The lines began to move, and a distance opened between them. The girl raised her voice. "We're near the Promised Land now. It's only a short journey from here. Open your eyes and your ears. The Kingdom is within your grasp."

The distance between them grew greater, and Margaret was glad for it. When the inspections were done, the men and the women were separated. A matron came up a flight of iron steps that was set into the floor of the hall. She directed the women to proceed downstairs, and stood aside, tapping each one on the head, counting aloud as they went. At fifty, she brought her arm down and stopped the line. Margaret was the last one in the group that passed. At the bottom of the stairs was a big room with brick walls that curved into a vaulted ceiling. It felt like a tomb. There were hooks on the walls and, in the middle, a long

copper trough into which two open spigots poured water. The
trough was surrounded by an iron railing on which was set small
trays that held balls of brown soap.

"Okay, ladies," the matron said, "we got no time to waste.
Hang your clothes on the hooks, and then it's time to scrub."
Two young girls spoke to each other in a language Margaret
couldn't understand. They giggled and began to undress. The
other women stood around looking bewildered. The matron
clapped her hands.

"Okay, okay, okay, let's get going. If you don't want to
spend the rest of your lives down here, then get them clothes off
and get into that water. It ain't gonna hurt." She clapped her
hands again. More women started to undress. The girl from Killorglin, the Rosary leader, stood by the stairs with her mother,
who still had her shawl drawn over her head, a small, bent
woman with no English at all.

"My mother can't undress," the girl said to the matron.

The matron continued to hurry the women with her clapping.
"Tell her she's got a choice," she said in a voice loud enough for
all to hear. "She can either wash or go back to where she came
from."

The girl went over to her mother and spoke to her in Irish.
Margaret began to undress quickly. She ran over to the trough
and stepped in. The water came up to her knees. It was so cold
it made her legs feel numb. She offered a hand to the old woman
and, with the aid of the woman's daughter, helped her in.

"Use the soap," the matron yelled, "that's what it's there
for."

A stout woman with her hair in pigtails squatted down into
the trough and splashed water over herself. The matron pointed
at her. "That's the way. Look at her, girls. This is the way to do
it." She rubbed her hands together and ran them over her face
and down her arms, a pantomimed cleaning.

They all started to squat down and splash, and their awkwardness gave way to a loud playfulness, the water cascading
onto the floor, the shouts of shock as they submerged themselves

in the water mingling with loud laughter. Margaret held the old woman's arm as she lowered herself into the water. Margaret looked at the other women as they went about their washing, girls with chests as flat as boys, women with full, hard breasts, the old woman's sagging downward, as if they had been sucked dry.

In a moment, the matron was telling them to get out, get their clothes on, get a move on. "We're outta towels," she said, "You'll have to use your clothes."

They dried themselves as best they could, and mounted the stairs a bit more confidently than they had descended them, a step closer to their new lives than the unwashed still lined up for inspection. They were given back their baggage and taken into a room off the main hall that had rows of long benches. For the first time since arriving, they sat. A clerk entered and stood in front of them. He quickly read aloud the contents of a sheet of paper he held in his right hand. "All tickets for travel outside of the city, whether by rail or by steamship, are to be purchased inside the hall at the windows marked appropriately. Upon leaving the terminal, those traveling in parties should make sure no individual is lost or separated. Don't converse or do business with strangers offering to carry your baggage, discount your tickets, or provide food or lodging. Hired cars are available to take you to the railway station, and the rates are posted by the door. The steamboat docks are on the North River." He gestured with the paper toward the door. "You can walk. It's just a couple of blocks. But be careful."

The room erupted in a loud babel of languages, the gist of the clerk's remarks given impromptu translation by whoever had enough English to grasp what he had said. Directly outside the room were the ticket windows, and beyond, down a short corridor, a large, open doorway, trees in the distance, steady stream of traffic, rumble of wheels, clanging of bells, voices, whistles, music, New York.

Margaret took her bag and walked down the corridor. There were no more clerks. The door was unguarded. The sun was out, but the air was wet and close, and she felt the perspiration run down her back. A few steps beyond the door she put down her bag and decided to wait for someone she knew from the ship to emerge. The English girl she had talked to earlier came out in the midst of about a dozen people, all the women holding hands, around them a rough square of men laden with baggage and trunks. The woman was clutching her book. They moved off into the city in search of the North River, the American Jordan, then west to Deseret, the Promised Land. More groups of immigrants followed, most headed for the river and the steamboat to Albany, tight knots of people determined not to be unraveled before they got out of the city.

Gradually, a number of the people Margaret knew from the ship came out and stopped beside her. They stood in silence. This was their destination. The discussions they had had on board had gone no further than this, the streets of New York. Delayed by engine troubles and fog, they had landed a day later than scheduled, and yet they had expected some welcome other than this, heat, noise, bustling crowds oblivious to their arrival. The full consequences of what they had done settled on them.

An inspector walked out of the doorway. One of the men asked him, "Sir, could you tell me the way to Pitt Street?"

"Sorry, I'm off duty," the inspector said as he walked by. "Try somebody inside."

A man and his wife and their six small children sat on their bundles. They were from Holy Cross, in Tipperary, and he had been the most active musician on the way over, forever playing his fiddle and singing. He stared glumly across the lawn around Castle Garden. The children grew restless and started to run about. His wife chased after them. He sucked on a tobaccoless clay pipe.

"I'm expecting me cousin to meet me," he said to no one in particular. The pipe made a gurgling sound. After a few more moments of silence, he stood and pulled a large bundle onto his back. His wife handed smaller bundles to the children and threw a large burlap sack over her shoulder.

"Ach," he said, "the Devil with waiting." They moved off,

and the old Irish-speaking woman and her daughter followed. With them as the vanguard, Margaret and the rest of the group that had collected by the door started toward the street. There was a policeman standing by a gaslight and another by the low iron fence around the park in which Castle Garden was situated. The ground was strewn with newspapers, rusted cans, and rags.

The first policeman twirled the baton he carried and hardly glanced at them. They moved slowly, nobody speaking. Up ahead, Margaret noticed a crowd of men, arms and legs draped over the fence. The second policeman was standing facing these men, his stick held in front of him. The men began to wave and hoot as the group approached, as if they saw someone they knew. Margaret fought the urge to turn back to Castle Garden. She let the momentum of those in front pull her forward. As soon as the immigrants left the park, the policeman walked away, and the men at the fence surrounded them.

She thought, or hoped, that they might be relatives of people from the boat, the cousins of the musician from Holy Cross, but he was already struggling with one of them, who had taken the sack off his wife's back and thrown it onto a derelict-looking wagon. As Margaret watched them fight over a trunk, she felt someone grab her bag. She gripped it with both hands. She was too frightened to scream, and turned to locate the policeman. He was moving down the path toward Castle Garden, his back to them. The man took hold of her arm. "Relax, sister," he said. "I'm only trying to help."

She pulled her arm away.

"Take it easy. Calm down."

She took a few steps backward, her bag clasped to her chest.

"There now. Easy does it," he said. "All I'm trying to do is see you get a ride outta here. That's all. That's what I'm here for."

The musician had given up his fight. His baggage and children were piled onto a wagon, and the driver was already off trying to coax or capture more business from the immigrants just leaving the park. Behind this first wagon was a string of similar vehicles, carts with broken railings, wheels missing spokes, sad, shabby horses, their hides covered with mange. The driver who had tried to take Margaret's bag had successfully snagged the bags of the old woman and her daughter.

Margaret was the only one still left on the sidewalk. The lead wagon pulled out. The man who had tried to take her bag looked down and reached out his hand.

"Room for one more," he said.

She took his hand. He pulled her up, took her bag, and tossed it behind. She had never seen anything like what she saw from their perch: thousands of coaches, carts, wagons, and vans packed together in two slow-moving streams that flowed up and down an avenue flanked with tall, imposing buildings, a rolling eternity of conveyances.

"I'm Bill Cunningham," the driver said. He smiled. There was a large gap between his teeth. He tipped his hat. His hair was gray, but he had the full, creaseless face of a boy. He untied the reins from the brake stick and patted Margaret's knee.

"No need to worry. I'll get ya where ya goin'."

Margaret moved closer to the end of the seat and held the railing tightly. Cunningham looked over his shoulder at an unbroken wall of traffic.

"Damn booly dogs make it tough for all of us, keeping us away from the Garden so youse gotta cart yer stuff all a ways from dere to here wid no help."

Suddenly he brought his whip down with a loud crack and jerked violently on the reins. The cart lurched forward, and the two women in the rear went sprawling onto the floor. The cart almost crashed into the tailgate of a barrel-laden wagon, but came to a halt just in time. The driver of the wagon shouted, "Bloody idiot, Goddamn donkey son of a bitch, I oughta break your neck!"

Margaret put her hands over her eyes. Cunningham ignored the driver. "Yeah, yeah," he said, "we all got cause to shout." He inched the cart forward, and when they had entered the stream of traffic, he said to Margaret, "People got no manners, that's the number one lesson for them arrivin' in this town. First come, first served, and don't stand in the way."

They moved slowly, stopping every few feet. Pedestrians wove through the traffic, trying to get from one side of the avenue to the other.

Cunningham said, "Where ya from?" He whipped the horses again, and the cart darted deeper into the traffic, cutting off another heavily freighted wagon. The wagon driver was standing, and almost lost his balance. He cursed loudly.

"I'm from Ireland," Margaret said.

"Neva woulda guessed. Thought you were a Chinee."

The driver they had cut off pulled alongside, next to Margaret. A burly man with a blond beard and a great wide hat, he looked over at Cunningham and pointed his finger at him. "You miserable little pimp, you ever try that again, I'll put my boot up your ass."

Cunningham stared straight ahead, as if he didn't hear what was being said. "Where in Ireland?" he asked Margaret.

Margaret watched the wagon pull ahead, and felt a surge of relief that Cunningham wasn't going to test the driver's threat. Cunningham tapped her on the leg. "I said, where in Ireland?"

"Cork City."

"Mayo for me, on my mother's side. She was an O'Dwyer, may she rest in peace. The Cunninghams are Galway people, that's where the old man was from."

They passed a small park. Ahead, the tangle of traffic became an impenetrable snarl. Despite the heat, people walked quickly, everyone in a hurry. Those leaving the buildings immediately picked up the pace, a crowd different from Cork City, not only in mass and momentum, but in dress, the cut of the clothing sharper, showier, the women's dresses tighter at the waist, wider at the hem. The men's coats were cut closer to their figures, the cuffs on the trousers narrower, better suited to the long stride of Yankee legs.

The cart crept along. Up at the next corner, a policeman waved the traffic on and blocked any vehicle from turning right.

When the cart was almost abreast of him, Cunningham whipped the horse, tugged on the reins, and swung a sharp right, almost knocking down the policeman as they rounded the corner. They shot forward, driver and passengers bouncing about. Behind, the policeman screamed for them to stop. Cunningham kept whipping the horses, and they careened down the street, scattering pedestrians as they went.

"Damn booly dogs," Cunningham said. "All they ever do is make a bad situation worse."

It was the second time he had used that phrase, and it struck Margaret as being wildly out of place: The boolies in the hills of Ireland were cool summer pastures where the livestock and their keepers retreated in the summer, as far from these streets as could be imagined. The big dogs who helped tend the herds were gentle and intelligent, lying in the shade next to the cows, their eyes half closed, tongues hanging out, bearing no resemblance to the policemen in their soft hats, blue tunics, and starched collars. But Margaret would grow used to the expression. Everyone did. Until, eventually, *booly* was shortened into *bull,* the pan-ethnic moniker for a city cop.

The impression of that first day never left Margaret. New York wasn't Cork City on a larger scale, which is what she had expected to find. It was a different order of existence. From the eminence of Cunningham's driver's seat she watched as aristocratic sunlit avenues intersected with streets in perpetual shadow. Right around the corner from grand churches and temples of commerce, their steps crowded with the faithful, were saloons and music halls going full tilt in the middle of the afternoon, slaughterhouses next to foundries, the acrid mix of blood, smoke, and horse piss hanging in the superheated air, acre after acre of sagging brick houses and slumping, wooden-framed tenements, the boulevards filled with fashion, the lanes crowded with dirt and misery.

She suspected that Cunningham was giving them an informal tour. She had given him the address of Mrs. O'Sullivan and was in no hurry to get there. As they drove on, the streets grew shab-

bier and more raucous. Children were in constant motion amid
the traffic; a wonder that they weren't run over instantly. There
were Irish-looking faces everywhere, the countenances of country
people and spalpeens, their clothing far less stylish than what she
had seen on the avenue near Castle Garden, but a Yankee swagger
to their step, the hustling gait that everyone in the city seemed to
share.

"Mostly our own kind here," Cunningham said. "Up a ways
are the Krauts. Further west, a sprinklin' of Italians. Ya can trust
the Germans. Thick as mud, but they're honest, which is more
than ya can say for the Italians. Few in number, but as shifty as
sand."

Margaret had lost any sense of direction. Each street they
entered looked exactly like the one they'd left, except perhaps a
bit more decayed and worn. It was as if the poverty of the Irish
countryside had been added to the worst degradation to be found
in Cork City, multiplied a thousandfold and set amid a grid of
coal-belching, iron-bleating factories.

Finally, in the middle of a street no better and no worse than
those they had passed through, Cunningham said, "You're
home." He jumped to the pavement and helped Margaret down.
The old woman and her daughter bid her good-bye. For the first
time since she'd left Ireland, she felt like crying, overwhelmed by
the thought of never seeing again these two women whom she
barely knew.

Cunningham told her that he would usually charge a fare of
five dollars for such a ride, but in her case, he was waiving it.
"Let's say it's on the house," he said, "as long as I can see you
again."

"You should be paid what you're owed. It's only fair."

"Don't worry about it." He picked up her bag and walked
into a grocery on the corner of the street. Margaret followed.
Inside, a girl was standing at the counter, her elbows on it, and
reading a newspaper. In the rear was a makeshift bar, boards laid
across barrels, two old men and a woman drinking whiskey.

"Which is Sixty-five Jackson?" Cunningham asked.

The girl kept reading the paper. She pointed with her thumb over her shoulder. "Building in the rear. Go down the alleyway next to here."

"You know if a Miss O'Sullivan lives there?"

She turned a page of the paper. "Ain't got a clue."

The woman at the bar in the rear called out, "Which O'Sullivan is it, Agnes or Tillie?"

"Tillie," Margaret said. The woman came forward, a short, slight, gray-haired figure with a flushed face.

"You've found her," the woman said. "Who are ye?"

"Margaret O'Driscoll."

"Ye were a little girl last time I saw ye." She looked over at Cunningham. "Who's this?"

"The man that drove me here."

Mrs. O'Sullivan took Margaret's bag from Cunningham.

"Come, then, let's get ye settled."

Margaret followed her. Outside, Cunningham remounted his cart and tipped his hat. The two women in the rear of the cart waved as it pulled away. Margaret hurried to catch up to Mrs. O'Sullivan. They stepped into the alleyway. Piss, a familiar smell. In Cork City, the privies were set behind the houses, but here there was no space. Three privies sat in the small courtyard at the end of the alleyway, their doors hanging open. The yard was filled with children, and though an open tap next to the privies had turned the ground to muck, they didn't seem to notice.

The tenement rose four stories, its façade covered with warped wooden stairs. Mrs. O'Sullivan stopped at the bottom step but refused to let Margaret take the bag. "How much did he charge?" she asked.

"He said the fare was five dollars."

"Five dollars! That bloodsucker will burn forever in the deepest pit of hell. Cost ye eight pounds to cross the ocean and he wants a pound to bring ye from the docks. Damnation to him!"

"But he didn't make me pay."

"Not yet, he didn't. But the likes of him never gave away a

drop of sweat without figuring on being repaid, one way or other."

Although Margaret didn't say anything more on the subject to Mrs. O'Sullivan, she was glad that Cunningham wanted to see her again, happy that someone would come looking for her. She felt she did owe him something, some kindness, not just in consideration of the fare, but in view of the time he took to get her safely to Mrs. O'Sullivan's.

When they reached the third landing, Mrs. O'Sullivan put the bag down. "Now let me have a good look at ye," she said. "You're the image of your mother." They entered a small, airless room, the only light coming through the open front doorway. Children's screams came from below, high-pitched and happy.

"I'd offer you tea, but there's no lighting a stove on a day such as this," Mrs. O'Sullivan said.

"No need," Margaret said, "I'm not thirsty at all."

Mrs. O'Sullivan walked into a back room. On the wall above where Margaret sat was a picture of Jesus pointing to His Sacred Heart. From behind, a shiny, brown-bodied insect scurried out, quick, furtive movements, something instantly repulsive about it. Margaret resisted the urge to reach up and squash it. Another one followed. They moved in a zigzag pattern toward the floor.

Mrs. O'Sullivan returned with a bottle of whiskey and two teacups. She poured a fingerful into each cup and handed one to Margaret. Margaret sipped the whiskey. A strange edge to it, unlike the whiskey at home. No great drinker of the stuff, but she had had enough to know this was different, watery, with a rough aftertaste. Whiskey made in haste, no hint of peat fires, no slow process of distillation; it was to be drunk, not sipped.

"Tell the truth," Mrs. O'Sullivan said. " 'Tis not at all like ye expected."

"No, but it's fine, fine, I'm grateful for it." Margaret thought that Mrs. O'Sullivan had been speaking of the whiskey.

"Haven't met a one yet ain't been nearly killed by the shock of the place. Don't matter how many times ye write and spell it out to them, there's no understanding New York till it's been seen with your own eyes, and that's why I didn't bother you with long descriptions. But don't worry, the time goes quickly and then one day ye wake up and can't imagine ever having lived anywhere else."

Margaret nodded. She was having trouble staying awake. Mrs. O'Sullivan talked on, a soft flow of words. The whiskey and shadows were overwhelming. The day felt as if it had begun a year ago. She hadn't slept much the night before.

She had slipped up to the deck and watched the lights of the city through the mist. What had she expected to find? A child's dream, already lost.

Mrs. O'Sullivan's boys were grown now, one a longshoreman, the other a grain shoveler in Brooklyn. They were patriots, too, she said, in the tradition of Margaret's father, attended all the meetings at Hibernian House on Prince Street across from the cathedral, and been sworn into The Organization by Michael Corcoran himself. Margaret made no mention of her father's transformation.

Finally Mrs. O'Sullivan said, "You must be tired. We'll talk business tomorrow."

She led Margaret through one bare, windowless room with a mattress on the floor into another about the same size, this one with a window that faced out onto a brick wall. There was a wide bed by the window, iron-framed, a prominent sag in its middle. Margaret undressed and lay down. Downstairs, someone was playing a fiddle. Music for a jig. The music of home. Voices and singing, the loudness of people when they drink. The noise died down a bit. She drifted off to sleep.

In the morning, the heat was so intense that Margaret thought the stove must have been lit. It hadn't been. Mrs. O'Sullivan had already left for work. The mattress in the middle room was occupied by a body beneath a sheet. Margaret moved past quietly. She opened the door to let the light in. The same crowd of children was playing around the privies. She went down and filled a pitcher from the slow-running tap, then went upstairs and lay down again. The heat was like a fever. She fell in and out of sleep, constantly waking from unremembered dreams. It was almost totally dark in the room when Mrs. O'Sullivan woke her up. They ate bread and salted fish by the light of a paraffin lamp. Mrs. O'Sullivan said that Margaret could share her bed for a dollar a month.

"What about the middle room?" Margaret asked.

" 'Tis taken."

"I know. I saw someone sleeping there when first I got up, but then she was gone."

"You'll hardly ever see her. Kathleen Leahy is her name. She cleans offices. Works nights, every night. A perfect tenant. If she ever decides to move, I'll give you first claim on her spot. It'll cost two dollars."

Mrs. O'Sullivan patted Margaret's hand. "Don't worry yourself about finding work," she said. "It's taken care of. I talked to the boss at the shirt-finishing factory where I work, and he said to bring you in. Says I, she'll be here first thing in the morning. One other thing," Mrs. O'Sullivan added. "Don't ever have this door unlocked. There's them would steal the pennies from a dead man's eyes to get the money they need for drink."

On the wall, above the picture of the Sacred Heart, at the periphery of the lamplight, Margaret could sense the insects hurrying along in the shadows.

They reported to work soon after dawn the next morning. The streets were quiet and empty as they walked to East Broadway, and it seemed to Margaret a different city from the crowded one she had seen from atop Cunningham's cart. The shirt-finishing factory was housed in an imposing building of red brick. They waited outside in a casual line of about thirty women, and Mrs. O'Sullivan introduced her around. A few of the women were German, but most were Irish. *Kathleen, Sheila, Anne, Maura, Angela, Lucy,* two *Peggy*s, there was no chance she could keep them all straight. Standing apart, by the gutter, were four colored women, the first Margaret had ever seen, three of them dark, one

light-skinned. Try as she could, she couldn't stop staring at the
darkest of them, a woman with skin that glistened, and high
cheekbones that made her face look as if it had been chiseled from
coal. She had wide, round eyes, and pupils the color of peat. None
of the other women in line so much as glanced at the colored
women, who talked among themselves, arms folded, their faces
alert and serious.

The doors to the building were thrown open, and they went
in single file past a man in a booth who handed each of them a
piece of paper marked with a number that matched one of the
numbered bags of newly sewn shirts piled in a room off to the
right. Each woman rummaged among the bags until she found
the one she was looking for, then took her bag over to a desk by
the staircase and handed the man sitting behind it the piece of
paper. He checked it against the bag, wrote the number in a book,
and had the woman sign next to it. The women carried the bags
to the second floor, a vast space with columns set at intervals, but
no intervening walls. There were iron tubs in rows on the side
of the room. In the middle were six steam boilers set on brick
bases, the fires beneath flickering behind iron gates. Black pipes
carried the steam up into the walls.

Margaret followed Mrs. O'Sullivan and watched her as she
opened the hatch on one of the boilers, her face turned away from
the steam that shot out, and shoved the shirts in individually.
Closing the hatch, she went over and brought back one of the
iron tubs. She pulled the shirts out, picking at them, shaking them
in the air. When the shirts were all in the tub, she took the tub
to the far wall, along the length of which ran a large sink. The
sink was filled with hot water and starch in which she soaked the
shirts. She wrung them out and filled the tub again. She and Margaret climbed another flight of stairs. The third floor was another
large space, but here there were clotheslines strung between the
columns. The heat almost knocked them over when they entered.
The women tried to string as many of the shirts on the line as
they possibly could. The sweat ran from Margaret's forehead into
her eyes. It blurred her sight.

"It's the hot air from the steamers," Mrs. O'Sullivan said as she hurriedly pinned shirts to the line. "Dries the shirts in no time, and come winter, you'll welcome the heat."

Margaret and Mrs. O'Sullivan went down to the first floor, took another bag, and repeated the process of steaming and starching. The shirts on the third floor were dry by the time they got back. They took them down and hung the new ones. They carried the tubs of dry shirts down a narrow hallway in which they had to stand against the wall to permit women coming from the other direction to get by. In a room half as large as the drying room was a big coal stove. There were a dozen irons resting on it, and ironing boards arranged around it in three rows.

From below came a pounding noise, a thunderous banging of machinery that made it almost impossible to talk as they ironed. Mrs. O'Sullivan stamped her foot on the floor and shouted, " 'Tis a shoe factory down there." She pointed at the corridor they had just come down. "That brought us across into another building." They carefully folded the ironed shirts and took them back to the first floor. The man who had handed out the numbered tickets gave each shirt a quick inspection.

"Missing a button," he said. He took one of Margaret's shirts and threw it aside.

"It was when I got it," Margaret said.

"Then you shouldn't have taken it." He wrote *14* on a piece of paper and handed it to her. "That's all you'll be paid for. We don't pay for damaged goods." She crammed the paper into the pocket of her dress.

They went back for another bag of shirts. On the second floor, Margaret burned her fingers on the steamer. They pulsed with pain. In the ironing room, the sweat ran down her legs, puddled in her shoes, soaked her blouse, and matted her hair to her head. She finished her next load and handed it in. The man didn't pull any out. He wrote *16* on a slip. A penny for every five shirts. Six cents so far. She sat on the bottom stair. The clock read 11:30. Quitting time was seven that evening.

In a room beneath the stairs, two of the colored women were

pinning shirts. The other two were moving up and down the stairs with buckets of coal and starch. They moved from floor to floor, keeping the stoves tended, the sinks full, putting the tubs, irons, and ironing boards in order, sweeping the floors, mopping where they were wet.

Mrs. O'Sullivan stopped where Margaret was sitting. The older woman's wet blouse clung to her breasts. "Better get a move on," she said. The muscles in Margaret's calves were taut and sore.

The dark-colored woman whom Margaret had admired earlier came down the stairs carrying two empty buckets. Mrs. O'Sullivan was blocking her way. The black woman stood waiting for Mrs. O'Sullivan to move. Mrs. O'Sullivan ignored her.

"You're in the way," Margaret said to Mrs. O'Sullivan.

"It's a white man's right to stand where he wants, and the last time I looked, I was still white."

The black woman stood with her eyes straight ahead. The perspiration dripped from her chin onto her dress.

Margaret stood up. "Very well," she said, "I'm ready." She made room so that the black woman could pass.

Mrs. O'Sullivan watched the dark-skinned woman go into the room with the other colored women. "You'll learn," she said to Margaret.

"To be rude?"

"No, about niggers."

"She was doing nothing but her job."

"She's here because she wants your job. Niggers will steal any job they can."

"She's got a job of her own."

"She's got a job because when they tried to bring niggers in to work with us, we refused to work, all of us, even the German girls. The niggers were willing to work for half what we get, and the owner said that was his business, that it was his right to strike any deal with an employee that he cared to. But we knew what it was. Soon as he had enough niggers he'd cut our wages, too, so we stepped down, the lot of us, and the husbands and brothers of some of the girls came and stood at the door with us, and we let it be known the first nigger tried to come in would get something else besides a job. Finally the owner agreed not to hire them except as pin girls and sweepers that get paid a daily rate, a child's wage, and more than a nigger deserves."

"They have to feed themselves, don't they?" Margaret said.

"Not on our bread." Mrs. O'Sullivan went up the stairs. "Don't waste your sympathy on them," she said.

On Sunday the factory was closed, and Mrs. O'Sullivan took Margaret to Mass at St. Mary's on Grand Street. Cunningham was waiting in front of the grocery when they came home. The day was warm, but not humid and oppressive the way it had been. Cunningham offered to take both of them for a ride. Mrs. O'Sullivan said no.

Margaret was delighted he had come back. He had his thumbs hooked inside his galluses and stood in front of his cart as if it were a coach. She didn't try to hide her enthusiasm. She put her arm through his and said, "I hoped you'd come." In the preceding days, as Margaret had walked to and from work with Mrs. O'Sullivan, sharing her table and bed, the two of them on the same sagging mattress, the loud wheeze of the woman's snoring keeping her awake, the hope had become progressively stronger.

Mrs. O'Sullivan stood with her missal in her hands. "Be careful," she said.

Margaret handed the older woman her own missal. "Take this for me, please." Mrs. O'Sullivan took Margaret by the wrist and whispered to her, "You owe him nothing, remember that, *nothing*."

They rode up Grand Street to Broadway, then north. To the east and west the streets gave way to sky and masts, here and there a glimpse of water, but the avenues unfolded into a steady vista framed in masonry. The traffic flowed at a faster pace than on the day Cunningham had taken them from Castle Garden. There were far fewer carts or drays, mostly coaches and traps with well-dressed occupants, a few with their attendants in livery. As they proceeded northward, the dense, unbroken blocks gave way to fields salted with lonely-looking houses. Cunningham named the churches and the squares they passed, the homes of the wealthy. They stopped in front of the new cathedral, massive walls of granite surrounded by a wooden framework. Cunningham helped her down. The watchman by the gate in the construction wall knew Cunningham, and he let them through. They walked up the stairs to the entrance and peered through the empty portals into the unroofed nave. It wasn't a church yet, not a proper one, still an unconsecrated shell, but already it had a holy feel.

They rode north again, along the eastern section of the seven-mile wall that enclosed Central Park. There was planking strewn about, and mounds of raw earth that made it look as if a great explosion had just taken place.

"The rich had it all set to build mansions on both sides of the avenue, with the park as their backyard," said Cunningham, but Mayor Wood stopped 'em, a man of the people, Mayor Wood."

"I'm not interested in politics," Margaret said.

"Here ya gotta be, at least a man does, it's his bread and butter. He can't afford not to be interested, especially the Irishman. We all got an interest in keepin' the likes of men like Fernando Wood in power."

"Mayor Wood is Irish?"

"No, but being a true Democrat he's careful to listen to the will of the people, and since a good number of the people in this city are Irish, he heeds our wishes."

Cunningham began to discuss the city's politics. Margaret admired the hills and meadows in the park, new stands of trees emerging from the chaos, ponds and lakes in the process of construction. Cunningham turned from the park, and after a drive through some half-constructed streets, they reached a real wood, wild and overgrown, with none of the landscaped symmetry of Central Park.

"This is Jones's Woods," he said. "A little ways up and we'll get a view of the river."

They came into a meadow that ran in a slight incline toward the river. Cunningham tied up the cart. Ahead was a wooden pavilion. A band was playing, and people were dancing. Cunningham went up the stairs without a word to Margaret. She stood outside, uncertain if she should follow. He came back in a few minutes with two mugs of beer. He drained his in one long gulp. They walked together to the end of the meadow, and it wasn't until they stepped up onto an immense outcropping of rock that the river came into view. It surged beneath them, a torrent of fast-moving water pushing toward the harbor.

"Over there is Blackwells Island." Cunningham gestured with his empty mug at the wooded shore opposite. The roofs of several buildings poked through the trees. "The workhouse, the city prison, and the lunatic asylum, they're all over there. New York's got two insane asylums now. You know a city is on its way to being something when it's got to have two madhouses."

They strolled back to the pavilion, and Cunningham kept going inside for more mugs of beer, and Margaret kept hoping that he would ask her to dance, but he didn't. They sat on the steps and listened to the musicians, Germans in purple uniforms with silver braid, and Cunningham talked politics. It was dusk when they finally left. The woods were already dark.

She half wished that he would kiss her, pull off into the woods, stroke her hair, embrace her, bury his head in her shoulder, confess some passion for her. She would kiss him back. She wasn't in love with him, but she felt so lonely she wanted to stay awhile longer with him, share some intimacy, words, gestures, even silence, open herself to the possibility of discovering in him a gentleness others didn't see and finding in herself the first stirrings of real attachment.

Cunningham moved the cart slowly through the woods. From behind came the faint sounds of the German band. "The Protestants love the niggers," he said. His words were badly slurred. "Take a nigger over an Irishman any day, even got a home for nigger kids on Fifth Avenue. That's because they know they can run the nigger's life, cuz he ain't got enough sense to run his own, and they're afraid of the Irishman cuz of the opposite. They know in their heart of hearts, even if they don't ever admit it, we're every bit as good as them."

At the word *heart* he thumped his chest the way the priest did when he said the Confiteor.

Mea culpa, mea culpa, mea maxima culpa.

The room was hot and close when she slipped into bed. Mrs. O'Sullivan was facing the wall. As soon as Margaret lay down, the older woman said, "Well, did he try to get back his fare?"

"He was a gentleman."

"Never was a cartman who was a gentleman. Either he had too much to drink or he was in a hurry to get over to Greene Street to get what you wouldn't give."

"He said he was going home." He hadn't told her where he was going. They had raced down the avenue and he had sung in a loud, drunken voice:

> *De Camptown ladies sing dis song,*
> *Doo-dah! doo-dah!*
> *Camptown racetrack five miles long,*
> *Oh! Doo-dah-day!*

"For some of them, Greene Street is home," said Mrs. O'Sullivan. "The whores are the only family they've got. Well, at least he didn't leave you with anything you have to carry into confession."

Margaret saw Cunningham twice after that. Both times they rode up to Jones's Woods, with the same result. He had too much beer, talked politics, and drove her home. Once winter came, she never saw him again.

The following fall, in 1860, a girl from the factory said she was applying for a job as a servant. The demand had picked up greatly, and the call for domestics was getting well ahead of supply. Mrs. O'Sullivan advised Margaret against following the other girl's example. "It's a kind of slavery," she said, "living your life under the eye of your master." But Margaret thought Mrs. O'Sullivan's view was influenced by the loss of the rent she would suffer.

Margaret bought a dress from A. T. Stewart's for her interview at the Society for the Encouragement of Faithful Domestic Servants. Though she got it at a steep discount, it had still cost her a month's salary.

Mrs. Bedford examined her application form as they stood in the vestibule of the house.

"I see you have experience as a resident domestic."

"Yes, ma'am." A small lie. She had cleaned houses in Cork City, but never lived in.

"I don't want an inexperienced girl. This is a well-ordered household, and it's important that any new help be able to master the routines."

"You can count on it, ma'am."

She cleaned the bathroom last, then relieved herself in Mr. Bedford's bowl.

Mea culpa. Another offense against Mrs. Oswald's Commandment No. III.

It was almost time to serve Mr. Ward his lunch. Glancing at the mirror, Margaret adjusted her cap. After lunch she would sweep downstairs and polish the hallway floors—a nearly impossible task to keep them shined and spotless, free of the grime and dirt continually tracked in on boots and shoes. As she came down the stairs, somebody gave the front-door knocker a loud rap.

She opened the door. It was a workman in overalls, standing with cap in hand.

"I'm here to check the gas connections."

"The connections?"

"The pipes. Make sure they're tight."

"All right. Go below and I'll let you in."

He put his cap back on and went down the stoop. Margaret

stood at the door a minute. Odd, a tradesman coming to the front door instead of going below, but nobody knew his place anymore. Miss Kerrigan's complaint, and there was truth in it, the way some of the merchants dunned Mr. Bedford about bills, coming right to the front door, like invited guests, and demanding to see him.

Miss Kerrigan was getting Mr. Ward's lunch ready when Margaret came into the kitchen.

"The gas man is here to look at the pipes."

Miss Kerrigan went about her work. "Sure, we have no problem with the pipes. Tell him not to waste his time."

Margaret walked to the front of the house and opened the basement door. The man was standing in the well beneath the stoop.

"The pipes is fine," she said.

He stepped inside and removed his cap. "This is an inspection, ma'am. Once every three years. You was notified by post."

He was on the short side, but taller than she. His dark hair was unparted and combed straight back from his forehead. He smiled at her, rows of white, even teeth, and blue eyes, a lovely soft color.

"It's getting warm out," he said.

An American from the sound of him. But it was an Irish face. What was the harm in having the pipes checked? She would stay beside him the entire time, never giving him the chance to take anything, which some workmen weren't above doing, although this one didn't look the criminal type.

"It is indeed," she said.

JULY 11, 1863

Let the Reader confess too that, taking one thing with another, perhaps few terrestrial Appearances are better worth considering than mobs. Your mob is a genuine outburst of Nature; issuing from, or communicating with, the deepest of Nature. When so much goes grinning and grimacing as a lifeless Formality, and under the stiff buckram no heart can be felt beating, here once more, if nowhere else, is a Sincerity and Reality. Shudder at it; or even shriek over it, if thou must; nevertheless consider it. Such a Complex of human Forces and Individualities hurled forth, in their transcendental mood, to act and react, on circumstances and on one another; to work out what is in them to work. The thing they will do is known to no man; least of all to themselves. It is the inflammablest immeasurable Firework, generating, consuming itself. With what phases, to what extent, with what results it will burn off, Philosophy and Perspicacity conjecture in vain.

—Thomas Carlyle, *History of the French Revolution*

I

Colonel Robert Noonan lay down to smoke a cigarillo, stretched out carefully, his head propped on two pillows, his boots extended over the bedside. He sucked in the smoke and released it just as the guns on the far side of Governors Island began to fire.

Boom, boom, boom, boom.

Big guns, they had been shipped to New York a year before, in the wake of the appearance of the ironclad *Merrimac* at Hampton Roads, and placed behind embankments dug by the Rebel prisoners held in Castle Williams. The North had been thrown into a panic, and although the *Monitor* had steamed out of the Brooklyn Navy Yard, south to the mouth of the James, and arrived in time to save the Union fleet, the city's defense had nonetheless been reconstructed. From Fort Schuyler to the north, on Long Island Sound, to Sandy Hook, at the eastern tip of New Jersey, new batteries had been put in place, with more and bigger guns and thicker and stronger fortifications. The batteries on Governors Island were part of this effort. They were silent for the first months. But in June, to reassure the city in the wake of Lee's invasion, General John Ellis Wool, Commander of the Department of the East, ordered them fired every morning.

The city was given no notice. The morning the batteries were first fired, some people thought the Rebels had entered the harbor, and took refuge with their families in cellars and basements. One man stopped a streetcar and forced the driver at gunpoint to race uptown, away from the Rebel assault. Mayor Opdyke appealed to General Wool to halt the firings. "Such cannonading," the

Mayor wrote, "is an unwarranted irritant to the peace and tranquillity of the population."

General Wool gave no reply other than to keep the guns firing each morning. On July 4th, 1863, the day the news of General Meade's victory at Gettysburg arrived, General Wool ordered the guns fired continually for two hours until they were so hot the battery commander silenced them out of fear of an accidental explosion. The following day they resumed their regular firing. People ceased to notice. By now, the booming had become as much a part of the city's life as ferry whistles, church bells, and the roar of traffic.

Noonan had come out to Governors Island the evening before and spent the night. Here, he was too close to the guns not to notice them. The windows of his room rattled. Except for his tunic, he was already dressed. There was nothing more to do. In a few hours the first names would be pulled from the drum, and the draft would be under way. He drew more smoke from his cigarillo. The original plan had called for a massive troop presence throughout the city the day the draft began, but the Confederate invasion had resulted in the city being stripped of troops. If the previous week had brought news of a Union defeat, the draft would have been postponed. Victory had made everyone confident that the machinery of the draft would proceed unimpeded. The guns boomed again, then ceased.

In his office in the city, in the St. Nicholas Hotel, Noonan had mounted a large wall map of the wards that contained the great bulk of the city's population. He outlined in red those that contained the largest potential for violence, a vast contiguous area that ran from the Second Ward to the Seventeenth and covered most of the neighborhoods east of Broadway and south of Fourteenth Street. People lived there crammed in among factories and slaughterhouses, in cellars, in tenements, in the decaying ruins of the city's ancient housing stock. To the north was the other potential trouble zone, the shantytowns. Noonan told each provost that the enrolling officers couldn't rely on voting records or the census to give them a list of eligible draftees. Half those enrolled to vote were, as Tammany called them, "the brothers of Martha and Mary," men as dead as Lazarus was before Jesus called him from the tomb. These new Lazaruses were summoned only on Election Day, when the likes of John Morrissey and company resurrected and reenfranchised them. In many areas the census was more a sampling than a summation. It avoided most of the hundreds of back-lot tenements reached through dark alleyways, and the cellars where four or five families shared a single room, and the wild terrain of the shantytowns, and the lodging houses where thousands upon thousands took their shelter one night at a time.

Noonan instructed the enrolling officers to visit every building, shanty, tenement, lodge, hotel, house, and cellar. The draft was to be fair. No one would be able to claim that only Catholics or Democrats were being enrolled. Just as Congress had directed, the enrollment would include every male citizen and immigrant aged twenty to forty-five. No exceptions.

Up until the enactment of conscription, the Provost Marshal's office had been charged with finding and arresting deserters, inquiring into treasonable practices and opinions, detaining disloyal persons, and apprehending spies. Improbable work in New York, where deserters could easily fade into the crowd, where disloyalty was praised by prominent politicians and preached by half the newspapers. But Noonan knew he hadn't been offered the job to see to those functions; Secretary of War Stanton had chosen him for the purpose of enforcing the draft, setting an Irishman to the task of conscripting other Irishmen. Stanton had telegraphed to see him in February, and despite the discomfort Noonan still suffered from the wounds he'd received at Fredericksburg in December, he had gone.

A trial lawyer accustomed to walking about a room as he talked, Stanton had received Noonan while standing behind a chest-high writing desk. The Secretary had his spectacles pushed on top of his head, and he used both hands to play with the ragged strands of his beard.

"I won't waste your time, Colonel," Stanton said. "In a matter of a few weeks, Congress shall have approved the Enrollment Bill. It has been a painful decision for the President, but there is no other way to bring this war to a successful conclusion."

Behind Stanton was a map of Virginia, Maryland, and the southern border of Pennsylvania. From where Noonan stood the print was too fine to read, but he knew much of the terrain from experience. Antietam, just below the Pennsylvania border. Manassas Junction, where the Manassas Gap Railroad met the Orange & Alexandria. Fredericksburg and the Rappahannock River. The dead piled up in heaps. Equipment strewn across the roads. A landscape of failure.

"The requirements we imposed last summer on the state militias led to a certain level of resistance. We told the states that in addition to the new levy of three hundred thousand three-year volunteers we were calling for, we were also imposing a levy of three hundred thousand nine-month men. The second proviso was merely a stick to encourage men to join and earn a bounty instead of finding themselves required to serve. We told the states we'd count every three-year enlistment as four men against the nine-month quota. It worked. The federal government didn't have to step in and decide the issue. But in some areas the states found it necessary to employ force in order to fill their quotas."

Stanton tugged at his beard. "Some of the worst incidents of violence were in the areas with heavy concentrations of Irish, particularly in the coalfields of Pennsylvania, where the situation threatened to get out of hand. I am a man without prejudice against any creed and have never thought of the Irish in particular or papists in general as disloyal or untrustworthy. Many have already proved their loyalty on the battlefield, as you have, Colonel, and the Irish Brigade is among the best fighting units we have."

"I resisted the idea," Noonan said.

Stanton brought his spectacles down from the top of his head onto the bridge of his nose.

"Resisted what idea?" he said.

"The Irish Brigade. After Bull Run, I told General Meagher I thought it would be better if recruits simply joined the regular ranks instead of being gathered in regiments distinguished by nation. Archbishop Hughes shared my views. He, too, felt we should fight as Americans, nothing more, nothing less, but we were overruled."

"I don't share your reservations. If I could raise a hundred regiments of Irish I would, or of Frenchmen, or of Mussulmen, whatever it takes to fill the ranks and crush this rebellion. That goes for the black man as well."

Stanton came out from behind his desk and walked over to the window. Several weeks before, General Sickles had stopped in to see him. The former congressman had painted a grim picture of what would happen if conscription were imposed on New York. "I know Paddy as well as anyone can," Sickles had said. "God bless his Democratic soul, he is as pugnacious and resentful a creature as God put on this earth, and don't let the veneer of musicality fool you into believing otherwise. In his heart of hearts, every Paddy believes the same thing: that the Know-Nothing–Abolitionist–Protestant Ascendancy has decided that in the contest between him and the nigger as to which will occupy the lowest station in American life, Paddy must win. Remember, the Paddies can be a poetical people when happy, but a murderous one when not."

"Do you have any objection to the enlistment of the Negro?" Stanton asked Noonan.

"No," Noonan said. "Although, again, I'm not sure of the wisdom of forming regiments based on race. The whole character and worthiness of an entire people will be judged on the performance of a handful of men."

"And you have no difficulty with emancipation."

"None."

"I am glad to hear that, Colonel. There is no question that emancipation has in some ways simplified the war and made it harder for the British to intervene, but it has raised fears among our own people, particularly in certain quarters of the laboring classes, where there is a general assumption the free black man will soon be competing for jobs."

"I am in favor of doing what must be done to win the war. Emancipation and conscription both serve that end."

"Of course I wish the administration had been able to obtain a better, purer form of conscription," Stanton said. "As it now stands, however, a draftee will have four choices. One, he can allow himself to be drafted. Two, he can refuse the draft and join up on his own, in a regiment of his choice, and thereby earn a volunteer's bounty. Three, he can pay three hundred dollars and remove himself from this particular levy, although he will be subject to future ones. Four, he can hire a substitute to go in his stead, which will permanently excuse him from the draft. Personally, I resisted these last two conditions. I maintained there should be neither exemptions for sale nor the use of substitution. But the argument was made that substitution is a venerable practice, and that since the Rebels have made it part of their conscription, we should make it part of ours. The three-hundred-dollar exemption, it was argued, would ensure that the bidding for substitutes would not get out of hand. It isn't a perfect law, but it is a necessary one. We'll continue to need a steady supply of men. We have all the materials we need, the guns, ships, shells, supplies, and we must ensure we have the men."

Stanton folded his arms and leaned with his back against the windowsill. That same morning, Frederick Law Olmsted of the Sanitary Commission had given him a recounting of his tour of the Western Theatre. Olmsted had been hopeful about Grant's chances of taking Vicksburg but wouldn't venture a guess about when. In terms of men, Olmsted had said, the price would be dear. Undoubtedly it would. But it must be paid. The war had its own momentum now, there was no stopping it, even if it meant arming the contrabands and drafting immigrant riffraff. By the end of the year, the three-year volunteers who had joined at the war's beginning would reach the end of their enlistments. If they chose to go home, what then? Better not to think about it. Concentrate instead on the campaign ahead, on the carrot of victory and the stick of conscription.

"We need leaders, Colonel," Stanton said. He paced back and forth in front of Noonan in the same manner as when he charged a jury. "And not just on the battlefield but on the home front. The draft is something entirely new to this nation, a mixing of chemicals whose result we cannot foresee. Enforcing it will be both delicate and dangerous. We are putting military men in charge of all the local departments. The biggest and most important department is in New York City. We need someone there who is reliable and decisive, someone who can be equally fair and forceful."

Stanton stopped and glanced at the map. Fields and rivers spotted with ruined reputations. McDowell. McClellan. Pope. Burnside. Mistakes. Botched battles. Lost opportunities. Perhaps even, in McClellan's case, treason. Maybe Hooker would prove the man. By this time next year the map would contain the names of once-insignificant towns, villages, and crossroads raised to fame because of the battles fought around them. That morning, Olmsted had been his usual pedantic, hectoring self, filled with complaints about the conduct of the war. He seemed to believe he was still in charge of constructing Central Park in New York and had talked as if he were giving instructions to some junior landscaper on the proper arrangement of rosebushes. Hooker, he had said, would be beaten by Lee. Said it with that same supercilious smirk with which he said everything, an expression worn by the whole insufferable crowd of New Yorkers who continually descended on the capital with unceasing complaints and unsolicited advice. If only the Union could do without New York.

Stanton already liked Noonan. A New Yorker with a smirkless face. A good sign. "Colonel, I have talked to a great many people about whom to put in charge in New York. Everyone recommends you."

As he did every time he told a lie, Stanton pursed his lips. He had tried to break himself of the habit but had never entirely

succeeded. He had only talked to a handful of people. Sickles had
made the case for one of his protégés, Duffy, but the man was
without real military experience. General Michael Corcoran had
put Noonan's name forward. "You won't find a better man or a
better soldier anywhere," Corcoran had said. Stanton had mentioned Noonan's name to several other officers. He had a fine
reputation. Been under fire. Wounded. Commander of the Sixty-
ninth New York. Best of all, an Irishman.

"What do you know about Colonel Robert Noonan?" Stanton had asked Olmsted at the end of their interview.

"Not much," Olmsted had said. "He is, I think, a prothono-
tary of Corcoran's circle, but while my personal knowledge of
Noonan is slight, my general acquaintance with the Irish of New
York is all too thorough. The leaders are as corrupt as their followers are ignorant."

Another point in Noonan's favor: Olmsted had nothing good
to say about him. "Colonel," Stanton said to Noonan, "I'm offering you the job of Provost Marshal for New York City. I will,
of course, give you several days to think about it, but I should
like an answer within a week."

"I accept," Noonan said.

"Here I've been trying to sell you something you were ready
to buy as soon as you walked into the room!"

"General Corcoran had already told me why you wanted to
see me."

"You're a joy to talk to, Colonel. A man who gives simple
answers to simple questions! But a word of advice: Get out of
Washington as quickly as you can before the mephitic vapors of
the Potomac infect you with the verbosity that sooner or later
fells all inhabitants of this city."

When his appointment as Provost Marshal was formally announced, Noonan was invited to the headquarters of the newly
formed Union League Club. Carpenters and plasterers were busy
transforming what had been a private home into a clubhouse. He
stood on the steps a moment. Union Square was empty except for

nannies pushing prams. On the other side of the park was the statue of General Washington around which a crowd of a quarter of a million people had swirled that first week of the war. Major Robert Anderson had been there, with the flag he had been forced to take down from Fort Sumter. Men and women had cheered and wept, strangers had embraced, Irishmen, Germans, and True Americans had stood side by side and sang "The Star-Spangled Banner." Noonan had watched from the stoop of a brownstone on the east side of the park. The crowd had reminded him of the great masses of people Daniel O'Connell had mustered in Ireland, men cheering speeches they couldn't hear, believing for this moment that the sheer weight of their collective desire was enough to bend the course of history. O'Connell had died a broken man, his crowds scattered to the four winds.

An Irish servant girl appeared at the door and conducted him across a trail of drop cloths to a small room in the rear of the building that smelled of fresh paint. A. T. Stewart, the city's leading merchant, and three other men Noonan didn't recognize were seated around a table. Stewart introduced them to Noonan, and they rose to shake hands. Stewart offered Noonan a seat on his right. The others sat facing them.

"Well, Colonel, our first order of business is to congratulate you," Stewart said. "We are honored to welcome you to the Union League Club in your new capacity as Provost Marshal. You're among friends. Anything you say will be held in strictest confidence."

Noonan heard the intonations of the Anglo-Irish Ascendancy in Stewart's voice, Ulster speech that had been tamed and trained at Trinity. He tried not to let it annoy him, but it did. "I have no need of such safeguard," Noonan said. "Anything I say here I could as easily say in the square across the street."

The girl returned with a tray of tea. They sat in silence as she poured. As soon as she left, Stewart said, "We know you are a busy man, and we have no desire to detain you longer than necessary, but we believe it's important that you comprehend the full gravity of the situation in this city. As Provost Marshal you know better than anyone the disgraceful prevalence of treasonous opinions in every level of the population." Stewart pushed his cup aside. He leaned his face close to Noonan's. The men across the table leaned forward. Stewart lowered his voice. "But, Colonel, what you might not understand is that mixed in with the Secessionist sentiment is something just as repulsive and, in the long run, perhaps even more dangerous." He pronounced the next word slowly, with great emphasis: "*Anarchy.*"

Stewart sat back in his chair. He took a deep breath as if he had confessed a secret that had been weighing him down. "We are living on the side of a live volcano, all of us. Each day the pressures grow and the rumblings beneath our feet become more ominous. Some choose to imagine the tremors are the random workings of nature, but we are not among them."

The others nodded in agreement.

"This Vesuvius is a creation not of nature but of men. Since the beginning of the war, there has been a growing agitation among the laboring class. It began with the grain shovelers. Five thousand of them tried to cripple the ability of the port to function. They left their jobs to stop their employers from using the new floating elevators that transfer grain from lighters to ships with efficiency and speed. Soon after, the employees of the Manhattan Gas Works walked off their jobs. When the Gas Works tried to fill the positions that the strikers had abandoned, mobs roamed the streets and chased away those hired as replacements. Next came the longshoremen, then the house painters, then the ironworkers, then the tobacco workers, carpenters, piano makers, machinists, until, by God, there is hardly an industry or business that hasn't been affected. In some cases the men have returned to work and the strikes ended, but for every one that is discontinued, another begins. At present, there are over thirty strikes in progress in this city. Yesterday, the tailors at Brooks Brothers walked off the job. Three hundred men employed in the production of uniforms for the Army." Stewart gestured toward one of the men across the table. "Mr. Atkinson is a partner in the firm, and he has something that might interest you."

Rodney Atkinson was a white-haired man with a round, pleasant, wrinkleless face. He took a pamphlet from the breast pocket of his coat, threw it onto the table, and pushed it across. Noonan looked at it but didn't pick it up. The title was in German, in big Gothic letters.

"I don't read German," Noonan said.

"No need to, Colonel," Atkinson said. "The usual rubbish, down with property, death to the rich, that sort of stuff. Was found in the drawer of one of the strikers' sewing tables."

"Each of us, no matter what our business, is being subject to such agitation and threats," Stewart said. "In one place, the demand is for more pay. Somewhere else, it is a change in the work rules. In my business of retail merchandising, there is now something called the Dry-Goods Clerks' Early-Closing Association, its supposed goal the reduction of the workday from twelve hours to ten."

"I'm sorry you are having such difficulties," Noonan said. "But the disputes between employers and employees are no concern of the Provost Marshal. If they interfere with the delivery of materials for the Army, General Wool, Commander of the Department of the East, will decide what should be done. If there are threats being made against you or your property, the police should be informed."

Stewart turned to face Noonan. "You are perfectly correct, Colonel. On its face, the labor agitation occurring in this city has nothing directly to do with the Provost Marshal. But beneath the issues of wages or hours or conditions there is another force at work, an insidious conspiracy of tightly organized revolutionaries who are fomenting an explosion of enormous proportions. These men view the war as the opportunity to attack the very foundations of property. All authority and all wealth are their enemy. They are traitors steeped in an inheritance of brutality and insurrection, and have dedicated themselves to the overthrow of our republican institutions."

Stewart placed a small square of paper on the table, unfolded it, and ironed it flat with his hand. "We have watched them carefully. We know who they are."

"If they resist the draft or advocate resistance, my office will look into it," Noonan said.

Stewart slid the paper in front of Noonan. "They are plotting far worse than that, Colonel."

"Perhaps. But I cannot arrest men on your word. They have a right to seek higher wages, especially in light of the increases in prices the war has caused."

"And a right to advocate the overthrow of every American institution, do they have that right, too? Are we to fight a war to free the slaves only to take the shackles from their wrists and place them on the wrists of men of property?"

Atkinson pounded the table with his fist. "Here, here!" he said. The others quickly joined in.

"Those who resist the draft will be arrested," Noonan said.

"Arrested?" Stewart said. "What good will that do? They will either be released by some sympathetic politician, Governor Seymour perhaps, or else turned into martyrs, their imprisonment splashed across the pages of the city's seditious newspapers, of which there is no shortage. There is only one thing to do with these scoundrels. Draft them!" With his finger, Stewart tapped the paper in front of Noonan. "Here are the names, Colonel. Each a known troublemaker, each a traitor. Put them in the Army and in one stroke you cut the head off the serpent."

"The draft will be conducted on the basis of a lottery," Noonan explained. "Those who provide substitutes will be permanently excused. Those who pay three hundred dollars will be excused from this round of conscription. Beyond that, it is not in my power, or in anyone's power, to determine the names which will be picked."

"Of course it is in your power, Colonel," Atkinson said. "And I daresay it is your duty. Without the slightest injustice to the others in this lottery, you could easily arrange for the selection of the names on this list. The country and city would be in your debt for such service, a debt those of us in this room would do their best to repay." Atkinson picked up the paper and extended it to Noonan. "Here, sir, look at these names."

Noonan took the paper. He folded it along the crease lines, ripped it into quarters, then into eighths, then dropped it into Stewart's teacup. "Gentlemen, I am grateful for your time." He stood up. "I will show myself out."

The day was Saturday. The evening before, Generals Wool and Noonan had come over to Governors Island to review the so-called Invalid Guard, sick and wounded men sufficiently recovered to serve in the light work of standing ready to arrest and remove any draft resisters, should they appear. The members of the Guard had paraded smartly. Major Ahearn had been in command. There were another 200 troops stationed in the forts around the city who could be called on in an emergency. In the city proper were the 150 men of the Provost Guard, the bulk of them lodged in the barracks in City Hall Park.

The evening was windless and suffocating. Even though the sun had slipped down to the horizon, the parade ground was broiling. Noonan and Wool reviewed the troops from General Wool's carriage. The perspiration streamed down Wool's face, and he panted from the heat. Afterward, they dined on the porch of the house that Wool used when he was on the island. It was a full meal of roasted venison and mashed potatoes, and Wool attacked it eagerly. Noonan barely touched his food. He drank ice water and smoked cigarillos.

At nightfall, a small breeze began to blow but quickly died away. General Wool had a suite of rooms in the St. Nicholas Hotel, where the War Department had its New York headquarters, but he often preferred to spend the night on Governors Island. The noise of the city carried across the harbor. Wool waved a paper accordion fan back and forth in front of his face.

"You'd think heat would smother a man's fighting instincts," Wool said. "If we was a logical species, we'd sit still in weather like this and wait until the autumn to do our killing, but unfortunately we ain't that smart. Greater the heat, the worse the killing."

Wool had taken his belt and tunic off. Unrestrained, the round bump of his stomach protruded from an otherwise thin body. He continued waving the fan with one hand and swatted a mosquito on his neck with the other. "Seems to me, though," he said, "the heat is particularly fearsome on city folks, makes them nastier and more unfriendly than they usually are, which ain't easy given the meanness they got naturally. A country man knows when it's time to sit still in the shade. But city folk keep right on moving and working, drowning in their own sweat, never stopping, and pretty soon they lose the ability to think straight. How else do you explain the silly ruction that the Mayor raised over them guns? The man presides over a town noisier than the workshops of hell. But the entire town gets itself in a lather over a little gunfire."

"We're all accustomed to different sounds," Noonan said. "I've seen soldiers sleep through artillery fire that would wake the dead, only to be awakened by the lowing of a cow."

"Had half a mind to turn them guns around and let the town have something more than just a report," Wool commented. "Lob a few shells down on top of 'em, give 'em a whiff of the real thing, specially those copperhead sons of bitches. Believe me, given the rightful provocation, I would enjoy nothing more."

Noonan had decided that there would be no troops present when the draft lottery began. The sight of them might be a provocation. Instead, he directed that the draft would start at the Ninth District office, on Third Avenue, in the Nineteenth Ward, in the upper reaches of the city, a sparsely populated area where any outbreak could be contained and brought under control. A large force of police would be on hand at the local precinct but would stay out of sight unless their presence were required. If there were no disturbances, then on Monday the draft would begin throughout the city.

General Wool dropped the fan into his lap. His head fell to

his breast, and he began to snore. He would be eighty on his next birthday, but didn't appear that old in uniform. Sitting in the chair, however, with his mouth agape, his jacket off, his posture gone soft, he looked to Noonan both tired and old. Noonan had two orderlies carry Wool to bed; he didn't awake when they lifted his chair and brought him inside. Noonan walked the grounds of the island and watched the city as the night grew deeper and most of the lights were put out. For over a week, there had been rumors gathered by the police and the Provost Marshal's office that an attempt would be made on Noonan's life. Saloon talk, mostly. Conversations overheard by informers. No suspect had been named. But Noonan had decided not to stay the night in his lodgings in Yorkville. It was important there be no incidents on the eve of the draft.

The noise from across the river had almost died away. The city was at its quietest. Noonan lay down in his room but couldn't sleep. He remembered the last time he had seen his father alive, an event he hadn't thought about in years. It was the spring before the Famine struck Ireland. He had returned to the farm from Dundalk, where he had secured employment as a clerk. His father's appearance had shocked him. A once physically powerful man who had raised himself from the subtenantry to a prime tenancy of ten acres, his father had shriveled into one of those ancient countrymen who sat by crossroads begging a coin in return for the stories and prophecies they routinely repeated. He slept on a low bed set next to the hearth. Noonan's older brother, John, still unmarried, saw to the farm.

Although it had been over a year since Robert Noonan had been home, his father barely talked to him. They sat and smoked the tobacco Noonan had brought. Noonan broke the silence by talking about the political turmoil Daniel O'Connell was causing in the country with his campaign for repeal of the union with Great Britain. His father made no response; then, after a long silence, he said, "I saw it in the sky. I knew someday I would. Every cloud that blocked the sun raised the fear of it in me, but now it's done, the sign appeared as she said it would, and it's the people brought it on themselves, with their wantonness and faith-lessness, God's judgment is on our heads."

"What sign?" Noonan said.

"The Black Pig."

John brought over to the bed a jar of whiskey and three cracked and dirty cups. He handed out the cups and poured. "It was a cloud he saw," John said to Noonan, as if their father weren't there. "A cloud like any other cloud. I saw it, too."

" 'Twas no cloud," their father murmured.

"His mind plays tricks on him," John said. "And he is near to blind."

"My mind is sound, and my eyes. 'Twas no more a cloud than the sun is a dish of butter. The cloven hoof, the tail, snout, ears, head—no cloud was ever shaped thus, exactly as the old woman said."

"What old woman?" Noonan asked.

John drained the whiskey from his cup and dragged his sleeve across his mouth. "In the name of God, stop this silly talk."

The old man cradled the cup in his right hand. The fingers were gnarled and bent; it seemed more a claw than a hand. He spoke rapidly in Irish, a language his sons had rarely heard him speak, and then reverted to English:

> *She lives by herself in the cliffs by the sea,*
> *As light and small as a bird is she;*
> *Her words are true words of prophecy.*

"That's how the poetry men described her. She was a tiny thing, with wild hair, we'd see her scurry about the cliffs when we hunted gulls' eggs, but she was a powerful creature, even the landlords feared her, and was over a hundred and twenty years when she died in 1791."

"No one lives that long," John said.

"Not today, but in olden times things were different, there was a strength in the people that is gone now, and she was no ordinary peasant's child but the daughter of a great Kerry chief, himself a man of seventy when he fathered her. There is no telling what age he would have reached if the foreigners hadn't come, laid siege to his castle for seven years, and finally stormed and burned it the day before the King of Spain arrived with troops and ships to drive the enemy away. The foreigners slaughtered the chief and all his sept, but when they went to seize his daughter she turned herself into a bird, flew through the air until she could fly no longer, and took refuge in the cliffs of Donegal."

John put down his cup with a loud clatter. "I can't stand to hear these fables anymore." He walked out into the yard.

"She knew what the weather would be, how the crops would fare, when a man would die and in what way. All the people came to her, even the priest, and brought offerings of food, mostly the sweet things she craved, and she told them what they wanted to know. Some went away in tears, others rejoicing, each knowing in his heart there was no escaping the future she described to them.

"One day, when the people were in the field hearing Mass, she appeared. The priest cursed her and told her to go away, but she paid no heed. 'Pray!' she shouted in a sharp voice, a bird's voice, 'Pray you may be spared the Day of the Black Pig, for when he appears in the sky, the final end will have come for Ireland, and the Devil will have his sway. The people will starve and stuff their mouths with grass to kill the ache of hunger, and though they flee across the seas, the Devil will follow them, and they shall drown themselves in distant waters and tear the flesh from each other's bones!' "

The old man was hunched over as though in pain. He spoke into the cup of whiskey, which he had not drunk. Noonan felt the urge to put his arm around his father's shoulders but held back. They sat silently until Noonan stood. "Ireland has already seen her share of hunger and death," Noonan said. "Perhaps the prophecy is already complete."

"Perhaps."

"I must be going now."

"Aye, then be gone. God's grace go with you."

Noonan went outside. His brother was standing by the wall in a slow but soaking rain.

"He's mad," John said.

"He's old, that's all."

"His mind is gone."

"He doesn't think as clearly as he once did."

"Little difference between the two, at least as far as I'm concerned, stuck here day after day with that raving relic of a man. Jesus, 'tis work enough to wring the rent out of this barren piece of land without having to carry him on me back. But how would you know? 'Tis neat and tidy work you do, done on paper, and never any lack of it."

"Work I took because this land was promised you, and there was nothing for me here."

John walked away without reply, crossed the muddy yard and the road beyond, into the fields. Noonan mounted his horse and set out for Dundalk, turning around only once, for what would be his last glimpse of home.

In the morning, after the guns had finished firing, Noonan put on his tunic and went out to General Wool's coach. Wool appeared a few moments later. He was stooped, and walked with a stiff, shuffling gait. He was already sweating profusely, and grunted loudly as he mounted the coach. He waved away Noonan's offered hand, falling into his seat with such force that he made the coach rock.

"Let us be off," Wool said. The sweat was beaded on his forehead and upper lip. "It is impolite to keep any man waiting, but to do so to the honored dead is downright insulting."

A private viewing of General Samuel Zook's body was scheduled for eight o'clock, in City Hall. He had been killed on the second day of Gettysburg. Before his body was offered for public viewing, his military comrades were to pay their respects.

"If you don't mind, General, I have offered Major Ahearn a ride with us," Noonan said. "He should be here momentarily."

"Damn you, Noonan, for turning my coach into an omnibus, and damn Acorn for being late."

"Ahearn, not Acorn."

"From the look of him, it would seem his pubes grew in the week before last. Nothing but an acorn, and he's a major already. We are awash in acorns, Colonel. We have been for some time. You see them everywhere, in business, the clergy, the Army, an endless parade of boys, none of them willing to wait, all of them in such a ferocious hurry. It is a dangerous thing when a country becomes all ambition and no wisdom, but it's what happens when experience is pushed aside and mere youth put in its place."

"Ahearn is an experienced officer," Noonan said. "I served with him on the Peninsula. He was wounded at Fredericksburg."

On the other side of the parade ground, Ahearn came down the front steps of his quarters. He walked with his head down, the same deliberate, plodding step as on that morning seven months before, when the Irish Brigade had crossed the pontoon bridges into Fredericksburg. The men had picked their way through the debris and smashed furniture scattered around the narrow streets. A storm of soft, fluffy goose feathers, the innards of disemboweled mattresses, blew about like snow. Noonan stood with Ahearn at the top of Hanover Street, the last protected space before the open fields that swelled in gentle waves toward Marye's Heights. In the northern sky, above the rooftops and over the river, was an Army observation balloon, a large white sphere as bright and prominent as the moon. As the Union guns began to pound the heights above the town, the tiny figures in the basket suspended beneath the balloon waved signal flags that told the gunners how to adjust their fire.

In a short while, General Thomas Francis Meagher came up the crowded street on horseback. The men stood aside to let him pass. Ahead was a small bridge that they had to funnel together in order to cross. Once across, the brigade formed into battle ranks, and when Meagher rode out onto the field, he was cheered. He leaned over a row of evergreen bushes, tore off a sprig of green, and stuck it into his hat. The men broke ranks. They clutched and ripped at the branches and stuck green sprigs into their caps. Noonan shouted for them to get back into line. Meagher sat facing the Heights, oblivious to the confusion behind him, and raised his sword. He yelled something that Noonan couldn't hear, and then the whole brigade went forward. They reached the first rise. The Rebels held their fire. Off to his right, Noonan saw Ahearn walking amid the ranks, encouraging the men, his face white and taut. As they approached the second rise, the thunderclap struck, Rebel artillery and muskets firing simultaneously; the entire front rank seemed to go down together, in unison, and the smoke rolled down on top of them. The gunfire was ceaseless. The sergeant in front of Noonan was hit in the mouth by a piece of canister that blew out the back of his head. Noonan fell over him, then stood and brushed off his clothes, aware of the ridiculous futility of his gesture even as he did it. He ran forward, sword in hand, and yelled at the top of his lungs. Through the smoke he caught glimpses of the Rebels: indistinguishable faces beneath slouched hats.

One ball hit him in the side and stopped him cold. The next one passed through his right thigh and lodged behind his left knee. He limped forward a few steps before he fell, and a soldier with a shattered chest fell on top of him, his eyes open and blood spurting from his mouth and the hole in his chest. Noonan rolled him off. He tried to stand but couldn't. He looked up and saw Ahearn go past, quickly disappearing into a curtain of smoke.

Wool looked out the window of the coach when Ahearn entered. He grunted in response to Ahearn's greeting. There were no more attempts at conversation. As the coach rolled off the ferry toward City Hall, the temperature seemed to increase appreciably. Hot as it had been on Governors Island, the city was far hotter.

At City Hall, Ahearn exited first. He offered his hand to Wool, but the old man glowered at him and came out unassisted. Noonan ascended the stairs of City Hall beside Wool. At the top, Mayor Opdyke greeted them. "Well, Colonel, I don't think we have anything to worry about, do you?" The Mayor looked ill. His hair was matted with perspiration. Around his eyes there was a Nile tint to the skin.

"I will be better able to answer that question this evening," Noonan said.

General Charles Sanford, Commander of the State Militia, came up behind Mayor Opdyke and put his hand on the Mayor's shoulder. "Pardon me for interrupting, but I wish to offer the Colonel congratulations on a job well done."

"We haven't begun yet," Noonan said.

"You've completed the enrollment of a hundred thousand men and established draft offices throughout the city, all without the slightest disturbance. I'd say you're well begun and half done, as the Greeks put it."

"The Colonel won't permit himself such happy thoughts," the Mayor said. "Perhaps he's just being superstitious, a not uncommon trait among the Irish, or perhaps he's merely being cautious, a necessary virtue among military men, I suppose."

"A good soldier must know when to be cautious and when to be brave," Wool said. "Noonan knows both." He walked away from them into City Hall; Noonan followed.

General Zook lay in state in a large rectangular room on the first floor. His catafalque was swathed in black bunting and banked with lily plants. Beneath, out of view, was a copper-lined vat of tightly packed ice in which the coffin sat. The heat was already causing the ice to melt. A steady drip fell, turning the red carpet around the coffin as dark as blood.

Zook had been dead over a week. Neither ice nor flowers nor the aromatic fragrances the undertaker had sprayed around the room could erase entirely the faint odor of corruption. Zook's face had been given a fresh dusting of talc to cover its sea-green hue. Zook had been shot at Gettysburg in the chest and the groin; he'd fallen from his horse and bled to death. Now his eyes were closed, as if he were asleep, but despite the undertaker's labors, the mouth was twisted rather than reposed, the final agony still on it. His gloved hands were crossed on the buckle of his sword belt, the gesture of the dead. Solid, reliable Samuel Zook. Noonan had last seen him alive on the morning of the assault on Fredericksburg. Zook had been supervising the repair of the pontoon bridges damaged by Confederate artillery fire. He wore spectacles at the end of his thick nose, and scratched at his frizzy brown beard as he moved back and forth. He looked more like a botanist gathering specimens in a spring field than a soldier in imminent danger of being punctured by a sniper's bullet. He walked back to the Union lines in the same deliberate way as he had paced the bridges, as though taking his daily constitutional. Noonan stopped to greet Zook as the brigade moved down to the river. Zook was sitting on a campstool, his head bowed in a silent grace before he took his breakfast. Although he had abandoned the pacifist tenets of his Mennonite faith, he was a rigorously devout man who refrained from alcohol, tobacco, and swearing, and who encouraged his men to do the same. "Sanctity Sam," they called him, yet it wasn't so much piety Zook radiated as the rock-hard holiness of a biblical prophet, a grim resolve to wear down the evil in the world.

Zook had moved from Pennsylvania to New York in the 1840s as the superintendent of the Washington & New York Telegraph Company. He was one of the few men in the business who was willing to hire Irishmen, and the first winter Noonan was in the city, Zook had taken him on as an assistant. Their days were spent running and repairing wires in the financial district. It was a boom-time business. New trading offices opened constantly, some of them little more than a desk and a telegraph key, and the brokers made a sport of cutting one another's wires. Zook liked to take his men out to drink after work, and the carousing often lasted until the following morning, when they went straight from the tavern to their jobs. Zook never seemed to tire of this routine, until the spring the cholera struck and carried away his twin sons, age six.

Noonan attended the funeral, at a Quaker church in the rural precincts of Brooklyn. Zook was crushed with grief. Noonan knew there were those who said that the cholera was carried by

the Irish, as endemic among them as popery and vice, and that
to associate with Paddies was to risk exposure to the onslaughts
of the disease. But Zook neither shunned nor condemned
Noonan. He simply stood by the graveside, the two small coffins
laid at his feet, and cried out over and over, "O Lord, I am a
sinner!"

Zook returned to work a changed man, reserved and
religious.

Noonan left the telegraph company the next year and didn't
run into his erstwhile boss again until after Bull Run, when Zook
arrived outside Washington at the head of the Fifty-seventh New
York, no trace left of his lighthearted, whiskey-loving days.

Now Zook was this lifeless husk. Noonan took his seat. He
contemplated that Wool had been wrong when he had described
the gap in the country as a matter of age, the ceaseless promotion
of youth. In truth, it was a difference less measurable, if just as
real. It was a contest between those like Zook, who understood
war for what it really was, the business of killing, and sought to
wind it up as efficiently as possible, and those who saw it as
adventure, glorious and invigorating, a contest that ennobled its
participants.

A minister read Psalm 25: "Unto thee, O Lord, do I lift up
my soul. O my God, I trust in thee: Let me not be ashamed, let
not mine enemies triumph over me." Zook's widow, a stout,
German-looking woman, wept quietly. At one point there was a
small commotion at the back of the room as late arrivals took
their place. The minister looked up without interrupting his reading. The service over, a diminutive man in black walked down
the aisle to Mrs. Zook. He spoke a few words to her, patting her
hand as he did. The undertaker, Noonan thought; then the little
man turned to come back up the aisle, and Noonan recognized
General George McClellan. Although in civilian clothes, McClellan was accompanied by a retinue of officers, who waited for him
by the door. He walked solemnly, at a deliberate pace, stopped
at the door, and greeted each mourner as he departed. It was as
if Zook had been a son or brother of his.

Noonan and Wool were last in line. Wool shuffled his feet impatiently as they waited. He whispered to Noonan, "I think our boy here is going into politics." McClellan seemed delighted to see Wool. "Ellis, old friend," he said, "how goes it?"

Wool's face was expressionless. "I'm doing my best, George," he said.

"No doubt of that, never was. We couldn't have had a Peninsula Campaign without you. If you hadn't saved Fort Monroe for the Union in '61, the door to Richmond would have been slammed in our faces."

"It got slammed anyway," Wool said as he moved on.

McClellan called after him, "That was the President's decision, not ours, Ellis. It was the President who decided to withhold the forces we needed to take Richmond."

Wool walked away without responding.

McClellan turned to Noonan. "Colonel Noonan, of the Sixty-ninth New York, adjutant to Thomas Francis Meagher."

Noonan was astonished that McClellan remembered him. They had met only once, a year ago, on Malvern Hill, on the morning of the last battle of the ill-fated Peninsula Campaign. Noonan had accompanied General Meagher. They had walked to the top of the hill, through a wall of guns, to a large field tent with its flaps raised. In the middle, atop a portable wooden floor, was an Oriental rug that had been confiscated from the home of some departed Rebel planter. Officers stood around, leaning over tables and examining maps. From the direction of the James came a galloping squad of horsemen. McClellan was in the lead. He held his hat at his side in continuous acknowledgment of the soldiers and artillerists who cheered his approach. He dismounted gracefully in front of the tent. Meagher stepped forward to greet him, and McClellan clasped Meagher's hand. Meagher introduced Noonan, who was struck by McClellan's boyishness, which was suggested not only by his shortness and his thick stock of black hair but by his smooth, soft face.

An orderly brought them hot coffee in white ceramic mugs. McClellan sat on a campstool.

"General," Meagher said, "I want you to know that your leadership has inspired us all."

"No, no," McClellan said. "It's my men. They're the real heroes of this campaign." He blew on his coffee and slurped it loudly.

"I can't speak for the other men," Meagher said, "but I can speak for my own, and we Irishmen are a race that looks to chieftains, it's in our blood, and when we find one with your combination of courage and skill, we'll follow him anywhere, even to hell."

McClellan stood. He stared down at the Oriental rug, a dizzying pattern of intricate coils and vines. He studied it as if it were a map, a place where he might find some clue to the devious stratagems of his Confederate adversary. After a moment, he looked up from the rug and its impenetrable designs. "You are kind, General Meagher," he said. "You also have the customary eloquence of your race. And because you have been so forthright with me, I will be the same with you. I have husbanded my troops and exposed them to risks only when I judged there to be an opportunity to break the enemy's line or the necessity to defend my own. In the face of overwhelming odds, and denied the reinforcements I had been promised, I have brought this army here with its honor and strength preserved." McClellan's eyes returned to the rug. "And yet, there are those ready to describe what I have achieved as treason. *Treason.* That is part of the villainous vocabulary being employed in Washington to impugn not only my competency but my loyalty."

"A man's deeds are his gold," Meagher said, "and yours are minted in the same imperishable metal as Hannibal's, Caesar's, and Sarsfield's."

McClellan looked up again. "Sarsfield?" he said.

"The greatest of Irish heroes," Meagher said. "He was a brilliant commander in the Williamite War. After the Irish defeat and the mass flight of the Irish soldiery to the Continent, Sarsfield joined the French army and died fighting with them, at the Battle of Landen in 1693."

McClellan's thick black eyebrows knitted, in something between puzzlement and a frown. He took a gulp of his coffee. An adjutant came across the rug. "General," he said, "I'm sorry to interrupt, but the enemy approaches." McClellan looked off to the James, toward the vast flotilla of flag-bedecked ships that had gathered to evacuate the army, and without another word he went outside and remounted his horse.

"I never forget my brother soldiers," McClellan said, "particularly my brave Irishmen. If I'd been given a hundred more brigades like yours, the war would be over today and the Union restored. But I wasn't. There were those who were willing to see the killing continue in order to deny me the victory. The words of this morning's psalm, then, rang with special meaning in my heart: 'Consider mine enemies; for they are many; and they hate me with cruel hatred.'"

Noonan said, "The brigade did its best for you."

"Of course, of course. The same may be said of the whole army. Its loyalty has been an inspiration. A mutuality of affection, I might add, for if it's true that never in the history of warfare has a commander had more confidence in his men, it's equally true that never has an army had more confidence in its commander. This latest engagement is the final, conclusive proof of that."

In the first week of July, the papers had reported that McClellan was in Albany helping with the organization and dispatch of militia troops to Pennsylvania. Noonan was sure now that McClellan had been nowhere near Gettysburg.

"Which engagement is that, General?"

"Gettysburg."

"You were at the battle?"

"In spirit, yes. Practically every dispatch from the battlefield reported that the troops believed I had been returned to command. The rumor was so universal it took on the force of truth, and the army went into battle thinking it was fighting for me. It was, if you'll pardon the expression, 'McClellan's ghost' who won the field. There will be no doubt of that when the histories are written. The evidence is overwhelming. I mean, George Meade is a decent enough sort, but to conceive of him beating Lee in a three-day struggle—really, it's preposterous on the face of it."

The undertaker approached. He was eager to replace the ice around Zook's coffin and to cover the wet carpet before the public viewing began. "Gentlemen, please, if I may ask you to step outside."

"It's been an honor to see you again, General," Noonan said. "But I must be going. I have business to attend to."

McClellan moved in front of Noonan as if to leave, but then stopped. He stood blocking the doorway.

"Gentlemen, please, if you don't mind moving outside," the undertaker said.

McClellan ignored the undertaker and stood his ground. "The papers make increasing mention of your business, Colonel Noonan."

"The news from Gettysburg and Vicksburg, which has been most welcome, has overshadowed our work," Noonan said, "but now it's our turn for attention." He could see Wool pacing the lobby impatiently.

McClellan put on his hat but didn't move. "If ever there were proof of the bankruptcy of the administration's policy, this is it. I know you're doing your duty, Colonel Noonan, as any soldier must, but the political strategy being dictated by the President cannot save the Union."

Instead of trying to outflank McClellan, the undertaker walked straight toward him. McClellan stepped out of the way. Noonan moved around McClellan's flank into the lobby. Wool had left the building and was slowly descending the steps.

"Remember what I tell you, Colonel Noonan," McClellan said. "The draft will not help us win the war."

McClellan out of the way, the undertaker closed the door to the chamber where Zook's body lay.

"But, General," Noonan said, "you yourself encouraged the President to impose the draft almost two years ago."

"Was a different war back then, a war solely for the Union, the Constitution, the national destiny. In such a struggle, conscription was not only conceivable but enforceable. The honest, patriotic mechanic and farmer could clearly see the necessity of it. But the administration has made this a war for the Negro. That is what we are asking our boys to fight and die for, the confiscation of the South's population of woolly heads. Before the administration can hope once more to have the support of the people, it must return to the one issue this war was begun upon. If it won't, the country will demand a new administration."

"I must take my leave, General," Noonan said. "But I make no apologies for the draft. To my mind, conscription and emancipation are both weapons that must be used in the winning of this war."

"I ask no apologies, but if you should wish to continue our conversation, feel free to come out to Orange Mountain. I'm returning there this afternoon and expect to spend the summer. The door is always open to my old comrades-in-arms. The war is far from over, and we must continue to concentrate our energies on finding ways to end it, in the political as well as military sphere." McClellan rejoined the group of officers he had arrived with.

Noonan caught up with Wool as the old man was entering his coach. Wool huffed from the effort. "Good, sweet, suffering Jesus," Wool said, "if that little bucket of slops could fight like he can talk, the war would have been over a year ago." He sat back in his seat. "What was on the mind of the American Napoléon?"

"Conscription and emancipation," Noonan said.

"Hell, that's all anybody in this town talks about. Eat with the Democrats and they spoil your meal by ranting about the worthless niggers. Eat with the Republicans and they can't stop going on about the shiftless Paddies. For my part, I've had quite enough of all of 'em, niggers, Paddies, Democrats, Republicans. I say to blazes with the lot. Get on with this God-blasted war, draft everybody, nigger, redskin, Chinee, white man, stick 'em all in uniforms, shoot those who refuse, hang every yellow-livered jackal who preaches compromise or defeat, one from every lamp-post in the city, and when you run out of lampposts, use the trees in Central Park, swing a traitor from every branch—and start with that Tom Thumb Caesar you were just talking to, put the hemp around his scheming throat, jack him up right in front of City Hall and let the body rot there till the stench reaches the nostrils of every copperhead in New York."

The coach traveled swiftly up Broadway. There was little traffic, and few people were about. Noonan took it as a good sign. The city was wrapped in a sweltering summer torpor. It drained the life from everyone.

Wool put his kepi on the seat next to him and ran his hand over his freckled, spotted pate, smoothing down the strands of hair drawn forward from the rear of his head.

"The problem isn't with the draft itself," he said. "It's the refusal of our legislative imbeciles to do away with substitution and the three-hundred-dollar exemption. A bad business, Noonan, but you're stuck with it, and my advice is to get on with it. I learned that lesson back in the thirties, during the Indian removals down in Georgia. Cruelest work I ever knew. Worse than war. Rounding up innocent, hardworking Cherokees, forcing them off their land, slaughtering their livestock, confiscating their homes, coercing them to move west to some distant destination beyond the Mississippi. But the cruelest part of all was doing it piecemeal, dragging it out, being unprepared, not having the men and supplies to get the thing done quick, with merciful dispatch."

"We're doing the best we can under the circumstances," Noonan said.

The coach pulled up in front of the St. Nicholas Hotel. Noonan got out first. Wool moved slowly. He crouched, put one hand on the door, and took Noonan's arm with the other. He grimaced as he stepped down. "Those Goddamn Tories," he said. He rubbed his thighs. "It's been fifty years since Queenston Heights, fifty years since them snot-eating British, them ass-kissing sons of Saint George, shot me right here." He patted his left thigh.

"The ball traveled through the leg and came out here." He patted the back of his right thigh. "My first time under fire. I was lucky that the ball didn't hit any bone, just passed through me like a knife through water, and them Englishmen and the Canadian toadies that fought for 'em never got their hands on me, good thing, since they enjoyed nothing more than finishing off the wounded, sticking a bayonet through you as you lay there helpless. But that's the British way, ain't it? Kick you when you're down. That's what they've been trying to do to us these past few years, taking the Rebels' side, just waiting for the right moment to step in and finish us off."

General Wool's coach moved off, but he continued to stand in the street. "Seems to me we got a score to settle with these royal bastards once this war is over. Might be a good idea to march north and take Canada. Should've done it fifty years ago when we had the chance, right there at Queenston Heights, it could have been a great victory, a second Yorktown, dropped the whole of the north country into our laps. But the Goddamn militia wouldn't cross the Niagara River into Canada. Did you ever hear of such a thing? Said they couldn't be forced to set foot on foreign soil. And the sons of bitches got away with it!"

A carriage drew up to drop off its occupants at the St. Nicholas, but Wool ignored it and stayed where he was.

"General," Noonan said, "please, step onto the curb."

"You know what those militia boys needed, Noonan? They needed a taste of the lash! Ain't no substitute for it! Been up to me, they each would have got a backful of strokes. My whole career in uniform, half a Goddamn century, I never hesitated to apply the lash. Never unjustly or out of spite. I had a man whipped, he knew he deserved it. And now Congress has forbidden its use. Worse thing those blockheads ever done, and God knows that's saying something. The lash is an irreplaceable instrument of soldierly education. Does more to instill the fear of God than all the military statutes and laws ever written. Never had any use for tying men up or hanging men by their thumbs or making them carry logs or knapsacks filled with stones. The longer a punishment goes on, the less of an impression it makes. Men grow used to cruelty faster than to comfort. But no man ever seen a whipping forgets it, and no man been stripped and whipped hasn't gone out of his way to avoid a repetition."

The driver of the coach that was waiting to pull up to the St. Nicholas motioned with his long switch at Wool. "Hey, General Washington," he said, "clear the way, I got people who needs to get into the hotel."

Wool looked up at him. "Was a time I would have had you dragged down from that perch and lashed senseless for such impudence."

"Was a time I woulda run you over without bothering to ask you to move. Now stave aside and let a man make his living."

Noonan took Wool by the arm and led him toward the hotel. Wool muttered to himself. He stopped at the door. "Perhaps we will win this war, but for the life of me I can't figure how," he said. "We've traitors for generals, and now we propose to turn sewer scum into soldiers. I wish you luck, Noonan. All the luck in the Republic." Wool began muttering to himself again. He and Noonan crossed the wide, elegant lobby of the St. Nicholas. At the bottom of the sweeping marble staircase were two of Wool's adjutants.

"Go ahead," Wool said to Noonan, "don't wait for me. It will take me a bit to mount this terrain."

Noonan went up the stairs. He heard Wool grunting behind him. A sentry saluted Noonan as he reached the second landing. The entire floor had been taken over by the War Department. Noonan walked down the corridor to the linen room that had been turned over to the Provost Marshal's office, the shelves for sheets and pillowcases removed, a simple desk placed by the window. It was far less comfortable and spacious than the regular offices on Leonard Street, but the War Department had a telegraph connection to Police Headquarters and so could receive reports from precinct houses all over the city. Noonan sat and smoked a cigarillo. Nothing to do but wait. He missed the distraction of Wool's voice. The sounds from outside were few, some wagons rolling along Broadway, no shouting, at least nothing like the usual discordant workday oratorio.

It was almost 9:00 A.M. In a few moments, Captain Jenkins would commence the draft lottery in the Ninth District office. Noonan had inspected the office the previous afternoon. Jenkins had formed a platform by putting two large tables together. He had placed the wheel containing the names of all the eligible men on top of it, 13,359 in number, from which a quota of 2,521 was to be drawn. Noonan had paced the office with Jenkins. There was a railing in front of the tables. Jenkins said he would place two policemen at it to watch the crowd. Noonan told him to have the police wait outside. "This isn't a courtroom," Noonan said. "There are no defendants and no prosecutors. The proceedings must be as routine and everyday as possible." If there was any trouble, the forces necessary to put it down would converge rapidly on the office, the police from the nearby Nineteenth Precinct and the Invalid Corps and the Provost Guard via streetcars from Police Headquarters on Mulberry Street. Jenkins was fidgety. He yelled at one of his clerks for misplacing his spectacles, then found them in his own breast pocket. Noonan was disappointed. He had picked Jenkins's office to commence the draft not only because of its uptown location but because Jenkins seemed to be a balanced, even-tempered officer who wouldn't panic. Noonan went over the details of the next day's schedule several times, and Jenkins seemed to grow calmer. "Invite anyone who wishes to inspect the lottery drum to come forward," Noonan said. "There are rumors that we have fixed the proceedings, that certain names have already been chosen. Make sure there's absolutely no hint of secrecy. If you wish, invite a spectator to tie the blindfold about the eyes of the clerk doing the drawing."

Now the draft was under way. The name, address, color, and age of each conscriptee was being announced and entered in a register. Noonan lit another cigarillo. An orderly knocked on the door and brought in a telegraph dispatch that had gone from the Nineteenth Precinct to Police Headquarters to the St. Nicholas:

DRAFT IS COMMENCED
FIRST 46 NAMES SELECTED
NO TROUBLE

The dispatches arrived on the half hour throughout the day. Noonan awaited them like a speculator anticipating some fantastic rise or fall in his stocks, and scanned the orderly's face for any hint of the nature of the reports as they were brought in. Noonan himself betrayed no sign of anxiety. He directed the orderly to place the telegrams on his desk, kept doing his paperwork until the orderly left, then slowly unfolded the paper. The messages reported the mounting number of names selected, and all ended the same way: NO TROUBLE.

In the early afternoon, General Wool stopped in to see Noonan. "It is done," Wool said. "The draft horse is saddled. Whether it will carry us anywhere remains to be seen." Wool shuffled off.

Noonan felt exhausted. It was more than just the previous night's lack of sleep or the months of hard work he had invested in the draft. It was also the sense of isolation he felt. On the pretext of keeping him informed, men would take him aside and tell him the latest lie, that he had married a colored woman, taken to drink, accepted a bribe, that he hid in his office all day, afraid to go about in public, that his friends had turned against him. He was told that General Meagher had said to a gathering of veterans, "Noonan is either an imbecile or a scoundrel." James McMaster, the editor of the city's Catholic newspaper, had published the announcement of Noonan's appointment as Provost Marshal on the front page. Beneath it, in a black-bordered box, was this legend: PROSTITUTION: THE PROFESSION OF ENGAGING IN DEBASING ACTS FOR MONEY. Noonan went to Archbishop Hughes to complain. Hughes dismissed it. "McMaster is a convert," he said, as if that somehow excused the man for employing New York's Catholic paper in support of the South.

Noonan threw the day's pile of telegrams into the wastepaper basket and straightened his desk. The room was very warm and close, the air stale, distasteful, filled not just with the relentless heat and the dust and dirt of Broadway but with a deathful stillness. It had been this same way yesterday afternoon, when they had finished the inspection of the district office on Third Avenue. He had stood with Captain Jenkins in the doorway and smoked a cigarillo. There was no breeze, no wind. It was as oppressively hot outside the office as in, the sky bereft of clouds, no sign that this weather would ever change. A lethargic flow of traffic moved on the avenue. They were about to go back inside when they heard people screaming. Up the avenue, a cartman's horse, overcome with the heat, staggered in its braces like a drunk. The vehicle veered wildly, knocked down a woman crossing the street, and mounted the sidewalk. People scattered to get out of the way. The driver was dragging on the reins, tugging violently, but the horse lurched ahead. The left wheel of the cart caught on a lamppost and ripped loose; a crate pitched to the ground. An enormous black pig struggled out of the wreckage. It squealed with terror, and its hooves clattered loudly on the sidewalk. Once free, it charged forward, head down, straight at the doorway where Noonan and Jenkins were standing, its short, stiff legs pumping furiously. Jenkins jumped back. Noonan stood where he was. He could see the blind, mad fear in the pig's eyes. Jenkins screamed at him to move. The pig came so close that its rough, bristle-coated skin brushed against Noonan, but it veered away from the doorway at the last minute and clattered down the sidewalk, hugging the side of the building as it went. It charged off the sidewalk, back into the traffic, its black bulk driving forward.

II

BEDFORD STOOD ON DECK, partly to enjoy the river breeze, partly to avoid being recognized by someone inside the passenger cabin. Uncanny how many times it happened in New York, despite the city's size and the numbers of people, the regularity with which you accidentally encountered someone you knew. "New York isn't a big city at all," Stark had been fond of saying, "but several dozen small towns piled on top of one another." On the other side of the deck was a band of cricketers, men in white, their female companions in soft, flouncy dresses, hats tied securely to their heads. Bedford scanned their faces to make sure he didn't recognize any from the small town that was Wall Street. He didn't.

The ferry docked in Hoboken. Bedford let most of the passengers disembark before him: baseball players as well as cricketers; respectable-looking clerks and their families, picnic baskets in tow; officers with their ladies—a crowd with means enough to afford the fare and spend the day watching ball games. He stopped at a tavern and had a glass of beer. The bar was only a few dozen yards from the water, but even at that short distance the wind died and the heat grew more intense. He ordered another beer—not his drink of choice, but he had worked up a thirst and the beer relieved it. The taverner was German and so was most of the clientele. They clucked and growled in their native tongue, and Bedford enjoyed his total ignorance of what they were saying, his freedom from being drawn into half-heard conversations.

After another beer, Bedford went out into the sunshine. The day was becoming blisteringly hot. His head swam a little, but the surrounding swards of greenery, the bleached blue summer sky, white sails on the river, made him feel in a festive mood, the first time he had felt that way in months. He walked a cinder path beneath the shade trees through the Elysian Fields, the parkland beside the river that had been set out years before by Colonel Stevens, the owner of the ferry franchises to New York, an attraction designed to draw a steady stream of fare-paying visitors who might otherwise never consider a journey to the wilds of New Jersey. He strolled at a leisurely pace. The path bent and twisted beside the river. At one point he saw a series of tents set up by the water, and soldiers scrambling over a barge. They sent a rocket blazing into the sky, a puff of smoke and sparkle that was only a test in preparation for the evening's fireworks, still another celebration of the twin victories of a week before, Gettysburg and Vicksburg, east and west, thundering blows against Secessiondom that made the final victory seem only a matter of time.

The trail of vapor the rocket left behind and the small smudge it made hung limply in the sky. Bedford felt his spirits sag. He had bought gold later than many others. He started at $144 an ounce and ended at $146, after a two-day frenzy of buying. He sold all the stocks through the Exchange he could manage to without appearing to be liquidating his business, and he fenced securities through Capshaw, everything he could get his hands on: his clients' holdings, and the Stark estate, which he managed for the heirs. He held back nothing. If he was to pay back Morrissey the money he owed him, a debt compounding at the rate of 25 percent per week, if he was to cover what he had already taken from his clients' accounts, if he was to regain the capital he needed for investment, there was no real choice. He put it all on a Union loss, on one final victory for Lee, a whipping in the style of Chancellorsville, except on northern soil, a fatal blow against the Yankee greenback.

Gold didn't move for almost a month. Just hung there at about $145, the whole country holding its breath. Bedford couldn't sleep. He wandered the house at night until the servants thought he was becoming unhinged. The cook brought him glasses of boiled milk. He'd douse the milk with whiskey, and drink the mixture in two gulps, but still he couldn't sleep. The heat settled on the city earlier than usual, and the early storms of summer, the lightning and thunder, jangled his nerves, reminded him of how his whole fortune now hung by one thread, the mass and accuracy of Rebel guns. Lee was apparently headed for Harrisburg. Once in possession of that town, he would be within equal striking distance of Washington and Philadelphia.

On the 30th of June there was a terrific storm in the middle of the night that blew through the house, ripping down curtains and scattering Audley Ward's papers across his room. The servants ran about, closing windows and mopping up water. Ward yelled for them to help him gather his papers. Bedford met Ward in the hallway. The old man was standing there in his nightshirt, his hands clasping sheets of paper. "My God," he cried, "this is a disaster!" He held up the soaking papers, the ink running down them in watery squiggles.

Bedford felt himself on the verge of seizing Ward and striking him, grabbing him by the collar of his nightshirt and dragging him down the stairs, throwing him and his soggy diary or history or whatever it was into the street, watching the pages wash away. He went past Ward without a word, down the stairs, through the pantry, into the cellar. He sat on the floor of a small, windowless room that was dank and cool. In it hung a row of winter coats wrapped in greased paper that moths couldn't eat through. He started to cry and, once started, couldn't stop. He sobbed for what seemed like an hour. He heard the door at the top of the stairs open and the hesitant voice of one of the Irish servant girls call out, "Mr. Bedford, sir, are ye down there? Is everything all right?"

He said in as steady a voice as he could, "Yes, fine, I'm merely looking for something I misplaced. Go away, please."

"Yes, sir." The door closed. He lay down on the floor, his face against the dank earth, and fell asleep. The next day, the heat was worse than ever. He bathed and dressed. He left without eating any breakfast. The mood in the Exchange was one of desperate anticipation. Everyone was fidgety and irritable. He went to Old Tom's at ten and stayed there drinking coffee and brandy until the early afternoon, then went home and climbed into the safe, soft familiarity of his bed. He drew his legs up to his chest and fell immediately asleep. The thunder woke him. It was nighttime again. He was wet with sweat. He heard the servants running about to close the windows and prevent a repetition of the previous night's damage.

The next morning's *Tribune* was filled with reports from a town named Gettysburg. An engagement had begun. The Union troops had caught the Rebels before they reached Harrisburg. Lee was on the attack. The news seemed to favor the Union forces so far, but that was to be expected; it always began on a high note, no matter how great a debacle resulted. He stopped at the Union League Club on the way home. The mood was no better than at the Exchange. The heat and anxiety made everyone sick with fever. Night brought no relief. Bedford went straight to his room. He hadn't eaten a proper meal in days but felt no hunger.

He was sitting in his office the next afternoon when he heard shouting in the street. He poked his head out the window. A boy was running about, screaming, "Vicksburg's fallen! Vicksburg's fallen!" People were emptying out of the buildings, and there was a tentative air of celebration. But within an hour the next edition of the papers was out, with no bulletin from the west. Bedford had a splitting pain in his head. He choked back tears. He told himself that he didn't care anymore; let Lee win or lose, but let the waiting end. Not wanting to go home, he stopped at the Union League again. The place was full of men who looked pale and ill. They were all in the same quandary. A few, he knew, were playing the same game as he, betting their future on gold and victory for Lee. He had seen them in the Coal Hole. Most were still in stocks and greenbacks, assets that would tumble in value if Lee succeeded. But they were all suspended above the same void, members of the same party of fear and unknowing. For the moment, at least, those like Bedford who had bet against the Union had no need to disguise their emotions, to pretend joy at a Rebel defeat or sadness at a Rebel victory. Everyone was equal in his fear.

Bedford slept well that night. There were no storms. He had no dreams. The church bells woke him at daybreak, a ringing that grew and grew in volume until it seemed certain every bell in the city had joined in. He knew in an instant what it meant. Lee had been defeated. Stopped by a nonentity like General Meade. Bedford lay still, relieved that it was over. He wasn't sure what to do now, although his choices were few, but the nervous tautness in his legs and back was gone. He was done with waiting. After a few moments, the windows rattled with the boom of the harbor guns, an incessant booming that saluted what had to be a great victory. He closed his eyes. In his mind he drew one of those allegorical sketches the papers would soon be filled with: A shell marked GETTYSBURG was traveling in a descending arc to make a direct hit on a fort marked SPECULATION. Rats in top hats were scurrying over the walls to avoid the explosion.

Bedford didn't bother to read the *Tribune.* The first time he looked at the gold quotations was on the following Thursday. Gold was at $130 and falling. That afternoon the note arrived from Waldo Capshaw. *We must talk.*

Bedford knew that Capshaw must have fitted all the pieces together: the losses at the faro table and the heavy debts to Morrissey, not exactly secret pieces of intelligence; the losses at the Exchange; the gamble on gold. Bedford didn't play chess, but he knew that there came a point, usually late in the game, where one player was reduced to a few possible moves that were discernible to everyone who understood the rules. He was at that point. He must now liquidate his gold holdings. If he gave Morrissey all he realized from the sale, it would still be but a fraction of what he owed. Morrissey would tighten the screws. Meanwhile, his clients must inevitably come to grasp how he had pillaged their accounts. If he tried to settle with them, to give them what was left, there was no telling what Morrissey would do, although he knew the rumors, how Old Smoke made examples of those who didn't pay their debts, bloated bodies fished out of the East River and the Hudson; the police wrote them off as suicides. And now Capshaw, whose intent was obvious. Even without having talked to him, Bedford understood the outlines of the offer that would be made. So much in payment, or the story of the filched securities would somehow reach the police. *And it don't matter to me one bit, Bedford, if you go ahead and try to tell the bulls that I'm the one fenced 'em for ya, because I got rid of 'em a long time ago, without a trace, and there's no way they'll ever lay a glove on me. You're the one will go to jail, Bedford. The only one.*

The perspiration soaked through Bedford's shirt and blotted the back of his jacket. He went up the hill past the Stevens mansion. Below, from behind a screen of trees, in the meadow near the river, he heard a roar of voices. A few moments of silence. A loud crack. More roaring. He took out his handkerchief, mopped his face and forehead, wiped his hands. He walked through the trees. A crowd of perhaps a thousand or more was standing around a playing field set out in the shape of a diamond.

Capshaw had named the time and place in his note. *Meet me at the baseball field in the Elysian Fields, at noon this Saturday, July 11th.* Bedford had come several times in the past to watch cricket matches and had seen other players engaged in baseball, an elaborate version of the town ball he had played as a child. He was surprised to discover that the baseballers now occupied this entire section of the Elysian Fields. There were no cricketers in sight. An umpire in a tall black hat walked up and down the line between the home plate and the first base. Whenever the pitcher threw the ball, the umpire would stop, crouch, and deliver a judgment in a loud voice. The crowd groaned or cheered at every call.

"Glad to see ya could make it." Bedford turned to his right. Capshaw had sidled up next to him.

"Your note was imperative."

Capshaw gave Bedford a sidelong glance. "If imperative means somethin' that can't wait, you're damn right. Anyways, I figured we might as well enjoy ourselves out here in the Jersey wilderness instead of sittin' cooped up in some Manhattan hellhole."

The player at the home plate swung with his bat and connected with the ball. The crowd roared. The ball seemed destined to reach the river, but one of the players standing in the far distance glided beneath it and caught it in his hands before it returned to earth.

"Come on, ya jacklegs," Capshaw yelled. "Jesus Christ, they haven't put a man on base."

"What is it you wish to discuss?" Bedford said.

Capshaw kept watching the field. "Now, now, Mr. Bedford, I don't think you came all the way over here without some fairly certain notion of what we need to talk about, but there's plenty of time for that. Right now, why don't we just try to enjoy ourselves?"

"When I wish to enjoy myself," Bedford said, "I seek amusements other than watching grown men play at field games."

"You mean you prefer the inside games, like faro? I woulda thought you'd enough of them kind of diversions." He smiled again. "Baseball is the safer contest, I'd say. Not that men don't bet on it." Capshaw nodded with his head toward a group of Army officers gathered along the line that led from the third base to the home plate. They clutched handfuls of greenbacks and bet on every pitch, the losers screaming at the umpire each time his decision disappointed them. "But the trappin's are more likely to help a man keep his head. Good Jersey air, sunshine aplenty, and the chance to walk about, you can't beat it."

"I appreciate your concern for my health, but I've business to attend to. I can't spend the whole day here."

The pitcher flung the ball. The player at the home plate swung and missed.

"That boy can hurl the ball, no doubt about it," Capshaw said. "Ain't ever seen anyone with the velocity he's got, and the true wonder is the spin he puts on it, the way he curves the ball away from the batter."

The pitcher threw with a motion that was something between an underhand toss and a sideways sweep, uncocking his wrist and snapping the ball as he released it. The batter tipped the ball into the air, and it was caught effortlessly by the player at the first base.

"That a way, Candy!" Capshaw yelled. He pointed at the pitcher. "A boy to watch," he said. "Name is Candy Cahill, the Candy referrin' to them sweet pitches of his the batters can't resist swingin' at. He's a Paddy, I know, and it's not my habit to cheer the likes of 'em, but there's no denyin' the way they take to baseball, like it was in their blood, the same as drinkin' and thievin' are."

Bedford watched Candy throw the next pitch. There was an undeniable fluidity in his motion, a disciplined agility that could come only after long practice. Bedford admired his gracefulness.

"He looks as if he could do this for his livelihood," Bedford said.

"He don't, not yet, but there are some that do, at least they take a good part if not all from playin' ball."

"I wasn't serious," Bedford said. "I didn't intend to imply I believed men are paid wages to play this game."

"Don't matter that was your intention or not, it's the truth."

"Men play and are paid? But by whom and for what?"

"Well, some of the big bettors is willin' to help make sure that the best players are in the game, and have been known to make up the wages a workingman might lose by comin' to play. And over in Brooklyn, the Union Baseball Club has put a fence around the field and is chargin' admission to see the game, ten cents a head."

"And people pay?"

"Four thousand of 'em at the last game."

"But why pay when you can see the same game played in unfenced fields and lots?"

"The best players is the ones taken to playin' behind the fences. They get paid from outta all those dimes." Capshaw turned and faced Bedford. "If I was looking to make a wise investment, it would be in baseball instead of gold. Seems to me the future of this game is a good deal more certain."

"We've touched at last on business," Bedford said. He felt a surge of anger as Capshaw continued to smile at him. "Suppose we go for a walk and discuss in private what is on your mind, and afterward you can return and enjoy the contest without distraction."

"All right with me," Capshaw said.

They walked away from the crowd, down a path that led back to Sybil's Cave. In some places the forest was so thick and lush they had to walk in single file. Sybil's Cave was nothing more than a long narrow hole that ran into the cliff beneath Castle Point. It was said that if you stood in its mouth and shouted a question, the echo would contain an answer, and because of that it was a trysting place for young couples who called each other's names into the darkness and listened as the sounds reverberated, the names mingled together. It wasn't until dusk, however, that the lovers came, using the darkness and foliage to their advantage.

Capshaw walked ahead. His straw hat was pushed to the back of his head, in the same fashion as Halsey. It rankled Bedford, the carelessness it implied, a contempt built on arrogance that Capshaw and Halsey shared, a visible assertion of pride in their own crudeness. Both of them had the habit of treating Bedford like some Knickerbocker aristocrat whom they enjoyed tweaking with their miserable manners. And both had helped bring him to this point, Halsey with his taste for faro, Capshaw with his eager willingness to pay cash for purloined bonds; each had led him to this path through a humid, airless forest.

"Jesus Christ," Capshaw said. He stopped walking. "Look at this mess." Directly ahead, the path dipped into a hollow that the rains had transformed into a small pond of fetid, stagnant water. Capshaw left the path and began to step carefully around the periphery of the muddy pool.

Bedford followed. The ground was wet and slippery. They grabbed at the branches of bushes and trees to keep their balance. A horde of mosquitoes hovered above the brown water and quickly became aware of the scent of warm blood, smell of sweat and lactic acid, aroma of hair oil. The mosquitoes buzzed in front of Capshaw's face. One flew into his ear. He shook his head violently, slapping the side of his head with his hand. He almost lost his footing. He stood still and beat the air with his hat. "Place is overrun with Jersey hummingbirds."

A large mosquito, if not as large as a hummingbird, landed on the back of Capshaw's neck. Bedford was close enough to see it prepare Capshaw's skin for its bloodsucking. Capshaw slapped his neck, but it was too late. The mosquito was gone. A small red papule and a smear of blood marked where it made its bite.

The squadron of insects had Bedford's bearings now. He flagged the air with his arms, and the mosquitoes moved out of range, some flying to his rear, others zipping about his head. He felt a small, sharp pain behind his ear. He swatted quickly and crushed a large mosquito with his hand, a mess of legs, wings, and blood. Capshaw stopped again. Bedford shoved him. "Move!" he yelled.

Capshaw slid and fell onto one knee. Bedford picked him up. The mosquitoes filled the air with their maddening, annoying, threatening drone, hovering around unprotected skin, looking for the chance to draw blood. With one blow, Bedford killed two that had landed on the back of his hand. He killed another on his cheek. Capshaw began to run. The ground had become drier and firmer, and Capshaw raced ahead in a half crouch. Bedford kept walking at his same pace. He struck at the mosquitoes methodically as they landed on his neck, face, and hands, killing them with increasing accuracy. He knew he couldn't reduce their number in any significant degree. For every one he killed there were a thousand eggs waiting for new rain to nurture them into larvae, the larvae into pupae, the pupae into winged adulthood, into bloodsucking, parasitical adulthood. But the toll he took brought him a small measure of satisfaction.

Capshaw was standing atop the rise where the path left the hollow. He beckoned Bedford with his hat. "Come on, man, run for it, there ain't a one of 'em up here." Bedford felt his heart thumping against his chest, but it wasn't from physical exertion. He didn't quicken his step.

It was only a hundred or so more yards to Sybil's Cave. They stood at the entrance. There was no one else around. Capshaw stuck his head into the cave opening and shouted, "Who'll win the war?" The last word echoed back at them. *War, war, war, war.*

"Well, according to Sybil, peace ain't as close as some people think," Capshaw said. "Maybe it makes sense to hold on to gold. No telling. Might shoot back up."

Bedford sat on a rock. Below, across the treetops, was the wide, majestic Hudson; beyond it, the masts and steeples of New York wrapped in a dirty haze of heat and smoke. At the point the city ended, where the hills were dotted with shacks and shanties, the river bent gently, beginning its course into the great hinterland, an avenue of water connecting to other avenues, canals and rivers and lakes, a ceaseless traffic of riches.

"What is it you are so eager to discuss?" Bedford asked. He watched the river and tried not to betray any emotion. His heart pounded so thunderously he wondered if Capshaw could hear it.

Capshaw stepped in front and blocked his view. "Look at me when you talk. I ain't one of your Paddy servants. I'm just as good an American as any self-appointed gentleman."

"You didn't bring me here to discuss your patriotism, I hope. If that be the case, I'll take my leave right now."

"You don't remember the first time we met, do you?"

Bedford thought he remembered it all too well. A sparsely appointed parlor in a desolate row of houses across from the shell of the papist cathedral. Shades drawn in the middle of the day. A brief haggling over price. A sickening tightening in his intestines, an intimation of final ruin.

"It wasn't when ya think," Capshaw said. "That wasn't the first time."

There had always been something distantly familiar about Capshaw. But it was an old problem for Bedford, this poor memory for names and faces, even of people he liked. "I'm sorry, then," Bedford said, "because I can recall no other meeting."

"We met at Bill Poole's funeral in '55."

"I wasn't at his funeral. I witnessed the procession, as everyone did, watched on Broadway as the cortège went by, but I didn't attend any of the ceremonies or the burial in Brooklyn."

" 'Twasn't at the ceremonies we met, but afterwards, at the lodge house of the United Order of Americans, at the dinner hosted by George Law."

"That I remember well," Bedford said. Stark had taken him, as always. A curious crowd. Around the bar were Poole's followers, the nativist street fighters of the Order of the Star-Spangled Banner, scarred veterans of the war against the Paddies, the last defenders of the besieged neighborhoods of True Americans that had been enisled by the incoming tide of foreigners. On the back of his hand each man had tattooed a spread-winged eagle, and around the eagle's head were the letters of the Order of the Star-Spangled Banner, *OSSB*. Gathered about a table in the corner were the officers of the United Order, men with no tattoos, at once the Saxon brothers and social betters of the men at the bar: John Harper, the former mayor's sibling; Rodney Atkinson, the merchant; and assorted ministers, brokers, lawyers, and a handful of judges.

Each group stayed in its own part of the room until George Law came in like a lion falling upon its prey. "Roarin' George," some called him in tribute to his vocal thunder, but to most he was "The Live Oak," a title inspired by his size and bulk, the trunk of his body as thick as a great tree's. Hod carrier and stone-cutter, he had saved enough to start his own construction company, and had made his fortune on the contracts he pulled down for the building of the Croton water system. Already known for his devotion to the defense of True Americans, when he had won the biggest prize of all, the contract to build the High Bridge, the seven-arch aqueduct that would cross the Harlem River, the longest and highest such span in North America, he claimed it would be built with 100 percent American labor—"which means," he said, "it will never fall to pieces."

The Live Oak bellowed his heart out that night of Bill Poole's funeral. His face was flushed with rage and grief, tears running down his cheeks as he drew the crowd around him.

"The scum," Law shouted, "the slime-eating Paddy scum, they've gone too far this time, given us no choice but to return blow for blow. I haven't a doubt this vile assassination was carried out by order of Morrissey and Hughes, Old Smoke and Dagger John, confederates in perfidy, and now they must be paid back, a pound of flesh for a pound of flesh. The Butcher died a True American! And that's how he must be avenged. Blood must flow!"

The crowd cried in unison, "Blood must flow!"

Stark and the other gentlemen didn't join in the yelling. They nodded and applauded politely. Although Stark had never said anything to Bedford about their purpose in visiting the lodge, it was obvious they had come not so much in memory of Bill Poole's life as in anticipation of George Law's future. Here was the spreading red glare of a rocket on the rise, the self-taught farm boy from Washington County who trod the plank road to Troy and found there the opportunities that would lead eventually to ownership of the Dry Dock Bank and of railroads and steamships, enterprises he tried to stamp with the mark of True Americanism, as he had the High Bridge.

The rush to California made his steamship business explode. But the Live Oak cared for more than profits. When the Spanish authorities in Cuba attempted to interfere with one of his ships and remove a passenger, he defied them, raised hell in Washington, called for war, invasion, the annexation of Cuba, *Let's finish what we began in Mexico and teach these monkeys a lesson once and for all.* Soon after, rumors of a presidential bid started. In Pennsylvania, the Know-Nothing majority in the legislature voted him their choice for the nomination in '56. "A combination of Croesus and Alexander" is how they described him, "with a true American heart."

"Let's not fool ourselves," the Live Oak said through his tears that evening in the lodge. "Let's speak the truth. Ireland has arrived in America, the entire nation transported here, lock, stock, and popery, and those of us who are descended from the brave Scots of Ulster, we know that can mean only one thing: War! Holy War! War to the death! No surrender!"

Stark left immediately after the speech, Bedford with him. They walked in silence for a few minutes, then Stark said, "Extreme language, but these are extreme times."

"Do you think he'll run?" Bedford asked.

"Who'll run?"

"George Law. Do you think he'll run for president?"

They were at the corner of Cortlandt and Broadway. Ahead was City Hall. Stark pointed at it. "That's where his interests lie."

"In being mayor?"

"In the charter for the Eighth Avenue streetcars. The com-

pany that possesses it is in default and is unable to proceed with
the laying of the track, and I'm told the Live Oak has planted
himself in the Common Council to spread his munificent branches
and offer the members the protection of his green foliage. Before
Bill Poole's mortal flesh begins to molder and his earthy memory
fade, our friend Mr. Law will bring his attentions to the business
at hand, which will not wait, the winning of the streetcar franchises and their proper exploitation in conjunction with the franchises he already holds for the Grand Street, Roosevelt Street, and
Staten Island ferries. A man can't attend to these affairs and run
for president at the same time, and it is my guess that Mr. Law
is more Croesus than Alexander."

Stark's judgment was proven correct. Law had directed all
his energies toward acquiring the goodwill of the Common Council. The franchises were given him. The talk of a run for the White
House faded away. Bedford saw Law very rarely at the Exchange,
where they had a nodding acquaintance, but while the memory
of that night at the lodge had remained vivid, he could summon
no recollection of Capshaw out of it.

"I was standing by the bar," Capshaw said. "We was introduced by John Harper, and I remembered you clear as could be,
because it appeared to me that we was around the same age. I
was impressed by the company you kept, the company of
gentlemen."

Bedford tried to re-create the tableau, but couldn't. Instead,
he felt a burning awareness of missed opportunities, investments
he should have made in ferries, streetcars, Manhattan real estate.
It had all been there, in front of his nose, gold beneath his feet
that was as real as any to be found in California.

"I'm sorry, but I don't recall. I have a weak memory for such
things."

"I always heard a gentleman made it a point of remembering
names, but maybe it's just the names of other gentlemen he troubles himself with."

"I think perhaps you have the wrong perception of me, Capshaw. I wasn't born to wealth. I was born to circumstances best described as humble, and I earned everything I possess."

"There are them say you used smooth manners to marry with advantage, that's how you came by your money."

"That's a Goddamn lie, but I didn't come here to argue my pedigree. You sent a note saying you wanted to see me. I'm here, let's get done with your business as quickly as possible. I wish to go home and bathe."

"Don't ride a high horse with me, friend. You're the one came seeking help, and I done what I can. But now seems people are poking around, putting pressure on me, asking questions, and I need your help to keep 'em at bay."

"What people?"

"Maybe they was bulls, maybe friends of John Morrissey. Couldn't tell."

"And the help you need is financial, of course."

"Yes."

"How much worth of help?"

Capshaw looked in the direction of the river. "Fifty thousand ought to do it."

"I don't have fifty thousand."

"Sure you do."

The day before, on Friday, Bedford had sold almost all his holdings in gold. He had the proceeds, over seventy thousand in greenbacks, in a carpetbag in his closet at home. He doubted Capshaw knew of the sale. This was merely Capshaw's attempt to determine the dimensions of his extortion.

"I have suffered severe losses on the Exchange, where most of my money is tied up. If I sold my stocks now, at their present value, I should incur a terrible financial reverse."

"Don't try poor-mouthing me, Bedford. I know where your losses have been, at Morrissey's faro palace and in the Coal Hole, and if you can't help me out, others can. The clients of Stark and Evans, for example, who would undoubtedly appreciate someone tellin' 'em to take a look at the firm's books. And Old Smoke, too, I'm sure he'd be interested to know that his number one client has gone and squandered that which properly belongs to the House of Morrissey on a losing speculation in gold. And the coppers, them also, they might confer a reward on him who turned in a man who steals securities."

"I can give you ten thousand on Monday, but that's all, I don't have any more."

"I got the afternoon to myself," Capshaw said. "Once I'm through watching the ball game, maybe I'll take the ferry back and pay a visit on Mr. Morrissey. Not a man with mercy or manners, none of the Paddies are, but a man of his word. When John Morrissey makes a promise or a threat, it's as good as gold. You can put it in the bank."

Capshaw stood gazing at the river, his hands pushed down into the back pockets of his pants, his hat at the same cockeyed angle as before. Bedford took out his handkerchief and wiped the sweat from his face and neck. Blood from his mosquito bites streaked the white linen. His heart raced. He felt like he might vomit. He grabbed hold of the trunk of a sapling and pulled himself to his feet. As he stood, a baseballer's bat that had been leaning against the tree fell to the ground. Neither Capshaw nor he had noticed it before. Perhaps it had been left behind by some baseballer who had come to Sybil's Cave with the girl of his affections, put down the bat that he might entwine her in his arms, and led her to a shadowy clearing in the woods, all but love erased from their minds. Or perhaps it belonged to a lone visitor who had come to enjoy the view and, lost in his own thoughts, had walked away without remembering what he had brought with him. But there it was, and as soon as it fell at his feet, Bedford had no doubt or hesitation about what to do with it. He reached down, picked the bat up, and raised it high above his shoulders. Capshaw had turned when the bat made its small thud on the ground. In the instant he saw Bedford pick it up, he reached behind himself, into the sheath hidden in the small of his back, and drew out a knife. "You Goddamn son of a bitch," he shouted, "don't come a step closer!"

Bedford swung at the hand that held the knife and hit it squarely. The knife sailed off into the bushes. Capshaw howled with pain. Bedford brought the bat down on the side of Capshaw's head. Capshaw staggered backward, his knees wobbling as if he were about to fall. Bedford had the bat up again, but Capshaw suddenly seemed to come to his senses; he turned and ran. Picking up speed and showing no signs of the blows Bedford had landed, he sprinted down the path. Bedford ran after him, as fast as he could. The distance between them didn't diminish. Capshaw raced down into the hollow, slipped at the fringe of the enormous puddle, and crashed into the mud. He immediately tried to get up, but slipped again. He was on his hands and knees when Bedford reached him. Bedford swung the bat like an ax, once, twice, against Capshaw's head. Capshaw collapsed facedown into the mud. Bedford poised to strike the back of Capshaw's skull. Capshaw shot forward and rammed Bedford in the groin with his head. Bedford slid backward and fell. Capshaw staggered to his feet, his face covered with a mask of mud and blood. He climbed up the side of the hollow, through the thick underbrush. Capshaw got only a few yards before Bedford caught up with him. Bedford swung wildly. He missed Capshaw and smashed a tree. Capshaw tripped over a log; this time he made no effort to get up. He lay there, panting, and covered the back of his head with a hand tattooed with an eagle.

Bedford stood above him, kicked the hand aside with his boot, took a deep breath, and pounded away with the bat until he lost any sense of how long he was at it, surrendering to the rhythm of the blows. Finally exhausted, he sat on the log over which Capshaw had tripped. The sweat ran down his face like rain, matted his hair, and soaked his clothes. The mosquitoes began to converge, buzzing furiously around Capshaw's body. Bedford felt them biting his neck and hands but made no attempt to brush them away or swat them while they sucked. He pushed Capshaw once with the bat. Perhaps Capshaw's last thought had been that it had been a trap, the bat planted there, the spot for his murder prearranged. It hadn't been. It had been a matter of fate, or luck, or destiny. (In reality, Capshaw had been less shocked by the discovery of the bat than by the willingness of a gentleman to use it in such a way. A gentleman couldn't take a knife and cut the throat of Mosie Pick, almost slicing off her head, the way he had. He had gone to her place to scare her off. She had been taking away his business, a Jewess the Paddies had come to prefer fencing their stuff with. They said she didn't have any airs about her and wasn't bent on cheating them, the way the Protestants were. She scoffed at his threats, sitting there, laughing, and didn't see him bring out the blade. He killed her with one swipe. One less foreigner to take enjoyment in the tribulations of True Americans. This morning, he had strapped the sheath to his belt the same way he always did, out of habit, no thought of having to use his knife, not with Bedford. Capshaw simply couldn't imagine a gentleman being capable of that, or of a deed such as this, using a bat to turn a man's head into a bloody pulp, right in the middle of a bright summer's day. It was unthinkable: Gentlemen were two-faced scoundrels, curs, cowards—not brazen murderers.)

Bedford decided to take the body to the edge of a cliff and drop it into the river, the resting place for myriads of New Yorkers—suicides, unwanted newborns—and of immigrant victims of cholera and yellow fever tossed silently overboard in order to spare the other passengers the purgatory of quarantine; a watery potter's field few inhabitants of which were ever fished out and identified. He dragged the body by the cuffs of the trousers toward the cliff. The belt snapped, and the trousers came off in his hands. He reeled and almost fell. He tossed the trousers away. He pulled the body by the ankles onto a narrow footpath and made rapid progress toward the river. At the edge of the cliff he discovered the river wasn't directly below. There was a ribbon of beach between the height he was on and the water. From the direction of the path that led to Sybil's Cave, he heard voices, a woman's talking and then a man's singing. He lay on the ground. The words of the song were clearly audible.

Ah! the hours grow sad while I ponder
Near the silent spot where thou art laid,
And my heart bows down when I wander
By the streams and meadows where we stray'd.

Bedford waited for the voice to grow faint as the couple walked toward Sybil's Cave. But instead it grew louder. They had left the path to the cave and were coming toward the cliff. He looked around for the bat. He had no idea what he had done with it. He rolled Capshaw's body to the edge and pushed it over. Then he ran. He crashed through the brush. Branches whipped his face. He ran until he reached a path. He followed it to a road that paralleled the river. He walked along its shoulder, in the shade of the trees, his head down. He was traveling northward. He kept moving. After a mile or so, he looked behind. The road was deserted. He knelt, washed his hands in the water, and plunged his head into it. He took off his cravat and coat. The sleeves were stained with the splatter of Capshaw's blood and brains. He rolled them into a ball and heaved them into the river. He had lost his hat but had no idea where.

He would make an odd sight, a man without a hat walking along a road beneath the summer sun, the kind of peculiarity someone might take note of and recall later for the police. There was no going back to the Hoboken ferry. He thought of waiting for dark, pushing a log into the river, and trying to paddle his way to the Manhattan shore, but the current would probably carry him out into the middle of the harbor. He lay down in the high grass but was too restless to sleep or even sit still. Toward dusk, he started walking again. When a wagon came by, as happened twice, he hid. He steered clear of the two ferry slips that he passed. He headed for the ferry below Fort Lee, in the shadow of the Palisades. It docked, he thought, at the village of Manhattanville. From there he could take the Hudson River Railroad back to the city. Money wasn't a problem. He reached for the billfolder in his breast pocket, then remembered his coat, a balled-

up clump of cloth hurtling through the air, making a slight splash
in the river water, the current catching it, unfolding it, pulling it
toward the bay, the cravat shoved into one sleeve and in the breast
pocket the billfolder. He rummaged the pockets of his trousers.
They were empty.

He kept walking. It grew dark. The road veered up a hill,
away from the river. Bedford left the road and followed a narrow
path along the river. Somewhere on the shore must be a fisher-
man's skiff that he could employ for his own use. He walked
through a hodgepodge terrain of dry earth, mud, and tidal ponds
filled with high grass. He found no boat. He thought he heard a
noise behind him, and turned. At a distance of several yards was
a lantern, a ghostly light that swayed in the darkness but exposed
neither hand nor face of whoever held it. Bedford walked fast.
The light was following him. He started to run. Ahead, from the
direction of the river, another light appeared. Bedford pitched forward into a watery hole. He couldn't touch bottom. He started
to swim. The prow of a small boat crashed through the high grass
and almost smashed into him. A lantern on a pole was extended
from the boat over his head.

"Over here, Sam," a voice cried out, "I got the cuss right
here."

The other lantern approached quickly. Bedford treaded water. "Give me a hand, please, I'm drowning," he said. He could
make out a figure standing in the boat. An iron spear with a sharp
hook set beneath the end almost touched the tip of his nose.

"Serves ya right, you damn Yorker," the voice said.

The other lantern came alongside. "Pull him in, Hiram, and
let's have a look. If we don't like what we see, we can always
toss him back."

The two voices laughed together. The side of the first boat
swung toward Bedford. He reached out to grab it but pulled back
his hand. Hung on lines that trailed in the water were the plump,
furry bodies of scores of rats, pink palms and soles shining in the
lantern light, muzzles opened to expose teeth with points like pins.

Bedford screamed. The voices laughed louder. The back of the boat came round so that Bedford could grab it. The man in the boat, Hiram, reached down and helped pull Bedford in. Bedford sat in the back. He trembled. Hiram sat across from him, spear in one hand, the pole with the lantern in the other. There were more rats lying on the floor of the boat. A few were still twitching.

"Suppose you tell me what ya were up to," Hiram said. His thin face was covered with a poorly trimmed beard. His shirt almost reached his knees. His pant legs were rolled up over his calves.

"I—I was seeking passage back to New York. I came over in a friend's boat this afternoon, a day's outing, and we became separated, and he, it appears, returned to the other shore without me."

The two boatmen laughed loudly. Hiram banged the end of his spear on the planks beneath his feet. "Ain't it always the way! Never been a Yorker born yet didn't have a pocketful of lies. The most brazen people on God's earth."

"And the rottenest," the man in the other boat, Sam, said. His lantern hung over the side. Bedford couldn't make out Sam's face but imagined it wasn't all that different from Hiram's.

"Ain't it the truth, Sam, they'd scalp a dead man, then charge his widow the price of a trim."

"I'm telling the truth," Bedford said.

Sam said, "Hiram, let's stop a-wastin' our good time. Throw him over and let's get back to work."

"Listen to me, please," Bedford implored.

"Let's listen," Hiram said to his unseen friend. "It's one of life's delights a-hearing a Yorker spin a ball of lies. No one on earth is as good at it. Now, go ahead, tell us how you got stranded all innocent-like and wasn't intent on poaching our muskies."

"Your what?"

Hiram poked one of the rats with the end of the pole. "Our muskrats, best there is, not like them poor starved, skinny handful you've got left on the other shore, your own fault, treatin' them the way Yorkers treat everythin', destroying all in your path, be it bird or beast."

A rat scraped the floor furiously with one paw. Bedford's teeth began to chatter. "I'm not a poacher. I've no interest in your muskrats or their fur. I'm lost and must get home. I've a wife and children who must think I'm dead. They'll be frantic with worry. If you've no pity on me, at least pity them!"

From the other boat, Sam's voice said, "Fur? This is July, the fur these muskies got on 'em now ain't worth the hair on a cat's ass. It's the meat that makes 'em worth the huntin', fetches a good price. The city folk can't get enough of it, even if they don't know it's muskies they're getting. 'Stew meat' is what the butchers call it."

"Sam," Hiram said, "if this Yorker thinks we're huntin' for fur, maybe he ain't lyin', maybe he's telling the truth."

"Maybe he's just stupid, Hiram. That's the case with plenty of Yorkers. They're dishonest, for sure, but they're also plain dumb."

"For God's sake," Bedford said. "I'm telling the truth. Please, I have no interest in muskies, none, all I want is to be taken to the other shore, to go home."

"Can ya pay?"

"Sure I can pay," Bedford blurted out, then remembered his coat swirling in the river's current. "I've lost my coat, it seems, and my money, but I will take your names and have payment sent to you as soon as I reach home."

The boatmen's laughter rang out across the water. Sam said, "Ain't they somethin', these Yorkers. They think no one this side of the river got a brain."

Hiram pointed at Bedford's shoes. "Tell ya what, friend, I'll take ya over, but the price will be those walkers you got on."

"My shoes?"

"Yep."

"But they're wet."

"Wet things got a habit of dryin'."

"I need them to get home."

"We ain't got all night. You can keep your walkers and swim home for all I care."

Bedford unlaced his shoes. As soon as he had the right one off, Hiram took it and put his foot in. "Fits perfect!" he said. Bedford removed the other. The rat scraped helplessly at the floor. Bedford brought his feet up onto the seat. "Do you wish the stockings, too?" Bedford said.

"Nope."

Bedford rolled the waterlogged stockings from his feet and tossed them overboard.

"Wait here, Sam," Hiram said to his companion. "I'll be back in but a shake." He put down his spear and lantern and picked up his oars. He rowed with steady, powerful strokes, and the boat moved quickly through the water. A few yards from the Manhattan shore, he said, "Out ya go."

"Can't you put me ashore?" Bedford said.

Hiram kept one oar in the water and brought the boat around. "This is as close to New York as I care to come. I'm a-headed home," he said. "Either ya get out or come back with me." Bedford swung his legs overboard and lowered himself into the water until his feet touched the slimy bottom. The water reached his chest. He swam toward shore. When it became too shallow to swim, he ran across the muck to where there was grass. He was somewhere above the city, how far he wasn't sure. He climbed through reeds and more mud, up an embankment to the railroad tracks. A hundred yards away was a cluster of shanties, a bonfire, raucous voices, the sound of fiddles. Saturday night in Paddytown, one of the countless collections of squatters' shacks that he had fleetingly seen in the days when he rode the train to Spuyten Duyvil and his meetings with Stark, glimpses of small children with burlap sacks for dresses, women smoking pipes, men with faces burned red from the sun. He walked south along the river side of the tracks. He heard the rumble of an approaching train, saw the headlight in the distance. He stood aside. He was ready to run alongside and grab on if it should slow, but it was a freight train that rattled and clanged as it rushed by. Fifteen minutes later, he heard another locomotive. This was a passenger train, only three cars, and it began to brake only a short distance away, slowing down without stopping completely. Two laborers hopped off the rear platform. The conductor waved to them.

"Good night, Pat," they yelled.

"Good night, boys," the conductor replied. He hung off the rear and waved a green lantern. The train gave a shrill whistle and started to pick up speed. The conductor went inside the car. Bedford ran alongside, grabbed the iron railing, and pulled himself up. At Manhattanville, he jumped off and ran into the bushes. Two or three people got off. The conductor waved his green lantern. As soon as he went back inside, Bedford climbed aboard again. At Thirtieth Street the train stopped, the steam engine was detached, and a team of horses was hitched in its place, ensuring that the train would move slowly as it traveled down the West Side to Chambers Street. The crew worked at a leisurely pace. Bedford hopped off the rear platform. In the middle of June, Bedford had received a secret missive from the clerk in Commodore Vanderbilt's whom he had been paying for tidbits of inside information over the last several years. The clerk had risen to a position of prominence in the Commodore's corporation, and was privy to important schemes. "I have news of breathtaking magnitude," he wrote Bedford. "The Commodore is planning an assault on the Hudson River Railroad, acquiring control through the accumulation of a majority interest in the capital stock. In the privacy of his office, the Commodore waxes about what he will do when he gets control. He talks of merging the New York Central with the Hudson, constructing a grand terminal in the midst of the city, and bridging the Hudson River at Rensselaer, which will bring our trains into the city of Albany. Now is the time to buy stock in the Hudson River Railroad. This will be the greatest killing since Theseus slew the Minotaur." Bedford had thrown the letter aside. He had been too busy with the short-term prospects for gold to bother pursuing such a tip. Morrissey on his back. His account books rife with fraud. Capshaw threatening him with blackmail. Bedford started to walk across the wet cobblestones. His bare feet felt cold and exposed. He took small, cautious steps.

"Hey, buddy, you just off that train?" A squat man in a vest and bowler hat was walking toward him. "Let's see your ticket." The man extended his hand. In his other hand he held a long locust stick that he tapped against his leg.

Bedford ran. The soles of his feet made loud slapping sounds on the paving stones. He charged into a street with saloons on both sides, men sitting outside to escape the heat. He stopped and thought for an instant of going back, but his pursuer was lumbering after him, the stick raised, a finger pointed directly at Bedford: "Stop that man!"

From both sides of the street men came out of the saloons. They were yelling. Bedford was sure one of them would try to tackle him, but they jumped out of his way as soon as he came near. He ran faster. He realized that the yelling was for him, a chorus of cheering, as if he were a runner in a race. He heard the shattering of glass. He turned. A barrage of bottles and mugs were crashing around his pursuer. The man had dropped his stick. He was covering his head with his hands.

"Hang the railroad scab!" somebody yelled.

The man turned in his tracks and headed back toward the river. A group of men set out after him, throwing more bottles as they went.

Bedford ran until his legs ached. He went through streets where despite the late hour the stoops and sidewalks were filled with people too hot to sleep. Thousands and thousands of Paddies. He sat on a curb. His white shirt had turned almost tan with dirt and sweat. His bare feet were bloody with cuts and lacerations, but he felt no pain, just a hot tingling. A workingman passed by, looking slightly tipsy. He threw some pennies at Bedford's feet. "Get yourself a whiskey," he said. "You look like you need it."

Bedford walked the rest of the way. He kept an eye out for the police. The wealthier the neighborhoods became, the quieter and more deserted the streets. He waited at the bottom of his stoop. All the lights were out, the bottom windows shut and locked. He had no idea where he had lost his keys. They were probably in his coat at the bottom of the Hudson. He considered trying to force a window but decided he had no choice but to ring the bell. He crouched in the dark of the doorway. He rang several times before he heard someone coming down the stairs.

As soon as the maid opened the door a crack, he pushed his way in. She looked startled and afraid. "Sacred Heart of Jesus!" she cried.

"Don't be alarmed," he said. He took her by the arm. He saw himself fleetingly in the mirror in the hallstand, the image of a man who had just escaped a burning, sinking ship.

"There was a terrible boating accident," he said. "A steam engine blew up." He steered her toward the stairs. "Fortunately, no one was killed." They walked up the stairs together. At the landing she pulled loose from his grasp.

"O my God, Mr. Bedford," she said, "look!" She pointed at the pale carpeting. He had left behind a trail of bloody footprints.

"You can clean it in the morning, Margaret. Now go ahead and draw my bath. Do it immediately."

She stood staring at the bloody tracks.

"Go ahead now, Margaret," he said. "I'm all right. I've cut my foot, that's all. The important thing is nobody was killed." He nudged her. "Margaret, please, draw my bath."

III

EVEN JOHN SKELLEY, steeped in the business of drafting, could barely keep up without spilling a portion of the brew. The overflow collected in a pail beneath the tap. Full, it was hauled by Mick Skelley, the last of John's seven sons, to a table on the side of Third Avenue and hawked at a penny a glass to the dust-

covered drovers and teamsters too thirsty and in too much of a
hurry to care that it was flat and warm.

"Skelley," a small toothless man shouted at the tap master,
"it's your kind of drafting the people are in need of."

In the crooks of his fingers John Skelley held three mugs beneath the tap and filled them one by one. Without looking up, he
said, "War or peace, the need will never go away."

"Beware the temperance men!" the toothless man said.
"They've their way, they'll do to drink what Lincoln done to
slavery, abolish it, such is their promise."

"Temperance and abolition, twin curses of the laboring man,
the same bastards behind both," Skelley said as he filled the last
mug. "But they'll have a harder time taking away a man's drink
than his slaves, I'd say."

"Ach," the toothless man said, "take all my niggers, but leave
me to drink in peace!"

Skelley placed the three mugs on the counter. The toothless
man grabbed one. One-Eyed Jack Cassidy grabbed the other two.
"That's the trouble," Cassidy said. "The laboring man isn't left
in peace but has his name tossed in a drum and, luck against him,
is forced to fight to free the niggers." Cassidy handed a mug to
the man standing next to him.

"Thousand in a single day, that's what Noonan will have
netted these past hours," the toothless man said. "That rate,
won't be long every able-bodied workingman is conscripted."

"Which of youse is payin'?" Skelley asked.

Cassidy tugged at the frayed, soiled patch that covered his
eye. "Payin' to get out of the draft, is it?"

The toothless man laughed. "The Union ain't so desperate it
needs the likes of Cassidy or me. Even if it was, where in the
name of Jazus would we find the three hundred dollars to buy
our way out?"

"Damn the draft!" Skelley said. "Which of youse is paying
for the drink?"

Cassidy removed his battered hat and tipped it toward the
man to whom he had just passed the mug. "Our friend here is

standin' us to drinks," he said. "And you should be aware of the honor he does this place by merely settin' foot in it."

"Honor enough to get paid," Skelley said.

The crowd at the counter was growing thicker and more restive. "Hey, Skelley!" one of them cried, "will ya have us die of thirst?"

"I've brought you the American song master himself!" Cassidy said.

"I don't care if it's Tom Moore risen from the grave. I've to be paid!"

Stephen Foster let go of the counter. He wobbled slightly as he fumbled in his pocket, took out a crumpled greenback, and tossed it onto the counter. How much had Jack Mulcahey lent him that morning in the bar of the hotel? An understanding man, Mulcahey had reached into his leather fold and plucked out several bills.

This should tide you over, my friend.

Only a loan, Jack. Once I deliver Daly his song, I'll pay you back.

A slight hurdle: The song was still to be written.

Foster took a long gulp from his mug. Ever since the rains around the Fourth, the week before, the temperature had climbed steadily, day by day, the city baking without relief, and the dryness in his mouth had grown worse until it penetrated his throat and bowels.

Cassidy put his arm around Foster, pulled him close. "Oh, what times!" he said. "The men of this city have their ears plugged with wax, but not to avoid the Sirens' sweet, destructive song. Done in the service of lucre, that's all that matters, only sound will draw attention, the chime of gold and silver. Ours is not an age for poetry. Yet, Foster, what the Sirens falsely claimed of their music might be truly said of yours: 'None that listened has not been delighted and not gone on a wiser man.' " Cassidy drained his mug and banged it on the counter. "Another round!" he shouted.

Skelley was back at the tap, filling mugs. "Cassidy," he said, "break that glass and it's yours to pay for!"

Foster took a gulp of ale. A pleasure to be in the enfolding gloom of Skelley's place. Blistering out on the avenue beneath a sun as cruel as found in the South, the South where he had never been, *way down souf, whar de corn grow.* A bitter memory: His brother, Morrison, had talked him into entering "Away Down Souf" in a song contest. It had received rollicking applause, but the judge awarded the prize to another song. Next day, Morrison discovered the judge trying to copyright "Away Down Souf" as his own. As yet unschooled in the knowledge that the world is filled with cheats and exploiters—that they are everywhere— Morrison and Stephen had been shocked.

"Lucky thing we met today." Cassidy said. "Nothin' save the chords funereal at Zook's obsequies. But the spectacle of con- scription, that's true musical stuff, a nation doin' what it must to fight a war, the resentment it raises among laborin' men. There's a 'Dixie' in this somewhere."

Dan Emmett's song. Another one-note hack. Knocked it out in an hour. Sounded it. Already be forgotten if not for the war. Foster finished his ale. He had bumped into Cassidy on the way out of Mike Manning's. Headed for General Zook's funeral. A fallen hero, a musical inspiration perhaps. Cassidy talked him out of it. They stopped in Mintern's on the Bowery, where the whis- key was served in glasses loaded with chunks of ice, Saratoga- style. Lost its charm after one drink. The ice melted fast and diluted the whiskey, and Mintern charged a double price for wa- tering down his drinks. Another cheat.

It had been Cassidy's idea to take a horsecar up the avenue and watch the conscription. The trip had been a pleasant one, the stir of air created by the movement of the car as close to a breeze as could be found in the sweltering city. They had left the horsecar at Forty-second Street and gone into Joe O'Brien's. The place was full with men who had come from watching the conscription.

Stretched out drunk on a table in the corner was Billy Jones, whose name had been the first out of the drum. Laid out like a corpse, red tablecloth over his legs and crossed mops at his head, Jones snored loudly, but nobody seemed to take much notice. After several whiskeys, Cassidy and Foster went back into the street. As hot as it had been earlier, it now seemed hotter. They walked up the avenue to Forty-sixth Street, the crowd growing thicker. At the corner of Forty-fifth Street, Cassidy met Pat McSweeney, a stooped, toothless wisp of an old man who quickly fell into conversation with them.

"Ah, Jack," McSweeney said, "say what you want against the draft, and mind you, I'm opposed as any man, but a short bit ago they called out the name of Councilman Joyce, and the thought of that jackeen in uniform ducking Rebel bullets is enough to turn a man in favor of conscription!"

"Be a blizzard in Hades before Joyce ever wears a uniform," Cassidy said.

Across from the Ninth District office, a horde of children played around the abandoned, half-built foundations of a house. Ragged and barefoot, they chased one another with sticks, seemingly unaffected by the heat. A pack of mongrel dogs followed, barking loudly. Atop a mound of dirt stood several women, soiled aprons tied around their waists. They ignored the cackling of the children and stared silently at the conscription office. Foster moved through the crowd and went up to the door of the office. Inside, it looked like the waiting room of a rail station: a large, undecorated space with a crowd milling about.

A man bumped Foster and pushed past. "To hell with the draft!" he yelled. "Three cheers for Ben and Fernando Wood!" No one took up the cry. McSweeney took a flask from the back pocket of his woolen trousers, swigged it furtively, and was about to put it back when Cassidy said, "What are ya, a bloody Republican? Hoardin' your treasure against the people? Share the wealth, man! The anthem of all true sons of the Democracy! Share the wealth!" The crowd took up Cassidy's refrain. "Share the wealth!" they yelled in a good-natured way, and McSweeney passed around the flask, a pained expression on his face as it went from hand to hand. When it reached Foster, it was empty. "We have been cheated, gentlemen," he said with a southern drawl. "There is no wealth left for us to share."

"Just as well," Cassidy said. "Heat like this, there's little whiskey can do to slake the thirst. Ale, that's what's called for. No other cure for the dust that collects in a man's throat."

Cassidy took Foster's arm, and they walked up to Skelley's. McSweeney trailed a few steps behind. "Ale it is," McSweeney said. He ran his tongue over his gums. Made a loud smacking noise with his lips. "Him who sees me to a draft will be doin' more than standin' me to a drink. He'll be savin' me from dyin' of thirst!"

"Then summon a priest!" called Cassidy over his shoulder. "That way you won't die doubly cursed—thirsty and unshriven."

McSweeney followed Cassidy and Foster as they pushed their way into Skelley's. His face brightened when Skelley drew three cream-headed brews and plunked them down.

"Know what we need?" Cassidy said.

"Another round?" McSweeney said.

"A song," Cassidy said.

"A lament?" McSweeney said.

"A ballad," Cassidy said. "At once sad and inspiring, in the manner of 'The Minstrel Boy,' the man gone off to war, wife left home to feed the children, inflation makin' it hard for them to afford the rent."

"Isn't it the truth?" McSweeney said. "A bit of mutton's gone from six to fifteen cents, and coffee from ten to fifty. God knows what coal will sell for when winter comes."

"Foster is the man to write that song," Cassidy said.

There was a commotion on the other side of the bar. John Skelley stood aside as two of his sons hauled a full barrel of ale from the cellar, pushed and pulled it up the stairs, and rolled it into place. The raucous waiting customers pinned Cassidy, McSweeney, and Foster against the bar and cursed Skelley for the interruption in the flow of ale, until Skelley's wife came in from the back, where she washed the mugs. She stood with arms folded, wisps of steel-gray hair falling across her red, perspiring face. Said nothing, just stood there, staring at the crowd. The shouting stopped. Once Skelley began to serve again, a space opened around the bar, and Cassidy, McSweeney, and Foster made their way out onto the avenue.

"An oven in there," Cassidy said to a man about to enter.

"Same everywhere," the man said as he went in.

The sun had moved across to the west side of the avenue, beginning its descent over Jersey, but there were still a few hours before it set, and the air was so baked, even night didn't promise much relief. Groups of sullen men continued to come from the direction of the conscription office, wives and children trailing behind.

"We should be goin'," Cassidy said to Foster.

"Suit yourselves," McSweeney said, "but I'd say you'd be missin' a grand show."

Foster was weaving about, having trouble standing. Cassidy took him by the sleeve. "Our friend," he said, "should be taken to his bed."

"You'll miss the Mad Maidens, you will. They say it's a spectacle not to miss, even better than anythin' at the Trump!" McSweeney said.

"What maidens are they?" Foster said. Cassidy tugged on Foster's sleeve, but the composer didn't move.

"See for yourselves," McSweeney said. "It's all free. Bill Cunningham makes the trip north each Saturday, hauls all who care to ride with him or can fit aboard, takes no fare but afterwards deposits one and all at Flanagan's shebeen. Flanagan is Cunningham's brother-in-law, so Cunningham keeps it all in the family, gets his reward from a cut of the proceeds from the poteen that's drunk."

"We've better things to do than go in search of mysterious oreads or drink home brew in some highland shanty," Cassidy said.

"Where is the chariot of Cunningham's?" Foster said.

"Be here any minute," McSweeney said with a wide grin.

They waited less than five minutes before Cunningham pulled up outside Skelley's. Boys and men jumped on, pushing and jostling. McSweeney mounted the cart and helped Foster and Cassidy aboard. The passengers yelled and shouted as Cunningham whipped his horse, and the cart jounced into motion. Foster sat on the floor, his back against Cunningham's seat. He rested his forehead on his knees. The rocking of the cart made him feel as if he might vomit. The wagon hit a bump, and his head struck hard against his knees. He leaned his head back, looked into the sky, empty as a blank sheet of paper, heard the grinding of the poorly greased axles, groan of the exhausted springs, clank of the harness chains, Cunningham yelling at his overburdened horse, loud creak of horse's traces straining against the load, several voices singing, one the verses, the others the chorus:

> Pat of Mullingar,
> She can trot along, jog along,
> Drag a jaunting car,
> No day's too long when sent along
> By Pat of Mullingar.

The cart left the avenue, followed a dirt road through a thick wood, shafts of sun falling through the branches. The grade grew steadily steeper, and the cart slowed to a crawl as it moved uphill. At one point there was a break in the trees. An expansive vista opened up, green sea of treetops, the river in the distance, white sails on blue water. Cunningham stopped the cart and called for volunteers to hop off. Several of the boys did. The cart moved faster, and at the top of the hill, the boys jumped on again.

"Good God," Cassidy said, "this better be good. We're being dragged halfway to Canada."

Cunningham drove awhile before he brought the cart to a halt. "Everybody out," he said. "And remember: Quiet. No yellin'."

McSweeney was one of the first out. He helped Cassidy and

Foster to the ground. "They say the Mad Maidens is a sight to see!" McSweeney said. They followed Cunningham and the others to the top of a small, wooded knoll. At a distance of several dozen yards was a stately three-storied building, a great stone hall with two flanking wings.

"They're not there yet," Cunningham said. "Good thing. I was afraid we was late."

"It's them that's late," another said.

"Ah, it's a grand sight," McSweeney said.

"What is it?" Foster asked.

"The Bloomingdale Asylum," Cunningham said. "And grand as it may seem, the lunatic population of New York is far outgrown it."

"Look!" one of the men said. "There they are!"

Three young women stood in a large, barred window on the second floor. They were dressed in identical charcoal-gray smocks. Two had wild red hair and looked as if they were sisters. The third was taller than the other two and had cropped black hair. As soon as they saw the men, they removed their smocks. They wore nothing underneath. One of the redheads leaned her head through the bars and threw the men a kiss. The other pressed against a bar, her large breasts sticking out prominently on either side.

The men waved their hats but didn't yell.

"I'm the one discovered them," said Cunningham to Cassidy. "Ridin' past one afternoon, I looked up and couldn't believe what I was seein'."

The black-haired woman got up on the sill and stood in the window in full view, one leg wrapped around a bar. She beckoned with her hand.

"Wouldn't I love to find myself behind them bars," McSweeney said. "'Tis a fine sportin' time I'd have."

"A shame it's an asylum for lunatics instead of imbeciles, or you'd have no trouble getting in," Cassidy said.

"The owners of the Trump have made themselves rich on a

view poorer than this," Cunningham said. "Set up a grandstand here and make myself a bloody fortune."

The black-haired woman was sitting on the sill, her feet hanging out the window, a black bar rising up out of the black triangle between her legs. She waved, and it seemed to Foster that she waved directly at him. He waved, and she waved back furiously, with both hands. Foster remembered the time Jane waved like that: They had been reconciled and he had stopped drinking and Jane was convinced that now, finally, they would have a settled, normal married life. They had rented a house in Hoboken, and he went off to New York every day, as if he were a regular man of business, and that first Friday evening, at the end of the first week, he saw her from the deck of the ferry as it neared the Jersey side of the river. She was standing by the gate, searching the faces on the ferry, and when she saw him, she began to wave with both hands so enthusiastically that she almost knocked the hat off the man standing next to her.

Go ahead, Jane. You're entitled to such moments. Precious few of them you've had. Wish it could last. Wish both of us could find what we are looking for.

In a loud, strong voice, Foster sang:

> *I dream of Jeanie with the light brown hair,*
> *Borne like a vapor on the summer air . . .*

The men all turned around, and in the window the women suddenly stopped their gyrating and stood still.

"In the name of God!" Cunningham yelled. "What the hell is wrong with you. You'll give us away!"

From the window came the voice of one of the red-haired women singing:

> *I long for Jeanie with the day-dawn smile,*
> *Radiant in gladness, warm with winning guile . . .*

In an instant, two matrons appeared and began pulling the women from the window; another was pointing and screaming at where the men were standing.

"Let's get outta here!" Cunningham cried, and the men scrambled off the knoll toward the cart. Foster sat where he was until McSweeney grabbed him by the arm and pulled him to his feet. Foster walked a short distance, tripped, and tumbled down to the bottom of the knoll. Cassidy and McSweeney helped him up and lifted him onto the cart an instant before Cunningham cracked his whip.

"Shoulda left the bloody idiot where he was," Cunningham said. "A lunatic is what he is, spoilin' everythin' for the rest of us. I've a good mind to dump him in the North River. Let him float out to sea with the rest of the garbage."

The cart rattled over rough, badly rutted roads until it pulled up in front of a windowless shanty; a goat was tethered in the yard. Three barefoot children ran inside as soon as the cart came to a halt. A small, bald man walked out.

Cunningham jumped down from the driver's seat. "They're all yours, Flanagan," he said to the little man, and then he went inside without another word. Cassidy and McSweeney helped Foster out of the cart, one on each arm.

"Has he had an accident?" Flanagan asked.

"The heat and the excitement," Cassidy said. "Between them he was overcome."

"Bring him in and we'll get him a drink," Flanagan said. "Should set him right."

A soiled piece of canvas divided the inside of the shanty in two. The children peeked out from behind. "Get back in dere!" Flanagan yelled, and their heads withdrew. He lit a lantern that hung from the roof. The men sat on the benches set against the walls.

"Welcome to ye all," Flanagan said. "I'd like to offer the hospitality of this house."

"The whiskey is free, is it?" said McSweeney. He and Cassidy set Foster down on the bench and sat on each side of him.

"A rich man I'm not," Flanagan said. "But though riches is beyond me, the price of drink in this establishment is fairly set. And here ye don't pay for the surroundings, just the drink."

"Was the surroundings we was payin' for, you'd be payin' us," Cassidy said. He spit on the earthen floor and kicked dirt over the globule.

"May not be the Astor House, but it's home to me and me family. And many the honest workingman has found welcome and comfort under its roof, so I'd ask ye to refrain from blasphemy or from expectoratin'." Flanagan stared at Cassidy as he spoke.

Flanagan went behind the curtain and returned with a tray of different-sized glasses and a large unlabeled bottle of whiskey. He moved around the room. Each man poured himself a large glass and dropped a coin onto the tray. When it came his turn, McSweeney nodded at Cassidy. "He's payin'," McSweeney said.

Cassidy dropped two of Foster's coins onto the tray and poured himself a glass. Foster sat crumpled against the wall.

"We should get some whiskey in him," Flanagan said.

"Needs a bit of dryin' out before any more goes in," said Cassidy. He put his glass to his lips. Suddenly, without taking a drink, he stood and pointed across the room at a chair placed in front of the canvas curtain. "Mother of God, what's that thin' there?"

Flanagan strode quickly across the room. "Them children of mine don't understand the meanin' of obedience. No gettin' it into them, even with a strap. Told them ten times I didn't want this left around. ' 'Tis not a toy,' I said." Flanagan picked up the object from the chair and cradled it beneath his arm.

"Give us a look!" McSweeney shouted. "We've paid good money for your drink, now let's have no secrets!" The other men banged their fists on the bench. "Give us a look!" they said in unison.

Flanagan hesitated a moment before he took the object from beneath his arm and extended it for them to see.

"Christ's mercy!" McSweeney cried. He made the sign of the cross.

Flanagan held a skull the color of earth. A row of brown broken teeth protruded from the upper jaw. The mandible was missing. He turned the skull around and held it up toward the lantern. The top of the cranium was shattered, a gaping hole in its middle.

"Jesus, Flanagan," Cassidy said, "I hope this isn't what the drink you serve does to a man." No one laughed.

"Was never a customer of mine, nor would I want the likes of him," Flanagan said. He put down the skull and picked up a small box. He lifted the top. Inside were half a dozen buttons, all black with tarnish except for one that had been polished and shined. He handed the button to Cassidy, who ran his thumb over the crown stamped on it and the letters beneath: GIIIR.

"George the Third," Cassidy said. "A button from an English uniform. Where'd you dig this up?"

"Did no diggin' at all," Flanagan said. "The children was playin' on the other side of the Bloomingdale Road, in them thickly wooded ravines and rocks where I've warned 'em never to go, and they stumbled on a passel of remains. Come screamin' there'd been a murder, and out I go with a shovel in one hand for protection, thinkin' one of 'em Bloomingdale lunatics is loose and commitin' mayhem. Then we reach this gully and there, sure enough, is the remains of the dead, but right away I knew they hadn't entered that state recently."

"There was more than one?" Cassidy said.

"Might have been two or three, but this was the only skull intact. Animals and the elements had scattered or destroyed the rest. There were bones all around, and the rusted barrel of a gun, and these buttons, one of which I polished up. Looks like new, doesn't it?" Flanagan took the button back from Cassidy. "Probably some of 'em English troops what chased General Washington out of the city met their end up here. The Yankees fought a rear-guard action somewhere around here, least that's what I've been told. Wounded and the dead fell into places and never found, till now."

"You sure this isn't the skull of a Patriot?" Cassidy said. "Could be his bones was mixed in with the rest."

"These are English bones, or those of their hirelings. The likes of General Washington would have never abandoned the bodies of the Patriot dead."

McSweeney walked over to the table where Flanagan had rested the skull. "You know," he said, "when I was a boy of four or five in Ireland, the army and the yeomanry came through our village in search of the United Irishmen. Was in '98, the time the French came to our aid. The countryside was overrun with rumors.

"None of the men of our village could speak English, except for a smatterin' of words, and though their sympathies was with the United Irishmen and with the French come to help them, they was too frightened to take any role in the rising. The army didn't care. To them, one Paddy was the same as the next. Forced us all out of our cabins in the middle of the night. Wrecked the places searchin' for pikes, but found nothin' save some tobacco wrapped in a broadsheet of the United Irishmen. Wasn't a person could read them English words that was printed on it, but the officer in charge said it was a sign of 'seditious intent.' Picked out four men from the village, my father among them, had them manacled hand and foot, and when dawn came, they was hanged from a tree just outside the village. 'Anyone tries to remove the bodies will be shot and his cabin tumbled,' the officer said, and there they hung till the ravens picked out their eyes and the wind stripped away their flesh."

McSweeney spit on the skull. "To hell with England," he said.

"And with the Yankee lickspittles who worship at England's altar, intent on keepin' the Irishman down and exaltin' the nigger over him," one of the men on the bench said.

"The bastards will take a nigger over an Irishman any day,"

Cunningham said. "Look at that orphanage they've put up for the niggers on Fifth Avenue. A mansion it is. And where do the Irish children go? Shipped out west or off to Randalls Island."

"The Irish people is in a sorry state, for sure," McSweeney said. "But we've ourselves to blame as much as the English or the Yankees. Every generation it's one of our own sells us down the river, traitors like Robert Noonan."

Cunningham said to Flanagan, "You should sell that skull to the Yankees. Same crew shit their pants with excitement when the Prince of Wales arrived would probably pay dearly to have some English relics to worship. Or they could gild it and present it to Noonan."

"Maybe I'm just a wishful old man," McSweeney said, "but seems to me the day of the Irishman bowin' and scrapin' before the Saxon is over. Won't the Fenians soon be ready to strike a blow for Ireland? And won't they have Thomas Francis Meagher at their head?"

"That's the holy war our boys should be preparin' for, stead of allowin' themselves to be drafted to die in the cause of the nigger," Cassidy said.

"Down the road lives Kate McGowan," Flanagan said. "Had two boys. The youngest killed at Antietam. The other's been wounded in Pennsylvania. She's sick with grief and worry, but I haven't seen any niggers at her door offerin' condolences or help."

"Not likely you will," Cunningham said. "Nor likely you'll see the nigger volunteerin' in the fight to free Ireland. But he'll soon enough take the jobs of them slaughtered to win his freedom."

Flanagan came around with the tray again. The bottle soon finished, Flanagan went to the still behind the shanty and got another. When he came back in, he roused the children from their beds, told them to scrounge all the kindling and dry branches they could find and heap it in the yard. A second and third bottle had been consumed by the time Flanagan interrupted the men's talking and singing and told them to come outside.

"Gentlemen," Flanagan said, "the time is after midnight, which means this is the twelfth of July, Orangemen's Day, and I think we shouldn't let such an occasion pass without some mark of our undyin' affection for our Anglo-Saxon masters!" He doused with kerosene the pile his children had collected and lit it. He brought out the skull.

"Let me do the honors," McSweeney said, and tossed it into the middle of the bonfire.

The men cheered. Cassidy yelled, "To hell with the draft!"

McSweeney lay still. He was unsure of where he was, a feeling he despised, distant memory of mornings in places better forgotten. He heard laughter, giggles, children's voices. He extended his hand, felt rough cloth a few inches away. Wherever he was, he wasn't alone. Slowly, the night before came back to him, dancing around a bonfire, swigging whiskey, cursing the niggers, the draft, the Republicans, the English, the English-lovers, the rich man's war. He opened his eyes: Cassidy lay next to him. Beyond, in the doorway, Flanagan's children were darting in and out, laughing.

McSweeney sat up and felt a sharp pain in his head. Next to Cassidy was another body: Foster's. They had spent the night on the dirt floor, the three of them, but McSweeney had no recollection of how they got there.

Flanagan came out from behind the curtain, and the children scattered. He stood in the doorway and screamed at them to stop their shenanigans.

"What's the time?" asked McSweeney.

"Past nine," Flanagan said.

"Jazus," Cassidy said without lifting his head, "could we have some quiet?"

"Is Cunningham gone?" McSweeney said.

"Long ago. Tried to wake ye up, but easier to wake the dead."

"Let's have some quiet so a man can rest," Cassidy said.

"How'll we get back to the city?" McSweeney said.

"Can't answer that," Flanagan said. "But I can tell ye that I'd be in my right to ask payment for last night's lodging."

Cassidy got up. "Lodging? You call the floor of this sty 'lodging'? Here's what I think it's worth." He spit on the floor.

"I've already warned you against expectoratin'," Flanagan said.

Cassidy helped McSweeney to his feet and pushed Foster's shoulder with his boot. "Get up," he said loudly. Foster stirred. "Charge us for lodging?" Cassidy said. "Well, you can try. But you better be good with your fists."

"Don't threaten me," Flanagan said. "Or I'll summon the law."

"Summon the bloody Supreme Court for all I care," Cassidy said. He reached down and put a hand under Foster. "Give me some help," he said to McSweeney. Together they lifted Foster to his feet and walked him to the door. Flanagan stepped out of the way.

The glare of undiluted sunlight made both Cassidy and McSweeney shield their eyes with the palms of their hands. They crossed Flanagan's yard with Foster between them and turned into the road.

"O Christ," McSweeney said, "we'll be walkin' all day before we reach the city."

"We'll go down to Manhattanville," Cassidy said. "Catch a train."

"We've money for that?"

"There's hardly a conductor on the line I don't know. Many the time they've extended the courtesy of a free ride."

After a while, Foster got his legs and walked without their help. They stopped at a farmhouse and were given permission to use the pump. They stuck their heads beneath the spigot, soaked their hair and washed their faces. Foster put his mouth to the spigot and kept it there. He pumped and pumped, drinking so much water that Cassidy said, "I'm surprised you haven't sprouted a hump to store it."

They went back to walking. The sun quickly dried them. Soon they were sweating heavily. In the late morning they reached Manhattanville, went down through the quiet Sunday streets, past the Christian Brothers' college, and sat on a log beside the tracks. The sun beat down hard. The pain in McSweeney's head grew worse. His stomach contracted, and the urge to vomit rose in his throat. He moaned.

"Are you all right?" Cassidy asked.

McSweeney shook his head. The contraction in his belly grew tighter. He stood and crossed the track to the high weeds on the other side. He bent over, gripped his knees, braced himself. Liquid gushed out of his mouth, splattering his trousers and his shoes. Sweat flooded his eyes. He pulled the sleeve of his woolen jacket over his hand and wiped it across his mouth. The sting of vinegar was in his mouth and nose. He ran a finger over the red ridges of his gums. He braced himself again and coughed so deeply that his ribs hurt. A small rush of vomit poured out. Sweat dripped across his face, puddled beneath his armpits, and ran down his sides.

In the distance was the whistle of a train. McSweeney walked back to the log and sat down. Foster had his head buried in his arms. Cassidy was up and standing by the track. As the train pulled in he walked beside it, looking for the conductor. But when the conductor descended the stairs of the middle car and jumped to the ground, Cassidy didn't approach.

"Wouldn't you know it," he said to McSweeney, "the only conductor I don't know and he has to be on this train. We'll just have to wait."

A cabriolet pulled up beside the log, and a tall gentleman in a frock coat got out of the passenger seat. There was a high polish on his shoes. His shirt and cravat were white and crisp. He looked at McSweeney blankly.

"Who do you think you're looking at?" McSweeney said.

The gentleman moved toward the train without answering. The whistle blew. He mounted the steps. Steam shot from beneath the car. He turned, grinned at McSweeney, and said something that was drowned out by the clatter and hiss of the train as it began to move.

McSweeney struggled to his feet and staggered. He shouted after the train, "Who do you think you're lookin' at, you three-hundred-dollar whore, Protestant son of a bitch!"

JULY 13-15, 1863

I saw the ramparts of my native land
One time so strong, now dropping in decay,
Their strength destroyed by this new age's way,
That has worn out and rotted what was grand.

—Francisco Gómez de Quevedo y Villegas (1635)

It is the common practice of the cultured portion of our populace to view history as it does the smooth and well-executed canvas. The gentleman enters the reverent hush of the *pinacotheca* and approaches the work of art. He sits on a small bench placed at the appropriate distance that he might have the proper perspective. Quietly, serenely, he regards the sweeping vista, capacious sky, the looming mountains with roseate peaks reflecting the candescence of a deathless sun that the gathering clouds of night can neither obfuscate entirely nor deny utterly. He sighs with pleasure at the symmetry of this design, an improvement on nature in the grand style of those majestic, irresistible panoramas executed by Frederick Church, all the savagery and brutality of the world's wildness tamed and contained by the aeonic mastery of the artist's *penicillus*.

Alas, dear gentleman, enjoy this fugacious moment, as false in its eternal aura as the peaceful creation depicted in this gilt-edged frame. Indeed, sir, incline your ear to the din that penetrates this asylum. Hark, the mob's howl! It rattles the windowpanes and reverberates in these marble halls. History, sir, is about to suck you in, true history, no painted version of the jungle but the real thing, a place you must crawl through, a steaming, muddy swamp. Wild hyenas snap at your heels, their teeth eager for your flesh. The fearsome python slithers amid the branches above your head. Aëdes buzz in your ear. Soon, sir, you will have no choice but to apprehend the trompe l'oeil of the historian and confront the terrible and inescapable truth of time's swelling and shallowing. This landscape belongs not to you or to your refined understanding. This is the eternal kingdom of the uncivil, the uncivilized, the uncivilizable; here rules the vile, the violent, the vicious; here holds sway forever the race of small-brained creatures, men with the minds of beasts, in whom beat the hearts of animals.

—From *The Ramparts of My Native Land,* by Audley Ward (unpublished manuscript; folio IV, 619–663; manuscript Collection, the Library of the City of New York)

I

DUNNE SAT MOTIONLESS in the lobby of the New England Hotel. He reread once more the note he had found waiting for him at the front desk the day before yesterday. The long-expected signal from Capshaw: *Father is dead. Please come home. Your dearest Mother.* He wiped his face with his sleeve. The heat lay like a blanket. Move or not, you sweated. Something was in the air. Odor of rotting fish and raw sewage. But something else besides. Been there for days. An expectation.

Last night, on the Bowery, outside the Atlantic Garden, a drunken plasterer, his clothes crusted with gypsum, fought an equally drunken soldier. No rare sight. But the sidewalk fisticuffs drew a large crowd, and when the soldier got knocked down the crowd set on him, kicked and screamed, people fighting one another for the chance to pummel him. Would have ripped him limb from limb if the Metropolitans hadn't appeared, and even then the mob didn't back away. A blizzard of bottles from a nearby rooftop knocked a few of the coppers senseless, and a gaunt, ragged old woman climbed atop the Garden's fence. Said any man didn't stand and fight had an empty space between his legs. Took a large squad of reinforcements before the police was able to drag the soldier to safety and bring some order to the street.

Outside, on Bayard Street, there were a few passersby. Unusually quiet for a Monday morning. Heat had everyone sitting still, at least for now. Maybe just jitters before a job. Nerves set on edge from waiting.

He had never trusted Capshaw. Figured it right away: Bring in the Paddy so he can take the blame. The scraps handed out by

Capshaw that April afternoon were enough to give a scent, but it was Cassidy who had pointed the finger at Jim Halsey, a name easily linked in the sporting places with Charles Bedford's. *The Faro Twins.* Halsey had turned out to be nothing more than a Wall Street flickertail, part of the speculating mob that scampers about the Exchange like a pack of rabid squirrels. A pimp to boot. Used his girl to get a piece of the Trump and then to get himself a commission in the Army. Must have figured that was the only way to escape Morrissey's clutches. Might be, so long as he kept on the move once the war ended and never showed his face east of the Hudson. Bedford was of a different stripe. Old name, old money. The kind sent Capshaw in a rage. Don't seem about to stuff all he had in a carpetbag and run for it, but Dandy Dan had put it right: *Despair sends men to places they never thought to be.*

The deal according to Capshaw: Apply the screws to Bedford. Pressure of blackmail added to Morrissey's threats, he'll put what he can in greenbacks and get ready to fly. Once he does, it's in and out, grab the wick, and Bedford still has to run, Morrissey and the Metropolitans both breathing down his neck.

Dunne folded the note and put it back in his pocket. Capshaw wanted to hold all the cards himself. The rat-noses' way: Play by our rules, or don't play at all. But no Paddy was quite as dumb as that, at least not in New York. Wrote another set. Tracked down Bedford. Followed him about in a casual way, him none the wiser. The Exchange. The Coal Hole. An occasional stop at Mrs. Woods's fancy house. Always home before the evening grew too late—one of them tall, imposing places makes Capshaw's look like a cabin. Housekeeper, coachman, a pack of Kathleens to do the cleaning and wiping. Waited till the missus was away and Bedford off to work. The beginning of June. Paid a visit in a sure and tested way. Went up the front steps, brazen as could be, the way a person of "larcenous intent," as the magistrates might say, would never.

The maid barely cracked the door; said, "Go to the tradesmen's entrance," as the rule book said she should. She opened the tradesmen's door and stepped aside, led the way past the narrow-eyed cook, suspicion dripping from her like drool from a dog.

"Since when do tradesmen knock on a gentleman's door?" the cook said.

"Way I read it, Lincoln's abolished such notions."

"He abolished slavery, not good manners."

The maid barely stopped to hear the exchange of words. She walked ahead. "These the pipes you want to see?"

"Sure are."

Time to do the job. Dunne took out a wrench, banged the pipes, turned the screws. Put an ear to the wall.

"Seen enough?" she asked.

"Got to check the pipes upstairs."

She chattered the whole time, watching in a distracted way the routine of pipe-rapping and jet-turning. In and out of every room.

The watchdog cook waited at the bottom of the stairs. Held a ladle like a booly dog's locust stick.

"We was never notified of any inspection."

"Must have been. Probably forgot. Happens all the time. Busy, hardworking people often do. Guess you could use more help in a house this size. Ain't it always the way? More you do, more they expect."

The cook shook her head. "Ain't more we need as them already here to show a willingness to work."

The maid let out a snorting sound. The tour resumed: rooms of old furniture, portraits of old relatives, long dead from the cut of their clothes, pictures too big and unwieldy to hide a safe. The only real storage right out in view, in the corner of the library. *Federal Certified All-Security Safe. Patented.* Seemed as easy a job as Capshaw had imagined, if this was where Bedford put his trust.

All the rooms inspected and the pipes given an official bang, Dunne asked to be shown to the door. Gave the cook a friendly good-bye that was returned with a grunt. Went out the tradesmen's route, the maid right behind, up the small flight of stone stairs into the sunlight. Dunne looked at her for the first time without the distraction of studying the surroundings, at the woman 'neath the uniform that wrapped every servant girl in the air of a nun, black and starched habit, hair tucked away.

She smiled in an open, inviting way. "You from New York?" she said. A pretty face.

"Wouldn't be from anywhere else."

"Where your people from?"

"Tipperary. Holy Cross, on my father's side."

"I come over with a family from Holy Cross."

"Hope they weren't relatives of mine. Got trouble enough taking care of myself!"

Her smile turned into a laugh. Straight teeth. Round, wide eyes: the deepest shade of green Dunne had ever seen.

Right then Dunne heard Dandy Dan's voice in his ear, as though Dan's shade was standing beside the stoop, fretting in the way he did when annoyed, moving his feet back and forth, his voice getting high and angry: *Get along, Jim! Want to see a woman laugh and smile? Take a week's tour of Greene Street once the job is done. The money will make the girls grin aplenty. Have all the sharebone a man can stand!*

Just a minute more, Dan.

The uniform couldn't completely hide what a fine, full figure she had.

She stood with her hands on her hips, a doxy's kind of pose. But Dunne felt there was something sweet about her, even an innocence. She talked on about missing her family, about the nature of her work, about the difference between what you expect of New York and what you find. Dunne lingered and listened. She had a gift for talking. Put a man at ease.

She paused. Seemed the moment to go. Dunne tipped his cap. "Best be off," he said.

"Yeah," she said, "it's getting warm. Soon the heat will be on us for sure," and she reached up and took hold of the stiff white cap about her head, lifted it off, and the red-golden hair fell about her shoulders, waves of it, startling bright as it caught the sun. She tossed her hair and took out the pins.

"They're all away, Mr. Bedford at work, his wife at the shore. What harm if a girl works without this pressed about her head like a crown of thorns?" She tossed her hair again, leaned her head from side to side, used her hand as if it was a comb, and the hair fell down her back, framed her face, rich ropes of it, thick folds of it, and the green eyes seemed even greener than before.

"Miss Kerrigan will have at me. But little joy there'll be in life to them who listen to the likes of Miss Kerrigan!" She glanced up at the sky. "At home, on days as hot and clear as this, little work be done or expected. But here there's no choice." She gave a look: half sad, half happy, oh well. Those eyes. "Good-bye," she said, and disappeared inside.

Dunne was alone on the sidewalk. He knew he should be gone, but he stayed. The ghost of Dandy Dan had completely disappeared, no echo of his voice, couldn't remember a thing he'd ever said. Dunne was unsure of what to do next, unsure in a manner difficult to explain. It was as if the weather had suddenly changed, although it hadn't, or as if the air itself was somehow different than before, although it wasn't; and he kept feeling like that, unsure, even when he went his way, and stayed feeling like that all day and the next, till Sunday, standing in the back of St. Stephen's, the church where the neighborhood servant girls hear Mass, he searched amid the crowd and saw the back of her fine head, her hair drawn up beneath a hat, her face leaned into a prayerbook. Just watching her gave him a stirred and happy sensation, although not the kind church was supposed to give.

He met her on the way out. She seemed to believe it was a stroke of luck, and didn't try to hide her surprise or delight. They talked on the steps till the other girls were gone. He walked her halfway home, and not knowing what else to do, gave a tip of his cap and said good-bye. He thought that seeing her once more would in some way help get his mind loose enough to think of other things. He was wrong. He spent the week with the same feeling as before, counting the days till he would be back in St. Stephen's, both content and excited with her in view.

The next Sunday she didn't pretend to be otherwise than pleased to see him again, and when they left the church, she led the way, in the opposite direction of where she lived, east, then north, up as far as the Central Park. Neither of them paid much attention to where they were.

They sat so close together on a bench that Dunne could smell the scent of the soap she used, fresh and flowery-like. A moment for saying what you feel if you was sure what it was and had the words.

"How long you been with the gas company?" The first time she asked a question like that. Nearby, a military band played a sprightly air.

"Too long."

"Steady work, is it not?"

"Been thinkin' of joinin' the Army. Have some adventure."

"And give up regular employment? Plenty of men in this city give whatever they got for a job like yours."

The band stopped playing. They sat a few moments, without a word. He walked her home and took a quick leave. He skipped Mass the following week, but the thought of her was never far away. Had thought to see her yesterday, but Saturday the message came from Capshaw. It was a sharp reminder of what had drawn Margaret to his attention in the first place. He went up to see Capshaw that evening. Place was locked and quiet as a tomb. *What game is the rat-nose playing now?* Dunne wondered. Instead of going to St. Stephen's on Sunday morning, he returned to Capshaw's. A maid answered. Said Capshaw had left the morning before without a word as to where. Hadn't come back that night. "Most unlike him," she said.

Dunne had been sitting in the lobby of the New England all morning. What next? Wait another day for Capshaw and give him more time to spring a trap? He rolled and lit a cigarette, picked up the newspaper, skipped over columns of war news and opened to the inner page. His eyes fell on a column story on the lower right-hand side:

MURDER AT THE ELYSIAN FIELDS—
BLOODY EVIDENCE OF A FATAL ENCOUNTER

The inquest upon the body of an unknown man found murdered on Saturday, on the beach at the Elysian Fields, was commenced before Coroner F. W. Bonenstedt, at Hoboken, on Sunday forenoon. After the jury had been impanelled, they proceeded to the Fields, and there examined the evidence of a fatal encounter. A short distance before Sybil's Cave, on the path beneath a leafy canopy, was found considerable blood spattered around, and indications of a deadly scuffle. There was a fresh mark upon a tree made with a blunt instrument, as though the person wielding it had missed his aim. Thence the body was dragged along, over rocks and ground, and, after the trousers had been removed, was hurled to the beach below. The back of the murdered man's skull had been crushed with repeated blows, and there are, also, severe wounds on the temple and forehead. Except for a tattoo on the right hand, of an eagle inscribed with the letters "OSSB," there were no distinguishing marks. As no person could give witness to the circumstances surrounding his death, and none could identify him, it was deemed probable he belonged to New York. Having inspected the scene of the crime, the jury adjourned its inquest until Monday. In the meantime the body will remain at the Coroner's Office, for identification.

Must be thousands had that tattoo. *OSSB.* Old Stupid Sons of Bitches was what every Paddy knew it stood for. Order of the Star-Spangled Banner what the rat-noses claimed it did. Dunne had seen it on plenty of hands. Still, Capshaw being missing the same time this story appears—maybe nothing more than coincidence, but maybe something more. Could be Capshaw was done in over in the Elysian Fields. Be a long list of candidates with reasons for doing the job. Bedford would be one.

Or maybe that body on the beach wasn't Capshaw's at all. Maybe he merely dropped out of sight to spring his trap. Could be he'll be heard from today.

Dunne put down the paper. He had waited this long. Give it another day, then pay a visit to the Bedford house. Unannounced.

11

BEDFORD FOUND THE STORY on the inside dexter page of the *Tribune*. It had been given no prominence. MURDER AT THE ELYSIAN FIELDS. He read it quickly until he reached the line "As no person could give witness to the circumstances surrounding his death, and none could identify him . . ." All he needed to know. He folded the paper and laid it on the floor.

Audley Ward sat at the other end of the table, absorbed in a book, the plate with the remains of his breakfast pushed aside. The maid appeared from the pantry. Bedford said, "No eggs today, Margaret, just coffee." He cleared his throat. "By the way, Audley, I've decided to join Sarah in Long Branch."

Ward looked up from his book. "Are you sure you're in a condition to travel?"

"A few days away from the frenzy of the financial markets, I'll be restored to new."

"Must have been a terrible experience. Any mention in the papers?"

"No, and don't expect there'll be. Boating accidents aren't sensational enough for our metropolitan sheets."

"But for an engine to explode and gentlemen to be thrown into the sea and almost drowned, my God, if that isn't worthy of reportage, what is?"

Bedford shrugged. "I'd think you'd be the last to be surprised by the poor judgment or bad taste of New York journalists."

"Quite so."

On Saturday night, home safe at last, Bedford had soaked for several hours in the tub. Exhausted, he had dozed off and awakened with a start to find Ward standing over him. "Charles," Ward had said, "are you hurt? There's blood on the stairs and I'm told you were in an accident. Shall I summon a physician? Have the police been notified?"

Bedford had sputtered something about accepting an invitation from an acquaintance to take a pleasure ride in his new steam-driven boat, a short jaunt around the harbor. They were returning to the pier when the engine suddenly exploded, hurling them into the water. Luckily, despite some superficial cuts and bruises, no one had been killed, and a passing ferry had plucked them from the harbor.

Ward shook his head. "The power of the steam engine is truly Mephistophelian. We regard it as our salvation, but it may well prove an instrument of damnation."

After his bath, Bedford went directly to bed, lay down wet and naked on the sheets, and fell into a deep and dreamless sleep that lasted into the late morning. When he awoke, he knew exactly what he would do. It would require no great preparation. Pack some clothes. Put the contents of the safe into a carpetbag. Travel light. No one must suspect.

"When are you leaving?" Ward asked.

"The noon boat. Have some business to attend to in the office, then I'll be off. Expect you'll make sure nobody runs off with the place while I'm gone."

"Have no fear," Ward said. " 'Care keeps his watch in every old man's eye; and where care lodges, sleep will never lie.' Remember me to Sarah." He went back to his reading.

Bedford gulped his coffee. He left the table, went into the library, opened the safe, removed the small wrapped stacks of greenbacks, and put them into a carpetbag. He walked quickly past the dining room. Ward's lowery face was buried in his book. Bedford stood by the front door, glanced at himself in the mirror in its gilded cartouche, took a peach-colored tea rose from the vase beside it, and made a boutonniere. Andrew, the coachman, came in, his coat already stained with perspiration. A faint whiff of horse manure clung to him. Bedford lifted his lapel to his nose, smelled the rose.

"Your bags, sir?" Andrew said.

Bedford pointed to the leather traveling bag that the maid had set beside the door. "That you may take." He put his hand on the carpetbag, which rested next to the vase of roses on the small Oriental-style table. "This I will carry myself."

Bedford stepped back into the hallway. He remembered the day he had arrived with Sarah and Ward. Her amazement and delight. A house to wonder at. How happy they would be in this place. How content. How quickly they had come to feel it was inadequate, too narrow and contained, unworthy of their aspirations. He put on his hat, looked once again in the mirror, made a last adjustment to his cravat, and went out. The coach was at the curb. Andrew held the door open. Bedford climbed in, set the carpetbag in his lap, wrapped his arms around it.

As the coach pulled away, Bedford looked back and glimpsed the façade a last time. How easy, he thought, to be deceived. Like so much of New York, his house seemed to have been there forever, but it was merely a piece of the ceaseless cycle of build up and tear down, today a towering rectangle of brown granite, tomorrow a decaying ruin in which fifteen families of louse-ridden foreigners slept in warrens jigsawed out of the old space. The day after that, who could know? A pile of rubble carted away as landfill for the city's ocean-eating shoreline, its place taken perhaps by some taller, grander building, the inhabitants deluding themselves into believing that the process of change had stopped until another wave of foreigners descended and the new structure, like its predecessor, ended its days as landfill.

In a moment, they turned onto the avenue. Bedford ran the morning's schedule through his mind, everything to proceed as usual: Read the mail, see to the appointments, visit the Exchange, pay a call at Old Tom's, same table as usual, same order, mutton chop, freshly baked bread, coffee with a shot of brandy in it. He had no taste for the new fashion in food, French sauces, sherbets, soufflés, the rage for champagne. That drink most of all. Bubbles. Who needed such reminders of the money business?

Just above Union Square, the heavy flow of traffic was brought nearly to a halt by a crew of Paddy workmen demolishing the walls of a squat, sagging structure that might once have been a tavern on what was then the Bloomingdale Road. It was dwarfed by the surrounding structures, the old country road having been transformed into a bustling artery of city life. The workers swung their iron bars into the walls and sent bricks tumbling down into the street. A cloud of fine dust covered the workmen in white, making them seem like ghostly inhabitants the demolition had exposed to view.

Bedford sighed at the thought of all the possibilities he was leaving behind. The new building would undoubtedly be several stories taller than the old. Perhaps it would have one of the new vertical railroads to carry people to the higher elevations. Who knew where it would stop? More possibilities by the day. In London, the Metropolitan Railway was operating underground trains that avoided the tangled chaos of the streets. People traveled in style, heavy carpets on the floor, richly upholstered seats, paneled walls, lighting supplied by incandescent gas drawn from India-rubber bags mounted on the roof. Cost two and a half million pounds to build. The profits would eventually be at least a hundred times that. How long before New York had a Metropolitan Railway of its own?

Below Union Square, the traffic began to move again, but there was soon another bottleneck and the coach swung onto Houston Street, following a familiar detour down Allen, across Division, through Chatham Square to Pearl. When they reached Chatham Square, the traffic was thick again. They came to a halt. Bedford tapped the pane high on the wall in front of him. Andrew's sweat-drenched face appeared.

"There's terrible congestion today, sir. Work stoppages and the like, a lot of people addin' to the normal delays."

"I'll walk the rest of the way," Bedford said. He got out, carpetbag in hand.

"Fierce day for walkin', sir, specially with a bag."

"Do me good. Go to the boat and deposit the luggage. I'll make my way directly there when I'm finished at the office."

"Whatever suits you, sir."

In front of a row of secondhand-clothing stores, clerks dragged out racks of jackets and pants. They unfolded canvas awnings to protect their merchandise from the sun. A squad of soldiers marched down Park Row in the direction of City Hall. Bedford remembered that General Zook's funeral was today: A fallen hero of Gettysburg, Zook had helped defeat a gold boom. Now, in death, he was helping foul up the traffic.

The office was quiet. Bedford put the carpetbag beneath his desk and rested his feet on it. He reviewed his calendar. Only one appointment. A broker from Philadelphia who had requested a meeting by letter several weeks before. The missive had been florid and overblown, promising an opportunity for instant riches "unseen since the days when the Phrygian king could, by mere touch, turn coarse elements into gold." When the broker was ushered in, he proved to be a match for his literary style. Ample of flesh, with a flowing mustache and a large pearl ring on his right middle finger, the visitor from Philadelphia spoke in a theatrical whisper, as if afraid someone might have his ear pressed to the wall. He began with an account of the recent cholera epidemic in his city and the ravages it had inflicted. His voice sank lower. The strangest phenomenon had occurred, he said. In one particularly dilapidated quarter, where the Paddies were all crammed together with their usual disregard for cleanliness or sobriety, a district where you would expect the cholera to thrive, there had been only a few cases, and those relatively mild. The medical authorities ascribed it to happenstance, a change in the wind. The Paddies attributed it to the Virgin and held a special service in her honor. But his interest aroused, the visitor said in a voice so small that Bedford had to lean forward to hear, he found both explanations inadequate and set out on his own to discover the true cause. He made a visit to the district and immediately noticed that it was dominated by gasworks, gigantic tubs of iron that commanded the eye and the contents of which demanded the attention of the nose. After several weeks of inquiry, he ascertained not only that the cholera had barely touched the neighborhood but that the incidence of dysentery and autumnal fever had approached zero. The broker sat back in his chair and paused, as if to let the facts he had related sink in.

Bedford suddenly had a deeper appreciation of the desperate nature of his own existence these past months. Sitting in front of him was a second-rate promoter in search of gullible investors. The thought that he had even bothered to respond to the man's request for an appointment, that the letter alone hadn't tipped him off to the confidence man behind it, made Bedford feel sad and a little depressed. How far he had fallen!

"You see, Mr. Bedford," the stout visitor said, "I have stumbled on an investment opportunity of huge proportions. If you'll forgive the pun, it's been right there beneath my nose all the time!" He leaned in close to Bedford's ear: "The salubrious properties of gas! Sir, it is as though the Sangreal itself has been dropped into my lap!" He stood and raised his hands to heaven, revealing two wet circles of perspiration in the armpits of his coat. He began to enumerate the blessings that would fall on those perspicacious enough to put capital behind his discovery.

Bedford sent the man off with the promise to give serious thought to his proposals. As soon as he was alone, Bedford deposited in the trash the ream of papers his visitor had left with him. He decided to forgo a last visit to the Exchange. He didn't want his ponderous sadness to be their last memory of him: the hunched shoulders and dolorous face shared by all those defeated on the Street. He went directly to Old Tom's and ordered his regular meal, but except for the brandied coffee, he left it untouched. The place was almost deserted.

Bedford paid his bill. The cashier was a young white man with a badly pocked face whom Bedford had never seen before. The cashier nodded toward the knot of colored waiters huddled in conversation in the corner. "Their nerves is all ajangle with the fuss over the draft. Was a drunken Paddy in here this morning screamin' how the time had come to set the nigger in his place." The cashier smiled as he spoke.

"The service was fine," Bedford said. "Same as always." He was unsure which of the colored men had served him. They all wore the same solemn expression. Old men with sugar-sprinkled kink, it seemed they had always been this way, as ancient and serious this morning as the day he had his first meal there.

When he came out of the cool interior of Old Tom's, the sun dazed him and made him feel faint. He grasped the carpetbag tightly and walked up to the corner of Vesey. By now the bag Andrew had put aboard ship was destined to sail alone to Long Branch. Bedford looked up at the clock in the steeple of St. Paul's Church. A half hour before the boat to Albany sailed. Connections to all points west.

Tears welled up in his eyes. An overwhelming sense of finality took hold of him, and a tremor ran through his body. The city he had set out to conquer had taken back everything he had wrested from it: house, business, wife, reputation, the respect of his peers. All gone. For an instant he felt paralyzed with fear, and then he remembered that years ago, when still a boy, he had stood on this very corner with Stark, who had pointed out this was where the great John Jacob Astor had once lived. "Was a step up in the world for the young German immigrant," Stark said. "But the dull Teuton and his plodding wife were not seduced by their progress. Though the surroundings were more substantial than they'd known before, they filled the rooms with foul-smelling furs and skins, boarded the windows against thieves, and relentlessly plowed their profits into real estate, money breeding money until it compounded into an imperial fortune!"

Bedford lifted his carpetbag, felt its weight. A good deal more than Astor had started with. His melancholy retreated a bit. Across the street, in the graveyard of St. Paul's, a row of green and gold flowers drooped with the heat, their heads bowed toward Wall Street. They did not toil or sow, but fortunes had been built on such as them. He recalled more of Stark's musings on the mysteries of man's relationship to money, how Europe had once been dotted with tulip exchanges that housed a manic bidding for bulbs. "The bubble burst," Stark had related, "but by then the wise had taken their profits and gone on to safer investments."

Bedford turned and walked toward the river. On a normal

day he would be on the floor of the Exchange at this hour, appearing confident and assured, no matter what. Never give in to fear. That was the first law of the market. And of life. The opportunities were always there for those who didn't lose their nerve. Fortunes to be made from fur, flowers, whatever was at hand. Who could know?

Across West Street, looming over the sheds that lined the waterfront, were the smokestacks and riggings of steamboats and sailing ships. There was movement everywhere, carts, horses, coaches, wheelbarrows, people. Families of Swedish and German immigrants watched as all their earthly possessions were lifted by the arms of the rusty cranes into the hold of the Albany boat. For a moment, everything they owned in this world was suspended over the dark waters of the Hudson, and they stood in studied, prayerful silence, their eyes rising and descending with the progress of the crane.

Bedford went up the gangplank. The boat vibrated with excitement. The purser took his ticket. Deckhands scrambled about and snarled at everyone to get out of the way, shouldering aside the unheeding. Bedford went up above to the first-class parlor. The hubbub below barely intruded through the thick red drapes and heavy carpets. Bedford had a glass of whiskey and went outside again. Everyone was aboard. The longshoreman were casting off the lines.

A whistle blew. One of the ship's officers cried out, "All aboard the *General Schuyler*!"

The deck shook as the great paddle wheel turned and the boat backed out of its mooring into the Hudson. People waved and cheered, threw bits of paper from the decks. Bedford put the carpetbag down between his feet. With its contents he would begin again. *Pay the bearer on demand*. Pay him whoever he is, wherever he may be, Denver, St. Louis, San Francisco, city, village, or frontier outpost. Without these notes and the specie they represented, what was the grandest and most substantial of residences but a monument to impermanence?

West again, Charlie! He felt gripped by the same spirit that had infused him as a boy. It had been misplaced, not destroyed.

Off in the distance, on the northeast fringe of the city, a heavy column of smoke swirled into the sky, as though an entire block were going up in flames. People crowded the railing to get a view. Bedford felt someone pushing persistently against him. He turned to confront a short, husky, pug-faced Irishman. "Sir," he said, "if you ask, I'd be happy to try to make room!"

"Don't bother tryin' to talk to him," a passenger on the other side of Bedford said. "He's deef as clam, and there's another around just like him."

III

FOSTER KNEW HE SHOULD NEVER have listened to Cassidy. Took all day to get home. Waited for a conductor to provide a free train ride. When that phantom never appeared, they hitched a ride with a cartman and didn't reach the hotel until dark. Bought a few rounds for Cassidy and the other one, whatever his name was. Wasted money, wasted time. Still no song for Daly.

This morning, a letter was delivered to the hotel and stuck beneath his door. *Dearest Brother.* The usual remonstrations . . . *the conduct of your life . . . the company you keep. . . . You are wasting your great talent . . . the wages of sin.* But no money. Not even any mention of it. Long on advice, short on cash. *Fraternally yours, Morrison.*

Foster bent over the washing bowl and splashed water in his face. He avoided looking at the mirror above the bowl, knowing what he would see: wasted eyes, wasted face, wasted everything. He dressed quickly, perspiring from the effort. Another brutally hot day. He searched about for something to write on, but there wasn't so much as a scrap. He ripped the back of the envelope from the letter and stuck it into his pocket. He went down the stairs and through the lobby, eyes straight ahead. Wasn't in the mood for conversation. As soon as he went out, the full glare of sunlight hit like the blast of an explosion. He groped his way along the wall until he reached an adjacent doorway that provided some relief. His legs trembled. He needed to sit. On the opposite corner, on the south side of Bayard Street, was a saloon he usually avoided, a Five Points way station filled with cutthroats and whores. This morning it looked quiet and deserted, its windows bathed in shadow, a cool retreat, a place to sit and rest. He would give himself another hour.

The saloon was as empty as he had hoped. He gulped a whiskey, took out the nub of a pencil from his pocket, put the envelope facedown on the bar. Thick, expensive paper. White, fresh, virginal. He poised the pencil.

The bartender came by and poured Foster's glass full. "On the house," he said.

Foster saluted him with his glass. For an instant he entertained the thought of missing his appointment with Daly. Drop a note and make another date. The coward's way out. He decided against it. Daly was a sociable Irishman, not merely talkative but agreeable, never pugnacious or threatening.

Be direct and honest: *The song is not yet done, but you will have it soon! You have my word on that!* He drained the glass and walked outside, steadier on his feet than when he entered.

The street was almost deserted, but from around the corner of Mulberry, down toward the Five Points, came a cheerful chorus of voices. A moment later a horde of cavorting children flooded the street. They jigged and twirled and twisted in a spontaneous dance, and tossed paper into the air. A ragamuffin of no more than five stopped directly in front of Foster, bent down, and laid a book open on the ground. He put his bare foot on it and with both hands ripped the spine apart, then tossed the book high into the air. The pages fluttered overhead and fell about the boy's feet. He ran on. Foster picked up the purple cover. It was inscribed with gold lettering. *The Five Points House of Industry: A Hymnal for Children.* A page of music was stuck to it. "Our Gentle Savior," by Geoffrey Graves. The bars and notes and clefs were all familiar. Foster hummed the music to himself. "Gentle Annie." His song.

Cheats and plagiarists everywhere. Even in the Kingdom of God. He threw the remnant of the book back down to the ground.

There was a tug on his jacket. A small boy had his hand in Foster's pocket. Foster grabbed the boy's arm and pushed him away. A second boy came up from behind and tried the same trick, but as soon as Foster turned, the boy ran off. The procession continued. More hymnals were ripped apart, their pages scattered. Behind the children came a band of laborers. They carried hods, iron posts, crowbars, axes, awls, whatever tools could be used as weapons. From a window above the saloon, an old man leaned out and shouted, "Where ye off to, boys?"

"To hang Robert Noonan!" one of the laborers yelled.

"Don't forget Horace Greeley!" the old man replied.

A laugh went up, and a detachment left the parade and filed into the saloon. Up ahead, the children spilled onto the Bowery and brought the traffic to a halt.

Foster followed in their wake. He crossed the Bowery and continued on Bayard. At the corner of Hester, a dozen Metropolitans looked about nervously, fidgeting with their locust sticks. Foster turned onto Attorney Street and followed it to Grand. The disorder was worse than on the Bowery. A barricade of broken crates and cinder barrels had been erected. A blizzard of ash sifted about the street.

A sprawling crowd was gathered in front of the buildings along the south side of Grand. Children darted around its fringes. On the steps of the Catholic church across the street, a short man in dirty overalls harangued the crowd. " 'Tis us who are the slaves!" he shouted. "If the rich man loves the nigger, let him fight to free him! And let us fight to free ourselves!"

A gray-haired harridan in a shawl came up beside Foster. "Ain't it somethin'," she said, "to see such a spectacle! Word is the uptown districts is taken by the people, and the police superintendent himself been strung up! And that black devil Robert Noonan is next! The people will make sure he pays for his treachery!" She spit on the ground and danced a small jig. "The same medicine for all them doin' the draftin'!"

The crowd surged forward. The door of a building gave way with a loud crash. People fought to get in. A moment later the windows were shattered, and the falling shards of glass rained on those below. A small girl was severely cut; blood spurted from her neck. She had barely been helped away when chairs, tables, and oak filing cabinets were hurled out the windows, crashing into the street.

Foster skirted the crowd. He made his way eastward half a block, to where Daly had his business. On the ground floor was a store with an overhanging sign in the shape of a diamond. Painted on the sign was "MOSES MEHRBACK, JEWELERS, EST. 1849." A tall, white-haired man stood inside, guarding the door. Foster went in the door next to the jewelers, up the stairs to Daly's. He knocked. No answer. He pounded with his fist. The door flung open. Daly stood there holding a cane above his head.

"What the hell are you doing here?" he said.

"The song," Foster said. "I promised to deliver it today."

"Piss on the song." Daly took Foster by the arm and pulled him in. He bolted the door. "There's a bloody revolution going on!"

Daly's assistant, a girl of seventeen, cowered in the corner. "It's all right, Maura," Daly said. "It's only Mr. Foster."

Daly went over to the window and looked out. "Just my luck. An enrollment office ten doors away. 'Course, they was gone the first sign of trouble, and now the honest businessman is left to shift for himself." He pointed to a table piled high with sheet music. "Taken me fifteen years to build this, Foster. Be damned before I'll let these bloody omadhauns take it without a fight."

The building shook with the force of a tremendous crash. Daly stuck his head out the window. "They're into Mehrback's!" he shouted. He unbolted the door and dashed out. In the corner, Maura cried softly.

Above Foster's head, the bulbs on the gas fixture shook with the vibrations from downstairs. Glass against brass. *Ping, ping, ping.* There was another resounding crash, and the vibrations increased. *Ping, ping, ping, ping, ping, ping.* Foster tapped his foot. A tune, but not one of his. *Ping, ping, ping.* One of Dan Emmett's. Heard it first in Cincinnati, an early piece; no great success, but it was an inspiration. The morning after he'd heard it performed he sat at his desk in his brother's office. Before him was the endless drudge of bills of lading, receipts, contracts, all to be entered on the empty pages of the ledger. Instead, he began to make musical notations, writing down what he remembered of Emmett's song.

Daly returned with his arm around Moses Mehrback, the white-haired man from the jeweler's shop below. There was a deep cut above Mehrback's left eye. Blood dripped down his face, and had stained the shoulder of Daly's shirt.

"Don't stand there, Foster," Daly said. "Give me a hand."

Foster pulled a chair forward. Daly lowered Mehrback into it. He took a handkerchief from his back pocket and wiped the jeweler's face, folded the cloth, put it in Mehrback's hand, and pressed the old man's hand against the wound.

"Hold it there, Moses," Daly said.

Maura was weeping. The building shook once more with the force of another crash.

Ping, ping. That day in Cincinnati, it had come to him. Emmett's music disappeared. There was a silence, a space, an emptiness, and then, like the tongues of fire that had descended on the Apostles at Pentecost, the music descended on him. *Ping.*

Oh! Susanna!

He scrawled it across the ledger. It was as though the music were in the air and he were the only one who could hear it, and if he didn't get it all, if he missed any part, it would be lost forever.

"Christ, Foster, what the hell's the matter with you!" Daly's face was only inches away. Foster felt the heat of his publisher's breath. "Wake up, man! Help me lift Moses up!"

"Of course," Foster said. He took one arm, Daly the other. Mehrback moaned. The blood had soaked through the handkerchief. It dripped onto Foster's sleeve. They moved to the door. Daly left Mehrback with Foster and went back and brought Maura to the door. She was shaking.

"Take her with you," Daly said. "You two go down first. Keep shouting 'Down with the draft,' loud as you can. I'll be with Moses right behind."

Foster took hold of the railing. Why had he ceased to hear the music? What had changed?

Daly's voice boomed in his ear. "Goddamn it, get moving!" A tongue of fire. Then a shove. Foster reached for the handrail but missed it. His legs swung out in a wide arc. His head struck the stairs, and his feet passed overhead. When the tumbling stopped, he lay still. A bearded giant with a crowbar stood over him.

"Down with the draft!" Foster shouted.

Before he could get up, Daly stepped over him, with Mehrback and Maura right behind. They went out the door. Foster got to his feet and followed them. There was wild mêlée in the street as people scuffled to grab the rings, earrings, and watches dropped or discarded by the first wave of looters. Daly pushed his way through, an arm around the jeweler. Maura hung on to the tail of Daly's shirt. Smoke billowed from the enrollment office and rolled over the street. The crowd closed behind Daly and blocked Foster's way. He saw the trio briefly again as they reached the corner of Pitt. Maura turned, like Lot's wife, for a last look. Daly grabbed her arm and pulled her away. They disappeared from view.

As the flames spread from the draft office to the adjacent buildings, the looting took on a new intensity. A table flew through Daly's window onto the street, and was followed by bundles of sheet music. Foster sat on the far curb, watching. His ears were ringing from his fall. A large lump had raised itself on his forehead, in the very spot where once, long ago, Dr. Mordowner claimed to have discovered the nation's most prestigious external disclosure of the Organ of Tune.

A gaunt, poorly shaven young man in heavy woolen pants and a filthy shirt plunked down beside Foster. He smelled as if he either worked in a stable or slept in one. Maybe both. He was drinking from an almost empty whiskey bottle.

"Da hast Du aber eine ganz schöne Beule!" he said.

"Pardon?" Foster said.

"Die da!" He pointed at Foster's forehead and laughed. He offered the bottle.

"I don't speak German."

"Egal. Nun trink schon!" He offered the bottle again. Foster took a drink and handed it back. The German stood, drained what was left, and tossed the bottle into the gutter. He pulled Foster to his feet.

Half a block away, a group of foundry workers had smashed open the door of a liquor dealer, and people were running from every direction to claim a share of the spoils.

"Ach was!" the German said to Foster. *"Lassen wir uns den spass nicht verderben."*

A laundry wagon turned the corner onto Grand. The driver, instantly aware of his mistake, pulled the brake and hopped off, leaving his load in the middle of the street. People swarmed over it. The cargo of carefully wrapped packages was ripped apart, shirt, skirts, petticoats, and handkerchiefs unfolded and examined, some donned, some thrown away.

The German took off his soiled gray shirt. He had a boy's physique, lithe, lean, taut. He put on a starched and spotless silk shirt. He rummaged through another package and found a pair of white duck trousers. He took off his woolen work pants, put on the pristine trousers, and pulled his work pants back on over them. He grinned at Foster. *"So bleibt Sie sauber für spater,"* he said.

The foundry workers passed from the liquor dealer's to an Italian tonsorial establishment. They smashed the shop window, rushed in, and commandeered the services of the owner and his staff. Half a dozen of the workers sat in the barbers' chairs, smoking cigars and swigging whiskey, as the terrified Italians tended to their hair and beards. A crowd gathered outside to watch. They laughed as the barbers began working on each mangy-haired, stubble-faced patron, and cheered as each left the shop looking as sleek and well tended as a lawyer.

The German hurled himself at the wall of spectators and barreled his way through. The crowd was in a happy mood and took his shoving good-naturedly. "Wait your turn, you crazy Dutchman," one of them said.

The German jumped into the first empty chair. The barber gave his hair a quick washing, wrapped his head in a steaming towel, removed it, lathered and shaved him. While the barber cut the German's hair, a tiny Italian manicured his nails. Finally the German rose from the chair. The stringy, straw-colored hair that had hung down over his face and ears was trim and uniform, slicked back and glistening with pomade. His forehead, newly revealed, was high and well proportioned. The wafer whiteness of his shirt made his skin seem the color of bronze.

Foster had watched through the broken window. The German came out, and they walked down to the corner of Chrystie Street and entered a lager-beer saloon that, in the interests of saving his property from destruction, the proprietor had thrown open, making the drink free to everyone.

The German chattered away with a few of his countrymen. Foster studied him in the mirror that hung high over the bar. It gave him a view as if he were hovering above, looking down like an angel on the mortals below. He was transfixed by what he saw. A beautiful, beardless youth changed by the tonsorial art from a hostler into a Hermes. The German glanced up and saw Foster watching him.

Foster felt embarrassed at being caught spying; he blushed. But he felt something else as well. An inner heat. Intimation of excitement. Music he alone could hear. A single line: *There is no beauty to equal thy face.* Where had he heard it before? Or was he hearing it for the first time?

The crush and heat of bodies inside the saloon made the room unbearable. The German gestured to Foster that he was leaving, and they joined arms, squirming and elbowing their way to the door. Outside, a large crowd milled about, seemingly unsure of what to do next, until from somewhere the cry went up: "To the Armory! To the Armory!" Suddenly the whole mass began moving north up Chrystie, toward Second Avenue, and people flowed out of saloons and side streets, swelling the procession as it passed each block.

The German stepped into the street. "*Los, mein Freund,*" he said to Foster.

"I'm tired," Foster said. "It's this heat. My room is not far from here."

The German shrugged and smiled, a wordless way of saying that he didn't understand, but it was a lovely smile. Foster wished it told him all there was to tell: a winsome, cheerful, charming young man eager for friendship. Maybe more. Foster joined the march. He walked beside the German up Chrystie. At the corner of Houston was the factory of a hat manufacturer, its roof occupied by scores of girls who threw confetti-like scraps of cloth and felt. They pointed north and cried, "Get the guns! Arm yourselves!"

Just across Fourteenth Street was another liquor dealer's. A group of boys worked hard at prying open the boarded windows. There was a stampede into the store. The German climbed in and emerged a few minutes later, cradling a bottle. Ahead, an immense sea of people, fed by rivers coming from every direction, surrounded a large brick factory building. Gunfire crackled from the upper floors. The crowd retreated, leaving a handful of corpses lying on the ground, but after a few minutes a new wave of attackers swept forward. They pounded on the iron shutters with hammers and crowbars, and a crew came at the front door with a lamppost that it used as a battering ram.

Foster and the German stood beneath the awning of a saddle store a block away. The windows were gone and it seemed to have been completely emptied of merchandise, but two small boys emerged carrying large saddles on their backs. They scurried across Second Avenue like two giant beetles. The German opened the bottle he'd stolen and put it to his mouth. His Adam's apple bobbed up and down as he guzzled it.

"*Gutes Zeug!*" he said, and handed the bottle to Foster.

Foster didn't take a drink right away. He listened to another line of music: *Dear is the light of your bright lovely eyes.* Was it old or new? He wasn't sure, but for now it was enough to know that the music was there once again, floating in the air. He took a long draft from the bottle. Still another line! *Dear friends and gentle hearts.* A new line for sure. He handed back the bottle and took out the scrap of paper and pencil from his pocket. Wrote the words down. The song machine was back in business! Maybe it was the fall that he had taken down Daly's stairs. Medical and musical history being made at the same time!

A roar went up from the crowd. The men with the lamppost cum battering ram had breached the door. People flooded in. The shutters flew open, and out poured chairs, tables, cabinets, a blizzard of paper. Without a word or gesture to Foster, the German ran to join the tide. He waved the bottle above his head.

Foster hid inside the saddle store and decided to wait until the German reemerged. He was still waiting when a large force of Metropolitans charged from the north and west, braving a hailstorm of bottles and paving stones. From where he was, Foster could see the flames as they burst through the roof of the factory building the crowd had seized. The fire must have reached supplies of kerosene because it ripped through the structure in a matter of minutes. People jumped out the windows, crashing into the street. A cordon of police formed, their backs to the burning building, but they all turned around when the roof collapsed and an eruption of smoke and ash shot into the sky.

More music was in the air. But this time it was old and familiar. Foster sang it aloud: "Borne like a vapor on the summer air . . . Floating like a vapor on the soft summer air."

IV

THE VOICES AND FACES were from the oldest nightmare that Alexander Turney Stewart could remember. Belfast. His childhood home. A winter's night. The wind screaming outside, clawing at the windowpanes, his uncle leaning toward the fire, the flames reflecting on his face. The children gathered around his chair by the hearth.

"*Scullabogue,* in county Wexford," his uncle intoned. "A name never to be forgotten. A warning to us all."

A horrible name, the very sound of it filled with the native's savagery. The children drew closer to the hearth light.

"The screaming popish horde drove the two hundred men, women, and children into the barn. Prodded them with pikes and scythes. Once inside, the people knelt and prayed for the strength to endure whatever might come. But even they must have found it hard to believe the papists were vicious enough to kill them *all,* babies and old women along with the men. Soon, however, the smell of smoke alerted them to what was in store, and the few who managed to claw their way out of the inferno died there on the grass of Scullabogue, their final taste of popish mercy a pike stuck in their necks or guts."

Alexander's sister began to cry loudly. Their mother came in from the kitchen. She upbraided her brother—the uncle whom Alexander had been named after—for frightening the children. "Look what you've done, Alex," she said. "Scared them half to death. Now they won't go to bed!"

He went to bed but could not sleep, and when he finally did, he found himself in a dark, cramped village in which a demoniac mob of whooping, howling creatures with apelike faces—the kind you saw on the country people or on the wretched beggars about the city—pursued him relentlessly. Hard as he ran, he barely moved. They were about to catch him. *Mammy! Mammy!* In a minute she was there, cradling him, cursing his uncle for disturbing her children's dreams.

The nightmare had recurred throughout Alexander Stewart's childhood, but it had been a very long time since he had dreamed it.

He leaned out the window of the coach. Today it was no dream, but as real and tangible as a paving stone. Twenty-third Street was filled with a multitude of New York's most wretched, drunken, imbecilic creatures. They marched beside a brigade of laborers armed with hammers and crowbars. Some carried railings ripped from the fence of a house on Fifth Avenue, graceful hatchet-headed iron shafts that looked like pikes. Pikes! The weapons of the papist revolutionaries!

The mob was marching west on Twenty-third and had blocked the flow of traffic on Third Avenue, both north and south. A few roamed among the stalled vehicles, demanding money. A gorgon with bloodshot eyes and a shock of wild red hair stuck her face into his coach. The very face of sin. Seamed with rum and depravity.

"Could you spare anythin' for a poor ol' soul such as meself?" Her eyes searched the inside of the coach. "Well, ain't you the one for travelin' in style!" she said.

He struck the ceiling of the coach cabin with the silver head of his cane. The coachmen just sat there, making no attempt to move. Another ghastly face appeared at the window, then another.

Here in the flesh: Scullabogue!

He struck the ceiling again. The coach didn't move.

The handle on the door rattled as one of the creatures outside attempted to open it. A second hand reached to grab the handle from inside. Stewart struck at it with his cane.

A howl went up. "You dirty son of a bitch!"

Stewart beat the ceiling hard, and suddenly the coach jerked backward, then shot forward, swinging into the north lane so quickly that he was almost thrown from his seat. The coach raced up the avenue. He wielded the cane like a hammer and pounded on the ceiling until the coach slowed and pulled over to the side.

He jumped out. The two of them sat up there in their red linen jackets and black stovepipes, faces awash in perspiration and fear. He shook his cane at them.

"Where in God's name do you think you're going?"

"Mr. Stewart, sir," the driver said. "We're lucky to have gotten outta there alive."

"And what of my store, boy? Do you think I'll run away and simply let the rabble have it?"

They stared down at him. Doltish, empty faces, mouths slightly ajar.

"Do you think I'll surrender the work of a lifetime to the likes of that crowd?"

As a boy, he had walked beside his father and uncle to the lighting of the bonfire, one in a chain that would burn on every hill from Belfast to Londonderry. The Eleventh Night. The sacred anniversary eve of the Battle of the Boyne. Smell of burning pitch. The insistent beat of the great drum thumping defiance. The straw-stuffed effigy of the Pope brought forward and thrown onto the orange flames. The crowd sang with one voice:

> Hundreds they've burned of each sex, young and old,
> From heaven the order, by priests they were told;
> No longer we'll trust them, no more to betray,
> But chase from our bosoms these vipers away.
> Derries down, down, croppies lie down!

He remembered little of the speeches, only a tall, imposing clergyman, with a mane of white hair that fell to his shoulders, who stood before the blazing bonfire and cried over and over, "No surrender!"

"Sir," the driver said, "the police will protect your store, but to return downtown is to put your life in jeopardy."

If the dolt had been in reach, Stewart would have grabbed him by his silk cravat and throttled him. Instead, he struck the side of the carriage with his cane, scarring the carefully polished ebony lacquer. "Idiot!" he yelled, "that store *is* my life! Now turn around and take me there by the shortest route you know."

He reentered the coach. He heard the coachmen's whispered debate as they weighed the certainty of losing their employment against the risk of losing their lives. To hell with them. If need be, he would walk.

No surrender!

The coach turned, crossed the avenue, picked up speed, and turned again, west toward Broadway. He took out a handkerchief and wiped his brow. He was bathed in perspiration. His hand shook like an old man's.

They had traveled only a short distance when a troop of Metropolitans blocked the way. The sergeant conversed briefly with the coachmen, then poked his head in. A pug-nosed, loutish creature bearing an uncanny resemblance to the rioters who had appeared at the window earlier, he tipped his hat. "Mr. Stewart," he said, "I was you, I'd be off these streets quick as possible. Word is, sir, the mobs is provin' themselves capable of all manner of outrage."

"And your job, Sergeant, in case you need to be reminded, is to seek them out and teach them a lesson about law and order. So may I suggest you abandon this little corner of tranquillity and go protect the lives and property of the good taxpayers who provide you a livelihood!"

One rap with his cane on the ceiling and the coach moved off. The driver went slowly, stopping at each corner to look down the side streets for any sign of the mob. As the coach moved down Broadway, more and more businesses were seen to be closed, windows shuttered or boarded up, doors padlocked and bolted. Stewart held his head. All he could think of was his store, situated there on Astor Place, America's grandest emporium, its doors open, its windows an invitation to one and all.

Those windows!

From whatever direction you approached, they were the first thing you saw, shimmering jewels in a cast-iron setting. He had discovered such windows on a trip to London in 1851. Shop fronts that sparkled in the sun, beckoned the passerby, demanded he pay attention to the spectacle before him. These were no narrow boxes that housed haphazard collections of wares, apertures as pinched as portholes. Here was a translucent invitation, a portal of welcome. And at night! At night they didn't become insignificant slits in the face of a dark and foreboding warehouse. At night the gaslight streamed through into the street, and the building became like a giant cathedral, windows ablaze with the power of a hundred thousand candles, a beacon of grace and hope and salvation.

Standing in that London street, he had remembered how as a boy in Belfast with only a ha'penny in his pocket he had pressed his nose against the window of a bakeshop filled with chocolate angels sitting on clouds of marzipan. He had always thought it was solely the sweets and swirled sugar that had made him part with the coin he had sworn to save. There, in London, he understood that it hadn't been the sugar that had first drawn him but the glass: the possibility of pleasure and satisfaction framed, contained, pinpointed by that thin pane.

He had decided right there, in London, that he would build a new cast-iron store that would proclaim the new dispensation. Walls of glass. A crystal palace by day, an illuminated temple by night. An irresistible display. It had taken almost twelve years to plan and build. Eight floors, each of two and a half acres. One hundred and five windows. Nineteen separate merchandising departments. An investment of $2,750,000!

On opening day, he had lined up the employees before the grand staircase that swept upward beneath a great skylight, a canopy of glass. They were arrayed in ranks: George Hobson, the general superintendent, at the head; the nineteen department heads behind him; and behind them, the rank and file of the store, 9 cashiers, 25 bookkeepers, 30 ushers, 200 cashboys, 470 clerks, 50 porters, 900 seamstresses dressed in identical striped smocks, 500 assorted delivery boys, boiler attendants, carpenters, and laborers.

Stewart stood at the top of the stairs. "You aren't merely employees of the world's greatest store," he said. "You are also participants in a venture as epochal as any since Marco Polo's day! And remember: As I have lived by the motto 'Honesty and truth are the surest aids in gaining a fortune,' so shall you. If you can't, leave now and seek your destiny elsewhere!"

No one moved. Hobson led the applause. The doors were opened, and a pride of dignitaries entered, General John Ellis Wool at their head. Stewart greeted them at the bottom of the stairs.

"On my soul, Stewart," Wool said. "You haven't assembled a store. You've built an army!"

The coach rolled through Union Square. There was an eerie quiet. A detachment of police stood in front of the Union League Club, but the normal daytime bustle of pedestrians was missing, and the regular rush of workday traffic had evaporated so quickly that a stranger dropped onto this spot might think the Sabbath was being observed. Fourteenth Street was also unusually quiet, but directly east, on Third Avenue, a trash fire had been set in the middle of the intersection. Hordes of people danced around it, moving in and out of the smoke. A witches' Sabbath.

The coach proceeded at the same maddeningly slow pace. Stewart slammed the head of the cane into the ceiling above him. "Damn you!" he yelled. As the coach neared the corner of Eleventh Street, with the Gothic bulk of Grace Church directly ahead, he could stand it no longer. He flung open the door and hopped to the pavement. He would settle accounts with the coachmen later. There would be a full reckoning. The louts could depend on it.

He could see the top floors of the store. No sign of smoke or flames. But he felt a stabbing pain in his stomach as he reached the corner of Tenth; then he got his first clear view of the ground floor.

Praise God, it was untouched.

He tried the doors on the northern side of the store, along Tenth, and all were securely locked. He tested the doors on the east and south. Locked as well. Hobson had seen to it. A stout-hearted, reliable man. Knew it when he hired him a decade ago.

Stewart relaxed a bit for the first time that morning. He shouldered his cane as if it were a musket, turned the corner of Ninth back onto Broadway, and approached the main entrance to the store. Ahead, the graceful spire of Grace Church reminded him of the twisting path by which the Good Lord had led him to this place.

He had set out to be a man of the cloth, had gone down to Dublin, enrolled at Trinity, and taken his degree in divinity. But as Daniel O'Connell and his fellow scoundrels made clear their intention to turn the country upside down with their agitation for Catholic emancipation, he had drawn the inescapable conclusion that the prospects for the Protestant clergy in Ireland would eventually diminish and grow narrow. He left for New York. Had it in his head to write a book. A novel. Pondering the idea, he took a position as a tutor in an academy on Roosevelt Street, in what was at that time still a respectable quarter of the city, and in the interests of making productive use of the small capital he possessed, he lent a portion of his funds to an acquaintance who wished to open a dry-goods store. The poor fellow failed completely. But as the psalmist said it, "The Lord putteth down one only to setteth up another," and in a moment of inspiration Stewart decided that instead of taking possession of the store and auctioning the stock to satisfy the debt, he would run it as his own. He scraped together what money he could and returned to Belfast, where he secured at low price a handsome supply of Irish linen and lace.

Returning to New York, he advertised "The Best Merchandise for a Fair Price, and for One Price," and they came by the hundreds, yea, by the thousands, till in the space of several days they had wiped out his inventory, and he began anew, advertising liberally, selling just over cost, piling profit atop of profit.

He began in a room measuring twelve by thirty feet and kept moving to bigger premises until in 1846, having accumulated every penny required to construct an emporium adequate to his ambitions, he built his Marble Dry-Goods Palace on the corner of Chambers and Broadway, overlooking City Hall Park. The edifice replaced Washington Hall, once a fashionable resort, now a disreputable watering hole for Tammany politicians, which in its turn had replaced the burying ground of some Negro sect that had for some long-forgotten reason abandoned the city.

When the foundation was dug, a number of remains were unearthed. Some said there was a curse on anyone who disturbed the bones of the dead. Some curse: the receipt box for the first day the Marble Palace was open contained $10,000, and it rarely held less than that afterward. Out of the store's earnings came the money to buy the Metropolitan Hotel and Niblo's Garden. When the war came, there were massive contracts to supply uniforms. Wonder of wonders, Stewart decided to do as Solomon had done and build a temple whose very grandeur testified to the good things God bestows on those He favors.

Mrs. Lincoln herself walked the aisles with him, her arm in his, and purchased $2,000 worth of linens and $1,500 worth of silver flatware, shawls, dresses, hats. A shining exemplar to all the ladies of America.

He had sent an invitation to General and Mrs. Grant to be his guests at the Metropolitan Hotel and to visit his store. He awaited their acceptance.

Stewart walked with purposeful step to the main entrance, on Broadway. A long journey from Belfast to this place, but mighty was the Lord who maketh straight the crooked ways. He would not abandon His servant.

The shades on the door were drawn. Stewart tapped with his cane. A face peeked out. It was Hobson's. The store's superintendent unlocked the door and stood back.

"You've secured every entrance, I see," Stewart said.

"Aye," Hobson said. "And I've a man hidden behind every window with orders to defend it at whatever cost."

Stewart knew that he had been hard on Hobson in the past, yelled and stormed at him, dressed him down in front of other employees, threatened his job, questioned his intelligence, left him quivering with indignation and humiliation. But this day he knew also that Hobson harbored no rancor against him. Whatever had passed between them, they were joined by history, tradition, the ancient awareness of a common foe. Hobson was a Londonderry man. That's why he had hired him in the first place. Thickheaded and stubborn, yes. But loyal as a hound and, if need be, every bit as ferocious.

"The hour has come, Hobson."

"Aye, Mr. Stewart, so it has."

The previous Saturday evening, in commemoration of the Boyne, the Loyal Order of the Orange Society of New York had held a dinner at the Metropolitan Hotel. An intimate affair. Only two dozen or so guests. Superintendent of Police John Kennedy had sat on Stewart's right, Hobson on his left.

They had discussed the successful introduction of the draft, which had begun that day. Stewart had mentioned the reports he had heard of agitators trying to whip up the crowd, shouting "Down with property!" and "Share the wealth!"

Kennedy had seemed unintimidated by such reports. He spoke admiringly of Robert Noonan. "He's the best of his kind," he said. "The fears about his abilities or loyalties seem to have been misplaced."

"Aye," said Hobson, "but we've yet to hear from the worst of his kind, and they be the bulk of it."

Thank God, Stewart had said to himself, for men like Hobson, who understood the nature of that brooding, uncivilizable race. It could not be thought otherwise. The evidence was there for all to see, from Scullabogue to the streets of New York, the same unchanging traits.

At the height of the Famine, fifteen years before, moved by the accounts he had read of the dreadful suffering in the Irish countryside, Stewart had chartered a vessel and sent it to Belfast loaded with foodstuffs. He had told his agent there that for the return voyage the agent was to arrange free passage for as many young men and women of good moral character as the ship could hold. Almost every single one was a Protestant, and the three who weren't had already announced their intention to convert.

At the end of the dinner, Hobson rose and proposed a toast. Though not a man given to public declamations, he spoke with passion, almost as if he sensed the disaster about to befall them. "In the days ahead," he said, "let us not forget the brave example of the thirteen apprentice boys of Londonderry who in closing the gates of the city against King James secured the sacred cause of liberty as well as their own immortality." The names rolled off his tongue without prompting or text: Henry Campsie, William Crookshanks, Robert Sherrard, Daniel Sherrard, Alexander Irwin, James Stewart, Robert Morrison, Alexander Cunningham, Samuel Hunt, James Spike, John Cunningham, William Cairns, and Samuel Harvey.

Standing in the vestibule of the store, there was little that needed to be said. Both Stewart and Hobson knew the threat they faced. Had known it all their lives.

Behind the inner door a crowd of frock-coated ushers strained to see what was going on. They seemed to Stewart an unimpressive band for conducting the resistance to a pike-carrying, bloodthirsty tribe of savages. But perhaps the apprentice boys hadn't looked much different when they slammed shut the doors of Londonderry.

Moved and shaken by the awareness that the God of Hosts had put them where the Reverend George Walker and the apprentice boys had once stood, right here, in the midst of New York, a city that bore the very name of the Great Apostate himself, James, Duke of York, the Traitor King, Stewart and Hobson embraced.

Stewart held Hobson by the shoulders and gently pushed him away. "I've always trusted you," he said.

For all the abuse he suffered, Hobson knew it was true. He alone had complete access to the books and managed not just the store but supervised the military contracts, a wondrous source of orders to fill. He sank to his knees and looked up into Stewart's face. Around the great bulbous nose the eyes were filled with a fine mist, and the gray pupils seemed to shade closer to blue.

"The day I hired you, Hobson, I knew you were a boy to be depended on!"

Hobson bowed his head. The cold tile of the floor pressed hard into his knees, and the ache turned into a sharp stab of agony. He tried to listen to the words of praise that Stewart was lavishing on him, but the pain drew all his concentration, and unable to bear it any longer, he tried to rise. His legs wouldn't unbend. In an instant of panic, he grabbed Stewart's arm.

Stewart pulled away and Hobson pitched forward on all fours. The ushers jockeyed with one another to see where he had disappeared. Hobson sensed that the stone gray had returned to Stewart's eyes. He pushed hard with his arms, forced one benumbed leg forward, and struggled to his feet.

"No surrender!" he shouted.

V

SQUIRT WAS TOO BUSY moving Mulcahey along to pay much attention to the press of people along the Bowery. Morning was not Black Jack's best time. Eliza and Squirt had spent half an hour rousing him and getting him out the door of the hotel. Mulcahey stopped. "Christ," he said, "they've cooler weather in the Sahara." He wiped his face with his sleeve and walked toward the entrance of a beer hall.

Squirt grabbed him by the tail of his coat. "No time, Jack," he said. "Mister Brownlee made it clear. You got four new minstrels in the show, and 'less you get 'em to dance when they's suppose' to dance and sing when they's suppose' to sing, he don't want you back. Told you that in front of everyone."

Mulcahey half recalled it from the night before: Brownlee's red face, loud voice, wagging head. *Don't make the has-been's mistake, Mulcahey. Don't imagine for a moment that you can't be replaced!* He felt Squirt's hands pushing him from behind. "All right, all right," he said. "Don't treat me like a mule."

"Don't act like one, I won't treat you like one," Squirt said.

They turned off Canal onto Broadway. At the corner of Broome, they stopped to let a caravan of beer wagons pass. A short distance down Broome, a saloon was already going full tilt. Someone was playing the piano. Mulcahey walked over and peered in the window.

"I thought so!" he said. "Nobody can play the piano like Mike Garvey. God, I haven't seen him in an age. Be insulted if he knew I was this close and didn't stop in to say hello."

Squirt took Mulcahey by the sleeve and pulled. Mulcahey staggered and almost fell into the gutter, but Squirt caught him and dragged him across the street. "Say hello later," Squirt said, "when you know you still got a job." Mulcahey followed Squirt the rest of the way without saying a word. They went into the alley beside the theatre, up the iron stairs. Mulcahey dropped into a chair. Squirt went to the basement, lit the stove, brewed coffee, and boiled a towel. He served the strong, black brew to Mulcahey. When Mulcahey was finished drinking, Squirt brought up the steaming hot towel and wrapped it around Mulcahey's face. Several times Squirt returned with freshly boiled towels and full cups of coffee, and by the time the rehearsal began, Mulcahey was on his feet, quick and alert and full of jokes. Good old Jack Jack.

Mr. Brownlee didn't show up until the rehearsal had been going on for over an hour. Mulcahey expected him to be pleased and happy. Instead, he appeared pale and shaken, barely taking any notice of the troupe. He told them that on the way downtown his coach had been stopped on Third Avenue by a gang of thugs who held a knife to his throat and plucked his watch and chain and pocketbook. "In the middle of Third Avenue!" he said incredulously. "In my own coach! In broad daylight!"

After a few minutes the manager came and whispered something in Brownlee's ear. Brownlee got up and left. The rehearsal

was called off. A stagehand told Mulcahey that a full-scale riot
had commenced in the northern part of the city. "The people is
on the warpath," he said. "Brownlee's a Republican and is afraid
of losing his scalp."

The box-office clerk came in and reported that there was a
crowd outside yelling for the minstrels. Seemed good-natured
enough, he said, but this day there was no telling what the likes
of them might be up to, and it was best if the troupe made an
appearance and sang a song or two to keep everybody happy.

Mulcahey led them to a small balcony that protruded over
the sidewalk. Stepping out, he was surprised to see that the traffic
on Broadway had almost completely disappeared. Down below,
gathered in a semicircle around the front of the theatre, was a
crowd of about two hundred, a mix of clerks and workingmen
who cheered when the minstrels appeared. Mulcahey launched the
group into "Old Dan Tucker" and followed it with "Who's Dat
Nigga Dar A-Peepin'?" He spoke the last verse:

> Now, ladies and gents, my song is sung
> And I'se hope you hab had some fun;
> If you want to keeps from sleepin'
> Come hear dis nigga here a-peepin'!

The crowd laughed and applauded. Mulcahey bowed and
told the minstrels to go inside. From below, a voice cried out,
"You got any niggers in there?"

"Who wants to know?" Mulcahey said.

One of the minstrels poked Mulcahey in the ribs. "Leave it
be, Jack," the actor said softly. "Let's go."

A boy in a blue errand coat stepped forward. "The people
want to know!"

Mulcahey strummed his banjo. "Well, boy, tell the people we
got coons galore. But none a good bath wouldn't bleach as white
as your ass!"

There was more laughter and applause. Mulcahey went inside. The box-office clerk met him on the stairs and said that

Brownlee had sent word to cancel the evening's performance. "All the theatres is closing," the clerk said. "The streetcars is stopped running, and there's mobs everywhere. Some is sayin' a Rebel fleet been spotted off Red Bank on its way here."

Mulcahey went to his dressing table. He took off his sweat-stained shirt, sponged himself with a wet cloth, and put on the fresh shirt Squirt had laid out. Squirt sat watching him.

"You'll have to stay here a bit," Mulcahey said.

"Figured that out for myself, Jack."

"All sorts of rumors floating about. Who's to know the truth? But seems certain there'll be trouble for your kind."

"Which kind is that?"

"It sure ain't redheads." Mulcahey reached over and rubbed Squirt's orange-colored nap. Done it a thousand times, before every performance, for good luck. Squirt never seemed to mind. Now he pulled back.

"Look, boy," Mulcahey said, "it's for your own good. Soon as I'm sure it's safe, I'll be back to fetch you. Meantime, you have the place to yourself. You can strut the boards like Edwin Booth himself. Just be sure to keep that woolly head out of sight."

Squirt walked away without another word and disappeared into the basement.

Mulcahey finished dressing and left the theatre intent on going directly to the New England Hotel and checking on Eliza. He hadn't gone more than a dozen yards when he met two players from the Adelphi. They were filled with stories of how the riot had started up at the Ninth District headquarters on Forty-sixth Street and was breaking out in other quarters of the city, almost simultaneously, and how the police were on the run, abandoning entire neighborhoods to the mobs. "Word is," one of them said, "it's all been planned ahead of time, and there's to be a coordinated attack this afternoon on Wall Street and the Sub-Treasury." He glanced nervously up Broadway. Without anyone suggesting it, the three of them went to Tom Kingsland's, which was packed with theatre people exchanging rumors and enjoying the prospect of a night's liberty.

It was nearly six o'clock when Mulcahey finally left. He had made several attempts, but each time a new patron would hurry in with some extraordinary report or rumor of what the mobs were up to. It wasn't until one of the other men from Brownlee's arrived with an eyewitness account of the Colored Orphan Asylum on Fifth Avenue being pillaged and burned that Mulcahey remembered his intention of checking on Eliza and reassuring her that Squirt was safely hidden away.

Canal Street had little of the traffic it usually did at that hour, but the Bowery was filled with people, many already drunk, some bedecked in frocks, hats, and dresses obviously plundered from fancy shops. More than a few were bleeding from cuts sustained entering those premises through broken windows. But the wounds did nothing to dampen the festive mood. Outside the hotel, a reveler wearing a ratty woolen shirt and a brand-new derby stopped Mulcahey and asked to borrow a handkerchief. Mulcahey handed it to the man, who wrapped it around a gruesome-looking gash on his arm and went off singing in a lighthearted way.

Eliza was sitting on the edge of the bed when Mulcahey entered their room.

"Jack," she said, "where's Squirt?"

"Safe as can be. Left him at Brownlee's just about an hour ago, when we was first informed there'd be no show tonight." He sat by her on the bed. "All the theatres is shut, my love, which means we shall have to find a way to amuse ourselves."

"There are mobs hunting and killing Negroes, and you left that boy *alone?*"

He took her hand, but she pulled it away and walked over to the door.

"How could you, Jack?"

"The boy is tucked in at Brownlee's for the night. Save for Squirt, it's empty. No one knows he's there but me."

"How do you know? How can you be sure a pack of them won't come and search him out?"

"Was leave him there or bring him here. Seemed sensible enough he'd be safer hid away than walking the streets. Squirt agreed." He walked over to her. "Let's not argue. There are better ways to spend our time."

"You could have stayed with him."

"To what good?"

"Forget it." She grabbed the doorknob. He seized her arm. "Leave go," she said.

"You can't go out."

"Remember, I'm a free colored person. You don't own me. I can go wherever I want, and I'm going to Squirt."

"Oh, for Christ's sake," Mulcahey said, "if it'll settle your mind, I'll go back and spend the night. Be more entertaining than listening to you. You know, Eliza, there are times you nag worse than a wife."

"I wouldn't know, Jack. I've never been one."

He put his hat on and left, slamming the door behind him. He stopped in at Tom Kingsland's on the way back, intending only a single drink, but it was approaching dark by the time he left. The shops and theatres along Broadway were shuttered and forlorn, but up ahead the St. Nicholas Hotel blazed with gaslight and activity. There was no sign of any disturbance. Turning into the alleyway beside Brownlee's, Mulcahey noticed light spilling through the open rear door. Beneath the stairs, figures huddled, their backs to him. They turned when they heard his footsteps. A body was stretched on the ground behind them, and though he couldn't make out any features, Mulcahey was sure it was Squirt.

A tall, square-shouldered figure came toward Mulcahey. He wore a waistcoat over a bricklayer's apron and approached cautiously, his right hand hidden behind his back.

"Lookin' for somethin' in particular?" he asked Mulcahey.

Mulcahey took a step back. "I've an appointment here."

"It's closed for the evenin'," the man said. His hand came from behind his back. He held a wooden bung mallet. Behind him, two others reached down, lifted the body from the ground, and brought it into the square of light framed by the rear door. "This who you come to see?" one of them asked.

Blood was pouring out of Squirt's nose. His eyes were open

but vacant and glazed. He showed no sign of recognizing Mulcahey.

"I'm here to see the manager," Mulcahey said.

"Try again another time," the man with the mallet said. He and the others carried Squirt to the fence that divided the alleyway and lifted him up.

"Look," Mulcahey said, "there's Metropolitans all over the place, and I saw troopers across the street. They're everywhere. Drop this boy and get outta here quick as you can!"

The man with the mallet sat astride the fence. "Sounds to me like you want this nigger for yourself," he said.

"Just don't want to see anyone get hurt unnecessarily."

The man leaned over and shoved the mallet into Mulcahey's face. "Then scat!"

The man and his two companions pulled Squirt over the fence. Mulcahey waited a minute before he followed. He caught up with them as they dragged Squirt feetfirst toward Crosby Street. "You know," he said, "it comes to me now that this boy is employed at Brownlee's. Bet they'd pay handsomely to get him back unharmed."

The trio halted. The man holding Squirt's right leg said, "What's your stake in this nigger?"

"My stake is in Brownlee's. I'm set to be hired there and want to make sure they offer the best show there is."

"Then do us all a service. Go practice your nigger-faced imitations somewhere you won't get in the way."

Crosby Street was far livelier than Broadway, and a parade gathered behind Squirt's body as it was dragged along. Mulcahey stayed close. At the corner of Spring, the man with the mallet was handed a clothes wire. He told the others to drop Squirt's legs and stand aside. He bent over Squirt, undid his belt, tore his trousers off, and tied the cord around his genitals. He put the rope over his shoulder and dragged Squirt forward. Squirt moaned loudly. People poured out of houses and saloons to see what the rumpus was about. Mulcahey lost sight of Squirt but pushed and shoved until he saw the orange kink of Squirt's head.

"The boy's had enough!" Mulcahey cried, but no one paid any attention. The parade stopped again. The crowd circled around Squirt. Mulcahey forced his way through. Squirt was directly at his feet. The boy seemed to have regained consciousness, his eyes flashing for an instant. He looked up and saw Mulcahey. A single word formed on his lips: *Jack.*

There was a gale of laughter and cheers as a boy opened his fly and urinated on Squirt's legs. A woman rushed out of the circle with a broken bottle and stabbed Squirt in the face. The crowd surged ahead and swept Mulcahey aside. Some men hauled Squirt over to a lamppost, and the next thing Mulcahey saw was Squirt's small, naked body rising above the heads of the crowd. It hung there limply, even when a burning torch was held beneath the feet.

Mulcahey turned and ran and didn't stop until he reached Tom Kingsland's. He ordered his own bottle and sat alone in a booth. He had it half drunk when he remembered the glow he had seen around Squirt's head several months before. Been so long ago. It had never happened like this before, the delay between the appearance of the light and death's arrival, never been more than a day or so. For a few moments it brought him comfort to think that what had happened to Squirt was foreordained and couldn't have been altered by anyone, no matter what they did, but when the image of Squirt's face lying in the street came back to him, the memory of his own name on Squirt's lips, Mulcahey started to cry, and the rest of the bottle couldn't make him stop.

VI

JIMMY DUNNE watched from the lobby of the New England Hotel as the dregs of the Five Points trickled down Bayard Street, the kind usually content to prey on one another, murdering for the sake of a drink or a bed or because the urge came upon them. One character in a wide Panama and a scarf about his neck

walked down the middle of the street, a hunting knife prominently displayed in his belt in the style of a frontiersman in a
Bowery melodrama. Seemed to Dunne the very image of Piker
Haggerty. But couldn't be, not unless the Tombs itself was giving
up its dead. Piker had slit his own throat the night before he was
scheduled to be hanged. He had confessed to killing a saloon-
keeper in the course of a robbery. "The fish insulted me," Piker
had told the court. "Wouldn't have stabbed him otherwise."

"You not only stabbed him, Mr. Haggerty," the judge said.
"You *slaughtered* him in the manner of a butcher in an abattoir."

"I teach a man a lesson, he learns it for sure," Piker replied.

Piker confessed to five other murders while he was awaiting
execution. Rumor had it that the priest who heard his last confession was never the same. A great throng of celebrants gathered
outside the Tombs in the hours before Piker was to be hanged,
and there was a near riot when they were brought the news that
he had taken his own life.

Piker's double spotted Dunne in the window of the hotel and
motioned for him to come out. Dunne hesitated a moment, then
went into the street.

"Piker?" Dunne said.

"None other." Piker lifted his hat, revealing the pointed skull
that had given him his nickname.

"I thought you was dead."

"That's what you was supposed to think!" Piker smiled. He
pulled open his scarf. Across his neck was a jagged, gruesome
scar. "Did it with a sharpened spoon. Doctor was paid afore to
pronounce me dead. Undertaker too. Whisked me out and
stitched me good as new. Been lying low since, but seems the time
has come to settle some accounts!" He retied his scarf.

Piker insisted that Dunne accompany him across the street
for a drink, and they reminisced about the old days, when the
Dead Rabbits held sway, and how John Morrissey had chosen
Piker as a boy suited for a career in politics. Dunne kept an eye
on the blade in Piker's belt, but death, though faked, seemed to
have softened Piker somewhat. He said that once he took care of

those who had betrayed him to the Metropolitans, he would leave New York, head west, and start over.

When Piker departed, Dunne went back to the hotel bar and drank sarsaparilla. The windows stayed shuttered all day. Only residents of the hotel were admitted, and they came and went trading the wildest sort of rumors, Confederate ships in the harbor, the water supply poisoned, the railroads seized and Rebel troops riding them down from Canada. Only thing certain was that the situation was out of hand. Didn't have to search for some remembered advice from Dandy Dan to know it was a day to stay low, don't risk a cracked head or a stray bullet from some panic-stricken militiaman. The condition of the streets confirmed the decision Dunne had already reached: A visit to Bedford's could wait until tomorrow.

Dunne went to sleep in his room in the afternoon and didn't awake until it was dark. In the distance was the sound of gunfire, like the pop of fireworks. The hot, lifeless air was laced with the smell of smoke. He heard people going to the roof, and went upstairs to join them. To the east, along Roosevelt Street, several buildings were in flames, and it seemed the entire block might go up. Farther in that direction, on Water Street, there were more fires. South, on the New Bowery, a single building was burning out of control. North, scattered around the city, were what looked like large fires. Dunne saw Eliza, Mulcahey's mistress, there, but she stood apart, in a corner, and went below without a word to anyone.

"Thank God there's no wind," the man next to Dunne said, "or the whole city would go up." A short while later there was thunder and lightning and a great downpour that dampened the fires and drove everyone downstairs.

The next morning, Dunne set out to scout Bedford's. There were no streetcars or coaches running, and the air was still thick with the scent of wet smoke, but except for the occasional rumble of what could only be artillery, he encountered few indications of any disturbance. It wasn't until he neared Sixth Avenue that he saw bands of toughs peering into shops, and a block away from

Bedford's he found the first signs of a riot, broken bottles and bricks strewn around, two bodies stretched out and motionless—it was hard to tell if they were dead or just unconscious. A longshoreman in a thick woolen shirt, his baling hook hanging from his belt, went from house to house, peering beneath the stoops. He almost knocked into Dunne. "We routed 'em!" he said with glee. "They ran outta here like a pack of hares!"

A dozen or so people converged on Dunne. At their head was a stout woman with a flushed face. She smelled of fish and held a gutting knife in her hand. "The booly dogs left with their tails between their legs," she said. "Some of 'em are hidin' hereabouts."

"Maybe you'd like to help us look for 'em," a boy said.

"Or maybe you'd like to make a donation to the cause," the longshoreman said.

Dunne unbuttoned his jacket and, making the pretense of looking for money, pulled a small revolver out of his pocket. "Seems I don't have a penny on me," he said. "Sorry, boys." He walked straight ahead. They let him pass. Turning the corner onto Bedford's block, Dunne slowed his step. At the west end, several hundred people were milling about. Dunne stopped at the bottom of Bedford's stoop. The small knot of people he had encountered at the east end had quickly grown to a hundred. Both ends of the street were now blocked. He hesitated a moment. Maybe he should keep walking, try to blend in.

The curtain in the window by the door parted. In an instant, Margaret opened the door. "Oh, come in, come in," she said. "I can't believe you're here. It's like the answer to a prayer!"

He went up the stairs. She grabbed him by the arm and pulled him in. Standing right in front of him was the cook, a frying pan in one hand, a meat cleaver in the other. "Stay right there," Miss Kerrigan said. "Don't come an inch farther."

"It's the gas man," Margaret said. "He's a friend."

"If he's a friend, let him go summon the police."

"O God, Jimmy," Margaret said, "it's been like a nightmare

since yesterday morning, when Mr. Bedford left for Long Branch. Seemed just a normal day till the grocer came with his delivery and told us to stay inside and lock the doors. Said there was a riot started uptown over the draft, but we hardly gave it a thought till Mr. Ward come back from visiting a picture gallery and his clothes is all ripped and there's blood on his face and he tells us he's lucky to be alive, that he was set upon by a gang of thugs who thought he was Horace Greeley. Poor man has been in the most fearful upset ever since, and then this morning these people begin showing up right outside the house cursing Horace Greeley and screaming for him to come out. The neighbors summoned the police, and a force of them appeared, and it seemed everything was going to be all right when suddenly there's a fearful noise, like wild Indians is on the loose, and the next thing the police is scattered and defeated and running for their lives."

"You've all got to get out of this house," Dunne said.

"I'm not movin'," the cook said.

"Where's Ward?"

"Upstairs, in his room," Margaret said.

"You two go out the back, over the fence to the neighbors. I'll bring the old man down and follow in a minute." Dunne eyed the door to the library. Would have the safe opened in no time. See if Bedford had taken it all to Long Branch or wherever he was gone to.

"It's not only Mr. Ward," Margaret said. "There's someone else. He's badly hurt." She led Dunne through the dining room and the pantry down into the cellar, to a storage room next to the kitchen. Lying on the floor was a man wrapped in a blanket, with a pillow beneath his head. Margaret knelt beside him and gently pulled back the blanket. The man wore the uniform of a Metropolitan. It was torn and tattered. His face was badly bruised, his nose crushed.

"We found him neath the stoop," Margaret said. "He'd been given a terrible beating."

"Bloody animals was searchin' for him like hungry dogs," the cook said.

"He's safe here," Dunne said. "Now go. I'll bring down the old man."

Margaret stood. In a slow, deliberate way she said, "If this man stays, so do I."

"Aye," the cook said. "We'll stay together and defend this house!"

"Oh, for Christ's sake," Dunne said, "help me move him."

The Metropolitan was a large man, and they had trouble lifting him. Dunne brought a chair from the kitchen, and they propped him up in it. Despite the battered condition of the face, Dunne was sure he recognized him. Dunne stood him up and threw him over his shoulder, staggering under the weight. Now he remembered: last April, during the trouble on the docks. Sergeant O'Donnell, the strutting leader of the Metropolitans, who promised him a taste of the locust stick if they ever met again.

"Get the door," he said to the cook.

"I'll go keep a watch on Mr. Ward," Margaret said, and ran out before anyone could say a word.

Dunne went to the back fence and dropped O'Donnell beside it.

"In the name of Jesus, be more gentle with him," the cook said.

"Climb over to the other side," Dunne said.

She stood for a moment, and looked at him. "Don't you touch a thing in that house, do you hear!"

He formed his hands into a stirrup. "I'll give you a boost," he said. She put her foot in his hands and went over with ease. He shouldered the policeman again and lifted him to the top of the fence. Some neighbors ran out and helped the cook lower him down.

Dunne dropped back to the ground, went through the kitchen and back upstairs. Outside the mob was chanting the name of Horace Greeley. He went straight into the library. The Federal Certified All-Security Safe was in the corner. He took the claw out of the inner pocket of his pants. He put his ear on the door and listened to the tumbler. Trick was to get within a few numbers, slip the claw in, and pry.

Margaret was calling from above, "Jimmy, are you there? Is that you, Jimmy?"

A brick crashed through the front window, followed by a barrage that tore the curtains from their rods. The whole house echoed with a rhythmic pounding and the front door tore from its hinges and crashed to the floor. Dunne gave the safe one last try. It didn't budge. He bolted up the stairs. She was peering over the banister, her hair hanging over her shoulders. She took him by the hand down the hall to a bedroom in the rear. A plump old white-haired man with a bandaged face lay on the bed. His eyes were open, but he seemed stunned and senseless.

"I can't get him to move," Margaret said.

Dunne heaved him over his shoulder. After O'Donnell, the old man seemed as light as a child. "How do we get to the roof?"

"There's a ladder beside my bedroom door."

They ran to the top floor. A ladder attached to the wall led up to a trapdoor in the ceiling. Dunne adjusted the load on his shoulder and took out his revolver. He handed it to her. "Go up and keep us covered. Anyone comes in the way, use it on them."

She climbed up, opened the trapdoor, and disappeared onto the roof. Her face peeked over the edge. "It's all clear," she said.

Dunne climbed up, holding tight to the old man. He reached the top, and Margaret helped pull the old man onto the roof. Dunne was about to climb out himself when someone grabbed his legs and pulled so hard he almost fell backward. He held on to the ladder and kicked. For an instant he was free. He heaved himself up, then his legs were snared again. He kicked again, but this time he couldn't break loose. He felt the sharp, hot pain of someone biting into his calf. Margaret grasped Dunne under the shoulders.

"Use the gun!" he yelled.

She took it from her waistband and held it in her hands, staring at it.

The biting stopped, but the weight around his legs was loosening his grip. "Use the Goddamn gun!"

She pointed it over his shoulder, down into the darkness, looked away, and pulled the trigger. It thundered in Dunne's ears. The drag on his legs disappeared. He climbed out and resettled the old man on his shoulder. They ran across to the roof of the next building. Dunne rested the old man against the chimney. Margaret handed him the gun. She was shaking.

"I'll be back in a minute," he said.

He ran to the ledge. Down below, the street was filled with people exiting the house with rugs, clothing, lamps, bedding, furniture. A fire had been lit, and they tossed on it whatever they didn't want: a piano, books, portraits of men in white wigs. Four men came out with the safe and pushed it down the stairs. They worked on it with a sledgehammer and crowbar, broke it open, and stood back. Dunne could see that it was empty.

VII

"YOU'VE NOTHIN' TO FEAR," Cassidy said. "The rich man and the nigger should be worried, not the likes of you."

Mike Manning mumbled something neither Cassidy nor McSweeney could hear.

"How's that, Mike?" Cassidy said.

Manning stood with his face by the corner of the shade that was drawn over the front window. He squinted from the slanted, unsparing sunlight. He walked back and sat beside Cassidy and McSweeney, his only customers, folded his arms, and set down his head. Had been like this for the whole time McSweeney and Cassidy were with him, well over an hour. They had banged on the window for ten minutes before he appeared.

"Maybe he's not there," McSweeney had said.

"And maybe the Pope's not in Rome," Cassidy had said, and kept knocking.

Eventually the shade had parted a crack. Seeing who it was, Manning had let them in but hardly spoke a word; he had poured them drinks and stayed by the window, his skinball face half hidden in the shade.

Cassidy patted Manning on the back. "If you'd like, we'll help you board the window up."

Manning raised his head. "Little good it'll do when the scum decides the time has come."

"You've got a right to your opinion," Cassidy said. "But I tell you, Mike, it'd go better if you opened the place. The police has given the order to close up? So what? Little chance of seeing a Metropolitan in this vicinity today! But the people will wonder why your door is shut. Person could put the wrong meaning on it."

"The people?" Manning said. "The people is nothin' but envious, jealous scum. Knock a man's head off, if he tries to raise it. A tribe of begrudgers. Bloody begrudgers. Forgive one of their own anything save success. That they never forgive."

"Words like that won't help," Cassidy said.

Manning shrugged. He went back to the window. Cassidy suggested to McSweeney they go someplace livelier where they might hear what was happening in the city, whether today would prove a worthy successor to yesterday. They said good-bye to Manning, who said nothing in return as he locked the door behind them. They walked up Catherine Street. On the north side of the street, the Brooks Brothers store was closed and shuttered. They stopped at Shugrue's Ale House, at the corner of Henry Street, which was packed with patrons enjoying the free drink. They were told that the battle was on again, especially in the Eighteenth Ward, on the East Side, and that on the West Side the crowds had taken control of the ferries. If the government was planning to send reinforcements, it would have to find another route.

McSweeney excused himself and went out back to the privy. His bowels were acting up again. A terrible ordeal. Started yesterday, when he awoke sweating, head throbbing with pain, mouth so dry it was hard to swallow. Felt as if he might foul the bedding and stood to go outside, but he knew instantly he would never make it that far, end up shitting his pants, so he squatted over the pail he kept in the corner for his night piss, felt the stream of liquid pour out, heard the dull, ugly sound when it hit the metal bottom.

"Jesus," his niece had said when he lit the stove to boil water, "do you want to kill us with the heat?

"My insides is acting up," he had said. "Tea is the only thing will quiet them."

"It's the drink that disturbs them in the first place. Mind what you put in one end, you won't be so bothered by what comes out the other."

His niece sat at the table doing her seamstress work. He drank his tea in silence. Lucky she was to have a tenant in the reeking basement of her Pitt Street hovel. Been there since he was let go from the shoe factory in '57, and if she showed him kindness in giving him a place to stay, he had never missed the rent, not once in all those years, doing whatever it took to see she was paid, cleaning up saloons, sweeping chimneys, running messages, and all she could do in gratitude was complain about a fire small enough to make a pot of tea. He returned to bed and spent the day.

The racket made by his niece's boys was what woke him up, their singing and shouting. They and their friends had come home loaded down with loot: scarves, belts, shoes, even a box full of dishes. His niece told them to get it all out of the house, said it was sinful thievery and she would have none of it under her roof. The boys laughed and started to pass around their spoils to the neighbors who gathered in the kitchen. The boys gave McSweeney some of the porter they had brought with them, and he drank it while listening to their accounts of the day's events.

The tea and rest and porter had restored him. Cassidy had stopped by in the morning to see how he was, gave his own extended and embellished account of what had occurred the day before, and suggested a visit to Mike Manning's.

Shugrue's was a far happier, convivial place, and when McSweeney finished his business in the privy and reentered, he found Cassidy entertaining a circle of longshoremen with his account of Monday's battles. "Mark my words," Cassidy said, "these days will never be forgotten by the people of New York. A hundred years hence our descendants will celebrate the time the Irish led the resistance to the draft!"

By the middle of the afternoon, Shugrue's was filled with reports of the renewed fighting on Second Avenue, the inhabitants of the Gas House District battling the Metropolitans and the Army. "Better to die here," someone said, "fightin' for your rights as an American, than down in Virginia, fightin' for the nigger." A sizable number of people left with the announced intent to join the battle, although Cassidy whispered to McSweeney that from the look of them he doubted they would make it past the next groggery.

Cassidy went on talking, and after a while McSweeney stopped listening. His mind went back to the same place and time it always did when the liquor took effect, the time of his youth in the rock-strewn field outside Spiddal, when he lay in the high grass, the time after the potatoes were dug and there were milk and butter and salt to eat them with, the time when the great rainless clouds swept in from the Atlantic, so close and so white that he imagined he could run up a hillside and jump on one, turn it around, and ride all the way to America, the time long ago before his teeth fell out and his bowels went sour, before the years of toil in that factory and the years on the docks, before the weeks of hell in the hold of a coffin ship, his wife dying at sea, before the eviction from the estate of Lord Kirwin and the blight descending on the fields like the judgment of God and the women keening over the rotted praties as though they were the carcasses of dead children.

Cassidy and McSweeney drank in Shugrue's all day and into the night, and it wasn't until word went around that three policemen in mufti had been caught trying to slip into the Brooks Brothers store that the place emptied out. Catherine Street was mobbed. McSweeney felt himself pulled along as the crowd moved south toward Cherry. Some boys ripped up cobblestones from the street and hurled them through the window of a plumber's shop. They rushed inside and came out with pipes and wrenches, which they handed around. Windows were suddenly shattered up and down the street, and the boys led a charge against Brooks Brothers, prying open the shutters and hammering down the front door.

McSweeney lost sight of Cassidy. He joined the rush into the store. People tore at one another to get inside. He trailed a washerwoman who used a long hatpin to make a path for herself. Once they got to a half-empty aisle, he set out on his own. He took two shirts, tied the sleeves together, and filled his makeshift sack with whatever he could grab. The numbers inside the store continued to increase. Fistfights broke out. The noise and confusion were deafening. McSweeney kept stumbling in the darkness as he made his way toward the door. The closer he got, the harder it became to make any progress against the tide of people coming in. By some streak of luck he found himself behind the woman with the hatpin and followed her out.

The pavement was festooned with bolts of cloth, plaids and stripes and solids rolled out like carpets, and a bazaar had sprung up beneath a streetlamp as the looters sought articles of clothing in their size or to their taste. McSweeney put his bundle beneath his arm and hurried up Cherry Street. He hadn't gone more than a few yards when the cry went up that the Metropolitans were coming. A moment later, a platoon of blue uniforms emerged from the shadows, and people scattered in every direction. McSweeney ran back to Catherine, and another squad of Metropolitans came charging down the street. Shots rang out. Stones and bottles crashed all around. A Metropolitan came straight at McSweeney, the locust stick poised to strike. McSweeney turned and ran. He dodged into a doorway and crept through a pile of broken chairs and tables. It wasn't until his eyes adjusted to the dark that he realized he was in what was left of Mike Manning's.

Beneath the roar of voices from outside, McSweeney thought

he heard laughter: a steady, continuous cackle from behind the bar. He crawled toward the sound on his hands and knees. In a small space between the sink and the wall was a body, arms and legs folded like a baby's in the womb.

"Be quiet!" McSweeney hissed. "The police is all over the place!"

The laughter grew louder. McSweeney crawled closer. Mike Manning stared out at him. Fat tears rolled out of the corners of his eyes and down his cheeks. "They've taken it all," he said. "Every shred. The dirty, rotten scum." He started to laugh again. When he finally stopped, it was quiet. The battle outside had ended. McSweeney put his bundle down and used it as a pillow. In an instant he was asleep.

McSweeney awoke at dawn. Mike Manning, still tucked in his hiding place, slept on peacefully. McSweeney took his bundle and slipped out the door. A line of Metropolitans stood guard around Brooks Brothers. McSweeney walked to South Street and followed it north. The docks were deserted. His niece's place was on Pitt between Broome and Grand, and he decided there would be less chance of encountering any trouble on Broome. He was right. Passed only one saloon that was open. His niece's boys and their cronies were standing outside. "Come on," they shouted, "we're goin' down to Roosevelt Street and hunt for niggers!"

He waved them off. He wanted to get home and open the bundle, see what he had. And why be bothered with this nigger stuff? Had little use for them, but always remembered how in his last year at the shoe factory, the owner had hired a nigger to sweep up under the workmen's lasts and they had all walked off their jobs, all except Dick Starkey, a former organizer for the Industrial Congress. The workmen surrounded Starkey when he left the factory, waved their fists and shouted, "Down with the niggers!" Starkey wasn't scared. He waited till they were quiet. "Boys," he said, "you got it half right. It's 'Down with Nigger-dom,' not 'Down with the niggers.' Down with the system that makes one man a serf and the other a slave, then sets them at each other's throat. Down with them who put us here to kill one another over who'll sweep the floor!" They hooted and booed, call Starkey a nigger-lover, but McSweeney stayed and talked to him, told him he liked what he'd heard. A week later the panic of '57 struck, and soon afterward, the factory closed and the men scattered. Never did find out what happened to Starkey, but his words stayed with McSweeney. Raving against the nigger was one thing, killing him another. Besides, if you took a long look at the state of the world, wasn't the nigger was the problem.

He turned onto Pitt and went up to the door of his niece's place. He noticed that despite the early hour, and the absence of crowds on the other streets, there was a large, loud gathering on the corner of Grand. He hesitated a moment, then decided to take a look. He reached Grand as a row of soldiers, having ordered the crowd to disperse, leveled its muskets and opened fire. A ball hit McSweeney in the right lung, shattered two ribs, and came to rest in his spine. He lay in shock. The last thing he saw before he lost consciousness was a priest in a purple stola kneeling over him. A thumb traced a cross on his forehead. Latin words.

McSweeney and the other dead lay there all morning. In the early afternoon, a woman came out of a tenement on Grand and threw some old sheets over them. At dusk, five policemen from the Essex Street precinct house came to have a look and reported back that after lying in the sun all day, the bodies were starting to give off a great bloody stench.

A little after ten that evening, the morgue wagon arrived with two attendants. As the men lifted the corner of a sheet, a single whiff was enough to indicate to them that these dead were beyond making any contribution to the surgical arts, their bodies employed to train young doctors in the use of scalpel and saw, their organs measured, weighed, dissected. The attendants rolled them in heavy canvas wraps. The bodies would be kept for twenty-four hours and, if unclaimed, shipped directly to potter's field, there to await being weighed in the scales of a more final judgment.

VIII

THE GUNBOAT *Unadilla* plowed north just as Noonan's carriage arrived at the entrance to Bellevue. Noonan could see the captain standing in the wheelhouse, in a chamber of yellow light, studying the darkness ahead, ignoring the waterfront that he had been ordered to patrol, the *Unadilla's* heavy guns a reminder of the measures the government was prepared to take to put down the insurrection. Noonan stayed in his carriage as the ship passed. He remembered reading somewhere how the ancient pagans believed that the souls of the dead were ferried across a river to the netherworld; the *Unadilla* seemed to him to have been lifted from that story, its black bulk moving off into the night, the light from the wheelhouse like a solitary eye, the pounding of its engines mournful and monotonous.

A detail of soldiers and police guarded the front of the building along Twenty-sixth Street. The soldiers snapped to attention as Noonan left his carriage. He went into Bellevue by the entrance nearest the river. Above the doorway, chiseled in the stone and limned with gilt, were the letters M O R G U E. Down a small flight of steps was a heavy iron door. He knocked. A center panel slid back, and two eyes looked out. An old man smoking a pipe opened the door and led Noonan into a brightly lit, low-ceilinged room of barren stone, nothing on the walls save a wooden board on which was painted a list entitled "THE RULES OF THE CITY MORGUE." He had barely had time to read the first ("THE CONSUMPTION OF SPIRITUOUS LIQUORS ON THESE PREMISES IS STRICTLY FORBIDDEN") when the attendant unlocked an inner door and ushered him through a room filled with a dozen open coffins into a smaller chamber in which there were eight marble slabs, corpses laid out identically on each, hands at their sides, loins covered with a white cloth. Gutta-percha tubes suspended from the ceiling dropped a steady trickle of water onto the corpses. The attendant saw Noonan looking at the corpses. "They got twenty-four hours to be identified and claimed. If not, we box 'em and ship 'em to potter's field," he said.

In front of them was a door marked WARDEN. The attendant rapped on it and pushed it open without waiting for an answer. A small man in a white smock sat at a desk eating a plateful of cold, greasy chicken. He stood with a startled look on his face and wiped his hands on his white apron. "We were expecting you, Colonel, but not quite so soon."

"Mr. Ahearn is very anxious to have his son's body. I told him I would see to it."

"Of course, but I must impress on you the abused condition of the body."

"I'm aware of that."

The warden took a key ring from his pocket. He escorted Noonan from his office into the corridor. "We have the Major in the latibulum. It's where we keep the most gruesome cases, out of public viewing, so there's no gawking by those morbid souls attracted by such spectacles. They come claiming only a wish to identify the dead, but their real intent is the most debased form of sensation. Unfortunately, our city has no shortage of these monsters."

They walked down a corridor paved with checkered brick. The warden unlocked an adjoining door and turned up the gas jet. The latibulum contained four stone slabs on which were laid bodies covered with wet sheets.

"I must remind you, Colonel," the Warden said, "we know it is the Major solely from the testimony of witnesses. The body itself is unrecognizable. Wasn't even a shred of clothing left on it."

"There were scars on his legs. He was badly wounded at Fredericksburg."

"Yes, I'm sure, but as I said, it's not that there is any question the remains are Major Ahearn's. It's simply that, well, the body's been as horribly mistreated as any I've ever seen." The warden took the corner of the sheet on the slab directly before them. He raised it slightly. "I feel compelled to repeat to you, sir, it is a hideous sight."

Noonan nodded. "Go ahead," he said.

On Sunday, July 12th, Noonan had left his quarters in Yorkville and traveled to the Provost Marshal's headquarters, on Leonard Street. The city seemed quiet. But the congregation of St. Andrew's, where he stopped to hear Mass, stayed its distance from him. A prosperous-looking man in a frock coat approached as he was leaving. "Why, Colonel Noonan," he said, "I'm surprised to see you here. I thought you'd be off celebrating with the rest of the Orangemen." He spit and walked away.

The reports waiting for Noonan at headquarters confirmed what he already knew. Much grumbling in the saloons and alehouses. Threats of retaliation. Talk of resistance. In the afternoon he met with the captains in charge of the district offices. Told them there would be no special guard detailed to any office on Monday. Defend one, you must defend them all. Better to proceed as they had on Saturday, as if this were the normal course of business, as necessary and unstoppable a part of the city's life as the delivery of the mail or the operation of the courts. Any resistance would be dealt with instance by instance, and the forces at their disposal would be brought to bear in a quick and concentrated matter. At dusk he picked up Major Ahearn at the City Hall Park barracks and drove to the Governors Island ferry. Nightfall brought no relief from the heat that oppressed the city.

Noonan awoke Monday certain there would be trouble but unsure how bad and widespread it would be. He took the first ferry back to the city and, Ahearn at his side, drove to the St. Nicholas Hotel. He waited for the telegrams to start arriving. He was surprised when the first reports reached him from Jenkins at the Ninth District office, where the initial draft on Saturday had gone off without a hitch. Noonan had presumed that whatever trouble there would be would arise in the lower wards, and even when it became clear something ominous and dangerous was occurring up on Third Avenue, he hesitated to commit the bulk of his small force lest he find that the real disturbance had begun downtown. He kept Ahearn at his side and sent a detachment of thirty men from the Invalid Corps to reinforce Jenkins.

By eleven o'clock, Noonan had received the police telegrams reporting that the Ninth District office was in flames, mobs in control of the entire area and the men from the Invalid Corps overwhelmed and routed, with several dead or missing. Ahearn asked permission to take the rest of the corps and attack the rioters. Noonan denied it. He dispatched Ahearn to Police Headquarters on Mulberry Street to coordinate possible use of the corps and other troops with the Metropolitans.

He went down the hallway to General Wool's office. Wool was dictating telegrams to every military commander in the vicinity of the city, requesting immediate assistance. He paused and stared out the window for some time before he spoke to Noonan. "Goddamn politicians and their draft. The situation is out of control. Mobs are attacking the rifle factory on Second Avenue, that so-called Armory. Owned by the Goddamn mayor and his son-in-law. The mayor was here a moment ago to inform me that there are at least a thousand rifles in the place primed and ready for use. Can you believe it? He waits till now to tell me. I should have him horsewhipped!"

"I'm leaving for Leonard Street to supervise the immediate removal and safeguarding of the records of the district offices," Noonan said. "I've sent Ahearn to Police Headquarters."

"Good," Wool said. "I've put General Sanford in command of all available forces. Consider any order from him to have my approval."

Noonan rode in a military coach to Leonard Street. In the late afternoon, he paid a visit to Police Headquarters. He set out on foot and passed the corner of Bleecker and Broadway moments after the Metropolitans had charged and dispersed a large crowd on its way downtown. Recognizing Noonan, the inspector in charge berated him for walking unescorted on the streets. "Superintendent Kennedy was set upon this morning near the Ninth

District office and beat near to death," he said. "They'd be more thorough with you. Wouldn't leave off till they made sure you was dead." Noonan thanked him for his advice but declined the escort the inspector offered him. He walked the rest of the way to Mulberry.

Police Headquarters was in turmoil. Wounded men lay in the corridors. Gun barrels poked through the upper windows. But it was far calmer in the Commissioners' Room on the second floor, where General Harvey Brown, the officer in charge of the federal forts in New York Harbor, stood with Commissioner Acton in front of a wall map of the city. Major Ahearn sat at a desk, writing down Brown's orders as he barked them out. Ahearn then passed them to a police officer, who carried them off to the telegrapher.

Brown showed Noonan on the map the various points where the police and troops were engaging the mob, and recounted the success they had had in evacuating several district offices. "It is a highly uncertain situation. Our forces are too thin to put an end to the matter, so we must keep the mobs contained and off balance until Washington sends us reinforcements."

"Have you talked to General Sanford?" Noonan asked.

"A home-grown McClellan," Brown said. "Be content to let the city be reduced to a smoking ruin as long as the state arsenals are safe and secure."

"Wool has put him in command."

"I've known old Wooly longer than I care to remember. A stuffed and blustery turkey-cock. Should have left the service after the Mexican War, but I doubt even he's dull enough to endorse Sanford's inane instructions."

"Tread lightly with Wool," Noonan said. "Bring him around by argument. He'll listen. What he won't abide is any challenge to his authority. His feathers are easily ruffled."

"Damn him and damn his feathers! There isn't time for such silliness!"

Noonan conferred with Acton and Brown for over an hour. He walked back to Leonard Street without incident and supervised the storing of the last load of records from the district offices. He was about to set out again for Police Headquarters when an officer arrived with orders for him to report immediately to General Wool's suite at the St. Nicholas. The General's carriage awaited Noonan in the street, along with a troop of cavalry.

The officer escorted Noonan up the stairs of the hotel. They heard Wool's voice as soon as they reached the top of the first landing, angry and impatient. The door to the suite was open. Inside, the main room was crammed with officers and civilians. The drapes were drawn, and a thick haze of tobacco smoke hung in the air. Wool sat in the corner, in a wing chair. Mayor Opdyke leaned on the chair, as if for support. General Brown stood in front of Wool, with Ahearn at his side.

"Insubordination is a court-martial offense!" Wool shouted.

"What kind of offense is it when the militia hides in its armories while mobs run amok?" Brown said. "Isn't cowardice a greater offense than disobedience?"

Wool pushed himself out of his chair. "Do I hear you right? Are you calling me a coward?"

"General Sanford's defense of the state armories is so ill advised that it exposes us all to such an accusation!"

"Impudence, Brown! It's in your tone and in your words!"

"Put the federal troops in this city under my command or a day from now it is the rabble and its leaders who will be sitting here debating how to divide their spoils."

Drops of perspiration beaded on Wool's nose and dropped onto his uniform. "Insubordination, Brown! I will not abide it!" He turned to an adjutant. "Where's Noonan? Goddamn him!"

The Mayor pointed at Noonan in the doorway. "He's right there!"

"Noonan, get in here," Wool said. "I'm relieving General Brown of his command. You're in charge of the federal forces in this city now."

"General Brown is a career officer," Noonan said. "His experience and knowledge are far ahead of mine. I think the plan he is already following has much to recommend it."

"Who asked you what you *think*, Colonel? You'll report to General Sanford immediately. Do whatever he says." Wool sank back in his chair. "Now get out of my sight, the lot of you!"

Brown and Ahearn were waiting for Noonan in the lobby. "The old fool," Brown said. "If Sanford has his way, the city will be lost."

"I've no intention of taking command. I meant what I said in there. You are the proper man. Let Wool calm down, then apologize. In the interim, go about your work. I won't interfere. When you've made your peace with Wool, keep doing the same."

"I haven't the stomach to ask his pardon."

"Have you the stomach to see New York reduced to a smoking ruin ruled by mobs?"

"Perhaps not," Brown said. He walked away without another word.

Ahearn leaned on his sword as if it were a walking stick. "They were talking about us before I arrived," he said. "I heard them as we came down the corridor. 'Can the Paddies be trusted to fight their own kind?' someone asked. 'Aye,' another said, 'remember how General Corcoran himself defied Governor Morgan and accepted a court-martial rather than march the Sixty-ninth in honor of the Prince of Wales.' "

"You've already proved yourself," Noonan said. "So have the Irish among the police and soldiers. We've nothing to apologize for. Wool knows that, as does Brown."

"The rioters are what the rat-noses will remember, not the soldiers or the police. They're disgracing us all. God pity the ones come within my sight!"

"Don't be led by your passions, Ahearn. Fight with your head. If there's any rule of warfare, it's that."

"They'll regret they ever started this," Ahearn said. He shook hands with Noonan and limped down the hallway, a tall, stocky figure with a red beard, very different from the boy Noonan had first met on the road to Bull Run, a thin, smooth face above a spotless white collar and a blue military tunic with green epaulets; the uniform had been the gift of Ahearn's father, who owned a small tavern in the lower part of Westchester. Ahearn had been expelled from the Jesuit college in Fordham after being found with a village girl in his room, an offense so serious that even the weeping and pleading of his father, and the offer of monetary atonement, could not win reinstatement.

That day on the road from Centerville, Noonan rode at the back of the column, trying to keep the regimental supplies and baggage in order as the vast military procession turned into a hopeless tangle of troops, artillery, wagons, coaches, cavalry, and sightseers. Noonan did his best. He roped the commissary wagons together and had the superfluous baggage stacked on the side of the road, but when the firing sounded in the distance, the soldiers scrambled out of line, running forward to get a taste of the battle before the victory was won. And then the momentum reversed itself. There was panic everywhere. Soldiers ran headlong, tossing aside coats, caps, blankets, canteens, muskets, whatever threatened to slow their flight. Noonan formed a group of stragglers into a platoon. Somewhere up ahead were Corcoran and the Sixty-ninth, and he was determined to reach them. Suddenly, out of the smoke, a company of late arrivals came marching across a wheat field in parade-ground formation. They pushed aside the retreating soldiers, and the young lieutenant at their head marched right up to Noonan. "We're here to reinforce the Sixty-ninth!" Ahearn announced in such a brash, confident tone that despite the chaos all around, Noonan burst out laughing.

Ahearn served with the Irish Brigade through the Peninsula Campaign and at Antietam. At Fredericksburg, his legs were riddled with encased shot and the surgeons wanted to cut them off at the knees, but he drew his pistol and threatened to shoot the one who tried to put a saw to him. They lay him in a corner to die, but he recovered and within a month was up walking. Two years of war washed away his boyishness.

Noonan went upstairs to the Provost Marshal's room. He sat in the darkness. His mind filled with the faces of the men from those early days of the war. The camp at Fort Schuyler. Eager recruits. Discharged. Captured. Wounded. Dead. General Corcoran himself had been taken prisoner at Bull Run. Held almost a year in various Rebel dungeons before he was exchanged. Corcoran was a skeleton when he returned, his eyes at once fearful and hard, a condemned man's look. The memory of the drummer boy's brains that had been splattered across his face, temporarily blinding him. Strong, iron-muscled soldiers clutching their stomachs and crying for their mothers. The knowledge of victory's brutal requirements.

Noonan slept all night at his desk. An orderly woke him. He read the first telegrams of the morning. This would be another bloody, dreadful day. Wool summoned him after breakfast. The old man looked exhausted. "Brown has apologized," he said. "I've returned him to his command." He spoke in a soft voice. "I had hoped to end my career in an honorable way. But the Yorkers have put that hope to the sword. A rotten city and a rotten brood of murdering thugs and traitors that inhabit it. I wish them all damnation to hell."

In the early afternoon, General Brown sent two officers with an urgent message summoning Noonan to Police Headquarters. They traveled in a closed coach. Brown was waiting for Noonan in the duty room. He drew Noonan in, closed the door, and sat behind his desk. "Ahearn is dead," he said. "This morning, without informing me, he went back to his lodgings on the East Side to gather his belongings. He went alone. I suppose he meant to demonstrate his contempt for the rioters. He was jumped from behind and set upon by a mob, some of whom were his neighbors. They treated him in a manner that would make a savage blush. A priest brought what was left to the morgue in a wheelbarrow. I am ordering an escort to travel with you at all times."

"We've too few men to waste like that," Noonan said.

"I thought that would be your response, so I ask that you please look at this." Brown opened the drawer of his desk, took out a thick brown envelope, and held it up. Scrawled across it in a crude, untutored hand was Noonan's name and a single line beneath: TRAITER TO YOUR KIND. YOUR NEXT. Brown opened the envelope so that Noonan could see the contents. Inside was a human ear.

"Mostly it's the Negroes been treated this way," the warden said as he lowered the sheet over Ahearn's remains.

On the way out, Noonan met Inspector John Murray of the Metropolitans. "There's something I think you should see," Murray said. He led Noonan into the room with the open coffins. A body, covered with a canvas tarp, lay in the corner. "We just brought this one in. Found him down on Second Avenue." He pulled back the tarp. A blond-headed corpse lay frozen in death, its arms reaching up as if to catch something.

Inspector Murray pointed at one of his hands. "Look at those nails, Colonel, all manicured and polished. And this shirt. Best quality. This was no ordinary workingman." Murray reached down and tugged on the man's trousers. Beneath the soiled outer pair was a clean white pair. "Ask me, we're looking at the body of a Confederate agitator. We've numerous reports they've been seen rousing the crowds. This seems to confirm the fact."

"Perhaps. Or maybe he's no more than a looter clad in some stolen clothes."

Noonan left the morgue and walked past his waiting carriage to the seawall beside the river. He smoked a cigarillo. The *Unadilla*, having circled Blackwells Island, steamed downriver, moving rapidly, the current now at its back. Noonan finished his smoke and threw the butt into the water amid a mess of sodden bits of paper, straw, and excrement. It bobbed upon the waves from the wake of the *Unadilla*, which slapped loudly against the seawall and, rebuked, slid back into the fast-moving waters and pulled the refuse along. Noonan said a prayer for Ahearn's soul. *Salve Regina, Mother of Mercy, our life, our sweetness, and our hope.*

JULY 17, 1863

Terrible is this place: It is the house of God, and the gate of heaven; and it shall be called the court of God.

—Introit from the Mass in dedication of a church

HIS IMAGE AND LIKENESS in the mirror: cassock draped on the emaciated frame like a coat on a scarecrow. *Terriculum.* A Latin word. Never been any good at that language. Enough to perform the sacred duties. But bits of what they had drilled into his head were still there. *Terriculum:* scarecrow.

Decades ago, still a young man, he wore a coat very much like the one on the scarecrow in the yard behind the convent of the sisters who ran St. Joseph's School; both were hand-me-downs from the students at the seminary. Could see that scarecrow from the sagging back stairs of the nuns' house. Stood with hat in hand, yellow straw, hard and brittle, worn every season, same hat as the scarecrow's and the slaves'. Suddenly, a face behind the tightly woven wire, black bonnet blending seamlessly into the darkness, her face floating in the air, disembodied, an image like one of those Roman women who appeared on holy cards, martyrs who went to some hideous death without fear or regret. Felicity, Perpetua, Agatha, Lucy.

"Yes, Mr. Hughes, what is it?"

"Mother Seton, I need your help." The brim of the hat turning endlessly in his hands, round and round like a wheel. Face burning as if from fever.

"Are you ill?"

"A priest, ma'am." Crimson-faced Paddy staring at the cracked and broken leather of his brogues. Afraid to look up at her, a convert already talked of as a saint. But her voice still all Yankee Protestant, sharp, clipped, superior.

"You wish to see a priest, is that it, Mr. Hughes?"

Tumble of words: desire to be a priest. Certainty of God's call.

The sharpness gone from her speech. Respect of the sisters for your habits of hard work. Edified by your devotion. "But, Mr. Hughes, a priest is more than just serious and sober. He must be a man of learning." Latin. A language in which he must think as well as pray.

Had a bit of the Latin in Ireland, Mother. Sure I could learn it. Already studying the books the sisters have passed on. Left unsaid: worn, tattered books, same as they used with the children of the slaves.

"It is not my place to recommend candidates for the priesthood. Talk to Father Dubois. He is a man of understanding and sympathy. He will do all he can to help."

Thought: an arrogant Frenchman. Impossible to talk to. Said: *Please, Mother, they will listen to you.*

"Very well, I will give it some thought. Perhaps there is some way I can help."

Wanted her to know how grateful. Face pressed to the screen like a little boy's. But the room is empty. She is gone. Scarecrow is the only witness, arms outstretched like Christ's on the Cross.

Ecce terriculum.

All gone. Mother Seton. Dubois. Years before. What was left? Only what the mirror beheld. An image to frighten birds, not men. No red hat. Half-built church. Sickness. Old age. Now this. Undone in a week what had taken a quarter of a century to build.

The Mayor, the Governor, the newspapers: You must tell the mob the Church is against them. Command them to stop.

As if they would listen. As if they would desist at one word from him.

What else did they expect him to say?

All my fault. *Mea maxima culpa.* Note of humility and contrition. Atonement for his arrogance, harshness, threats.

Nineteen years before, in 1844, they expected the same. Philadelphia in flames. Two Catholic churches burned. A Catholic library destroyed. A dozen people dead, scores wounded. A nativist delegation on its way to New York with a bloodstained flag. Fliers everywhere: *Rally to Be Held at City Hall Park! Papists and Foreigners Be Warned!*

Went to see Mayor Morris. James Harper, the Mayor-elect, also there. Twin smirks. Can't hide their glee that the chief Paddy has come to beg their protection. Don't even offer a chair.

"Are you afraid that some of your churches will be burned, Reverend Hughes?" the Mayor asks. A serpent's solicitude.

"No, I'm afraid some of *yours* will be."

They rise together out of their chairs.

"Is that a threat?" asks Mayor-elect Harper.

Only a fact: If you countenance a nativist demonstration in this city, the consequences belong to you, and if a single Catholic church is burned, *New York will become a second Moscow.*

They turn in unison to the window as though the conflagration might already be under way. Park Row can be seen through swaying, leafy branches. Bustling, not burning.

Mayor-elect Harper: "I have never encountered such villainy in a clergyman! It is intolerable!"

Chief Paddy: "Sir, if I wished a lesson in villainy, I should think of no better teacher than a publisher like yourself who is so ashamed of printing the vile and lurid lies of the likes of Maria Monk that he sets up a separate publishing house to spew such anti-Catholic filth. Good day, gentlemen. You are forewarned."

Words burned in their brains. The prophecy of Dagger John: *New York will become a second Moscow.*

Now it was.

Rumble of artillery, pitched battles in the streets, murders and mutilations, lynchings, looting, mass drunkenness, arson, larceny. Cries of newsboys: *Massacre on Second Avenue! Terrible Battle in the Fourteenth Ward!* "The Arch-Hypocrite himself," Mr. Horace Greeley proclaims, "let him tell his people to stop!"

Just like that: Jesus telling the waves to be still. Did Greeley and the others know the lie of it? Was that what they wanted to see? For him to say "Stop" and for it to continue? A public humiliation. Or did they really believe that the mobs would halt in their tracks and go to their homes at a word from Dagger John, the High Priest of Paddydom?

Dictated a statement to Corrigan. *In spite of Mr. Greeley's assault upon the Irish, in the present disturbed condition of the city, I will appeal not only to them, but to all persons who love God and revere the holy Catholic religion which they profess, to respect the laws,* etc.

Published it. Not enough, they said. Some of his own priests come to him. Walk the streets, they pleaded. Make an appearance.

In a few moments he would step out onto the balcony. Could hear the voices below. Needed help in order to walk. Would have to sit as he spoke.

Not enough, they would say. Waited till Friday, when the army had the situation in hand.

Damn them all. What did they know?

The day Hughes had met with Morris and Harper, he'd walked out of City Hall down Park Row, barely aware of where he was headed. It was midday, and the crowds grew thicker as he approached Chatham Square and the Bowery, the saloons more numerous. A block away, the Five Points was as filled with revelers as it would be at midnight. Whores beckoned from doorways. Street musicians and beggars competed for the sidewalk. In the middle of the block, two muscular Negroes carried on a pugilistic demonstration. A semicircle of spectators egged them on, tossing pennies as the bigger of the two beat the other to his knees.

Farther along Chatham Street, at the corner of Roosevelt, a horde of dirty, half-naked children gamboled around a trench that overflowed with garbage. Old men sat on rickety wooden steps and talked with one another in Irish. Women shouted out of windows at the children in the street. Hughes crossed to the other side. A horse lay dead, its head on the curb. Two small children squatted beside it. Little more than infants, dressed only in sacks, they clapped with delight as two older boys stuck crumpled newspapers under the horse's tail and mane, and set them on fire. None of them saw Hughes as he crossed the street. He grabbed the biggest boy by the collar and spun him around. The threadbare collar ripped loose, and the boy fell backward on the sidewalk. The other boy ran away, and the infants began to cry.

Hughes straddled the boy. "What's your name?"

The boy tried to stand. Hughes drove a foot into his chest. "You aren't a savage!" he shouted. "Your parents gave you a name!"

"Toss, me name is Toss Brady."

Hughes took away his foot and helped him up. "Get out of my sight, Thomas Brady, and don't let me see you near this animal again." The boy took the wailing infants by their hands and hurried away. The air was filled with the acrid smell of the horse's burned hair.

A second Moscow.

He had measured the reaction in the faces of Morris and Harper to those words. Their rat's noses twitched with fear. They believed he could give the order and it would be done, the Paddies emptying from shebeens and cellars to do his bidding. But these streets contained the truth of the diocese of New York. A mass of people, few of whom knew him by sight, the most wretched of them in loose contact with the Church and the handful of priests he had to tend them. He would never apologize for what their oppressors had made them into. He must goad, push, guide them all. He knew what they were now, destitute, disorganized, and without discipline; but they were flesh of his flesh and he knew what they could become, and he would show the way, clear their path, so that they might be exemplars of the Holy Catholic and Apostolic Church, the moral superiors of their Yankee tormentors, the light that would lead America to the True Faith. Let the priests tend them in their particularity, consoling the broken and the doomed, baptizing, forgiving, burying. He would tend them as a flock, thousands upon thousands, use their strength of numbers to see to it that their hunger and exile, their suffering and sacrifices, their mourning and weeping in this vale of tears, weren't without consequence in this life as well as the life to come.

*

"Your Grace, it's time," Corrigan said.

His sister crossed the room, stood beside them, picked the lint off his sleeve, swept his shoulders with her other hand. Saw her in the same mirror as himself. Both in black, birds of a feather, more crows than scarecrows.

Took Corrigan's arm. Flabby, without muscle.

A few days before, Father Kavanaugh had stood in this very spot, tears in his eyes. Went on about the treatment of the Negroes. "What is being visited upon these people is shameful beyond words."

Sent him away. The cheek of him. What other priest had ever worked beside them in the fields, shared the same cup of water? Or written a poem as he had, in their defense, a poem that was published years ago in a newspaper in a small town above the Maryland border called Gettysburg?

> Wipe from thy code, Columbia, wipe the stain;
> Be free as the air, but yet be kind as free,
> And chase foul bondage from thy southern plain;
> Oh, let Afric's son feel what it is—to be.

Youthful dreams. Let freedom be. In America, things were taken, not bestowed. Shove your way in, shoulder against the door. The Negro had his friends. Let them help him. He would speak for his own people. Before the children of Africa were conquered and enslaved, hadn't the Saxons plundered the kingdom of Ireland? And though slavery rescued the African from his pagan superstitions and gave him the light of Christianity, hadn't Ireland's conquerors tried to extinguish the Faith, to uproot the foundations of northern Europe's oldest Catholic realm? And though the Yankees wept and ranted over the sin of slavery, what tears had they shed over Ireland's oppression, the exodus and mass starvation of her children, the destitute women and children left to die in ditches or to beg some small sustenance? What abolitionist had offered them a single crust of bread? What true friend of humanity had extended them a hand? Or had anything in his heart for them save derision, ridicule, disdain?

Let nobody lecture him about the Negro or the war.

What bishop had done more than he?

He had preached the war and the draft from the pulpit: "For my own part, if I had a voice in the councils of the nation, I would say, 'Let volunteers continue and the draft be made!' This is not cruelty; this is mercy; this is humanity—anything that will put an end to this spilling of human blood across the whole surface of the country."

Gone to Europe at the behest of Seward and Lincoln, to press the country's cause with the French Emperor and the Pope. "You speak their language," Seward said.

In Paris, the Emperor hardly said a word. Sipped brandy and watched the Empress as she leaned toward Hughes and pointed to a small scar next to her eye, a tiny crease in her milk-white skin. "Here, Bishop Hughes, here is a souvenir of the Republicans, something I have to remember them by, a sliver of iron from one of their bombs. They came close, but they forgot that it is not the gendarmerie who protects the Emperor, but God!"

"The Republicans in American don't throw bombs," Hughes said. "Our President upholds order, he does not subvert it."

"Not throw bombs! Mr. Lincoln not throw bombs!" The Empress's cheeks turned red. "Why, I wonder what Monsieur Davis and the good people of Virginia would think of your assertion! And tell me, Your Grace, is it a love of order that brings Mr. Lincoln to support Juárez and his Republicans in Mexico? They butcher priests and nuns, expropriate private property, and run out on the country's debts, but I suppose from your point of view, Juárez has the interests of the Church at heart."

In Rome, Cardinal Antonelli swiveled slightly in his chair and turned his profile toward Hughes. The image of Mother Seton jumped into his head, a memory from long ago, her severe profile behind a screen, image of a virgin martyr. Antonelli's face was the other side of the coin. Imperial nose and forehead, the smooth features of a Roman emperor: a maker of martyrs.

The Cardinal folded his hands together in front of his face, the index fingers joined together and pointed upward. He leaned back in his chair and glanced toward the dark and distant recesses of the ceiling. "Pardon me, but I am perhaps a little confused," he said. He unfolded his hands and held out his left palm. "On the one hand, you are a true supporter of the cause of the Holy See, which no one can doubt. But on the other, you travel on the business of President Lincoln, a friend to the Holy Father's enemies, and you take it upon yourself to visit the Emperor, to insult both him and his wife, and in so doing to endanger the very future of the Church." Antonelli moved each hand up and down as if it were part of a scale unable to come into balance. "Where is the true weight of one's loyalty?"

"I insulted no one. I conveyed to the Emperor the President's wish that we avoid war between our two countries. And who dares accuse me of disloyalty to the Holy Father?"

A cold smile from the Cardinal. The face of a gombeen-man, a scheming seminarian who had mastered the papal books and, without being ordained, fixed it so that the Pope couldn't buy a pair of socks without his approval.

"My friend, you are loved and respected in this city, but, well, because of the great distance between Rome and America, a certain confusion has been allowed to arise, and essential matters have become obscured and blurred. It is regrettable but not incurable, I assure you. The time is coming when the Holy Father will dispel all doubt, when he will clarify his authority for the educated and uneducated alike, and there shall be no trying to disguise error as truth, and disloyalty will be expunged."

"Who is it who says I am disloyal? Give me one name!"

"Please, Your Grace, we must go. We have placed a chair on the balcony." Corrigan again. Pudgy folds of the neck protruding around the starched and immaculate collar, a nun's labor.

Outside, a Roman sun, pitiless. Across the way, houses shuttered against the rioters, against the sun, perhaps against him. He sat, felt the humiliation of it as soon as he did. Gripped the balustrade, tried to pull himself up. No strength in his arms. This would have to do.

Cheering from below.

"They call you rioters, but I can't see a rioter's face among you . . ."

Christ, it was all a jumble, words, ideas, past, present. "If I could have met you anywhere, I should have gone. But I could not go. My limbs are weaker than my lungs . . ."

The pulpit in the cathedral would be as high as this balcony. A marble perch. It would face a great rose window in the western façade, a circle of light, the eye of God, the unblinking Judge.

O Christ, what sin was so great that You should turn away Your face and abandon Your servant like this?

JULY 30, 1863

How we joyed when we met, and griev'd to part,
How we sighed when night came on;
How I longed for thee in my dreaming heart,
Till the first fair coming of the dawn.

—Stephen Collins Foster,
"Our Bright Summer Days Are Gone"

I

Margaret woke to a black sky, suffocating heat. In the east, over Brooklyn, a low streak of red signaled day. There was no wind. From below came the noise of wagons and drays, the city's day already begun before the first light. Across the rooftop, other bodies began to stir, people rising up and becoming silhouettes against the dawn. She gathered up her bedding and went downstairs to Mrs. O'Sullivan's, where she had been staying since the destruction of the Bedford house. The air was thick and stale and feverish. Mrs. O'Sullivan stirred but did not wake. Margaret grabbed a pitcher and went down into the yard. She pumped it full of water, took it back upstairs, and sponged herself. Her hair had come undone. Pieces of hair hung down her back. She would have to brush it and braid it again. She sat at the table by the stove.

She had spent that night after he rescued them in his room. He lived in a hotel. She wanted him to ask her there, and he did. Next day he took her to Mrs. O'Sullivan's. Said he would call on her in the next few days. Two weeks had gone by. She had heard nothing. Never believed that story about him being with the gas company, at least not after that first day he had come to see the pipes. Miss Kerrigan was right. He was up to something. Maybe he had come to spy on Mr. Bedford, who had been acting most peculiar in recent times. Maybe he was intent on the shenanigans Miss Kerrigan accused him of, on burglary, but no common thief would have rescued them the way he had. Whatever he was, she didn't care anymore. Just wanted to see him again.

She thought she was pregnant. Felt it from the first minute.

Wouldn't be absolutely sure for another week. But her flow was already late. Hadn't worried about it at first. Told herself he would come back, they would get married, no one would ever know. Mrs. O'Sullivan saw the change in her mood. "Look, dearie," she said, "if you're puttin' any faith in ever seein' that one again, you're invitin' a terrible heartbreak."

Margaret lay her head against the wall. In the corner of the ceiling, almost directly above, a spider worked intently on her web. Her front legs flashed in quick, certain motions. She moved back and forth, up and down, spinning the silken thread out of her stomach, weaving a crisscross pattern of self-created wire. She worked furiously, laying wire atop of wire, until Margaret realized it wasn't just a web that she was constructing but a cocoon, a nest in which to hatch her eggs.

Margaret dressed quickly. She was working as a day servant now. Easiest work to get since the riot, and so many employers not wanting to have the Irish living under the same roof. Still, they couldn't do without the help. Support herself till she became too big to work. What then? How desperate would she become? What help was there? Out of her stomach, life. But, Mother of Mercy, where was the web to sustain it? She went downstairs. At six-thirty, Dolan would slow his cart at the corner but not stop, and she and Maureen and Sheila would jump on for the trip uptown, save three cents each over what the horsecars charged. Be at work at seven and begin the cleaning right away.

They were there on time but Dolan was late. Maureen and Sheila chatted away. She didn't hear what they were saying. She stared at the corner, praying for Dolan to appear. Can't afford to lose this job. And then, instead of seeing Dolan, she saw *him* walking up the street, slowly, looking about suspiciously, hands in his pockets, so serious and, God, so handsome.

II

CATHERINE STREET SHOWED LITTLE TRACE of the riot. Brooks Brothers' windows were nailed shut, pine boards hammered in place of the iron shutters the mob had ripped away. The glass in Mike Manning's front window and the door had been replaced. A newly painted sign hung above: GERAGHTY'S SALOON. Dunne looked in. Nobody to be seen. Geraghty apparently didn't have his predecessor's ambition that this be the first place opened on the waterfront each morning, whiskey-baited pot laid on the sea bottom to snare those denizens who couldn't crawl from bed to work without a glass or two.

Dunne stood in the gloom of the doorway. A few laborers appeared out of the morning mist and hurried toward the docks. They glanced around warily. Dunne stepped out and crossed the street. He turned and looked behind. Never knew, not after what had transpired during the riot and its aftermath. The booly dogs were still trying to catch the scent of those who had played a part or stashed some loot. Notices of reward posted everywhere. Troops still pulling people in. He hurried past Brooks Brothers, north on Cherry.

The sun began to burn away the mist. More people were about. Draymen hauled the day's first load from the docks. Newsboys trotted toward the ferry-houses, hands and clothing smeared black from the freshly printed papers beneath their arms. Dunne looked behind again. Getting to be a habit. He had checked out of the New England the day after Mulcahey had run amok and smashed up the hotel bar, demanding to know where his girl, Eliza, had gone. She had left the hotel the morning the news of Squirt's murder was brought by a stagehand from Brownlee's. The stagehand said he was taking up a collection to give the colored boy a Christian burial, and when Eliza asked if he had seen Jack, he said, *Sure, Jack is safe and sound, holed up in a saloon on Grand.* She went out the door, pushed aside those who tried to stop her, without a word to anyone. But when Mulcahey showed up, he couldn't be convinced she hadn't told someone where she was headed. The Metropolitans had to be called in to subdue him. They clubbed him to the ground and hauled him away. Weren't taking any chances these days. A few of them stayed behind and poked around the lobby, stopping people, asking questions.

Dunne left the next morning. Moved into a sailor's hotel on Pike Street, a rickety, flea-ridden whore's paradise, but it had already been raided and searched by troopers and seemed safe for now. Dunne knew he should be planning another job, a quick and easy piece, but he hadn't been able to bring his mind to it.

A squad of Metropolitans passed down Scammel Street on their way to the waterfront. Never saw a booly dog alone these days. Didn't go anywhere unless as a pack. Dunne slowed his step until they went past. He had traveled this same route every day, promising himself if he didn't see her this time, he would never come back. Same broken promise every day. Margaret had agreed to come back to his room that day he got them safely out of Bedford's. Left the old man and the Metropolitan with the neighbors. The cook looked at Margaret and him with the same mixture of contempt and suspicion. Didn't seem impressed with the rescue Dunne had just performed. "What was it brought a gasman back to our door at such a time?" she asked. Dunne didn't answer. Margaret didn't seem to care. When they were alone, he held her so tight he surprised himself, almost as if he were clinging, and later, when they lay down on the bed in his room, she cried for a moment, and he kissed her as gently as he could, and she took the pins from her hair and it spread across the pillow like a shawl. They made love once, the first time for her. She rose and washed herself from the basin on the bureau, and they made love again. She fell asleep. He listened to the whisper of her breathing and lay awake till dawn.

He was glad she left the next day without a fuss. He walked

her to the bottom of Jackson Street, said good-bye, some words about seeing her again, but was happy to be free once more. Had to get back into business now that Capshaw's scheme was bust. She went up the street, stepped into an alleyway, and disappeared from sight. But she hadn't gone away. She was still there, in his head, all the time. He hadn't found a way to get her out.

He knew where she was living. He could go and knock. But he couldn't. How to put a kind face on a trade like his? He was sure that the truth would drive her away, unless he didn't try to explain, said nothing save that he had left his job and planned to join the Army, and if she were willing, they could get hitched, take the bounty he got for signing up and add it to what he already had. Be enough to see her through. Once the war was over, they could start fresh.

He was thinking all these things, same as a hundred times before, when he came around the corner of Jackson and saw her standing with the other girls. He was startled. He thought at first that she was waiting for him. But in an instant the cartman arrived. The two other girls got on. She stood on the pavement watching him.

"Margaret, for Chrissake, get on!" the cartman yelled.

Dunne tried to force himself to approach her at a slow, deliberate pace, to remember all the words he planned to say.

"Hello, Jimmy," she said.

He had his hands in his pockets, eyes on the gray paving stones. He felt the girls in the cart staring down at him. "I've things I must talk to you about," he said.

"Leave or stay, Margaret," the cartman said. "But tell me which it is."

"I can't talk now," she said. She took hold of the rail. Dunne took her other hand and helped her up. She stood in the back of the cart, the green eyes above him now, looking down. He tried to read what was in them but couldn't.

"I'll be here when you get back," he said.

"It'll be late. After eight."

The cartman cracked his whip. The cart began to roll. Margaret sat. Dunne walked beside the cart. "No matter. I'll be here. I've got plans for us."

The cart gathered speed and made a fast turn onto Grand. Just before it went around the corner, she looked up and waved. A happy wave, Dunne thought.

He stood where he was. He would wait. However long. He had plans. Whatever it took.

JANUARY 16, 1864

The Towers of Manhattan

The dust is the dust, and forever
Receiveth its own;
But the dreams of a man or a people
Forever survive;
These builders, their crimes and their curses,
Their greed and their sordid endeavor,
Lie in the dust,
Dead in the dust,
But the vision, the dream, and the glory
Remain.

—Don Marquis

I

MORRISON FOSTER couldn't sleep. He had been listening to Jane's crying all day. Still was. It came through the door of the most expensive hotel in New York, a pine door shaved and shaped in Albany by a machine that could cut a door as thick or thin as was desired. The St. Nicholas had ordered its doors cut thin. The city's first hotel to cost over a million dollars, but the owners had skimped on details such as doors and windows. Morrison was more annoyed by the thought of such disregard for the principles of solid construction than by Jane's crying. She had been sobbing for days now. He was almost used to it. She started as soon as he came and gave her the news. *Stephen is dead.* She let out a cry and fell into his arms. Might have hurt herself badly if he hadn't been there to catch her. And he had spared her the full tragedy. He didn't have to. He could have been blunt, told her what else he had read in the personal and confidential message expressed to his office by the New York undertaker. *Died by his own hand.* But that wasn't Morrison's way. Never had been.

From the beginning Morrison had been responsible, serious, considerate of the feelings of others. They made the mess, he cleaned it up: Papa's drinking, Momma's moods, Stephen's irresponsible, flighty, self-indulgent ways. William, a cousin whom Papa and Momma had raised as though he were their son, had left home in 1826, the year Stephen was born. William was often a help, but from a distance. It was Morrison who went to the door when the landlady was looking for the rent, when the grocer came with his unpaid bill, the tavern keeper, the shoemaker, the teacher looking for their sister, the minister, the immigrant with

the ugly grin who said Stephen owed him for the performance of
an unspeakable act, said it loudly, right there on the steps where
the neighbors could hear.

Morrison threw off the covers. He took his robe off the chair,
stuck one arm into the air, then the other, and slid the sleeves
over them. He tied the robe around his middle, hugged himself.
It was freezing. The hotel provided no heat after midnight; more
skimping. He walked away from the thin door and the sound of
Jane's sobbing. The wind struck the window hard, rattling pane
and sash. He pulled aside the drape. Below, on Broadway, the
lampposts created small pools of light. A drunken man helped a
woman over a heap of ash-blanketed snow. She fell, and he fell
on top of her. Their high, happy laughter echoed in the street.
They got up and struggled against the wind across the trafficless
avenue, Broadway at 4:00 A.M., quiet and vacant at last.

Jane's sobbing sounded more inconsolable than ever. At this
point she is weeping for herself, Morrison thought. He had wept
at the news of Stephen's death, wept for almost an hour over
Stephen's life, the unfulfilled promise, the sins, the shortcomings.
But long ago, as a child, he had studied the weeping of the be-
reaved, and it seemed to him that though a portion of their tears
were for the deceased, most were caused by the sting of being
reminded of a common oblivion, the emptiness and futility of
resisting it, the certainty that all would be swallowed in the same
conclusion, everything lost and gone forever. Though faith taught
that this end was only another beginning, even faith, Morrison
observed, trembled in the presence of death, wept, cowered, at
least in those first glaring moments when the truth of human fra-
gility was too fresh to be explained or softened by words, no
matter how sacred their source.

Would Jane weep harder if she knew how Stephen died?
Morrison wondered. He spared her the truth, as he had spared
everyone. He took the undertaker's message and burned it. He
went to her home, wrapped Jane's child in his arms, rocked her,
reassured her, arranged for her lodging and care while they were
away in New York. The child was distraught over her mother's

weeping. She had no memory of her father, and Morrison didn't mention Stephen's name to her. He held her small hand, patted it. "Momma has lost a dear friend. That is why she weeps. She grieves over a friend's death. There, there, child."

Morrison arranged all the details of their journey, or at least saw to it that William Millar, his secretary, did. As manager of the Juniata Iron Works and as brother of the late William Foster, vice president of the Pennsylvania Railroad, Morrison was extended every possible courtesy by the lines they traveled to New York. They left Pittsburgh in the morning, via a mail train, in a closed compartment of their own. Lunch was brought to them. Jane ate nothing. She sobbed incessantly. Morrison enjoyed his food, but the closer they drew to their destination, the more he worried that a crowd of New York journalists lay in wait for them at the terminal in Jersey City. One or two might be bribed into silence, but as a pack the smell of scandal made them implacable. There was no one waiting for them on the platform except the clerk from the railroad's New York office, who saw them to the ferry and said that a coach would meet them on the other side and take them to the St. Nicholas, where arrangements had already been made. All went smoothly. They arrived on the 15th, just after dark. The maître d'hôtel met them at the desk and escorted them directly to the dining room. The hotel table was as grand as ever. Five courses were on the evening's card, beginning with shrimp-and-asparagus soup. They had barely begun to sip it when Jane had another fit of crying. The maître d'hôtel was most understanding. "The war has caused such tears to be shed far and wide," he said. Morrison put a gold coin in the man's hand and nodded, as though the war were the reason Jane was dressed in widow's weeds.

They ate no breakfast the next morning. They left the hotel and entered a waiting coach that took them to the undertaker's. Morrison was glad for the harshness of the weather, the drab skies and ice-tipped winds that had the whole city traveling with collars up, mufflers wrapped tightly about the face, hats down over the eyes. There was no one at the entrance to the undertaker's. They hurried out of the coach and inside. Winterbottom, the undertaker, was waiting for them in the vestibule. He shook Morrison's hand, bowed to Jane, and escorted them into a dignified oak-paneled room with large chairs upholstered in green leather. It seemed to Morrison that it might as well have been a banker's office as an undertaker's. An attendant took their coats. Jane sat and cried into her handkerchief. The attendant returned with a silver tray on which were two cups of hot cocoa and a bowl of whipped cream. Morrison was about to take a cup when Winterbottom motioned for him to follow. They went out a side door, down a stone corridor, into a small cold antechamber.

Winterbottom rubbed his hands. "Mr. Foster," he said, "this is a most delicate matter."

"You have handled it well," Foster said.

"The man who brought your brother to the hospital implied he might go to the police. He said that, well, the gash in your brother's throat wasn't the accidental result of falling upon a piece of crockery. He said that it was deliberately self-inflicted; that your brother told him so; and that it was a civic duty to report such an act to the authorities."

"Where is this fellow now?"

"He has taken a trip to Rochester. His expenses were all paid, and he was given something additional. I saw to it."

"I'm deeply grateful." Morrison's words turned to puffs of steam. He shivered. "May I see my brother's body?"

"Of course," Winterbottom said. He didn't move. "But it wasn't that fellow alone, I'm afraid. There was the coroner as well, and a nosing journalist from one of the city's most disgusting sheets. Showed up here several days ago making inquiries. Threatened to run a story about 'the songster's suicide'—his phrase exactly—and I had no choice. He had to be paid. It was a substantial sum."

"You did well and shall be remunerated in full, as I said in my note. You received it, didn't you?"

"Most definitely, but I was just making sure, Mr. Foster. I wish I could report that in the shadow of death all men shun duplicity or insincerity, but such, sir, has not been my experience."

"Same in every business," Morrison said.

After he saw Stephen's body, Morrison fetched Jane and escorted her in. She fell to her knees and prayed a long time.

The shroud was drawn up to Stephen's chin, leaving only his face in view. Morrison was prepared to restrain her if she attempted to lift the sheet and expose the gruesome blue-and-yellow gash across Stephen's throat, the thick, irregular stitches adding to the horror, but after gazing at Stephen awhile she turned away and put her head on Morrison's shoulder, and he led her out. She had never questioned Morrison's explanation of her husband's death—that he died in a fall—and didn't do so now.

Morrison left Jane in the oak-paneled room and returned alone to Winterbottom's private office. He took out a blank bank draft and laid it on the desk. "What is the full amount for your services?" he asked.

Winterbottom handed him a bill. There were no items, just a total.

"Does this include shipment of the body?"

"Everything is included, Mr. Foster."

Morrison filled in the draft and signed it. He handed it to Winterbottom, who stared at it a moment before folding it and putting it in his pocket.

"What should I do with the possessions that were on your brother's body?" Winterbottom said.

"What is there?"

"His clothing."

"Dispose of it as you wish."

"And this." Winterbottom handed Morrison a small purse. Morrison snapped open the clasp. It contained a handful of copper coins and a folded scrap of paper. Morrison took out the paper. It looked as though it had been torn from the back of an envelope. On it were penciled five words: *Dear friends and gentle hearts.*

"This I will keep," Morrison said.

*

Morrison took the coverlet from the bed and put it around his shoulders. He sat at the desk by the window and lit the oil lamp. He removed a thick folder from his briefcase. If he couldn't sleep, he would work. He had turned many a restless night to his advantage in this fashion, harnessing the anxiety or dread that drove him from bed to a useful purpose.

This past June, as Lee had approached Harrisburg with the obvious intent to destroy the Pennsylvania Railroad's bridge over the Susquehanna and break the link with the West, Morrison had lost all desire for sleep. He had worked night after night, ceaselessly reading maintenance reports and requisitions, until he had cleared his desk entirely of any business and started on his personal correspondence. He had written a long-overdue reply to Stephen's request for yet another loan. Now Morrison felt a mixture of regret and sadness at the memory of how he had turned his brother away. It was the last note he had ever sent Stephen, the final words between them.

Morrison opened the folder that had been given him by a director of the Pennsylvania. It contained a confidential account of the Pennsylvania's negotiations with an assortment of New Jersey railroads to unite their various tracks into a single consolidated line from Philadelphia to Jersey City. It would be managed, of course, by the Pennsylvania. Tantalus's prize was at last in reach: the fruit-laden bough of New York Harbor, an endless supply of freight and immigrants to be hauled west, an insatiable demand for the raw materials of the interior to be consumed or exported. There were ten pages of item-by-item estimates for the lading that could be expected from a consolidated line, ten more on the specific investments in track and equipment required to create such a line. An engineer's report was appended. Morrison skimmed over it to the last paragraph, which described the Jersey City terminal he and Jane had passed through yesterday. "Today it is nothing more than an oversized barn with a galvanized iron roof," the engineer had written. "In the event of consolidation, a grander, more permanent terminal should be contemplated, a structure that would testify to the power and position of the Pennsylvania."

Morrison pushed aside the folder. There was no sound from Jane's room. She was either asleep or giving her grief a rest. He reached into the pocket of his robe and took out Stephen's purse, opened it, and withdrew the scrap of paper. *Dear friends and gentle hearts.* He wished for a moment he had some of Stephen's talent that he might compose an ode or song that used these words to open a tribute to his brother. But his abilities had never extended to the poetical or musical. "Morrison is the practical one, the Foster with sense," his father said on more than one occasion, said it with a half smile on his face, as if amused.

Muffled sounds came from outside. Morrison stood and pulled back the drapes. It was dawn. The traffic was flowing once again, vehicles and pedestrians moving resolutely up and down the avenue. The relentless bustle of New York. He ran his hand across the sill. It was cracked and peeling, covered with soot. Poorly installed, poorly maintained. The hotel was barely ten years old and was already falling apart. Everything did unless you stayed on top of it, paid constant attention, repairing, cleaning, rebuilding. Poets and artists never worried about such matters. They smiled and sang, and left the work to the practical ones, ironmongers and smiths, merchants and businessmen, workmen and engineers, men of sense and responsibility. Morrison stuck the scrap of paper into the folder to mark the engineer's report. He would refer to it again, he decided. On the journey home, he would take a careful look at the Jersey City terminal, make some calculations, draw a preliminary sketch. It must be a useful, efficient structure, but the engineer was right. It should also be large and magnificent, able to withstand the assault of time, a monument to lasting things.

EPILOGUE

History isn't a record, a factual, objective, reasoned account of what occurred. History is a collection of remnants, shards, fragments. Make of it what you will. History is detritus.

—Audley Ward

THAT SUMMER OF 1863 is etched indelibly into memory. It commenced with the news of Lee's movement north, which, to appropriate Dr. Johnson's phrase, "concentrated wonderfully" the attention of the nation. Unlike New York City, however, our town never harbored doubts about the outcome. We all believed that right would triumph, as it did, and the threat of a Confederate invasion led not to panic but to a new burst of patriotic fervor. A wave of volunteers flowed into the recruiting hut beside the town hall. My eldest brother, Frederick, who was nineteen at the time, was among them. How I remember the day he and his comrades departed! They marched in loose formation to the terminal on Newark Avenue with the German Society Band at their head. We small boys trailed behind. Our hearts beat with the knowledge that these warriors were not the stuff of distant legends or ancient history, but our brothers and cousins and uncles, and though they arrived too late to participate in the glorious triumph at Gettysburg, we were sure that the very word of their approach helped put Lee to flight.

Two events from that time stand out in my mind. The first was a murder that took place in the old Elysian Fields, the report of which spread like cholera through the town, striking terror everywhere. The sacred precincts of play had become home to the sin of Cain! Outside the valiant contest of war, and sometimes even in it, the taking of any life is a gruesome transgression, but when the killing is murder, and not murder of the ordinary sort, a single shot, a solitary stab, but a brutal and ferocious assault that leaves the corpse unrecognizable, an icy chill enters the human heart. Of such a type was the murder in the fields.

For me it was made all the more disturbing by the fact that the corpse of the slain man rested in the basement of our house, in which my father maintained the town coroner's office. I was cursed with nightmares and shivered in my bed. My mother came and stroked my head. She said that the slain man as well as his slayer were undoubtedly Yorkers. She meant to comfort me, but instead inspired the fear that lurking in every corner of the night were Yorkers of murderous intent. My sleep remained disturbed!

As great as was my dread, it was insufficient to keep me or my comrades away from the very fields that haunted our dreams and that our parents had expressly forbidden us to visit. Drawn rather than repelled by the prospect of danger, as boys will always be, and undeterred by our parents' threats of punishment, we ventured into the Fields, to the very area in which the murder had occurred.

The hour was near dusk. The shadows in the woods turned deep and ominous. Running up the path to Sybil's Cave, we panted from a mixture of fear and physical exertion. We tarried at the cave's entrance nary a minute but flew back down the path, each inspired by the desire not to be the last in the pack. I led the way, running as with winged feet. I hurtled so fast that I was unable to negotiate a turn and, sliding on a muddy patch, crashed into the brush. I scrambled frantically to my feet. As I did, my hand closed quite fortuitously about the stem of a baseball bat, as though Fate itself had decreed that I should not miss it. With bat in hand, I resumed the race, eventually regaining my place in the lead.

It was not until we reached the halo of a streetlamp at the fringes of the fields that our anabasis came to a halt. Delighted with our safe return, we joked and laughed, pretending we had never been frightened at all, and I, quite proud of my find, held it up for the others to see. There, in the glow of gaslight, Ken Curtin, a tall red-haired lad who claimed to be Welsh but whom we mockingly accused of being Irish, noticed a clump caught in a fracture at the thick end of the bat. He reached up and pulled it loose. He held it for a moment in his hand. Horror crossed his face. "My God!" he said with alarm. "This seems a piece of skull and human hair!" Suddenly the shadows filled with

Yorkers. Ken dropped the bat, and we resumed our race.

Upon reaching home I informed my father what we had found, and he, after promising retribution for my disobedience at being where he had forbidden me to go, went off to fetch Sheriff Eisman. Together they went and retrieved the bat. What we had taken for a fragment of human scalp they discovered was a piece of tree bark with moss upon it. Yet after careful examination, they speculated that the bat may well have been the deadly instrument employed in the fearsome murder in the fields.

I expected no reward for making such a find, but hoped, perhaps, that because of it my father might forgo the punishment he had promised. I hoped in vain. That night, as he prepared to put the strap to me, he said, "Sin is sin, and as it is written 'Thou shalt not kill,' so it is written 'Honor thy father and thy mother.' " I learned my lesson well. The perpetrator of the murder, however, was never found.

*   *   *

In all the years after, there never was heat like that summer. My grandfather blamed it on the war. The same heat had oppressed his boyhood home in Königsberg, he said, the summer after Napoléon's victory at Jena. Heat or no, the murder in the Elysian Fields brought the cold presence of death into our midst. "What is the world coming to?" was the question most frequently upon our elders' lips, and almost within hours of the murder, the infamous and awful draft riots that commenced in New York City seemed to give them their answer: *The world is coming to ruin.*

The riots were the second memorable moment of that July, and though, thank God, our town was spared any of the carnage and savagery that were commonplace across the river, the blood-red fires that rose up in the night sky and the terrified exiles who landed on our shore were awful reminders of how close we were to the volcano. That knowledge inspired formation of a local defense force that stood guard throughout the week. On Wednesday and Thursday, the first units that had been hurried back from Gettysburg to put down the insurrection arrived by rail. The town cheered lustily as the heroes of the Union boarded the ferry to cross the Hudson, and we boys watched in awe and amazement as these sun-burnished giants entered the terminal. We knew for sure the nefarious Yorkers were about to meet their match!

It was Sunday morning of that infamous week, when the soldiers had done the work we had expected them to do, that the loudest echo of the riot was heard in our town. As was his custom, my father was late in dressing for church. The whole family sat waiting in the parlor when Sheriff Eisman arrived and told my mother he needed Father right away. My father came downstairs, and the Sheriff informed him there was trouble in the fields and summoned him to join a detachment of citizens on its way to deal with it. With no more explanation than that, off they went, and I, pretending I could not hear my mother as she shouted for me to come back, trailed behind.

The Sheriff and his men proceeded directly to the area of the fields occupied by the playing diamonds of the base-ballers, their sport, though the Cooperstown Chamber of Commerce may loudly protest otherwise, a homegrown product of Hoboken. That day the fields presented a most remarkable sight. Everywhere you looked were the crude tents of pathetic families of Negroes who, fleeing the violence directed at them in New York City, had set up impromptu camp.

Now, however, the teams of baseballers had approached, intent upon their Sunday sport, and the Negroes had refused to move. It seemed the madness across the river was about to spill over, and a riot to ensue! The Sheriff's men immediately imposed themselves between the would-be combatants, but the exchange of words between the players and the refugees grew more heated and threatening until a strikingly attractive Negress of the lightest hue stepped forward. In a voice so rich and dramatic it might well have been found upon the stage, she averred that the players would soon have their fields back.

"Give us this single day of peace," she declaimed. "We shall use it to gather our possessions and tend to those who have been hurt, and then we shall leave most gladly, shaking the dust from our feet." When the grumbling of the baseballers continued, she drew a small pickaninny to her side and said, "You who call yourselves Christians, can you find it in your hearts to give this child a few hours free from persecution?"

The baseballers stayed awhile longer, and some continued to protest the loss of their fields, but gradually they melted away and the Negroes were left in peace, guarded by a small number of the Sheriff's men. The next day, as the Negress had promised, her people were gone and were never seen again.

—Kurt Bonenstedt, *The Town Across the River: Hoboken as It Was* (New York: The Metropolitan Press, 1935)

❖

In its early years, New York was notoriously inhospitable to the dead. The Dutch and English settlers routinely desecrated the burial sites of the Native Americans. They ripped open the earth to plant crops and sink foundations, and had about as much regard for the bones and bodies they came across as for the dirt they found them in, maybe less. Soon enough, many of the original settlers met the same fate as the Native Americans they had displaced. As the city began its relentless march up Manhattan Island, tombs, monuments, and family plots once situated in wastelands, or on hilltops, or in the corner of some green field became part of a bustling, hurry-up metropolis. Some early graves were probably respectfully removed. Others, more likely, were simply obliterated.

Gradually, life improved for the dead. Churchyards and formal cemeteries well north of the settled areas (a development mightily encouraged by the Rural Cemeteries Act of 1847) offered a secure resting place. But the dangers to the dead did not entirely abate, especially with the rise of a professional medical establishment and its voracious appetite for human specimens for examination and dissection. New York Hospital, for example, did a wholesale traffic in cadavers, permitting its students an endless variety of opportunities for sawing, chopping, cutting, slicing, dicing, and otherwise practicing the medical arts of the time. The practice was so extensive that in 1788 there was an attack on the hospital by a disturbed and outraged citizenry. The militia was called out and ended the affair, but not before it added five more citizens to the supply of the city's dead.

In death as in life, it has always been advisable to be rich instead of poor. New York's indigent dead learned this the hard way in the mid-1820s, when the city fathers reconsidered the placement of the municipal potter's field. In 1797, a piece of property outside the inhabited region of Manhattan had been set aside for the purpose and, in an early example of mixed land use, was also designated for the performance of public executions. In the interim, however, the city had undergone one of its periodic growth spurts (a horizontal expansion that would later turn vertical), and the necropolis of paupers, which by this time contained at least ten thousand souls, stood squarely in the way of progress. For well over a generation, here was where the city had dumped the nameless victims of cholera, yellow fever, and typhoid, as well as drunks, prostitutes, criminals, and other of the disreputable dead. It wasn't exactly an inducement to the respectable classes to settle nearby. But neither for the first time nor the last, the city's real estate developers and its public officials put their heads together and came up with a rewarding solution. The potter's field was closed, trenches were dug to let any buildup of gases escape, the rot of the dead was exposed to the air and elements. After a period of time, the potter's field was sealed up again, resodded, and reseeded, and a park was laid out there. Fed by a wondrously rich compost, the flowers and shrubs were soon abloom, and within a decade the new expanse of greenery dramatically boosted land values. The park was quickly surrounded by handsome, stately residences in the Greek Revival style, and in 1837 the neighborhood became home to the University of the City of New York, today's New York University.

Even wealth, however, has been no guarantee of eternal rest for the dead New Yorker, a lesson learned the hard way by the family of Alexander Turney Stewart, the Belfast-born merchant whom many credit with the invention of the department store. By 1848, Stewart was one of the most successful merchants in the city, and he built a grand new store at the busy corner of Chambers and Broadway, the Marble Dry-Goods Palace, which later served as the headquarters of *The Sun* and which still stands to this day.

In order to build his Marble Palace, Stewart not only had to demolish Washington Hall, which stood on the site, but to dig deep into the earth to lay the foundations of the massive new edifice. This meant uprooting a part of the old Negro burial ground that Washington Hall had been built upon. There were those in the city who thought Stewart might insist the architects devise a way to leave the dead undisturbed. It was widely rumored that the ghost of the man who had built Washington Hall roamed the vicinity, loudly lamenting his decision to disquiet the bones of the Africans. He could find no peace, the ghost told those who took the time to listen.

Stewart scoffed at such an idea. With the levelheaded practicality of the Scotch-Irish, he brushed aside the cavils of the superstitious and went about his business. His immense success seemed to refute any notion of a curse. He prospered greatly, and in 1863 opened an even grander emporium between Broadway and Fourth Avenue. More than a store, Stewart's Cast-Iron Palace was a door to the future, the Gate of Heaven, the portal through which the masses passed from a world in which shopping was an everyday necessity into one in which it was a glorious activity, a carnival of choice, a cornucopia of pleasure.

The profits poured in. Stewart diversified. He purchased theaters and hotels. He became a close confidant of President Grant's. He built a home that cost the incredible sum of two million dollars. He filled it with a million dollars' worth of artwork. He purchased a large tract of land on Long Island and built a planned community on it, Garden City, and thus, along with consumerism, helped set in motion that other engine of the American Dream—suburbanization. And then, in 1876, he died.

He was laid to rest in the yard of St. Mark's-in-the-Bowery, the Episcopal church at Second Avenue and Tenth Street, in a ground-level vault covered with a marble slab that gave only the family name. But almost from the moment he entered the ground, the city abounded with rumors that he would find no rest. Why this was so is difficult to ascertain. As disturbed and violent a place as New York was in those years, with bloody incidents like the Draft Riots of 1863 and the Orangemen's Riot of 1871 exposing the city's vast netherworld of poverty, resentment, and ethnic hatred, the violation of burial sites and the ransoming of corpses were almost unheard of. Many rich and powerful New Yorkers, the potential targets for such acts, had died and were left to enjoy their quiet, unending sleep. Why wasn't Stewart? Perhaps it was because of where he was buried; not in the bucolic precincts of Green-Wood or Woodlawn, but on the very fringe of the city's vast caldron of seething slumdom. Or perhaps it had something to do with the curse that Stewart had ridiculed and disregarded. Who can say with certainty?

In any case, on October 8, 1878, two and a half years after the merchant prince's death, the sexton of St. Mark's discovered that the marble slab above the crypt had been moved, though the grave itself was undisturbed. The church took precautions against the intruders' returning. The slab was moved to a new location and the real grave covered over. But the ghouls weren't fooled. A month later, on the evening after the temporary watchman had been dismissed, robbers uncovered the real grave, and removed Stewart's body. Stewart hadn't made it easy for them. Once in the crypt itself, the thieves had to unscrew the cover of a great cedar chest, cut through a lead box, and break open the copper coffin, a job they somehow performed without rousing any alarm in the densely packed neighborhood around the church.

Although they had no suspects, the police were desperate to take some action against the criminals who had violated the tomb, that sanctum sanctorum of Victorian propriety, so they pulled in anyone who was known to have expressed ill will against Stewart while he was alive. There were many: the small merchants he had undersold and put out of business; the clerks and seamstresses he had sweated and squeezed, frustrating all their attempts to unionize; the legion of petty thieves caught and arrested in the store, and prosecuted to the fullest extent of the law. Meanwhile, a small army of guards was hired to protect the resting places of those with names like Astor and Vanderbilt. But Stewart remained the only member of New York's golden circle of nabobs to endure involuntary resurrection.

Finally, using the alias of Henry G. Romaine (a play, perhaps on the name of a variety of lettuce—"lettuce" was current New York slang for money), the body snatchers contacted an intermediary and demanded $250,000 for the return of Stewart's body. Stewart's executor indignantly refused. He made a counteroffer of $25,000. The negotiations collapsed. It wasn't until two years later, in 1880, that Stewart's distraught widow insisted the negotiations be reopened. She had been unable to sleep. Her dreams had been haunted by the image of her husband wandering about the streets outside the Cast-Iron Palace, vainly seeking to gain entrance.

The word was circulated that the Stewart estate was ready to pay, and the body snatchers once again got in touch with an intermediary. Mrs. Stewart said she was willing to pay $100,000. The body snatchers said they would take $200,000. The two sides seemed to be making progress. But the executor stepped in again and said that the estate of Alexander Stewart would make a once-and-final offer of $20,000. If it wasn't accepted, the possessors of Stewart's mortal remains were free to keep them forever.

A few weeks later, on a deserted country road in Westchester, a relative of Mrs. Stewart's met with three masked men who gave him a gunnysack filled with human bones and a piece of cloth cut from the lining of Stewart's coffin to prove that the bones had, indeed, been lifted from St. Mark's. The masked men took the $20,000 and ran. They were never seen or heard from again. Mrs. Stewart regained her ability to sleep. The bones, whether they were Stewart's or some substitute's drafted to the purpose, were packed off to Long Island, there to sleep in heavenly peace amid the suburban fastness of the Garden City Cathedral.

—Richard Blaine, *Ghoul's Night Out: A Short History of Grave Robbing, Tomb Looting, and Assorted Mayhem Against the Dead* (New York: The Center for the Strange, 1990)

———— ◆ ————

A BRAWL IN GERICH'S TAVERN
LEAVES ONE DEAD,
TWO WOUNDED

ACCOUNT OF THE EVENT BY
AN EYEWITNESS

ASSAILANT STILL AT LARGE

At 10 o'clock Wednesday evening, a member of Monaghan's Grand Cake Walk and Minstrel Burlesque Company, which is engaged at the Fremont Theatre this week
and next, was shot dead in the barroom of Gerich's. The
deceased is identified as Mr. John Mulcahey, of New York
City, age approximately 60. The two wounded men, Louis
Anderson and Michael Farrell, also members of the theatrical troupe, were shot in the hand and leg respectively.
Both were treated by Doctor Horstwine, whose office is
next door to Gerich's.

Deputy Andrew Dusenberry of the Sheriff's Office, who
was called immediately to the scene, reports that Mulcahey
was struck between the eyes by a single round and died
upon the spot.

According to Widley Armbruster, a clerk with the Western Union Company and a patron of Gerich's at the time
of the incident, the minstrel trio arrived soon after giving
their last performance of the day, exactly as they had done
for the last several evenings. They consumed "copious
amounts of whiskey," says Armbruster, "and sang in a loud
manner." A man whom Armbruster describes as "stout and
well-set, wearing the jacket and cloth cap of a sailor,"
asked the trio to stop. A shouting match ensued. Mulcahey
and the unidentified man traded insults, which led to an
exchange of blows.

The combatants were separated by the other patrons of
the barroom. "And then," says Armbruster, "just when it
seemed to be over, the fellow turned around and shot the
three of them."

Dr. Horstwine says that neither of the two wounded men
is in any danger.

James Gaffney, the manager of Monaghan's Minstrel Company, described the deceased man as "a respected and admired practitioner of the black-faced art." He added that "despite this tragic loss, the abundant talent found in our show means we can proceed with all our scheduled performances."

The Sheriff's Office requests that anyone with information on the identity or whereabouts of the assailant make himself known to Deputy Dusenberry.

—*The San Francisco Republican,* November 12, 1897

———◆———

The American Irish Historical Society
254 West 42nd Street
New York City
December 4, 1899

Hon. Stuart R. Stover
The State Historian of New York
The Capitol
Albany, New York

Dear Mr. Stover:

Per our discussion of September last, you will find enclosed the manuscript containing a description of the formation of the Irish Brigade. It also represents, I believe, the most detailed account ever given of the 69th Regiment's role at Fredericksburg, Va., in December, 1862. I hope it will fill in the gap that has, up until now, existed in the Official Records of the Rebellion and bring due honor to the Irish New Yorkers who so bravely fought to preserve the unity of our Nation.

As you suggested, I interviewed as many of the survivors as could be located, but though the Old Guard never surrenders, most of its members are dead! The few still alive, however, offered a vivid and lively account of that day they crossed the Rappahannock. It seemed to them as fresh as if it happened yesterday.

Whilst I had some difficulty locating Colonel Robert Noonan, Commander of the 69th on the fateful day, after some investigating I found him living in Brooklyn. Again following your suggestion, I have written the narrative as though it were all from the mouth of the Colonel himself, and, in accord with the practice of the Official Records, have signed the Commander's name to the article, for which he has given his consent.

Ironically, in view of these facts, it was Colonel Noonan who was the least communicative of all with whom I spoke. I interviewed him on several occasions, but he seems a man whose constitutional bent toward taciturnity is exacerbated by advanced age, exceedingly poor health, and the particularly deteriorated state of his eyesight, which has left him nearly blind.

When the work was done, and the manuscript near to its final form, I took the precaution of reading it aloud to the Colonel, telling him to stop me at any part of the narrative that he felt needed to be either amended, or shortened, or expanded.

The Colonel sat silently through most of my reading, several times loudly clearing his sinuses, which I mistook for a signal to pause, but he waved with his hand, signalling for me to read on. He did, however, stop me at the point in the account of the engagement at Fredericksburg wherein it is related how Father Willet, Chaplain of the 69th, blessed the men as they prepared to undertake their heroic assault. Recounting the event in Noonan's words, the text reads as follows (p. 16): "Although not a Catholic myself, I was the first man to receive the good Father's blessing."

The Colonel said in a tone I can only describe as challenging, "Who told you that?"

I replied that several of those I'd interviewed had made a point of mentioning he was a Protestant, but I assured him there was no intent to raise the issue of religious sectarianism. The only purpose was to underscore the unity that existed in the Regiment. I read on (pp. 16–17): "He [Father Willet] then went along the lines blessing each man, Catholic and Protestant alike. As soon as the Father had finished his religious duties to the regiment, I [Colonel Noonan] placed in his hat a sprig of boxwood which I had received from General Meagher, telling the men of the regiment that I would make an Irishman out of the Father that day—the good Father being a French Canadian—and the men had a good laugh for themselves, then stepped as cheerfully to the fray as they would into a ballroom."

At this point, the Colonel seemed taken by some sort of seizure of the brain. An incoherent flow of words sputtered from his lips, and his face turned a vivid shade of purple. I summoned his nurse immediately, and she ordered me from the room. She emerged several moments later to inform me that the very delicate state of the Colonel's health, and the severe turmoil that sometimes clouded his brain, required an end of my interview. I told her of our deadline, and she then instructed me to leave the manuscript with her. She informed me that as soon as the Colonel seemed recovered she would read the remaining part to him, carefully noting any reactions, and send it to me directly.

She has proved as good as her word. I received the manuscript last evening, and as you will see, there isn't a mark upon it. In the end, it seems, we passed the Colonel's muster, and so added a missing chapter to a brave and noble history.

> Sincerely,
> Michael R. Patterson
> Librarian-Historiographer

Proceedings of the State Historian, Comprising Reports to the Legislature, Correspondence, and Other Papers, Vol. XXIII, published by the state of New York (1900)

——◆——

ALBERT J. MAXWELL

> 65 Wall Street
> New York City
> December 3, 1903

Mayor-elect George B. McClellan
297 East 36th Street
New York City

Dear George,

Mayor-elect! What satisfaction it gives me to put those words before your illustrious name! I know that in the flush of your resounding victory you undoubtedly find yourself besieged by an army of office seekers, petitioners, etc. I hesitate to join that rogues' gallery but my dearest Lolly has prevailed on me, insisting, in her words, "I know George, and he will do his best!" It is at her bidding, then, that I write, and if this letter be judged a breach of friendship or good taste, let the blame be on the distaff side of our union!

During her recent convalescence, Lolly was attended by a most capable and industrious nursing companion by the name of Mrs. Sheila Noonan. Good-hearted Lolly, as is her wont, managed to drag out of the woman the details of her life story and, worse, to involve herself in rectifying any and all injustices. (Poor Lolly will ever be the victim of her Huguenot blood!) As it turns out, Mrs. Noonan, a widow, has for some time been seeking to collect the military pension of her late husband, a man many years her senior, who served under your father in the Peninsula Campaign, as a member of the 69th New York. Her husband, Mrs. Noonan says, was a full Colonel, with a distinguished record. His later years were apparently spent in a severe state of physical depletion, which exhausted their funds and greatly strained the capacities of Mrs. Noonan.

The unyielding pressure of uxorious concern permits me no alternative but to put this matter before you. Lolly will not rest until Mrs. Noonan's cause is recognized by the government of the United States! And she won't allow me to rest, either!

I will be at the Manhattan Club for the Christmas Eve reception should you wish to discuss the matter. And be forewarned! Since this is the one evening of the year the club is opened to spouses, Lolly shall be there, too.

Sincerely,
Bert

H O N .   G E O R G E   B .   M C C L E L L A N

The House of Representatives
Washington, D.C.
December 19, 1903

Dear Bert,

Your letter of the third has been forwarded to me here in Washington.

I should love to oblige both you and your lovely bride. Unfortunately, I discovered a very long time ago that if I tried to give a hearing to all the various claims of those who served, or claimed to have served, with my father, I should have no time to do anything else. Besides, I leave Congress now, to attend to the fortunes of our fair city, and such matters are best taken up with my successor or the War Department.

I look forward to Christmas' Eve, but let us all agree ahead of time that we shall discuss topics more suited to the season than Army pensions.

Yours,
Geo.

The Correspondence of the Hon. George B. McClellan,
Mayor of the City of New York; Vol. 1: 1903–1905,
published by the city of New York (1914)

◆

DEATH CLAIMS COLONEL VAN WYCK
CIVIL WAR VETERAN AND BUSINESS
LEADER SUCCUMBS AT AGE 91

Colonel Ezra Van Wyck, 91 years of age, Los Angeles business and club man, Civil War veteran, and prominent supporter of many philanthropic causes, died yesterday at the Clara Barton Hospital after a brief illness. The cause of death was given as high blood pressure and uremia. His body was removed to the Rupps Funeral Chapel, 824 South Figueroa Street, where funeral services will be conducted at a date to be announced later.

Colonel Van Wyck had been identified with a number of business and financial concerns in various capacities during his more than five decades of residence in the state. At the time of his death, he was still actively engaged as a director of the California Trust Bank, the Jefferson Union Fidelity Investment Corporation, and the Arcadia Motion Picture Studio. He was a respected and beloved member of several clubs, fraternities, and social organizations.

Born in Albany, New York, on May 13, 1835, the descendant of ancient Dutch families (his mother was a Van Vliet), Colonel Van Wyck built a successful lumber business in that city before the Civil War. As the Colonel himself often told the story, he might never have participated in the War Between the States if he hadn't lost his business during a card game. "It was the luckiest loss I ever had," the Colonel told a convention of Elks last March in Santa Monica. "I lost a fortune but found my country."

In the fall of 1863, he joined a local regiment being raised in Albany. He saw much action during the Battle of the Wilderness and Grant's campaign against Richmond but emerged unscathed. At war's end, he decided that rather than return to Albany he would seek his future on the frontier. Prior to his arrival in California in 1870, he was a partner in several successful trading companies in the territories.

Upon first arriving in California, Colonel Van Wyck settled in Sacramento, where he met his wife, Emma Curtis Van Wyck, the daughter of Marcus Curtis, himself a well-known member of the State Bar and a director of the Union Pacific Railroad. Mrs. Van Wyck survives her husband.

A resident of Los Angeles for the past twenty-seven years, Colonel Van Wyck was sergeant at arms of the California GAR from 1912 through 1915 and was a staunch supporter of the movement for national defense and closer cooperation between the U.S. Army and the National Guard. He was also a member of the First Americans Society, a Shriner, and a member of the Masonic Lodge of Sacramento, the Santa Monica Lodge of Elks, and the American Legion.

Described by all who knew him as a vigorous, gregarious man, much admired for his patriotism, good judgement, and business acumen, the Colonel was working at home on Monday last when he was removed to the hospital, suffering from a high fever and severe abdominal pain. He died the following night in his sleep.

Besides his widow, Colonel Van Wyck leaves two sons, Bedford, 49, and Charles, 46, both of Los Angeles.

—*The Los Angeles Times,* December 16, 1926

◆

AMID PAGEANTRY, FORDHAM
INSTALLS NEW PRESIDENT

A BRONX NATIVE

Sunday afternoon, in a ceremony of pomp and circumstance presided over by Patrick Cardinal Hayes and attended by two bishops, ten monsignori, and the presidents of several other Jesuit colleges and universities, Fordham University inaugurated the Reverend Augustine J. Dunne, S.J., as its twenty-fifth president.

The ceremony was conducted in the auditorium of the University's splendid new building, Keating Hall, which was recently completed at a cost of $1,343,000 and whose clock tower has become, almost instantly, a landmark of the Fordham neighborhood.

POLITICAL DIGNITARIES IN ATTENDANCE

After a Mass of Installation in the University Church, the Cardinal led a procession into the new hall. In attendance were also a number of political dignitaries. Included were: Bronx Borough President James Lyons; Bronx District Attorney Samuel J. Foley; Congressmen Patrick Fitzsimmons, Michael B. Brady, Francis X. O'Hara, and Vincent A. Hickey, all of the New York delegation; Justices Aloysius Flynn, William Purcell, and James P. McManmon, all of the State Supreme Court, First Department; Assemblymen John J. Hanley, Robert E. Murphy, Peter M. O'Donnell, Ignatius O'Rourke, and John Jude Francis Cassidy; New York City Police Commissioner John Moore; Fire Commissioner Morgan Kennedy; and Commissioner of Docks and Terminals Charles Parnell O'Brien. Many of the dignitaries are graduates of the University or its law school.

WORDS FROM FATHER DUNNE

The invocation was given by the Cardinal and was followed by a rousing rendition of the national and university anthems by the Fordham Glee Club. The heads of each academic department made an address of welcome.

In his response, Father Dunne, who served previously as the Regent of the Fordham University Law School, thanked all in attendance. He said that in deciding to found a Catholic college in what was then "a small village on the far periphery of New York City," Archbishop John Hughes had shown "prophetic foresight."

"First of all," Father Dunne said, "Archbishop Hughes knew in his heart what today is obvious to every eye: This neighborhood would become once and forever Irish." This remark was greeted with warm applause and laughter.

"Second, the Archbishop understood that as New York rose to prominence among the cities of the world, it would require institutions that rested not upon the shifting sands of opinion but upon the Rock of Truth."

ANCESTOR WAS RESTAURATEUR

Father Dunne is the first native son of the Bronx to be made Fordham's president. Born in 1890, in what was then referred to as the Annexed District or the North Side, he attended St. Luke's Grammar School and Xavier Academy before entering the Society of Jesus. He is the son of James A. and May Dunne, both now deceased. His father, longtime leader of the Tecumseh Democratic Club, owned and operated the Morrisania Insurance Brokerage. His grandfather was a well-known restaurateur in the lower part of the city.

—*The Bronx Home News,* September 1, 1936

◆

Opened in 1961, the Van Rensselaer Shopping Center was for a brief period the largest such retail operation in the Capital District area and represented a milestone in the county's economic development. The Center's success, as is often said in the retail trade, was guaranteed by three ingredients: location, location, location. Situated beside the juncture of an interstate highway and the main county road, and anchored by two major department stores, the Center did over $500,000 in gross sales on its opening day.

The Cannon Development Company of Garden City, Long Island, oversaw construction of the project, which was conceived, financed, and built in under two years. A prime reason for this expeditious completion was the enthusiastic support received from the county government. In light of the controversy that came to surround the selection of the site, this support was invaluable.

The land on which the Center is constructed had been taken up by a small cemetery and a derelict church. Though familiar landmarks to the long-term residents of the area, few knew the true history of the property, which had for many years belonged to a sect of Negroes that had purchased it sometime after the Civil War. Although never officially incorporated, the small community of houses built around the sect's church was known locally as Midian's Well, the same name as the church.

Most of the residents of Midian's Well worked as waiters and menials in and around Troy, and there is a passage in one of Phyllis Conner's turn-of-the-century short stories (which are often set in Rensselaer County) that gives us a vivid, if fleeting, picture of these Negroes:

> In the rear of the drafty horsecar that rollicked up the Schuyler Road was the usual band of silent, dignified ebony creatures, who sat with hands folded as if in prayer, their eyes cast upon the tobacco-stained floor.

There is also a mention of the Negroes of Midian's Well in the police report published in the Troy *Record* of December 19, 1889:

> *Negro funeral turns disorderly.* Death of local woman, "Mother Maria," results in illegal ceremony in front of church that blocks road. Warning issued. No summons or further action undertaken.

Beyond these fragments, nothing is known of the sect or its practices, except that sometime around the end of the First World War the last of its members either died or moved away, and the houses fell to ruin. The church itself was taken over by Negro Baptists and was still in use as late as 1941. Soon after, it, too, was abandoned and, along with the adjoining gravesites, became little more than a rendezvous for local youths on Halloween.

The condemnation proceedings completed and title to the site transferred to the sponsors of the Van Rensselaer Shopping Center, the work seemed ready to begin. The first step was the removal of the occupants of the graves to a specially designated section of Evergreen Cemetery. On the day the process was to commence, the Reverend Thomas Montgomery of the Mount Pisgah Memorial Church organized a protest. The demonstrators lay down and refused to move until a public hearing was held on the disinterment.

The sponsors agreed to such a hearing and it was held within a week. Speaking against allowing the disinterment, the Reverend Mr. Montgomery said, "We must not and will not sit idly by while the bones of these holy men and women are wantonly and needlessly disturbed. They are our ancestors in faith and in hope, and their memory must be honored, not obliterated."

Replying on behalf of the county, Norman Sandwaller, an attorney with the Office of Deeds and Titles, pointed out that the bodies would be reinterred in dignified and appropriate surroundings. "Subsequent development of the site," he said, "would benefit Negroes along with everyone else."

The County Commission subsequently confirmed the decision to allow full clearance of the site by a vote of 7 to 0. A week later, on April 14, 1961, construction began.

> —Calvin A. Hutchinson, *New Frontiers: From Mohawks to the Modern Age: A History of Rensselaer County* (Albany: The State University Press, 1965)

---◆---

> *Each belongs here or anywhere as much as the welloff . . . just as much as you,*
> *Each has his or her place in the procession.*

> —Walt Whitman, *Leaves of Grass,* 1855 edition